OLIVE GROVE

Bhupendra Gandhi

authorHOUSE®

AuthorHouse™ UK Ltd.
500 Avebury Boulevard
Central Milton Keynes, MK9 2BE
www.authorhouse.co.uk
Phone: 08001974150

First published by AuthorHouse 10/1/2010
This book is printed on acid-free paper.

ISBN: 978-1-4520-7129-9 (sc)

Contents

OLIVE GROVE

Woman of Straw

Woman of Substance

CHANDA (Village Anarkali)

LETTER OF DESTINY

SISTER USHA

KISMAT(FATE)

Chance Encounter

APPENDIX

ACKNOWLEDGEMENT

My first book, *"Ivory Tower"* was well received by the readers, although I can not say the same on the financial, commercial front. Then I do not write for profit. It is a hobby, a therapy that keeps me busy, my mind occupied and keeps the depression at an arm's length, especially when some one is more or less confined to one's home.

Ivory Tower has thirty one wonderful short stories. All these stories have different theme, background, location and suspense, especially at the end. The main reason for achieving such diversity was that it was written over a number of years, during changing political, social, financial and cultural environment, starting in Dar es Salaam, my birth place and a heaven on earth, beginning at a time when I was still at school.

But it is more or less impossible to replicate, to reproduce such diversity on a regular basis, especially in such a short period of time span. So my new book *"Olive Grove"* has only eight short stories compared to thirty one in Ivory Tower.

As couple of these stories are well over fifty thousand words and some seventy pages long, it may be inappropriate to call them short stories. The final story *Olive Grove* that gave the book its title was written after my younger brother Yogendra passed away at the relatively young ago of sixty three.

We were like twins. We came to London together and had lived together for some thirty five years. Most of us believe in orderly departure. So when some one younger passes away before his time, it would be difficult to take it in, come to terms with the tragedy. We say time is the healing factor. But at our age, time is not on our side and healing is a relative word!

In many ways Olive Grove reflects our lives. It contains many factual events, the holidays we had taken together, visiting Wales and our tranquil life in Tanzania. It reflects pain, happiness, love and ambition. No wonder it is the longest story I have written, some one hundred and fifty pages long. It could be printed as a book on its own.

As it would be difficult to read such a lengthy story at one go, while travelling on a train or a bus to work, I have divided such stories into short chapters where the readers can take a break and start afresh without losing the thread.

As I have already thanked every one who has been associated with me, with my writings and helped me climb the ladder of journalism, I would not repeat their names and take up valuable space.

Instead I would like readers to enjoy one of my favourite poems that I wrote when I was a student. The theme of the poem is close to my heart, as we were practically born on the sea. The message is as much relevant today as it was some fifty years ago.

We more or less learned swimming before we learned walking, as our parents were progressive and the beautiful, warm waters of Indian Ocean were just a stone throw away from our home in Dar.

We can see the sea from our balcony where I used to sit and do my homework, writing and listening to BBC, as television was still on a drawing board, as far as us, in Africa were concerned.

CRY FOR HELP

I saw a shoal of whales
Small and large, happy and content
Swimming in the span of mighty ocean
As free and happy as could be

One of them, the leader of the shoal
Swam out to me and said
"Hi! My friend, can I speak to thee
Please lend me thy ear, as I may not be here

You humans are suppose to be kind and clever
God made you supreme, to be our guardian angel
Then why you act like teenage, mindless thugs
Behave like a raging bull in a China shop

You humans make our lives living hell
Look at my family, some twenty and two
Young and old, suckling and strong
A picture of health, happy and content

No worry, no enemy in our ocean paradise
Except greedy humans, the ultimate parasite
I am afraid, I will be caught one day
A big powerful harpoon, all steel, sharp and solid

Fired from a Japanese, Norwegian whaler
Will explode on impact, if lucky, will kill me outright
My heart will torn to pieces, destroying my soul
A river of blood will pollute thy ocean

Lingering death, undignified end of a magnificent mammal
My lifespan, one hundred years of joy and fun
Reduced to no more than twenty and two
By the act of unparallel human thuggery

Ducking and diving, having no respite
Having fun, you must be joking!
It is a struggle for life, a day to day survival
Taking each week, each day at a time

Can you ever see the tears we shed by a bucket full
Hear our cry of pain, anguish, hurt and ghastly death
I wonder why thee humans, the master race
Do not hung their heads in shame

Roaming the seas, visiting North and South Poles
Bathing in the lukewarm waters of Gulf Stream
Feasting off the beautiful Hawaiian paradise
Now no more than a distant dream, a fading memory

What have we done to offend thee humans
That you want to hunt us to obliteration
Rubbing the salt in our painful wounds
Calling the cruel cull, a research science

Ending on your dinner plate, in a five star restaurant
A pleasure anomalous and mystifying
We fail to understand, to apprehend human taste
Why human stomach do not churn in pain

At the sight of the slaughter of the majestic mammals
To feed your young, on the flesh of the innocent
In fact feasting on mothers in milk and innocent babies
That should put human race to utter shame

I have only one message for thee humans
Leave us alone with Mother Nature
So that we could have some fun, some respite
Spend some time with family and Mother Nature

Our family needs some breather, some space, some respite
A new lease of life form human excesses
Hopefully a long, happy, contended and fulfilling life
If we become extinct, it will be a Herculean tragedy

An irreplaceable loss to so clever a mankind
Your children and grandchildren will be the losers
Who would never see s spouting spectacle
An unrivalled magic show, a spectacle supreme

On the vast, unending waves of ocean stage
This is our gift, our sacrifice to thee undeserving humans
To this beautiful green, green planet earth
That sustains us, keeps us all in good health and wealth.

Since beyond the time of Lord Rama and Krishna
Sadly we are coming to an unglamorous end
As a result of human vandalism, human excesses
That will be the last nail on the coffin of Mother Earth.

OLIVE GROVE

Chapter One

Goodbye to Jolox

It was a daily routine for **Kiran** to stand on the raised veranda, in front of the entrance door, at day break when the sun may be struggling to break lose and stare at the distant mountain peak, ***"The Sierra de Ronda*** mountain range with the majestic peak touching the sky at some 4600 feet, towering over the surrounding landscape.

The peak is affectionately known as ***Montana Baja*** which means a steep or not so high a mountain. This term is widely used throughout Spain, especially in ***Canary Islands*** to describe various peaks and mountain ranges.

The Sun and the peak were half hidden in the morning mist and early cloud cover that was the daily routine, especially during the winter months when days are short and nights cool and longer.

The wet, rain bearing clouds so often incorporate the rainbow colours with silver lining that would block the Sun appearing early, especially during cold and wet winter months, thus prevents the Sun from spreading its warmth and light that is so essential to banish the early morning blues, the rosy cold that is the hallmark of any hill station.

In a way Kiran was like a helpless deer caught in the glare of a powerful, intruding pair of headlights from the four wheel drive, a favourite vehicle of the mountain residents. Then it was the only transport that would take the villagers around, can negotiate steep and so often muddy tracks.

Neither the sun nor the mountain would change the habit for any one, as it was embalmed in nature, a God's creation, a long established routine since time immemorial. We are all children of God and depend on the **ALLMIGHTY** for our daily existence, our happiness, our survival.

Kiran had to get used to the late appearance of the sun and lack of warmth during winter months. Then this at least give them four seasons, a welcome break after the scorching heat of the summer months when mountain slopes become a fertile ground for forest fires that could destroy so many people's homes and their livelihood.

On the other hand, the tiny hamlet of **Tolox,** in the most beautiful province of Spain, **Andalusia, the Lake District of Spain** hardly deserves to be called a hill station.

Traditionally hill stations are hot spots for the rich, to spend their summer months, escaping from the oppressive heat of the coastal plane. But mercifully winter months are short, no more than four months in a year that qualify to be called winter months.

The summer months of July, August and September are more oppressing with long days and summer heat that raises the temperature to uncomfortable level of 45* centigrade and above.

But Tolox is spared such an uncomfortable variation, with cool nights that give respite from the days' heat. However forest fires on the mountain slopes, among the pine forests are a constant hazard villagers have to live with during those tinder dry summer months. Then it is the same every where, especially California and Australia where bush fires are a menace one has to put up with.

In Hindu mythology, the sun reigns supreme. It has a God like stature, as without sun, the life as we know would not exist on this beautiful planet called Mother Earth. We call sun **"Surya Dev"** or simply Sun God!

It is not uncommon for many Hindus to get up early and pray as the Sun comes out. It is in Hindu ethos that the Sun arrives each morning and leaves each evening in a chariot driven by sixteen white horses. Every Hindu knows the famous Sanskrit words, **"Tamaso Ma Jyotir Gamaya** which simply means **"From darkness to Light"** a little phrase with so many hidden meanings.

Although Kiran is not a religious person, perhaps he was unconsciously following in this tradition practiced by his forefathers back in India, an oasis of enlightenment, knowledge, culture and the mother country for most East African Asians who were brought to East Africa, the federation of three countries, **Kenya, Uganda and Tanganyika** to build the railways and open up the fertile interior.

The tiny village or rather a gathering of a few dwellings with some acres of arable land that gave the scope of creating orchards of grape fruit, orange and lemon trees along with tiny vineyards that produced a small quantity of wine.

But it was a quality wine that was in great demand from top restaurants and super rich residents from the surrounding areas, mainly from **Malaga** and **Marbella**, the only notable towns, yet in infant stage of development, in those pioneering days when Spain was a dictatorship.

Tolox Montana Wine, fresh and crispy had an enviable reputation and a loyal client list who would pay a premium to acquire a year's supply of this life sustaining nectar that even God would envy and enjoy!

But the income, however small for most farmers was sufficient for the meagre needs of the residents. The lack of hectic life style personifies the village of Tolox in more ways than one would like to believe.

People were not money oriented and needs were so basic that it was practically impossible for any one to go hungry, in the land of the plenty where the philosophy was to share and share alike.

Human values, friendships, integrity and family ties were more important than material wealth or the fat bank balance. How the times have changed and certainly not for the better!

No wonder the older generation is lost in the maze of technology, jargons, lack of respect; devious money making scheme that drives them to despair! Then every event, advancement has a purpose and every setback has its lesson.

It was a daily routine for Kiran to stand here early in the morning, come hell or high water and watch the Sun rise from behind the mountain peak, dispersing the mist and spreading the sunlight, heating up every acre of land in its path.

The Sun especially graced Kiran's home or rather his wife's home, as he and his wife **Olivia** had inherited the estate from Olivia's father when he passed away some twenty years ago.

Naturally he left every material possession to his only off-spring, a lovely, kind and caring girl affectionately called Olivia, as her traditional Spanish name was too difficult to pronounce for Kiran, at least in the beginning. But every one knew her as Olivia, a sweet and popular name in Spain.

Olivia was the apple of her father's eyes. Olivia and her family gave Kiran a new lease of life when Kiran was down on luck and nearly out of his mind with a family tragedy that would have destroyed a lesser man.

No wonder his heart was heavy, filled with sorrow and silently shedding tears from within, trying to appear strong and resolute outwardly for the sake of his beloved Olivia who had given Kiran every imaginable happiness in their long and happy married life.

Kiran knew that he may never set foot in this village again, once they have moved out to be near their children and grand children.

Such a move would bring quantum improvement in their family life; self satisfaction and motivation levels that were getting stale without purpose, without aim or reason in their retired but comfortable life. It was time to make a move before it was too late, before the old age set-in in earnest.

The serenity and calm, peace and fulfilment in their life made them senile in a way that would make Kiran restless and eager for a change. His body may be feeling the ravage of the approaching old age but his mind was alert and as young as when he set foot on this beautiful ranch, farm or *"The Olive Grove"* the name this place was known as to the locals.

It was a beautiful piece of farmland on the outskirt of the village of *Tolox,* standing on the slopes of sierra range, the mountain slope, some what isolated but views, scenery that would heal any wounded heart.

Kiran focused his eyes on the rising sun, the spreading rays that caste long shadows which were diminishing by the minute, as the sun climbs out of the mountain cover, mountain shadows, gain height and like Lord Krishna, spread his wisdom, light, heat and comfort into the hearts and souls of his devotees down below, a majestic king, an emperor looking down on his subjects with love and affection!

No one could have given Kiran more love, affection and support than Olivia and her family who bestowed every kind of love and affection on Kiran, taking place of the son the family had lost in the *Spanish Civil War.*

Kiran was a precious, princely son in law for Olivia's father, a God send gift for the family in their hour of need. Indeed Kiran gave *Senor Martinez*, Olivia's father the reason to live, work and even prosper, as now he had a family and perhaps grandchildren to look forward to.

If there is heaven on earth, this is the place to be in, at least when Kiran first set foot in Tolox, a very long time ago that turned out to be a minor miracle, as Kiran had given up any hope of living a normal life, getting married, having children and be happy.

Kiran happily traded his exciting London life for the serenity of this place, a heaven in the making! God brutally shut down one door for Kiran but opened another at the right time. God indeed works in mysterious ways, beyond our understanding, our comprehension.

As we say, the justice in the court of God may be delayed but never denied! But then, justice has many faces, different meaning to different people. It would be difficult to pin down the meaning of the word justice.

The mountain air, the sunlight and heat sustained Kiran's Olive and Orange Grove and the tiny but well maintained and productive vineyard that gave them some what a comfortable living standard with money to spare for the good, charitable cause which normally means the Roman Catholic Church that looked after the needs of the village people.

In fact the church ruled the roost; the priest presided over his congregation like an Emperor over his subjects and settle minor disagreements in the family, the community and his words were final, respected by one and all.

The church was the centre of excellence in every way, morally, culturally, socially and physically as well. It would make sure that no one goes to bed hungry, sleep rough, without a roof over one's head or in need of medical attention. Most nuns were trained to provide First Aid, albeit for the basic ailments only but would arrange the transfer to a Medical Centre in case of emergency.

The simple village life means that there was not much distinction between simply surviving and really thriving. The inequality of city lives was less meaningful and more marginal in such places. Villagers were endowed with the capacity, the ability of making such differences unimportant, unwelcome and morally unacceptable. It was a commune living without giving it any name tag. It was certainly not a Kibbutz.

It was on such a charming morning that Kiran met Olivia, a twenty year old village beauty, an exquisite girl, a charming and sensual village lassie trying to come out of the shackles of her youth, her galloping hormone and her bulging body who literally took Kiran to her big and bulging bosom.

Kiran fell for Olivia, hook, line and sinker, as soon as he laid his eyes on her or rather on her voluptuous body and expanding chest line with olive colour skin, as smooth and delicious as virgin olive oil that can last a thousand fries! Then with Kiran's appetite, a thousand fries would not last that long!

But on the intellectual front, Kiran and Olivia were as different as chalk and cheese, as apart as the classical creation of Austrian master composer Wolfgang Amadeus Mozart and the American legend, one and only King of Rock Elvis Presley.

But that does not mean Mozart's music is more pleasant, more interesting, more elevating than Elvis Presley's.

It is just different and gives us a choice to play a different music on different social, religious and cultural occasions. Perhaps these opposite attractions were the mainstay of their success on the domestic and marriage front.

However once in bed, with the curtains drawn and the lights turned off, then the only thing that matters is the warmth of the voluptuous body laying next to him.

The darkness gives the opportunity to make the most of affection and the desire of one's partner, give and take as much out of their partner as they could, making every night a honeymoon night, at least during their first few months of their married life.

After all we are young and energetic but once in a life time. Blink too often and the opportunity is gone. Youth is like flowing water. It flows in one direction only, the downward flow. So one has to catch, drink the sweet and fresh water while we can!

Olivia had so much to offer, her full, voluptuous body with broad thighs, bulging chest and olive skin. Yet Kiran's unenviable, unexpurgated and untenable sexual desire so often drove Olivia to the brink of despair, albeit for a moment or two only, as she enjoyed this attention as much as Kiran did, perhaps a bit more.

Olivia never complained or tried to stop Kiran when in full flow. Then perhaps it would not have been easy or even possible to stop such a young, healthy and strong man when he is in his stride, a bull in a china shop, china being Olivia's bulging body.

There were more than enough signs of a bull ravaging the brittle china to make Olivia uncomfortable the next day when she had to wear long and covering garments to hide the previous night's excesses.

Lines were drawn early in their married life and each knew exactly what their limitations were and what was expected from either of them. There was a clear divide that kept the disagreement to a minimum. Then Olivia was such a kind, caring and soft person that she would give in even before their conversation turn into an argument.

Obviously these village girls were not in need of plastic surgery to make the most of their assets. God's blessing, clean and fresh mountain air and nutritious organic food was enough to develop these girls into desirable beauties in their own right.

They were voluptuous but not portly in any sense. They were mountain mermaids with a difference! They could swim in mountain air rather than in sea water and riding such a maid was a pleasure in the extreme.

Clouds were their chariots to roam the wilderness. Kiran had the pick of the bunch, perhaps more by chance than by choice, although Kiran firmly believed that life's decision should be based on choice rather than by chance. One should never be the prisoner of the past but an architect of the future! Every dawn is a new day to the one who is enlightened.

Unlike today, it was not necessary for girls to have paper thin figures to make the grade. Perhaps no one would have taken any notice of today's beauties like Kate Moss, Julia Roberts, Victoria Beckam, Naomi Campbell and their likes. They are a kebab without meat, a risotto without sea food.

Perhaps for Kiran it was sexual attraction at first. But he soon found out that it was much more than her attractive, even mouth watering body that was making Kiran fell head over heels for her, invigorating Kiran in her presence, like a knight sitting on King Arthur's Round Table. Yet the Round Table was not the main attraction.

Olivia's appreciation of Kiran was the fragrance that the roses shed on the hands that pick them up, crush them and turn them into perfume that delight so many hearts and souls. So often such a bottle of perfume given to a raging beauty is the beginning of the romance, ever lasting friendship and inevitable reunion at the altar!

In those bygone days when Britain, indeed European countries like France, Portugal, Spain, Germany, Netherlands and many more ruled the world, ruled the roost and their subjects, mainly in Asia, Africa and Latin America were considered some what inferior human beings. Liaison between a white girl and a coloured boy was a taboo not many would like or dare to breach.

Marrying a white girl, even though she may be much lower in etiquette and social standing was never the less considered to be a step in the right direction, climbing social ladder and attracting envious attention in our ultra conservative Indian community.

Then all the communities, even the British, European communities were conservative in one way or another! Such nonsense stopped lovely Princess Margaret marrying her sweetheart Peter Townsend, thus ruining two lives for ever.

But our youngsters who went to England for further education, advance studies and came back highly qualified with their white, young, beautiful and charming British brides were the girls they met at the college.

They were their fellow students and were of equal status, with high standing and blessed with affluence, beauty, charm and good manner in every respect.

These young brides were indeed a credit to their Christian culture, liberal tradition and social values that would surpass our Hindu ethos in some respects. The shibboleth of Western culture was well respected and admired by all.

The rot had not yet set in any way. Those were the romantic, pioneering days when love was real, sex was a tonic that would bound the married life. Freedom was like a loving house that one has to build brick by brick. There was no pot of gold that one can chase! It was worth remembering that armatures built the Ark, the professionals built the Titanic!

So often these girls would marry Indian boys against the wishes of their parents, perhaps being rebellious or just to prove that they were not living in medieval time, or out of ontological circumstances.

But most of these marriages were as happy as could be, even under most trying circumstances, as living with their Indian in-laws in an over-crowded home was not always easy, accommodating or fulfilling.

In a way Olivia was no match for Kiran who was well bred, highly educated, tall, slim and financially independent person with good manner, indeed a very desirable young man who would steal any girl's heart.

No wonder Olivia was smitten and was eager to please him in any way she can. Then Olivia had descended from heaven who literally saved Kiran's life without even realising that Kiran was in a precarious and fragile state who badly needed reassurances and comfort in the bosom of a kind and caring female company.

Although when Olivia walked down the village path, wearing a skimpy dress in the hot midday sun, her bulging body parts fighting hard to remain hidden under her inadequate attire, she would turn every young head with ease and often with envy and jealousy from her female friends.

For strangers, it would take some time to get used to such beauties. She was popularly known as **Senorita Olivia, una chicka muy Bonita y amable**, Miss Olivia is a beautiful, kind and caring girl.

Unfortunately there were hardly any young men in her class, in the same league that would raise her pulse, steal her heart or fulfil her ambition, no matter how limited those ambitions may be, let alone sweep Olivia off her feet.

Most eligible young men would leave the village for the nearby towns and coastal holiday resorts of Benalmedena, Fuengirola and Torremolinos which were developing fast.

These developments also provided jobs and a taste of life away from the tiny hamlets. The city lights were burning brighter than the twinkle of the stars or the cool light of the moon on the deserted horizon of tiny villages like Tolox.

In the beginning, some did return to find brides who would have a pick of the bunch, a choice but this tradition soon died down, as more and more boys picked their own partners from where they work and live.

In any case village girls also started to follow into the foot-steps of their male counterparts and would leave the village, either for further education or jobs in the fast expanding coastal belt of **Costa del Sol,** the sunny coast.

So Kiran was a God send gift. He was an early Christmas present for Olivia. Perhaps Kiran was the penultimate young man for Olivia who was running out of options.

She was by now losing hope of meeting some one of her stature in the village but was unwilling to lower her standard or expectation. She was not the type who would marry in haste and repent at leisure or leave her father alone in the village and move to the city, as he had already lost his only son, Olivia's brother, in some what tragic circumstances.

It was not difficult for Olivia to attract Kiran's attention, interest and raise his blood pressure by showering him with love, attention and taking care of his every need bar sexual ones.

But that does not mean Olivia would not tease Kiran in a way that would give him sleepless nights, dream of her body and soul and perhaps lose his self control which may not have offended Olivia in any way! In fact Olivia was getting frustrated at Kiran's self control, no matter how admirable it may be.

It would not be lady like for Olivia to take the first step, however shy Kiran may be. She can only tease and hope Kiran would lose his self control, come out of self imposed exile and lay down his soul at the feet of Olivia!

It was only a question of when and not if, as it would be impossible to keep apart two young and robust souls for long, either in the cool of the night when body comfort and heat is a God send gift or the steaming heat of the day, especially during the sizzling summer months when bare flesh was on display in abundance, especially under the cool shower after a hard day's work.

The scorching heat would practically make it impossible to work in the field or the vineyards, pruning and stalking the young vines without removing most of the cloths. The **Sombrero** or the large Mexican sun hat, hot pants and loose tops were the main attire for the working women.

Olivia looked so sexy in those attire, especially without under garments or the garments with holes and cuts at the most delicate places that would give Kiran the glimpse of her natural assets, her over bearing thighs right up to the junction and expanding breasts that he would like to kiss and massage till the cows come home! Perhaps Kiran was too naïve not to try!

But Kiran was too much of a gentleman to take advantage of her love for him, put her under any pressure, cross the Laxman Rekha, a line drawn by Laxman, Lord Rama's brother in order to protect Lady Sita, Lord Rama's wife whom Laxman loved and respected so much.

They were obliged to spend fourteen years in the jungle to fulfil the promise Rama's father gave to Kaikai, Lord Rama's step-mother.

She wanted her son Bharat to be the king instead of Lord Rama, the eldest son and heir apparent to the throne of Ayodhia, the capital city of King Dashrath's vast empire.

Still it was a restrictive, primitive and primordial social atmosphere, some what like a Dark Age in pre Second World War Europe, compared to our present day freedom on most fronts, including sexual front where youngsters first live together, have children and then get married, like an after thought?

The villagers who were mostly Roman Catholics had a strong code of conduct and sex before marriage, before tying a knot and making a life long commitment was a taboo no parent or priest would allow. There was no elitist nonsense or fascist cyber warriors to challenge the code of conduct laid down by the church, for the common good.

In a way priests who were held in high esteem, in fact as respected and elevated as prelates, had great influence whose advice was sought and taken into consideration on such family occasions, like birth of a child, marriage and the death, a tragedy in the family.

Priests were not merely religious Gurus but they were faith healers, counsellors, psychologists, marriage brokers and even financial advisers, although very few would possess such an abundance of wisdom to serve the community on all these fronts.

But as we say, one eyed Jack is the king in a kingdom where every one is blind; a single thorny bush is a beauty, greenery in a sea of sand! Olivia was used to this routine, Kiran getting up early to watch the sun rise from behind the mountain.

Kiran could not help but remember the famous words of Julius Caesar when he first stepped ashore, English shore and said, "*I stopped, I thought, I wrote, Vini, Vidi, Viki.*

Initially Kiran rented the cottage standing amongst the trees, a short distance from the bungalow for just one month. But he soon found out that this is the place that would sooth his bleeding heart; heal the deep wounds.

The place has the beauty that would conquer the beast, mend his broken spirit and tame the monster of hate, anger and rage that was tearing Kiran apart, destroying him from within.

This was the monster that circumstances, the nature or even the God heaped upon him without reason, without cause and certainly without any justification. So often life's greatest setbacks also revel life's biggest opportunities. But no opportunity was worth such a sacrifice.

Perhaps Olivia was such an opportunity. Waking up every morning with the voluptuous body of Olivia, smelling of roses, the touch, the friction with an olive smooth skin, spreading next to him with an open invitation would tempt any young man, create turmoil in any heart.

So why should Kiran be an exception! He had the same desire as any young and healthy person. He was no different than ordinary people. *Senor Kiran no es mas diferente que las gente normal.* Living in Spain for so long that Kiran was more at ease in Spanish than either in English or Gujarati, his mother tongue that he had nearly forgotten.

Today Kiran was not alone, standing on his favourite spot and looking at the rising sun. Olivia was standing next to him, holding him tightly with her hands firmly round his waist and looking at her husband, her hero, the man she loved so much, would die for him, her Prince Charming!

Although it was a clash of two cultures, both some what rigid in certain aspect, there was never an incident that would send any one up the gum-tree.

There was no hallucination, only the realm of reality, faith, trust and intense love that would conquer all, move a mountain and dam a river! Not every marriage is blessed with such serenity, such spirituality!

Kiran who was lost in thoughts, oblivious to the surroundings, suddenly grabbed Olivia, drew her close so that her breasts were pressing hard against his chest, gave her a long, lingering kiss that almost choked Olivia. But she did nothing to push Kiran away or disengage from his shackles.

It was like the first kiss they shared under an olive tree all those years ago but still as fresh in his mind as the rising sun appearing from behind the mountain peak.

Even at their age, they did enjoy making love, having sex and romantic liaison, albeit with restrain, purpose and gentleness. Kiran so often wondered why he was still so eager to kiss, cuddle and play with Olivia's breasts after some forty years of love making when this has been a daily routine for most of the time! Would he ever slow down and leave Olivia alone?

The wilderness of youth when they searched and exploited every inch of their bodies, even the most inaccessible private parts, without limit, without hesitation or any embarrassment that was the part of the youth mentality, the flower power, the hippy culture that was long confined to dustbin with the approaching age and the wisdom of limitation.

It was a past relic laid to rest with the changing nature and passage of time, like the flowing water that would not stand still for any one.

Yet who can say what today's' youngsters do behind closed doors when pornography is so easily available, even rules the roost in so many young and corrupted minds and hearts!

But passage of time does relieve the body of certain physical and sexual desire that may be unthinkable in our youthful days. The time does not stand still, either for a prince of a pauper. There is no fruit that would give immortality, a fairy tale we read so fondly in our youthful days. The age gives us good judgement and the good judgement comes from experience and experience comes from bad judgement! Is it a vicious circle!

Olivia, to her credit, had maintained her figure, her attractiveness and was as sexy as ever, with fuller body and even larger, over-bearing breasts that Kiran could not resist, even at his age and so often felt guilty about his excessive demands on Olivia. Then resisting Olivia was an exercise in frustration! A mind never loses its lustre on any front, especially on imagination front. Even the age can not dent it.

But he knew that for Olivia, he was Eros, the son of Aphrodite who in Greek mythology is the God of love. Eros is identified with the Roman

Cupid. Eros has the freedom on the love and an extension on the sexual front.

Olivia was a tough woman with a high threshold for pain, especially when the pain is as a result of love making. She would never stop Kiran from enjoying her body to the full, even bearing wounds, love bites with admirable restraint.

But these token of love would prevent Olivia from wearing revealing clothes that would show her misdemeanour and raise eyebrows in the village, even though by now they were married, living as husband and wife with a licence to do what they like on sexual front, albeit behind locked doors.

Perhaps Kiran would have gone much further than just kissing Olivia passionately as his hands were already searching, protruding on to her breasts. But the sound of the approaching vehicle alerted them. It was their taxi to take them to the Malaga airport.

* * *

Chapter Two
Reminiscing the Past

The ride from Tolox to the Malaga airport was short but captivating, especially the descent from the height of some four thousand feet to the coastal plain of Costa del Sol.

The Costas have now become a heaven on earth for holiday mad Britons who worship sea, sand and sangria, not forgetting the cheap and degrading sex on the beach but surprisingly they miss out on the beautiful, slim and culturally rich Spanish girls! Then there is no saying for taste!

As Spain is a strict Catholic country where religion still rules the roost, it has kept out the sick British and North European pederast tourists who flock Asian countries like Sri Lanka, Thailand and Philippines in search of innocent, young boys to satisfy their sordid sexual pleasure.

Perhaps shallow British cultures acquired recently would make the Brits second class citizens on all these cultural, religious, family values and good manner fronts. How the mighty have fallen!

There was a time when Britain, British people carried certain cachet, decorous, ruled the roost on all fronts, including decent and chivalrous behaviour so lacking in the present day generation.

In those days mountain slopes were covered with eucalyptus and pine forest, olive and orange groves as well as vineyards with breathtaking views, with narrow corridors, well trodden lanes that people use as a short cut from one farm to another. This was the coexistence between humans and nature at its best, a sustainable way of life in perfect harmony with Mother Earth.

It also provided a heaven to walkers and nature enthusiasts. The slow pace of life in these mountain villages personifies the old tradition, the old ways, the honourable ways that kept the society civilized.

Roads were narrow with twists and turns and to add to the joy, hazards and excitement of such a roller coaster ride. There were horse drawn carriages as well as donkeys laden with all sorts of agricultural produce blocking the road, not to mention occasional wild life crossing the road without regard to Zebra Crossing! But this was the cornerstone of life, daily existence, a charm in adversity!

Not a dull moment or a time to close your eyes. Kiran and Olivia wanted to enjoy the beauty, charm and excitement of their last taxi ride from their home to the airport.

After all they had sold their home with all the land to a developer who may turn it into a holiday complex, a theme park. But now it was not their concern. It was a decree absolute that gave them the freedom to move away, as far away as Australia, a world down under, a prehistoric land with such wild life not found any where else in the world. Perhaps their euphoria may not be justified. Only time will tell.

But no matter what, the inhibition of what would happen, how this beautiful part of Spain may be ravaged by developers will always linger on in their subconscious mind. After all no one can live in a place for more than forty years without forming some form of attachment to the place, the land and the people they may know.

It is but human nature. After all it is mother earth we are destroying in the name of progress but in reality it is the human greed. As Gandhiji said, the ***mother earth is able to provide all our needs but not our greed***.

The thoughtless and indiscriminate destruction of Amazon rain forest so essential for the well being of our eco system, atmospheric balance, to control the carbon dioxide is the prime example of human excesses that may one day make us all homeless on the beautiful Mother Earth that we may have destroyed in the name of progress and greed. The slow process of euthanasia has already begun. The only question is whether we would stop it before it reaches a point of no return.

The corrosion of culture, decent values and humanity had already set in. It was only a matter of time before Spain would enter the rat race that is already bleeding America, a land of plenty that is fast becoming industrial, cultural and financial desert.

Naturally Kiran and Olivia were both lost in their own thoughts, taking a dip in their own pool of wisdom, experience, the world of pleasant memories and heart breaking tragedies, occasions that nearly brought Kiran to the edge of precipitous.

It was time when life had no meaning, no purpose, no reason or attraction after he lost his entire family in a tragic accident, leaving him all alone, like a new born lamb that has just lost her mother to a pack of marauding wolves! Yet oblivious to the future that the All Mighty may have already charted for him! We may just be a prototype of God's will.

The flight from Malaga airport to *Madrid,* in an old *Falker Friendship* plane was short and uneventful. But in those pioneering days, no air travel was uneventful.

So often it was rough, tough and tumbling, especially in small aircrafts that could not climb higher than twenty thousand feet, thus unable to avoid air turbulence.

After a two hour wait, they *boarded BOAC Comet,* the most advance jet passenger plane in operation at the time. Yet the flight from Madrid to *Perth* in Western Australia was a long and tiring journey with several stops.

Although there were several flights from London to Australia, there was only one flight a month that would touch at Madrid, as not many Spanish people were moving to this vast and beautiful country, not too dissimilar to Spain, except in vastness and variety of climate zone, from tropical Northern Province with the main city of *Port Darwin* to *Tasmania*, as cool and frosty as Britain!

Travelling from Spain to Australia en masse was still in an infant stage, an enigma for most Spanish people who were not as entrepreneur as their British and American counterparts, at least not in recent time.

One may wonder how such a docile nation once ruled most of South America, at times rivalling the British Empire! Then all great nations had their ups and downs.

Bharat was once the centre of culture, learning, art and science. It was Bharat at its best, under Chandragupta and Ashok that spread Buddhism throughout Asia without firing a single shot in anger.

Egypt had her glory under Pharaohs Ikhnaton, Tutankhamen and Ramses II, Greece and Roman Empires during Sumerian and Aegean period and last but not least the once mighty British Empire!

Yet some of these once mighty nations are no more than relics of the past, fossilized into nonentities that beggars' beliefs, beleaguered at the bottom struggling to survive. Britain, Italy, Spain and Portugal are the prime examples of the once mighty nations that have fallen, reduced to a pitiful existence.

Being first class passengers with all mod cons available at the time, made their journey not only bearable but some what enjoyable as well. Air travel was much leisurely and pleasant at the time compared to present era that is more like cattle herding than a pleasant trip!

After all very few people could afford to travel by plane to Australia, let alone by first class especially when travelling a long distances that would cost an arm and a leg!

This was a luxury reserved for a few rich and privileged people. Blackpool and Skegness were the favourite holiday destinations for most Britons who could afford to take holidays, as paid holidays, annual leave was not yet invented.

Olivia and Kiran were treated like VIPS. Drinks, hot and cold, snacks and hot meals were served often, as well as drinks available on request. To their surprise, they were served some of the best Spanish wine on offer, mostly served in five star restaurants in Spanish cities like Madrid, Barcelona and Seville.

But for the majority, the basic passenger ships were the main mode of travel, especially from one continent to another, from Northern hemisphere to Southern hemisphere. The assisted passage for British migrants, from London to Australia with full board was available for just ten pound, a six to eight weeks sailing depending upon where one would disembark in Australia.

The most sought after destinations were Sydney, Melbourne and Perth, in the far flung corner of Western Province, still in the early stage of development but a stunningly beautiful city where Kiran and Olivia were flying, where their children have settle down and were building their future in the new world with more or less unlimited resources.

Australia has a huge land mass, mineral wealth with coal, iron ore, gold and perhaps diamonds as well. It is a dream land, a heaven in the making. Yet practically empty, desolate and waiting to be explored if not exploited.

After an hour or so, chatting with Olivia, who in any case was not a repartee at witty conversation, Kiran was out of topic for prolonging the conversation. After all he was married to Olivia for nearly forty years and there was no dissimulation of any kind between them.

She was a woman of few words but plenty of action on all fronts and that is how Kiran preferred her. Perhaps that was her main charm, beauty and attraction! After all who would like to have a cool and docile woman when he could have a beautiful, charming, mischievous and sexy Menka sleeping next to him! Olivia was Kiran's Menka when he first laid his eyes on her.

Going back to his slumber, the old memories that Kiran had managed to suppress were flooding back, no matter how hard he tried to divert his mind. Perhaps this upheaval of moving from Spain to Perth in Australia was too much to take in at this time in their lives. But then it was now or never, as they were not getting any younger.

Kiran was going back in memories to his Indian roots, his culturally rich and accommodating Hindu religion that in fact had never left him, although going or rather accompanying Olivia and her family to Church was a routing he had observed since he got married to Olivia. It was out of necessity rather than change of beliefs. Then most Hindus believe that there is only one God we call *Ishvar* but there are many paths that lead to the ***All Mighty!***

It was a happy time and Kiran embraced every moment of his time in Tolox, a blessed land with charming atmosphere, kind and accommodating people, with Olivia and their two children.

It was like watching the stars dancing in a moonlit sky, a magical slumber after a hard day's work, an honest work in a field, a grove, a field, the land that gives us our daily bread!

There was no temple nearby for Kiran to visit. In any case a Hindu would not hesitate to say hallelujah to any God, to Lord Jesus Christ who many Hindus would consider the reincarnation of Lord Rama!

Yet like all Hindus, Kiran had created a small temple in his home with the images of Lord Krishna, Lord Rama and Lord Shiva or rather his ***Shivelinga,*** an oval stone that represent the all inclusiveness of abstract divine source, the earth being part of universe, the ultimate creation of the All Mighty.

Shivelinga is the symbol of omnipresence of God. Many believe that Hinduism is the ultimate omniscience of religion, being the oldest religion and all new religions have their roots in Hinduism. Most Hindus believe in living an austere but fulfilling life of prominence and privileges under their rich cultural heritage.

Even Olivia and their two children would often join him in saying prayers, although it would be too much to expect them to understand the intricacies of our complicated Hindu religion.

But they took every thing in our stride, especially on the cultural and religious front. The daily, early morning prayers after a hot shower, in front of the tiny temple, gave Kiran the sense of inner harmony and prayers watered the lush garden in his fertile and active mind!

Like most Hindus, religion was not an issue for Kiran and never will be. Hindus can assimilate with any culture, tradition and like a honey mixed with milk; it produces a mouth watering drink of cultural mix that enriches every life, the nectar fit for a king or even The Lord!

This is in sharp contrast to some other culture and religions which are indigestible under any circumstances except with total surrender, a humiliating give in, all in the name of love for one particular God! Some times, such a God may only exist in one's imagination.

Kiran's father was a doctor, in fact a heart surgeon while his mother was a Principal, what we would call a "Head Teacher" of a girl's school in the beautiful town of ***Mombassa***, gateway to ***Kenya and Uganda,*** the British colonies.

Mombassa is one of the most beautiful seaside towns, an important port on the African continent, with miles after miles of sandy beaches with pure white sand and crystal clear, blue waters of the Indian Ocean on our doorstep.

After Madrid, the first stop for refuelling and restocking the kitchen with exotic food stuffs was Cairo, the centre for Islamic studies and Middle East melting point, the gateway to the mighty desert of ***Sahara*** and beyond.

It was a two hour stop. So passengers were only allowed to roam the airport lounge, reserved for BOAC passengers, as the sun was still shining, rising on the British Empire, the greatest conquest in human endurance and ambition, surpassing even the Roman Empire by a mile.

There was not much to do at the airport except visiting a collection of heterogeneous, Sumerian artwork, some taken from the tombs of the ancient Egyptian kings, pyramids and the temples of Abu Simbel. The break gave Kiran and Olivia an opportunity to exercise their legs, take a walk and relax in the open air.

Although there was mouth watering food on the menu, in the lounge restaurant, Kiran and Olivia had no appetite, as food and drinks on the plane were more than sufficient to satisfy every one's need, taste and variety. No wonder Kiran and Olivia were back on the aircraft well before allocated time, as it was much cooler and relaxing on the aircraft than in the airport lounge.

* * *

Chapter Three

The Success on Educational Front

The next stop, one of the main stops was Bombay where they landed just before midnight. It was a one night stop, to let them recharge their batteries. They were taken to a four star hotel for the night, to have a good night sleep, a shower and a cooked English breakfast in the morning before boarding the plane at midday, a postmeridian flight.

It was a God send break, very much appreciated by all the passengers. It stopped the rupture of their core with a good night's sleep and hefty if not healthy breakfast.

No matter how good the food may be on the plane, it can never compete with the fresh food cooked on a traditional cooker, the oven and served in a vast dinning room in four or five star restaurants, with smartly dressed and polite ***camareros,*** (waiters) attending to one's every need. It was like living a life of rally!

It was difficult for Kiran to go to sleep, as it was a long, moral sapping and extremely tiring day. The night was hot and humid, the mind and the body abstracted, in suspended anti-animation in an enchanting fantasyland.

There was air-condition, but it did not suit Olivia's otherwise delicate framework! She preferred a ceiling fan instead. But a fan can only give a marginal relief. It can only circulate the hot and humid air, not cool it or change its texture! Moreover it made a cracking noise that irritated Kiran at first but it became rhythmic and resplendent to his mind and soul as the night progressed.

While Olivia was fast a sleep, Kiran was wide awake. Olivia was in magical slumber after a long and weary day. Then Olivia never had any problem with sleep. She would enter a dream like colony as soon as her head hits the soft pillow! Could it be her charming, innocent and carefree nature that had such a repertoire with the Goddess of sleep?

Perhaps Olivia's naked body, as voluptuous and sexually luring as ever, especially in the heat of the night, was making Kiran nervous, in case he may want her, disturb her sleep, a well earned rest Olivia thoroughly deserved, a sapient lady in the nicest manner.

Then Kiran live in an oasis of enlightenment and the sun would always dance on his colourful horizon, on his fantasyland. Kiran did not believe; give credence to Eastern, Hindu or Buddhist morality that sex after certain age is morally wrong and physically a taboo, against social conventions.

In a way our body is like a fertile garden and for it to flourish, one has to nurture it daily. In the words of Benjamin Disraeli, the secret of success, longevity is constancy of purpose!

Even at their age, Kiran and Olivia had kept their routine of giving a hug before going to sleep and Olivia had a body full of sexual amenities that would go to waste if not utilized.

So often a hug may lead to a passionate kiss, a romantic liaison. It is a common knowledge, a medical fact that sex at any age is a quantum improvement in one's satisfaction and motivation level, a distinction between simply surviving and really thriving!

But one has to act one's age in sexual encounter, as in any field. After all most sportsmen and sportswomen retire by the time they are forty, some even in their early twenties, like swimmers.

But sexual masochism and masquerading was long put on ice by Olivia and Kiran. In any case tonight was not the night, ***perhaps not tonight Josephine, as Napoleon Bonaparte would say?***

Naturally Kiran's mind drifted in the past, taking up from where he left while on the plane. Kiran and his younger sister Kalpna, a beautiful Hindu name when loosely translated means imagination, desire or even a sweet dream, were born in the coastal city of Mombassa.

Gujarati is a culturally rich language where most words have double, even treble meaning, can be translated in many ways, depending on the sentence, circumstances and of course one's own imagination where even the sky is not the limit!

Kiran's parents were from the province of Gujarat, on the Western coast of India, one of the most prosperous parts of Bharat with adventurous, ambitious and educated people. Many have migrated to Africa, Europe and America. In fact a Gujarati can be found in any corner of the world.

Kiran distinctly remembers his last main holiday when they went to Canada, flew to the beautiful and culturally rich city of Vancouver, a starting point for a cruse to Alaska.

One of the stop, port of call was Anchorage. When Kiran visited a nearby village, a place called Palmer if Kiran remembers it rightly; he was introduced to the local Mayor by the name of Pravin Patel, a fellow Kenyan, a Gujarati from the same part of Gujarat as Kiran's parents!

Indeed Gujaratis are an accomplished community who could even make the desert bloom? Gujaratis are the adherent supporters of enterprise and capitalism with rare acumen!

Gujaratis are averse to abstention when it comes to gathering wealth, climbing social ladder and educating their children.

As in common with most Hindu families, Kiran's parents valued education very highly. Naturally his father wanted Kiran, his only son to follow in his foot-steps and become a surgeon, especially a heart surgeon.

It was understandable, as heart disease, heart attacks were so common among the Indian community, even in those days but due to lack of knowledge and treatment, most heart attacks went unnoticed, unrecorded, thus did not appear prominent on the medical chart or the statistics.

In that way Kiran can not only earn a good living but also provide a good service to the close knit community, as his father did, working one day a week free, in an Indian Community hospital, run by the community, a charitable trust, looking after the most venerable people, charging a small fee, a fraction of the cost one may incur in a private hospital.

Although the cost of living was low, the earning, the pay was even lower and hardly any one had a saving, not even a bank account. It was literally a hand to mouth existence for most people. But it was stress free, without worries or complications.

Only a few super rich, mostly businessmen who could save and afford a private treatment that so often required a visit abroad, to India or to the capital city of Nairobi that could provide most treatment, so often in private hospitals run by a religious order, free to the faithful, albeit with a large donation!

The rest were obliged to pay the commercial rate. But at least the treatment was available on the door-step, saving a fortune in travel cost. London was out of bound for every one, including the super rich. It was the age of austerity in more ways than just financial.

Kiran was the odd one out in his family. His sister Kalpna wanted to follow into her mother's foot-steps and become a teacher, teaching science subjects like biology and chemistry.

But she was much more ambitious than her mother, as she wanted to do her Masters degree and then PhD, if the circumstances were right, if there was no pressure from her family to get married by certain age that was the norm at the time.

Kiran's ambitions were more in line with his Hindu community. He was more business minded than his family. He was told that his great, great grand father was the head of the treasury, a financial adviser to the Princely State of Nava Nagar.

At the time Gujarat was divided, indeed fragmented into so many tiny states, some no more than a tiny principality with few villages and a population of less than one hundred thousand people.

So when Kiran told his parents that he would like to qualify as a Charted Accountant, they were neither surprised, disappointed nor agape, as they knew how good Kiran was at maths, economics and English language. Science was never his strong subject. In any case this was not an aberrant ambition in any manner or expectation. Kiran was an aerobatics performer on the educational front! Success in any field is more or less guaranteed.

They also knew that as a Charted Accountant, Kiran could earn a good living, have affluent life-style, almost as good as a doctor and could look after his family financially.

This is the dream, ambition and aim of most parents, that is what they want from their off-springs, financially secured, morally upright and happily married!

Success is about sense of independence, not the conquest. It is not about seeing the world but seeing the light, able to distinguish between right and wrong, being helpful and creating hindrance. Success is not about ability to create definitive dogmatic and rigid state but it is about unfolding the thought of process of dialogue and continuum.

But as a Charted Accountant, Kiran could never be as affable, could leave afterglow as a doctor who enjoys a God like stature in our Indian community. But Kiran would never trade the riches of his soul, the virtues of honesty for a fat, overflowing bank balance, a beach house facing the mighty Indian Ocean, only a few feet away from the golden sands and frothing, murmuring waters that has thousand tales to tell.

Even in such a demanding, manipulate profession; Kiran would never alienate any one. It was not in his nature, in the family tradition. He was a naturally born psychologist, an angle of delight, not Turkish but Indian delight!

Kiran's parents were glad that at least Kiran was not studying agronomy, not that agronomy is in any way a less important than any other study, achievement or profession.

But deep inside Kiran could sense that his father was a bit disappointed, as he knew how clever Kiran was, that he could be any thing, study any subject, even rocket science and come out on top.

But to his credit, he was willing to back Kiran, send him to London and let him study what he would prefer, where he would feel at ease.

He knew that Kiran would chart his future with the care and accuracy of aeronautics. The education that gives eternal happiness is more important than any other success, on any front, although it was difficult for a doctor to understand how dealing with figure work all day could be interesting or soothing to the soul!

This kindness, understanding and full support from his family without question made Kiran even more determined to succeed and make his parents proud of his achievement.

So when it came to choosing subjects for his HSC (Higher School Certificate) the present equivalent to "A" level, Kiran chose four subjects rather than three which was the norm, the requirement but much harder and more intensive than A levels.

Kiran's chosen subjects were maths, higher maths, economics and English. These were the more difficult subjects but Kiran obtained distinction in all subjects, a school record, as no one had obtained such good marks, distinction in Economics and English language, as after all English is a foreign language for most Indians. This achievement made his parents proud and even more supportive in whatever Kiran would like to study.

Kiran carefully laid his plans; explained his ambition at a traditional family meeting that was the norm when it came to making an important decision.

Kiran's parents would always take into consideration their children's point of views and so often would act accordingly, a joint decision for the good of all. In that way children learnt to stand on their own feet, responsible for their action, success or a failure of their own making! Of course their parents were always there for advice and support, as Kiran and Kalpna were after all children who needed a guiding hand now and then.

They always tell Kiran and Kalpna that they should never compare themselves with any one, not even their parents, as every one is an individual person with a gift, ability in one particular field, may it be sport, music, science or art.

If they do compare, then they are insulting, under-estimating themselves, their own ability to succeed. It is like when you start judging people, then they will have no time to judge themselves or love them!

It is like imposing their wrapped politically correct views on others. We all know what that would mean or where it would lead, take us. The mind is a wonderful servant but a terrible master! So beware the **Ides of March!**

Kiran wanted to go to Oxford before doing articles for accountancy, studying maths and economics that would give him exemption from most exams bar the final ones. But it was not an idée fixe, just an inspiration.

In that way Kiran could become a Charted Account within a year or two, having a pick of the best firms, internationally renowned firms to do his articles. This would guarantee his future, earning even more than a doctor!

In those days, one has to pay a premium to enrol in a good firm to do the training. But not if one has a degree from one of the prestigious universities, like London School of Economics, Oxford and Cambridge, the peak of the bunch for further studies.

Unlike today, there were very few firms of Charted Accountants that were allowed to take students to be trained as Charted Accountants. That was one of the reasons for paying a premium.

Even though Kiran's parents were able to pay for his studies, the community awarded Kiran a scholarship, in recognition of his father's charity work and Kiran's brilliant exam results. That would cover most, if not all of his study cost.

Kiran sailed through his degree course with flying colours and even completed, passed his few exams in a record time, to become Charted Accountant, as these prestigious firms gave their students all the help they may need, study leave and paid for their expensive revision course as well.

In any case Kiran was good at modulating, change the flow, the perception when the circumstances demand. He would see the world, not as it is, but as he would like it to be. After all any Tom, Dick and Harry could live a normal, aimless life but to be Gandhi or Mandela, one has to be special, follow the wonderful Mantra of success and self belief, even under most difficult circumstances.

Then our religion, our culture is blessed with such mantras, gurus and beliefs. That is the reason why Hindu culture gave the world prominent personalities like Lord Rama, Lord Krishna, Lord Buddha, Mahavir, Guru Nanak, Ashok, Chanakiya, Gandhi, Shivaji, Tagore and hundreds, if not thousands more noble men and women.

Bharat was the Bastian of civilization and human excellence long before Christianity became the prominent religion and Lord Jesus Christ one of the noblest son to grace Mother Earth.

No wonder these accountancy firms had 100% success rate, as they chose their intakes with diligent, examining, scrutinizing their background and family tradition. This was indeed an elitist profession, a close door for most but a privileged few. It was as difficult as gaining a place at Oxbridge.

If some one becomes an articled clerk, a trainee, it would normally take five years to pass all the exams and complete the training. But for a university graduate, especially from Oxbridge, it would take no more than two years, with intense training and exams every six months.

The day Kiran was admitted to the Association of Charted Accountants as a fully qualified account, with a practicing certificate, was the happiest day in his life. His life mission, at least on the educational front was accomplished, his dream became a reality. The lush garden of his mind has at last blossomed; the orchard was full of trees laden with fruits. What more a young man want?

Now it was time to go home on a long, relaxing holiday, spend few days relaxing on the golden sands of Milindini beach, with pure white sands, clear blue, shallow, warm waters that one could trod on, drink water from green, fresh coconuts which was Kiran's favourite drink but did not have a sip for some six years.

It was time to meet his parents and hug his baby sister Kalpna whom he missed most, as they were very close. She must have grown into a beautiful and charming young lady. How his heart would fill with pride and joy when he takes his sister in his strong arms and not let her go!

* * *

Chapter Four

The Shattering News

Kiran knew that as soon as he goes home, his parents would press him to choose a girl and get married. That is the ambition of every parent to see their children get married at the right time, at the right age and in all the right circumstances. One could never marry in haste, as it would lead to repent at leisure.

Kiran was not averse to getting married or had a dyed-in-the-wool attitude towards local girls, especially as he would have the pick of the bunch of the desirable girls. There was no shortage of good, well educated and beautiful girls in his community that was in the forefront when it came to providing life partners, as the community was united, prosperous, progressive and well educated and blessed with beauty, wealth, light skin and a kind of superiority bordering arrogance.

This kind of attitude, mentality and superiority complex would not be tolerated in this day and age. But it was the norm then in every community, every culture and religion. It was part of the culture, establishing roots and not to be under the shadow of an ovate community, equally progressive and prosperous communities.

They had already chosen few girls for Kiran to meet, get acquainted and make the final choice, take the ultimate decision which would be his decision and no one would put any pressure on Kiran, at least not his family, although a girl's family may indirectly try to influence him if they feel he is a good catch for their daughter. But that is understandable, a normal concern for a girl's parents in any culture, tradition or religion.

This was the tradition then and even today not much have changed, except parents would not hesitate to look beyond their own community for a good partner for their son or a daughter.

However the present generation do not need such a helping hand from either their parents or the community. Internet is a great help if every other avenue fails. Indeed internet is the first avenue for many youngsters, as it is like a love marriage, a self made match, marriage made in haven or rather a computer, to be a spoil sport!

The two girls Kiran was interested, was friendly with before he went to England were petit Rekha and dynamic Divya. Kiran had known both girls since childhood. In fact they were in the same school but being a few years younger than Kiran, were in the lower class, along with his sister Kalpna.

Kiran particularly fancied Divya, as she was one of the most beautiful girls in their school. She was tall with shoulder length brown hair, always left loose, floating in the air.

She was mischievous, a hobgoblin with inquisitive nature, gnomic in conversation, pale smooth skin, like their female ***English teacher Anna*** who used to teach English language and literature. Divya was full of self confidence, indeed not an iota of self doubt or pessimism in her beautiful, fast developing body and mind!

Now looking back, Kiran realised that perhaps Divya was not too dissimilar to Olivia, except that Olivia had much fuller body with curves in all the right places, while Divya was much slimmer, a bit taller and being young, was still developing her natural assets. She was indeed blossoming in front of his eyes!

While Olivia was very much sexier with kind and of submissive nature, Divya was perhaps more intellectual, clever, mischievous and a perfect match for Kiran, practically on every front.

Moreover, like Kiran, Divya would climb the ladder, be on the podium, on educational, social and marital front. She was as ambitious as Kiran. The two working in harmony could have conquered the hearts and minds of the community with ease and affluence. They would be a perfect couple on every front, in any situation.

The arrival of English teacher Anna gave Divya a moral boost, made her realise that a girl can be as successful as a boy on educational and profession level. The elitist nonsense of some male teachers was confined to dustbin. They were no more than fascist cyber warriors.

Kiran distinctly remembers that many boys used to choose English literature as their **GCSE or HSC** subject so that they could be in Anna's class. At their age, it was not unusual to have a fixation, obsessive interest in their female teachers, especially an English teacher, who in colonial era enjoyed a semi God like status amongst Asian population.

Kiran used to tease Divya, calling her his Anna. It was the compliment Divya enjoyed and appreciated most. In fact any girl would enjoy such a compliment, as Anna had a Goddess like stature among the students.

Anna was the favourite teacher for all, boys and girls alike. But such complements Kiran could only dispatch when they were alone, in his home, when Divya would visit his sister Kalpna, who were best friends. No wonder Divya would look after Kalpna as if she was her younger sister!

Even at that young and innocent age, Kiran knew how to praise a girl, raise her ego, boost her self esteem, pay compliments to girls he liked and Divya was one of his favourite and she knew it. Perhaps he was a born flatterer, a Romeo, a philanderer in the making.

Then Divya was not exactly shy. She would tease Kiran that he fancies Anna that he is in love with her to which Kiran would retort in his witty manner that he is in love with one girl, his dream girl and her name begins with D and not A and one day, he would marry her! Even for Divya, this was a bit too much! She would retreat feeling happy and elevated.

These were innocent, happy and loving relationship that they had, they enjoyed and would treasure until their dying days. It was an innocent philandering at its best. Yet a scintillating experience never the less, for Kiran and especially for Divya. They were in a way grown up **Milky Bar Kids** of their time, era and generation!

In turn Kalpna would tease Kiran, that he liked Divya, he is in love with her, but only when they were alone. Kalpna had a wicked sense of humour in the Wellspring of youthfulness. After all she was Kiran's sister, two peas from the same pod.

Kiran was perhaps a Supremist, may be due to the family's standing in the community, a leading light, proud member of this small but prosperous community. Kiran used to tell her sister that one should not marry with some one they can live with, but should marry some one they can not live without.

Was Divya such a girl who would fit the bill?

As in any situation, any field, a good judgement comes with experience and experience comes from a bad judgement. But in selecting a life partner, one can not afford to make a mistake, as one only gets one chance, one opportunity and have to live with the mistake for the rest of their life.

There were no divorces or separation except due to death. Losing a life partner in child birth was one of the most common causes for a young and healthy woman to lose her life.

So in a way, Divya was one girl Kiran can not live without. Even when he was in England studying, Divya was always on his mind. So often Divya and Kalpna, both the girls would gang up on Kiran, to get the better of him.

Four hands made light work of Kiran's resistance. It was an exercise in frustration for Kiran. No wonder some times they even succeed when Kiran would give up and take them out for a drink, a bottle of coca-cola, a favourite drink in the hot sun when the temperature would touch 45*C.

How sweet and satisfying these drinks were! Then any thing in moderation will always preserve its status, be object of one's desire, the nectar of life.

The use of the word love in that context was, more or less a taboo. But then Kiran and Kalpna were very close and like twins, they can read each other's mind, thoughts and even desire!

So Kalpna was not wrong, as Kiran indeed fancied Divya and one day would be happy to marry her, his childhood sweet heart, perhaps without realising it!

But today Kiran was hearing Divya's raspy, honey smooth voice while he was drifting between sleep and wide awareness, sadness and sorrow, regrets and guilt but rigmarole in view of what followed; success and happiness on the ranch, in Olivia's bosom who gave him a wonderful family his parents would be proud of.

In a way Kalpna would love to have Divya as her Bhabhi, an elder brother's wife, a sister in law, although they were very young and the marriage was on the distant horizon, a mountain too far. It was definitely a silver lining on the distant cloud.

But then there is no harm in dreaming, building castles in air if not in sand. We all have dreams from time to time that keep the wheels of life on track, in harmony and perpetual happiness. After all dreams are dreams, not realities, even if they may be day dreams!

This liberal atmosphere in their household was the influence of their parents who believed in giving them all the freedom they deserve. They can bring all their friends to their home, boys and girls but always in a group, a boy and a girl can never be alone in a home or a in a confined space.

31

That was the unwritten rule, the tradition all would observe and respect without any one telling them what to do or how to behave. It was the influence of the social atmosphere of the time. It may sound oppressive today but it was the norm that installed discipline in young minds.

This innocent liaison between boys and girls was more fulfilling, more exciting than today's freedom of sleeping around with Tom, Dick and Harry and yet chasing that elusive pot of gold on the sexual front.

Kiran's parents were well ahead of time in every sense. After all their marriage was a love marriage. They met on a ship while going to Bombay for further education. It was the normal, the only mode of transport for East African students going to India for further studies.

Such ship romances were not that uncommon, as for most students, this was the first taste of freedom, liberty and independence. Those who had made this journey before, having visited their parents during holidays, college breaks, were expert at taking advantage of girls who may be on their first, the maiden voyage and feeling some what lonely and lost without their friends and family members nearby. It was time to discover DNA of self-enlightenment.

It was the first opportunity of living with unbridled exhilaration after a long period of self-confinement. The ship romance was some what like the Second World War romance between American boy soldiers and young English Roses who fell hook, line and sinker with the charm, deep pocket and cock-a-hoop attitude of these some what loutish soldiers, many with Jekyll and Hyde personalities who had never set foot outside their home towns, let alone cross the mighty Atlantic Ocean and land in Europe.

It was indeed a strange and fascinating love story, as Kiran's father chose to study medicine while his mother did BSc in science, and a master's degree, MSc in biology and chemistry.

They were in different Universities but not too far away, as in those days, even in Bombay, there were very few establishments for higher education. Most would be satisfied if they reach, pass standard twelve, the hall mark of achievement, especially for girls.

After going out for nearly seven years, they finally got married. The match was indeed made in haven, the marriage that would last till death do them part. Indeed even the death, when it came could not separate them.

They were cremated together and their ashes scattered in the winds on the slopes of Mount Abu, their favourite place where they enjoyed their honeymoon and the last holiday, the final resting place for three wonderful people Kiran loved, cared and would have willingly died for.

Kiran was making an arrangement to go home, after a long and some times a painful separation. But the reunion would be a big celebration, an all out party and a wonderful event to follow that is if Kiran could get married to Divya who he understood has turned into a very beautiful, sophisticated young and desirable woman, at least according to his sister Kalpna who was still dreaming of having Divya as her Bhabhi.

While Kiran was busy giving a final touch to his plans, his parents and sister were on a short holiday in India, to go to Mount Abu, visit the world renowned Jain temples, the most beautiful temples any where in the world.

The temples are situated high up Mount Abu with breath taking scenery to match the beauty of the marble temples, carved out of big slabs with love, care and unique craftsmanship, intricate design that took more than thirty years to build. This was the tribute to the symphony of nature, to explore the realm of extraordinary.

Each pillar took more than two years to build, to carve, with up to ten stone masons working twelve hours a day. These temples would put even the much hyped up Taj Mahal in shade!

The road journey from Mount Abu Railway Station, at the foot of the mountain to the top is in it self an unforgettable experience.

The road building was a marvel feat of engineering, the road turning and twisting all the way after a few miles from the station, with ever changing views, scenery, deep gorges, valleys and waterfalls that make the journey excitable but dangerous as well.

Road accidents were common. It would take only a one unguarded moment to go off the road, end up in a deep valley or a fast flowing stream, a disaster of unimaginable proportion. The wild life, especially deer, foxes and occasional pack of semi wild dogs added to the hazards.

No one can imagine that such a tragedy could strike them. It is always for those who are not careful, even reckless for their own good. We are too careful, too sensible to take such risks, to be victims of such a tragedy!

But such belief, self assurance is of no consequence when travelling on such a dangerous road, so often a bottleneck with every sort of transport using the road, even pilgrims on foot.

Kiran's parents were as responsible, as sensible as one could be. They had even hired a four wheel drive vehicle with an experienced Nepalese driver who had ploughed these roads for more than twenty years without a single mishap.

After all roads are even more dangerous, hair-raising and at greater height in his native country, the most beautiful nation on earth, the Himalayan kingdom of Nepal, with the tallest mountain in the world, mount Everest lurking in the background.

But when the time is up, nothing, no body can help, save us from the impending disaster. Their vehicle, a converted army jeep went off the road, on a rainy day and ploughed some five hundred feet into a ravine, instantly killing all four people, Kiran's whole family wiped out in an instant, along with the Nepalese driver who never had an accident?

When Kiran got the news, he was struck numb, find it difficult to take this tragedy in, still believing that it must be a mistake, that his family is well and alive. All Kiran's friends and colleagues were equally shocked, stunned, tried desperately to consol Kiran. But how could any one help.

There are no words to express in such a sorrow. It was beyond Kiran's endurance, any one's endurance. It is difficult to believe that God is capable of inflecting such a pain on any human being, let alone on Kiran, who had not set a foot wrong, harm any one in any way. Kiran even considered whether the life was worth living, have any meaning. Could it not be easy, a way out if he join his family in heaven.

But first, it was his duty, his obligation to give his parents and baby sister a fond farewell, cremate them and disperse their ashes from the highest point on Mount Abu, let them float in the wind, let the wind carry the ashes as far and as wide as possible and come down on the mountain slopes, the forest and the beautiful lake, the Sunset Point where tourists gather at sunset, to see the red, hot globe sink in the distance.

Let the ashes drop on their final resting place, the place they loved and visited as often as they could. As an eldest son, it was his solemn duty and expectation to perform these last rites, no matter how painful it may be.

How Kiran managed to retain his sanity and gave his family the last rights is the question Kiran has been asking ever since. But some questions will always remain questions, no matter how long one may live. Perhaps we are better off not knowing the answers.

* * *

Chapter Five
Performing the Last Rites

Kiran was fortunate that his best friend Ramesh, a fellow student whom he only met when he joined the firm stood by him throughout the ordeal, as like Kiran, he also had completed his studies and obtained the membership of the association.

He was at a lose end, not sure whether to go home or settle down in London and make it his home, follow in the foot-steps of so many East African students who were not willing to go home permanently, as the political situation was changing fast, with independence looming on the horizon. They were not sure whether they can fit in the new environment, live peacefully in the changing environment of Africanization.

Kiran and Ramesh took the first flight to Bombay, travelling by as direct a route as possible. Yet it took them four days to reach Mount Abu, cremate the bodies in front of just ten people. If it had happened in Mombassa, hundreds, if not thousands would have attended this funeral.

In a way this was a more appropriate goodbye, a personal farewell. Kiran was too tired, too emotionally drained even to shed a single tear. His body was numb with pain, torture and mental, as well as physical fatigue and the inner upheaval that no one could explain or understand.

After performing the last rites, Kiran flew to Mombassa while his friend returned to London, still in a dilemma what to do next. It took Kiran three months to wound up his parents' estate.

Kiran's uncle, his father's eldest brother and his wife were there to give Kiran every support he may need. But they themselves were elderly and in poor health. Moreover two brothers were very close, like twins, even though they were as different as chalk and cheese, day and night, sun and moon, gainsay all but in blood relations.

While Kiran's parents were on top of the educational ladder, his uncle was not even a graduate. Then they were brought up in different circumstances, different environment. In a close knit family, the eldest son has to make all the sacrifices in order to let the younger one to realise his potential. It was the dream of the family that their youngest son become a doctor who could be an asset to the whole joint family.

Moreover Kiran's uncle had no children. So in reality Kiran and Kalpna were like their own children, their family.

In a way they were fiduciary to these lovely and caring children, Kiran and Kalpna. In return Kiran and Kalpna were brought up to respect their uncle and aunt more than even their own parents.

Such was the respect accorded to the family elders, especially to those who have made sacrifices for the family. So Kiran's uncle was as much shocked, affected and down hearted as Kiran, if not more. At their age, there was no time for wounds to heal, to lay to rest the painful memories. When some one, especially of older generation loses the will to live, then the end comes more swiftly than expected under normal circumstances. It is a medical fact and not a fiddle-faddle as some would like to believe.

By the time Kiran had dealt with his parent's estate, sold their family home, cashed various insurance policies along with provident funds, as both his parents were in high flying jobs, at the top of their profession, Kiran was indeed a young, rich person.

Yet, money had no meaning. Kiran felt he had collected a bounty. It was a blood money that would only bring misery, not happiness in his life. Kiran would have willingly donated every penny just to have one week with his family, to see a smile on his sister Kalpna's face. His heart was riddled with guilt, as if he was some how responsible for this tragedy.

Kiran asked this question a million times. Why did he go to London? Was it more important than staying with his family in Mombassa or even going to Bombay where his sister went for further studies? If he had gone to Bombay, then he would have been in that car with the rest of the family. There were million and one questions but not a single answer. His mind, his thoughts were getting gnarled day by day.

Kiran's uncle wanted him to stay in Mombassa where his friends and remaining members of his family were. But every street, every house, every corner, every person he met reminded him of his past, his parents, his sister, what he had, what he could have, what he lost.

Even Divya, who was back in Mombassa, after gaining a Master's degree in commerce and business administration, who was by now even more beautiful, charming, sexy and desirable woman but even she could not persuade Kiran to stay.

Kiran had a perfect reason to return to London, as he had to give one more year to his firm who had given him all the support to qualify as a Chartered Accountant.

So after some three months, Kiran was back on his desk, struggling to settle down in his daily routine, to be back in the grove. After struggling for four months, Kiran and his immediate Bose realised that it was impossible for Kiran to concentrate.

It was not fair on Kiran, the firm or the clients, as his work had detracted due to lack of concentration, interest or effort. In the end Kiran had a long chat, heart to heart talk with the Senior Partners, offering to buy the remaining period of his contract, to compensate the firm for not being able to fulfil his part of the agreement.

Kiran was a good, hard worker, popular with clients before the tragedy. Even Senior Partners were shocked and in disbelief, would not accept a penny and let Kiran go, as what happened was beyond any one's control, with the promise that he would be welcome back at any time if he could recover from this tragedy, sort out his life and would like to make a career in accountancy. It was an honourable discharge.

After all it was the time, the age, the era when friendship, loyalty, hard work and comradeship were acknowledged and appreciated. Money did not rule the hearts and minds of the people as they do today. Money was not the roots of all evil, contrary to common belief.

Now that Kiran was free to do what he like, go where he please and financially secured, he was at a loss what to do, how to chart his future. He even thought of returning to Mombassa but by now his uncle had passed away. His heart could not stand the burden of this tragedy. He died of a broken heart.

Divya, who could be one person to mend his heart, give him hope, lead him out of darkness, gloom and doom, had got engaged to a doctor, a son of a prominent businessman. So there was nothing for Kiran to go back to.

Kiran took the time out to recuperate, mediate, heal his mind and body and find out what he should do next, where he belong! Kiran's favourite place to visit, especially when he needed guidance, divine help and intervention, was the Hare Krishna temple in the city.

Kiran had a friend, Shri Bimal Krishan Das who was a wise, matured, well educated person from a well to do family, at ease with himself after going through a hard fought, tumultuous and painful divorce and became a victim of his wife's cunningness, dishonesty and scheming. He lost every thing, including his two beautiful children.

In the end he was left penniless, without hope, without future or any chance of being happy in the near future. This was the time when he joined Hare Krishna Movement, became a disciple of Lord Krishna and a temple worker, a priest in the making.

One option for Kiran was to join *Hare Krishna Movement (ISKCON)* and devote the rest of his life to their cause. But as Kiran was also eager to roam the world for a year or so, his friend Bimal Das persuaded Kiran to fulfil his last ambition first and then join ISKCON, which would require a life long commitment to serve Lord Krishna.

In any case the city temple was small and had more volunteers than they could use. However there was a talk that one of Hare Krishna devotee, a member of Beatle Group wanted to donate his Watford mansion in the green and beautiful English county of Hertfordshire with some ten acres of green and fertile land.

ISKCON can create Lord Krishna's Vrindavan just a stone throw away from the heart of London, one of the most beautiful, dynamic and multicultural cites in the world.

Here cows can roam freely and the devotee could reap the harvest of milk, cheese, butter, ghee (clarified butter) plant fruit trees and grow seasonal vegetables to make the settlement financially viable and independent.

They can create a small, self sufficient settlement with donations flowing in, particularly from the Gujarati Hindu community who worship Lord Krishna whose birthday, *Janmastami* which falls in the month of August, is one of the most important day in Hindu calendar, after Dipawali and New Year. The attendance for the midnight arti, the time Lord Krishna was born, is the highest for such a festival outside India.

As the temple would be located in the heart of countryside, there would be plenty of opportunity to buy the surrounding agricultural land and expand it to make it one of the biggest, grandest temples, settlement outside India.

Kiran, being a Chartered Accountant, could join their management team and be an asset, help in planning, charting the future of ISKCON, applying for Government and Council loans and grants, preparing cash flow forecast and annual accounts.

This was a wonderful dream to recreate Lord Krishna's Vrindavan outside India, a legacy for the younger, future generation and Kiran could be a part of this dream.

But it would require willpower, toughness, dynamism, dedication, life long total commitment and sound mind, mentally fit to engage in such a challenge to turn the dream into a reality. Perhaps Kiran was not in right frame of mind at the moment.

After all ISKCON is a Gnosticism that is saturated with spiritual knowledge one may struggle to find any where else. Then Hare Krishna Movement is not short of such dedicated volunteers, is indeed blessed with such manpower that makes it the most dynamic but utterly peaceful movement in the world.

But there is no place for delusion of secular sainthood that unfortunately ravages the Hindus in their motherland Bharat where there is little difference between the saints and the sinners in religious awareness, religious loyalty and adherence. The masses are impregnated with religious listeriosis by the corrupt to the core politicians. Religion was the opium for the masses, a tool to control them, to create a vote bank and exploit them at their will.

Living a monastic life that include getting up at day break, to pray, milk the cows, till the land and clean the temple, the premises is a challenge that could not be taken lightly. This is clearly neither the life for Liebfraumilch drinking city wiz kids nor a launderette where one may come to wash their inner misdeeds, like a confession box.

Neither Hinduism nor ISKCON believe in superfluous washing of one's sins. Integrity and intellect are the two main ingredients for cleansing of the soul, in readiness to serve Lord Krishna or Lord Rama, the two pillars, the two most popular deities in Hindu religion.

It requires sound mind and healthy body with unwavering lifelong commitment, accompanied by a sense of inner harmony, in the lush garden of one's mind that has the power to attract the spiritual and mental harmony.

Perhaps Kiran was not ready, not in the right frame of mind to commit to the ISKCON cause. Perhaps his inner core, his trust and spiritually was ruptured by these tragic events. He needed a break of a year or so, go, wonder and visit as many countries as he could until the lava in his heart cools down.

Kiran has to regain his composure and is ready and willing to lead a normal life with serenity, angelic in nature and enlightened in substance.

It was difficult for Kiran to strike back, utter vaporous sermons, preach hatred or plot revenge when there was no visible enemy, when the enemy was abstract rather than a materialistic object.

Perhaps visiting Himalayas, experiencing the solitude, spending some time in a monastery, the ***Shangri La of Lost Horizon***, taking a dip in the holy waters of ***Mother Ganges*** may lead to the elevation of the soul and will make Kiran feel at ease with nature, with Mother Earth. After all Kiran can not and should not live in the post-tragedy guilt. A time will come when the alleviation of his soul will come with inner peace.

The winter was nearly over. The sweet smell of spring flowers was filling the cosy atmosphere with romance, hope, anticipation and excitement in young hearts. After all every one is young but only once in a life time!

The Cherry trees were in full blossom, the bright yellow and white daffodils with red and pink centre, neatly laid in flower beds, as well as scattered on the road verge and roundabouts, with tulips and wall flowers scattered every where gave the city a romantic interlude.

Birds were out in droves, pigeons, swallows, buzzards, common sparrows, magpies, wood pigeons and even parakeets, the recent arrival on our door-steps due to climate change, were fluttering in the gentle, warm air, the spring sunshine that comes as a breath of fresh air after the winter blues.

The flutter of butterflies of various shape, colour and size, in many parks that littered all over London created most ebullience, cheered most hearts, young and not so young, the ebbing hearts, the romantic hearts, even the bleeding hearts!

The silent show of panache and elegance put up by butterflies eclipsed the more robust lasers of the feathered friends that monopolize parks and open spaces at this time of the year.

The young ones without partners were flying aimlessly, making a nuisance of themselves, while the mature adults were busy building nests for the arrival of the young ones in mid-summer, one responsibility that can not be taken lightly.

* * *

Chapter Six
Day Dreaming on the Plane

It was a long hot night for Kiran. He had been drifting in and out of sleep all the time while Olivia had, as usual, a restful night. They did not get up until the phone rang, an early morning call at 9am in the hot and humid morning when most of the people would be at their desk!

As the pick-up time was 10am, they ordered a room service which arrived in just fifteen minutes, even before Kiran could shower and shave. But this was a mixture of Indian and English breakfast, the Indian one for Kiran which he really enjoyed, as he was eating paratha, dry potato curie along with Spanish omelette, plenty of toast, potato wafer, mushrooms and baked beans with tea, coffee and freshly squished orange juice.

Even Olivia enjoyed paratha and potato curie, as this cooking was far better than what Kiran could cook, as Olivia could never get the hang of Indian cooking.

Then again, Kiran was not a bad cook either. But even Kiran could not compete with fully qualified cook in a four to five star hotels, cooking such food day in, day out. Cooking Indian food to perfection is an art that comes with plenty of experience, under an expert guidance of a master chef.

The bus arrived on time to pick them up and they were on plane well before the time. As Kiran relaxed in his first class leather bound, reclining seat, he was back in his dream world. The next stop was Singapore, a long way away. But there was a short refuelling break at Colombo, the capital city of Ceylon, now better known as Sri Lanka.

Olivia knew that Kiran had a restless night. So she did not insist on talking and let him drift into his dreamland. By now she was familiar of Kiran's past, his tormented life before he met her and his habit, unwilling, uncontrollable urge to go back into his past, visit the pleasant as well as his haunted past. In a way this was beyond Kiran's control and he has learnt to live with it.

Soon Kiran was back in London, in his bitter sweet world of day dream, taking it from where he left off when he got up in the morning. When Kiran finally decided to travel, roam the world, what surprised every one, especially his friends, was the mode of transport Kiran chose, a powerful 500cc Triumph Tornado motorbike, the latest model with most up to date gadgets and of course the latest safety devices as well.

It would be much easier to travel, to visit the remotest parts of the world on a motorbike than in a car where roads are just tracks, a simple path formed by every day usage, trodden by no more than human feet and donkey rides.

No wonder amongst seasoned travellers, such a mode of roaming the world is better known as Bailey bridge travel brigade! Kiran did now want his first enterprise not to be a forlorn hope, a hopeless enterprise.

Normally Kiran is a cool and calm person who did not believe in taking unnecessary risks, whether it is in finance, moral or physical obligation or even on romance!

He would prefer to stick to the tried and tested methods where the risk of going wrong is small. So why such a sudden change in his attitude and personality? Kiran's Armani-clad shoulders were now bearing the weight of the leather jacket and the helmet on his head which was a complete transformation from a city office whiz kid to Romany existence.

This question of summersault in life style was prominent in the minds of every one who knew Kiran, including Kiran himself. The only answer Kiran could come up with, an honest answer after searching his soul was that deep down, he would prefer a death in the same manner as his family; that is if he has to lose his life.

Some how he held himself responsible for this most tragic accident. His conscious was guilt ridden and he would like to make amend if he can, but how, when and in what manner he was not sure. Then Kiran was not alone in feeling this way. Every one who loses a close family member in such tragic circumstances would naturally feel the same way.

But Kiran would take every care, every precaution so as not to be a victim of a road rage! Slowly but surely he was beginning to come to terms with this tragedy of Hercules proportion.

He knew it would take a very long time for wounds to heal, for him to live a normal life. But he now realized that even his family, his parents and his little sister would not like him to remain angry, sad, unhappy and miserable all his life.

What happened has happened but life, the show must go on. When one's time is up, no amount of money, influence or power can buy even an hour more than what is written in our Kismat, the destiny. Any thing else would be a futile exercise in frustration.

Kiran may come to terms with his misfortune but frolicsome he would never be. His life would always be frappe if not frozen. This event would always be like a ***Frankenstein's Monster*** back in his mind.

No amount of self denial or turning his life into a sacrifice paddock will help or change the fact, turn the tide or set the time back. Water at the mouth of the river can never return to its original source, neither can an event in one's life.

Spring was the right time to explore Southern Europe, countries like Spain, Portugal and Italy, before the onset of summer when it would be too hot, too uncomfortable to travel, especially by motorbike with all the protective cloths and head gear Kiran would have to wear.

Kiran thought it would be better if he first tour the beautiful Wales, a charming and hospitable country with long and sandy coastline, Pembrokeshire National Park, a jewel in Wales' crown, its tourism, high mountain peaks, valleys, lakes and waterfalls Kiran would enjoy, appreciate the beauty before he ventures into Europe where they drive on the wrong side of the road?

In those distant days when tourism was in its infancy, there was hardly any traffic. Even the big Lorries were not that obvious, as most of the heavy goods were transported by rail and river barges.

In a way this trend made roads more dangerous, as empty roads encourage drivers, riders go as fast as they could. Moreover there were no speed cameras and police patrol cars were more meant for town centres than motorways.

Kiran made a point not to ride, on the road for more than four to six hours a day and take a break after two hours. This would enable him to travel, on average between 100 to 200 miles a day in good weather, on faster roads.

But if he is in the right location, he would stop, have a cup of tea or coffee at road side cafes and chat with the local people as often as he could, thus restricting his travel to just fifty miles.

Kiran would also stop at beauty spots, special observation platforms, viewpoint, vantage point and what they call in Spain *"El Mirador"*. Then he was not in a rush to catch a train or a ferry. Time had no meaning as such when there is neither a beginning nor an end.

One of Kiran's hobbies was photography. So Kiran always kept his expensive Pentax camera handy and captured such sceneries with ease and enthusiasm of a child playing with his first toy!

After all, meeting locals was the main aim, the purpose of his travel, to roam the world, meet and greet people, learn their culture, tradition and make friends, however short such a friendship may last.

Kiran was and still is a methodical person who would like to organize every event to minor detail, compartmentalize his priorities. He would not like fear and emotions muddled with his project, be hindrance in any way, let the corrosion set in.

As usual, Kiran charted his Wales adventure to near perfection. He knew exactly where he would like to go; what to see and where to stay but also play by the nose, construe and make an instant decision. He has to show the courage of his conviction and make an instant decision where it merited.

Kiran was ready to be flexible, as so often some of the most beauty spots, old ruins, forts, cathedrals and monasteries are not even charted, on the tourist map. Only the local people know and could guide Kiran to such beauties, especially for some one who is Romany at heart!

So on a bright, warm and sunny day, late in April, Kiran took off on his ***Magnificent Machine,*** a dream machine, an object of envy and desire for the less fortunate on the financial front.

Kiran bade farewell to London one early morning when most Londoners were asleep, enjoying the rest day. Kiran wanted to be as far away from the city traffic as he possibly could.

As the roads were deserted so early on Sunday morning, Kiran was able to leave the traffic behind in less than half an hour, enjoying the solitude of the motorway as if it was built specially to take care of Kiran's need.

Even with two half an hour breaks on the motorway, Kiran was on the outskirt of Cardiff, the capital city of Wales in the early afternoon. He decided to spend the night in a farmhouse, in the beautiful ***Vale of Penarth.***

Kiran had an early night, as he had an early start in the morning. The next day, he had a leisurely breakfast. The Wales if famous for its food, a healthy, fresh and appetising food right on the door-step, from the local farms and the hospitality of the Welsh people is legendary.

Kiran, being a vegetarian could not touch thick, juicy pork sausages or crispy bacon. But he had Spanish omelette, with mushroom, baked beans, fresh oven baked bread and fresh fruit salad with coffee. There were two other guests who were friendly and inquisitive about Kiran's mode of transport, as he did not look like a motorbike type wanderer.

It was a long time since Kiran had a good night's sleep, without waking up, without having nightmares and being soaked in perspiration, having panic attacks. Kiran even enjoyed his food, the breakfast, especially organic lightly fried crispy mushrooms.

The fresh country air, the farm house atmosphere with cockerel waking him up early in the morning, the singing of birds and the farmer busy feeding the pigs, milking few cows and goats made Kiran to forget his problems for a while.

Cardiff is a city of culture and art and home to Welsh rugby team. But Kiran was not a sport person. His first and only stop was the museum overflowing with Welsh art effects, its culture and history.

The Welsh people are mostly the descendants of the Celts who once dominated Ireland and Scotland and are closely related to the Bretons. The Welsh language is related to the ancient Celtic language and widely spoken in rural areas, especially in the North.

The Welsh literature goes back some 1500 years. The Welsh calendar is full of festivals with music and poetry known as **eisteddfodau** which are held throughout the country where Welsh tradition is paramount with carol singing as its main attraction.

Kiran spend some three hours in the museum and by the time he had a coffee break, it was time to move on. His wandering urge, spirit was fast gaining control over his normal sedate routine.

His next stop was the historic town of Carmarthen, the town with overbearing fort or rather the ruins that attacks so many visitors. After a late lunch, Kiran was on his way to the little port of St. David's where he stayed at a Bed and Breakfast establishment, overlooking the sea at **St. Brides Bay.**

This part of Wales is a heaven for wild life without equivocation, for bird watching, with numerous islands, practically all small, most even tiny and all but one uninhabited.

This isolation, along with the warm ocean current, the Gulf Stream originating from the warm waters of the Gulf of Mexico, made these islands a perfect heaven for colonies of sea birds, sea gulls, puffins, guillemots, razorbills and kittiwakes, a few amongst many varieties who have colonized these islands and turned this corner of Wales into a heaven on earth for all, wild life and human adventurers, the walking enthusiasts, the ardent supporters of nature who endorsed and envisaged the advantage in preserving this unique heritage for the future generation.

Many have made a lifelong pledge to take care of this piece of heaven on their door-steps with financial contribution and voluntary work who may be on call throughout the year whose endeavour is paying a rich dividend.

Kiran observed that the Welsh people could be divided into three categories, those who are sport mad; support their clubs to no end, the hard working people like miners who would like to spend their time relaxing in pubs after a long day underground and those who were mad about Welsh culture, arts, wildlife and nature who belonged to so many voluntary organizations to encourage, protect and preserve this proud and precious tradition, the centuries old heritage.

The islands Kiran wanted to visit, leave his foot-prints were **Ramsey Island, Grassholm, Skomer and Skoholm Islands**, part of the Pembrokeshire National Park, a Nature Reserve.

Next day, after early breakfast, he left for the tiny port of St. Davis, St. Martin's Heaven, a sailing point to board ferries to visit these islands. Kiran took a comfortable, two Decker Ferry, a whole day sailing that would take him to all these main islands in one visit.

But they will only be allowed some free time on one island, the **"Skomer Island"** where tourists are allowed to land, spend up to three hours among the birds, grey seals and bird colonies under the watchful eyes of a well trained guide familiar with local wildlife, flora and fauna, on the pay of the Pembrokeshire National Trust.

One has to move slowly, never to leave the well drawn, well marked, well worn trodden path, observe complete silence except the occasional clicks of cameras.

The island is full of burrows and tunnels which may collapse under human weight and would kill the birds, destroy the eggs underneath. The visitors were well versed while on the boat, before they land to avoid such an incident.

Fortunately the birds, the wildlife were habituated of human presence and came to realize that they pose no threat, either to them or to their young ones. Yet visitors had to keep a healthy distance, especially during breeding season, as birds are more nervous and protective who may even attack some one who may venture too close to their chicks. Then the wildlife guides were fiduciaries for these birds!

It was a pleasant sailing, especially to visit Skomer Island. The sea was translucent; almost transparent that would enable the sunlight to reach the sea-bed.

One can see deep down through the crystal clear turquoise waters with swarms of fishes of all shape, size and colours, with occasional group of dolphins.

Even basking sharks making an appearance at the right time of the year was not out of question, so would loggerhead turtles, the giants of the oceans who would unfortunately not come ashore to lay eggs.

Perhaps the sands are too cold for these tropical mammals that prefer warm beaches of Cyprus, Kerala and Cuba than Wales. Who can blame them? Wales is not and never can be a heaven, at least not for humans who have experienced the pleasure of living in tropical paradise?

The Skomer Island is a heaven on earth, especially on a day like this, with clear blue sky, sunshine and warmth made the sailing a pleasant experience, especially watching from the top, away from the sea waves that occasionally drench those who sit too near the edge, in front. But practically every one was wearing a raincoat to protect them from sea drenching.

It seemed the visitors were well versed in visiting these islands and most were regular tourists or rather enthusiasts, nature lovers for whom this was an annual pilgrimage. This was their Costa del Sol and the Caribbean put together. The landing was a bit awkward but the new jetty was already under construction that would make the island accessible, even to less mobile tourists, enthuses.

The island is full of burros where the birds incubate their eggs. Kittiwakes and puffins soar purposefully over the vertical cliffs, in cloistered stillness. The burrows were skilfully built so as not to be flooded during heavy rains. But occasional mishaps, mortality were inevitable.

Nature may occasionally hinder but it is the human intervention that is normally responsible for the disappearance of so many life forms all over the planet.

The island was covered with dense but low bushes, undergrowth, the dense indigo of bluebells quickly floods across the gentle slopes like a new laid carpet, one of the most spectacular display of wild flowers one could see, enjoy any where in Britain. This is nature at its best.

All these islands come under the National Nature Reserve of Pembrokeshire Coast and managed by the Wildlife Trust of South Wales.

This beautiful part of Wales has been the home of many famous sculptors, painters, photographers and writers who have been inspired by the stunning natural beauty of Pembrokeshire coastline, made this place their inspirational home and left their legacy.

The name that readily came to my mind and so often readily and affectionally mentioned by the locals was that of poet and writer ***Dylan Thomas,*** a noble son of Wales whose name is on every Welsh tongue. Dylan is their Shakespeare. His play ***"Under Milk Wood"*** describes with wit, humour, charm and compassion, a day in the life of the residents of a small fishing village on the Pembrokeshire coast.

One could not help but wonder what height he could have reached, what mountains he could have climbed if he had not passed away at the tender age of 39, just when he was in ascendancy on the literary front!

* * *

Chapter Seven
Solva, the Hidden Jewel

It was late afternoon by the time Kiran returned to the mainland, at St. Davis Point. He wanted to visit, see the tiny port of **Solva** all locals were talking about. So Kiran turned south instead of going north.

This tiny place is situated on **St. Brides Bay** with a safe, well protected inlet. Kiran stopped for a cup of coffee at a café on the top of a cliff overlooking the inlet. It was sheer luck that Kiran had a coffee break in this café, completely cut-off from the main road.

Although the mist was setting in and obscuring the view, Kiran instantly knew that he had discovered a jewel in Pembrokeshire's crown but the place was hardly known outside its perimeter, outside the local community.

The café with an enchanting, unusual and charming name *"Gateway to Heaven Café"* was run by a middle aged couple, husband and wife who introduced themselves as Martha and Martin. As this was an off beat place, they never had the opportunity to welcome some one like Kiran in their spacious café.

So they were as curious about Kiran as he was about them. Martha was a kind and caring woman in her early forties who did all the talking, attended, served the customers, managed the business and was a chatterbox, as some one serving customers has to be. In any case, human company, especially an intelligent and intellectual one was as rare as a sighting of a cuckoo in the middle of winter.

Martha was certainly not a handmaiden. Her husband Martin, a man of few words, cooked, cleaned and did the hard work in the kitchen, behind the counter, in a separate room which served as a specious kitchen.

This was indeed a lucky break for Kiran, as they had a flat, an apartment with three bedrooms over the café with stunning views of the tiny port of Solva and the surrounding landscape, the Irish Sea and the roaring Atlantic Ocean in the distance.

The murmur of the waves and the shrikes of seagulls were drowning all other noises, even during day time. Then there was hardly any traffic, as the road or rather a narrow lane ended at the café. So only those who want to visit Haven Café would use the lane.

As visitors were few and business at subsistence level, they had converted two bedrooms as guest house, available as bed and breakfast to occasional visitors.

Kiran always had dinner included with B & B, as it would be difficult for him to leave and look for an eating place once he was back from the day's outing.

In any case additional income was always welcomed in such places where tourists were as rare as gold dust. It would be a pleasure to have a company of additional paying guests at dinner time.

Kiran was pleased to have a break here. After an early dinner with Martin and Martha, they chatted for a long time. Kiran developed an affinity towards the couple, as Martha bestowed her elder sister like affection on Kiran without intention or awareness, making it as natural, as real love between a brother and a sister as one could imagine. In essence Martha was a ***Good Samaritan***.

The couple had no children and as Martha had passed the child bearing age, they had come to terms of living a life without an offspring. These God fearing people had immense faith in their Catholic religion. They would travel a long distance to attend the Sunday morning mass, come hell or high water. They live by the gospel, the teaching of Lord Jesus Christ, a type of *glasnost* encouraged in USSR under ***Mikhail Gorbachov***.

The vast, spacious walls of the diner were the resting place for some beautiful paintings, photographs of natural scenes and writings, sayings of some famous philosophers, authors and politicians. The one attracted Kiran's eyes and had never seen before was ***"Church* is *not a finishing school for saints. It is a nursery for the sinners!"***

The other slogan Kiran had come across many times was the famous words of the late President John F. Kennedy, the first descendent of the

Irish immigrants to occupy such a high post. *"Do not ask what your country can do for you but ask what you can do for your country!"* How true? We would like the State to provide free NHS, old age pensions, free education, retirement homes, and nursing homes, a few examples of our dependency on our country, our motherland.

Then there were: *"It is never too late to have a happy childhood. But the second one is up to you and no one else. Burn the candle, use nice sheets, wear the fancy lingerie. Don't save it for a special occasion. Today is the special occasion. No one is in charge of your happiness but you. So stop complaining and start enjoying life before it is too late."*

This brief encounter with Martha brought back the happy times, the wonderful memories Kiran had with his sister Kalpna. But this time he was not led back, drawn into sadness and sorrow that would bring back panic attacks and sleepless nights.

Perhaps this was the interlude Kiran needed to escape from the gloom and sorrow, self pity and blaming game, the guilt trip and the witch-hunt his mind could not escape from.

Although Kiran always gets up early in the morning, a habit he acquired back in Mombassa where the sun would rise early throughout the year, Mombassa being situated just south of equator, Kiran now preferred to get up late, at 8am instead of 6am his usual time, as time had no meaning.

It was a pleasant choice and not a Hobson's choice. In any case it was warm and comfortable early in the morning when the sun's rays decorate the bedroom, disturb his privacy and make an entrance without invitation.

By the time Kiran was ready for breakfast, after shower and shave, it was nearly ten o'clock. Martha and Martin were down in the café where Kiran preferred to have his late breakfast.

Kiran did not realised how spacious, well furnished this diner was, with a sitting capacity for some thirty people, with plenty of space between tables, if squeezed, it could easily accommodate up to fifty people.

The triple glazed glass frontage gave protection against the cold wind without minimizing the fantastic views down below, especially when Kiran looked through his tiny but powerful pocket binoculars.

It was too early for passing trade, the tourists to walk in. But there were a couple of hitchhikers, walking enthusiasts who were warming their bodies after a long and satisfying walk, with a hot pot of tea and a breakfast of thick pork sausages, bacon, eggs and the usual trappings that goes with the traditional Welsh breakfast.

Kiran was spoilt for choice to sit, as most window tables had fantastic views. Kiran chose the one that had a straight, nearest view of the tiny Solva harbour, well away from other occupied tables and plenty of direct sunlight to warm any one's heart, mind and body.

Without asking, Martha brought a pot of coffee, full of fresh percolated, filtered coffee with goat's milk and some toasts, marmalade and goat milk cheese to start with. By the time Kiran had finished breakfast, he wondered whether he would be able to eat any dinner, let alone lunch.

After three days on the roads, Kiran thought it was time to reflect, take stock of his desire, wish and future ambition, to chart his future, where to go and what to do.

So he was not in a hurry to leave this place. When Kiran first planned his glob trotting journey, he promised himself that he would keep a detailed diary, write it every evening before going to bed.

But it is easier said than done; as the day spent on the road do take its toll on body and soul. Kiran even envisage that perhaps he could publish a book that may help others in his situation, with plenty of beautiful photographs taken by him.

He would call it ***"Hitchhikers' Guide to Paradise"*** or ***"Hitchhiking to Paradise"*** or ***"Hitchhiking from Hell to Heaven,*** some thing similar. So today was the right time to start writing.

Kiran spent some three hours glued to the table, writing in detail a day's events, including miles covered, where he stayed, whom he met, the places he visited and what he learnt, what was his opinion, linking them with photographs he may have taken.

As there was no one who needed her services, Martha pulled a chair and sat in front of Kiran, asking all the routine questions.

She was a bit surprised that Kiran spoke such eloquent English. His words and phrases were right from the English dictionary. It was indeed a sonorous language but it came out without effort. It was natural. After all Kiran had a degree in English language from one of the most prestigious Universities in the world.

Now and again Martha would leave to attend a customer or just to leave Kiran alone so that he could proceed with his writing. Every now and then Kiran would take a break to look at the fantastic scenery below.

He noticed that the harbour, the tiny inlet was full of water last evening, being high tide. The boats some anchored in deep water while others tied up at the jetty, gave the impression that this was indeed a place for the well-off, as some of the boats looked grand, at least in contrast to the surrounding, posh and expensive, like mini yachts one would like to sail to the far off places like Madera, Canary Islands as well as Channel Islands on our door-step, if not as far as South Seas, Samoa, Hawaii and the Maldives!

This morning the tide had ebbed, laying a large part of the inlet bare, without water, except in small pockets, the depression in the sands. Many boats were resting on the seabed, fast stuck in sand. Others were far at sea, just a tiny speck on the distant horizon.

Kiran remembered his childhood when they used to go on picnic, on a small island off the tiny village of Malindi, often spending a night or two on the sandy beach, as pure as gold and as beautiful as paradise. But they were too young, too innocent to appreciate and understand what paradise meant!

It was an experience to sleep in the open, under a star-studded sky with moon playing hide and seek with the thin clouds that could not hide even a needle. The warm turquoise water with frothing waves was reflecting and magnifying every twinkle of the distant stars a million times.

They would be all alone on the island, as if they were the sovereign, a kingdom without subjects, without any form of dictate! These were the happy, innocent days without a worry, a cloud in the sky. How Kiran's world changed in a blink! Who said that a life can change in a blink, but do not worry, God never blinks!

Getting up in the morning with the sound of sea gulls, crows, cooing of wood pigeons, grey parrots or ***Kasuku in Swahili*** and a flock of parakeets that would even disturb the sleep of Kumbkarna, the God of sleep difficult to wake!

Kiran's life and that of every one else was as serene and mystic as the one in Jules Verne's fictitious but pleasant and adventurous world, a lost continent, in ***James Hilton's*** imaginary heaven on earth ***Shangri La,*** the place where the time had stood still for the last two hundred years.

The rustic atmosphere was wrapped in a silk cocoon and isolated from reality, from the rest of the world, protected from the aftermath of the gruesome two world wars that had engulfed the continent of Europe twice in less than three decades.

In a way this tiny port of Solva was as isolated as Kiran's tiny island where he had spent many a happy days. No wonder Kiran was not in a hurry to move on, leave Solva, the wonderful view and kind and caring woman Martha behind in a hurry.

He spend the entire day in the café, except an hour's break when he rode to the sea below and had a closer look at the harbour where the fishing boats were offloading their cargo of fresh fish caught during the night. In a way Solva was a fishing port, a working port, alive with human presence and endurance, although on a minuscule scale.

Then people's needs were not that high either. One could easily, comfortably survive on less than a pound a day. Most bed and breakfast establishment charged less than five pound a week, so often throwing dinner free and in Wales with a glass of wine as well.

Although Kiran was a vegetarian, he was not averse to a glass of wine, port or sherry now and then. This stood him in good stead later on while touring Spain and Portugal.

In Mombassa Kiran used to love walking with bare feet, on the wet sand when the tide had receded, looking at the small pool of water in sand depression where tiny fishes were trapped, at least until the water rush in at the high tide and free them, that is if they survive the onslaught from ever present seagulls looking for an easy meal.

Kiran took off his shoes and wandered on to the sand and the sea bed lay bare by the receding tide. But the sand was too cold for comfort. Kiran soon retreated back to his motorbike and to the comfort of his favourite café from where Solva looked like a heaven but in reality it was a cold heaven he would find it difficult to get used to, especially during hostile winter months with storm force wind blowing in from the Irish Sea.

In sharp contrast, the sand in Mombassa, on the tiny island off Malindi was so hot that Kiran could only walk on it if the sand was wet, making it much less hot and bearable. What a sharp contrast? Then Mombassa and Solva are miles apart, on different continent, almost on different world.

Kiran was welcomed back with a smile and a mug of coffee, laced with some brandy, as Martha realised how cold Kiran was feeling, as he was rubbing his hands and face.

The coffee, rather the brandy gave some warmth to Kiran, sitting in his place in the company of Martha. This time even Martin joined in, having closed his kitchen, as he knew no one was going to order food tonight.

While Martha had coffee like Kiran, Martin preferred a pint of cold beer, a Welsh beer with full flavour and with 7% ABV, indeed a strong beer for most but normal for the Welsh who are used to alcohol from an early age.

As it was too early to retreat to the comfort of the flat, they drank and talked. Even Martin opened up, had as much input as Kiran. Martin even offered a glass of beer to Kiran who thought there was no harm in trying.

The taste was bitter, not to his liking but it had a wonderful effect on him. He became cheerful, talkative and comfortable in the company of this wonderful and caring couple who were not in any way a fiddle-faddle people. Then the life is strange, especially when on the move.

One day we meet a saint, next day a sinner who would not hesitate to double cross a saint or sell an innocent girl into slavery.

Kiran came to knew that this was only a summer business. The café would remain closed for six months, from October until March. The real business would start during Easter holidays.

During winter months, Martin would seek a job on the fishing boats, as they were always short of sailors, especially during the bitterly cold, wet and dark winter months that would make the life of fishing boat crew difficult and dangerous. Only the toughest would survive in such a profession, yet crews are paid a pittance!

Martha may have a job as a maid servant or a chamber maid in Fishguard, less than an hour's drive from Solva. But on most part, accommodation was provided with the job. Yet these jobs were uncertain, irregular and low paid. So they would have to register as unemployed from time to time to make the ends meet. It was inevitable with seasonal jobs.

Kiran could not help but ask Martha how she could live alone in such an isolated place when Martin would go to sea and she may not have a job. Martha jokingly asked Kiran whether he would like to move in as a permanent paying guest, to which Kiran replied that he would definitely consider it when he retires! These were genuine, kind and caring people, not the sanctimonious dimwits' city dwellers.

Those were trouble free times when ghoulish behaviours were unknown and ladies were treated with respect and honour. In traditional Indian, Hindu culture, such ladies are well respected and accorded the honour they deserve.

Martha was impressed at Kiran's politeness, his willingness even to help in the chores and the financial advice he gave after examining their books.

It may surprise many that how could some one open their books to a complete stranger, but there was hardly any profit, any asset to hide and being CA, Kiran commanded their respect.

It would not be difficult to distinguish between gibberish and a professional person, even for down to earth people like Martha and Martin.

They were not the people who would chase that elusive pot of gold. Martha was a kind of rose that if you touch, it will leave a little bit of fragrance clinging to your hands.

Next day, after a stay of two nights when Kiran bade farewell to Martha and Martin, Martha gave a big hug to Kiran, her eyes wet with emotion. On Kiran's part, for a second or two he thought he was hugging his sister Kalpna.

Martha extracted a promise from Kiran that he would not only stay in touch but will definitely return one day, when his lust for wandering is over, his pain subsided and he is back to his normal best. This was a journey of roller coaster emotions. Perhaps, in a strange way, the beginning of the long and arduous healing process that would last many years.

* * *

Chapter Eight
Beauty of North Wales

Kiran spent more time in Solva than expected. But it was time well spent. Martha was a tower of strength but now Kiran will have to be a road gazelle or a cheetah to make up for the lost time.

Perhaps this was the prototype of the life Kiran would lead, the people he would meet when on the road. Perhaps Martha was a protégé! Kiran would have to emulate the life-style of a real, a true hitchhiker. Kiran would have to go through the dialysis of a life on the run, on the road, as such encounters would make him streetwise and extrovert, one quality Kiran lacked and is the main ingredient for success, to stay one step ahead of trouble.

After leaving Solva early in the morning, Kiran took the coastal road so as to enjoy the beauty of the Pembrokeshire coast as long as he could. But then this was the only road, unless Kiran wanted to move inland, the road he had marked for his return journey.

Kiran had three short stops before reaching his destination of *Lake Bala.* He passed the costal villages of New Quay, Aberystwyth, Borth and Barmouth before Kiran moved inland.

It was a leisurely ride of some six hours before he reached his destination. Near the lake, on the outskirt of the village of Bala, on Road A494, there was a caravan park where one could either park one's own caravan or hire one on a day or a weekly basis. Kiran booked in straight away.

As it was still early afternoon with sun shining, Kiran had a time to explore. He took the picturesque tourist railway, a steam railway that would carry tourists round the lake. It was a wonderful outing, short, sweet and relaxing.

The starting point is the Bala Station and it ends at Pentrepoid. The railway hugs the four mile long and a mile wide lake at various places, thus enriching this fantasy line with superb scenery of overflowing clear, blue water, boats laden with tourists as well as tiny fishing boats for the fishing entrusts. The lake is rich in fresh water life.

The lake Bala, (Welsh name Llyn Tegid) is always full of water, being constantly fed by rivers and streams, the prominent being Afon (river) Llafar, Afon Tryweryn, Afon Twiven and many more.

Kiran made a good use of this time, visiting various other lakes, as this region of Wales is like an **English Lake District.**

Two other lakes worth a short visit are Llyn (lake) Celyn fed by river Afon Tyrweryn and popular as a water sport destination, with rafting, canoeing, water skiing and fishing being the main attraction.

This turned out to be a long day for Kiran. He had left Solva early in the morning and by the time he took to bed, it was ten o'clock at night, after being on the road for some ten hours, albeit with numerous breaks, for a cup of coffee as well as train ride, a boat ride and stopping at vantage points.

After a wonderful company and homely atmosphere in Solva, the caravan was a bit of a let down. He felt some what lonely but the sleep came to his rescue, as Kiran was physically and mentally tired, too exhausted not to go to sleep straight away.

When Kiran opened his eyes in the morning, a bit late but completely refreshed, as he had a sound, ten hour sleep at one stretch. After his daily routine of shower and shave, Kiran left the caravan, had a breakfast in a small café on the caravan park.

Kiran's routine of having breakfast so often became his salvation, in spirit if not in soul! Today was no exception. As the tiny café had very few tables, sitting places, Kiran was obliged to share a table with a tall, slim girl, wearing a torn jeans, at all the right places, bearing the flesh, soft white skin, in most inappropriate places, a sign of affluence and matching denim blouse, a typical dress for a hitchhiker.

Kiran's lighter dark skin, Indian looks and unusual dress sense for a wanderer always created a stir and interest, especially amongst his fellow female hitchhikers. So often Kiran was a tall, dark and handsome hero for a female to know and talk to. Perhaps an Indian prince, a son of a Maharaja back in India.

So Kiran was not surprised when the girl started talking with him, as if she had known Kiran for a long time. Then it is so easy to make friends amongst your fellow travellers. The roads are a lonely place indeed!

As it turned out, they had much in common. She introduced herself as Penelope but preferred to be called **Penny**. She was a Cambridge graduate in maths. Penny had an affluent background. Her father was a **Conservative Member of Parliament from Cambridgeshire South.**

As Penny was uncertain what to do, whether to go and work in the city, join a firm of Charted Accountant as an apprentice or work for an insurance company, a bank or similar financial institution, or even become a teacher. But until she acquires acuity, wisdom to make a right decision, she had taken a year off to hitchhike the world!

Naturally her ultimate aim was to follow into her father's footsteps and enter the House of Commons. She was already active in politics while at the Uni, being a Vice President of the Cambridge Student Union, a prestigious post indeed.

As Penny was on her own, without a transport, Kiran invited her to join him for a day or two to tour, to explore this beautiful part of Wales. After all two heads are better than one and many hands make a light work. Penny readily accepted Kiran's offer, as she was as much impressed with Kiran's background and qualification, as he was with Penny's.

Kiran wanted to explore the Snowdonia National Park, a rugged place but in sharp contrast to Pembrokeshire National Park along the coast where the sea was a constant companion.

Within two hours Kiran and Penny were in Mount Snowdonia and Snowdonia National Park. Their first stop was the Snowdonia Railway Station from where a narrow gauge railway takes tourists to the summit of one of the highest mountain in Britain; Ben Nevis in Scotland is the highest mountain in Britain.

On a clear day, one can have views of all three countries, England, Wales and Ireland. Kiran and Penny were a bit early for the clouds to disperse completely. But they were dispersing, thinning out fast, as the sun's rays gained ascendancy, melting the mist like flakes of snow in the midday sun!

The Irish Sea was visible, through the hazy mist, on the West to Caernarfon Bay and North to Colwyn Bay with the tourist port of Llandudno a famous landmark. The awesome sight from the summit was a tribute to the symphony of nature. One could explore this region to the realm of extraordinary.

The powerful binocular at the Mirador, viewing point was so helpful. Kiran had his own good quality Pentax binocular to look at the valleys and forest, at bird life and lakes and streams.

It was a wonderful train journey to the top, the summit at 3560 feet, passing through breathtaking valleys, gauges and fast flowing streams, so often fed by the melting snow that makes water fresh and crisp, a drink one would enjoy without worrying of upset stomach, as most rivers, even streams are polluted, water undrinkable without boiling.

The range and variety of flora and fauna was impressive. They had an hour's break before the train would depart for the downward journey.

The *"Summit Café"* was a perfect place to sit down, have a cup of coffee in the company of a charming, scintillating, intellectual and lively person like Penny, an exuberant girl who instantly reminded Kiran of Divya, the girl he was in love with.

How Kiran wished there was a bed and breakfast accommodation on the summit, on the flimsy café building! In reality, it would need a sturdy, well built building of bricks and stones to stand firm against the fierce winds and rain that hit the summit, especially in winter.

Like Kiran, Penny was also a methodical person. She knew what she wanted to see, the places she wanted to visit. Only her timetable was uncertain, as she had to depend on the generosity of motorists for a lift. Kiran thought it was unwise for such a charming and beautiful girl to take risks, trust drivers who are complete strangers.

Kiran could not help but wonder how Penney's parents may feel, have any misgivings about their charming daughter who could give her any mode of transport, including a small car, but she prefers to hitchhike!

But Penny was full of confidence and very careful indeed. She would not accept a lift from a lorry driver and would always carry an alarm that would deter any one. She was a sensible girl who had taken all the precautions to make her as safe as possible. She believed in Kismat, what may happen, happens for a reason.

The mountain and the surrounding areas with peaks like Tryfan, Aran, and Cader Idris are turned into National Park with Welsh names like **"Eryri"** which means **"Place of Eagles"** give this place Wild West feeling.

The name Place of Eagles is perhaps more evocative of the magnificence of the rich cultural heritage, natural beauty and varied, lively wildlife, unspoilt and untamed, spectacular vistas, Miramar, slopes covered with forest with pine, oaks, silver birch, sycamore trees in prominence, rugged highlands, fast flowing, indeed cascading water falls, water being as fresh as rain water one can drink to one's heart content.

Twenty percent of the Snowdonia National Park (SNP) is specifically designated area of beauty and national heritage by United Kingdom and European Union (EU) under European Habitats Directive as a special area of conservation.

The whole area is rich in wild life with wild mountain goats, hares, mountain deers, foxes, badgers, wild pigs and beavers being the main wildlife.

Then there is variety of birds with mountain eagles, falcons, wood peckers, wood pigeons, kingfishers, owls and similar birds giving mountains a sort of aura that naturalists love. No wonder the place has one of the highest concentrations of caravan parks in Wales.

When Kiran and Penny sat on the bike, it was only early afternoon. There was plenty of time to visit the surrounding places. They visited the tiny village of Betws y Coed, with a waterfall nearby, as well as Pistil Waterfall, one of the most beautiful places of natural beauty in Wales. The road leading to the waterfall was so narrow and hair raising that made Kiran realizes the advantage of a two wheel drive rather than a car!

They had an early dinner in Bala before they returned to their Caravan Park. Penny suggested that they should hire a double birth caravan, as it would be much cheaper and more comfortable than single ones.

Penny offered to share the expenses at every turn but so far Kiran paid for their food, breaks at various cafes. But Penny would not let Kiran pay the full amount for the caravan.

It was indeed a much comfortable and luxurious caravan with a shower and two tiny bedrooms. They both had showers before going to bed, as it refreshes body and soul for Kiran.

The goodnight kiss was a bit lingering and on the wrong spot! But both, Kiran and Penny were too tired to read any thing more than just a kiss, perhaps a trivial misdeed! This was not the time or a place to peculate affection!

Next day, after a leisurely breakfast, Kiran and Penny rode South, through Mid-Wales. This is a different Wales, more rolling hills, gentle valleys and small, shallow lakes than North Wales.

The Brecon Beacons is the most beautiful part of Mid-Wales, covered with rolling hills, numerous cascading streams, spectacular waterfalls, rivers, **Black Mountain Range** with a peak **886 meters high**. It forms the natural border with Herefordshire in England.

They visited a stately home, near Llanwrtyd Wells, a small town on the banks of River Irfon, overlooked by the ***Epynt and Cambrian Mountains*** but more like high hills, in the ***Secret Heart of Wales***.

There are series of Hills known as ***"Fans"*** This is a ***Red Kite Country*** overflowing with plenty of water as well as vast and varied wild life, as the vast variety of flora and fauna, woodlands, hills and caves provide a natural, varied habitat for all forms of wild life.

In medieval times, the place even had wolves and black bears, now long gone due to human colonization. As usual, humans are a threat to every living organism, plants and wild life.

The mid Wales is a heaven for sport mad younger generation offering full range of activities, rock climbing, abseiling, caving, potholing, gorge walking, white water Kayaking, open canoeing, mountain biking and similar activities that keeps one young at heart, body and spirit.

Kiran thought this was a perfect place for Penny, as she was indeed young, adventurous and a little bit foolhardy, a perfect combination for adventure, a thrill seeking person who would not mind taking measured risks.

Kiran and Penny visited ***Brecon Beacon National Park,*** on the outskirts of the town of Brecon, which is a natural watering hole for one and all, with Caravan Parks dotted around, some providing a real luxury living.

They visited villages and places of interest like Abergavenny, Ebbw Vale and Builth, a recent, modern town going back to Victorian age, before they reached Cardiff and spend the night at a luxurious B & B establishment.

Penny had a sharp eye for good accommodation, at a reasonable price. The place was practically deserted and the TV room, with a primitive, black and white Phillips TV the star attraction. Those were the pioneering days when radios rather than TVs ruled the hearts and minds of people.

Kiran and Penny relaxed in the lounge, with a bottle of wine and a packet of crisps and nuts, watching ***Coronation Street*** and ***The Dixon of the Dock Green***, a favourite programme at the time.

Relaxing on the sofa, Penny knew that Kiran was too shy, a real gentleman to make a move on her. Kiran's serenity and peaceful nature made him appear so shy but extremely desirable. So Penny gently sleds on his chest, arms, as natural as a lioness seeking the protection from a male lion, the king of the forest.

Kiran was at a loss what to do but he did not try to stop Penny seeking comfort in his open shoulders and stretched chest, gently kissing him and encouraging him to massage her breasts, in fact any part of her body.

Kiran knew that even in his days at Oxford and Cambridge, there was a culture of drinking, pot smoking and having sex between students, some times even with young, handsome but some what naïve professors who could not resist advances from their young, bright, mischievous female students like Penny who would not hesitate to lay bare their body and soul!

After all these were the romantic days of love, sex, wild parties, student politics and of course dens for spies working for the Soviet Union, for their ideological advancement, not financial gain.

It was a foregone conclusion that Penny was not a virgin girl. But then virginity was a hindrance rather than a help or pride at Cambridge. Kiran had an hour of kissing and cuddling, pampering and massaging Penny that gave so much pleasure and satisfaction to both. But it made Kiran nervous as well, as he felt he may want more and could not restrain his urge. Would Penny resist him, stop him if he wants her badly, go all the way?

After early dinner, they went to bed in their own rooms, Penny, while teasing Kiran said, "Kiran do not forget to lock your room or you would wake up next to me, next my voluptuous, naked body. But I am not going to lock my room. So the choice is yours."

It was obvious to Kiran that Penny would not be averse to sleeping with him. But he would not feel at ease with such an encounter, adventure after such a short, a brief friendship, although it was natural that every ounce of his body desired Penny but his head overruled his heart!

Kiran's nobility was a turnpike, a barrier when it came to enjoying life at the Uni. What a pity, an expensive truancy, Kiran now thought! But today, he did not lock his door.

Penny was at least a voracious person, an honest, straight forward person in every way. She would not take advantage of Kiran's generosity, would willingly share, pay her way, as she was not short of money. Perhaps she was better provided than Kiran.

The next day, after breakfast they had to Part Company. Penny invited, rather dared Kiran to give her a passionate kiss that would linger on into her old age. By the time Penny let Kiran out of her hold, her embrace, both were out of breath, with wet lips and stretched tongues, as well as sore nipples for Penny, perhaps wet under garments as well!

Penny pleaded with Kiran to stick with her, join her to roam ***Devon and Cornwall***, visit ***Land's End and Lizard Point***. When she realized that Kiran was eager to return to London and go to Europe, she joked.

"Kiran, I know why you do not want to join me. You know that after two weeks in my company, I would become irresistible. Perhaps you may have to ask me to marry you, as you can't live without me. Who knows, I may even say yes, that is if you treat me like a lady and keep me in the lap of luxury I am accustomed to?"

Kiran indeed liked her company, her wicked sense of humour and knew that if he joined her, he would be sleeping with her before the sun would set and she would indeed become irresistible, physically, sexually and above all intellectually.

"Penny, if we had met at Uni, under different circumstances, perhaps I would have asked you to marry me. You are such a wonderful, kind and caring person I know I could not resist you too long.

Intellectually we are a perfect match. But whether I could keep you in the lap of luxury is a million dollar question! Then again the word luxury is a multi-meaning word. I am sure I can keep you in luxury, in heaven in my heart, give you pleasure that you can only imagine. You know what I mean, Penny!"

"Kiran, you are a naughty boy but you forgot to mention the words, sexy, adventurous and desirable girl, one in a million! That is what most boys would tell me, then you are different, a cultured person who is not after sex, unlike most boys. Then again I may be wrong. Looks are so often deceptive, aren't they?" My breasts are hurting and nipples are sore! But who is complaining?"

"That is your attraction, why I like you, trust you and want you as well. You are endowed with the capacity for being genius." Penny really wanted Kiran to change his plans. She was already falling in love with Kiran, without even realising it. But then it was a mutual feeling. Some how Penny had a magnetic power of the mind to attract and influence every young heart that would cross her path.

It would have been a privilege for Penny to shape Kiran's mind, made him mould into her dreams and be part of her success on social and political front. This would have been an act of catalyst of Penny's own dreams, ambition and sexual pleasure.

There was no need for Penny, a liberated soul, to bow down to her Western, Abrahamic morality, which had been confined to dustbin in her family a long time ago.

Kiran could not help but smile serenely. After a heart searching half an hour, Kiran bade farewell to Penny. Kiran was glad that in a way, he had managed to retain the depth of his dignity when it would have been tempting to walk into her bedroom, share her bed without a murmur from Penny and have a honeymoon night?

Even today, after a gap of nearly fifty years, it made his mouth water. He could not help but put his arms round Olivia, drag her by his side, to the surprise and delight of Olivia.

Then in many ways Penny was an oasis of enlightenment, especially for some one who had lived a sheltered life in the calm waters of the colonial era. It seems life's greatest setbacks reveal life's biggest opportunities. Kiran had a mountain of setbacks but only hills of opportunities.

Now it was the time for his luck to change, to climb the summit of serenity. Perhaps this brief encounter with Penny made quantum improvement in Kiran's self esteem.

Kiran never had any communication from her, nor was he expected any, as Penny was the girl who would not dwell too long on any one, any situation, would easily move like a butterfly, from one flower to another.

Even today Kiran could not help but wonder where Penny may be, what is she doing, did she enter politics and became an MP and above all, what would have happened to him, if he had joined Penny and got married to her.

Perhaps all the thoughts, romantic liaisons that lay dormant for so many years were surfacing from his subconscious mind when Kiran was drifting in and out of sleep, day dreaming.

Perhaps life could have been interesting, living in a fast lane but may be too turbulent, full of unpredictable uncertainties. Definitely not a sea of calm and ebbing tide that is what Kiran deserved and got from Olivia and her family. Then life is full of ifs and buts.

* * *

Chapter Nine

Final Farewell to London

Returning to London after a whirlwind tour of Wales was like coming home. Kiran had learnt more in just a week than in his five years' stay in London. He had stayed in all sorts of accommodation, from YMCA hostel to hotel, caravan and B & B on farms.

Kiran met vast and varied people, hippies, backpackers, adventurers, and students, rebellious off-springs who came from rich and influential families. Then Martha and Martin were the gems of humanity and of course mischievous, marvellous, gorgeous and very desirable Penny who could have changed Kiran's life for ever!

In just under a week, Kiran became from an ordinary straight forward guy to a street-wise person who could handle any situation! This was a good baptism for more ambitious travel on the world stage, especially on a motorbike! After all, we the Indians are more family oriented and hippy lifestyle is as alien to us as carnivorous diet! The word Romany or a hippy is not even in our vocabulary!

Without such a tragedy, Kiran would have settle down in daily routine, would have gone home, find a decent, well paid job, perhaps in those well established English companies with overseas branches.

Kiran may have got married to a girl like Divya and lived happily ever after! But this tragedy had broken camel's back, thrown Kiran's life in disarray, in turmoil. Kiran merely existed from day to day. For Kiran, passing a week was an achievement, a relief, a gift from God! Even a good night's sleep was as rare as sighting a rainbow in Sahara desert.

Perhaps every cloud has a silver lining; every tragedy opens a new avenue. A star is born out of an explosion and there is no gain without pain, although Kiran's pain could not be defined or could be categorize in any way, in any manner. It was beyond human endurance, even beyond imagination.

It was a sheer luck to meet Penny, a pleasant encounter Kiran will remember and cherish for a long time. Perhaps it was an omen of future events to be unfolded. All his friends were so happy and elated to see him. Now they were not only his friends but they were his family members as well. Ramesh, who had shared every tragic minute with Kiran, was particularly happy to see him.

This was the first time since the tragedy Kiran some how felt at ease with the world. Perhaps with the passage of time and finding right company, even a right partner; Kiran may come to terms with his loss. But it was a big **PERHAPS!**

But in the end, whatever that does not kill you make you strong. It is never too late to have a happy second childhood or even the second adulthood. But the second time around, it is entirely up to you and no one else. You make or break your life, your future.

Deep inside his heart Kiran was glad for this second opportunity to make a go of his life. But he was too guilt ridden to acknowledge it openly. After all if one gives up when it is winter, when trees are bare and ugly, sunshine in short supply, than one will miss the promise of spring when trees are spouting buds, eager to come out of the winter blues, a child trying to take its first step.

Then there is beauty of summer when trees are decorated, painted with blossoms, ready to bear fruits that would sustain many lives. Come autumn, "*The Fall*", trees are laden with life giving fruits and berries, a prelude to winter survival. The hibernation is but one part of life. The warmth, sunshine and spring inevitably greets us when we come out of hibernation.

One should not judge life from one encounter, no matter how painful it may be, not to let the pain of one season destroy the joy of the rest of the year. After all it is nature, to be here today, gone tomorrow. No one is in charge of one's happiness but oneself!

When Kiran returned to London from his Welsh adventure, he was eager to leave London while he was still normal, before he was dragged back into self pity and depression, panic attacks and nervous disposition, before he lose the urge to roam the world. But after Welsh adventure, it was unlikely. His appetite for travel, for adventure was wetted, raised and primed.

Kiran had become more philosophical. Perhaps he realised that what has happened, has happened and there is nothing he could do to change it. He will have to live his life, as best as he could. Frame every disaster with the words, "would this matter in ten years' time?"

The sky can not remain laden with dark clouds. The sun has to come out sooner or later and even a rainbow may appear on the horizon. It would be better to live in hope than die in despair, to hope for the best but to prepare for the worse, be watchful and then go with the flow! In Kiran's case, he had seen the worse. The life could not be more tragic than he had already witnessed.

Within two weeks of returning to London from his Welsh adventure, Kiran left London one early morning. He knew this time he may be away for a long period. Perhaps he may never come back. It would not be out of bounds for Kiran to join a monastery in Spain or Greece, become a Buddhist monk in Ceylon, Tibet or Thailand.

Kiran may even find a **Guru** and end up in an **ashram,** some where high up in the Himalayas, the mystic land, the abode of **Yeti**, the source of holy river **Ganges** and **Lord Shiva,** one of the three Gods who manage the Universe, Lord Brahma, the Creator, Lord Vishnu, the Administrator and Lord Shiva, the Destroyer.

When Kiran boarded the ferry at **Southampton**, his heart was heavy, in turmoil and his eyes wet. He was leaving a place that was his home for the last six years, where he had made good friends and knowing well that this could be the final farewell to this green and beautiful land, the kind and caring English people. Kiran took a deep breath to calm his mind and fill his lungs with English air!

In those days, ferries were just ferries, not a mini cruise liner that we have today. Yet the ferry Kiran boarded was some what luxurious in relative terms, as it had a few cabins for premium paying passengers, with showering facilities.

It was a leisurely three day cruise to the Spanish port of Santander. The passage through the choppy waters of **Bay of Biscay** was stomach churning, at least for most passengers if not for Kiran, as Kiran had sailed through even choppier waters back in Mombassa.

It was indeed an unforgettable experience to sail to the beautiful spice islands of **Zanzibar and Pemba**.

It was even more fascinating to sail to heaven on earth, the serene, lay back islands of **Seychelles,** a welcome to another world, a lost world, with miles and miles of sandy beaches, a group of some one hundred fifteen islands with unique flora and fauna, some belonging to prehistoric era.

This is an archipelago of legendary beauty. Some seventy five islands are low-lying coral atoll and reef islands on the outer rim. They are uninhabited and most probably will disappear under water in the next fifty years or so, climate change raising the sea water to its highest level for some two thousand years.

The other forty one islands, many inhabited but visited regularly to harvest coconuts, cashew nuts, cassava and such naturally growing edible food, a gift of nature, are the oldest mid-oceanic granite islands on earth. The main island with international airport is Mahe with capital Victoria.

The omnipresent bird life is unique, a paradise for naturalists, bird watchers as well as lonely heart tourists, as we were told people, especially ladies were so friendly and accommodating! Fortunately sex tourism was in its infant stage and people were religious, church influence widespread and paramount.

For us, Seychelles was famous, a star attraction for the giant coconuts, unique fruits, similar to our star fruits, lynches, guava and their likes which were so different from the ones we had in Mombassa.

These fruits were only grown or rather grew naturally in these islands and animal life, giant tortoise that children could ride! As these islands have been cut-off from the mainland, they have preserved their prehistoric heritage of flora, fauna, birds and animal life.

In those days, ships were not equipped with stabilizers that keep modern liners steady in the roughest seas. Today's cruse ships are more like five star hotels on the sea, a floating resort with ever changing scenery.

There were as many Lorries and cars as passengers. Most vehicles were commercial, carrying British manufactured goods, even brand named cars like Austin, Morris, Hillman, Rover, Ford and Jaguar, a few among many famous British names, now just a faint memory. How the time has changed?

Those were the days when the words **"Made in Britain"** meant something, denote quality, craftsmanship and pride, a real value for money. Today no one wants to touch any goods made, manufactured in Britain, a sick man of Europe when it comes to manufacturing industry.

The ferry perhaps sarcastically named **"Pride of Britain"** was a basic ship where the only place to meet, eat, drink and socialize was the bar cum lounge, with a restaurant. In the evening it provided entertainment, by the crew, passengers and any one who has the slightest talent for singing, telling jokes or dancing to the jukebox music.

There was a simple, macho atmosphere where every one could feel at ease, provided they are not too fussy about the company of hardened, well built and a bit noisy people whose hearts were much softer than their looks. It was the case of never judge a book by its cover.

But it was certainly not the place to be eccentric or the company to be polemic, discuss politics or the religion. Their main topics of conversation were their families, girl friends, sex, food and weather. The intellectuals would have to remain on the sideline, wait for another day, another company.

Lorry drivers and others may sleep rough or in their vehicles, some Lorries even had comfortable sleeping compartments, well equipped cabins with most amenities, even paraffin run hotplates, so as to save on the hotel cost as well as useful when stranded in snow or strike which was a frequent occurrence in France.

Kiran met his fellow ship mates in the morning while having a breakfast. On his table for four, besides him, there were two lorry drivers and a **Gap Year Student** who introduced himself as **Robin**. As he was not sure what to study, which Uni to attend, he opted for a year's break and travel the world, or rather Europe. Robin was an idealist. He wanted to change the world single handed!

Kiran immediately felt at ease with Robin, as he was, like Kiran, from London. Robin had attended the school in London Borough of Harrow, which boasts one of the best **Grammar Schools** in London. Even famous and privileged sons of India like Pandit Nehru and Mahadavebhai Desai had attended boarding schools in Harrow.

Robin was planning to hitchhike throughout Europe, including Communist states in Eastern Europe, Poland, East Germany, Bulgaria and Romania where Robin may not be welcome, even if he had the visas. Hitchhiking was a novel concept, a free ride, a Romany lifestyle the Communist regime would not like to encourage amongst their younger, well disciplined generation. Then Robin was a determined person who would not mind chasing a rainbow, a shadow! One can not fail a test; an exam unless one takes a test, sits an exam!

Robin's final destination was **Israel** where he would like to live and work on a **Kibbutz,** a communal collective settlement, with collective ownership of all properties and earnings. It was a self run, self governed, self financed mini state, a modified version of **Moshav Shitufi,** similar to collective farms in USSR but without State interference.

The farm is owned and run by its inhabitants, sharing every thing. In those days such an adventure, a life in the desert oasis was not only fashionable but in great demand.

In reality the life was tough and the existence was basic, to say the least with strict discipline and back breaking farm work.

Then the Jewish State was formed out of tragedy that nearly wiped out the entire Jewish population of Europe. Some six million Jews lost their lives, mostly in concentration camps run by Gestapo, Hitler's army of Secret Service. They learnt the hard ways that cowards are the food, the fodder for the braves as well as the fanatics. An ounce of courage, practice is better than a ton of theory, begging for mercy.

The Kibbutz life was a pleasant experience, especially for the Jewish youngsters who were flocking to these settlements, to work on the farm, till the land from early morning until late evening, with a break in the afternoon, as it would be too hot to work outdoor between 1pm to 4pm.

The evenings and week-ends were free to enjoy, meet the local Jewish boys and girls. Some youngsters even stayed for some time and came back with beautiful, gazelle like young Jewish brides, nimble on their feet, difficult to catch!

Their golden tan, slim figure and humble outlook, as most had lived a sheltered life on a Kibbutz; under the watchful eyes of their parents and community leaders was the main attraction. In comparisons, most of today's youngsters have a social skill of a Dalek looking forward for the next fix.

They are more like Milky Bar generation who had failed to grow up? The saying that every Saint has a past and every Sinner has a future some how sounds hollow when applied to these whiz kids who have only one ambition, how to get rich in the shortest time span!

The Gnosticism or the Gnostic atmosphere of the Kibbutz's gnarled life style had its own rugged charm! There was no gazumping in love, comradeship and loyalty, to the family, kibbutz or the nation. The patriotic action always leads to the elevation of the soul. These are the noble principle that has laid the foundation of the State of Israel.

Israel was a proud nation in those early days when the future was unsure, uncertain, as every Arab state was eager to destroy the State of Israel, as they fervently believed that the creation of Israel was an imposition, an occupation of Arab land.

Jewish people were equally firm in their belief that it was the land of their ancestors, going back five thousand years, well before the onset of Islam. Then politics and religion is always complicated, more than meets the eye, one subject one should avoid in a confined place and unfamiliar company.

It was an idealistic concept more appropriate for the time when Europe was still reeling from the atrocities of the Second World War and Israel was struggling to build the nation that would be a safe heaven for the Jewish people.

Israel had to be an advanced nation, a super military power, a well educated state where every one has a degree or two, with the finest and well equipped army, loyal, dedicated citizens, a military might to recon with. Jewish people had learnt the hard way that they could not depend on any one in their hour of need. They have to be self-reliant in each and every way. The might is always right and the might must be always on the side of Israel.

It is a pity that Jewish people have more or less forgotten their past, gone soft and physical labour is shunned in the State of Israel. They are unable or unwilling to live in peace and harmony with their neighbours, although the neighbours are not that accommodating.

Jews were like Nomads, Romanise people persecuted universally for being enterprising, hard working, well educated and successful businessmen with higher living standard, well above that of the local people, the masses who had the upper hand when it came to democracy or even dictatorship. It was not the time to be prophetic.

Before Kiran disembarked at the Spanish port of **Santander,** he became friendly with Robin who was much younger and less experienced than Kiran. Robin looked up to Kiran, like an elder brother, admired his achievement on the educational front, as well as his good nature and his determination to succeed in whatever enterprise he may embark on.

It was inevitable for Kiran to invite Robin to join him on this journey to a fantasy land. For Robin, it was a God send gift, as he could be a back sit passenger, rather than a hitchhiker standing on a roadside in all weather trying to hitch a lift.

Spain is the most interesting country in Europe, blessed with high mountains, snow covered peaks, deep valleys, rivers and fast flowing streams. Spain is a historic land dotted with churches, castles, cathedrals, museums and ancient buildings with a rich heritage of arts and crafts, with the name Picasso shining brightly above all.

The climate is variable, from long hot summers in the South to cool, mild temperate climate in the North, bordering France, as well as rugged interior with mountain ranges like Sierra de Gredo, Sierra de Guadarrama, Sierra de Demana and many more.

Where there are mountain ranges, there are inevitably fast flowing streams and rivers, lakes, ponds, dams and varied and vast flora and fauna, birds and animals, wildlife in abundance. There was a hint of African beauty and wilderness in this vast and exciting country.

* * *

Chapter Ten
The Spanish Adventure

The port of **Santander** is the gateway to Spain for those who sail from North Europe. Kiran, in company of Robin spend two nights at a caravan park. Although Robin was a decent boy, Kiran badly missed the company of Penny who was street-wise, well educated, well read and a charming fellow traveller. Then it is so romantic to have a female company when on the move, especially on motorbike!

Kiran even thought for a moment whether he made a mistake in rejecting Penny's offer to be with her, roam Devon and Cornwall together. In any case it was too late to regret. It was water under the bridge, perhaps a missed opportunity. Kiran soon put her out of his mind and concentrated on the job on hand.

Santander is the capital city of Cantabria, located between Asturias and the Basque country. It boasts eleven clean and long sandy beaches. It is also the home of the magnificent coastal resort of **El Sardinaro,** the resort well known and favourite among the Spanish upper class but not with the Brits.

As the northern coastal resorts of Spain are on the Atlantic coast, unlike Mediterranean coast, Santander beaches are cold and windy until well into summer months of June to September. Even then sea water is too cold for most but the bravest and the children

The places of interest are as usual parks, churches and cathedrals and excursions, especially fishing and dolphin, sharks and whales watching or rather spotting from the comfort of the luxurious boats equipped with most essentials.

Two days seemed to be too long to spend in Santander. So they were eager to move, travel east, along the border with France. The first stop, only a four hour ride, was the city of ***Bilbao,*** a thriving town in its own right.

As no one speaks English in this part of Spain, Kiran had to buy an extra phrase book, as the one he bought in London was too basic. Kiran spend at least a couple of hours a day learning Spanish since he boarded the ferry. Kiran was naturally good at languages and Spanish was no exception.

Bilbao was a tiny settlement on both the banks of river ***"Ria del Nervim"***

(Estuary of Nervim) The name Bilbao was given to this settlement in 1300AD due to its geographical importance, as a commercial and maritime centre.

There are numerous places of interest, a well worth stay of two nights in a Spanish National Tourist Board run hotels known as ***parador*** which were excellent, a good value for money on most part.

So often these accommodations are in castles or even old palaces, more like five star hotels than guest houses, beyond reach for budget travellers. But prices are well marked and accommodations well documented.

There were plenty of places of interest and that include numerous churches and cathedrals, Iglesia San Antonio and Cathedral de Santiago, Edifico (building) de la Bilbao, Palacio (palace) Ibaigane, Universidad (University) de Deusto, Casa (house) Mentero and Ayuntamiento (Town Hall) a few among many buildings, churches and historic places of interest, too numerous to visit or to mention.

Our next stop was the tiny enclave of Andorra, a beautiful place with wonderful mountain scenery. It was a long and tiring journey with no towns or even villages of significance on the long route from Bilbao to Andorra.

As it was mountainous country with no proper roads, only lanes and paths, it took Kiran two days to reach Andorra. Two nights they spent on the way were interesting.

They were sheltered from the bitterly cold winds first by a Spanish family in their modest farm house, with three beautiful, lovely mountain lassies, daughters with interesting names, ***Margarita, (daisy) Marina (sea) and Mariposa (butterfly).***

The youngest one was Mariposa and she did float like a butterfly. Robin was really taken to her, as she had a rugged beauty with over developed breasts, as well as the rest of her lower torso well out of proportion but never the less sexy, with mischievous outlook, haunting eyes, a perfect company for cold nights!

The girls liked Kiran, with his broken Spanish with English pronunciation and his effort to be kind and appreciative.

When Kiran said to girls, *"Me gusta todos tres nombres. Ellas estan muy encantadorias.* (I like your all three names. They are very beautiful.) Mariposa, the giggling lassie could not help but comment.

"Senior Keran, es usded no menos attractivo. Como Yo deseo que Yo puedo encarcelar en mi habistation y echo la llave. (Senior Keran, you are no less attractive. How I wish I could imprison you in my bedroom and throw away the key?)

Kiran though that although these girls were attractive, friendly and fun to be with, but their parents were strict and sensitive. It would be better if he leave, say good night as soon as possible; otherwise he would be as helpless as a deer caught in the glare of an intruding pair of headlights. Three against one was not a contest!

"Senoritas, no me comprendo mucho, para buenas noches y adios haste manana. Que suenes con los angelitos! (Girls, I do not understand much but good night and see you tomorrow. Sweet dreams!)

"Que pena, Que lastima! Adios haste manana temparana, nuestras novio! (What a pity, goodbye until early tomorrow morning, our sweet heart!) With three girls blowing kisses from a distance, Kiran, with Robin retreated to their lonely bedroom with cold mattresses!

But to their surprise, they found hot water bottles under the blankets. It was better than nothing! These gorgeous girls were a mere pot of gold, look but do not touch; a silver cloud on the distant horizon. Kiran could not help but wonder, how wonderful it would be if Penny was sharing his bed tonight?

Kiran felt that the household routine was a bit shambolic with too much going on at any time. But then these three amorous girls in their prime with overflowing hormones, what could he expect! Certainly these girls were pleonastic but not loud mouthed!

They were like gushing mountain streams fed by the melting snow, water as pure as melted Artic ice! Could he lose his serenity, his calm, his sense of right and wrong in the presence of not one but three such voluptuous bodies! Could they be extremely desirable as bed partners, especially on cold nights but not as life partners?

Would his mind develop a mentality of an uncaged monkey, rushing from one branch to another, from one beauty to another, from Margarita to Mariposa!

But Kiran had by now mastered the psychology of making friends and winning encounters with opposite sex! In a way this household was an oasis of enlightenment in more ways than one can imagine.

Kiran could not help but wonder what life would throw at him if he could spend a month in this house! It would definitely make a quantum improvement in his satisfaction level; perhaps not if his hormones breaks lose in the night and he had a loot mentality! Perhaps it would be no more than an exercise in frustration! It was time to give his imagination a rest!

Kiran was eager to ride away after early breakfast. As the next day was Sunday, the family got up early to go to church some distance away. So Kiran and Robin had an early breakfast and left at the same time to the giggles and slight disappointment for the girls.

"Adios y tenian el viaje seguro". (Goodbye and have a safe journey) the girls giggled.

"Adios y muchas gracias por su ayuda." (Goodbye and thank you so much for your help, hospitality) Kiran replied in his imperfect but sweet Spanish.

The three girls, to their delight and surprise, saw Kiran produced three beautiful half open red rosebuds, plucked from their garden! He gave one rose to each girl and in return he got a kiss on each cheek from the girls, dressed in their Sunday best, in front of their parents who had a soft smile on their faces! It seemed Kiran had the knack of attracting affection and respect. Kiran was sure that he would have got a long and lingering full blown kiss from each girl if there parents were not there.

It was obvious that the parents knew about their girls being flamboyant and flirtatious but as these young, charming and beautiful girls hardly meet any eligible, smart and cultured, desirable young men, they tolerated their flippancy, over eagerness, the innocent fun! After all, they were young and ambitious once.

In any case the modern youths from cities would consider these girls plebeian, only fit for fun and sex, not as life partners. But to Kiran, they were more than plausible and deserve much better than a lonely life in a forgotten corner of the country. At least Kiran had not lacerated them in any manner. Kiran's flattery was innocent, compassionate and genuine. Then Kiran was by now a master of kidology.

There were no mobile phones; even land-lines were more like grapevine that would go into hibernation at the slightest excuse. So how can they grudge some innocent flirtation for their three lovely lassies! After all they were young ones.

The second night they spent in a ***pension***, a basic hotel for the weary traveller. Kiran would indeed be relieved when they reach Andorra, as roads were mere tracks, slippery and so often with blind curves.

Robin was perceptive and percipient, an asset, as he kept his eyes open, read signs and now and again urged Kiran to slow down.

Kiran had, by now got used to driving on the right side and taken to his powerful bike like a duck to the water.

Perhaps it would be more arduous, dangerous ball game if Kiran has to navigate city roads, city traffic, ride his bike in Madrid and Barcelona, especially without Robin as a passenger, navigator and advisor! But Kiran hoped that by then he would be indeed an experienced rider, even on Spanish roads with its moody, passionate and tempestuous drivers and high mortality rate.

After his Welsh experience, Kiran had thrown away his caution to the wind; detail planning abandoned in favour of a free ride, roam where his heart would take him and stop, break the journey at the most unusual places.

This gave Kiran a sense of freedom, unplanned unique pleasure and strange encounters, the feelings that he is an explorer, a present da***y Marco Polo, even Vasco de Gama*** who discovered sea route to India, a land of milk and honey, granary for the hungry Europe at the time. How the time and priorities have changed!

Riding motorbike gave Kiran the choice and freedom of taking unknown, unmapped, uncharted roads or just paths inaccessible to other mode of transport except hitchhiking and his financial security, freedom helped him to stay in places out of bound for most budget travellers.

Robin showed his appreciation time and again, as Kiran would not let him pay for petrol or rather gas in Spain, tea and coffee, meals in roadside cafes they frequently stopped at, to break the monotony of riding a bike with great concentration.

Kiran has now become an expert at making friends, especially with the opposite sex, as he was a tall, dark and handsome young man most girls would give an arm and a leg for!

Kiran realised that friends are the family we can choose ourselves and discard at our will. So there is no need to be miser when it comes to making friends, fermenting friendship. Life is indeed a lonely place without good, honest friends who would stand by us in our hour of need. But we have to be careful before we cement the friendship.

It was a long and tiring ride from the small town of Candanchu to Andorra. But they passed through some magnificent mountain scenery, scattered with purpose built *"Los Miradors"* or *"Observing Platforms"*.

The mountain peaks with romantic names like Pena Collarada, Punta Vigenma and Pico de Aneto were the few mountains, reaching a height of well over six thousand feet that Kiran had to navigate.

The tracks were wet, slippery and so often blocked by fallen trees which was a death trap if not spotted from a distance. The whole journey was a race between a tortoise and a snail. There were no winners, only the determined finishers.

They had at least ten stops, to have a hot drink, taking in the magnificent views, mountain scenery or even observe wild life at close hand and listen to the orchestra of nature on full blast! Kiran's camera was clicking all the time, so often out of sheer enthusiasm than justification, as there may not be enough light or the scenery may be shrouded in mist and drizzle.

Among the vast and varied wild life were mountain goats that can climb a sheer vertical slope that would be a death trap for any other animal, even mountain lion or rather a kind of leopard and black bears which were the only animals that can pose danger to humans.

But these shy creatures usually stay well away from roads and human habitation, as they were nearly hunted to extinction for their furs and skin. Goats, cattle and sheep belonging to local people had bells tied round their neck, as the sound of bell could lead the shepherd to them when the mist engulf the mountain slopes and visibility is very much restricted.

It was a hazardous job to gather these animals and herd them to their pens. Without the sound of bells, their job would be impossible. The shepherds were so expert that they could identify each and every animal from the sound of bells, whether it is a sheep, a goat or a cow and their names, as each animal was given a name in family tradition.

The whole journey was a big learning curve for Kiran and Robin. The climate, roads, scenery, wild life and even people were as different as chalk and cheese from the rest of Spain, especially the coastal resorts and the big cities. Then this is the beauty of Spain! This is unity through diversity, although the fiercely independent Basque people would like to be an independent nation in its own right.

Chapter Eleven
Andorra, Mini Switzerland

Before Kiran and Robin could enter Andorra, the plane landed at Singapore airport. Kiran was brought back to reality with a bump. This was a long flight from Bombay to Singapore with a stopover at Colombo. Again it was midday and the stopover involved spending a night in a five star hotel,

"The Imperial Hotel" was mainly at the disposal of English guests and always fully booked, as Singapore was and still is the gateway to *Far East,* to the eastern most corner of British Empire, *Hong Kong, North Borneo, Malaya*, *Portuguese colony of Macao and Australia and New Zealand*, a serene part of British influence*,* from home to home for the British people.

As usual *BOAC*, the world's leading provider of air services had the pick of the hotel rooms, as nearly one third of the hotel guests were from BOAC flights.

By 2pm, Kiran and Olivia were having lunch in the posh hotel dinning room, on the 10th floor, overlooking the *Straight of Singapore* and the *Batam Island,* clearly visible through a powerful binocular on a clear day.

As Kiran had a peaceful and relaxing flight, day dreaming all the way to Singapore, he was relatively fresh while Olivia was some what tired, as she could not relax much on an aeroplane.

Kiran and Olivia both had wonderful, tasty and varied lunch and dinner, a mixture of English, Indian and Chinese dishes, variety of cuisine that would satisfy any one's taste buds, even that of Olivia.

Olivia particularly enjoyed late dinner, especially risotto type basmati rice with prawns, her favourite dish that she could cook to perfection and that also include vegetable biryani, Kiran's favourite dish. Then practically every Spanish girl could cook paella and prepare the famous Spanish drink Sangria. That was the minimum requirement to get married in those days!

The rice tasted really nice and appetising when cooked by Olivia, with home grown fresh vegetables that Kiran had introduced, on his own small plot of land where he grew brinjal, cauliflower, ginger, garlic, fenugreek (green methi) green turmeric, okra or lady's finger, green hot chillies, gourd (duthi) coriander, bitter gourd (Karalla) spring onion, spinach, sweet potato, yam, mint and vetch, (Guar) a few of the exotic vegetables Kiran had managed to grow. Then Spain has such a tolerable climate that it is not too difficult to grow seasonal vegetables.

Kiran had taken to farming like a duck to water, an Eskimo to Igloo, a German to beer drinking and Spaniard to Sangria! Later on when Indian food became popular in Spain with British tourists flocking to Costa de Sol and the Baleares Islands of Majorca, Ibiza and Minorca, Kiran managed to build up a valuable clientele in the restaurant trade, supplying them these exotic vegetables, thus providing a second income to supplement the main income derived from olives, grapes and holiday lettings.

By the time the plane climbed into clear blue sky over Singapore, it was well passed midday. Today Olivia was lethargic, as she had a rare sleepless night. So Kiran had no option but to slip back into his unfinished journey into Andorra with Robin.

Kiran had to pass through *Basque* country before they reached Andorra, deep in the Pyrenees Mountains. There was a tiny check point, a Custom and Immigration post where their passports were checked and stamped with a month's visa.

Andorra is a mountainous municipality, an independent country with breath-taking scenery where the film *"Sound of Music"* the best musical ever was filmed in 1970s that put the country on the tourist map and made *Julie Andrew* a household name. Indeed Andorra is the second highest country in Europe, after Switzerland. Like Tibet, Andorra is the roof of Europe.

But back then, just after the war, it was an unknown tiny semi-independent nation jointly administered by Spain and France who had the right to influence the nomination of the *Chief Minister* and *Head of the Church (Bishop)* alternatively.

Andorra is also a ***"Free Trade Zone"*** without any tax or duty on the goods. Thus it is a heaven for those who are addicted to shopping, love chocolate, spirits, cigarettes, perfumes and such luxury items taxed to the hilt in their own countries.

As a teetotaller and a non smoker, Kiran had no interest in shopping but the high cost of living was a burden on backpackers on a shoestring budget. The only shopping Kiran did was to buy a gold chain with a beautiful Cross, with bit of soil from holy land, the birth place of Lord Jesus Christ, in a cavity in the cross and covered with glass, as a sign of good luck, from the monk, although not the ***Monk who sold his Ferrari!*** (Title of Robin Sharma's famous and illustrious book worth reading)

This was my first gift to Olivia and she is still wearing this chain, her good luck charm with pride!

Kiran thought the money would go to a home in need, for a good cause. Perhaps this charm did work, for both, Kiran and Olivia. Kiran found love, happiness and purpose in life and Olivia, her Prince Charming!

As we say, faith can move a mountain! Surely Kiran's mountain of burden, guilt and self pity was now in the distant past, buried deep in his subconscious mind, laid to rest after a long struggle.

Before they could reach the town of Andorra La Vella, the only town and administrative centre, the darkness, the mist, the damp and cold weather descended on this isolated heaven in a hurry. Few stars brave enough to make an appearance could not stamp their authority on the empire of darkness. Perhaps Dracula, the Prince of Darkness was lurking behind every tree, every shadow and the dark, haunting castle!

It would be dangerous and foolhardy to continue on a motorbike in the dark, with cold and fierce wind piercing their bodies, especially Kiran's, as the rider in the front take the full force, as an added obstacle for the rider.

Kiran saw a light in the distance, a tiny twinkling light that would come and go, appear and disappear, as if playing hide and seek, the only sign of life, an indication of human habitation in this desolate heaven. Kiran sincerely hoped that it was not an illusion, nature playing a trick on him!

Although Kiran was not sure, he had no choice but to ride in the direction of light and hope for the best. In ten minutes' time, they were knocking on the doors of a monastery, built like an ancient castle, a fortress.

A monk opened the door and when he saw the plight on these two young men, strangers shivering in the cool of the night. He invited them in for a meal, a hot supper they were about to have. It was a simple meal blending with the surrounding of the building and its inhabitants.

The starter was an onion soup with coarse wheat loaf that tasted really sweet, specially with churned butter and fresh marmalade, followed by meat dish but hard boiled eggs for Kiran, mesh potatoes, various boiled vegetables and a glass of strong wine, or rather a big mug of wine with home made, textured goat cheese that made Kiran drowsy, the wine, not the cheese and in need of a bed even before the meal was over!

This was the best meal Kiran had for a long time, full of warmth, energy, satisfaction and fulfilling. Then they were hungry, cold and exhausted. Any food would have tasted like a king's buffet, a meal fit for a queen, a meal in a five star restaurant.

The haunting atmosphere, loneliness, the pitch darkness and the hauling wind like a wailing cry of a desperate child gave this dark and dingy place an atmosphere that would sink any heart. It was like entering the castle of Dracula where he would imprison his victims, usually young and beautiful girls.

There was no electric light, only the candles and kerosene lamps of the bygone era. Was the atmosphere romantic! Not in the least, not tonight. In fact the interior of the monastery matched the cold and gloomy atmosphere of the outside wilderness.

Kiran went to sleep as soon as he hit the soft, warm and surprisingly comfortable bed. When he woke up in the morning, at around 8am, his usual time, Kiran felt fresh and full of energy. It was a new dawn, a new day and a fresh start. He had an undisturbed sleep for nearly twelve hours! No wonder he was feeling fresh and energetic.

The monastery looked completely different in daylight. At these height, the sun's rays heat up the place fast. Kiran called it *"Shangri La."* The monks would have breakfast at 9am, after getting up at the break of dawn and putting in a few hours' hard labour before breakfast.

It was a daily routine to milk cows and goats, collect eggs and churn milk to produce butter and cheese, wash and clean the stables and let the cattle out, put them to graze, all on empty stomach or rather on a big jar of hot milk sweetened with honey and their special mixture of herbs and nuts that was really nourishing and gave them enough energy to perform these arduous tasks before day break, in semi darkness.

It sustained them until breakfast that is after having a shave and a cold shower! There was no hot water as such, although guests were provided with buckets of hot water.

The monastery stood on twenty acres of rolling, fertile land that would easily sustain some thirty monks whose needs were basic. The building was an old castle converted for habitation but with bare walls, long, dark and cold corridors and rooms with tiny windows, it was more like prison cells than bedrooms and parsley decorated, mostly with quotes in Latin from the Holy Bible.

There were some thirty five monks of varying ages of twenty five to sixty five, as the monastery would look after their old and the infirm monks when they are unable to put in a hard day's labour in the field.

They would switch to administration work, become foremen and look after the finances to make the settlement self-sufficient.

There was a well furnished crafts room where monks with special skills in wood-work, painting and jewellery making have a free reign to design and produce work of art for sale in the local shops. This is the place from where Kiran bought the gold chain with a Holy Cross.

The monk, who opened the door when Kiran knocked, was Father Fredrick, a young man in his thirties. He spoke fluent English, Spanish, Catalan and French, the four most widely spoken languages in Andorra, although Italian was fast gaining ground.

Kiran and Robin were requested to address him as Brother Freddy, perhaps his nick name. He was a lively person, full of knowledge, enthusiasm and charm. As usual Kiran's name, his dark skin and Hindu background created some interest, a bit of curiosity but not for long.

After a healthy breakfast with hot milk, porridge, eggs and bread but without tea or coffee, Brother Freddy took us on the tour of the land that belonged to the monastery.

The land was divided into three sections, one for the vineyard to harvest grapes that would produce wine and provide some income, as the wine had a good reputation in the area.

The second section was planted with serials, wheat, maize and barley. The crops provide the food all year round and the stems were fermented, soften and used as a cattle fodder in winter as the ground would become bare if over grazed.

The rest of the land was for grazing cows and goats whose milk was turned into butter and cheese, buttermilk and milkshakes in the hot summer months.

Within the monastery walls, there was a big central courtyard where stood a spacious glass house that produced fresh vegetables like tomatoes, potatoes, onions, cabbage, cucumber, lettuces and their likes all year round, as it was heated in winter months.

After the tour, Kiran and Robin went on a sight-seeing tour of the area. The area is littered with ruins of castles, Romanic churches, medieval bridges, expensive royal houses, mansions belonging to French and Spanish millionaires and unparallel natural beauty with fast flowing streams, lakes, ponds and grazing land where cattle could roam in freedom.

Andorra is indeed a Christmas card country with dotty villages, snow covered landscape and charming mountain peaks that would cool an angry heart and troubled mind! This was the right place for Kiran to be in.

There were no boundaries, as most of the land was a common land belonging to the State with a few vineyards in private hands, mostly in the hands of religious establishments and Noble Lords with small well kept castles incorporating guest houses.

Yet Andorra is indeed a tiny nation with just 488 sq. km in area. It is a God's gift to humanity. It would take just fifty minutes to travel from Spanish border in the South to French border in the North.

The population is just under sixty thousand, yet it has some 140 nationalities. But the vast majorities are native Andorrans, Spaniards, French, Portuguese, Italians and the British.

* * *

Chapter Twelve
Roaming on Monastic Lifestyle

When Kiran and Robin returned to the monastery for lunch, they decided to spend a week at the monastery; that is if the **Head Monk Father Joseph** would let them stay for a week.

Kiran was told, to his surprise and delight that they could not only stay but they will be provided with free board and lodge in exchange for working on the farm half a day. The labour was indeed scare and very costly as well, as most Andorrans were reasonably rich, well-off people, if not millionaire and averse to hard work.

It was the planting season. As the summer is short at this height, the monks would raise maize, wheat and barley plants under the glass and plant them in the field when plants are sturdy and well established.

It was hard work in the field to create raised base, a row of lane with drainage to plant each one in a row with a bamboo cane support and water them from the stream that was flowing through the monastery ground.

The ground was fertilized with cow dung and such natural manure so as not to lower the quality of flowing water with chemicals and artificial fertilizers. The monks were well versed in soil management. They planted a red rose bush in front of every row of grapevine.

When Kiran asked the question, what was the purpose of a rose bush, he learnt that roses and grapevines are infected with the same fungus. But rose bushes catch it first, well ahead of grapevine. So as soon as the rosebush shows the sign of fungus, they can take the precaution, spray the vines with a solution of vinegar and other ingredients that would save the vineyard before it is too late!

It was obvious that there is no need to use chemical fertilizers or pesticide to control fungus and such other hazards to farming. There are many natural remedies but they are time consuming to implement and labour intensive, thus making it commercially impractical!

It seems mother earth comes a poor second to human greed, business and intensive farming on the cheap. Then with bulging human population, it would be difficult, if not impossible to feed billions on sustainable farming methods! What we need is birth control and reducing human population. But no politician, especially in democracy, has the courage to tell the truth.

There was a deep well to supplement the stream water in late summer months when the water from the melting snow would dry up. The area was also fenced off to keep the cattle out, especially goats, the most destructive animals but most rewarding as well.

Kiran and Robin were not obliged to get up at day break but would have an early breakfast before starting work, cleaning stables before moving on to land, hard labour indeed.

They would help until one when they would shower and have lunch. The afternoon was free for them to roam the land to their heart's content. The dinner time was 7pm and bedtime 9pm.

As there was no electricity, there was nothing much to do at night except go to bed early. Ostensibly even taking, having monks' company was in short supply. They were practical men lost in their own routine, their world. In some ways they were like zombies, mechanical robots programmed to perform certain tasks. Then perhaps Kiran was being harsh, as there were some intelligent, intellectual monks who administer the monastery well, make it self sufficient.

Perhaps they sincerely believed in the saying ***"Early to bed, early to rise, will make you healthy but not so wealthy and surely a wise a monk?"***

So often Kiran would joke to Robin that they were being ostracized for their past sins! They were obliged to live like an ostrich with their heads buried in sands, where no peccadilloes were permitted!

But in reality, these monks were kind and caring to Kiran and Robin, especially as Kiran had spent some money in their gift shop where he bought the chain. They knew that Kiran and Robin were not free riders and they indeed worked hard on the farm.

It was just that they had no room for oscillation in their life-style. They could not vivify their daily existence. After all they were the servants of

God and children of Mother Earth and they would like to live in harmony, as we would like to with our parents, our family members.

So often the logic of despair can seem so compelling. So often these monks, their life-style and such religious places are looked upon as askance for no other reasons than mistrust and ignorance.

Some may think that monks are a beleaguered community. But in reality, they are the enlightened ones who have come out of bunker mentality; a stereo-typing on our part is due to ignorance and lack of knowledge. So often human mind is a closed shop. We are creatures of habit, familiarity and set in our ways.

These monks have triumphed over adversity to establish such a peaceful heaven when the world around them is fast crumbling into political chaos, economic meltdown and moral values confined to dustbin. In a way these monks, God's children are surrogate apologists for human sins. Their saintliness is the best revenge on the rest of the spoilt world.

Andorra is indeed a small nation, just 488 sq. km. in area. It would take just fifty minutes to drive from the Spanish border in the South to French border in the North.

It was an ideal arrangement for Kiran and Robin to have four to five hours off in the afternoon. There was more than enough time to travel to the farthest place, to any corner of Andorra.

Kiran was no longer a methodical person who would like to plan every step of his journey. Pettifogging was left behind as soon as he entered Spain, a laid back country where every job is done tomorrow but Manana (tomorrow) never comes. It always remains manana!

Instead Kiran had armed himself with a detail road map, atlas of Andorra that was marked with every tiny road, lane and even the path used by local people, no more than a narrow trodden track formed by constant usage, walking, treading by human feet.

Every morning, before they set out, they will spend some ten minutes with Brother Freddie who would instruct them where to go, what to see and how long it would take riding a motorbike. The town of Andorra la Vella was less than half an hour's ride on a bike and their first stop.

They spent one entire afternoon in the town, as it has some beautiful parks; the main one is Central Park with some fascinating lakes and water areas. The town is surrounded by mountains on three sides with breathtaking views below.

Andorra is indeed a Mirador country, a photogenic place where one could not help but click one's camera to one's heart content. It seems photography is as addictive as alcoholic drink or smoking, if not more.

With so many mountain peaks, rivers, fast flowing streams, ancient churches, catacombs, bridges dating back to Roman times and parks with water features, it was not difficult to understand why Kiran wanted to spend a whole week in Andorra.

Many buildings are carved out of mountain-side, built in harmony with the location and provide stunning views. Some are just hanging from the mountain sides in such a precarious position that one may hesitate to enter.

The places Kiran and Robin visited, photographed and categorized were "Mirador" of Andorra la Vella, Juclar Lake, Tristaina Lake, Casa de la Vall Gardens, Romanic church of Santa Coloma, Sant Vicens castle, Pas de la Casa ski resort, some what deserted in the height of summer.

They went up the Cable car at Pas de la Casa, Pica Comapedrosathe, the highest peak at nearly 3000 meters, many glaziers, the ski Resort of Ordino-Arcalis, one of the most popular one with breath taking mountain scenery, worth a visit in winter.

Then there was the village at the foot of Pas de la Casa, Church of Santa Eulalia and Sant Miguel, Sant Joan de Caselles, Romanic church of Santa Filomena de Aixovall and Santa Victoria, a few of some twenty churches and cathedrals Kiran and Robin visited in a week.

Kiran enjoyed the magnificent ludic-sport complex of Caldea with hydro-massage, sauna and swimming in the warm waters of the ricers in natural scenery, in the open, fresh air, under the blue sky.

The week passed away before they realised. But they covered a lot of ground; saw most on offer, as Andorra is such a small country, nothing more than half an hour ride to reach any part, any place of interest and any tourist attraction.

They felt it would be worth a visit in winter when the snow would cover most peaks and provide romantic Christmas card scenery that we normally associate with Switzerland and Austria. But this monastery would be a difficult place to be in, as it would be extremely cold, dark and damp during winter months.

It was some what a sad goodbye, as the monks had treated them well, provided them with food and shelter, gone out of their way to make their stay as comfortable as possible. They were not subjected to monastery rules on most part. Contrary to public assumption and belief, monks are not a haemophiliac society in any way.

Perhaps they may be fiduciaries for human sins, human excesses and may live a disciplined, anti shambolic life that most of us are not capable of. This is a blessing and not a setback, definitely not a boil on humanity! Their lifestyle is an antidote to our lose morals and loot mentality.

Just before leaving Kiran was granted ten minutes in the company of the Head Monk who rarely saw any one in private. Kiran felt he was with Dalai Lama, the noblest son of Tibet, if not the world.

Dalai Lama is a kind, caring and learned human being, persecuted by the Chinese in his own homeland Tibet, another beautiful country, the roof of the earth, brutally occupied and savaged by Chinese, one of the cruellest people on earth!

Kiran, who is a Hindu on his father's side and a mother who was brought-up as a strict Jain, did expect monastery to be non-violence and a no go area for meat eating or a place free from carnivorous diet. So he was surprised to notice that most monks were not vegetarians. It shows how little we know about such places, establishments, sects and communities some have been with us for hundreds, if not thousands of years. Hare Krishna movement, the most law abiding, peaceful, caring and knowledgeable movement is still a mystery for most Westerners!

Kiran and Robin were given an open invitation to visit them at any time; a warm welcome would always await them. For a moment or two Kiran felt like joining them, become a monk. But in the end his urge to see, roam Europe was stronger than the attraction of the serine life of a monastery.

Kiran had no experience of either a monastery or ever met a monk. He thought that their lives were lackadaisical, lack purpose but not any more. He developed a healthy respect for the monks and their way of life. Kiran could not leave without a good donation, in appreciation of the welcome they received.

* * *

Chapter Thirteen
Attractions of Costas

Kiran and Robin left early, as their next stop was the beautiful and cultural city of **Barcelona,** the capital city of **Cataluna.** At the time there was no motorway between Andorra and Barcelona, the roads were primitive, hazardous and few, more suitable for the primitive mode of transport than the mechanical age, present age dominated by cars and vehicles.

The country just south of Andorra is hilly, mountainous but after crossing **Sierra del Cadi** range, it was a pleasant ride, hilly but not mountainous.

The land, the valleys were covered with fertile soil, with Olive Groves and fruit orchids that produce fruits like oranges, grapes, lemons, pomegranates, as well as apples and pears, plums and nectarines at various heights. This is one of the prosperous regions of Spain.

As usual, Kiran had many tea and coffee breaks, at the roadside cafes, in villages where they would venture now and then and even in a private house, now that Kiran was able to speak the language **bastante bien,** fairly well.

As usual, there were more women than men in the village and the house where they had coffee with some home made bread served by a beautiful but married girl whose husband was working and living in Barcelona.

"Buenos dias Senorita O Senora! (Good Morning Miss or Mrs!)

"Soy Senora. Tengo un marido. Pero el vive en Barcelona. (I am Mrs. I have a husband but he lives in Barcelona)

"Que pena? Tiene un tipo estupendo, como la actre, esbelta y de buen talle! (What a pity. You have a very good figure, like an actress, slim and shapely!)

In those days with only the radio to keep company, Hollywood ruled the roots. Actors and actresses, like John Wayne, Gregory Peck, Kirk Douglas, Rock Hudson and actresses like Audrey Hepburn, Sophia Lauren, Rita Hayworth, Doris Day and Elizabeth Taylor were every one's favourite, to emulate and to follow in their footsteps.

"Senor, ha estado muy feo pero muy guapo tambian! Como yo desio que mi marido fue querer usted! (You are very naughty but you are also very handsome! How I wish my husband was like you!)

As the girl was on her own, Kiran could pull her leg. With slim figure, she did look juvenile, underage to be married. Kiran would not like to pay compliments in presence of elders who are respected in the Spanish society, a Gnostic society in many ways.

But the society was haemorrhaging slowly but surely in the post war era that was impregnated with brutality and hangover from the dark days of the most brutal conflict in human history. It has turned people into mignonettes, thorny human beings. At lease Britain was showing the signs of harbouring a sense of post-imperial guilt.

Kiran also noticed that Spanish girls were no different to English girls. They do like, indeed appreciate a bit of teasing and flattery. Then flattery is a universal language.

Kiran's boldness has triumphed over his blandness, his heart over his mind. Even an ounce of flattery, praise and appreciation is better than a ton of theory, false promises and decisiveness or to be a surrogate apologist for any cause or concern. Unlike Muslims, Hindus are born surrogate apologists!

But Kiran was careful that his praise, teasing does not involve any physical contact except kisses on both the cheeks when leaving, in the presence of family elders. That is the tradition, especially in the interior, amongst villagers where old traditions die hard. Even the strictest of the parents would not grudge such a respect for their daughters, especially when some one is leaving, parting company for good!

It was a leisurely ride. Yet by the time they reached Barcelona, it was well pass lunch time. As usual, their first task was to find an accommodation. This time it was a youth hostel, like our YMCA but more specious as well as a bit luxurious, that is having an attached bathroom rather than having it in a corridor and sharing it with all the residents, so often queuing up early in the morning for a shower!

As Robin was on a tight budget, Kiran had to compromise on the dwelling he chose. But he was not fussy, as he had stayed in all sorts of accommodation while touring Wales. Then these are the places where he could meet people, find a good company, make friends like Penny. Perhaps another Penny, a Spanish Penny, a Pillar was waiting in the wings!

Every place, every accommodation has pluses and minuses, rights and wrongs, positive and negative points. It was up to Kiran how to make the best use of any situation, any opportunity and by now Kiran was able to make the most of even bad situation, bad company and accommodation.

They had decided to stay in Barcelona for a full week. Next day was given to sight seeing, by bus, tram and train rather than by motorbike, as Kiran wanted to avoid city traffic. They wisely bought a weekly combined ticket for bus trains and trams.

There first stop was the Barcelona Colon Monument, a sixty meters high figure with the statue of Christopher Columbus at the top, hardly visible from the base. The Port building opposite and Maritime Museum were certainly photogenic.

The seaside was not too far, Rambler del Mar where numerous boats, yachts of different size and price tag were berthed. Civtadella Park and Museum de Zoologia with lakes, fountains and picnic area took some time to enjoy and recharge their batteries.

The next day was reserved for Barcelona F.C. Camp Nou Stadium, one of the best and biggest in Spain, home of the famous and very successful football team in Europe.

If some one is a real football enthusiast, it would take a whole day to see all that is on offer. Kiran and Robin joined a group of Spanish visitors so that they can have an organized tour.

As the guide was speaking to the local people, Kiran could only pick up a few words, sentences here and there. Now he realized how difficult it is to master Spanish language.

They visited the Trophy Room, laden with silverware, Photo Gallery or Jugadors Internationals (International Players) with the photographs of their famous players. Even in those early days, there were some South American players on their book, but today it is a different story, a different atmosphere, different era.

The Art Room and the shop were, the Coffee Bar and the Rest Room as well as the pitch and the seating accommodation with five star seating in special luxury boxes were out of bound for most but the cream of the business and political world.

All together they spend some three hours. The football mad Chelsea supporter Robin was over the moon. He could proudly write home that he has visited ***Camp Nou Stadium; the home of Barcelona F.C.***

Kiran hoped this would make quantum improvement in Robin's satisfaction and motivation levels, as Kiran had noticed that although Robin was a bright and intelligent boy, he so often lacked the urge and determination to reach the top.

As we are all endowed with the capacity of being genius, Robin may one day become Pele, the Brazilian genius, the best footballer the world has even

seen.

It was like going on a sightseeing tour of Buckingham Palace! This was an experience of a lifetime for Robin, a football mad sports fanatic. He must have thought Lord Buddha, Lord Rama and Lord Jesus Christ must have blessed him for this precious moment in his otherwise sheltered life.

It was like a pilgrimage to the holy city of Mecca, Medina, the Wailing Wall in Jerusalem, Vrindavan, where Lord Krishna spent his childhood, looking after cows or taking a dip in the holy waters of River Ganges!

It would be difficult for some one who is not a football fan to understand this finalism. It is the opium for sport mad fans. It is worth remembering Bill Shaklee's famous words. Football is not a matter of life and death. It is much more than that! Friendship built on football terraces is as important, as ever lasting as friendship built on the college campus, in a class-room.

Robin embraced every moment, every minute of his time in this exotic land, the home of Spanish football. Robin was in a magic slumber while Kiran felt he was in a fantasyland.

There was still time to visit MNAC Museum, near Maji Fountain of Montijuice, with night laser display in high season. The park is dotted with beautiful statues, work of art.

Next day was for Park Guell, unusual and interesting. The park is dotted with unusual columns, pillars, some support the pathway above while others are just for decorations with plants on the top.

One place for relaxing that caught Kiran's eyes was a large seating area with picturesque design, decorated with colourful tiles, mosaic and colour, built by Joseph Jujol.

The Gate House with white and blue tower with a Cross at the top was attractive and some what different to the multicolour Mosaic Dragon

Fountain. Each day provided with wonderful sights of parks, museums, work of art and street artists. But it involved a lot of walking. So early dinner and bed was the routine, as getting up early was essential to gain the maximum out of a day.

The most important monument or rather a church still under construction after well over one hundred years is the "*The Church of the Holy Family.*" It has been under construction since *Saint Joseph's Day, 19th March 1882.*

It was the brain child of the architect *Francisco del Villar* who initiated, laid the foundation stone. However in 1883 *Antonio Gaudi* took over the construction of the crypt in neoclassical architecture, the popular style at the time. The iglesia was intended to be the symbolic Church of Christ but would be more of a showpiece than a place of worship on a daily basis.

The project would have three architectural masterpieces of three monumental facades representing the Birth, the Passion and Glory of Christ. Each façade would have four very high towers that would symbolize the twelve Apostles.

The showpiece central spire symbolizes the Saviour with four towers representing the four Evangelists. The apse or the arched recess has another spire representing the Virgin Mary.

Inside the recess, there is a complete model of the church, what it would look like when finished and the crypt where Gaudi is buried. There is also a museum dedicated to Gaudi's work, models, plans and photographs of his vast and varied work, projects.

After the sight-seeing tour of Gaudi's masterpiece, *The Church of the Holy Family*, the rest was an anti-climax.

However Kiran visited the Zoological Gardens first opened to the public in 1892, the Aquarium, the old port, the Royal Shipyards, the Opera House and many famous statues, old buildings.

There is also a special Walk, the artist's Avenue where young and upcoming painters paint, exhibit and sell there work. In the end the week was just enough to explore this historic city, the most artistic and beautiful city in Europe.

As Kiran had since then visited Barcelona on several occasions, with Olivia and their children, Kiran had a mix memory of his first visit.

One memorable outing that would always remain deep in Kiran's heart and soul was the train journey to one of the holiest place in Europe, the

Montserrat. It was a memorable train journey, a narrow gauge train passing through some breathtaking scenery.

The Black Madonna of Montserrat is a wooden statue that has some what turned black due to thousands of candles lit at her feet. It was a humbling experience to hold the hand of Madonna that protrudes out from the glass cabinet.

After sight-seeing in Barcelona and visit to Montserrat, Kiran was eager to move away from big cities and see the true Spain, the Costas that Spain is famous for. They took the coastal route, the road hugging the Mediterranean Sea, stopping for tea and coffee at the coastal resorts of Sitges and Vendrell before spending the night at the regional capital town of Tarragona.

Their two stops before reaching Alicante were Castello de la Plana and Valencia, a big city and the regional capital.

But Kiran did not explore the city, as he was eager to reach Malaga where he wanted to spend a week or two, exploring the interior as well as relaxing on the famous beaches of Benalmedena, and Fuengirola. The Balearic Islands of Majorca, Minorca and Ibiza were also tempting, well worth a visit.

Kiran rented a caravan for a week but payable on a daily basis in Fuengirola before visiting **Gibraltar,** the rocky outpost that is British through and through, in every sense.

In fact people in far flung British colonies like Falkland Islands, Bermuda, Malta and St. Helena are more British in outlook, tradition and loyalty to the British Crown than people of Britain themselves. People of Gibraltar were no exception.

The importance of Gibraltar is its location on the tip of Spain overlooking the narrow Straight of Gibraltar, guarding the entrance from the Atlantic Ocean to the Mediterranean Sea. Gibraltar was also called **"The Pillars of Hercules."** The two peaks of the Rock, the Calpe and Abyla dominate the Straight.

There is only one main street, a close resemblance to any British High Street, with familiar names like Marks & Spencer, Woolworth, BHS, McDonald, Pizzerias and many more.

Besides the Rock and its famous residents, the Apes of Gibraltar, (Macaca Sylvanus) are a must on many tourists' itinerary, there is not much to see except for those who are interested in history, arts and museums.

The Cathedral of Holy Trinity, the Naval Dockyard and The Great Siege Tunnels with magnificent views over the Isthmus that separate

Gibraltar from the mainland Spain are worth a visit if there is time to pass. St. Michael's Cave and the Moorish Castle were other attractions Kiran and Robin visited.

In those days, Gibraltar was a busy working port with fishing boats plying the Mediterranean Sea, the Naval Dockyard and the British cargo ships sailing to India, East Africa and the Far East clogging the port.

While having a coffee break near the dockyard, a café frequented by sailors and dockyard workers, Kiran met a young man from Liverpool who was a chef on the cargo ship with a catchy name *"Catherine"* which was unusual for a cargo ship.

The ship was sailing to Cyprus in two days time, then to Israel before passing through the Suez Canal and onward to Colombo and Australia. There was a vacancy for a deck-hand.

This was a God send gift for Robin to sail to Israel, although it would be a hard work being a deck-hand. In a way it was a Hobson's choice but Robin was young and a strong, healthy boy.

After spending some four weeks with Kiran, Robin did not fancy standing at the road corner and asking for a lift. Kiran's company was an oasis of enlightenment that had taught Robin so much, especially how to be street-wise and to grab an opportunity when it knocks on your door. So Robin readily agreed to work his way, his passage to Tel Aviv. Robin fell for it hook, line and sinker at the notion of cursing to Israel. But this would be cursing with a difference.

Perhaps with Robin's luck or lack of it, this may turn out to be a galley ship propelled by oars in the medieval times, the Roman times!

Pity Robin did not have a gander before jumping into a frying pan! Perhaps as most of the crews were lascar, Robin, with his white skin and English background, may get a preferential treatment.

As soon as they returned to their caravan in Fuengirola, Robin packed his bags or rather a backpack and moved to the ship in Gibraltar. So now Kiran was on his own and free to roam, go where he desire, where his heart would take him. Surely this freedom would make quantum improvement in his travel plans! Would he miss Robin's company?, well not as much as he missed Penny's!

* * *

Chapter Fourteen

The Olive Grove

Kiran decided to explore the hinterland, the mountains only a stone throw away from the coast, from the beautiful beaches of Benalmedena, Fuengirola and Torremolinos, as he felt this part of Spain was attracting more tourists than any other part of Spain, a heaven on the planning board! An investment some where on the Costas could never go wrong.

Although these were early days and there were hardly any hotels on the beach, Kiran's business mind anticipated that it was only a question of time before sun starved Britons would discover the beauty, charm and all year round warm climate of Costa del Sol. Kiran's sombreness was replaced with boyish enthusiasm. His face lit-up at the money making opportunity. But he was not in a hurry. Time was on his side. First he has to embrace every moment of his time in this exotic land with panache and enthusiasms.

A couple of months in summer, months of July and August may be too hot for most Britons, so a cool hinterland was an advantage, an added attraction for those who would like to move to Costa del Sol and make it their permanent home, retire to spend their declining years in a warm and friendly climate, away from the ravages of cold, damp and dark winters when so many elderly, the weak and the disable people lose their lustre, their lives.

Mijas, a tiny village less than an hour's ride from Fuengirola was his first stop. It was an unspoilt village with a beautiful church and few shops serving mainly the local farming community. But it had a rugged charm that was hard to ignore in a hurry.

After spending a couple of hours, Kiran moved on, as he felt a bit lonely in such a tiny place. Perhaps the lack of a young, beautiful and friendly face made all the difference. Now Kiran was enlightened in substance if not the Spanish way of life, Spanish wisdom!

Kiran's next stop was another mountainside settlement, a tiny village of **Tolox,** at the foot of **Serrania de Ronda**, a mountain range with a peak well over six thousand feet high. It was a place worth a visit according to some of his fellow travellers in the Caravan Park.

There was no direct road between Mijas and Tolox. So it was a guess work whenever Kiran had to leave the charted roads and take to unmarked tracks, known only to the local residents. This is where his motorbike came in its stride, made all the difference.

Even though Kiran had prepared his own road map from the information he gathered from those who had been to Tolox, it was not long before he was lost in the hilly, unmapped, unsigned countryside. To make the matter worse, the sky was getting dark, the wind chilly, an indication of approaching tropical storm that so often brings rain and relief at this time of the year.

It may be a relief from the heat but to be caught in a storm in the open may not be wise or desirable, as such storms are accompanied by thunders and lightening. In the unknown, on an uncharted way, a tiny lane, Kiran suddenly saw the sign *"Gasolinera."* It was a petrol station with a tiny shop cum café, a God send gift for Kiran.

On entering the shop, Kiran could not see any one. But there was a bell on the counter which Kiran rang and after a long pause, an old lady, perhaps in her fifties with a bulky figure but kind face came out.

"Hola, Buenas tardes. Puede ayurdarme por favour? Estoy perdido." (Hello, good afternoon. I am lost. Can you help me please?)

"Buenas ttardes Senior." Then after a long pause, she shouted *"Pedro, viene aqui pronto. El Senior quiere su ayuda.* (Pedro, come here quickly, the gentleman wants your help.)

Kiran wondered for a moment whether she could understand him. He was sure these people would not understand a word of English. So it was not even worth trying.

After what seemed to be a long wait, a young man, perhaps in his mid twenties came in, with a tray and three cups of strong coffee, with a bowl of sugar and a mug of fresh milk.

"Un café Senior?" It seemed he did not believe in formalities.

"Si Amego, con leche y una cuchara de azucar. (Yes my friend, with milk and one spoon sugar.) As the spoon was really big, Kiran requested one spoon sugar rather than two he normally take.)

"Es usted el turista, verdad?" **(You are a tourist, aren't you?)**

"Si. Soy de Londres. Me yamo Kiran y muchas gracias por un café. (Yes, I am from London. I am Kiran and thank you for coffee)

"De nada. Me yamo Pedro" (It's nothing. Don't mention it. I am Pedro)

"Hay cerca la pension O casa de huespedes? (Is there a hotel, a guesthouse nearby?)

"Lo siento, hay no pension cerca, pero hay una granja, el rancho con chalets por alquiler. (I am sorry. There is no hotel or a guest house nearby but there is a farm with cottages for rent.)

"Estupendo. Donda esta el rancho?" (Great, where is this farm?)

"La routa esta un poco complicado. Pero esta no problama para me. Bebe su café Y puedo llevar al rancho." (It is a bit complicated. But don't worry. It is not a problem for me. I can take you to the ranch)

Pedro was really friendly. Even the woman, who introduced herself as Maria, was smiling at Pedro! But it was not a normal smile, a wicked smile, a mischievous smile!

After a leisurely coffee break, Pedro opened the shed and out came a *Vespa Scooter*, a tiny scooter, a basic form of transport, very cheap to maintain and run and indeed very popular as well at the time.

Kiran had his motorbike filled with petrol for which he paid some two hundred pesetas but coffee was on the house!

Pedro was right. The road to the farm was a bit complicated. But a good map, a drawing would have done the trick, as the farm was sign posted all the way. Kiran soon found out why Pedro was so eager to show him the way!

Within ten minutes they were at the farm gate. There was a big board at the entrance gate, *"Olive Grove"* *(Las casitas para alquiler)* cottages for rent. The farm building was set well inside, some two hundred meters from the gate.

Pedro rang the bell and after a wait of some five minutes, a lovely Spanish girl opened the door. Being height of summer, she was appropriately dressed, in a body hugging tea shirt and a short, flowery, loose mini-skirt that showed her inappropriately broad thighs. It seemed Pedro was more interested in her bulging breasts rather than her mini skirt that barely covered her some what long red knickers, let alone her over bearing thighs,

"Buenas Tardes Senorita Olivia, mi Novoia, mi la amor. Tengo un visita que alquilar su chalet. Estupendo, verdad! (Good afternoon my friend, my sweetheart! I have a guest who would like to rent your chalet. It is marvellous, isn't it?)

Now it was obvious to Kiran why Pedro was so eager to come with him and show the way and why Maria was smiling at Pedro. She knew from the beginning that Pedro would accompany Kiran to Olive Grove.

"Gracias Pedro Y adios haste manana. (Thank you Pedro and goodbye until tomorrow.)

"No vaso de vino para me?" (No glass of wine for me?)

"Hoy no. Esta muy ocupado. Quiza manana! (Today no. I am very busy. Perhaps tomorrow.)

It was clear to Kiran that Olivia was not keen on Pedro but he would not take no for an answer. When some one says manana, than manana never comes. It is always manana, always tomorrow, not today in Spain!

Pedro left grudgingly blowing kisses and Olivia reciprocated the gesture so as not to disappoint Pedro too much. After all he had brought a client.

Kiran could not remain silent. "Muchas gracias Pedro Y da me llama tan pronto como quando yo arribar su casa por favour. Hace un poco lluvia ya. (Thank you Pedro and call me as soon as you arrive at your home. It is already raining a bit.)

"Gracias Senor Kiran. Es usted muy amable. (Thank you Kiran. You are very kind.)

Olivia closed the door and led Kiran to a tiny room which was a sort of office, an all purpose room. She asked Kiran to sit down and said, *"Encanda Senor, soy Olivia y vivo aqui con me padre Martinez.* (Please to meet you sir, I am Olivia and I live here with my father, Senor Martinez.)

"Encando Senorita. (Please to meet you Miss.)

"?Soy de Inglaterra? (Are you from England?)

"Si, soy de Londres, Inglaterra. (Yes, I am from London, England)

"Pero usted hable Espanol bastante bien? Por quanto anios tiene aqui en Espana? Es usted no hispano-americano, verdad! (You speak Spanish fairly well. How long you have been in Spain. You are not a Spanish American, are you?)

"No Olivia. Yo no hispano-americano y estoy aqui en Espana por ocho semanas solomante. Pero me gusta aprender las idiomas. (No Olivia, I am not Spanish American and I have been in Spain for only eight weeks. But I am good at learning languages.)

Ay! Es usted a universitario, academico, verdad! Estoy mucho impersionar! (So you are an academic. I am very much impressed!)

Kiran found Olivia sweet and charming and above all he had made the right sort of impression.

It took just ten minutes to fill in the forms and pay a deposit. As usual Kiran requested half board, which means breakfast and dinner included. Of course, he had to pay extra. But he did not mind. In any case, it was either that or cooking. There were no cafes nearby.

They only let the chalet on a weekly basis. So Kiran had to be here for a week. But looking at Olivia's voluptuous body, her over bearing figure and charming manner, Kiran thought a week would not be too long.

In any cast it was time for Kiran to have some rest, respite and a sense of belonging to a place. This place was as good as it comes.

The chalet was a one bedroom accommodation, with a lounge, fully equipped kitchen and a shower with ceiling fans, fitted cupboards, wardrobes and a storage room. It was a specious accommodation for a couple or a one child family.

The views were superb, over looking the Olive trees and a mountain peak in the distance. Kiran felt oneness with the surroundings even before he had settle down. This could be his oasis in his world of stress and misfortunes. Kiran could visualize his ideal week.

Kiran met Senior Martinez at the dinner time. In his usual manner, taking his hand and bending a bit, Kiran said,

"Encantedo Senor Martinez. Tiene una buenas las granjas y su hija Olivia as muy amable!" (Please to meet you Senor Martinez. You have a nice farm house and your daughter Olivia is very kind and helpful.) In return Senor Martinez wished Kiran a happy and enjoyable stay. Even he was impressed at Kiran's ability to speak Spanish more or less fluently, at least for an Englishman, as English people are famous at being lazy when it comes to learning foreign languages.

Dinner time is a special event of the day in Spanish families. The dinner is served normally late, between 8pm to 10pm. It always involves a three course dinner, the soup to start with, the main dish and a sweet dish to end the dinner, with a cup of coffee and the wine is a must, mostly red wine with the dinner, the main course. It was a challenge for Olivia to prepare a vegetarian dinner. But as Kiran was fond of rice, a favourite dish in Spain, she knew that Kiran would like her cooking.

Senor Martinez was obviously impressed with Kiran's manner and his youthful appearance. But according to Senior Martinez, youth is not the time or the age of life. It is the state of mind.

One can be an old man even at the age of twenty! He immediately knew that Kiran must have a good upbringing and he comes from a well respected family with traditional values that Spanish people appreciate and adopt.

Then Senor Martinez was an old, experienced man, in his early sixties. He had the wisdom that goes with the age, experience and the sufferings that some had to undergo in life.

Good judgement comes from experience and experience comes from bad judgement. There was plenty of scope to make bad judgements in the preceding decade.

Spain had just come out of a brutal civil war that had shattered, ruined many lives, many families. Like our Indian tradition, a family is not complete without a son and in any case Spanish families were large with at least three to four children. So Olivia being the only child was a bit unusual and definitely involves a family tragedy. Perhaps Olivia may have lost her mother at childbirth, the most common cause of death amongst child bearing women. It is simplistic but never the less true.

The breakfast time was at 8am. Kiran was promptly in the dinning room at the designated time. Normally Spanish breakfast is in continental tradition, that is breakfast is cold and not a cooked one that would include sausage, bacon, baked beans that Englishmen are accustomed to.

But with tourists flocking the country, especially from Northern Europe where the hot breakfast was the norm, the Spanish tradition was taking a back seat, adopting the new way of life, although it was still in the infant state, as only a few privileged could afford going abroad.

The Continental breakfast normally include bread, rolls, cheese, butter, marmalade, boiled eggs, cereals and tea, coffee and milk. But Olivia had specially prepared Spanish omelette with spring onions, green chillies, grated potatoes and slices of mushrooms.

It was a tasty omelette, perhaps prepared with care and for a special guest. It was a leisurely breakfast with weather the main topic of conversation, as last night was a bit stormy with thunders and lightening accompanying the rain. Such occasional thunder storms keep the countryside green and forests free of devastating fires. But such storms are few and at long intervals.

As it was wet and windy, there was no work on the orchard. Olivia was free, except some house work and to milk a few goats and feed the chickens. So Kiran was not surprised when Olivia joined him in his chalet just before midday, ostentatiously to ask Kiran whether he would like some sandwiches for lunch, as she was preparing some for her father.

As Kiran had no provision, had not done any shopping, he readily agreed. Olivia promptly arrived at midday, dressed for the weather, with jeans and a top with plenty of cleavage that certainly made Kiran hungry.

Was the hunger for food or for some thing more intense was a question that would remain unanswered for some time. Kiran thought for a moment that he should not leave the quality of his hunger to chance. He should make the effort to be his choice!

Olivia, for her age, she had big and bulging breasts that would protrude from any top. No amount of cloths would corrode her sex appeal. She was corpulent, plump but certainly not fat or overbearing. She was pleasing to eyes, refreshing to mind and turbulent for heart, a real, unwrapped Turkish delight!

She had brought with her cheese and tomato sandwiches for Kiran and ham and cheese for her. There was coffee, tea, sugar and milk in the fridge. That was the norm for all guests.

Kiran was writing his journal. It has become his daily routine to make notes of the day's event before going to bed and when he is free, he would write a detailed account, a sort of travelogue, putting in his innermost thoughts, feelings and incidents.

When Kiran told Olivia what he was doing, in answer to her inquisitiveness, she mischievously inquired whether she would feature in his book, his travelogue.

Kiran said, "Well Olivia, you will have to wait until my book is published. But I can tell you that perhaps I may give my book the title *"Olivia"* or *"Olive Grove."* Would you like that Olivia?

Olivia's face brightened up and she said in a sweet, teasing voice, *"Claro Senior Kiran. Me gusta esta mucho! Pero que para me fotografica? Soy no un poco hermosa y seductora tambian, verdad? "* (Of course Senior Kiran. I would like that very much. But what about my photo? Am I not a bit beautiful and sexy as well?)

Kiran was taken back a bit with her boldness. But he soon gathered his composure and said, "Of course you are beautiful and desirable as well. As I am a gentleman, I would not use the word sexy! You are naughty but nice, like a bucket full of wine. But you have a boy friend Pedro, aren't you?"

"Oh no Senor. Pedro no esta me novio. No me gusta Pedro mucho tambian. (Oh no sir, Pedro is not my boyfriend. I do not like Pedro much)

Kiran like to tease Spanish girls. They were different from English girls. They were more straight forward and passionate. They would not hesitate to express their opinion, call spades a spade and when some one pays a compliment, they like it, especially from foreigners!

Olivia told Kiran in no uncertain terms that Pedro was not her boyfriend and never will be. He is a village idiot, a village Romeo who is after one thing and has one track mind. I am surprised that such an intelligent person like you thinks that I may fall for Pedro.

Kiran realised that he had touched a raw nerve and will have to grovel a bit to be in Olivia's good book. But by now, he had learnt what button to press, how to flatter, pamper a girl's ego.

"Olivia, I am very sorry. I was just teasing. I knew that you are not interested in Pedro when you gave him marching orders yesterday. Please forgive me for hurting your feelings. In any case now that you have made it clear, I can be your bouncer, your knight in shining armour when it comes to Pedro, can I?"

"Well Kiran, I got you, didn't I? I knew you were just pulling my legs. So I wanted to give you the taste of your own medicine. I may be a village lassie but I am not that naïve! I may be a prototype but not that innocent. You city slicks think we, the village girls are idiots. Don't you!"

"This is my precinct, my area of domain and as for Pedro; I can handle him with kid's gloves." There was a twinkle of mischief in her eyes. Olivia was so naughty, yet innocent and pleasing with glint of anger that would melt any one's heart. She was like an angle for a foreigner who may be lost in a strange, foreign land.

Kiran knew that he would have many such boisterous brushes with Olivia that would make life interesting in this cool, calm and harmonious household but lacking a bit of turbulence that could make life interesting, fulfilling and satisfying.

There was a broad smile on Olivia's face, a smile of satisfaction, a triumph of an ordinary girl over a well educated city yippee. For a moment

Olivia forgot that Spanish is not Kiran's mother tongue, that he could not understand her properly.

Perhaps that gave her the boldness to express herself as freely as it could be possible in such a short time, such a short acquaintance. If some thing goes wrong, she can always say that it is a misunderstanding, without losing face! This is the philosophy of the wicked.

"Olivia, you are naughty but nice. You are my ***Turkish delight***, a sight for sore eyes and a thread to mend the broken heart."

"Kiran, you are so wise. You know all the right words to say to a girl and that also in a foreign language! I am impressed. I am sure we will get on well, like a house on fire! Kiran, but I can not imagine you could have a broken heart. You are the one who could break many a girls' hearts. But I hope I won't be one of them. Could you break my heart Kiran?"

Although there was a mischievous smile on Olivia's face, Kiran could not make out whether she was serious or just pulling his legs. But she was right. Kiran could never break her heart.

"Olivia, how could I ever break your heart? But I am sure you are in the hearts and minds of many people and that include me as well!"

When Olivia prepared two cups of coffee, she politely asked Kiran's permission whether it was all right for her to eat ham sandwich with him, as he was a vegetarian.

Kiran was surprised how easily Olivia can change a topic of conversation, from being naughty and mischievous to being polite and obliging, as if she was in the presence of Dalai Lama or the Pope?

How can such a charming, beautiful, clever and above all a sexy girl, a reincarnation of the mythical girl ***Menka*** could be single, although she was hardly in her early twenties, perhaps twenty one, twenty two or so. She was certainly capable of making fireworks in any heart, just like all those courtroom pyrotechnics.

Although Kiran had a lengthy chat, an hour long conversation, he realised that when it came to serious conversation, his Spanish was too basic to make headway. Even referring to dictionary and an advanced phrase book made little difference.

So Kiran asked Olivia whether she would like to be his teacher, teach him the finer points of the language and in return he would teach her English or perhaps vegetarian cooking.

"Kiran, if you would like to learn proper Spanish and speak like a native, then it would need more than a week or two, no matter how many hours you may put in. But I am ready if you are serious. Please wait and eat my dinner before passing judgement on my cooking skill."

"As for me learning English, you will be wasting your time. I am not that clever a girl, not academic minded. But if you would like to bang your head against a brick wall, I am ready and willing.

After all I can never have a better, more charming teacher than you. Perhaps I can become a teacher's pet, as we say in Spanish, *"la preferida da la maestra."*

"I am your student. I am all yours! If you could teach me English, if I could speak English, a universal language, my father will be very much impressed with you Professor Kiran and perhaps he may grant your wish as well!"

What wish Olivia was hinting, Kiran could just guess and wonder! There was a wicked smile on Olivia's face, showing her pearl white set of perfect teeth.

"Olivia, don't underestimate yourself, I don't. You are much cleverer than you would like me to believe. I am a good judge of character. I am sure in no time you would make me eat out of your hands."

"I have noticed how clean, how well kept your house is, with inflorescence, art effects and décor of the highest order. It is like palatial and I can not find fault in your cooking either. You are not a nether girl in any manner. But you have to go on a personal odyssey of self discovery." Kiran was at least truthful in this respect.

But he wondered Olivia could understand him, as this conversation was getting more difficult, a way beyond Kiran's grasp of the Spanish. Then perhaps Kiran was more expressive, expressing, using gesture to make a point.

"Kiran, as I said before, you know how to inflame a girl's ego, how to sweeten up a maid, perhaps a mermaid like me. I like you, even though you may be a flatterer! You know how to cater to the vanity of an innocent girl like me. But you are irresistible. You are my hero. **Me gusta Senor Keran muchisimos!**" (I like Senor Kiran very much) Now it was time for Olivia to be sincere and honest.

Perhaps for a moment Kiran thought this could be the ploy to keep him in this place as long as possible, as tourists were hard to come by. But he soon realised that neither Olivia nor his father were money minded, business people who would like to keep him for the rent.

In any case the rent was minimal and if Kiran could speak the language like a native, there would be quantum improvement in his satisfaction and motivation level while travelling the length and breadth of the country. In Spain, learning language, speaking the local dialect was the shortest way to a girl's heart, her affection and much more!

Olivia was an added attraction. Just chatting with her all day would make a lot of difference in his motivation, the barometer of his satisfaction level. He made a mistake in not taking up Penny's offer. He should not repeat, make the same mistake twice. He should rather embrace every moment of his time in such a charming company, in an isolated place that could become Kiran's *"Shangri La."*

Kiran knew he could make Olivia eat out of his hands soon. This was a lesson in the psychology of winning a woman's heart and mind. Who knows how this friendship may develop or what could be the end result?

Perhaps the *"Olive Grove"* could become an oasis of enlightenment, a paradise in the making, a place with substance where Kiran could let lose the riches of his soul. Kiran strangely felt that his life had just begun to flicker, a ray of hope and expectation on the far off horizon, a rainbow, a silver lining on the distant cloud. Well, if necessary, Kiran could bow down to Western, Abrahamic morality and why not?

Lord Buddha is at last smiling on his favourite pupil Kiran! It was up to him to make the most of this God given opportunity. As we say, when the Goddess Laxmi, the Goddess of wealth comes to put a Tilak, a mark on your forehead, one should not keep her waiting!

* * *

Chapter Fifteen
Port Darwin, Gateway to Australia

The loud announcement by the Captain that the plane was landing at **Port Darwin** brought Kiran out of his slumber, out of his day-dreaming and back to reality. Then reality was as interesting, as exciting as any moment in his life. After all Kiran and Olivia were being reunited with their children.

Port Darwin is the main stop-over where the passengers flying to Perth have to disembark. They are transferred to a smaller plane, so often it is Falker Friendship or Boing 707 aircraft, while the Comet would fly on to **Sidney,** the main destination for majority of the passengers.

Australia is a vast country, indeed a small continent made up of only one nation. The distances between major cities scattered from North to South and East to West are vast indeed and flying is the only viable way to travel, even though flying was in its infant state and a privilege for the few, unless one has plenty of time on hand and infinitive patience to use road or rail which is rare in this day and age. We are all rushing around as if we are going to miss the last train, the last bus.

It was nearly a forty eight hour or two day stop. While the Comet took off within two hours, Kiran's flight would not take off until midday, the day after tomorrow. That means the next day was completely free, set for sight seeing, as Port Darwin is indeed a beautiful city, a tropical paradise but prone to the mayhem from frequent hurricanes during rainy seasons and tidal waves that sometimes bring havoc to this tropical paradise.

The hinterland is exciting with tropical rain forest, fast flowing rivers, lakes, gorges, valleys and mountains inhabited by wild life as different as docile hippos and aggressive tigers! It is full of crocodiles, wild buffalos, wolves, antelopes and variety of poisonous snakes, on land as well as in water. It was indeed a **Crocodile Dundee Country** no one would like to venture into without a trained local guide, a Crocodile Dundee in the making.

Port Darwin, popularly known as just Darwin, is the capital city of the Northern Territory, the most northerly city with sub-tropical climate. It is situated on the **Timor Sea.**

The nearest country to Australia is the Island of Papua and New Guinea, only a couple of hundred miles of sea; **The Torres Strait** separating these two countries, although Indonesia is not too far away, a country that is a staging point for illegal immigration to Australia from the Far East and the troubled land of Afghanistan, Iraq and Pakistan.

The population of Darwin was under 75,000 at the time, although now it is well over one hundred thousand. It acts as the Top End's regional centre. The city has grown from a pioneer outpost, a tiny port to a modern, multicultural city.

Its proximity to Asia, East Timor, a country ravaged by war, just liberated from the clutches of Indonesia, makes it an important gateway for many Asian countries bulging with human population, in sharp contrast to Australia, practically an empty land with huge potential.

The city is built on a low bluff overlooking the busy harbour, a working port, a fishing as well main connection with outside world, an important port on the shipping lane connecting Timor Sea with Coral Sea, Indian Ocean with Pacific Ocean.

Darwin receives the heaviest rainfall in Australia and many tiny, seasonal as well as ever flowing rivers flow into Timor Sea. It has only two seasons, a wet and a dry season. There are no winter months as such, although months of June, July and August are some what cooler than months of December to March, a summer season for most Australians.

On 9th September 1839, **HMS Beagle** sailed into Port Darwin area, under the command of **John Clements Wickham** to survey the coastline. The port was named in honour of the great seafarer Charles Darwin, although his scientific achievements came later in life.

However the first visitors to land on this coastline were the Dutch, way back in 1600 who created the first maps of the area and gave the Dutch names like Armhem and Groote Eylandt.

The gold rush of 1870s at **Pine Creek** gave Darwin a permanent settlement and transformed from a tiny port into a place of importance, a future capital of Northern Territory.

Darwin was first called Palmerston after the then British Prime Minister Lord Palmerston. In 1870, the first Overland Telegraph Station was opened in Darwin, in a wooden shed like building, still standing and preserved as a national monument.

Between 1500 and 1900, British people were adventurers, seafarers, conquerors and one of the most able administers and inventers in the world. How the mighty have fallen! Today we are a nation on the verge of bankruptcy.

Not many people know that Darwin was one of the most heavily bombed cities during the Second World War. Australia stationed ten thousand Allied troops in Darwin in 1940 in order to defend the Northern Territory from the Japanese occupation and in retaliation.

As a result, it suffered a wave after wave of aerial bombardment from Japanese naval air force, the same fleet that bombarded the Pearl Harbour. Two hundred forty three people lost their lives and large parts of the town were flattened.

These were the first of many raids on the town. In a way, the war and the attack on Darwin helped in its development, with road and rail building, improving infrastructure and linking it with Alice Springs in the South and Mount Isa in the south-east.

Kiran and Olivia decided to take an excursion to the charming city of Katherine. As it was a long day, an indeed some fourteen hour excursion, in a specially adopted four wheel drive Land Rover that could easily accommodate up to ten people, they went to bed early.

When they came down early for a light breakfast, all packed and ready to go, they found their driver cum guide by the name of **Jolly John**, all ready and waiting.

There were only four people beside the driver. So Kiran and Olivia had plenty of space to spread their legs and make themselves comfortable. The other couple was from Adelaide who had travelled from Adelaide on the Ghan Express.

As they had disembarked at Alice Springs and visited Ayers Rock, they flew in from Alice to Darwin. Being retired and plenty of time on their hand, they wanted to see as much of Australia as they can, while they were fit and healthy for their age.

After initial introduction, John gave a detailed instruction of what to do and what to avoid. He was fully prepared for any emergency, although in his ten years as a guide, he had never lost a client?

Well, that was reassuring. But there is always first time. John had plenty of water and food, fuel and first aid box, as well as ropes, shovels, flares and such handy tools that could be life saving in an emergency.

They were told not to leave the vehicle until John tells them it is fine to disembark. Never to go off the road or the well marked trail, especially with tall grass and not to go near bushes, pick up any plant, flower or berries and not to eat, no matter how tempting the fruits may look.

They must always move in a group, not get separated and led by John who will walk in front, armed with a riffle. He will stop every two hours to stretch legs or when some one makes a special request, to answer nature's call that could not wait!

The road was passing through ever green scenery, changing landscape and numerous streams and crossing river Adelaide was an experience and a sight to behold.

The surrounding areas on both sides of the road, although void of human presence except a few tiny aborigine settlements, were teaming with wildlife, both mammals and birds, especially reptiles.

Crocodiles were a constant nuisance but only near water. Then there were numerous streams, small lakes and ponds that would easily harbour crocodiles. Then crocodiles are always hungry and humans are the easy prey, unable to run or fight back unless armed with firearms.

Then there were snakes, both land and water snakes, some of them poisonous in deed. But they will only attack in self defence. If we leave them alone, they would not bother humans.

But it could not be said of dingoes, the wild dogs that would attack any one. As they hunt in a pack, they are very efficient and successful hunters. Then there are wild camels, kangaroos, wild buffalos and other wild animals that may be dangerous if provoked or if they are guarding their off-springs.

Once they left the tropical wetlands and entered the arid, hot and hostile Red Desert, the scenery was routine with desert plants, cacti and ground hugging bushes with tiny leaves and big thorns.

The first village they stopped, had a break, was at Noonamah, just before leaving the wetland. It was more than a village with some three thousand residents. They had a coffee break in a pleasant Café run by a couple known to John, as this was his usual stop.

Other stops were at Hayes Creek and Pine Creek, famous for its gold-rush and one time capital, administrative centre for a few years during the war when Darwin was regularly bombarded. This inland place was safe from Japanese bombers based on their aircraft carriers. Surprisingly, Japan had some of the best aircraft carriers at the start of the Second World War.

They had an early lunch at Katherine, a beautiful town that made its name and money manufacturing concrete railway sleepers which were badly needed to replace wooden ones, a famous and popular munching snack for the termites who were eating away wooden sleepers fasters than they could be replaced!

Here they had the opportunity to see the town, visit some shops and taste tropical fruits, as fresh as they come and that include mangos, guava, pineapple, papaya, Jack fruit, dates, berries and green coconuts, a slightly different variety than the ones normally found on the coast. They were much smaller but water much sweeter as well.

The local wildlife include blossom bats, slow moving Aussy lazy lizards, a nice way to pay back Aussies who always called English Pommy and mass of colourful, tropical green parrots, budgies, wood packers and the usual assorted birds residing in parks and gardens.

After visiting the ***Nitmiluk National Park,*** Kiran or rather the party had several choices. Visit the twenty five million year old Katharine Gorge by the vehicle that had arrived in that would be a limited excursion, fly over the inter connecting gorges, that is if the helicopter flight was operating or cruise down the Katherine River, although Cannoning was an option but only for the young and very fit persons that automatically ruled them out,

In the end, after some deliberation, they came to the safe and interesting conclusion, to cruse the river in a safe and some what luxurious boat. It was a fascinating trip, having a look at the ever changing river and its banks, sometimes just rocky, steep bank without a bank and at other times too wide for water to reach both banks, thus having wide, deep and long sandy beach.

All these pleasure from the safety and the comfort of the lounge, sipping the Australian lager, the amber nectar that is indeed much better and tastier than most English or Continental beer. The Australian snack of mixed nuts and thick crisp would go well with the beer, although Kiran missed the pressed and seedless olives. It was a relaxing experience, a well worth excursion.

The return journey to Darwin was uneventful, as most were too tired to stay awake, preferring to take a nap in the comfort of the air-conditioned vehicle.

After consuming a few more bottles of beer, Kiran had a late dinner but early bed, as next day was again a long day. But the flight was not taking off until noon, thus giving them plenty of time to rest and recuperate. Kiran was looking forward to spending a long time in bed with Olivia and he warned her in advance!

The coach ride to the airport was on time and without a hitch. In those days there was no security or lengthy check-in process. Within no time they were airborne and in their own dream. Perhaps the last night was a memorable one that had drained their energy.

It certainly was a long time since they made love in this manner; recreate their youth and early, romantic life when only the imagination was the limit on love, sexual front! Perhaps Olivia would never have imagined that at her age, she would have to nurse her breasts or hide love bites! But then the old age is in reality a mind game!

* *

Chapter Sixteen
The Beginning of New Era

After spending a couple of hours, Olivia went back to the farm house, in a relaxed and happy mood. Kiran moved back to his writing, in some what pensive mood.

Perhaps his inner most thoughts, his restless mind or call it a premonition, but a positive one, was in a way stirring his conscious, feeling that this may be his penultimate, even his final destination, his ultimate resting place where Lord Shiva found his Menka or perhaps Lord Krishna his Radha, as Menka's love was more disruptive than the pure, golden affection of Radha.

The place was surrounded with beauty, the charm of the mountain, the forest with pine trees and the hospitality of the people with Olivia icing on the cake, the ultimate winning factor.

Kiran did not have to wait long, be on his own for long. Within an hour's time Olivia returned to Kiran, but this time her father was accompanying her, walking in tandem and spring in their foot-steps.

For a moment or two Kiran thought the worse. Could he have offended Olivia in any way? But the smile on Senor Martinez's face was more than reassuring.

"Bienvenido, Senior Martinez Y Senorita Olivia en me casita."

(Senor Martinez and Olivia, welcome to my little house!)

Kiran did not have to wait long to find out the reason for his visit. He came straight to the point. Then he was a man of few words, at least until he comes to know the person better.

"I am glad my son that you would like to learn proper Spanish. If you would like to live here in Spain, make this country your home, then it is obligatory for social etiquette to learn the language."

It seemed Senior Martinez has already assumed that Kiran would perhaps like to make Spain his home! Perhaps he was thrilled that an Englishman would like to make this tiny, unknown village his home. It was like Gandhiji coming to Dandi from where he began his march to freedom!

"Then you are a very clever young man who would pick up the finer points of Spanish language in no time at all. I do not mind Olivia teaching you Spanish. But knowing my daughter, you will learn cooking Spanish food well before you master the language. Mind you, I would like you to remain a vegetarian as long as possible. I am myself not that fond of meat diet."

"Olivia knows that the shortest route to a man's heart is through gastronomy and flattery and Olivia bless God, is expert in both!" This brought smiles on all three faces.

But interestingly for Kiran, there was not even a shade of embarrassment on Olivia's face. Then father and daughter were very close, more like friends than relations. Kiran instinctly knew that this relationship between father and daughter will stand in good stead if he would like to come close to Olivia, be her Knight in shining armour, if he would like to sit on the Round Table of Senior Martinez.

Then the brevity, the lack of inappropriate verbosity was the secret of their good father, daughter relationship. There was no two tire relationship. There was no cold dish to serve. Father and daughter were now living in an oasis of enlightenment and harmony. As Senior Martinez had no son, Olivia was naturally his protégé! The farm was Olivia's precinct, her domain with Senior Martinez a mere figurehead!

Losing Olivia's mother, the life's greatest setback for Senor Martinez had revelled the life's greatest opportunity, that is to tie the knot of love and affection with his only offspring, only blood relative that will last as long as they both live.

His only sorrow, regret was that he will precede Olivia and he would like to see Olivia get married, settle down and perhaps give him a grandson before his departure.

He knew how pretty, clever and exciting Olivia was, although he could not describe Olivia as sexy out of respect for his daughter, although he could not fail to notice that all young men would naturally be attracted to her bulging, over bearing breasts that Olivia was not shy to expose and exploit.

Then why should she be obliged to do so! God had given her such a figure with some purpose in mind. Some are blessed with brain, radiating health, enchanting, sweet voice, gift to play musical instruments, physical strength and sexy body.

They all use their strength, natural gift in one way or another. Even educated people take pride in putting behind their names the letters showing their academic excellence or the letters of Honour, the reorganisation of their achievement in various fields by the government, elevating them to Knighthood with the title of Sir, Lord and Baroness.

Kiran realised that although the old man seldom smiled and was in pensive most of the time with a tinge of sadness, he was also very fond of Olivia, his only child and would bend backward to see her happy.

As long as Kiran could keep Olivia happy and contended, the old man would eat out of his hand. Then Kiran was a practitioner of hope, expectation and courage that would rub on any one close to him. But Kiran was clever enough not to stare at Olivia's breasts or her thighs when the old man was around, out of respect if nothing else.

"But to be serious, I would like to introduce you to our local priest, **Father Joseph**. He does not say much about his past but I feel he is originally from England, although he has been in charge of the Parish for the last thirty years. He speaks perfect English and Spanish and he would be glad to teach you our language."

"Of course you can teach Olivia as much English as you can. I have been telling her to learn English from Father Joseph for a long time. Perhaps she would listen to you more than to me! She is a clever girl, although she is a bit lazy when it comes to acquiring academic excellence."

Senor Martinez stayed for half an hour and before he left, he gave Kiran few books in Spanish to make a head start. Fortunately for Kiran, the day after next was Sunday. He wanted to strike iron, shape it while it was still hot and flexible.

They had two services on Sunday, an early morning one at 9am and the second one at midday. As it lasted only for an hour, every one preferred the early morning one, so that they could have the rest of the day free.

But this Sunday, Senior Martinez attended the midday service, so that they can have a long and meaningful conversation with the Father Joseph after the service. Besides the three of them, there were only six other people, three middle-aged couples.

Olivia and her father only had a horse drawn, two wheel buggy that can take two people. While Senor Martinez came by buggy, he let Kiran go first on the motorbike with Olivia, so that she can guide him, show him the way.

It seemed Olivia was not new or averse to such a transport. The helmet suited her. She hold on to Kiran tightly and joked, "Kiran, if you find my grip too tight or can not breath freely, let me know and I will loosen my grip"

"Olivia, if I can't breath, it won't be because you hold me tightly. It would be because you let me go in the first place. Believe me Olivia, it will be a great loss for you!"

Olivia did not say any thing but gently sink her teeth in Kiran's back, leaving her marks. Kiran felt like telling her it was the wrong place to bite, but he wisely kept quite. After all they were going to church!

The service was forceful, on the topical subject and refreshing, like a gushing stream overflowing after a sudden bout of tropical rain at its majestic best. But the service was over within half an hour.

When every one departed, Senor Martinez introduced Kiran, as some one from London, England and living in one of his chalets who was eager to learn Spanish.

Father Joseph presumed Kiran would not speak a word of Spanish. So he started the conversation in perfect English. Kiran, to his surprise and delight, replied in perfect Spanish and they had a lengthy conversation in Spanish before they reverted back to English for a short time only, as it would be impolite to speak in a language Olivia and her father could not understand.

"Senior Martinez, your guest speaks good Spanish but as he would like to speak like a native, like a Spanish person, I can give him a crash course, two to three hours a day, every day except Sunday, for three to five weeks and he would be as good as gold in Spanish, as fluent as one can be in such a short time.

Kiran was indeed a bright young man, well educated and with good upbringing." Father Joseph looked at Olivia who was in her Sunday best clothes and gave her a smile.

Even Father Joseph could not resist looking at Olivia now and then, as she was looking stunning indeed in her white attire and red, silky hat, with her long, reddish hair left untied to flutter in the mountain air that gave her an air of elegance, appearance and good manner.

Olivia was making full use of her fuller, well developed figure, although there were no eligible young men in the congregation. Perhaps it was for Kiran's benefit or taking the advantage of the opportunity to dress well, as they do not have many events to look forward to except going to church on Sundays and on religious festivals.

When Kiran was alone with Olivia, he could not help but remark that Olivia indeed looked like a bride, well dressed, beaming and indeed beautiful, her posterior thigh muscles giving her backside a sexy figure. Then Olivia would look sexy in any dress.

"Kiran, what a pity there is no bridegroom around! You should stop paying compliments and start acting! After all words are just words. An ounce of action is preferable to a ton of words, theories and good intentions!"

As usual Olivia was quick off the block, like an Olympic runner at the sound of the starting whistle. Perhaps teasing was in her nature, may be she was receiving such complements all the time.

It was agreed with Father Joseph for Kiran to be there every day except Sunday, from 2pm to 4pm for Spanish lessons. Father Joseph had all the books Kiran would need to learn Spanish. But conversation was more important.

Whatever Kiran would like to say in Spanish but could not, he can say in English and Father Joseph would translate it into Spanish. It was up to Kiran at what speed to learn, how many hours he could put in as home work.

On Monday, after breakfast, Olivia and her father worked on the farm. They had some ***thirty acres*** of land where they had planted olive trees and grapevines. Olive trees did not need much looking after, except at harvest time. But vineyards needed pruning, tidying up and watering.

Olives were harvested in late summer and transported to a nearby mill, where olives were pressed, oil extracted, filtered and bottled as virgin olive oil. Some mills use heating process that yield more oil but cold pressed olives give a superior quality of oil which was more in demand, especially from well established restaurant industry, as well as exported overseas, to Northern Europe and America.

Then there was a vegetable patch and flower garden, with roses, hibiscus, pink rose, daisy, magnolia, lilies and many more flowers native to the region. Olivia was fond of cut flowers. She had a vase of fresh flowers in every room in the farmhouse.

Olivia encouraged Kiran to join them on the farm, teasing him that city boys were too lazy to put in a hard day's work, get their hands dirty. This was a challenge Kiran could not resist. It was a mind game and Olivia exploited Kiran's background, lack of physical labour to her advantage.

In any case Kiran had experienced this sort of labour in Andorra while staying in the monastery. This time the added attraction was Olivia, as she put in half a day's work, dressed in body hugging shorts and an open top.

She really looked sexy. But as her father was working with them, her open top was not that open, except after Senor Martinez withdrew a bit early and left these two alone.

At times Olivia was tantalizingly provocative, knowing full well that Kiran was a gentleman and it would not be easy to break down his resistance. Olivia had full confidence in her ability to get her man without using underhand tricks!

Then she was not averse to use her full charm, her sexiness to breakdown any resistance Kiran may display. It was a challenge for Olivia she would not like to lose, come second best. For Kiran, he could not lose. He was in a win, win situation, head you win, tale you lose!

They would work on the farm two to three hours in the morning except Olivia who would put in a couple of hours before breakfast, milking goats, feeding chickens, collecting eggs and cleaning pens, stables and let the horse loose on the fenced grazing area, along with goats.

Kiran would leave after lunch. Olivia was encouraged to join Kiran by her father, to her and Kiran's delight and surprise, ostensibly to learn some English.

Father Joseph was also pleased to see them both, as he was only expecting Kiran. Then Olivia was every one's favourite in this tiny village where human company was at a premium, especially a female company, a charming company!

It was decided that Kiran should spend the first half an hour teaching Olivia English before father Joseph would join them.

Olivia soon realised that it was a waste of time to sit on the Spanish lesson, as she would not understand a word of English, the conversation between Kiran and Father Joseph who was indeed an Englishman who had settled in Spain.

So for two hours Olivia was left on her own to learn English from the plenty of books in Father Joseph's armoury. Moreover Kiran had prepared a book of some five hundred simple Spanish words in every day use with its English meaning, English words and short, simple sentences.

As Olivia was eager to learn English, Kiran had set a target of two hundred English words for Olivia to learn each week, that is less than thirty words a day when Olivia was able to spare some five hours a day for her study. This was a simple task for any one and Olivia was certainly not any one, not any Tom, Dick and Harry!

Kiran wanted Olivia to build up her word dictionary, vocabulary. The grammar would come next, as English grammar is a child's play compared to complicated Spanish grammar.

After two weeks, it was time for Kiran to look back and appraise the achievement on two fronts, his own progress and that of Olivia. As Kiran had so much time on his hand, putting in some five to seven hours a day, he had made tremendous progress, learning all the finer points of this sweet and sophisticated language.

Father Joseph was contended that within four to six weeks Kiran would be as fluent as some one who has been living in Spain for a long time. Even Olivia was making more progress than any one had dared to hope. Then home is where your heart is. With the right incentive, even Mount Everest is not out of reach for the determined.

Olivia was putting in long hours, seven days a week, almost as many as Kiran if not more. She could now converse with Kiran in Basic English, to the surprise and delight of Senor Martinez who was slowly but surely coming under Kiran's spell.

He knew that this was Kiran's influence, that Olivia was falling head over heals in love with Kiran. But he was not complaining. He knew Kiran would make a wonderful son in law, perhaps he could get his son back, in the form of Kiran, the reincarnation of his son ***Dominique*** whom he lost in tragic circumstances.

Although Olivia's father was a liberal and broad minded person, he had some misgivings, as Kiran was after all a foreigner. But for the time being, he kept his doubt, his misgivings to himself, except reminding Olivia not to bring shame on the family that would make his life intolerable in such a small and close-knit community.

Olivia's answer was that she would rather die than bring shame on her family, although Olivia was not sure she could keep her words, her promises if it came to a crunch. But if she has to choose between Kiran and her father, Kiran would always come second best, no matter how much she may love Kiran. It was No Contest and Kiran knew it well. He would never put Olivia in such a difficult position.

Then Kiran was her Prince Charming. She had no intention of letting him go. After all it is not that often that a peacock would visit this part of Spain that often. It would be a folly to let such an opportunity slip by. If she fails, it would not be due to lack of trying.

There were no pills or contraceptives to protect a girl if she loses her self control, except the age old French connection! But she had tremendous faith in Kiran; that he would never allow such a scenario, a girl becoming pregnant outside marriage, no matter how great the temptation may be.

Kiran had grown taller, planted deep roots in the last few months since the tragedy and he knew how to steady the ship, to control his urge, his desire and how not to rob the girl of her self respect for momentary madness, skin deep pleasure, loss of self control. But if Menka could entice Lord Shiva, so could Olivia entice Kiran.

Kiran knew that such an action will always have a reaction that may ruin many lives. In a way Kiran personifies the strength and nobility of his upbringing, the principles installed in him by his parents. Kiran was and has always been perseverance in his beliefs. He knew the difference between right and wrong, being moral or immoral, being a cheap Romeo and a responsible Lord Rama!

Kiran would always contemplate in solitude, at night when he was alone, the pros and cons of his life on the farm, the way Olivia was attracted to him and his love for her, his desire, paternalistic, marital and sexual.

Olive Grove may not be Shangri La but it may be the right place to heal the scar of the Mount Abu tragedy. This is the place where his odyssey may come to rest, free him from the guilt trip and rebuild his life.

After all even Lord Krishna had to leave the sanctuary of Vrindavan and start afresh in Gujarat, building the wonderful city of Dwarka, on the shores of the mighty Indian Ocean.

Perhaps Kiran may be able to return to his roots one day. After all the exile is a dream of glorious return with all the trimmings accorded to a homecoming hero!

But Kiran was practical. He knew the dream inevitably fades, the imagined return stops feeling glorious, as so often there is nothing to return to except faded memories and the changed landscape on every front, especially on the social front, so often the land is unrecognizable in any manner or style.

In Kiran's case, every one he loved had left this world or moved on, leaving Kiran just a dot on the memory lane. The exile was more palatable than the home coming?

The nature had peculated, robbed Kiran of his glorious past. Now Kiran was pertinacious in his determination to build a new life, in a foreign country, among unknown people where he could start afresh, lay a new foundation. The recent perpetual struggle between life and obliviousness must come to an end. He should make Olive Grove his Vrindavan.

* * *

Chapter Seventeen
Decision Time

The four weeks Kiran promised Father Joseph that he would give his undivided attention to his studies were almost over. Indeed Father Joseph was pleased with the hard work Kiran had put in and his command over the Spanish language. Kiran could speak fluently. Any one would think that he has been living in Spain for few years rather than few weeks.

It was a soul searching time for Kiran, whether he should move on and roam the world to his heart's content or settle down here with Olivia and make Olive Grove his home. Perhaps he may never get a better offer. This was his D day! So why was he dithering!

Olivia was an added attraction that made the situation a bit intricate. Kiran was now so intimate with Olivia that they so often made gentle love, Kiran holding Olivia in his arms, gently playing with her hair, touching her breasts and kissing her on desirable parts of her body.

If Kiran would like to leave, now was the time, a few more weeks and he may not able to leave, even if he wanted to. Even now he would break Olivia's heart and that would trouble his conscious, as Olivia had given him love, hope and a reason to live, even prosper.

But Olivia was made of sterner stuffs. She was a born survivor. But the question was would Kiran meet some one as loving, caring, beautiful and sexy as Olivia? Moreover *"Olive Grove"* was an oasis of peace, tranquillity and enlightenment where the most restless souls, even Lord Buddha would find peace and salvation. The surroundings were as pleasant, mystic and peaceful as could be imagined. It was difficult to imagine such an opportunity would come Kiran's way in a hurry.

Olivia could provide Kiran a lifelong meal ticket, although such thoughts would never influence Kiran in any way. Kiran had already missed out on Divya and perhaps on Penny. Could he afford to lose Olivia as well?

Olivia had already made quantum improvement in Kiran's satisfaction and motivation level. He was almost back to his normal self. Besides Olivia, there was her father Senior Martinez and Father Joseph whom he came to know well.

Both liked Kiran and treated him as their son, some one they could trust, confide and pass on their life's savings, made him a beneficiary in their will! They knew that Kiran was endowed with the mental ability and moral authority for being genius, a guardian angel for Olivia and the Church if he could be persuaded to join the Church, be a part of the congregation.

But all that changed in the blink of an eye. Men may propose God may dispose! When Kiran and Olivia returned after their Sunday classes with Father Joseph, they found Senior Martinez on the floor, in pain, unable to speak or raise his hands and his face slightly distorted.

Olivia was shocked, taken back and almost paralysed, in trance, unable to act in any way. Kiran had to take charge of the situation. He knew that Olivia's father was having a stroke.

Kiran slapped Olivia gently to bring her back to reality, as he needed her help, to find out what medication her father was on, what they had in medicine chest. Kiran pushed two aspirin down the throat of Senior Martinez to thin the blood so that the clot may dislodge by itself and rang for the ambulance.

Normally it would take a long time for an ambulance to arrive in such a remote and isolated place. It would be much quicker to take the patient to the nearest hospital. But with horse and buggy as the only means of transport, it would be impossible.

But Kiran and Olivia were fortunate that the ambulance was dropping a cancer patient in the next farm, after being discharged from the hospital in Marbella, the nearest town with a decent hospital.

The ambulance arrived within ten minutes. The paramedics thanked Kiran for his quick thinking in giving aspirin that may have saved his life or at least it stopped the clot from damaging the brain. Olivia accompanied her father in the ambulance while Kiran had to follow on his motorbike.

By the time Senior Martinez was well settled in cardiac ward, it was getting late in the evening. Kiran wanted to stay in Marbella, in a bed and breakfast accommodation but Olivia said that the animals needed rounding up, locking up in their pens and to be fed next morning.

Fortunately it was only an hour's ride on motorbike with clear roads. Yet by the time they had their dinner and went to bed, tired and exhausted, it was nearly midnight.

After the initial shock, Olivia had composed herself, at least that's what Kiran thought. Kiran decided to sleep in the farm house, in the guest room rather than go back to his chalet, to the relief of Olivia. As soon as he hit the pillow, Kiran was fast a sleep, as he had done a lot of riding, creating mental stress as well as physical exhaustion.

Normally Kiran was a sound sleeper. He could sleep eight to ten hours at a stretch. But today he woke up and looking at the watch, it was 3am and still dark, even on a midsummer night.

Then the mountain always caste a shadow on the area, giving it a different character than what could be considered normal on the coast.

Before Kiran could drift back to sleep, he thought he heard some noise downstairs which he should investigate, in case they may not have locked up properly. There was no fear of burglary or any sort of violence. But an open door may encourage wild animals, especially foxes to enter homes in search of food.

When Kiran came down, he found Olivia sitting in the dining room with a cup of hot chocolate, crying silently, her face covered with smudge, with tears running down her rosy cheeks.

Kiran could not envisage another such tragic, helpless day so soon in his life. Kiran had become not only caring but also strong and resilient person. Yet seeing Olivia crying did stirred his conscious, his heart and his feelings.

Even in such tragic circumstances, Kiran was stunned looking at Olivia in her short, all revealing nightie without much underwear, as the night was so hot and humid. Fortunately Kiran was wearing his boxer's shorts that protected his modesty.

Kiran could not help but take Olivia into his arms, her body, her breasts pressing hard against his bare chest. He held her for a long time. It seemed words were neither necessary nor important but Olivia who was sobbing uncontrollably in the arms of Kiran, soon calm down. It seemed Kiran's gentle stroking her long and silky hair, his occasional words of encouraging calmed down Olivia.

After both had hot drinks, Kiran led Olivia upstairs. When he paused outside her bedroom, expecting Olivia to leave him, she showed no sign of letting Kiran go.

They both ended up in one bed, more out of seeking comfort and solace than any for any other reason.

"Olivia, please don't worry. Papa will be fine and will come home soon, that is my promise to you." Kiran was sure that the worse was over. Senior Martinez will get better and will come home, although he will ever be able to work on the farm was a different question.

"Kiran, this is the first time you have called my father papa, (a common word for father, both in Spanish and English) I don't know what I would have done without you."

Kiran was tempted for a minute to say that Olivia could have called Pedro who would have come running. But this was neither the time nor the place to joke, especially when Olivia was in such a fragile state of mind.

As Olivia trusted Kiran so much, she was able to share his bed without the fear of being taken for granted, being lent upon in any manner or intention.

Olivia spent the night clinging to Kiran who found it difficult to fall a sleep. Both were wide awake and lost in their own thoughts, drifting in and out of their own world. Suddenly Olivia turned around, took Kiran in her strong arms, in her vice like grip, gave him a gentle kiss and said, "Kiran, do you love me?"

This was the time for Kiran to come clean, not to rest his finger in different pies.

"Of course I love you Olivia. Can any one resist you?" Kiran was at least sincere in wanting her.

"Then why don't you ask me to marry you? You know how much I love you, want you and you want me. Why waste valuable time sleeping in separate beds, behaving like strangers on the sexual, physical and emotional front?"

"It is only a question of time before I lose my cool, we may lose self restraint and have our honeymoon before the time, before we get married! I am sure you don't want that and I am in complete agreement with you. But we are both young, in our prime and in close proximity. I know how you look at me when I am working on the farm, in shorts and loose top!"

"We can not keep our feelings, our desire under lock and key too long." Olivia was frank but she had never said so much. Now she was able to say half of it in English as well. Olivia had made as much progress on her English as Kiran had on his Spanish.

The difference was that while Kiran had so many people to talk to in Spanish, Olivia only had Kiran and Father Joseph to talk to in English. Father Joseph even joked with Olivia that being in love works wonder on the education front as well, that she is indeed a very bright girl but until now lacked motivation; let her literary talent go to waste, but no more! Kiran was her Prince Charming!

He even encouraged Olivia to bring Kiran amongst their fold. Kiran would be an asset to this dwindling community, being deserted by the young and upwardly mobile local lads who prefer city life rather than working on their family farm.

Kiran thought for a while and then said, "Olivia, you are right. But this is neither the time nor the place to start making plans, charting our future.

When papa comes home and is much better, then I will ask for his permission and I will go down on my knees and propose to you, asking you to be my darling wife."

In reply, Olivia gave Kiran a passionate and lingering kiss that almost chocked Kiran, before letting him go, loosening her vice like grip when she realised that Kiran was massaging her breast, twisting her nipples that was raising her blood pressure to a boiling point. It would be better to let him go before it was too late!

Was this weary visitor from across the sea a Hercules in disguise? Would he tame her before she could bring him under her domain, gain mastery over his soul, mind and body?

Kiran now realised that to try to keep Olivia away, deny his feelings and desire was an exercise in frustration. He will soon be consumed by hunger for more such encounters without perimeter. Once the dam is busted, then water is free to roam any where. The walls of Kiran's inner perimeter enclosing his heart, his feelings and his desire may not last long, stood firm against the tide of emotions. He has to stop sitting on the fence and come down on the side of his happiness.

Olivia was well built, muscular and a very strong girl indeed, more than a match for Kiran in physical strength who was himself a tall, well built, strong young man.

He could not help but wonder, what their honeymoon night would be like when they are free to do what they like, hurt each other as much as their fancy may dictate, have sex in any manner that may please them, every which way bar none!

Soon Kiran and Olivia drifted to sleep, at least in much better frame of mind than when they came back from the hospital. These mountain people are, on the whole healthy people. Neither Olivia nor her papa had been admitted to hospital before.

When Kiran woke up, he was alone in the bed. Olivia must have woke up early, at her usual time of 6am, to feed the animals, let chicken, goats and the horse out of their pens.

When Kiran came down, the breakfast was on the table, with Kiran's favourite Spanish omelette and button mushrooms ready and waiting for him on the sturdy wooden dining table.

The farm was more or less maintenance free. The weeds were controlled by spreading straws along the ridge. Even watering was done automatically, labour free, as was the practice throughout Spain. They lay rubber pipes at the base of a plant, bush or the tree with holes and switch on the tape for an hour or so until the soil is well soaked.

On the farms in coastal regions where summers are excessive, it is a common practice to soak the land by tankers filled with water, just before the summer heat.

This is equivalent to some five inches of rainfall and will keep the plants, trees healthy and well watered throughout the summer months, until the rainfall in winter.

This weather pattern is known as Mediterranean climate, suitable for wine and olive crops, as well as citrus fruits like oranges, lemons and pomegranates.

After breakfast, Kiran joined Olivia on the farm, as many hands make light work. They were back in the house in less than two hours. As the visiting hours were from 2pm to 6pm, Olivia and Kiran spend the time concentrating on their studies. But both realised that their minds were not geared to study, not this morning.

By the time they reached hospital, it was tea-time. Senior Martinez had a restful night. There were no complications, no visible rupture of hair like blood vessels in the brain, due to prompt action by Kiran, thinning of blood on taking aspirin.

As there is no treatment as such for stroke, Senior Martinez was kept under observation for three days before allowed home where he would have to carry out prescribed exercise to regain the loss of movement on his right side, particularly right hand. A physiotherapist based in the nearby village would visit him on alternate days.

Olivia was pleased, was over the moon to see her beloved papa well and back home, although it had not yet sunk in, realised that it was a long and arduous task for Senior Martinez to be back to full health, to regain his original mobility, that his life on the farm may never be the same again.

When Kiran started calling Senior Martinez papa, on the insistence of Olivia, he soon realised that Olivia and Kiran have made a good use of his absence, cemented their love and affection for each other.

After a week when Kiran asked for his permission to marry Olivia, papa was over the moon. He could not help but pull Kiran's leg, asking him that he has not put Olivia in the dock, that he has no option but to marry his lovely daughter out of sheer necessity!

"Papa, do you really believe that I could behave in such a dishonourable manner! I love Olivia and respect her as much as you do.

I have found a father whom I can call papa and you have found a son in law who is prepared to be your son as well! You know that Olivia has never been so happy in her life. This is a blessing in disguise for all of us."

Kiran was absolutely right. Olivia had never been so happy in her young, short life, confined to this tiny village. Going to church early on Sunday morning was the highlight of the week!

One place where they like making love was under their favourite giant olive tree that was three times bigger than normal trees but hardly bear any fruits.

What it did give was shelter from the midday sun and clean, open, sandy place underneath its vast canopy where Kiran and Olivia would rest, have a drink and make love after their morning shift on the farm, to their hearts' content.

Could this tree be the off-shoot of the tree Lord Krishna planted in Vrindavan, his favourite place where he spent many a happy years with his consort Radha!

As papa was not allowed on the farm and there was no other human presence, Kiran and Olivia could make love with hardly any clothes on. Then they were engaged and on the verge of getting married. So why worry about such hindrance, unnecessary restrictions when they could enjoy the nature by being one with mother earth.

One incident they will linger on in their memory for a long time was when Pedro suddenly arrived on the farm with a Spanish couple who wanted to rent the chalet for a week.

While the couple stayed in the farm house with papa, Pedro came looking for Olivia who had just finished her shift. It was indeed a hot and humid day with temperature well above 45*C. Olivia whose clothes were saturated with perspiration was down to her skimpy G string red knickers that could hardly cover a few inches of her most private part.

They were under the open shower for the use of farm workers on such a hot and humid day. Today Kiran and Olivia were under the shower.

Normally they use the portable shower screen but as Papa was confined to home and no one else was working on the farm, Olivia could not be bothered bringing out the screen. The cold water was really refreshing for body and soul.

Although they started showering in their underclothes, they soon caste off all the clothes, as Kiran and Olivia started enjoying the shower, their not so innocent mischief making and for Kiran, Olivia's voluptuous body, kissing, cuddling and making love to their heart's delight.

Pedro's arrival was in a way divine intervention, as they may not have stopped half way. Olivia wanted to be a virgin bride on her honeymoon night and this escapade would have destroyed her dream and would have made their honeymoon that much less of a honeymoon, a tiny bit less special.

These may be outdated, old-fashioned and obsolete views in our present day and age when we have confined morality to dustbin, but these virtues were still fashionable, desirable in those days when every one would go to church on Sundays, keep meat off the menu on Fridays and sex before marriage was as rare as sighting of a swallow in midwinter.

It was in no way an appeasement or weasel words, a pathetic effort to please any one. It was a genuine atmosphere at the time, a democratic tradition for younger generation to care and respect their elders, their age old traditions that have served the society well.

Pedro turned around and walked back to the farm house, perhaps thinking what he had missed, although not for lack of trying, followed by Kiran and Olivia. It is needless to say that Pedro never sat foot on the farm again nor he attended their marriage, even though Kiran and Olivia personally delivered the wedding invitation. Poor Pedro! Who can blame him? He must be regretting the day he brought Kiran to Olive Grove!

Olivia had tremendous faith and trust in Kiran and knew that this will be a union of not only two bodies but two souls, until death do them part! This was a union, a marriage of two different people, two contrasting lifestyle, culture and ambition. So it was vital for Kiran to have Olivia's unquestionable support and trust which she readily gave.

Within a month Kiran and Olivia got married in the church. The ceremony was conducted by Father Joseph who was as delighted as Senior Martinez and was now looking forward to baptise their children as soon as he can!

The way Kiran and Olivia were making love every night, exploiting their bodies to the threshold of imagination and pain. Olivia becoming pregnant was inevitable.

Kiran was glad that Olivia had a modern outlook when it came to making love, having sex. So often Olivia made all the running to the surprise and delight of Kiran.

Their night was an Arabian night, a night of magical slumber after a long and weary day that inevitably brought improvement and motivation in their lives. Kiran was rejoicing in the beauty and splendour of this tiny slice of Heaven called Olivia!

Kiran became a willing victim, a sex slave with a difference. One concession Olivia had to make was to give up wearing low cut tops and mini-skirts, as her breasts and thighs were covered with love bites, bruises all the time. Did she care! Not a bit except not to show the sign of her bedroom adventure to her papa, out of respect.

Then Papa was young once. He would not grudge such attention or pleasure Olivia was getting out of her marriage, a match made in heaven. But it was nice and comforting to know that children or rather young adults still respect their adults.

Then it was the age, an oasis of enlightenment that is so alien to today's generation! Then perhaps this generation has stopped bending to the demands of social pressure. Perhaps it may not be right for the mind to be always a part of and in unison with the community.

* * *

Chapter Eighteen
The New Beginning

Now that Kiran had made the commitment, he was determined to succeed on all front, on his family front, show Olivia all the ropes, train her in the art of etiquette, etymology, give Olivia a lifestyle she deserves and papa what he wanted most, a grandson. ?*Si Dios quiere?* (God willing!)

Kiran wanted to expand and make business profitable so that he could support the lifestyle he had envisaged for all of them and that include their children, an expanded family, as and when it may happen.

Olivia was already getting proficient in English. Now she was learning business acumen, economics and appreciation of wealth, what benefits it could bring to their sheltered lives.

She was beginning to appreciate the meaning and usefulness of being rich or at least well-off. Financial standing automatically brings other benefits, such as respect and invitation from people they may have never met!

Olivia was changing fast, from an ordinary, innocent village beauty, a sensuous Venus of Roman era to a clever, modern, sophisticated and equivocating business woman in the making!

Her endeavour was much appreciated by Kiran. Papa felt Olivia was taking over the duty and the function he would have expected from his son. He could not hide his delight, joy, exuberant and long suppressed aspiration and emotions. He knew that Kiran had managed to bring out the best from Olivia. Where did he fail?

But Kiran was hoping she would not change too much, that she would retain her innocence, sense of fun, that include fun on sexual front as well as on social and domestic front. Olivia was indeed a joy to be with, either in the orchid, farm, kitchen, house or in bed!

Fortunately for Kiran, Olivia had tremendous faith and trust in Kiran that he would never let her down, come hell or high water. He would look after her not only during the time of plenty but during famine as well, although famine was never even a remote possibility in the reign of *"King Kiran, King Richard, The Lion Heart!"*

The business, *"The Olive Grove"* was trotting along at a subsistence level at best. But as there were no mortgages, no borrowing, people could survive on whatever they earn. Papa and Olivia were more than comfortable as their needs were so meagre.

They did not have even a car or a scooter, as the horse and buggy served their meagre transport needs well. Horse was an appreciating, all purpose assets rather than a car, a depreciating asset that would become a liability with age and usage.

Kiran's first step would be to invest some of his considerable fortune in buying up surrounding agricultural land that he could have for next to nothing. With his expertise in accountancy, his business brain and now his mastery over the Spanish language, his and papa's close friendship with Father Joseph, sky was the limit for his dreams, his aspiration and his Empire building ambitions, as these people were neither business minded nor ambitious enough to thwart his plans, raise obstacles or become rivals on the business, commercial front.

This was the prevailing atmosphere at the time, especially away from cities. With his upbringing in an ambitious and educated family, as well as London education, Kiran would be an odd man out. He could tower over the rest; become a Lord of the Manor, although he was not Manor-born but he very much wanted his children to be.

His first task was to take papa and Olivia onboard, register a limited company and transfer Olive Grove to the newly formed company which he named *"Olive Grove Enterprise."*

Although Olivia was responsive to the idea of setting up a limited liability company and transferring Olive Grove, putting it on Company's assets, papa was naturally a bit concerned, some what apprehensive. After all he had known Kiran for less than six months.

As Kiran's intentions were honourable and he was willing to give the majority of the shares in the limited company to Olivia, papa eventually came on board.

Papa was a wise and careful person. He had a long and heart to heart talk with Father Joseph who reassured Senior Martinez that Kiran's intentions were not only honourable but he was a wealthy person in his own right.

He explained Kiran's plans, that he was willing to invest a considerable sum of his own money, after examining Kiran's investment portfolio and especially his bank accounts. Now Olivia and Kiran had papa's full and unconditional blessings to expand Olive Grove as they wish.

In a village community, the church is the hub, the centre of all activities, social, religious, financial, communal and business. Father Joseph was a trusted figure and Kiran would always have his blessings.

Every one would consult him on all matters. Father was a marriage counsellor, an estate agent, marriage broker and a judge and jury to settle domestic disharmony. Family break-up was rare and divorce unheard, as it was a taboo in Catholicism.

This was basically Gnostic society, community. It was of utmost importance for Kiran to keep Father Joseph on board at all times In any case Father Joseph loved Olivia like a daughter and Kiran was a fellow exile from the green, green shores of England, a land of hope and glory, milk and honey, opportunities and advantages.

Kiran became a regular churchgoer and Father Joseph's right hand man, sugared with generous donations flowing from his heart and business for good causes, for charities that Father Joseph would like Kiran to support.

But there was no nepotism in their friendship, just the need to help every one and one another, the old type of netherism, pure and simple, without hidden agenda or ulterior motive. This was the age of shivery, human values and true and trusted friendship.

One such project was an orphanage appropriately named *"Shelter"* which would take in women and children who had fallen on hard times, due to the loss of a bread winner in a family.

The tragedy was brought on by the brutal civil war that turned father against son, brother against brother and family against family that left so many people destitute, without a bread winner, as some quarter of a million men died in this carnage.

Kiran so often would visit this orphanage, taking father Joseph in his newly acquired VW Beetle car and work with the father, give his love and affection to children and play football with them. Kiran had added a car and a tractor to his farm implements, car for comfort and tractor as labour saving investment.

But it was his generous donations that made Kiran popular and a heartthrob to some of the teenage girls who find Kiran irresistible, a knight in shinning armour, a messiah specially dispatch from heaven by Lord Jesus Christ in answer to their prayers.

Kiran was an angel masquerading as human being. This was the time, the era when generosity, saintliness and human values were appreciated and acknowledged. Masochism had no meaning, no place in the hearts and minds of the people, in the ultra conservative society.

These charming, innocent and neglected girls really envied Olivia who would occasionally accompany them. So Olivia was aware of how much Kiran was in demand, appreciated by these teenage beauties, Kiran's own personal followers, his kamikaze army! Then Olivia had acquired awareness and enlightenment, at least as far as Kiran was concerned and she was not without her admirers as well!

Kiran was a pied piper to these mesmerised teenage tearaways! These children were in no way nihilist. They were just the victims of social and political upheaval. They were nestlings who were not able to fly for one reason or another. Shelter was indeed glad to have some one like Kiran and Father Joseph as their patrons.

This was the era when a role model was hard to find except on the Hollywood set. Sport personalities and politicians were not even on the horizon, unlike today, as their faces stare at us from every angle, plastered on billboards, newspapers and TV.

Kiran soon added some two hundred and fifty acres of prime agricultural land, most of which was planted with olive trees and grapevines. He built five more chalets and made an arrangement with a British Holiday Company to let these chalets to British tourists with wine tasting scheme.

The vast basement under the farm building was converted as a wine storage and testing place where tourists could not only taste wine but could buy bottles of wine with the proud label of ***Vino del Casa de Olivia.*** (Vine from the house of Olivia)

Kiran even smartly designed grape, fruits and olive picking holidays with subsidized accommodation. In return he obtained free labour that was getting scarce in villages, as the young men and women were moving away from farming to less physically demanding jobs in cities and coastal areas which were fast developing as tourist resorts.

Such working holidays were becoming popular with Spanish families living in cities, as they wanted their children to have the taste of farm, village life they had left behind, so often with regrets later on in life.

Cities may look bright, shining and glamorous from a distant. But all that glitters is not always gold. City life can become lonely and depressing; especially in old age when children have flown the nest and one partner may have departed early.

This makes life indeed lonely and unbearable. Kiran remembered the saying he learnt back at home, ***"Make a new friend but preserve the old, as new is silver, old is always gold"***

The Beetle car was mainly for the comfort of papa who took a back seat, spent most of his time playing dominos, cards and socializing, organizing church events. Such activities made quantum improvement in papa's life, in his satisfaction and motivation level.

Indeed Papa and Father Joseph get on well, like two peas from the same pod. Olivia was the common factor in their bond, now cemented with the arrival of Englishman Kiran.

Father Joseph always try to raise the spirit and self belief in every one who come close to him, move within his inner circle. He genuinely believed that we are all children of God.

We are all endowed with the ability, the capacity to be genius in our chosen field. It is only a question of trying, believing in one's own ability. Olivia was the prime example. Kiran believed in her.

Kiran knew that Olivia could climb Mount Everest, be on the podium and live in a palace. Until now, no one taped in her reserved strength, gave her an opportunity. If Kiran had not turned up at Olive Grove, Olivia could never have learnt English, mastered the business intricacies and turned herself into a shrewd business woman.

This was the demonstration of Kiran's intention to be part of the community. He had the *"finca"* that is land, property, real estate in the countryside and willing to work on it, pruning, irrigating and harvesting the crops.

With the help of a local expert, a redundant farmer by the name of **Lopez,** introduced to Kiran by Father Joseph and whose farm of some fifty acres Kiran bought, Kiran was able to reorganize his farm, all the land he had bought and still buying as and when it came to market, made available at a reasonable price.

Besides olives and grapes, Kiran had set aside some fifty acres of land to plant orange, grape fruit, Satsuma, tangerine and pomegranate to give him diversity and choice, fresh fruits going straight on to the supermarket, ***supermercado*** shelves, under their brand name ***"Olive Grove Enterprise"***

In business Kiran had the power, the foresight of perceiving things beyond normal acumen. He was indeed a clairvoyant. Even his business portfolio in London was doing very well indeed, as the business was booming, building the infrastructure and manufacturing industry that was neglected during the Second World War when all resources were targeted at winning the war.

Kiran had two types of Olive trees, the ***Hojiblanca*** and ***Manzanillo*** verities. The Manzanillo variety ripens first, in October. It is an art to harvest olives with as little physical labour as possible.

Nets are fastened at the bottom of the trees, using other, nearby trees as fastening poles or stakes firmly driven in the soil.

Then branches are combed, using plastic or wooden combs to loosen the olives that drop into the nets below. So often branches are gently shaken to get to the stubborn olives that refuse to be combed!

The olives are then collected either in big jute sacks or open plastic baskets and taken to the village mill, ***"The Molino Panda Rosa"*** in the appropriately named ***Plaza del Oliva*** or the Olive Square.

As Kiran now had a tractor that can drag a cart filled with olives, it was much easier than using a horse drawn transport. It still required a few trips to carry all the olives to the mill.

There the olives are off loaded into big metal or plastic containers and labelled with owners' name and the name of the farm, as usually the mill press olives from different farms, producing different variety and quantity of oil. While most farmers would need a few hours time, Kiran would need a day or two as his land and harvest keep on increasing.

The process of extracting olive oil would start on a floor-level grid which feeds into a hopper. The olives then pass through a chute and are shaken to remove leaves, twigs and branches. This stage of preparing olives for oil extraction can take up to three hours, depending upon the quantity and quality of picking.

In the final stages, the cleaned olives are fed into vats which have a manually operated taps. The pressed olives deliver oil starting with a drip and ending in torrents, filling twenty five to fifty litter drums, as many as two to five hundred drums.

The olives grown on Olive Grove were the types that yielded virgin oil. Olives were large, firm and juicy that would yield a good quantity and quality of oil by just pressing. The oil is known as, **Cold Pressed Virgin Olive Oil,** as no heat is involved that normally reduce the flavour and vitamin contents of the oil.

Then there are olives that are smaller, drier and much firmer, known as *"La Aceituna Dura"* These olives have to be treated, processed under hot steam to make them soft in order to extract oil. This oil is of poor quality, mostly used for frying while virgin oil is used as a dressing, in salads and as an added ingredient, even as a dip for certain first course dishes.

These hard olives are also used as snacks, especially good with beer and wine. Spanish people eat them in the same way as the British who would have crisps and peanuts with their beer and ale. But olives are much healthier than crisps and available as hard pressed snacks in brine or vinegar with stones removed; a must for most Spaniards.

It is a pity that although Brits are flocking Costas as their summer holiday destination, they have not yet taken olives to their hearts. Such snacks are not available in British pubs and restaurants where they serve alcoholic drinks.

Kiran would sell oil drums to a wholesaler who would bottle it and sell it to supermarkets and retail outlets, as a produce of Olive Grove. In the same manner grapes were sold to a vinery that would press and bottle the vine. Kiran would buy back some stock to sell to the tourists who come to the farm on a wine tasting, olive picking excursions.

Kiran was already planning to install a mill and a vinery. But as he may only use it a few weeks a year, the capital outlay may not justify the cost. The owner of the mill, *"The Molina Panda Rosa"* was already willing to sell the mill to Kiran at a knock-down price.

But the machinery was too old and the process too laborious to justify investment. Instead Kiran would book couple of days for his sole use, paying a small deposit in advance that would guarantee him the days he needed.

Kiran was indeed grateful to Olivia for her full and undivided support. Olivia was in a way heart and soul of this enterprise. Papa was happy but getting increasingly eager and restless to play with his grandson while he was healthy. That would indeed illuminate his life; fulfil his dream, his final years. After the age of sixty, every year is a bonus that one must enjoy to the fullest.

Kiran and Olivia had given two years to put their business in order and bring the farm building to the comfort level Kiran wanted, desired for his family before making Papa happy, give him what he wanted, although it was not entirely in his hand to make Olivia pregnant.

While building wine cellar and a very spacious, all purpose warehouses in the basement, Kiran renovated the house which already had five spacious bedrooms.

He completely redecorated the whole house, in a way he had envisaged as soon as he realised that this is his permanent home, his dream home.

Kiran put down wooden floorings throughout, a new kitchen with the latest facilities, gas cooker, Kelvinator upstanding fridge freezer, wall to wall cabinets and made three bedrooms en-suit with fitted wardrobes in laminated wood, the latest design to come on market.

These improvements with a new roof and a wood and glass conservatory at the back entirely changed the look and the comfort of the farmhouse. The open view of Olive Grove and the mountain peak in the distant more than doubled the value of the house. Now the house was fit to bring up children in comfort, indeed in the lap of luxury.

As there were two full time employees, a farm-hand and an all purpose maid to clean the villas, stables and the rest, Olivia was made more or less redundant. Then there was farmer Lopez who came in now and then, whose advice and knowledge was indeed valuable to Kiran.

Olivia took over the running of the business, write books and keep records while Kiran devoted his time to sell the products, visiting nearby towns, hotels and supermarkets, dealing with holiday companies, wholesalers and distributors, middle agents. As common to most Western economies, there was a thick layer of middlemen in Spanish businesses that would keep the price of most produce artificially high.

Kiran had laid foundation, made perfect arrangement for the business to succeed, to prosper. Now it was time to try hard, to concentrate on having a family. But Kiran and Olivia were both worried that although they were not using any form of contraceptive, Olivia had not conceived after two years of marriage.

On consulting doctor, a gynaecologist, they were assured that there was nothing wrong physically in either Olivia or Kiran. Perhaps it was the pressure of work, the unintentional desire not to conceive. An interlude away from it all may help.

But the doctor did prescribe some hormone tablets for Olivia to aid the nature, to give a helping hand. But above all, they were told to relax and have sex at the right time, a shambolic sex, not a scrupulous one, as well as sex per chart prepared by Olivia who knew when she was at her best! Then for Kiran, she was at her best all the time.

* * *

Chapter Nineteen
The Good News

Olivia did not have to keep Kiran waiting for too long. Within three months of their visit to gynaecologist, Olivia was proud to tell Kiran and Papa that she was pregnant. Both Kiran and Papa were over the moon, the last missing link in creating a whole family, a perfect home for all the family in this wilderness was at last taking shape, bearing fruits. After all there was a light at the end of the tunnel, especially for the old man, for Papa. Kiran could not help but feel that some one from up there was looking after and taking care of them.

While Papa wanted a boy, Kiran was keen on a girl, a little Olivia who would grow into as beautiful and as charming a little girl as her mother. Olivia had never seen her Papa so happy. The squabble, pulling each other's leg was the highlight of the day. At last there was a smile on the old man's face, a weather beaten face that has witnessed so many tragedies in his life.

Kiran would like to pull Papa's leg, "Papa, you are not the most handsome man in the world. So let us pray for a girl, a carbon copy of her mother Olivia, the most beautiful girl in Spain?"

Papa would counter Kiran by showing him his old photograph in National Service uniform, at the tender age of eighteen! But his main thrust was that a child, a boy naturally takes after his father. Is Kiran not the most handsome man in the area? My *"El Nieto"* (Grandson) will be an exact copy of his dad, clever, good looking and handsome!

How could Kiran counter such an argument! Kiran had no answer to Papa's triumphant disposition. The old man had the last laugh, to the delight of Olivia, as she had rarely seen her Papa smiling. It was indeed a pleasure and a delight to see a smile on Papa's wrinkled and sad face. He had aged beyond his years.

It seemed the God was at last smiling on the whole family. When the time came, Olivia gave birth to a twin, a boy and a girl, to the surprise and delight of every one, especially Papa and Kiran!

Normally twins are of the same sex, either two boys or two girls, as they are developed from the same embryo that may split up due to some reason. But once in a while, especially when the woman is on fertility drugs, she can give birth to a twin, developed from two different sperms.

It seemed God was kind to Olivia, as she would have dreaded to see either of them disappointed. Naturally Papa and Kiran were on the high, with Champaign flowing freely at the special celebrations arranged by Father Joseph, after baptism.

These were Kiran's desire and wish to thank every one in the village and the community at large. This was his way of thanking every one for their tremendous support and encouragement to Kiran when he was a new arrival, a stranger, struggling to establish his roots.

Now there was harmony, love, commitment and happiness not only in Kiran's household but in the community as a whole. There was no shibboleth between Kiran and the rest of the community. He was no longer an outsider but a valued member of the congregation, the village community, in perfect harmony with the community, the Church, Father Joseph and Mother Nature, the landscape that was a hidden heaven, a jewel, a sight for a sore eyes for a city dweller.

After so many years, Papa was at last at peace with his conscious and the world at large. One day when Kiran and Papa were enjoying a bottle of wine from their vineyard with pressed, seedless olives, Papa suddenly brought out an old album that he would never do in presence of Olivia.

He picked up a fading photograph of a young boy and said in some what shivering, stuttering and trembling voice, "Kiran, I have not opened this album or talked about my son for a very long time. I am only telling you now, as I know you have undergone such a tragedy in your own life. So you will understand my pain, my despair and my desire to block out this tragedy.

The greatest tragedy in parent's life is to bury their grown up children who depart before their time. I lost my only son when he was hardly out of his teen, in the civil war that tore this country apart. In a way it was a war between different nations, different ideologies, fought on Spanish soil.

The Spanish people were made the scapegoat, used as a cannon fodder and discarded after the war.

You are too young to remember the Spanish civil war, which was more like an all out conflict, indeed like world war, as more than fifty nations were involved, pouring in thousands of war planes, tanks, artilleries and professional soldiers from Hitler's Nazi Germany, Mussolini's Fascists Italy to the Soviet Union, the Bastian of Communism.

Then there were USA, Britain, France, Mexico and many more nations. If I go into detail, it will be bigger and longer than your, Hindu's Holy books of Ramayana and Mahabharat put together.

But it would certainly lack the wisdom of the most revered book in Hinduism, the book of Bhagwad Gita, the words of wisdom spoken by none other than Lord Krishna. Perhaps Lord Jesus Christ was a reincarnation of Lord Rama and Lord Krishna.

So I will give you a brief history of the Spanish Civil War. The seeds were sown way back in 1902 when Alfonzo X11 assumed power. In 1931, to his great credit, he allowed free, fair and democratic elections.

People overwhelmingly voted for a Republic. The king reluctantly went into exile on 14th April 1931. In 1936 at the next election, the country was bitterly divided into two main, opposing groups, to fight the election. Both parties were hell bent on winning the election at any cost, by any means, fair or foul. It was more like a war than an election.

On one side, led by **Manuel Azana**, were socialists, Communists and their allies, united under the banner of **Popular Front. (PF)** They were anti monarchy, anti Roman Catholic Church who wanted Spain to adopt Soviet Union style Socialism.

Opposing them was the right wing coalition under the banner of **National Front, (NF)** made up of Republicans, pro Roman Catholic Church, army generals, landlords and upper, richer class who believed Socialism and Communism was the ultimate decline of this once strong and mighty nation who was a world power in the bygone era, conquering practically the whole of South America, the way Britain colonized North America.

The Popular Front won 263 seats out of 473, a clear victory for the left. The PF upset the Conservatives and the right wing army generals by freeing left-wing prisoners, transferring Right-wing Generals to Spanish Overseas Colonies and failing to protect churches that were firebombed and came under constant attack from the Communists. Burning and looting churches was an every night event.

The wealthy people began to transfer vast amount of money and gold to Switzerland, thus causing economic crisis and military uprising. The PF government distributed arms and ammunitions to left wing trade unionists, party members and other such left leaning organizations, as they did not trust the loyalty of the army, even though they had installed puppet, inexperienced Generals on the mainland Spain.

While most European governments wanted to remain neutral, the PF government and their policies were popular amongst the masses, especially ideologically influenced younger generation.

They saw socialism as the classless society where every one was equal in the eyes of law and in the society. They fervently believed that capitalism was an elitist nonsense, fascist cyber warriors, while the religion was the opium for the masses, another way to keep the working class subdued and obedient.

This was the romantic era on the social and political front, as people were so ruthlessly suppressed by the rich ruling class who now wanted their revenge, wanted a pound of flesh, more freedom and above social equality, a classless society that only Socialism and Communism can give, at least in theory, as Communists had their own elite, privileged class in the loyal party members.

This gave birth to *"International Brigade"* a hotchpotch of a volunteer army, a heterogeneous collection of young talents but ill trained, ill equipped idealistic youngsters whose main weapon was their beliefs rather than fighting skill, military training, who were fighting alongside the people who were armed by the PF government.

They were a genetically engineered fighting force. But they were not trained soldiers, just committed, brain washed volunteers with their iconoclast beliefs and loyalty to Soviet Union.

General Franco, who was exiled to Canary Islands, became the leader of the NF forces to fight the Communist takeover of a Catholic country where most of the people were religious and regular church-goers.

He launched his attack on Spain from the Spanish African Province and was quickly joined by Generals who were removed from their post by the PF government.

Portugal, under Antonio Salazar also supported General Franco, thus closing its border which was a supply route for the PF armies. In September 1936 General Franco became the Commander of the entire NF army, united under his leadership.

He ruthlessly purged the army of any anti Franco elements and in return received full support from **Hitler's Nazi Germany and Mussolini's Fascist Italy** who poured in well trained soldiers along with planes, tanks and armoured vehicles.

The only support PF received was from the Soviet Union. The West was paralyzed, not able to decide who the foe was and who was the friend, who to support and for what reason? While the West would never support a Communist takeover of Spain, the right wing army generals were in the pockets of Nazi Germany.

It was like choosing between devil and a deep blue sea, King Kong and Godzilla. General Franco's rampant army soon gained the upper hand, capturing one city after another. The capital city Madrid came under heavy bombardment from Luftwaffe.

The surrender of the capital brought the end of the civil war in 1939. General Franco was now in complete charge. He carried out a ruthless purge, executing more than one hundred thousand prisoners and many more died in concentration camps.

All together Spain lost some 4% of its population through execution, fighting, hunger and disease. This civil war was Frankenstein, a foreign creation who lost control and was let lose on the innocent, unsuspecting and some what naïve people of Spain.

My son died in Alicante, another city that resisted until the end and was heavily bombed. One of his friends, who survived the bombing and the starvation, brought me my son's final letter, along with a few of his possessions, his watch, wallet and the chain with a Cross and a locket with our photo inside.

I was not even able to say final farewell or lay his body to rest He was buried in a mass grave along with his comrades. He was not yet twenty one" Papa's voice was chocking with emotions.

My son was an idealist young man, more passion than common sense. Many of us did not join the war, the carnage, as we felt that we were being used, made fiduciary, fighting a proxy war on behalf of Communism, Capitalism and Fascism. Influencing young and developing mind was much easier than influencing, fooling people like us.

I tried to remind my son that this political ideology was extremely ephemeral, *sic transit Gloria mundi* (Thus passes the glory of the ideology!) as we say in Latin. As a result of this brutal civil war, our Spain, a beautiful country full of sun, sand, sangria and fun, was fossilized into silence. People were turned into zombies, family members spying on each

145

other, neighbours turned against each other, many on the payroll of the State.

After a short break, he continued, "Olivia was born a year after his death. But unfortunately we lost her mother in childbirth. She was as beautiful as Olivia if not more.

But we were both broken people, surviving from day to day. Olivia was the only reason that kept me going. I got some solace, comfort from my religious belief and Father Joseph was a God send gift for the community when his wisdom and support was most needed.

I understand Father Joseph came to Spain as a member of the International Brigade and joining church, becoming priest was the only way he could have escaped persecution, even death. His loyalty to church stood him in good stead, proving that he was not a Communist.

Father Joseph never talks about his past, nor would we ask him any questions. I am just glad that he survived and since his arrival, he has been a tower of strength for many villagers who lost their children in this brutal civil war. He was a God send gift to our community. Being so highly educated made him humble, caring and grateful to villagers who took him to their heart in no time at all."

"So Kiran, now you know every thing about my family, why Olivia is so precious to me and why I am so grateful to you for making Olivia happy, giving her every thing that I could not, transforming her from a simple village girl to an intellectual, a tall and confident person who can take care of herself."

Papa was clearly in distress. He had never spoken so much or opened his heart to any one. Kiran could not help but took Papa into his arms and let the old man cry, lessen the burden, share his pain that had remain buried deep down in his heart.

The old man was made of sterner stuff. He soon regained the composure and resumed their drinking and eating snacks. But he warned Kiran not to say any thing to Olivia.

"Papa, you don't have to worry about that. I do not want Olivia to learn much about our past, your or mine. She is a happy go lucky girl and I would like her to retain her innocence, her kind, caring and playful nature for ever! I am also very grateful to you Papa for giving us your permission to marry"

"Kiran, my life was lackadaisical before your arrival. You know that you are a God send gift not only to me and Olivia but also to Father Joseph and the whole village community.

You are the second gift from God, after Father Joseph. You know the kidology, the ideology of being popular and that will stand you in good stead in this small, well-knit community who is already eating out of your hands!"

You can even make me frolicsome if you try hard. You know how to butter an old man, how to make me happy.

You are a rain maker in waiting. Now I can depart peacefully, meet my makers, my boy and Olivia's mother when the time comes. What more can I ask from you or from my God! Hallelujah!"

There was a broad, sad smile of satisfaction on the weather beaten, gnarled face of Papa. Kiran's heart was filled with a tinge of sorrow, as well as joy and happiness. Kiran thanked God for making him the instrument in making Papa happy, give him the gift that he always wanted.

It was like a rainy day, a drizzling day with bright sunlight appearing and disappearing with the rainbow saturating the sky with brilliant colours that would transform even a gloomy day into a shiny, joyful, playful day with hope and expectation in the air!

* * *

Chapter Twenty
The Happy Family

With two children to look after, Olivia had more on her plate than she could handle. As usual, Father Joseph came to their rescue. He found a lovely girl by the name of **Pillar**, a popular and common name amongst Spanish girls, who became the live-in nanny, a valuable addition to the household.

She was only a few years older than Olivia. Unfortunately she got married at an early age. Her husband who went to the city never came back. That was more than six years ago. Such incidents were not that unusual, especially if the wives they leave behind were neither much educated to fit in a city life nor beautiful enough to captivate their husbands, although beauty is in beholder's eyes.

Although Pillar was a simple, ordinary, honest and hard working girl who neglected her personal charm and beauty, she had all the curves in the right places with well developed body. Moreover, she was tall and well proportioned. Her short, boy-cut hair was allowed to grow waste long, regularly washed in a silky shampoo and let loose to flutter in the fresh mountain air.

Her long, old fashioned clothes were discarded in favour of sleeveless tops, at least during hot summer months that gave her breasts much needed uplift. Her mini skirts in her favourite red colour and high heeled shoes to go with her yellow tops, Pillar was a completely transformed woman who could win any one's heart. Olivia, who was by now fashion conscious and discarded her clothing on a regular basis, gave Pillar an enviable collection of fine dresses in her own wardrobe that would make any one proud.

148

Pillar learnt and accepted Olivia's generosity with enthusiasm and gratitude. Olivia was like a smiling Lord Jesus Christ looking upon his favourite disciple Pillar with favour and blessing. Then Olivia was by now a Spanish Sloane Ranger in her own right, although a bit shambolic and disorganised, a privilege of the rich and the influential with true blue blood running in her veins! After all, nobility is man made, not a creation of God! Lord Jesus Christ was not a noble man by birth, yet he became the noblest man to grace this planet.

In no time at all Olivia transformed Pillar from an ugly duckling into a beautiful swan, from a weakling foal to a graceful mare. Pillar's presence would grace any occasion. No wonder Papa was so fond of her!

Pillar was able to turn many heads, create flutters in many hearts, rather older hearts, as there were hardly any young, eligible men Pillar could be interested, go on date with.

The demise of the old Pillar gave birth to a new and confident girl who could hold her head high in any company. In certain ways, Pillar had even more commanding personality than Olivia, although Pillar certainly lacked Olivia's sex appeal. Then sex appeal is a personal choice, like one man's food is another man's poison! Sexiness ebbs with age while personality remains intact at any age.

Pillar was a God send gift to the family, especially to Olivia. She would not only look after the children but Papa as well, although Papa was fit and healthy but after the minor stroke attack, Olivia and Kiran would not like to leave Papa alone in the house for too long.

In any case Papa had a slight handicap that he would jokingly describe as a cock-and-bull story. Papa would rather die than admit his disability. Papa would describe his handicap, the loss of strength on his right side as minor health misdemeanour. Then such a positive attitude helped Papa to recover fast and enjoy his life as best as he could.

The children were given English names, **Richard and Rosanna**, **Rich and Rosie** in short. But they both have Krishna as their middle names. The name Krishna is common to both, a boy and a girl. It was Papa's wish, as since Kiran's arrival, he had taken keen interest in Hindu religion and learnt much about it from Father Joseph who was a scholar in eastern religions.

As a young boy, while studying English at Oxford University, Father Joseph had read many of the books written by famous German author, **Hermann Hess**, winner of the Noble Prize for Literature.

His works include such famous titles like **Glass Bead Games, Peter Camenzind and Siddhartha**, based on Buddhism, the mystic religion that caught the imagination of young, university graduates, ever since James Hilton wrote the famous novel **Lost Horizon**.

Hess was a pacifist and a conscious objector during the First World War. He became a Swiss citizen in 1923 and was a pacifist opponent of Hitler. This made him a darling of the young, left leaning students on university campuses.

The business was by now well established. The farm had more than four hundred acres, planted with grapevines, olive and fruit trees, oranges, nectarine, plums, peaches, apricots and pomegranates.

Kiran had three full time employees to look after the farm and a maid for chalets. The farm was only labour intensive during harvesting time, in the months of September to November when grapes and olives, as well as fruits are harvested and in need of seasonal farm labour.

Kiran had a good portfolio for clients with long term contracts to supply wine, olive oil, fresh fruits and juice to supermarkets which were just becoming fashionable but still a tiny dot on the retail horizon. Local retail shops and restaurants were the main customers.

Now that Papa had come out of his shell, his self-imposed period of mourning, he would laugh and joke with every one. He would even pull Pillar's leg that if he was a few decades younger, he would have chased her around the house and asked her to marry him!

"No way Papa I would have accepted your proposal. I like Olivia as a sister, not as my step-daughter!" The house was once again buzzing with laughter, joy and children's innocent bullying of Pillar, Papa and Kiran.

Olivia was the only voice of sanity. For a moment Kiran thought he was back in the coastal resort of Mombassa, in the company of his little sister Kalpna and her two naughty but nice friends Divya and Rekha. It was a happy house, a contended household full of laughter, happiness, love, unity and joy.

Having sold the livestock, the horse, goats, pigs and chicken, the life was at a stand-still on the farm during winter months. Kiran and Olivia would take frequent holiday breaks, city breaks to the beautiful towns and cities of Madrid, Alicante, Cordoba, Seville, Cadiz, Granada and Barcelona. Kiran loved the history and the Gothic style of architecture that dominated the mainland Europe from the 12th to the 16th centuries.

At last Kiran felt that he was no longer a gypsy or an expatriate. He was at ease with Spain and its rich cultural heritage, the country where he had planted his roots, ensign, just like his parents who considered Kenya and Mombassa as their home.

On longer holidays to Balearic and Canary Islands, Madera and Portugal, Papa and Pillar would often join them. By now Pillar was not only popular with Papa and children but she was indeed a valued member of this vibrant, extremely well-off and caring family.

Olivia would often tease Kiran that if some thing ever happens to her, he should marry Pillar, as she would look after him and the children even better than her.

Kiran had a ready made answer. "In some society, culture and religion, a man is allowed to have more than one wife. So why wait! After all having Pillar when he has passed his sell by date would not serve the purpose!" Olivia would laugh at this suggestion, a mischief making answer.

Such holidays were interludes for Kiran and Olivia, between their work, extremely busy life and their enjoyment with Papa, Pillar and children. If nothing else, Pillar had certainly taught every one how to be humble, kind and caring beyond the call of duty. She would massage Papa's arms and legs, as Papa never regained full mobility after the stroke.

Kiran had learnt a long time ago that a man has the right and indeed obligation to look down at another person, only when that person needs your help and assistance to get up, to stand on his own feet.

Kiran and Olivia had plenty of time on hand to play with children and go out on picnics, visit beauty spots as a family, in their brand new Land Rover, a four wheel drive vehicle in great demand in those days.

These mountains were indeed a busy place during summer months when the town folks would desert their hot, humid and overcrowded places in search of cool breeze, peace and calmness of these not too far-off and mostly deserted mountain slopes.

Four wheel drive transport was the only one Kiran would trust to drive on mountainous roads. After the tragedy that robbed him of his entire family, Kiran was extremely cautious. His car was custom built with steel roads added to the frame that gave an added security.

Kiran would never drive after having even a glass of wine or when it is raining; roads are wet and slippery or at night, in the dark when even familiar roads become unfamiliar, strange and dangerous, so often wild animals crossing the roads who when caught in a vehicle's headlight, freeze, become sitting ducks for drivers as well as hunters, as hunting was permitted throughout the year with the exception of protected species.

The roads in the vicinity of Olive Grove were not that steep with sharp bends, as mountains were not so high. But roads were primitive and slippery during rainy seasons. Mercifully accidents were rare, as there were hardly any motorised traffic and drivers were on most part elderly, careful and responsible road users.

Although there was a regular flight between mainland Spain and Canary Islands, passenger boats, so often car ferries or cargo ships with up to 30 cabins for fare paying passengers was a preferred mode of transport.

It was a leisurely way to move from one place to another, that is if time was not the essence, the main ingredient. These ships may not be able to compete with modern day cruse ships, especially when it comes to food and entertainment. But it had its won charm, beauty and atmosphere, especially if there were first class cabins for privileged few with room service, not so common at the time.

It was a real relaxation, nothing to do except relax, read, drink in the bar and have breakfast and dinner. They had to pay for every bit of luxury, not all inclusive holidays like we have today.

But in many ways it was more fun, as passengers were so few and forced to stay on board for a long time without shore leave! That brought them together, created a family type atmosphere, a friendship bonded on such a holiday so often lasted a lifetime. Many young ones fell in love and got married. This was a holiday romance with a difference.

It was not meant to be a quick fix, loose romance that is the order of the day where the main aim is to get drunk, to bed as many girls as possible and every thing, every one is quickly forgotten as soon as the plane takes off from the holiday destination. No one differentiates between love and lust, between a long term commitment and short term exploitation on sexual and social front.

Then gazing at sea, over a bottle of beer in the bar watching occasional shoals of dolphins, sharks and whales or just sitting and taking in the sun through the double glazed windows with a book like Lost Horizon, A Town Like Alice, For Whom The Bell Tolls, Moby Dick, The Old Man and the Sea and Farewell to Arms was altogether a different experience.

Then perhaps it may not interest today's generation or their yuppie lifestyle. Laptop computers and mobile phones are more important than classic books that played such an important role in the development of younger generation, their culture, their way of thinking and their ideology.

Every youngster of reasonable intelligence was a believer either in socialism, communism or capitalism. But capitalism was so tainted that practically no one would touch it with a barge pole on the university campus.

Even playing cards, dominos, chess and such games with children, often the Ship's Captain joining in gave a completely different prospective to the holiday. It was like a big, extended family where every one knows you and you know every one.

As children started growing up and Papa growing old, such holidays became less frequent except during school holidays. But Kiran and Olivia were able to go away on short breaks leaving children and Papa in charge of Pillar and Father Joseph.

Papa had a wonderful time with the children, spoiling them rotten. Then the old man was entitled to his pound of pleasure and an hour of happiness after losing his only son and his beloved wife Victoria and going through hell.

Although their primary schooling was in Spanish, in their local village school, children were expertly tutored by Father Joseph in English language and literature. At home, while they spoke in Spanish with Papa and Pillar, Kiran and Olivia would only talk to them in English.

Both children were at ease in two languages. For their secondary education, they had to go to a school half way between the village and Malaga where English was one of the main subject, even medium of instruction if students prefer it.

Papa passed away at the ripe old age of eighty seven when Rich and Rosy had graduated from the Madrid University, with a first class science degree in biology and chemistry. These universities are as prestigious in Spain and the Latin World as are Cambridge and Oxford in Commonwealth, the lose association of former British colonies.

Papa was able to attend their graduation ceremony, his proudest day since the birth of his first child. As we say, the sun will always shine for those who have the patience to weather the storm and the rain. Papa certainly did wait until the storm in his life was over.

It is always difficult to appreciate the beauty, the happiness and contentment that are on our door-step. We all would like to live on a mountain top so that we can have fantastic views, without knowing that the true happiness come to us while we are on the mission, on the path to the summit. There is much more pleasure in travelling than arriving at the final destination, just like thinking, waiting, dreaming of a honeymoon night is more exciting than the honeymoon itself.

Both Rich and Rosie were eager to continue their education, do medicine in England, follow into their father's footsteps and go to Oxford, the spinneret of educational excellence.

As overseas fee paying students with proficiency in two languages and science degree behind their names from the foremost and prestigious university in Spain, it was not too difficult to be accepted at Oxford, a citadel of education excellence.

This was the beginning of Rich and Rosie's career in medicine that would take them at the top of their chosen profession. Kiran's chain of thoughts, his immersion in the past, the pleasing past came to an abrupt halt with the plane landing at the tiny airport at Alice Spring.

* * *

Chapter Twenty One
Town Like Alice

Kiran first read the book *"A Town Like Alice"* when he was still at school in Mombassa. The book deals with love affairs between two prisoners who were interned in Malaya by the all conquering Japanese army and reunited in ***Alice Springs*** after the war. This is a heart warming love story with an unusual beginning and a fascinating ending.

The book is so well written that it is a classic in its own right. Kiran saw the movie based on the book, as well as the TV serial ***Tenko*** loosely based on the book but neither the film nor the TV serial managed to capture even half the romantic interlude, periodic atmosphere, the rustic charm of the book, the long trek that killed so many prisoners of war.

It was especially gruesome for women prisoners who were so often brutally raped and starved. Most Japanese prison guards had inferiority complexion when it came to European women and it gave them sadistic pleasure to see them reduced to no more than beggars, destitute, prostitutes begging for food, rest and lenient treatment.

Kiran would put this book in his list of all time great novels, along with Gone with the wind, Dr. Zhivago, For whom the bell tolls, War and peace, Snows of Kilimanjaro, Lost Horizon and a few more.

So Kiran was eager to visit this place, a wonderful tiny town or rather a village in the middle of nowhere. He had read and gathered as much information about Alice Springs as could be readily available. Even the most ardent residents would hardly know, scratch the surface with Kiran when it comes to knowing Alice Springs inside out.

Alice Springs which is simply known as *Alice* is the second biggest town in the *Northern Territory* with less than twenty thousand residents. The biggest town is of course Port Darwin, popularly known as simply *Darwin.*

Alice is geographically at the centre of Australia, on the southern most borders of Northern Territory and equidistant from *Adelaide*, the capital city of *South Australia* to *Darwin,* the northernmost town of any significance.

The traditional name of Alice, as known to aborigines was *Mparntwe*, inhabited by the *Arrernte* tribe who occupied, lived in this area for some fifty thousand years. Now they form only a tiny percentage of the population, living a nomadic existence.

The town of Alice Springs straddles the usual dry *Todd River,* stands on the river bank. The river is only flowing for a couple of months after the rainy season which is patchy, the rainfall varies vastly from one year to next and so often rain never materialise. So water is a scare commodity. It is supplemented by deep artesian wells, in common with most settlements in the desert like landscape of the interior.

Alice stands one thousand eight hundred feet above sea level. The *McDonald Mountain Range* is just south of Alice with a peak some three thousand feet high. Alice is a hot place in summer with an average day temperature of 36*C while winter months are cool when the temperature is in the region of 10*C.

Alice is a half way home, equidistant from Adelaide, the capital city of South Australia and Darwin, the capital city of Northern Territory. In 1861, John McDonald Stuart led an expedition through central Australia, thus opening a route from South to North and opening a telegraph station, a great advancement and achievement in those pioneering days when a letter posted in Australia would take up to six months to reach England.

Alice is a half-way house. *Alluvial Gold Rush* in 1887 gave Alice a permanent settlement. The settlement was known as *Stuart* until 1930 when it acquired the name Alice Springs. The *Todd River* was named after *Sir Charles Todd* who was Post Master General of South Australia.

The pioneers started moving to hinterland after the gold rush, first using the hardy animal, the Afghan camels and then the interior was opened up by the narrow gauge railway from Adelaide to Darwin, appropriately named *The Ghan Express.*

Alice became an important tourist destination from where tourists, at first Australians and later on from Europe took excursions to Ayers' Rock or just spending a week on a sheep farm, having a taste of the outdoor life, going camel riding, hunting wild dogs, the dingoes and kangaroos.

Kiran remembered reading an article titled *The Last Frontier.* It was about the railway journey on Ghan Express. The part of the article that stuck in Kiran's memory was about the group of four people who break the journey at Alice and spent a week on a sheep farm appropriately named *Paddy's Hideout.*

It was a humorous piece, very well written. All the camels were given names, referring to famous people and that include John Kennedy, Churchill, Mandela, Charles de Gaul, John Wayne, Rock Hudson and Napoleon for male camels.

The female camels attracted the names like Joan of Arc, Queen Elizabeth, Marilyn Monroe, Rita Hayworth, Audrey Hepburn, Mrs. Simpson and Sophia Lauren, along with Hitler and Mussolini, names given to those camels which were difficult to control and only fit for riding for seasoned handlers.

How Kiran wished he could get the opportunity to mount Sophia, Marilyn or Doris Day, his favourite actress after watching her famous comedy films like Pillow Talk with Rock Hudson.

It was exciting, tough and hot to body to spend a week on such a farm, but a great experience, a glimpse in the lives of those hardy pioneers who opened up Australia for the present day generation.

It is even difficult to imagine what these people have scarified, suffered or how hard their lives were when it would take some six months by ship to reach Australia from England.

The ships were small, even tiny and during storms and rough seas, no one could even eat or drink due to sea sickness. Many would die of various diseases, especially scurvy, disease caused by lack of fresh fruits that gives vitamin C, an essential ingredient to maintain a good health.

Those who are old enough to remember the MCC tour of Australia in 1936, known as Bodyline Series, the technique of bowling at batsmen's body to hurt them rather than get them out was perfected on the ship that took the English team, under the captainship of Douglas Jardin, to Australia, a three month sailing that gave them plenty of time to hatch-up this most unsporting, ungentemanly cricket matches in the history of this noble game played by gentlemen.

The red soil structure gives Alice a unique location. Ayers Rock is located south west of Alice and is the starting point for excursions leading to the rock, the largest single rock formation in the world. It is a challenge, even for the fittest to climb and circumnavigate the rock, a popular test for the macho tourists.

Unfortunately for Kiran, this was only a two hour refuelling stop that only allowed Kiran and Olivia to visit the bar and have an ice cold Australian lager. Like Germans, Australians are famous for their love for the amber nectar!

Although this was a short break, Kiran felt the need, the urge to visit this place for a longer duration, as while climbing, the pilot flew over the town, giving passengers a bird's eye view of the place, with dried-up river bed and sheep farms as big as some countries!

It looked so desolate yet a compelling countryside with a rugged charm of its own that could not be put into words.

Kiran was soon in his slumber, in and out, dreaming and day dreaming, reminiscing his past. Rich and Rosie had a wonderful time at Oxford. Being gifted pupils, they had to work much less on theories. So they were able to put in more time on practical part of their studies.

They soon qualified as doctors in their chosen field, specializing in heart conditions. While Rosie became a consultant, Rich chose to be a surgeon. So it was a perfect arrangement, for Rosie to see a patient first, make diagnosis and if the patient needed surgery, a bypass, valve replacement or even transplant, she would refer him to Richard.

After working at the world renowned Harefield Hospital in London, visiting their parents in Spain as often as they could, both decided to emigrate to Australia, as this vast and beautiful country would not only offer a better living standard with warm climate, it was more like home, more like Spain and Olive Grove.

They also wanted to be reunited with their parents, with Kiran and Olivia, as Papa had briefed them, told them what their parents had sacrificed, gone through in their lives.

They felt it was their duty, indeed their obligation to look after them in their declining years. Their only regret was that Papa was not there to share in their dream, their success.

It would be unfair, they will be failing in their duty if they let their parents remain alone, neglected of love and affection and above all deprive them the pleasure of playing with their grand children. Papa was the main influence in their lives and they wanted Kiran and Olivia to be the main influence in their children's lives, as Papa was in theirs.

The fast developing yet practically sparsely populated city of Perth was their choice to settle down, although Sydney was the favourite of most professionals leaving England to go down under, for the sunshine of Australia.

Naturally both Rich and Rosie were offered high posts in the **Perth Community General Hospital,** a centre of excellence and the main hospital in the Western Province, bigger than Great Britain and Ireland put together, almost as large in area as Spain?

Moreover life was at a slower pace in Perth, almost like a village, what they had in Olive Grove and properties were less than half the price one would have to pay in Sydney and Melbourne. So it was possible for them to recreate their beloved *"Olive Grove"* on the Australian soil!

Kiran was a multi millionaire yet living a simple life, in the same village, same house, too large for three of them. Although by now Pillar was surplus to requirement, she was more like a family member than an employee or even a guest.

Pillar had given the family her best years. She was indeed more of a mum to Rich and Rosie than Olivia. Now it was their time, their duty, indeed their obligation to look after Pillar, the way she looked after them, Papa and the children.

Moreover Kiran preferred Pillar's cooking than that of Olivia, as Pillar had turned vegetarian after visiting an abattoir with the children when they were forced to watch cattle being killed in the most inhumane manner.

No wonder all three, Pillar, Rich and Rosie turned vegetarian overnight, to the surprise and delight of Kiran. That encouraged Pillar to learn cooking vegetarian dishes, from various cookery books Kiran had in his possession.

Now Pillar can cook vegetarian pilau rice in so many different ways, fried rice with jeera (cumin seeds) egg fried rice, mushroom, peas and mixed vegetable fried rice or just simple boiled rice and roti and nan, plain nan, garlic nan, bullet (very hot) nan with green chillies and stuffed paratha with spicy mashed mess, peas, spring onion or various roughly grounded nuts with raisins, a Peshawaria nan fit for a king's dinning table.

Pillar's vegetable curries were made from fresh potatoes, cauliflower, runner beans, aubergine, okra or ladies' fingers, maize as well as dal, the Indian soup but much more spicy and taken with food, especially rice rather than as a starter. The dal is made from lentils such as comfit, green gram or mung, lentil.

As Kiran had planted his own vegetable patch, all these ingredients and that also include green garlic, spring onion, fresh green chillies, ginger were available fresh, grown organically that gave her cooking a special flavour that could not be found in restaurant food. Pillar learnt cooking most of these dishes from Kiran.

Then she started experimenting, creating her own recipe, using fresh tomatoes, coconut milk, yogurt and various Spanish sauces that would blend nicely with the Indian culinary.

Now except Papa and Olivia, every one else was a vegetarian and that put a special responsibility on Pillar. Kiran who himself was a good cook, gave it up after Pillar took the responsibility of winning the hearts and minds of every one through her cooking skill, the gastronomy!

Now Kiran was Pillar's ancillary, even analgesic in the kitchen, as Kiran had learnt cooking out of necessity rather than out of love. Kiran was a Bailey bridge when it came to cooking. Could Kiran be avuncular to Pillar?

Olivia tried her best to persuade Pillar to join them in Perth, as by now Olivia and Pillar were more like sisters and Pillar was now as fluent in English, as clever as Olivia, with even better figure and sense of humour.

Understandably Olivia was reluctant to leave Pillar behind. But she can not force her to join them. As a parting present, Olivia brought Pillar a two bedroom modern flat in the village centre so that she would not be completely alone or lonely.

By now the village centre, ***The Plaza de Oliva*** was a busy place at most times, with regular bus services to all parts of coastal belt, Malaga, Benalmedena, Fuengirola and beyond. Moreover there were all sorts of shops, restaurants and taverns. Pillar who was assiduous, soon found a part time job in a tourist office, as her command of English was a great asset when trying to find a job when a very few Spanish people were bilingual.

Pillar was a great help to English speaking tourists who were interested in spending a few weeks in self catering accommodation that is Olive Grove? Who knows Pillar may find another Kiran.

She was beguiling and charming. She had a kind of animalism, sensuality that even used to disturb Kiran on some occasions. It was Pillar's euphoria, her dream, her final wish to find some one like Kiran but it was not her destiny. It is difficult to judge God's intention. God definitely works in mysterious ways!

But Pedro was still there, still single and all alone! Poor Pedro! He had a gold mine in his grasp, on his door-step. Yet he gave it away to Kiran! Olivia and Kiran so often felt sorry for him, his self inflicted wound, his euthanasia! In reality, even if Kiran had not turned up, Olivia would never have married Pedro.

Then perhaps there comes a time when one has to accept the reality and stop living in a dream world, waiting for her Prince charming that normally exist only in one's imagination.

One has to wake up one day and start living in the real world. Olivia was indeed very fortunate that Kiran appeared at the right time and Kiran would never let her forget it!

In all honesty, Olivia knew that she was no match, not in the same league as Kiran, at least to begin with. But then she was on the home ground, on familiar territory, in her own country while Kiran was a visitor, a guest who over stayed his time, his welcome, for the love of his life! Kiran was the benefactor in Spanish feudalism, Papa being the Lord of the Manor!

* * *

Chapter Twenty Two
The Arrival

Although Rosie who was married to Raj, a fellow doctor whom she met in London, she wanted her parents to stay with her. But it was more practical for Kiran and Olivia to stay with Richard and his charming wife ***Marie***, who was a full time housewife looking after their two children, eight year old ***Peter*** and five year old ***Pretty*** who were a handful and took up most of her time.

Rich met Marie when he was a surgeon at Harefield hospital. She was a theatre nurse in charge of the operating theatre. What attracted Rich to Marie was her extremely kind and caring nature, always able and willing to help others.

With her glorious, almost bewitching looks, with long, blonde hair touching her knees, she was a favourite date for every doctor, even consultants who were mostly married or in steady relationship. That precludes them from Marie's dating calendar.

Being Catholic and brought-up in convent, she was different from most nurses who would compete with each other when it came to dating or rather bedding doctors.

Rich and Marie were different in that manner, with different priorities and principles that brought them together. Marie's austere and serious attitude towards sex and loose living was in sharp contrast to the general trend, what her fellow nurses' wanted and desired.

This was the beginning of the binge culture and single mum scenario that has blotted western culture and destroyed family values, decency and encouraged state dependency, benefit culture, some thing for nothing attitude.

Once Marie came to know Richard's background and went with him on holidays to Spain, to Olive Grove, she fell for Rich, hook, line and sinker. Although most nurses considered Marie a lucky person for bagging such a handsome and up-coming consultant, most doctors were envious of Rich, as Marie was indeed a stunning beauty, although on educational front Marie may not be his equal.

Then Rich never wanted an ambitious, highly qualified colleague who may be his equal who could compete with him on carrier front. Even then, Marie's qualifications were not that irrelevant. Her qualifications, skill and experience were in great demand in Perth where she worked as a Matron in charge of the surgical ward until the birth of their first child.

Rich knew the difference, the gap in education between his mum and dad. He felt that was the reason for their success on all front, happiness in their domestic life. He wanted his own married life to be as happy, blessed and contended as that of his parent's.

Rich was not wrong in his assertion. Marie loved, even worshipped Rich in the same manner as Olivia loved Kiran. For Marie, Rich was her knight in shining armour, her Lord Krishna who would look after his Gopi, his Radha!"

Rich was a God send gift to her, a star on the horizon. Marie was a religious person, a rarity in medical profession. She had great faith in the **Black Madonna of Montserrat,** her patron saint, whose blessings she would seek before she would embark on any adventure, make an important decision, a life-long commitment. What commitment could be more life long than getting married and staying together till the end?

Then Black Madonna is held in high esteem amongst Catholic faithful and Montserrat is only second to Lourdes in France, famous as a healing place, the holy water that comes out of the wells is so precious to the pilgrims that thousands of bottles are sold to pilgrims every week.

Montserrat was the first place they visited after their marriage and spent three nights in this charming, holy and blessed heaven Marie loved and worshipped this hidden jewel in the mountain.

As a frequent visitor, Marie even knew the Head Monk whom she had met several times. It was indeed an honour to be granted an audience with Father Francis. Then very few can resist Marie's charm when she is at her best.

Rich and Kiran, father and son were very close indeed. On the advice of Kiran and Olivia, Marie did not return to work. Instead she preferred to devote her time looking after Rich, their two lovely children and there house, their farm, also named ***Olive Grove!***

It was a spacious property, with six bedrooms, three en suite, a large lounge, fully fitted kitchen with luxurious, air-conditioned conservatory, a large patio with out-houses, couple of stables and thirty acre monstrous garden or a farm, a mini forest, whatever one would like to call.

Being brought up on 450 acre ***Olive Grove*** in Spain, Rich was fond of open space. In any case there is only so much land on earth. The land-value will always rise in the long term as human population keep on expanding. At one time, one could buy an acre of land in the outback for less than three pound an acre. Then again, even a pound was a lot of money.

This luxurious and spacious property was partly financed by Kiran and Olivia. The most interesting room in the house was in the attic, an observatory with a powerful state of the art telescope that would enable Rich to look deep in the galaxy.

Astrology and astronomy were Rich's hobbies, along with riding, forestry, bird watching, walking and like his father, growing vegetables, as they were all committed vegetarians! With warm and sunny climate and plenty of water, Marie's vegetable patch was an envy of every one, as she had some thirty different varieties of vegetables, not including the herbs. Even Kiran was not familiar with some of the varieties and most impressed with Marie's green-fingers.

There was a large, deep and well stocked pond in the middle, the water being regularly supplemented from the artesian well and the tiny, ever flowing spring, thus providing a watering hole for wild life all year round.

It was indeed a heaven in the scorching heat of summer months, the forest being over populated with all sorts of birds; many migrating varieties while others just seeking shelter from the heat.

Forest fire is the main hazard one has to guard against in those tinder dry summer months. But with frequent patrols, a watchful eye and well managed forest, with wide paths dividing the forest and clearing the ground of dry grass, bushes and dead trees, had enabled Rich to keep forest fire off his patch.

It is all question of good management. Most such fires in Australia are started by human beings, either due to negligence or deliberately, for a short lived thrill that may ruin so many lives. Occasionally thunderstorms with lightening may be the cause. But this is rare.

A couple of acres were utilised for flower beds and vegetable patch, a tennis court, swimming pool and cricket pitch, a must for sports mad Aussies who may have plenty of space in their outback!

The rest was tastefully allowed to be a natural forested area with mature trees by the previous owner who was a Forest Officer. It was an exquisite piece of land, a forest where even Lord Rama would be happy to spend fourteen years in exile, in the company of Lady Sita and brother Laxman.

The popular and ever-green trees that covered some thirty acres were eucalyptus; the variety **Eucalyptus Rhodantha or Rose Mallee Tree** has spectacular grey foliage.

It is a multi-trunk tree with large pinkish red flowers, **Weeping Myall Wattle** or **Acacia Pendula** with lovely grey leaves that reaches the ground, thus providing a good ground cover for flightless birds like guinea fouls.

Then there are various types of palms, in fact **57 Varieties** that may have encouraged Heinz to have **57 verities of tinned food!** The striking Beautiful **Banksias or Giant Candles** is a sight for sore eyes when in full bloom, a favourite tree for birds and bees alike.

Acacia and a couple of varieties of olive trees gave a good mixture, not forgetting fruit bearing trees like guava, orange, banana, grape fruit and peaches, planted near a tiny spring flowing through this vast garden paradise. This spring, entirely on Rich's land, appears from no where, spouting cool, fresh, pure drinkable water and disappearing underground at the edge of the forest.

Then there were olive trees that grew well in this climate, but the poor soil structure, especially for olive trees meant they would not produce edible fruits. Olives were left on the trees for birds to feast on.

Rich had also allowed patches of land to be covered with bush, ground hugging plants that would be a perfect habitat for so many birds, some flightless and other form of wildlife.

But these bushes had to be well away from the house, as they also shelter snakes and Australia has some of the most poisonous and deadliest snakes in the world and that include venomous snakes like Eastern Brown, Tiger Snakes and Coastal Taipan. But Sydney Funnel Web Spider is the deadliest of all.

In reality deaths from snake bites are rare and compared to countries like India, Thailand, South Africa, USA and Mexico, the figure is negligible. Snakes are a shy creature.

They would prefer to run away unless cornered, trampled upon or some one try to catch a snake when they attack in self defence. If you leave them alone, they would not bother you! There are no spitting cobras in Australia. But snake fear is instinctive. More people are killed from honey-bee bites than snake bite! Yet we never treat bees as dangerous!

Fortunately the Environment and Forestry Department provided a regular patrol to check out undergrowth and make them safe, removing any snake to a safer area, away from human habitation. Then there were mongoose that would drive away or kill any snake!

There were more than thirty varieties of birds who were permanent residents of this mini Vrindavan and with seasonal migration; it could easily reach some one hundred varieties. The star attractions were peacocks and guinea fouls specially introduced by Rich and Marie.

Rich was a wildlife fanatic, making good use of his father's wealth. He built observation platforms, often well concealed in big, leafy, evergreen trees, out of sight that would provide a perfect opportunity to observe these birds at close length.

The varieties Rich had counted on his patch, including some sea-birds as well as fresh water loving birds, as the coast is only twenty miles away and Perth is perched on the banks of the Swan river, include occasional appearance of giant Royal Albatross, Sea gulls, White Ibis, always popular with ordinary bird-watchers the Black Swan, a rare visitor compared with white swan, Crowned Heron, Pelican and Kingfisher, a few among many water loving birds.

Other varieties include Storm Petrels, Asian Doe twitchier, Australian Grebe, Great Bustard, Garnet, Reed Warbler, Shelduck, Robin, Wood Ducks, Bar-breasted Honeyeater, Petrel, Barn Owl, Swallows, Black Bittern, Black Kite, a popular visitor to the large pond, Cuckoo, Tern, Finch, Rock Thrush, Burke's Parrots, Sandpiper, Cuckoos, Cockatoos, Egret, Gosh and many more birds, not counting the common birds like Raven, Pigeons and their likes.

After Kiran and Olivia had rested and recovered from the long flight, although with frequent breaks in luxurious hotels, it was not too demanding neither on the body nor on the soul.

Marie took them on the tour of the forest, in a special four wheel powerful buggy, like a beach buggy, visiting various interesting viewing points, the lake and the spring.

Kiran, being a born businessman, was already thinking how to maximise the use of this wonderful Vrindavan in the Australian wilderness. Perhaps he could have half a dozen chalets built and rent them out to holiday firms, in line with his business back in Spain.

But Kiran knew that neither Rich nor Olivia would support his plans, as Olivia has so often mentioned to Kiran that they are rich, indeed loaded beyond their wildest dream, after the sale of their Spanish ranch Olive Grove.

They had enough money to last not only their own lifetime but several generations. Kiran being Kiran, he could not help dreaming about business adventure. He was a born businessman. It is the thrill, not making money that kept him going.

Kiran would not let Olivia forget that he turned a twenty acre farm, into nearly five hundred acres of olive grove, vineyard and orchard, into multi million dollar business that enabled their two children to attend one of the best university in the world, climb the ladder on the educational and professional front beyond any one's wildest dream or expectation. It all needed financing on a grand scale!

His only regret was that Papa passed away before Rich and Rosie could reach their professional peak, play with his great grandson. Then Papa had very happy and fruitful decade or two before he left this world!

Rich and Rosie were living in the same area of Perth, only half an hour by car. Although Rosie's house was more luxurious with all the amenities, including an outdoor and indoor swimming pool, state of the art gym, Jacuzzi and a spa, their garden was a mere two acres, covered with lawn and trees that needed minimum maintenance.

Then Rich was only a stone throw away if her children needed more space! In any case they all spend week-ends together. It was the family tradition and after all they are twins who are naturally very close.

As both Raj and Rosie were working, leading a busy life, they had no time to look after the house and the children, let alone acres of space. Then Rosie had a live-in nanny, a Pilipino girl in her late twenties who would look after their two children. Rosie clearly remembered how well they were looked after by Pillar, their nanny whom they still miss and were in constant touch with her.

One condition Kiran and Olivia put forward before they agreed to move to Perth was that they would live an independent life, in their own bungalow. So Rich was obliged to buy a four bedroom bungalow, half way between their two homes, equidistance from Rich and Rosie, just fifteen minutes ride on either side that would suit Kiran and Olivia fine.

* * *

Chapter Twenty Three
The Happy Ending

It took some three months for Rich and Kiran to bring the bungalow up to their expectation, with a small garden, large patio and vegetable patch with no more than half an acre of garden. It was in sharp contrast to Olive Grove, both in Spain and in Perth.

The bungalow was built with future in mind. It was wheel-chair friendly throughout, with broad, fireproof doors and extra bedrooms for a live-in carer or nurse. Although Kiran and Olivia were in their early sixties and super fit for their age, they knew that health and wealth can never be taken for granted. It is liable to change in the blink of an eye. Moreover with three doctors in the family, they have to respect their judgement.

Marie would not let them spend much time in the bungalow, on their own. The love, relationship between Kiran and Marie was a perfect reflection of what Kiran had seen, observed between Papa and Olivia.

Now Kiran was Papa in need of love, affection, care and consideration! Olivia could not help but tease Kiran, pull his leg that he is now a geriatric who needed constant care and attention.

She even presented Kiran with a ***Zimmer Frame*** on his ***60th birthday?*** But she was indeed happy and grateful that Marie was such a caring person who had taken Kiran under her wings. God forbid but if any thing happen to her, if she had to go first, she knew Kiran would be well looked after. In fact two ladies, Rosie and Marie would spoil him rotten! It was such a caring, loving and united family, as rare as an iceberg in the Australian desert!

Before they moved in their own home, Marie took them on the grand tour of Perth, showing them all the beautiful places this city has to offer to the young and the old, the retired and the active.

Top of her list was the King's Park, four hundred hectors of virgin bush, city gardens, barbeque on the beach in purpose built corners, shielded from the wind, the cool sea breeze, Perth Zoo and cruising **Swan River** on the doorstep of Perth.

The port of Fremantle was also not that far away. The northern beaches are practically deserted, like *"Eighty Miles Beach"* But they are too far away from Perth, except by air or an idle short cruse holiday in it self. No wonder these shores are a heaven for sea wildlife, for sharks, whales and for a fishing enthusiast, a heaven on earth, on Perth's door-step.

A boat trip to **Rottnest Island** was the highlight for Kiran, as it reminded him of his childhood spent in the beautiful city of Mombassa, right on the shores of romantic and majestic Indian Ocean that they loved so much but never appreciated.

Then we seldom do what is free, easily accessible and on our door-step until we have to move away from such a heaven. As we say, familiarity so often brings contempt, ignorance and lack of appreciation.

Kiran was more of an expressionist than an idealist, a 20th century virtue. He finished his book; a novel based on his own personal experience and simply titled *"Olivia"* with a stunning cover portraying Olivia at her best, in scanty attire, having a shower after a hard day's labour, under an olive tree, under faint protest from Olivia who thought she was looking too sexy for her liking!

But she looked so different now that there was no way their grand child or any one who had not seen her at her sexist best, could recognize her. Kiran was proud of her beauty and sexiness and he saw no reason to hide or use a model for the book cover. Moreover the cover photo was deliberately covered with mist, water spray so it would look natural and elegant but without revealing too much!

It took three months after moving in their own bungalow, working up to ten hours a day, seven days a week to finish the book and send it to a publisher.

It was a mammoth novel, some one hundred chapters, one thousand pages and a million words, beginning with his life in Mombassa, London, the tragedy on Mount Abu and his arrival at Olive Grove, falling in love with Olivia. Kiran did not miss a single character, however big or small part they played in their lives.

Naturally Papa, Father Joseph, Pillar, even Pedro and their darling children Richard and Rosanna were the main characters and finally moving to Perth, one of the most beautiful and specious city in the world. But Olivia was the star, from beginning to the end.

Kiran did not let corrosion of any character, including those who shaped his early life, his parents, sister Kalpna and her friends Rekha and especially Divya who was in a way his childhood sweetheart, whom he would have married if the Vidhata had not been so cruel to him. Then there were his friends in London and the people he met in Wales, Martin and Martha in the tiny port of Solva that began the process of healing his wounds.

Then there was Penny who stirred his feelings, his sexuality who could have even changed Kiran's life! Some how he resisted her charm and moved on, the decision he could have regretted if he had not met Olivia!

With Richard and Rosie's rich and influential client list, it was not difficult to get the book publish. Now Kiran was waiting for a Movie Mogul to turn up at his door-step and produce another **Gone with the wind** type movie and put him and Olivia in the limelight! Perhaps it may happen one day with television ruling the roots with miniseries and producers running out of creditable plots, books and storyline.

Moreover Australia is fast becoming a centre of excellence when it comes to discovering new talents like Kyle Minogue, Crocodile Dundee actor Paul Hogan and producing TV serials like Home and Away and Neighbours that has given Australia a mini Hollywood stature.

Australia has wonderful, sunny climate, rugged scenery, white, sandy beaches, state of the art buildings, studios and above all plenty of local talent. So Kiran was not wrong in his assumption that it is only a question of time before his novel would turn into a mini TV serial or a block buster movie like **Titanic!**

His worry was who would play Olivia and Kiran! Was there any actress who could do justice to the role of Olivia or even Papa, who was in many ways the main character, the star attraction! There were a few but not entirely perfect match. Jody Foster is a good actress but she does not have voluptuous body Olivia had at the age of twenty one!

Kiran's favourite would be **Kate Winslet** who gave the film Titanic a lift! **Leonard Di Caprio** is as handsome as Kiran was at his age. Then James Cameroon is a must who practically single handedly produced the film, made it a great box office success.

Gloria Stuart portrays the elderly *Rose* who narrates the film. *Olivia* has to be narrated by one and only Papa, or to give a twist in a tale, by *Father Joseph* if his character can be given more prominent. The permutation is endless. But Kiran should not jump the gun.

It may never happen. There may be hundreds if not thousands of novels written by talented but unknown authors that remain unpublished, as they have neither the finance nor the connection to help them go to print.

Then there is no harm in day dreaming, living in a make-belief world. Kiran's own life-story is beyond belief, stranger than fiction, some thing, a storyline that can only be credible on a cinema screen.

Kiran clearly remembers one of his favourite films, *"The world of Suzie Wong"* heartfelt bitter sweet romantic drama, set against the backdrop of exotic and exciting colony of Hong Kong during the height of British colonial era, featuring the charismatic American star William Holden.

He portrays a struggling painter with high ambition who embarks on an unlikely and tumultuous relationship with a young, witty and a beautiful Chinese prostitute whom he employs as a nude model. Nancy Kwan who plays Suzie Wong gave a memorable performance and made the film extremely watch able.

Today was the anniversary of the day Kiran and Olivia landed at the Perth airport. Rich and Rosie, brother and sister only needed an excuse to have a party or rather a barbeque at Rich's place where children can run wild, but always under the watchful eye of *Marina*, a Spanish speaking Pilipino nanny who was, like Pillar, a part of the family.

Rosie and Raj had obtained a work permit to bring her all the way from Manila, as she was fluent in English as well as Spanish, the two languages Rich and Rosie wanted their children to be fluent in.

The past year was one of the happiest years in their lives. Their time spent between two families, four adults and four children was a sea of waves, not tranquillity, a gentle breeze, not hurricane. But today was a special day in more ways than one.

As there were no neighbours within an ear-shot, they can play music, Spanish, English and Indian, as loud as they would like. After a long and eventful day, they all retired to the house, children who were active all day, fell a sleep and adults had a glass of port or whisky to end the day.

As usual, Kiran took the central stage and gave a short speech thanking every one and the Lord. Then he called Rich, gave him a hug and let Marie handed him an envelope.

Rich was speechless when he saw the documents inside. Kiran, with the help of Marie and Rosie, had managed to purchase two hundred acres of adjourning land, to add to Kiran's already vast outlay. It was Kiran's wish to expand this estate and make it one of the best in the area, if not the Western Province.

This was not all. Kiran handed every one a copy of the document, a trust-fund he had created for his four grand children. Their financial future was secured. They would be free to study, even go to Oxford or Cambridge if they wish.

Kiran being an accountant, a tax consultant, wanted to minimise death duty. So he wanted to distribute his vast wealth before it was too late. Yet he had retained nearly half of his capital so as not to be dependent financially on their children. After all Kiran and Olivia may have a long life, some twenty years or even more.

This was the day Kiran felt his life's mission was complete. He could now take a back seat and let every one manage their life. He would be there in the background if needed. Could Lord Krishna ever take a back seat!

* * *

Epilogue:

In all these euphoria, sense of elation and garden full of sweet smelling roses, Kiran and Olivia, especially Olivia felt some thing missing in their lives, a corner of her heart empty, a link in the chain broken.

Deep inside their hearts they experienced a sense of guilt that they felt should be addressed if they want to be really happy, contended and live happily ever after.

That missing link was Pillar. How could Olivia be happy when she knew that her elder sister who practically sacrificed her family life, her happiness and her young, emotionally tormenting years to take care of Papa and their two young children was now all alone in Spain, in the tiny village, working part time to make the ends meet while they were living in a lap of luxury, surrounded by their loving, caring family members.

So after a long and protruded correspondence and numerous telephone calls, Kiran and Olivia were able to persuade Pillar to join them with the threat that if she refuses, they would return to Spain to be with her. Rich even went all the way to Spain to persuade Pillar and to wind up her life, settle her financial affairs and to accompany her to Perth.

Although Pillar knew that Kiran and Olivia could never do that, abandon their family, it was wise not to put it to test. After all she was missing Olivia and Kiran more than they would miss her, as they were surrounded by their loving family members while she was all alone and lonely.

Today was the day, the happiest day, as Pillar would be landing at Perth airport, to join Kiran and Olivia in their bungalow and they were all at the airport to welcome Rich and Pillar.

The reunion, although tearful, was the best gift **God** could give to Kiran and Pillar in their advancing years. When Olivia greeted Pillar, hugged her, it was difficult for her to let her go.

Tears were freely flowing from their eyes. But they were the tears of happiness, joy, reunion and fulfilment of a dream that all three, Kiran, Olivia and Pillar would grow old gracefully, in the company of each other and only God could part them from each other when the time is right.

As we say, all's well that ends well. There could not be a better or happier ending for either Kiran or Olivia. How glad Papa must be, watching his brood on the ground while perched high up there in the heaven, with his beloved son and loving, caring wife, Olivia's mother. It was time to say Halleluiah! Praise to All Mighty!

* * *

Woman of Straw

Chapter One
Welcome News

When Nirav opened the morning post, he received a pleasant surprise, the good news he was waiting for a long time, at least a long time for him, as he was madly in love with his lovely, shapely, mischievous and not so tiny **Tina,** his wife of just six months.

Nirav could not put her out of his thoughts, even for a night and how could he, after the stormy romance and the wonderful ten days they spent together and now to look forward to a stormy honeymoon Tina has promised him, the trappings of getting married to such a lovely, sensuous and extremely smart girl. Tina was an oasis of sexual enlightenment. Then Nirav deserved the best, the smug and perennial fruits of hard labour he had put in qualifying not only as a doctor but settling down in America with all important **"Green Card."**

Tina knew not only how to keep her promise but how to please Nirav, especially when it came to love making. She would tease him, tantalise him and even frustrate him. But in the end she would more than compensate Nirav for all her mischief, for being a forbidden apple, albeit for a short time only. After all it is human nature that we do not enjoy any pleasure in life that come easily, without effort.

The reason of Nirav's jubilation, his joy and exultation was the letter, a document he received from the Home Office, granting his wife Tina permission, a visa to come to USA for permanent settlement, renewable every year until she is granted the all important **"Green Card"** that opens most doors for industrious and ambitious Indians, mainly Gujaratis.

It is said that blue blood runs in the veins of every Gujarati. Although Gujaratis, like Punjabis, Sikhs, is a small community, numbering some fifty five millions, they are prominent in every walk of life, especially in the West.

Nirav, who is a doctor, believed, perhaps erroneously, mistakenly and unjustly that all Indian (Hindu) American girls are too westernized, liberated and career minded to become a good wife, a fitting life partner on the domestic front, become an integrated part of our Hindu family.

It is wrong to generalise, to place all American Indian girls in one category, in one basket, paint or rather tarnish them with one brush, a book can not be judged by the cover or one's personal experience, however bitter it may be. All that glitter is not gold, nor every thing white is sweet milk-drink. Nirav learnt that lesson through a bitter experience. Good judgement comes from experience and experience comes from a bad judgement. Unfortunately Nirav had to learn it through the hard way.

Nirav is the only son, although he has two elder sisters, now married and well settled. One in London and the other sister preferred to stay in Mumbai, not too far away from where his parents live.

As Nirav was bright, a clever child, good at studies; he was encouraged by every family member to become a doctor, a hallmark of success, not only for him but for the whole family. A father is always proud to say "*My son is a doctor.*"

Surely Nirav did not let any one down. He passed all his examinations with flying colour and after completing his internship, he was appointed a Registrar, in the same hospital within two years, a rapid promotion indeed.

Then Nirav is not only a bright student but he has the personality, temperament, good nature and aptitude to go with his brain. Indeed he has a mature head on young shoulders, young and developing body.

Nirav is six feet tall, well built with fair skin, an attractive young man blessed in every sense, in every department, in every faculty. Perhaps his family reflected true blue blood without realising it.

Every Hindu is proud to say that he is the descendent of Lord Rama or Lord Krishna? However on most part, their deeds do not match their aspiration, their claim of divine ancestry. Moreover they are reluctant to wear their ethnicity or faith in public as most Christians and Muslims do.

In Mumbai, among bright and ambitious doctors, especially Gujarati doctors, it was and still is a craze, perhaps an obligation, a step in the right direction to go to America, a distant land supposed to be paved with gold, with golden opportunities to further one's knowledge, social standing and of course the all important bank balance.

So, even though Nirav was the only son, his parents were the first to encourage him to go to America, add a degree of two behind his MBBS, become a specialist, perhaps a surgeon and come back to Bharat where he could walk into any job, in the most prestigious hospital, an object of idolization among his work colleagues who could not go to America or Europe, could not say they have London or New York experience.

That would indeed be a feather in Nirav's cap and his family's reputation. His dad Manubhai and his mum Nimuben will be proud parents, well respected in the community, an illuminated family.

So often these young, ambitious doctors are reluctant to return to Bharat, to their roots, preferring to settle down in America and make the country their home, especially if they get married with an "American girl. After all America is the most advanced, rich and sophisticated nation, a heaven on earth for well educated and ambitious professionals.

The God has blessed USA with every kind of prosperity, every convenience a human being may want and desire and that include a variety of climate, cold, temperate climate in the north, hot desert in the centre and mild, warm, dry, wet and arid, tropical climate in the Southern states of Florida, Texas, Arizona, New Mexico and California. It is a rich and self sufficient country in practically every aspect that humans may need to survive and prosper.

But the excessive use and over exploitation has indeed robbed the country of oil, gold, silver and other minerals that the country has to import in vast quantity, thus draining the financial resources of the richest nation on earth, but not for too long, as Americans spend twice as much as they earn. They live on bank overdraft, the generosity of others.

It is a recipe for financial disaster in the long run. In so many ways, Americans are adopting Indian mentality, that is, eat, drink and be merry. Who knows what is round the corner, here today, gone tomorrow?

* * *

Chapter Two
A Time for Home Visit

Within three years of moving to San Diego, Nirav was offered a well paid permanent post in the local hospital and acquired the all important Green Card, as he was well on the way to becoming a heart surgeon, the most prestigious, sought after qualification in the medical profession. Indeed Nirav was a young star, a rainmaker in waiting, the Northern Star that brighten ups the sky at night.

Although Nirav was happy in his life, with a good expatriate friend circle, he was never the less lonely, in need of a female company, a wife who could share his life, his joy, his success and his triumph, some one who is a friend, a companion and a confidant, a pleasant face to come home to.

It was time to take the next important step in his life, which was to get married and settle down. In any case, his parents were eager for him to come to Mumbai and get married there, as he would have a pick of the bunch, highly educated, smart and beautiful girls from respectable families, even millionaire's daughter if he plays his cards right, uses his faculties in a wise and gainful manner, a triumph of foreign attire over the local apparel.

This is known as the psychology of winning. After all the news of the arrival of some one like Nirav, a prospective son in law extraordinary spreads like wild fire, through the grapevine that binds the Gujarati community in Mumbai, aright to opt for the best that his achievement deserves.

Nirav had no problem, no inhibition in getting married in Mumbai, where he was born, brought up and educated. It was a normal step to take; especially as he knew how smart and beautiful some of the girls in his college were. India is in the forefront when it comes to choosing a beauty, a Miss World.

They were Gujarati, Hindu girls from elevated background that would put Nirav in shade if he was not so brilliant at studies and well built hulk of a student! Nirav enjoyed, treasured every moment in this exotic, electrifying college, Uni atmosphere where he had acquired a special standing, through his hard work and physical stature that stood him in good stead on the sports field. He was a champion swimmer, a Tarzan to his fellow competitors.

So when he returned home to Mumbai, albeit for three weeks only, his parents had made all the arrangements to meet as many girls as the time would allow, the circumstances would permit. Nirav's insouciant assumption seems to be that his mission would simply work out without much effort on his part, as he was a pied piper, a beehive overflowing with honey, a queen bee, the pick of the bunch.

It is a normal practice for an expatriate coming home to get married, to put an advert in the local paper, usually a package of three adverts which include a weekend and the letters from the parents of eligible girls would drop on the doormat in droves. It is not unusual to receive a thousand letters if advertised in more than one or two newspapers.

After going through, reading and cogitating some four hundred responses from just three adverts, Nirav's parents prepared a short list of some fifty girls, discarding all those who were not educated in English medium, who were less than five feet three inches tall and those who did not sent their photos with there letters or did not have similar education, that is only one in eight applicants were deemed to meet the primary criteria.

Nirav was not particularly interested in doctors, but a Master's degree, an MBA or even a PhD in information technology, finance, business and similar subjects would be desirable, a great help when looking for a professional post or going for further education for a year or two to come up to the Californian standard, the most advanced and prosperous state within USA.

As most if not all Nirav's friends were professional people, Nirav naturally wanted a professional life partner who would integrate easily and effortlessly within his inner circle of friends who were all highly qualified, the cream of the expatriate community.

As soon as Nirav landed at the Mumbai airport, meeting, interviewing girls, going out, entertaining or being entertained became a clock-work routine, some times meeting three to four girls in a single day.

Not only Nirav had to go through the list of fifty girls but there were many girls who were among his relations, daughters of family friends, acquaints and relatives who all knew that Nirav was coming home to get married and perhaps to lay down deep roots if and when he decide to come home after qualifying and gaining experience in his chosen field of heart surgery and transplant. A father in law with good contacts, connections and a fat bank balance would certainly help him to settle down quickly and make his mark on the medical front.

In the first week, Nirav saw, met some thirty girls, mostly from the list prepared by his parents. But Nirav could not honestly say that he could marry and take any one from the bunch, with him to America.

Yes, some were very beautiful girls indeed, some even highly educated but they were either too young, too old, too naïve, lack smartness, could not speak good English or were even too ready to throw themselves at his feet while some were arrogant beyond belief, daughters of millionaire parents who had lived the lives of prominence and privileges whose philosophy was that money could and should buy every thing, including a doctor husband from America, with a Green Card! Nirav had no time for such spoilt girls, however smart, well educated they may be.

Most girls were more interested in going to America, in obtaining a Green Card through the back door by getting married to Nirav so that in future, they can sponsor their own relatives, brothers and sisters who may not meet the criteria, get a Green Card on their own merit.

Then by chance or destiny, Nirav met **Tina** whose real name was **Tulsi,** a sweet but old fashioned Hindu name associated with the holy shrub found in every Hindu temple and most Hindu homes as well, as this plant has some medicinal value as well, to get better if suffering from cold, mild fever and sore throat.

Tulsi was the birth name only. Every one knew her as Tina, a bold, charming girl full of self confidence and self belief, natural grace that would soon attract any one's attention.

It was Sunday. They were invited to a wedding; a friend's daughter was getting married. Normally Hindu weddings, like Italian and Greek weddings are grand occasions, celebrated with panache and pomp, spending a fortune that many could not afford. It is like to celebrate in haste, repent, regret and pay up later, at leisure, that is if there is any leisure in the hectic pace of life in the ever busy, fast moving life that personifies modern Mumbai, the financial, commercial capital of India.

But this celebration was on a small scale, a bit muted, as both were getting married for the second time. This was a rarity once but not any more. As there were only some one hundred and fifty guests, not five hundred, most guests were as tumescent as young stallions. The venue was posh, in a five star hotel conference room.

Nirav's mum knew that there would be many girls of marriageable age, as such functions, events are inevitably used to show off wealth, parents parade their marriageable offspring with pride and cunningness.

Even mega business deals are concluded if parties involved are prominent businessmen. In fact such occasions are religious, cultural, political and business occasions, all rolled into one?

* * *

Chapter Three
Chance Meeting with Tina

As soon as Nirav and his mum **Nimuben** entered the hall, the bride's mum took Nimuben aside and whispered in her ears. When they sat down, Nirav was told that a lovely girl called Tina would like to meet him.

Within fifteen minutes, Nirav was having a drink with Tina in the hotel lounge where most youngsters gather to escape the long and some what repetitive, tiresome marriage ceremony that may last for several hours. Only very dedicated and close family members would sit through such a ceremony, certainly not the younger generation who would say "This is not my cup of tea!"

Nirav was glad to have Tina's company, as he did not know any one else. From all the girls Nirav had met, Tina was the best, most suited, a prospective life partner, the one who could settle down in America with ease. Who said that all good things in life come when least expected. Surely it could be true in this case, as Nirav had not come expecting to meet some one like Tina.

At five and a half feet, Tina was indeed a tall girl, at least for a Gujarati girl, as normally Gujarati boys are hardly that tall. At fix feet, Nirav was an exception. Then both his parents were reasonably tall.

Tina was wearing a light sky blue colour sari, with a matching blouse, that is usually a bit darker in colour compared to the sari, giving uplift to her upper torso, a normal tradition, a clever dressing sense to make the most of their curving assets.

It was a sleeveless blouse, hold together with a series of strings at the back, the recent trend in the fashion where the girls need the minimum of the material to maximise the fashion that leaves very little to imagination. Tina was slim, with the sari hugging her attractive figure but without much curves, a sign of a busy, active life that keep such girls slim and extremely active, giving them statuesque figure, a cat walk build that most fashion models admire and possess.

Tina's most striking feature was her long, dark, silky and fluffy hair, kept loose to flutter in the air, only a pair of dark sun glasses expertly resting on her head, keeping her hair in the right place.

Normally girls use a plastic bend or a cotton ribbon to keep the loose hair in place. But apparently it was the modern trend, the latest fashion among the trendy girls to use sun-glasses that gave them a kind of superiority complex, an air of affluence, make them stand out in a crowd.

Nirav found her charming and attractive, although her obvious assets were not that well developed. Her long arms, protruding from her bare armpits were slim and long. She was wearing a low cut blouse with a minimum material content but she was wearing an uplifting bra with expertly hidden falsies that gave her small breasts a big lift. So often small is beautiful, big is cumbersome, obstructive! Well beauty or even sexiness is in beholder's eyes. Nirav certainly found Tina attractive and sexy!

According to the famous Indian film song, "Fashion badthi jaya, kapda ghadata jaya" that is as the fashion advances, it needs less material, more some one shows her bare flesh, more fashionable she is considered to be.

How true it is in today's fashion world, in the mini skirt era when a tennis top or a blouse which needed no more than the material of couple of handkerchiefs is the height of fashion, unless the girl has an over bulging breasts, uncommon among young working, professional Indian girls.

Every girl knows that her best assets that draw instant male attention are their breasts and boys like big, well developed breasts, at least on most parts, that keep plastic surgeons in the lap of luxury. But most have to do with padded bra to attract the wondering young eyes.

Nirav found Tina extremely charming, even without sexy curves. She was clever, well educated with teasing smile, sweet voice and provocative manner that would be hard to ignore. Her self-confidence was bordering to over confidence, even arrogance; but well hidden behind her charm, beauty and natural grace. Tina was indeed a rainmaker or even a Kingmaker in waiting. After all every king has a queen!

Tina had a certain grandeur that distinguished her from the rest of the lot Nirav saw, experienced at first hand. Her each word was some sort of test, an invitation or a challenge that a boy of Nirav's intelligence could not ignore. Her every sentence had a purpose, an invitation in a teasing manner that some one with less self assurance would find it hard to handle!

So often women inspire men to great things, self beliefs but prevent them from achieving them? It was Tina's calibre, the dress sense, her bare flesh and self belief that first attracted Nirav, not her cooking skill! Perhaps she was an archetype of a female personality. Her academia denoted female, sexual intelligence that would be hard to ignore. Even Lord Krishna and Shiva fell prey to such fatal female charm.

Nirav and Tina spend three long hours together. They knew that this chance meeting was a set-up job to bring them together. So there was no need to pretend otherwise or to beat around the bush.

Moreover Tina had full confidence in her own ability, as she came from a well to do family. Her father was a doctor and mother a high ranking civil servant. She had two brothers, one elder than her and the second younger, who was still at the college, studying law.

Tina had a BSc and MBA in finance, banking and information technology. Having attended St. Javier College with English medium, her command of English was good enough to settle down in America without going through hard time, without the struggle to master the language that normally makes the life difficult for the new immigrant, especially the girls who have studied in colleges where the medium of instruction may be Gujarati or Marathi.

What impressed Nirav was that Tina was not after his Green Card. Yes, she would like to settle down in USA but with the right partner. She would be equally happy to settle down in Mumbai. The person was more important than the place, be it Mumbai, London or New York, at least that was the first impression Tina projected. But so often it is dangerous to judge the book by its cover.

Nirav and Tina even went out for a walk. Occasionally holding hands and on one occasion when her sunglasses fell down, Nirav picked it up and put it in his pocket, as he loved to see her hair flutter all over her face, arms and chest, giving him the opportunity to stroke her hair while trying to flick them back, in the right place.

Well, Tina was not the only one who knew all the tricks of the trade! Nirav always believed not to leave the quality of life to chance but to choice, especially when selecting a life partner and with his stature, education,

Nirav was in a prime position to exploit even a half opportunity, overwhelm any female, no matter what privileged background she may have.

Although it was their first meeting, both felt at ease. So when they parted company, it was inevitable but to exchange their mobile numbers, meet again as soon as possible.

Seeing Nirav happy, with a smile on his face, Nimuben realised that at last Nirav may have found a girl that he may like, could marry and take her to America. After all it may not be a wasted journey.

Although Nirav was a doctor, a highly educated person with modern outlook, he did not have a girlfriend as such, in Western sense, where living and sleeping together was the norm, although he had many female friends during his college days but was not close or intimate with any particular girl to share his flat, his bed. Perhaps he was concentrating too much on his studies, his future to have such a distraction.

So it was but natural that he could not get Tina out of his thoughts when he went to bed. Her charming face, smooth, silky hair, lovely figure, her dress sense and teasing but pleasant manner haunted him throughout the restless night.

Next morning, when he got up late and by the time he had gone through his daily routine, it was nearly mid-day. On the pretext of buying a newspaper, Nirav left the house and phoned Tina, who was eagerly waiting for his call.

Tina jokingly said, "Nirav, I thought you may have skipped the town, thinking that I am after you."

"Tina, I will only skip the town when we elope?" Nirav felt at ease in answering Tina in her sweet, teasing manner.

* * *

Chapter Four

Shivaji Nature Reserve
(Mumbai's Garden of Eden)

They agreed to meet the next day, near Shalimar Holiday Complex which was for Nirav only twenty minutes ride by a taxi. When Nirav came to the hotel complex, waiting in the car park, he saw some one riding a scooter waving at him.

The scooter stopped near where Nirav was standing and when the rider removed the helmet, Nirav realised that the rider was she. In fact she was none other than Tina, his dream girl!

Although it is not that unusual for a girl to have a scooter in Mumbai, Nirav was, never the less surprised but not unduly perturbed. As usual, Tina was wearing a pair of black trousers with a snow white sleeveless blouse. Only her long fluttering hair, yet to be pegged down with sunglasses and a very light make-up may give away her sex.

When Nirav came closer, Tina gave him a big smile, revealing her smooth, shapely pearl white teeth that are normally a prerogative of the super rich, film stars and people in public domain who are willing to spend a fortune at special dental clinic.

Tina's perfect teeth were natural, not a gift from a dental surgeon. But she took a great care of all her natural assets that God gave her and that include her beautiful hair, smooth skin, pearly teeth and her lean, slim figure, going to a gym at least twice a week, finding time from her busy life style.

While still sitting on her scooter, holding the helmet in her lap, Tina said with a broad smile, "Hi Nirav, did you sleep well?" then continued, "Would you like to have a coffee in the Shalimar Garden or prefer to go to a nearby nature reserve and have a light picnic in the wilderness?"

Tina was still smiling; perhaps enjoying the dilemma she had posed to Nirav, a smart, high flying doctor from San Diego, California but a captive audience for tempestuous Tina.

Nirav took his time to reply and then said in an inquisitive, unsure voice, "Tina would you like me to ride this scooter?"

"Of course, unless you would like to walk." Then reassuring Nirav, she added, "Nirav, I am not only fully insured, but I have never been involved in an accident. Moreover you are a VIP passenger.

I absolutely guarantee your safety. My life, my happiness depends on it." Tina was indeed full of confidence, self belief and self assured.

Nirav sat behind Tina, put on the spare helmet and slowly they rode out of the Shalimar car park. As there was so little space, Nirav had to sit close to Tina, touching her back side.

Within five minutes, Tina stopped at a quiet road-side and said in some what serious voice, "Look Nirav, it would be dangerous for both of us if you do not sit very close to me and hold on tightly to me. Don't worry; I will not hold it against you. It would be a prize piece of hypocrisy if I do."

Tina could not help but tease Nirav sweetly. But he realised that it was a serious matter, sound advice and there was much truth and wisdom in what Tina said. He should better listen to her.

So Nirav sat as close to her as he possibly could and hold her tightly, as if his life depended on it. But it posed a bit of a dilemma for Nirav. If he put his hands high, they might rest on her breasts, if low, then on her thighs, on her lower stomach.

In the end he thought it would be wise and perhaps less tempting to keep his hands as far away from her breasts as possible, even though her breasts were tiny and not that sexy. Then for Kiran, every part of Tina's body was sexy, even her stomach where his hands eventually rested.

Scooter is the best mode of transport on the busy, over crowded Mumbai roads but it is also most dangerous, as it claims the lives of more youngsters than through any other cause or illness.

Tina was a careful and capable rider. She would never take the scooter on the fast, dangerous roads where most of the fatal accidents occur.

Within twenty minutes they entered the ***Shivaji Nature Reserve,*** an island, an oasis of peace and tranquillity, the Garden of Eden and full of greenery, vast open space and fresh air in the heart of over populated, over paved, polluted concrete jungle affectionately known as Mumbai.

In some respects it was similar to Hyde Park in London and Central Park in the heart of New York. While New York and especially London is littered with parks and open spaces, in every area, every borough, numbering more than two hundred major open spaces, Mumbai distinctly lacks such open spaces, due to bad planning, ignorance and corruption.

The park is occupying an area of some one thousand acres. It is a heaven, the last retreat for wild life, especially birds, as city is over flowing with humanity with hardly any open space for birds to nest and bring up their young ones.

It is no wonder that bird variety here in Shivaji Nature Reserve is staggering, with common and rare birds like bulbul, cockatoo, dove, eagle, falcon, hawk, kite, lark, magpie, martin, nightingale, parrots, peacocks, quail, raven, skylarks, swallows, thrush and woodpeckers of various shape and size are seen regularly, many occupying the artificial nests provided by the Green Lobby, one of better import from the West, who take care of such parks and nature reserves, turning them into bird sanctuaries.

This is indeed the Indian, Hindu tradition that lost its lustre during the British Raj when it was more fashionable to hunt, to kill rather than save, nurture and preserve our heritage, our wild life and forests where famous sages used to live and meditate.

Peacocks and guinea fouls are observed with interest and curiosity, running wild, adding excitement to the calm and peaceful atmosphere enjoyed by a tiny percentage of the population, as most live from hand to mouth, working all God given hours to provide a roof over one's head and two square meals a day and these are the lucky ones. Gandhiji's perception of Ram Rajya, meaning a land of hope, glory, wealth, truth and equality is just a distant dream that will never become a reality.

Slum dog millionaire is but a Bollywood dream, an escapism from reality, for a couple of hours while watching a film in an air conditioned cinema. We are mere puppets controlled by twin strings of joy and hope. Mumbai is the most famous den of inequality where most residents are unwitting part of unanimity. Yet the city is a magnet for village dwellers, a fool's gold, a hen that lays a golden egg but only for a very tiny few lucky ones who are born with a silver spoon.

The lake in the middle of the reserve never dries up. During the worse summer excesses, the lake is fed, the water is supplemented by tankers to keep the water level high and give the water birds, like ducks, cranes, swans and stork a permanent place to reside.

The small island in the centre of the lake was full of trees, bushes and greeneries where water birds build their nests and retreat for the night. It was the only place out of bound for humans, even the rowing boats were not allowed to go within the boundary marked by the floating nylon cones.

The lake adds beauty and charm to this oasis of peace, tranquillity and natural beauty. This park is also a retreat for human beings, especially for young at heart and courting couples who need space and solitude which is in short supply in the bustling city.

Today Tina did not come here to observe wild life but hopefully to be one of the courting couples. She wanted to impress, to mesmerise and captivate Nirav, with her charm, tenacity, attractive figure, her different but unique sex appeal and her sheer personality, so that Nirav would not meet, interview, socialize with any more girls who could steal her Lord Krishna from under her feet. It seems any move; any liaison is fair in love and war!

Tina knew what a flood of response an eligible boy like Nirav, a young hulk of a doctor with a Green Card would receive. But she had tremendous confidence in her own ability and she already knew that Nirav was very much interested in her. He only needed the final push to make up his mind. Tina was almost irresistible and she knew it. She utilized her lethal attraction, the fatal charm to the utmost. After all Mumbai is a city where only the most ambitious and ruthless survive, make their marks, sit on the podium.

That is why Tina had brought Nirav to this romantic and isolated place, favourite location for young at heart. Tina was wearing a sleeveless, low cut blouse with uplifting bra to give her diminutive assets a lift to attract Nirav's attention, in a subtle but very visible manner. After all Nirav was a man with common need, obvious attractions, no different than any other man when it comes to female attraction.

Tina parked the scooter in a secured compound, immobilised it and chained it to the pole in the parking bay before going in the nearby office where she handed in the two helmets and received a ticket with the registration number of her scooter printed on the ticket. Now no one can steal, retrieve or ride away on her scooter without this piece of paper.

Nirav could not help but admire her thoroughness in every thing that she would do. There was an air of affluence and self belief around her, in her every move, a typical city girl brought up in a well to do family. She was equal to Nirav without a trace of inferior complexity that Nirav did not expect in an Indian girl. Then Nirav did not have that much experience when dealing with girls, especially Indian girls. One may say he lived a sheltered life for a doctor when it comes to mixing with the opposite sex, especially as bold, demanding and forward as Tina!

It was a kind of bravado one would not associate with Indian girls. Then perhaps Nirav was living in the past. It was not the age of Goddess Ambika but the actress Ashwaria Rai, the queen of Bollywood and the most beautiful girl in the world. Nirav was not a fan of Indian movies.

The household names like Ashwaria Rai, Rani Mukerjee, Shilpa Shethi and their likes did not particularly register with Nirav.

After a ten minute walk, they came to a small café cum shop where Tina was greeted by the owner like a friend, an old customer. Tina brought some cold drinks, nuts, crisps and sandwiches and borrowed a jute mat and a plastic sheet to spread on the grass, to sit down on.

She handed this small bundle to Nirav to carry while she took charge of food and drinks. It seemed she knew the routine well, how to make one self comfortable without carrying all these items all the way from home. In the land of one eyed Jack, Tina had the advantage of two eyes!

Nirav was more or less a spectacle, as Tina had taken charge, as she was on a familiar territory, a frequent visitor to this beauty spot. In a way Nirav was happy for Tina to take charge, have self confidence which will stood her in good stead when she lands in a strange and foreign country.

A further five minute's walk brought them to a shady area, at the edge of a forest or rather a cluster of trees, a perfect isolated place on a hot, sunny and humid day with temperature touching 40C*. The cool breeze from the forested part of this vast park made the heat bearable.

Tina spread the jute mat and the plastic sheet on the grass that was already brown, under the onslaught of this fierce heat rather than looking green, its normal colour after the monsoon, before the arrival of this oppressive summer months' excesses. But then the monsoon was just on the horizon. But it was already too late for Nirav.

Tina took out a packet of wet tissue, gave a couple to Nirav and cleansed her face, neck and arms. Some how Nirav was engrossed in thoughts, fossilized for a moment. He was watching Tina rather than to follow her in wiping his face and hands.

191

When Tina jokingly offered Nirav to help, he came back to reality, using the tissues before they dry up in this intense heat. Tina could not help wondering what was going through Nirav's mind. But it was obvious that she was making an impression on this very clever and charming young and an incredible hulk of a man! Would life be a one, long, sweet dream with Nirav, an every day picnic!

* * *

Chapter Five
Love in the Afternoon

As soon as they were settled, Tina opened a bottle of cold drink, which they shared, drinking from the same bottle with two straws? Nirav enjoyed this sharing, as their faces were touching each other, the heavy breathing, gasping for air, mostly on Nirav's part giving away the game, the state of his mind, letting Tina gauge his feelings for her. Tina knew how to act as a catalyst of her own dream, achievement and progress.

Nirav was mesmerised by Tina, by her antics that were the part of the daily routine for these high flying, great achieving youngsters? This was the new Mumbai, not the one Nirav left behind some five years ago! One may wonder how a city, youngsters change so much in such a short time. Then this modern world is moving at speed of light. If you blink, you are left behind. This is called social highway that moves at the speed of light.

Whatever Tina did had a purpose, panache and style. She had a grace of a gazelle and the speed of thoughts of a cheetah. It seemed she was well groomed in etiquette, good manner and some how knew, could almost read Nirav's mind to ascertain his likes and dislikes, his weak and strong points and act accordingly.

It is the wisdom, goodness of the God to give us five precious qualities, freedom of speech, freedom of action, freedom to shape our lives and freedom of conscience and the prudence never to practise any of them! What wonderful words of wisdom first uttered by the great Chanakiya!

After they were refreshed by drinks and the biting, Tina said, "Nirav, I am a bit tired, as I did not sleep well last night. It was so hot, humid and suffocating? I would like to lie down. Is it all right if I rest my head on you?

Tina said casually. It was a simple, understandable request. But could any action, any deed or words be simple or without hidden meaning, agenda in Tina's world?

"Tina, I thought you would have brought the air pillows as well, as you are so organised?" Nirav could not help but praise or tease Tina.

"Well Nirav, for an American boy, you are so naïve? Why should I bring a pillow when I have you?" Tina said with a teasing smile. Nirav realised that it would not be that easy to get an upper-hand over Tina. But he felt that even in defeat, he was victorious when dealing with Tina.

She was indeed extremely witty, clever and always had the right answer for any question, any situation. Tina was perhaps a born expressionist.

She was not the one to buy redemption with a caution. Perhaps her hectic pace of life personifies the new, younger generation. Nirav could not help but wonder how such a young and naïve girl has such a pool of ancient wisdom personified by Narad Muni, a mischief making monk who had answer to every question, in our Hindu mythology.

"Tina, I would like to lie down as well. Like you, I did not sleep well at all but it was more than the oppressive heat that kept me awake. But you can rest your head on my chest."

"Can I play with your hair? Do you know that you have the most beautiful hair I have ever seen on a girl's head?" Nirav said it almost like an after-thought.

"Well Nirav, we are both adults. If you like my hair so much, please feel free to enjoy your self. My aim is to please you in any way I can. But I am sure being a gentleman, you will not take advantage of my venerable state of mind. Would you?" There was a soft smile, enough to show her pearl like perfect set of teeth.

Nirav removed her sunglasses as soon as Tina rested her head on his chest. He lifted her head momentarily, to bring her long, smooth and silky hair, expertly washed and shampooed with a tinge of sandalwood, in front, resting, covering her upper torso.

As her hair were spread all over her chest, Nirav could not help but occasionally touching her tiny breasts, her black bra that was more or less completely exposed, as Tina was wearing a skimpy tennis top with a frontal zip, pulled well down. In this heat, any piece of clothing was one piece too many on the body.

There was a golden silence, broken only by the light wind, blowing through trees, some of them were whistling trees, a kind of tropical pine trees that grow throughout South East Asia and Africa.

When the wind passes through the leaves of these trees, it makes a romantic sound, like a sweet whistle or rather a flute played by Lord Krishna to attract the attention of Gopies bathing in the holy waters of River Jamuna.

Sage Valmaki, who wrote the famous holy book of Ramayana once said that human imagination has no limit, no boundary and no constrain. Indeed human mind is a free spirit that no one can cage. Only a body can be a prisoner, not the soul or the mind!

There were occasional coos, soft murmur, mews, chirps, croaks, cockles and shrikes, bellow and Koyal's sweet singing, adding romance to the already pleasant and romantic surroundings. But one has to listen carefully to catch all these nature's musical notes, played in perfect harmony. No wonder this place was a lover's paradise where young hearts meet, enjoy each other's company, explore the unknown and make plans for the future.

There was hardly any one around. Where could one get such a romantic atmosphere, solitude and a shelter from prying eyes in the heart of overflowing humanity?

No wonder Tina had brought Nirav here, a romantic Vrindavan, Lord Krishna's favourite place where he would like to meet Radha, a dream girl that even Lord Krishna could not resist but admire and enjoy her company, a spiritual reunion of two souls. Was Nirav Tina's Lord Krishna, be part of unanimity? Well, only time would tell.

Tina, a chatter box at most times, was silent, almost tongue-tied, lost in deep thought. Nirav could not help but wonder what was going through her mind, as he became bolder with his hands, pulling the zip even further down, playing with her bra, expecting Tina to admonish him for his misdemeanour and zipping up the blouse.

But Tina was silent, letting Nirav carry on stroking her hair and playing, pressing her bra, her now pulsating breasts, the excitement running through her entire body.

Perhaps there was no need to disassociate, be alien to Western, Abrahamic morality that Nirav may have immersed himself while in America! It would be difficult not to be a Roman when in Rome, especially if one is in the company of Helen of Troy!

Nirav wanted so much to unbutton her bra and play, stroke and kiss her tiny breasts but being a gentleman, he would not like to take advantage of the romantic situation, the heat and the loneliness. Although Nirav was every inch an American, the inbred Indian culture stopped him from being an iconoclast.

But the next time when he touched her breast, resting his hands on her bra, Tina seized his hands, pressing them hard against her breasts. Then she slowly turned her head towards his, until her broad, wet lips rested on his, breathing heavily, the aroma of sandalwood and sweat was so overwhelming!

Forgetting his manner, that he was a doctor and a gentleman, Nirav gave her a long, lingering kiss, unbuttoned her bra and pressed her breasts, twisted her nipples as hard as he could that hurt Tina and made her grunt, squeal and gave a muted cry of pain and pleasure that normally disturbs the peace of a honeymoon suit.

She in turn squeezed his tongue so hard that Nirav thought it was going to come out for good? This embrace, snug and intense cuddling, kissing lasted some ten minutes before they both ran out of steam and felt a bit embarrassed.

Nirav was the first to disengage, to apologise, begging her forgiveness for this momentary madness, loss of self control. But Tina was quick to point out that it takes two to tango, that they were both equally guilty or innocent, as one's perspective may be, adding that she indeed enjoyed it and have no regrets. Neither was in a position to preach modesty, virtue of self control and why should they?

But philosophically Tina added, "I hope you will not hold this momentary madness against me. After all I am a fully blooded woman in my prime who appreciates being loved and cuddled, especially by my heart throb!"

If it was meant to reassure Nirav, it certainly worked. But Nirav had to reassure Tina that he does not think any less of her for this intense encounter of most pleasant nature.

Perhaps the thought may have crossed Nirav's mind that this could be the beginning of the corrosion of the so called superior culture, the typical Indian mentality under the Abrahamic onslaught!

It is like every one would prefer to go to heaven but we do not want to believe in heaven or hell, nor do we want to chart our path to heaven! It is indeed a waste of time, like building castle in the air!

Every event, every action has a purpose and every setback has its lesson, adds a bit of wisdom and makes the person better prepared for the future. Was this a setback or an advancement of Tina's dream! After all Tina was an ambitious, shrewd and calculating girl, a typical Mumbai babe!

They spent three more hours in the park, having picnic lunch, talking or just enjoying nature, each other's company, even hugging and cuddling but within bounds of decency, a bit wiser second time around. Perhaps they have acquired the sense and sensibility of inner harmony, in the oasis of enlightenment!

Surely their dalliance was more appropriate to the Indian culture rather than Eurasian one second time round.

Perhaps in such a brief encounter, they have mastered the art of mind control and spiritual awareness or was it a mind game! It seems every action is fair in love and war. It was love, the Helen of Troy that launched a thousand ships!

Nirav even zipped her blouse up to her neck to avoid any temptation, but it was too hot a day and Tina had to lower it up to a point where it would not expose her black bra that Nirav found so attractive and raised uncontrollable urge to play with her breasts, although there was no reason to bend to the demons of social or cultural pressure, not in this wilderness where the symphony of nature extended beyond the realm of extraordinary. Self acknowledgement is the DNA of self-enlightenment that Lord Krishna gave the world in our holy book of Bhagwad Gita.

It is the logic that nurtures the opinion of what is right and what is wrong; one person's food may be another person's poison. Surely Tina's serenity made her appear angelic in nature, enlightened in substance. Could looks be deceiving! If so, Nirav was well past it.

"Tina, why do you always wear a sleeveless, low cut blouse?" Nirav could not help asking the obvious question but with a mischievous smile on his face to make it a light hearted question.

"Well Nirav, I would like to wear a bikini in this hot weather but we are not that Westernised." Then Tina added her own question. "If it makes you uncomfortable Nirav, then I do not mind wearing a polo neck top, although it would be a torture in this hot and humid weather and a bit uncomfortable for me. But I do not mind making a scarify to please my Lord Krishna.

After all I am a simple girl, a Gopi from Vrindavan who would willingly rest at the feet of her Lord." It seemed Tina could play with words as well as Nirav but it was a mixture of English, Gujarati and Hindi, with occasional Marathi words that Nirav would not understand.

But let me tell you what we girls think of wearing a low cut blouse. A good girl loosens a few buttons or the zip when it is unbearably hot while a bad girl loosens, unzips her blouse to make it hot for others! Nirav, in which category do I fall?" Nirav could not help but admire her wicked sense of humour. After all very few Indian girls have such sophisticated sense of humour.

This will stand her in good stead in San Diego, amongst his intellectual friends. It was obvious that she could hold her own, be heart and soul of any party, either here in Mumbai or even in America.

"Moreover you will have noticed that most girls do wear sleeveless, low cut blouse, even those who have big, bulging busts, bosoms, so often even without a bra, along with mini skirts or short dresses that may even show their knickers? I wear jeans or trousers.

I do not show my legs or rather my thighs and yes, I wear black knickers and they are tiny, keeping up with the modern fashion. But my aim is to please you. So let me know your preferences. Your command is my wish!"

Tina was back to her best, could not help teasing Nirav but whatever she said, made sense and had an element of truth and practicality that Nirav had to acknowledge, however grudgingly.

For Nirav, Tina was like a hobgoblin, a mischievous creature in fairy tales. Tina was an extremely shy sycophant, a perfect put-up job but knew the time and the opportunity when to press the right buttons to gain the maximum advantage! Was this the sole prerogative of the girls residing in Mumbai, especially if they come from a privileged background!

"Tina, perhaps you have taken it the wrong way.

Not only I do not mind but I would like to see you in a mini skirt as well." Then added, "You have to forgive me if I can not keep my hands in my pocket. But I promise that I will try my best, will be on my best behaviour from now on and will not rock the boat. Moreover I give you my permission to admonish me if I misbehave in any way."

"Nirav, do not give your words or make a promise that you can not keep! In any case I do not want you to get frustrated" Nirav could not make out what Tina meant but did not have the courage to ask Tina to clarify herself.

It was time to make a move. Tina got up first, gathered her belongings and then turned to Nirav and said, "Nirav, can you please keep a watch. I would like to go behind those bushes to freshen up."

The ecstatic sensation and the hot weather had wetted her knickers and her thighs were wet, sticky and moist. She took her make up bag, a few moist tissues and paper towels and disappeared behind the bushes.

The place was so isolated that there was no fear of any one peeping, especially behind such a canopy of nature. Tina took off her jeans, removed her soaking knickers, cleansed and dried her private parts, her thighs before putting a fresh pair of knickers on and the same, some what dusty pair of jeans.

Tina emerged from behind the bushes in ten minutes. But it sounded like an hour to Nirav who was patiently waiting for her to reappear.

It seems he would be lost in this wilderness without his guide, his mentor and companion, the tempestuous Tina.

During these two meetings, Nirav came to know all about Tina and her family while Tina wanted to know all about life in America rather than about his family, as she seemed to know it already.

When Nirav returned home, he told his mother that he would not like to see, meet or interview any more girls. He would rather spend the remaining ten days or so, knowing Tina better.

Nimuben was pleased that Nirav has at last found a girl he may like to marry and take her with him to America. As the two families were of equal status, Nimuben felt that her son was not marrying a misalliance girl, some one beneath their status, although it would have made no difference, as now a days boys and girls choose their own partners and parents have to go along, unless there is religious difference.

Caste, creed or social standing is no more an obstacle between two young loves. It seems the Indian, the Hindu society is at last moving in the right direction and perhaps casteism will soon be confined to social dustbin for the good of the community and the nation.

* * *

Chapter Six
Marriage Proposal:

Two *days* later, while having a coffee in Shalimar Hotel Rooftop Garden, by now a favourite place for Nirav and Tina to meet, talk and plan for the future together, Nirav proposed, going on one knee, to the surprise and delight of the onlookers and to the joy and delight of Tina. Hallelujah, exclaimed a couple of Americans from the Deep South. Perhaps it was anno Domini, the year of tempestuous Tina, the day her dreams came closer to become a reality and for Nirav, he has found the mysterious and elusive ocean beauty, the Mermaid!

In many ways the Shalimar Rooftop Garden was a relaxing, exciting, romantic beauty spot. It was on the seventy fifth floors, some eight hundred feet from ground level but well over a thousand feet above sea level, as the hotel was constructed on a raised land, a natural elevated plateau of more than five thousand square meters in area.

This elevation enabled the building to have a deep and strong foundation that seventy five storey high building will need, especially in Mumbai where the water level is just below the surface in most areas, as Mumbai is like an island surrounded by sea on all sides.

The whole city is built on a marsh land that is not immune to occasional flooding during monsoon months. This place was a tiny slice of heaven, indeed an enchanting fantasyland where one can rejoice in the beauty and splendour unmatched any where else in the overcrowded, over developed and over populated city. This was indeed an oasis of peace, serenity and tranquillity in the ocean of filth, super rich and extreme poverty. It was a different world, a Jules Verne's world, the Lost Horizon for a lucky few amongst the overflowing humanity.

As most of the land in the vicinity of the hotel was owned by the conglomerate, the hotel was at a distance from the city precinct. Moreover there were no footpath dwellers or corrugated iron shacks with open sewage drains that normally pose health problems, especially for the children of the NRI who visit their motherland but lack the immunity to deal with such health hazards that the children born in the city acquire naturally.

So there was no pollution and absolutely no mosquitoes or other insects in the roof garden, even though the entire place was covered with plants and vegetation.

The hotel owner, the billionaire Shah brothers who owned a chain of hotels throughout Bharat and South East Asia and now fast expanding in Western Europe and America, had spared no expense in making this hotel, the Shalimar Garden Hotel and Beach Complex their show piece hotel, a bench mark others had to follow, to emulate in this cut throat business where only the fittest, most imaginative and adventurous would survive. But if you succeed, the reward is mind boggling!

It was a seven star luxury only for the NRI and Westerners as well as super rich Indians. There is no scarcity of rich Indians as India has more millionaires and billionaires than any other country in the world. Indian society is a society of the extreme with filthy rich who travel by their own helicopters and jet planes while millions who live on the footpath and have to struggle for one square meal a day!

Shalimar Roof Top Garden is frequented by film stars, leading cricketers who are semi gods, businessmen, wheeler and dealers and Westerners that include NRIs. The Garden is so tastefully decorated that one may feel they are in a Ross Garden, a perfumery, a Mogul garden in the days of the affluence.

The garden was tastefully divided into some fifty enclaves, with rose hedges, ratrani, (Night Queen) a typical Indian plant that flowers at night with sweet smell and numerous other plants, such as hibiscus, periwinkle, michelia or Indian magnolia, chaplet, jasmine, pink-rose or karan and many more. It had the inbuilt floor air conditioning as well as heating for few cold winter nights that Mumbai enjoys, especially at such a height.

There were several fountains that spread, throw up rose water and at night colourful lights gave this place a unique atmosphere, an unparallel lap of luxury with one waiter for every two tables. Then in Mumbai exclusivity is expensive.

The wonderful, advanced technology even enabled each and every cabin to be covered with a glass wall with the touch of a button, giving complete privacy as well as comfort against weather extremes. Even the worse excesses of the monsoon would not dampen or damage Shalimar Garden. It was an outdoor garden with all the comforts of an indoor one, immune to weather extremes at most times.

The view from the top was breathtaking, out of this world. The distant tiny islands with famous elephant caves dating back two thousand years were clearly visible on a clear day, as the sky is normally free of smog at this height and in this particular area with low density of human habitation.

It would be impossible to find a table in the evening, unless one is a regular visitor and knows the manager or have a permanent booking available only to their permanent or life members who have joined the Spa and Sporting Club with annual subscription of one hundred thousand rupees, discounting the joining fees. Yet there was a five year waiting list.

During lunch time, it was not that busy. Moreover Westerners and NRIs get a preferential treatment. It was Nirav who would take charge and feel at ease here rather than Tina, as English seemed to be the natural language for communication rather than Hindi, although all staffs were at ease in all three languages widely spoken in Mumbai, English, Hindi and Marathi. Tina could speak all three languages fluently with added advantage of Gujarati, while Nirav lack the fluency in Marathi.

Nirav, by now a full blooded American, naturally had an egalitarian attitude, especially with their fellow guests who were on most part NRI and Westerners. Nirav's concentration was at the root of mental mastery that would open many doors in most unexpected places.

Nirav and Tina made a perfect couple, each complementing others and together they could deal with any situation, prosper in any company, tackle any one without feeling inferior in any way, even in the company of super stars and multi millionaires.

Nirav loved to have a bottle of kingfisher beer with their special bitting, lightly roasted sparingly spiced nuts of various type with unique flavour and taste, cheese bites, chicken wings, mini meat samosa and Kashmiri kebab with their special sauce no one can reproduce, while Tina would have a cup of coffee, an occasional charlotte, especially apple charlotte, spending a couple of hours in peace and solitude unmatched any where in Mumbai.

It would cost Nirav some three to five thousand rupees, a month's wage for many local people but only half an hour's pay for Nirav who was surprised how Tina knew such wonderful places, out of reach for all but a handful of residents and friends in their circle. Perhaps Tina could ignite the flames of her personal potential that would produce startling results.

If Nirav ever decide to come back to Mumbai for good, then such luxuries would play a major part in his decision to return to his birth place. Nirav had the magnetic power of mind to attract spiritual and material abundance, even in a city like Mumbai.

Mumbai had changed a lot since his college days. Even San Diego did not have any hotel, any place remotely similar to match this wonderland.

It was just out of the world. But one has to be enlightened to be part of this jet set age Mumbai where privileged few lived with unbridled exhilaration.

Now it was race against time to get Registry Wedding out of the way, to get the all important documents, the marriage certificate so that Nirav can apply for a permanent visa for Tina, as soon as he returns to America.

There was no time to undergo the Hindu marriage ceremony which both families wanted to be on a grand scale, as for Nirav's family, it was the last marriage in the family and for Tina's family, it was their first opportunity, her father being a doctor, there was a long list of guests they would like to invite on this auspicious occasion, having enjoyed the hospitality of others when their children got married. It was time to reciprocate the favour, the hospitality and the honour bestowed upon Tina's family by friends and relations for so long.

It was decided that Nirav should come back for two or three weeks when Tina's application for a permanent visa is approved, based on the marriage certificate issued by a registrar after a civil ceremony. Normally it takes some six months to obtain such a visa in America where every application is thoroughly examined and checked, as bogus marriages are common just to get a Green Card.

Those ten days between meeting Tina and returning to America were the most enjoyable period in Nirav's life. It was no problem to get a slot for the civil marriage, as there are agents who can arrange any thing, solve any problem at a right price.

A NRI doctor from America can demand and receive VIP treatment from most civil servants, police and even judges and politicians, albeit through a third party, that is through a special agent. Money and influence can and do solve most problems in India. Whom you know counts more than what you know.

Bank balance is more appreciated than character references. One has to be careful of Snake-oil salesmen that abound in the upper layer of this privileged society. There is a huge difference between well being and being well off.

The cradle of civilization has become a cradle of corruption that oils the wheel and makes life comfortable for the rich and the influential and that include most returning NRIs.

No wonder some of the NRIs wish that life could be that simple, that accommodating in the West, that by paying the agent a small amount, all documents could be delivered to one's home!

After the registry marriage, Nirav proposed to Tina that they should go on a short honeymoon. After a long pause, Tina said, "Nirav, here registry marriage is not considered a proper marriage. It is a necessity rather than a holy occasion. Registry marriage is not the union of two souls that marriage is all about."

"Our families, especially mine, will not feel at ease or feel comfortable if we go on honeymoon before we get married according to Hindu tradition. But I leave it to you. My fate is in your hands. If you want honeymoon that badly, then I am all yours, soul, body and flesh."

Tina knew how to manipulate Nirav, how to make him agree with her way of thinking, even without putting any pressure on him. Well, she was a Menka who conquered Lord Shiva by her panache, beauty and sex appeal.

So Nirav was no match to Tina's subtle smiles of enlightenment unfolding across her lips. Nirav was already a prisoner of Tina's manipulating sexual charms that only an actress of considerable talent could project.

It seems residing in the West is not an advantage when it comes to understanding women, their innermost desire or how to avoid becoming a prisoner of charm, beauty and sex appeal! Who can tell what grows in the lush garden of a woman's mind! It could be desert cacti or the sweet smelling English Rose!

If Tina puts the ball in Nirav's court, he can not kick it away into the touch line without her participation? It seemed innocent looking Tina had a matured and calculating head on her young shoulders, that she can twist Nirav and get away with it. Tina was a Menka who could make Nirav dance to her tune, a puppet on a very long string?

Nirav thought for a while but took Tina's advice. Even without honeymoon, Nirav would have Tina all to himself, to play with her body in every way he want but without consummating, riveting the marriage, without performing the final act.

Then so often the journey to a dream destination is more exciting that the arrival, a mountain looks magnificent from a distance then when one may try to climb.

Love making, exploring every inch of Tina's silky smooth body gave Nirav more pleasure than he could have in sex, the final act that would end in retreat, the body and mind having lost its lustre, even if for a short period only.

The ten days before his departure were the most enjoyable period in Nirav's life. Besides monopolising the Shalimar's Roof Top Garden, they visited the Shivaji Natural Reserve several time and made love to their heart's content. Tina even wore miniskirts showing her legs, rather upper thighs that raised Nirav's blood pressure. They did every thing that a honeymooning couple would do without consummating their marriage.

For Nirav, there was no need for restraint or feel guilty in any way, hold back his desire, as they were legally married in the eyes of the law. They were husband and wife. Even Tina's pleas were not sufficient to hold him back, stop him giving her love bites on her most private, inaccessible parts of her body.

So the goodbye at the airport was a sad, painful separation, especially for Nirav. Numerous love bites on his body were the bitter-sweet memories he was taking back with him. He could not help but wonder how many more such bites Tina was nursing, especially on her tiny breasts and high up on her thighs, out of sight but hopefully not out of Tina's mind.

The letter of visa approval for Tina in to-day's post brought these memories flooding back to the surface. It was time to return to Mumbai for the final ceremony, the final stamp of approval from the society, family and friends and especially from Tina.

Nirav knew that tonight's telephone call to Tina will be a long and protruding one but a pleasant one none the less. Soon his enormous telephone bill will come down when he returns to San Diego with beautiful and bewitching Tina at his side, as her newly wed bride, hopefully after an unforgettable and stormy honeymoon that he has been dreaming ever since he met Tina at a friend's wedding.

* * *

Chapter Seven
Return Visit: The Date with Destiny

This time Nirav could get only two weeks leave. So it was a bit hectic. Nirav arrived in Mumbai only three days before the marriage, on Thursday, while the marriage was on Sunday.

The marriage ceremony was held in a temple, in the presence of a few family members and close friends, followed by a reception in a hotel, attended by some five hundred people, mostly on Tina's side, although the expenses were shared by two families.

This is a new but a welcome trend, as in the olden time, the burden fell on the bride's family. The marriage is more and more becoming a democratic way of life where all decisions are taken after consultation rather than bridegroom's family dictating the terms, a moment of sober reflection, addressing the bride's family with respect and civility.

By Monday Nirav and Tina left for a week's honeymoon, in the honeymoon hotpot, the favourite seaside resort of Goa. They were booked in the famous five stars Kohinoor Sea and Sand Resort, with its own beach, extensive gardens and state of the art facilities of every type imaginable, with indoor and outdoor pools, sauna, hot whirlpools and extensive gardens with running stream, free fall pools with waterfalls and state of the art gym, not to mention various sport facilities and range of restaurants to cater for every taste, carving and appetite.

This beauty of a resort is a much favoured destination for honeymooners, especially for Westerners, as the local people who are super rich have now targeted Mauritius, a jewel of an island in the heart of the romantic Indian Ocean, off the coast of South Africa.

Nirav and Tina would have liked to go to Mauritius but the lack of time and the long distance travel, some ten hour flight from Mumbai to Mauritius made it impracticable, as their flight from Mumbai to San Diego would take up to twenty hours, with a long stop at Heathrow airport and a change over at Los Angeles or a long drive to San Diego. So Mauritius was a No Go destination, at least this time.

So Goa was the next best destination, especially as Kohinoor Resort has every facility that one may wish, with special suits and service for honeymooners, what Nirav and Tina wanted most.

For Nirav and Tina, the main attractions were each other, their bodies, sexual excitement and intellectual company. Nirav was 27 and Tina just 24 years old. Yet these were their first sexual experiences, their first sexual partners which would be a novelty in the Western culture.

Although Nirav and Tina had enjoyed each other so much in Shivaji Nature Reserve, this was the real thing, without inhibition, without guilt or restrain of any kind. Now they do not have to chase that elusive pot of gold. It was on the beach, on their doorstep and in their bed, in any spot their hearts may desire.

In the Western society, it is hard to find a virgin boy or a girl over the age of 18 and the age is rapidly coming down. The sexual filth on the TV, phonographic magazines and lack of any parental supervision on most part has severely dented Western moral standard.

Sex is as free, as common as drinks and drugs which cheapens marriage, especially honeymoon. Some newly wed Western couples even go on their honeymoon with their children?

No one is a virgin on a honeymoon night in the West. So often both partners have children before marriage. Honeymoon has no real meaning, unlike in Indian culture where a girl would find it difficult to be accepted if she is not a virgin on her honeymoon night.

Although the attitude is changing, especially amongst the young Indians born and brought-up in the West where cohabitation between youngsters is slowly gaining ground but still rare indeed. It is too early to say for the good or the bad, what harm it may do to the society or it could be a blessing in disguise?

The breakdown of the family, single parenthood and the spread of sexually transmitted disease (STD) is becoming the scourge of the Western society. Indian community in the West is at least free from such self inflected wounds and as a result, their children get the best of both the world, excelling at studies and occupying high posts with much better salaries and a higher living standard than the national average.

The Indian community has gained an enviable reputation as the most educated, law abiding, hard working people welcomed by most Western nations, including Australia and New Zealand which were the bastion, parapet of the white race. Any other colour of the skin was considered inferior, an inbreed attitude without any justification.

This is in sharp contrast to the reputation gained by India's neighbours where economic stagnation, religious, ethnic cleansing is the order of the day.

Nirav and Tina, although highly educated but still climbing the ladder on all fronts, were primarily educated in India rather then in the West.

Nirav and Tina, as a newly married couple on honeymoon, had wisely chosen Kohinoor Beachside Resort as their honeymoon destination, especially as they were allocated a beachside bungalow, reserved for honeymooning couple, an isolated place, away from the hustle and bustle of the Complex life.

Nirav and Tina were more interested in exploring each other's body, physically, mentally, sexually and intellectually. But they were also determined not to lock themselves up in their luxurious bungalow but to explore the ground, the deserted beach and all the facilities on offers which were considerable.

Nirav and Tina knew that although seclusion, privacy and obscure location specifically designed for honeymoon couples was important, a God send gift, they will have all the privacy they want in their San Diego apartment. But such an opportunity to enjoy the nature at its best may not come their way that often.

Honeymoon night that one may stretch into a week comes but once in a life time, at least for most of us. Nirav knew that once they return to America, they both would lead a very busy and hectic life, working, studying and laying the foundation for their future happiness and financial wellbeing.

After all, Indians are materialistic people. The phrase, keeping up with Johns and Smiths has been replaced by keeping up with Patels and Shahs, at least in the Indian phrase book. Perhaps that may be one of the reasons why hard workings Indians are welcome with open arms in the West.

Nirav would not rest until he becomes a consultant, a heart specialist, a surgeon and Tina would love to add PhD behind her name, her other qualifications of BSc and MBA. This would enable her to put the word Doctor in front of her name.

Why should she lag behind Nirav? After all Tina was as good as Nirav at studying and turning her dreams into a reality. We are all empowered with the capacity to be genius. It only takes determination and single mindedness.

But her motives were different, not noble. Tina wanted to paddle her exclusionist ambitions and to serve her sanctimonious, self-righteous ambitions for her sole benefits.

Ambition, goal, hunger for success and building empire, financial empire in this day and age drives and inspires people. At one time British people were the most ambitious and enterprising people that enabled them to build an empire, ruling one third of the world population, stretching from Hong Kong in the East to British Guiana and Falkland Islands in the West. Now China has taken up the challenge, the old British hunger and the British mantle to become a global power without parallel.

Indians are a bit late developer when it comes to love making, become sexually active, even though the ancient India gave the world the first book on sex, the one and only book the Kamasutra that has influenced all the modern books and writings on sexual matter.

Nirav and Tina were the prime example, as both were virgin on their honeymoon night. Getting married naturally boosted their sexual drive, their desire and confidence. Nirav was determined to make the most of this lovely location, romantic atmosphere and the warm, blue sea.

Although Nirav and Tina had kissed and cuddled, made love passionately, they had never seen each other without cloth that is until their honeymoon night.

Although Tina was shy or pretending to be shy, she could not dare to stop Nirav when he was in full flight. Moreover Nirav was too strong and too deep in love with Tina to hold back his feelings, his affection, his love and bodily desire, not that Tina wanted it any other way. It seemed Nirav still had atavism, the primitiveness in him that had disappeared from humans as they advanced on the evolution stage.

Tina hardly wore any cloths, certainly not her favourite black, half moon shaped bra while they were in the cottage. For a couple of days, they only left their luxurious and isolated abode to go out to the hotel dinning room for meals rather than have a room service, on the insistence of Tina, as she needed a respite and a break from Nirav's love making intensity and insatiable appetite for sex.

The vast extensive grounds were so artistically manicured and the beach covered with silky smooth and warm sand as well as athul blue waters of the Arabian Sea were so tempting that Nirav and Tina soon decided to keep love making confined to the period of darkness, thus enabling them to take advantage of the beautiful surroundings and the excellent facilities.

They walked bare foot in the hot sand and took a dip in warm water, Nirav admiring Tina coming out of the sea with body dripping, looking like a mermaid that ancient mariners used to dream about, when they used to be on the high seas for up to six months at one go.

Tina, the beautiful, sexy and mesmerizing belle was looking stunning in her all white, all black or canary yellow bikinis that Nirav loved so much to see her wear. But it restricted Nirav from giving her love bites in the exposed parts of her body and that left a tiny small area of her body that Nirav can kiss to his heart's content.

But seeing, watching, observing Tina in such beautiful bikinis more than compensated Nirav for not able to kiss Tina all over her body. The extensive love making had already left her breasts sore and the tips soft and some what swollen, which made Nirav feel guilty, although Tina did not seemed to mind or complain, at least not with conviction.

In fact Tina so often matched Nirav's intensity, made Nirav groan with pain and retreat, backed away to nurse his own wounds, the sharp bites that Tina had inflected on Nirav.

But for Nirav, she was a replica of Ursula Andress, as seen in the 1962 movie Dr No, as she wore similar bikinis, her slim figure allowing her to wear the tiniest of the upper bikini while the lower part of the bikini was punctuated with dots and leather like belt with a buckle as worn by Ursula.

Tina looked as stunning as Ursula, if not better, coming out of water with dripping long wet hair sticking to her body and teasing, permanent smile on her lips. Nirav could not stop clicking his digital camera. They wanted to embrace, treasure every moment in this exotic ancient land that God created in His leisure time.

But Tina could not help but feel beleaguered against the brute, over welling strength of Nirav, who was indeed a strong person physically. But it was about to change in the most unexpected way.

* * *

Chapter Eight
An Excursion with a Difference:

While talking to the chambermaid, exclusively assigned to a couple of honeymoon bungalows, Nirav learnt that there was a dream excursion, not yet on the tourist map, not offered by any tour operator and known only to a handful of taxi drivers who have been in this trade for some time, who were adventurous enough to go where no man has gone before, taking the phrase from the famous series ***Star Trek.***

These pioneers of rare and out of the way excursions have taken Western tourists to the far flung corners of this tiny but beautiful state within Indian Union, with vast, varied and interesting marine life, bird sanctuary, rivers and waterfalls that most of the Western tourists fail to visit, preferring to spend their time on the beach or near the swimming pool, sun bathing, reading and drinking excellent Indian beer, Kingfisher and Cobra.

But fortunately, most NRI tourists do not fall in this trap. They prefer to see as much of the country as possible that is if their social engagements allow any time away from their local relations!

Nirav talked to Sandip, the taxi driver who was the cousin of the chambermaid. He was so convinced that this trip would be an experience to treasure, that Nirav and Tina would cherish as long as they live, that he even offered not to accept any money if they did not like the trip, that if they feel it was a wasted journey.

Sandip's confidence and his description of the excursion more than convinced Nirav and Tina to take a couple of days off from their intense sexual escapade that so often reduced Tina to tears, that is tears of joy, satisfaction, expectation and occasionally unintended pain that is inevitable during a honeymoon period. Even Tina's grunts in that raspy, honey smooth voice excited Nirav. Tina was more than a match for Menka!

Their destination was an old Maratha-Mogul fort on the border with Maharastra and Fort Terekhol hotel on the mouth of a tiny but ever flowing river. As it was a long drive, they left early in the morning, at about 5am, to avoid local traffic, to be as far away from the bustling tourist resort as possible, before the morning rush hour starts in earnest.

The taxi, as usual in Goa, was a specially manufactured vehicle, more like a small Volkswagen Combie than a Saloon car.

Four people can sit in comfort with ample luggage space or a travelling aid who would sit unintrusively at the back and provide all the assistance, all included in the excursion price. But on this occasion, Nirav and Tina did not request such assistance. So Nirav, Tina and Sandip were the only occupants with plenty of spare room for a nap or a cuddle?

Tina, as usual was thorough and had packed an overnight travelling bag and emergency ration, including First Aid Box, in case they have to spend a night away from the hotel.

They travelled through emerald countryside, full of paddy fields, cashew nut trees and fruit orchards. The road so often hugging the distant hills, which looked even more characteristic, romantic and majestic from a distant but the hills inevitably, disappointed us when seen from an arm's length. Then there is an appropriate saying, a proverb in Gujarati that "Mountains are pleasing to eyes from a distance, not when one has to climb it?" How true!

After all Goa is not famous for hill stations and the land is flat on most part, at least on the coastal plain. The Journey was like a slow boat to China, roads were primary once they left the main road network, tourist facilities non existent and in some villages people came out to greet us, as if they were welcoming VIPs, as hardly any one from outside ever set foot in these remote region. Occasional passing tourists were *Marko Polo's* of the modern world.

This was such a remote, off beat place, not far removed from the Nobel Literature Prize Winner author *Rudyard Kipling's* beloved country, his famous writings set in the 18th Century Bharat.

The scenery, the atmosphere and the environment was in perfect harmony, matching the one described in the *Jungle Book*, only the animals like Share Khan, the tiger and Muglai the bear were missing and of course the wild boy Sabu was not seen any where!

The leisurely paced journey took us across the swift, fast flowing rivers, with ancient, antiquated bridges, only used by non motorized vehicles, ready to collapse at the first excuse? No wonder Sandip asked us to walk across while he drove the car over the bridge.

We entered the district of Penem, after crossing the river at Colvale, on the south bank and Macasana on the north bank where we had a well deserved half an hour's break.

Our driver who spoke fluent Kokni, the local dialect spoken throughout Goa, as well as Marathi and English, took us to a nearby village, where we had a cup of traditional Indian tea, heavy on milk and spice and boiled for a while, a favourite of Tina and in fact all Indians but not Nirav's cup of tea who would have an English cup of tea at any time? However Americans prefer coffee over tea, their national drink. But it would be too much to expect coffee in such a remote place.

As it was only 9am in the morning, it was a tea break, although it sounded more like a lunch break, with fresh chapatti, local Nan bread, cooked in clay oven, and fresh vegetables grown in their own patch of land. The food was hot but tasty, consumed in a private house, enjoying the hospitality of the village people at first hand.

As these villages were near the border of Maharastra and many villagers were from Maharastra, they spoke Marathi, beside Kokni. Tina who spoke fluent Marathi and understood Kokni, was at ease and happy, as she was able to dress in her usual attire, the sleeveless, low cut white blouse, with black bra and long trouser and of course her trademark sunglasses, a perfect attire for these villagers who would easily confuse her with their Indian movie heroine!

Moreover she was at ease with women and children who loved some one from a city, especially if she can speak their language fluently. They were curious but impressed looking at Tina, her cloths, as all women wore saris, even at night when they go to bed! This is real India, real Bharat of Lord Rama and Krishna's time.

For these simple villagers, Nirav and Tina were the VIPs who had graced their humble dwelling and refused to accept any payment. Accepting money some how would put a blemish in their tradition, their hospitality.

But Sandip who knew the tradition, had brought with him plenty of old cloths, saris, blouses and skirts, as well as sweets, ball pens, note books, rubber bands and such other presents for children, spending some of the deposit money, advance payment that Nirav gave him.

However on leaving, Tina pressed a note of Rs.200 in the hand of a lovely young girl and no one could ignore Tina's wishes. She was a towering figure, a dominant but pleasing personality who would steal any one's heart.

After leaving the town of Pernem, they left the civilization behind. From here onwards, roads were primitive, rather dirt tracks which ultimately dropped them at the door of *Fort Terekhol hotel*, the only hotel around, within the radius of at least seventy five miles.

Chapter Nine

Fort Terekhol Hotel and the Haunting Fort:

The hotel was built by Marathas in the early 18th century, for the royal families and their guests, to take a break on the sea side, during the oppressive summer months when the temperature routinely touched 100*F inland. The cool breeze from the sea kept the temperature bearable and one can always take a deep in the cool waters of the Indian Ocean!

The hotel, with ten double size en suit bedrooms, three specious suits upstairs, overlooking the estuary, where far below, fishermen in their outriggers, long narrow canoes, struggled furiously against the treacherous swirling current, to earn a subsistence living.

We had a short, two hour's sailing, exploring the river rather than exploring each other, in a small canoe, crisscrossing a maze of shallow, fast flowing waterways, past tiny villages, where adult and children alike rushed to the water's edge to wave at us.

It was Rudyard Kipling country at its best. Nirav had never experienced any thing like this before, nor was he and Tina are likely to experience, encounter, enjoy it again in near future, unless they take a trip down Amazon River in Brazil.

It was getting dark and they were born tired. Moreover the hotel was too tempting to be ignored. Nirav and Tina stayed the night in the upstairs suite, one of the most rustic and unusually romantic place on earth, with two servants to a guest, besides Nirav and Tina; there was only one German couple who were staying for three nights.

There was an hour's grace before the dinner was served. The bar, actually a ting fridge freezer was full of local beer and a few bottles of red and white wine. Nirav had a couple of large bottles of Cobra beer while Tina had a small bottle of red wine before the dinner was served.

The dinner was a real treat, a fresh harvest from the sea; a tuna steak was the main course but not everyone's cup of tea. They enjoyed the fresh vegetable soup, accompanied by garlic nan and fresh mix salad.

As for the main course, the nan, rice, two types of vegetable curries, one a dry bhindi bhaji with onion gravy and the other potato and peas curry in thick tomato puree, accompanied by tomato and onion salad, green salad, yogurt mix, followed by fresh fruit cocktail, thick sweet yogurt lassi (drink) were more than adequate after a long and a hard day on the road.

The drinks and the hot bath before they went down for dinner was the highlight of their stay at the Terekhol hotel if not the excursion, the big circular bath with lukewarm water enabled Nirav and Tina to share the bath, make love to their heart's content, enjoying each other's body until the water became too cold to stay in.

This was the first time after their marriage that Nirav and Tina made love in a soft and gentle manner, Nirav cuddling and kissing every inch of Tina's body that even Tina enjoyed and encouraged Nirav not to stop when Nirav struggled to reach her most inaccessible organs.

In a way this hotel was romantically haunting place. The wind blowing from the sea, passing through every crack, tiny opening, gap in windows and doors and the complete darkness, associated with ghostly silence broken only by hauling of the wind and occasional cries of wild animals.

It provided unique, haunting atmosphere that made Tina cling to Nirav all night, yet they both had sound and refreshing sleep not enjoyed since Nirav landed at the Mumbai airport. In fact it was a perfect honeymoon night, in a four poster luxurious bed, perhaps last slept in by a Mogul Emperor.

Could it be Shah Jehan and his most beautiful bride Mumtaz who inspired him to built Taj Mahal in her memory? Mumtaz gave him nine healthy children and three still births. He found it so difficult to be away from Mumtaz that Shah Jehan used to take Mumtaz with him while he was leading his army in a quest to conquer Rajasthan and Maharastra.

The next day they left the hotel at 9am, after a hefty breakfast and above all a long, sound and peaceful sleep. Nirav could not help but think how wonderful it could have been if they had spent their entire honeymoon week here in the wilderness! They made a point to spend at least three nights here on their next visit to Goa.

The next stop, the object of their desire was the 16th century Maratha Redi Fort, just across the border in Maharastra, once a summer retreat for both Marathas and Mogul Kings, although it was difficult to ascertain where Goa ends and Maharastra begins.

The fort must have been a magnificent structure, a superb piece of architecture in its heydays, with tall soaring towers, deep moat and ramparts with stone parapet. Some of the towers were even equipped with clay ovens to boil water and pour it over the enemy below!

They certainly knew where to build their forts. This fort was overlooking a shallow lagoon, edged by a dazzling white sandy beach, completely deserted, which must put Goa's celebrated beaches into shade.

The fort was in ruins, a sleeping beauty castle, covered with wild vegetation, thick stone walls crumbling with age and neglect. Certainly the modern day Bharat does not know how to preserve their precious and unique heritage, historic monuments of great beauty and importance, that is until some Western charity come and give them a helping hand, a lesion in preserving the past for the future generation.

After browsing through the courtyard, holding on to Tina tightly, occasionally kissing his Mumtaz, while soaking the silent atmosphere, akin to Shah Jahan's tomb, spirit wondering in search of one of the most beautiful and sexy woman Noor Jehan, the Aphrodite of Indian history, sad, silent yet some how fulfilling that would completely drain a young and romantic couple emotionally.

Nirav and Tina had a long stroll, clinging to one another, as if to make sure that no one could separate them, snatch one of them away into perpetual separation.

After the Fort, they had a leisurely stroll on the near empty beach, before they left Maharastra for their beloved Kohinoor Hotel and Beach Complex.

This was one of the most remote; fascinating excursions Nirav had experienced in their travel any where in the world. It was completely off the tourist map and rarely visited by people from other parts of India, even Goa and Maharastra, let alone by tourists from the West.

One can not help but wonder how long it will remain hidden when it has so much to offer, wonderful, unspoilt sandy beach that would put the celebrated beaches of Goa and Kerala in the shade?

For a couple of days Nirav and Tina experienced Rudyard Kipling feelings or rather travelling in the spaceship Enterprise, going where no one has gone before, even forgetting that they were on their honeymoon.

When Nirav said, Beam us up Scotty and nothing happened, they realised that it was real, not just a dream!

When they disembarked at their hotel, Nirav could not help but give Sandip a big hug and a sincere thank you, giving him Rs500 above their agreed price, although Sandip was reluctant to accept it, saying that his price was inclusive of every eventuality, but helpless against Tina's persuasive smile and mild leg pulling, as he was a single person, still in search of his Mumtaz, or perhaps Anarkali, the famous beauty and a courtesan in Emperor Akhbar's court.

Their rest of the stay at the Kohinoor Beach Resort was, in a way an anti-climax, after their excursion into the unknown. Even their love making, to the great relief of Tina was mild, civilized and restrained, that gave Tina's delicate breasts and other private parts of her body some time to recover from the soreness and the bites, some so openly visible when wearing a bikini.

Now Nirav was admiring Tina's beauty, her slim figure in a bikini, her beautiful hair from a distance or gently making love in the soft sand and the athul blue waters.

Tina could not make out what has damped Nirav's enthusiasm. But she was not duly disturbed, as the gentle love making had more passion, real love than the wild orgies.

Chapter Ten

Goodbye Mumbai, Welcome to San Diego

Within two days of returning to Mumbai, Nirav and Tina left for America, as husband and wife, where they were met by Nirav's close friends Anand and Anupama, doctors *and **Prem and Priya***, Prem a senior research pharmacist working in the same hospital as Nirav.

Priya, a shy, petit, kind and caring, an unobtrusive girl, a mother of two lovely children, was a psychologist and a psychiatrist, but commonly known as a shrink in America, a slang word for psychiatrist, in a small private clinic, not too faraway from where Nirav and Prem were employed.

In America, psychologists are in great demand. All professional people, like high flying lawyers, financial experts, surgeons, actors and sport personalities all have their own psychologists, like ordinary people have a GP and a dentist in London.

Priya loved Nirav to bits. He was her younger brother Sanjay who was a diplomat, posted all over the world. He was in Malaysia, acting as a Deputy High Commissioner at the time.

It was difficult for Priya and Sanjay to meet that often but they inevitably talk to each other on the phone practically every week. They were the only children, both highly educated and in demanding profession and happily married.

Prem and Priya came to America a few years ahead of Nirav. So they were well settled in a beautiful, five bedrooms house on the outskirt of San Diego, in an exclusive development, a ***Mount Sinai Residential Complex,*** in a well sought after location, the ***Mt. Helix District,*** in the Orchid Grove Residential Area.

The Orchid Grove is a safe distant away from the coast but Freeway 8 is on the doorstep that would take one all the way to the coast, to the Ocean Beach Park, Golf Course and all the beach facilities, including warm, clear blue water of the Pacific Ocean, a welcome retreat in the summer heat. It is an hour's drive outside rush hour, when motor ways are clear and driving becomes a pleasant experience.

All the houses, a thirty in all were built on a five acre individual plot, with huge garden or backyard. As Prem and Priya were the first to put the deposit when the scheme was publicized, they were able to choose the best plot, a corner one that had more land than the most. It was also backing on an open land, a park, a desert beauty spot that gave them a wonderful view from their bedroom windows.

The swimming pool, the barbecue and the large patio artistically constructed, using local granite was the main feature, not forgetting nearly two acres of matured cacti garden, an artistically created wild area, as if untouched by human hands, with valuable desert plants.

It was the pride and joy of Priya, who had green fingers and was a natural when it came to growing, nurturing rare plants. But in Pedro, they had an excellent gardener who knew every plant native to this region and to his native country Mexico as well.

Priya had one great advantage. She had a deep bore, artesian well that provided all the water needed for such a vast garden and the swimming pool. Although desert plants are hardy, some do need water during the summer excesses when the temperature routinely reaches 50*C. The summer extends at least six to eight months in a year.

For Priya, it was a hobby, a passion, as at the time in California; it was a craze to grow, to collect cacti and similar rare and very old desert plants. As these plants take such a long time to grow, to mature, as some may grow only an inch or two in a year and may flower but once in ten years or even once in a life time, they were in great demand, from botanists, naturalists, self appointed guardians to this wilderness and super rich as wee as conversationalists.

Such high demand led to the reckless digging up of these precious plants from the desert, in the wild where they may be growing for hundreds of years, to be sold on the black market; that is until the State brought in draconian laws making it illegal to dig up any plants growing in the wild, with a one hundred thousand dollar fine and up to ten years imprisonment, not only for the thieves but for any one who buys them from unauthorized, illegal dealers.

That soon put paid to illegal digging up of plants from the wild, a profitable side business for many criminals. Mercifully America does not have many bleeding heart politicians, unlike Britain. The State shows no mercy to habitual criminals; even death penalty is legal, although sparingly used in worse cases. Most Americans are devoted, church going Christians who believe in *"Eye for an eye"* type of justice.

Even planning permissions for housing developments were only granted with strings attached, that is to protect any desert plants which may be more than twenty five years old.

Prem's extensive garden boasted many such expensive plants, some planted by Priya but most were there when this exclusive housing project was inaugurated with just thirty very spacious houses in a plot that can easily accommodate one hundred, but with much smaller gardens or outback that is the trademark for such an eco friendly development.

Pedro had brought many such plants from over the border, as Mexico is just on the doorstep, when it was legal to import plants from Mexico. But today even that route is closed by the Mexican government, following into the footsteps of California.

But by now Priya had build up an enviable collection of desert, semi desert and imported plants that would grow well in this region, with some two hundred feet elevation and dry, hot climate.

Their collection included plants like Acacia Constricta, Sonoran Tree Catclaw, Acacia Pendula Boree that grows to a height of 40 feet, Skunk Tree, Blue leaf Waffle, another tall plant, Big Honey Suckle, Living Rock Bush Cacti, Goat's Horn Cactus with sweet smelling flowers, Aloe Jucunda slow growing plant with pink flowers, Anacacho Orchid Tree, White California Bird of Paradise, Old Man's Cactus, slow growing but can grow up to fifty feet, like a bean poll without leaves, Mediterranean Fan Palm, twenty feet high, pampas grass with long, white flowering stem and Red Torch Cactus with beautiful red flowers.

These are the few of one hundred varieties growing in Priya's vast garden, a nature reserve, a paradise for the wild life, especially the birds. It was the best kept garden, not only on the estate but in the area, occasionally winning prizes, that is when Priya would bothered to enter in such a competition.

This area is famous for poisonous snakes, especially rattle snakes. But the wall surrounding the complex and regular inspection by the wild life expert employed by the Complex management kept all the creepy spooky and crawly creatures out, in the desert where they belong.

Yet Priya would never allow ground hugging plants to cover the land where snakes can hide. She preferred tall, slim plants with clear ground underneath, covered with well cropped short grass that could not give shelter to even a frog, let alone a poisonous snake.

These rare and long growing plants were one of the reasons for five fold increase in house prices in this area. Only rich and professional people at the upper end of the ladder could afford to buy a house in this exclusive complex.

Not only Prem and Priya was such a couple but Prem came from a very wealthy family who paid the substantial initial deposit, to the slight displeasure of Priya. But parents always like to help their children, especially when they have more money then they can ever use.

So often Prem would tease Priya that she married him for his or rather his family's money and Priya would tease back that Prem wanted a highly educated, petit and pretty wife. The life is never a long drawn honeymoon, a permanent holiday. But Prem and Priya's life came pretty close to being a match made in heaven, just like a smiling Buddha raining his blessings on his favourite disciple, in this case his favourite couple!

The whole complex was protected by a ten feet high perimeter fence and regular security patrols with only one entrance manned by an armed security guard, 24 hours a day, seven days a week.

Prem and Priya were one of the highest earning professional couple in San Diego. No wonder they could afford such high living standard with a living in nanny, a petit Mexican American girl, a fluent bilingual, to look after their two children and to teach them Spanish, as some one speaking fluent English and Spanish has a distinct advantage in every walk of life in California, the state flooded with Mexican Americans who are hard working and dependable workforce.

Nirav was indeed very fortunate to have such good, loyal, kind and caring friends, especially Priya who loved Nirav to bits, in the absence of her own brother Sanjay. She transferred, bestowed all her sisterly love to Nirav.

Prem so often teased Nirav that he comes second best in Priya's esteem. Prem and Priya were like close family members for Nirav, whose success on all fronts Nirav wanted to imitate, to emulate.

Within two weeks of their return from Mumbai, Prem and Priya threw a grand party in their vast backyard, to celebrate the holy union, the marriage of Nirav and Tina, inviting close friends and work mates.

The Indian community in San Diego was very small but as Los Angles is just a three hours drive once on the motorway, their friend circle include many doctors residing in the big city.

Tina, who normally is the heart and soul of any party, was quiet and subdued. Then perhaps this was a big change in her life-style. She naturally felt a bit out of place, although every one tried to make her feel at home, comfortable and part of the crowd. Tina felt at ease with Prem who is an easy going person who can get along even with the devil. He took Tina under his wing and introduced her to every one.

But in sharp contrast, Priya was a cautious person who will take her time to know a person, give her seal of approval. But once the person gains her trust, she would go out of her way to be nice, friendly, helpful and hospitable.

It took a long time for Nirav to gain Priya'a trust but now Nirav was her younger brother who could do nothing wrong. She would go a mile for Nirav and he knew and appreciated her loyalty.

The love, friendship, admiration, esteem and respect between Priya and Nirav were the prime example. They were like twins, a brother and a sister who would understand each other perfectly, like telepathy, like reading each other's mind, thoughts.

The party was a great success. Every one liked Tina, admired her dress sense and above all loved her long, dark, silky hair, as most hard working professional girls could not afford the time or the effort to look after such long hair, as it has to be washed, shampooed, nourished and arranged all the time to keep them healthy and growing.

They congratulated Nirav for unearthing such a jewel, a Bombay beauty and bringing her to San Diego. With love bites fading fast, Tina was able to dress normally, that is her sleeveless and low cut top but with midi skirt rather than trouser, as she was not yet familiar with the local dress sense.

Tina soon found out that her dress sense was not out of place in this hot and dry climate where temperature routinely touch 40* in summer months After all Tina was a connoisseur, an expert at socialising.

* * *

Chapter Eleven
Settling Down in Daily Routine

Slowly but surely Tina and Nirav were getting into their daily routine. Tina found a part time job, teaching IT to deprived children in a City College and attending advance English classes with the intention of doing PhD. Tina was now as busy as Nirav, laying the foundation of her future in America.

The time flies when one is busy. It was difficult for Nirav to pinpoint but he felt that they were, slowly but surely, even systematically drifting apart. Tina was polite but indifferent. Their love making lacked passion, the intensity and adoration that should be natural in a newly married couple was lacking.

Nirav also noticed that it was Tina and not him who was changing. Nirav was as eager as ever to cling to Tina, be passionate, rekindle their honeymoon spirit if not the intensity but it was impossible to do so when Tina was trying to disengage, opt out, move away from Nirav, in a tactful but determined and upsetting manner.

Nirav new that if he fails to tackle this problem, get to the root of Tina's strange behaviour, he may be trapped in a marriage without love, passion, sex and happiness.

Nirav loved Tina too much for such a situation, such a scenario to take roots, become a norm. Nirav wanted his life, their lives to be an oasis of enlightenment, enmeshed in love, care and happiness without bounds. Nirav wanted to feel oneness with his domestic life, pay tribute to the symphony of nature, to explore the realm of extraordinary in a marriage with his dream girl with whom he fell in love at first sight.

It would be impossible to plan for the future, to settle down, buy a house and start a family, although it was too early to think that far ahead. Nirav wanted his married life to mirror that of Prem and Priya, full of love, devotion, fun and happiness. But Tina's attitude made it impossible. Nirav's serenity and angelic nature was perhaps taken by Tina as a sign of weakness, some one she could manipulate and deceive, use and misuse. Nirav would like to resolve this situation before it became the San Andreas Faults that is permanent, ever present, one situation no one could resolve.

Nirav decided to open his heart, to air his problem to Prem and Priya. If any one can help him, Priya can and definitely would. She would go a mile; do any thing humanly possible to bring a smile and happiness in Nirav, her brother's life.

So one day, three of them met in Priya's private, consulting room when all three had a half day off. Priya encouraged Nirav to open his heart, to tell her every minute detail, not to feel nervous, hold back or feel embarrassed in any way. Priya's training helped Nirav to open up, talk openly and frankly.

It took Nirav two hours of almost non-stop talking to open his heart, tell Priya every minute detail that so often brought tears in Priya's eyes. For Priya, a trained psychologist with PhD to add to her other qualifications, it was a daily routine to listen to her patients.

Yet her eyes were wet, her heart filled with emotion, while listening to Nirav, her baby brother who was the apple of her eyes, the most important person in her life, after Prem and children.

Prem was lost, did not know what to make of this tragic situation. Priya had her doubts as soon as she laid her eyes on mischievous, attractive but sweet and tantalising Tina with multifarious personality.

She now knew what mischief, what game Tina may be playing with Nirav's life, how much she can hurt Nirav if allowed, given a free hand. For Tina the marriage was an acquisition, a conquest, not the merger of two souls till death us do part. Nirav was handicapped right from the start. This was any thing but a summit of serenity for Nirav whose euphoria, happiness was extremely ephemeral. They were definitely not on Mount Sinai!

After some deliberation and when she gained her composure, Priya said, "Bhaiya, (brother) it hurts me so much to see you unhappy. I know exactly what is going on, what Tina is doing, that Tina is taking you for a ride. I have come across many cases like yours before.

But I would not say any thing now. Let us meet after a week or two, here in my surgery, as it is the safest place to talk. Whatever any one says who is my patient remains confidential. Not even a court can demand to see my files. But as you would have noticed, I have made no notes, not taped this conversation. So there is absolutely no record of this conversation ever taking place.

Bhaiya, here in America, we have to be ultra careful. Even the walls of this office are sound proof and no one can hear us outside, no bugging device works here. That is why we should only talk in this office. But Nirav, be careful, do not let Tina even to suspect that you have opened your heart to me, let alone talked about her, your problem, the state of your marriage.

Let us play this game as she would like you to, let her think that you are naïve, you are madly in love with her, that she is the apple of your eyes, that you would put up with any of her antics"

Then looking at Prem, she said, "Prem, be careful when you talk to her, on phone or in person. If Tina suspects any thing, then Prem will be her first target, the most obvious person to squeeze, as you not only work with Nirav but are also married to me. "Then added with a smile, "Tina is much more intelligent than both of you put together. But she does not know me well.

That is to our advantage." That brought a smile on Nirav's face and said, "Thank you sister for your confidence in me, my darling sister."

Nirav had blind faith and trust in Priya. He knew no one can fool Priya or hide any thing from her prying eyes. This was her professional training and Nirav's confidence was not misplaced in any way.

If any one can help Nirav, Priya can and will. But he was taken back at Priya's assessment of Tina, who was like a female scorpion who would sting her partner to death after making love, having sex.

* * *

227

Chapter Twelve
Tina's Past Catches Up

Nirav was eagerly waiting for their next meeting. He did not have to wait for long. But this time Prem preferred to remain in the reception area and let Nirav and Priya discuss, resolve, solve the problem. He knew that the problem, the situation was far from idyllic as it once appeared to be, the one that could be resolved with a cuddle and a cup of tea.

Although Prem was outwardly jolly, easy going and carefree, in reality he was sensitive, unable to handle such mental pressure, inner pain of the heart and mind. In deed he was a gentle giant with a heart of gold whose motto seems to be embracing every moment of his time in this exotic land, charming wife and loving family. He was living in an oasis of enlightenment, fulfilment and sheer joy and happiness.

It is part of human nature to pretend, to kid our selves that we are capable of handling any and every problem, any eventuality that the nature, the society throws at us. But in time we realise, acknowledge the time of shared endeavour, strive to share, lessen the strain and pain in a way only humans can.

We seek comfort in drinks, drugs and counselling. I wonder who wrote that after twenty five alcopops, even mother Superior would take her bra off! Is it human mentality, our strength and weakness to laugh off our misgivings, our problems, our shortfalls in a way that no other living creature can!

Priya was in pensive mood. Without beating around the bush, Priya said, "Bhaiya, it breaks my heart but I feel it is my duty to warn you, to tell you the truth, however painful it may be. I knew Tina when she was in the college. When Tina was in the first year, I had just completed my master's degree in psychology.

I stayed on to teach, a real honour for me, as such a privilege is only granted to the most brilliant students. Even then Tina was well known for her provocative dress sense; sleeveless white cotton low cut blouse and black uplifting bra, so often accompanied by a mini skirt in true crinoline fashion that would easily show her black knickers as well.

No wonder she was able to create turmoil in so many male hearts with provocative dress sense as well as her physical mischief-making. God had given her the most wonderful assets and a playful nature to make any man weak at the knees.

She had irrepressible personality, even for the most confident and self assured males on the university compound. She was a gregarious, irresistible personality by nature. Men would be attracted to her like bees to a honey bearing flowers.

The insouciant assumption was that the liaison with Tina would be an experience to treasure, to cherish later on in life, in old age.

Tina was always surrounded by desirable males and she knew how to manipulate one against the other, to keep them all dandling on the tenterhook with bated breath. Men were mere boys, puppets on a long string who would dance to her tune.

In the last two weeks I have gathered a lot more information on Tina. She was a popular student, always seen in the company of most eligible boys. Moreover she was good at sports, especially tennis and swimming where she excelled. No wonder she was known as mermaid!

Even young professor used to fancy her and that boosted her confidence, not to mention her success on the educational front. She used her charm like agronomy, like a bulging bank balance regularly replenish by an underground water reserve.

I understand that before Tina left the college, she fell in love with a handsome boy who was also the son of the college principal, Dr. Ravindra Sharma. Most probably she is still in love with him and perhaps this marriage is a sham, to come to America, to get the Green Card that will enable her to bring her boy friend here later on.

I wish I am wrong, that Tina is simply passing through a bad phase, a difficult time in her life. But some how I know that not only I am right but it may be the tip of the iceberg. So far, bhaiya you have seen nothing of her evil intention, cunning plan that may ruin you for ever.

But I have a plan to thwart her evil scheme that will only work if you can fool her, let her go on believing that you love her, trust her and nothing has changed. Every plant in the garden is in the bloom and your relation with Tina is as idyllic as ever. But you have to prepare yourself, as if you fail to prepare, then be prepared to fail, which is not an option for you.

The spark of life should flicker as bright as ever. Any sarcasm in your heart should not come to surface. This will be your personal odyssey of the self. I must keep in the background, not seen too often with you. Otherwise it will be ominous for your wellbeing in every way imaginable"

"Above all, be your normal self, keep to your daily routine and do not do any thing out of the ordinary. Try to look, keep busy until you get the opportunity to find out what her plans are.

If her intention is evil, in any way detrimental to your wellbeing, then dump her like a hot potato, before she realized what hit her. If I am wrong, then obviously she will never come to know about this meeting. This is the first lesion in psychology of winning."

"Believe me Bhaiya, there is no such thing as perfect crime. She will slip up sooner or later. This is a mind game, a game of chess, of wits and the person who is cool, calm, calculating and cunning will win in the end. I hope that person is you and I will be with you all the way."

Nirav had never seen Priya so serious but she was cool, calm and determined. They had heart to heart talk, discussed the plan in detail for two hours before they joined Prem in the reception.

Now Nirav realised why Priya did not want Prem to know their plan. It would not be fair on Prem to be burdened with such a secret, as he was not a trained doctor, a psychologist.

Although revelation about Tina came as a shock and a surprise, Nirav was cool, calm and determined to find out what Tina was up to. He also knew that Priya is seldom wrong in her judgement, in her assessment. In Nirav's case, she would go an extra mile to come to a right decision, right conclusion. If there was any doubt in her mind, then she would have kept quiet, tried to help Nirav and Tina to come closer, save their marriage. But she knew Nirav's present problem was a tip of an iceberg.

It was now up to Nirav how to tackle, to execute the plan and be free of Tina and teach her a lesson she will not forget as long as she lives. It would not be nice, pleasant in any way but this was not a game. Indeed it was a gamble, do or die situation no one faces in real life.

The opportunity Nirav was looking for came a bit sooner than he expected. But he was ready, fully prepared.

Chapter Thirteen
Time for Payback!

***In** less* than a year since Nirav and Tina got married, Tina received fantastic news. Her elder brother Shyam was getting married. That means Nirav and Tina will have to go to Mumbai, as Tina was the only girl in the family, the only sister to her two brothers, one elder and the other younger than her.

Nirav, as brother in law, has the right, the privilege to act, to deputise as Shyam's, the groom's best man. That is the Indian tradition. By now Nirav had taken over most of the responsibilities to run the home smoothly, so that Tina could concentrate on her work and her studies, as Tina was eager to add PhD behind her name and the word doctor in front of her name.

Tina was working, studying hard, as busy as a bee! That also gave her the reason to keep a bit of a distance, not to let Nirav climb all over her all the time. But Nirav was determined to give her one tormenting night, now and again, so as not to raise any doubt in her mind that Nirav may be drifting away from her, although that would have pleased her in a strange way. This was a mind game, a game of two halves.

This seemed a perfect arrangement for Tina, to enjoy one stormy love making session but being free for the rest of the week, even a fortnight. After all she was a young and a healthy girl who needed love, sex and sexual excitement in her life now and then. Nirav was, in any one's esteem a good catch, a handsome, highly educated person any girl would be proud to have him as her husband. Tina was aware of her good luck.

Nirav and Tina agreed that while Nirav should go for two weeks, as he had used up most of his leave, his holidays, Tina could remain in Mumbai for four weeks, so that she can spend some time with her parents, especially with her ailing father who was in poor health.

Tina would also like to know her Bhabhi (sister in law) as she may not get another opportunity for some time. Moreover she can continue her studies, as it mostly involved research and writing thesis that can be done from any where, with the help of a computer and a few books.

She was writing thesis on applied economics, particularly the effect of rapid development of San Diego, as a desirable residential area and a centre for medical excellence. The local university would love to publish such a book, written by a local student.

The town was expanding very fast, with residential and retirement complexes, shopping malls, medical centres, holiday resort, nature reserves, reforestation to make the land green that would attract more tourists.

After all San Diego was only a few hours drive from the bulging and polluted city of Los Angeles. The residents of LA would like to get away from the pollution to the clean and crispy air of San Diego, with vast open spaces, desert scenery and nature at its best. Most wealthy Los Angelis residents would prefer to have a second, a holiday home in the vicinity of this great, fast expanding town, on the verge of acquiring the status of a city.

If fast train, a bullet train that travels at more than 200 mph and connects the main two cities of Tokyo and Yokohama, could be built to connect San Diego with Los Angles, then this small sleepy town will soon become an extended suburb of the bulging city of Los Angles, a town on the commuter belt, as with modern technology, most people can work from home, popping in the office may be once or twice a week.

The information technology works wonders, distance has become irrelevant and a bedroom in the house can be converted into an office, saving rush hour travel time and the inconvenience.

This arrangement suited Tina right to the ground. It will give her a couple of weeks to be with her boyfriend; although outwardly she protested that she would miss Nirav so much. But Nirav was ready, taking Tina in his strong arms and giving her a passionate kiss that almost suffocated Tina, Nirav said, "Tina I will miss you ten times more than you will miss me. After all you will be with your family, while I will be alone here."

"When you come back, I want a repeat of the night we spent in the Fort Terekhol Hotel when we spent the whole night in each other's arms. Now you are more beautiful and sexy than ever. Even your breasts are much fuller and turgid while your buttocks do show up. I find it difficult not to pinch them when you come out of shower!"

"I know I am going to enjoy so much. There is so much more of you for me to give you love bites. I have almost forgotten how sexy you look in your bikinis. Perhaps we can go to Mount Laguna Nature Reserve for a long week-end to rediscover each other. It is time we discover some of the most beautiful spots right on our door-step, within a few hours' drive from San Diego."

This flattery reassured Tina that Nirav was still as mad, as madly in love with her as ever, that she had not lost any of her charm, wit or her sexiness. Indeed her breasts were much fuller now that she had put on some weight, making her curvier sexier, more visible, as she was too thin before. Who says flattery works but once? In Nirav's case, it worked every time. Then again Nirav was sincere almost to a fault, most of the time. Nirav's blandishment was at its best as he knew this was game he could not afford to lose, as he would lose his life's savings, his endeavour and his happiness for ever if he fails.

Shyam, Tina's brother was getting married to a girl in Baroda. The night before the marriage party's departure by special train, Nirav was violently sick with vomiting and diarrhoea. So Nirav was unable to travel with the party in a special, air conditioned compartments popular with Western tourists.

It upset every one, especially Shyam and Tina who even offered to stay behind to look after Nirav. But Nirav knew how important this occasion was for Tina. Nirav convinced every one that this was just a case of bad food poisoning.

He does not want to take any chances by travelling a long distance, cooped up in a railway compartment. But he would be as good as gold within the next two days and if necessary he would not hesitate to admit himself in a hospital and go on a drip. But it was most unlikely, as he was drinking plenty of fluid with mineral supplements.

The visiting doctor, a family friend was of the same opinion and that reassured every one, including Tina and Nirav's parents. He even confirmed that Nirav will be able to fly to Baroda in two days time. There was no reason not to be optimistic.

The marriage was on Sunday but the party, consisting of some fifty people would leave Mumbai by train, in a first class air conditioned compartment, on Wednesday, so that Shyam can have a Stag Night on Friday and be ready for Sunday ceremony.

Shyam and his wife had arranged an unusual honeymoon. They would fly to Trivandram, stay at the Palm Beach Resort and sail the Kerala backwaters for three nights, in a converted rice boat, specially prepared for honeymooning couple.

It would be much larger than the ordinary boat, having a double bedroom and a rooftop deck, as well as a comfortable deck at the back that will give complete privacy that a honeymooning couple may need.

This was a new concept and may not be a cup of tea for every newly wedded couple but in the middle of a lake, the privacy would be more assured than in a hotel.

The way Nirav and Tina spent their honeymoon, made love and climbed over each other, perhaps would have been difficult in such a confined space. But then Sanjay and Sarita were having a two week honeymoon.

So they can afford to be gentle to each other for three nights only? More over, these boatmen or the crew are well trained to be unintrusive, out of sight, almost invisible and will only appear when called upon. This tiny boat could be as luxurious as a cruse liner with more attentive staff and only two passengers?

As the train for Baroda would leave at 2pm, it was agreed to meet at the Mumbai Centre at 1pm sharp. Nirav's mum and dad and Tina left the house at 11am by taxi, giving them one extra hour to counter traffic or any emergency, such as accident.

Nirav touched his parents' feet, hugged Tina and said in an emotional voice, "Tina, I love you. Please do not worry. I will be there on time and take care of my parents. I will text you with flight details on Saturday morning. I will go straight to our hotel by a taxi.

But keep your mobile on all the time once you reach Baroda and have settled down in the hotel. Have a wonderful trip. After all such an auspicious occasion comes but once in a life time. Make the most of it." Nirav's voice was chocked with emotions. He knew this was a goodbye and he would not see either Tina or his parents for a long time.

Nirav sounded so genuine. Perhaps he was feeling guilty about what was going to happen to Tina, an earthquake in their lives and only one will survive, come out on top. That would be Nirav.

"Please give me a ring when the train leaves the Mumbai Central. Once I receive your call, I will take Valium and go to sleep but not before I have spoken to you."

Nirav had really taken Priya's advice to heart. Failure meant the end of his dream, a life long humiliation, out smarted, out thought and mugged by a smug, heartless woman with deadly intention. Failure was not an option for Nirav. Failure would be like a lingering death, a death of thousand cuts.

* * *

Chapter Fourteen

The Perfect Execution of Nirav's Plan

Not far from Nirav's home, there was a travel agent's office, who was the main agent for British Airways and a couple of American Airlines.

As soon as Tina and his parents left, Nirav gave a ring to the travel agent, on his mobile, so as not to keep his land line busy, to find out if there was any direct flight to Los Angles later that evening.

The only flight available was with BA, one leaving at 8pm. It will reach Heathrow Airport at 6am in the morning, Mumbai time. There will be a two hour wait before it will take off for Los Angles. But only business and first class tickets were available. All economy class tickets were sold out, unless Nirav would like to be on the stand-by.

Nirav reserved a business class one and promised to collect the tickets by 3pm at the latest. Nirav knew that he could not leave the house until the train departs for Baroda and he receives Tina's phone call.

Fortunately for Nirav, the train was on time. Tina rang him at ten to two, telling Nirav that they will soon be on their way. Nirav requested Tina to pass the phone to his mother to say the final farewell.

The Indian railway station is like a fish market or a stock exchange where every one is shouting at the top of their voices. There are all sorts of voices at the railway station but the human voice normally drowns all other noise.

After talking to Tina and his mother, Nirav was satisfied that they were indeed on the train and on their way to Baroda, out of touch for at least twelve hours, more than enough time to leave Mumbai without any one knowing it. Surprise and secrecy was the name of the game, a win or lose situation. For Nirav, it was like a Hobson's choice, miss it and it will be the end of his dream. There will be nothing left to ponder, to build the life on.

Nirav's suitcase was already packed, as he had only taken out the essential items, as and when necessary. But Nirav removed all unnecessary items, such as extra clothing. He wanted to travel light, pass the custom quickly and without any questions. He even left behind his cameras.

Now all Nirav needed was their passports, return tickets which will seal Tina's future. Passports and tickets were in the safe. Nirav also opened Tina's suitcase and checked it thoroughly. He found photocopies of their passports, including the pages stamped by the US authority giving Tina the permission to stay in the country indefinitely.

Perhaps Tina was just cautious, in case their passports may get lost or stolen. Nirav had himself taken out photocopies and kept them in the file. Tina had just picked up some of these and brought them with her.

He destroyed, burnt these copies and put the passports, return tickets in his briefcase before he went to the travel agent to pay and collect his one way ticket to Los Angles.

As usual in Mumbai, NRIs, especially the Americans receive a VIP treatment. As soon as Nirav sat down, a peon brought him a cold bottle of Pepsi. The agent by the name of Piyush, encouraged Nirav to take up a first class ticket, as the difference was only $500 and that also include the privilege of using VIP lounge, special counter to pass the Customs and boarding first, with all the food and drinks included. As less then one third first class tickets were taken up, the agent was eager to sell one to Nirav.

VIP lounges are really luxurious, providing all sorts of facilities that include tea and coffee, shower and shave and privileged boarding without queuing. But the best advantage was that Nirav would be able to sleep comfortably all the way to Heathrow and beyond.

As Piyush came to know Nirav better and realized that Nirav was not in good health, he went out of his way to help Nirav. After spending some twenty minutes on the computer and on the phone, he came up with very good news.

Nirav could disembark at Miami airport and there was a connecting flight from Miami to San Diego, right at Nirav's door-step, thus saving him a four hour journey by car, from Los Angeles airport to San Diego. It was a God send opportunity that Nirav took it with gratitude, even though it cost him $200 more. But this time spending money was the least of his worries. The God was indeed smiling on Nirav, as every plan went without a hitch.

Nirav readily accepted the offer to upgrade his ticket to first class. Piyush who by now was like a friend, also arranged an air conditioned Mercedes car for just $40 to pick him up from his house four hours before departure, making it sure that nothing could go wrong.

Nirav knew that he will get but one opportunity, the only chance to secure his future, miss it and his life will be hell. The cheating, lies and deception on the part of Tina have been so constant that Nirav's anger, his desire for revenge was like a smouldering ember burning quietly, slowly gathering the energy, the power before revealing the full extent of its destructive power that would chard every thing that stood in its path. It would be like a volcano exploding.

When Nirav returned home, he had just one hour to rest and recuperate, recover and convalesce. He made a few quick telephone calls, to his sister, a friend and the doctor, reassuring every one that he was fine and not to worry, to phone or to disturb him, as he may take a sleeping pill and sleep until late next day. He will ring them if he needs their help or assistance. As Nirav himself was a doctor, every one knew that he could take care of himself.

Nirav left a short note on the dining table for Tina that he has gone to a nearby hill station with a friend and will give her a ring soon. Nirav wanted to keep his plans, that he had left Mumbai a secret as long as he could, even after he had reached America.

With the help of Piyush, the travel agent and his first class ticket, Nirav sailed through the customs with ease, negotiated all obstacles, immigration formalities without a hitch. These agents are so influential who would help in each and every way to a favoured client!

* * *

Chapter Fifteen

The Home Return with Difference?

In less than half an hour Nirav was safely resting in the VIP lounge. His first act, before he sat down with a cup of coffee and a newspaper, was to go to the conveniences, the wash room. He tore out two pages from Tina's passport, the one with her name and details and the second one with USA visa, the immigration stamp, confirming her residential status.

Nirav could not dare to burn these pages, in case it may trigger the fire alarm. But he cut them into numerous tiny pieces with a scissors borrowed from the VIP lounge attendant and flushed them down the toilet. It took three flushes for all the pieces to disappear.

Now Nirav knew that there is no way Tina could return to America, to mess up his life. She had no passport, no ticket, no papers and no friends in America who could help her.

In a way, Nirav felt sad and guilty. Although Nirav had a short married life with Tina, they had some wonderful time together, in Shivaji Nature Reserve, Shalimar Roof Garden, Kohinoor Beach Resort and the excursion into the unknown, the wild and exciting love making that so often reduced Tina to tears. But they were tears of joy, pain and satisfaction. But this mischief on the part of Tina was not peccadillo, a trivial mischief that Nirav could forget and forgive in a hurry.

The doubt only surfaced during the last few months when Tina's mood changed. Nirav realised that her heart was not in their love making. Although she tried her best, she was not able to fool Nirav, a trained doctor who can judge the change of mood, the underlying fault-line and differentiate the real joy with a put-up job.

But the file Tina kept on her computer was dynamite. If Nirav had been caught napping and their divorce had gone to court, it would have ruined Nirav's life for good, even branded him a sex pest, cruel and unfit to practice medicine. This was a foul pigmentation in Tina's character that Nirav could not comprehend, as Tina was by no means a plebeian girl who would be overwhelmed by the glitter of America.

Perhaps Nirav may even be forced to leave America if Tina had succeeded in the execution of her near perfect plan. Nirav shivered, a cold sweat covered his forehead at the thought of the consequences of Tina's action. Was the ride that is his brief but extremely satisfying encounter with Tina on the sexual front worth the fall? Not in a million years.

The plane, a Boing 747 was as luxurious as any one could expect. Nirav converted his front row seat into a comfortable bed. The air steward could not be more helpful, more sympathetic, especially when Nirav told her that he was a doctor and was suffering from a bad attack of diarrhoea and vomiting for the last two days, that he was on a four hourly medication, required to drink plenty of fluid with dioralyte, a mineral supplement to replace the loss of minerals due to diarrhoea.

Nirav had a comfortable night, albeit with the help of a 10mg Valium. When he woke up early in the morning, he was a bit lethargic. But there was no sign of diarrhoea or vomiting which was, in a way, self inflicted wounds, to avoid going to Baroda with the marriage party. So the cure was simple, in his own hands.

The VIP lounge at Heathrow Airport was indeed comfortable and well furnished. Nirav showered, shaved and had a hefty breakfast. He phoned Prem and Priya, gave them the good news and requested them to meet him at the San Diego airport which was in any case right on their door-step, saving them a long and tiresome drive to Los Angeles.

The flight from Miami to San Diego was uneventful, in a small plane with a capacity of some fifty passengers, but as usual, it was only half full, giving Nirav all the space he needed to lie down and relax.

When Nirav landed at San Diego airport, both Prem and Priya were there to meet him. He hugged Prem and could not let go Priya, with tears freely flowing from his eyes. He could not decide whether the tears were of joy, sorrow or just the relief, as he escaped a close shave, an encounter with the devil.

Priya let Nirav to empty his tear tank, let his heart which was in turmoil for some time, to settle down, feel the relief before saying, "Bhaiya, I am so proud of you and your courage. You have out thought, out manoeuvred and defeated a very clever, beautiful, sexy but determined, vindictive and a wicked, cruel woman."

Then looking at Prem, she continued, "I don't think my Prem could have successfully carried out this plan."

Now it was Prem's turn to comment, "You know Nirav, Priya is absolutely right. I do not have even half of your patience or temperament. I am glad that I have married one of the kindest, cleverest and a loving woman in the world. Next time you should leave it to us to find you a nice girl."

"I do not think there will be a next time, at least not for a long time." Nirav said with a sweet bitter smile. Then added, "

"Bhaiya lets wait and see, not jump the gun." Priya tried to reassure Nirav who naturally sounded so bitter.

There was no way Prem and Priya would let Nirav go to his empty flat, full of memories. Prem had collected most of his essentials as soon as Nirav rang him from Heathrow and that included all his important files and papers, books and statements, on the advice of Priya, who would not under estimate Tina under any circumstances. She had read her diary.

The guest room was already prepared in anticipation of Nirav able to accomplish the tricky mission, a difficult mission if not impossible one. So when they reached their home, appropriately named "*Casa Grande*" a Spanish word which means a Grand or a big house, it was 10pm Mumbai time. Nirav had undertaken a gruelling journey of more than 24 hours, with two stop over, at Heathrow and Miami.

It was a wise decision on part of Nirav to travel first class, that enabled him to rest and sleep all the way. Yet he was shattered, physically, mentally and emotionally.

Although it was midday in San Diego, Nirav went straight to bed, to the disappointment of children who were so fond of uncle Nirav, as he loved playing with them, taking them out to park, McDonald and Pizza Hut, spoiling them rotten to the slight annoyance of Prem and Priya, who were although kind and caring parents, were never the less disciplinarian.

They would not like to spoil them rotten as most American parents do. When Nirav handed an envelop to Priya and said, "Priya, this is my gift to you, the most charming and caring sister any one could have," there was pride and satisfaction in his heart.

Priya opened the envelop which contained Tina's passport but without her name or any detail. Priya burnt it over the gas cooker with a smile of satisfaction and gave Nirav a hug and a smile of relief.

Chapter Sixteen

The Dawn of the New Beginning

Next day when Nirav got up at down local time, having slept some eighteen hours, he felt a bit less tired, relaxed and free, as if a great burden was lifted. It was Friday. He checked his mobile for messages but there were none.

Nirav was now fully recovered from his self inflicted wounds of diarrhoea. He spent the day sitting in the garden, under the shade, drinking lemonade and fruit juices, keeping away from beer, his favourite drink, at least until his tummy was back to normal.

In the afternoon he had a nap and before going to bed late at night, Nirav sent a simple text to Tina, "Darling, I can not make it. I can not get a booking, as the flight is full. But I am fine, in good health and miss you. Have a fun and see you soon." Nirav did not want to rock the boat, at least not until they return from Baroda on Tuesday, as his parents were with Tina, in her care.

By the time they return, Tina would realise straight away what has happened. But even Tina, a resourceful, self confident person of immense ability indeed could do nothing; could not harm Nirav in any way, without her passport, papers and her return ticket. Indeed Nirav had put her where she belonged. She would need Nirav's cooperation, his affidavit even to submit any papers.

Nirav still had one week left before he has to resume duty. He decided, with the encouragement of Priya and Prem not to return to work early but not to let any one know that he was back in San Diego.

It was a half term holiday in school. With children at home, they were the perfect antidote for Nirav to banish Tina out of his mind, out of his system, and rebuilt his confidence, his trust and faith in his fellow human beings.

But looking at Prem and Priya, Nirav knew that Tina was an exception to the rule and not the norm. Without Prem and Priya, Tina could have taken him to a cleaner. Priya guided and advised Nirav every step of the way and gave him the courage to carry out the plan that involved the nerves of steel and cunningness of a fox.

Every cloud has a silver lining, even a cumulus cloud. One can not go through life on a bed of roses. Occasionally a thorn does pierce, prick one's finger. It is part of life, the way of nature. Could any one have better friends than Prem and Priya? The God dealt him a bad card in Tina, perhaps by mistake or that Tina may have fooled even the God.

Who said that after all, God is human? Was it the Chinese philosopher Confucius or the Greek Socrates?

After all one can not go through life crystal gazing. Perhaps this was a lucid period in his life. Nirav remembered a joke he read some where, a long time ago, that perhaps match his misfortune? A middle aged woman was badly hurt in a car accident. She thought she was going to die. But one night the God came into her dream and told her that she still has thirty five years left, to live and enjoy her life.

Soon she got better and having received a good compensation, she decided that as she has so many years left, why should she not spend this money on her, making her look beautiful, sexy and attractive.

She visited a plastic surgeon and had a breast enlargement, fuller lips; all her wrinkles were removed that gave her a smooth face with silky skin to match her already near perfect slim figure, hair transplant, so that now she had a head full of long, blonde and beautiful hair, in place of short, light brown hair.

She employed a fitness guru, a personal trainer to keep her in good shape. She looked stunning, at least ten years younger and every one commented about her transformation, from an ordinary, middle aged, unintrusive woman no one would look at twice, to a charming, attractive, self confident woman that would turn many heads.

One day, while crossing the road, wearing a high hill shoes, she was run over by a bus and got killed. When she asked God why this tragedy, when the God promised her a long life, the God apologetically said that she had changed so much that he failed to recognize her. So no wonder Nirav failed to recognize Tina with all her charm, beauty, sexiness and inbuilt deceitful nature and she did not even need a plastic surgeon?

Nirav was determined to make the most of his free week to sort his life. He knew that whether he likes it or not, he will have to write, get in touch with Tina, as without her cooperation, he would not be able to get a quick divorce. But before he visits a lawyer for advice, he must write, draft a letter to Tina and show it to his lawyer before posting it.

* * *

Chapter Seventeen

The Final Goodbye and Farewell to Tina

After a long deliberation, soul searching and a push from Priya who helped him to draft the letter, Nirav managed to write to Tina a lengthy letter, explaining her why he did what he did. She had left him with no choice.

"Tina

As you know I was madly in love with you the moment we mat at a friend's wedding reception. For me, it was a love at first sight, although it was a completely different matter for you. But you played your part to perfection. Perhaps you may have a long training, a good teacher or you are a natural, a born actress! Then our mythology is full of stories with beautiful, sensuous women like you bring down honest, decent, even sages and the supreme God Lord Shiva!

There was impalpability in your every move, beyond the grasp of an innocent person like me. You made the use of kidology like an expert. Perhaps you belonged to ossified traditions. Every thing you said, did was hypocritical masquerading as sincerity and sentimental rhetoric disguised as truth. It was indeed the tyranny of improvised thinking expertly executed.

You had the charm and the attraction of the fatal and chaotic Kennedy Clan. I became the victim of the same fatal attraction. I can not help but wonder whether your entire upbringing was carefully orchestrated to put you on the highest pedestal by any means, fair or foul.

But then your family is too decent to install such crap values in their children. Perhaps you are an exception to the rule, the only scandalous liaison, the only skeleton in the cupboard.

It is beyond any reasonable doubt that you suffer not from credit crunch, but moral, decency crunch, a character that is so foreign to most Indians, especially to our charming and beautiful Indian girls who on most part are morally superior to your Western counterpart. Then there is always an exception to the rule, a single rotten egg in otherwise a basket full of nutritious ingredients.

I passionately believe in the Hindu doctrine known as Karma, one reaps what one sows; a patriot action leads to the elevation of soul. Perhaps I may have planted the wrong seeds in my previous life, or could it be the other way round?

In a way, you were my first girl friend, the first girl I kissed so passionately, in a romantic picnic spot, the ***Shivaji Nature Reserve*** you took me on your scooter. I was so excited. I was over the moon, believing that I have found my soul mate, my Anarkali, my Juliet, a babe-in-the-woods, unearthed a diamond in the form of trendy, tiny but gorgeous Tina, a dream girl who would share my life till death do us part.

I do not have to tell you how wonderful our honeymoon was. The love we made was unbelievable and you participated in it as enthusiastically as me. So often you were more aggressive, more demanding, more daring than me. I just could not understand how could one be so deceiving, play act or heartless! Then even God is unable to judge a woman, measure the depth of her heart, her feelings.

Today, I am not even able to put the word "Dear" in front of your name. You have hurt me so much, taken advantage of my trusting nature, my innocence, my love for you so that you can come to America as my wife and get a Green Card and then dump me. You wanted to be a surrogate breadwinner for your useless boyfriend, a wonderfully Gladstonian action without parallel.

It is unbelievably cruel, heartless and evil. We all have heard or even experienced a Credit Crunch but this was, at least for me a Conscious Crunch. Perhaps I was time-wrapped in a morality that no longer exists in today's materialistic world, like the patriotism that Indian people lost with the departure of the British. India will never have any one like Gandhi, Sardar and Bose ever again. Then again Lord Rama, Krishna, Buddha and Nanak were unique, a one off gift to the world.

But I believe that every event has a purpose and every setback has its lesson that makes a better person. Life is not a cradle of roses. Some times one has to cross a desert, even if to reach an oasis, the only ray of hope in a vast desolate desert without heart or soul.

I did not even want to write this letter, have any thing to do with you. But I am not a vindictive person. I believe, I feel duty bound, that I owe you an explanation, the reason why I abandoned you the way I did in Mumbai. So this letter, my last piece of commutation may be a bit long, as I would like to pour my heart out and let you know how evil you have been to me.

It was heartless for me to abandon you but deep in my heart I am sure that there is no need for me to explain, as you already know the reason. I am sure you would not even blame me for my action.

But what must come to you as a great surprise, a terrible shock is that how I came to know your plan, your deceit, your evil intention, as you are indeed a very clear girl, expert at computer technology. You took extraordinary care to hide, to conceal your evil plan.

But you made one big mistake, that of under-estimating me and my friends. You forgot that I am a trained doctor. It is part of our training to observe our patients, to know when they are not telling the truth, concealing some thing, are evasive, hiding behind lies.

I also exploited, took advantage of the time, place and the situation, your state of mind, when you were lost in a sea of happiness, your guards were down, you were most venerable, oblivious to any danger. It was my chance to ostracize you, to banish you from my life for ever. I know this was an odious act, a thuggery mentality on my part. But I had no choice. I had to do it to safeguard my future. It was the question of the survival of the fittest or rather the most ruthless.

But then, you were playing the same game with me since the day we got married. So why should I be any different. I first suspected that there was some thing wrong, that you are hiding some thing from me when we started living as a husband and wife, making love, having sex like normal, newly married couple do. It was capricious, at least on my part. But that alerted me, ringing the bell of impending disaster. After all it is nearly impossible to pretend, to play-act day in, day out.

It was obvious that your heart was not in it, in our marriage. You were just going through the motion, performing your duty as a loyal and devoted wife, especially in front of my friends and colleagues. But then you sounded so genuine when we first met, got married and went on our honeymoon. I could not help but wonder how did you managed to fool me. You should have become an actress, as Bollywood is so devoid of actress with natural talent.

It was unusual, uncharacteristic and out of normality for a girl like you. Ordinarily you are a bright, bubbling, fun loving girl who would take the lead, teaching me a trick or two, exploiting the sexual pleasure to the limit, encouraging me to explore every inch of your body.

So why this sudden change as if we have already celebrated the golden anniversary of our marriage and raised half a dozen of our children! It just did not made sense?

The obvious reason for such behaviour is simple, at least to a trained doctor. It is that you do not really love me; your heart is some where else, with some one other than me. I am a third party in this marriage, a necessary evil to put up with, a means for the end, a meal ticket for some one else.

Once I realised that, I was determined to find out who that person may be. It was obvious that this person was not here in San Diego but in Mumbai, a figure from your past, from your Uni days.

Two can play this game of hide and seek, sun and shade, appear and disappear. By showering you with my love, attention, trust and kindness, I wanted you to lower your guard, to slip up.

But you were too careful, too alert, on guard all the time to give me any clues. But I became a sycophant, a kind of sugar daddy to retain your trust. I played the part of Naradmuni, the fictitious character in our holy books, a perfect fall guy and a charmer at the same time.

Your unbelievable secrecy, being alert all the time meant only one thing, that the stakes are high; you are playing a dangerous game. You even bought prepaid telephone cards to call your boy friend in Mumbai so that these calls do not appear on our bills.

One observation I made was that you were spending a lot of time in our computer room, especially when I was away, on duty. You even persuaded me to buy you your own PC with convincing arguments that you need it for research, to write your thesis for your PhD course work. I even let you impose your form of dictate on me, with considerable ease.

Perhaps you may have thought that I have a social skill, a nature of a Dalek looking forward to the next fix?

So the answer I was seeking may be stored in your computer. Luckily I resisted the temptation of buying you a laptop that you could carry every where with you. Instead I told you to borrow mine at any time, as I hardly use it.

I even volunteered to take off your hands some of the household choirs when you took up a part time job in the University to teach IT, as a part of your PhD course, that enabled you to Spend a considerable time away from me, even attending English classes to bring your English to my, to American standard.

That meant that you have come here, to USA to stay for good. You had a loot mentality in a literary atmosphere. Secretly I could not help but to admire your tenacity and determination to put your life on the highest pedestal, to grab the opportunity with both hands.

No matter how careful one may be, it is impossible not to make a tiny mistake once in a while. One day while emptying the waste paper basket in our computer room, I found a heap of papers torn into hundreds of tiny pieces, along with normal letters and posts.

No one would go to such a length unless these papers are important. It was practically impossible for any one to put them together. It was a tiny mistake, a bit of negligence, carelessness on your part, as in the past you used to burn them. Perhaps it was overconfidence I managed to install in you with my own persistence and perseverance.

If there is a will, there is certainly a way. God help those who help themselves. No crime is fool proof, provided one may want to solve it badly, willing to toil, give time and energy. Underestimating your enemy is a recipe for disaster, a defeat and ultimately will lead to humiliation.

I took all these heaps of papers to a friend's house. It was easy to separate posts and other letters, as they were not torn that badly. But it still left me with hundreds of tiny pieces.

It was a tedious, mind-boggling job only a determined person could do. Then it was a matter of life and death for me. If I could solve the riddle, then perhaps I may get my lovely, sexy Tina back or at least I will know what I am against, what surprise you are planning for me, that you will not be able to lead me to a slaughter house, at least not without a fight, a bloody nose.

After spending hours and days, we at last managed to put together your torn letter. It gave me the name and address of your boy friend back in Mumbai and above all, your email. It was so well concealed, a mixture of letters and words that it would be impossible for any one to guess, even for an expert. Then you are an expert in IT and you used this knowledge expertly, to your best advantage.

Now all I needed was the password which I knew would involve the name of your boy friend or a family member, such as your brother Sanjay. I was right. So the next time when you were away for the whole day, on a Uni excursion, I also took a day off and spend the whole day on your computer, with a friend who was like you an expert in IT.

It was not that difficult for him to find the password and to go into your files. I was amazed at the amount of materials you had stored on your computer, all your email exchanges, love letters, even your photos, some in compromising pose, phonographic in nature, topless, in sensuous pose in your boyfriend's arms that leaves little to imagination.

I could not even imagine that an Indian woman from such a cultured background would dare to bare, to pose in such a provocative manner. The photo that offended me most was the one showing your boyfriend kissing you between your legs. Even in Western culture, such photographs are rare. It was an Aladdin's cave for me, for my case, for my defence if you ever face me in court.

When I tried to take your photos wearing a very revealing G-string bikini, more or less topless that I persuaded you to wear on our honeymoon, you stopped me saying that it would be inappropriate to keep such photos in our album, in our home. What a hypocrite I thought, as some of the photographs on your computer were not only topless, but bottomless as well!

I felt so hurt, sick, humiliated and determined to get rid of you at any cost. I was in such a pain that it would be difficult for you even to imagine. But in a way, pain is a powerful teacher. To transcend the pain, I had to experience it first hand. As they say, don't be angry, get even. After all Anger is only one letter short of Danger!

It gave me strength and the courage to overcome my love and affection for you. After watching those photos, making love to you was a nightmare. But I had to keep up the charade and you helped me by being aloof and keeping your distance!

If any of these photographs fall in the wrong hands, it will cost you your dignity, respect of your friends and the family and you may become a victim of a blackmailer. I will only use these photographs if you contest our divorce, if we end up in court. I can not understand how an intelligent and smart girl like you ever got in such a mess! It must be long time corrosion in your character to sink so low that no one can even gauge the depth of your wickedness. Perhaps your evil is bottomless, your greed measureless and your stupidity timeless.

Do you know what hurt me most, that nearly made me confront you and throw you out of my flat? It was the day to day diary you wrote, kept on the computer. It was full of lies, half truth and character assassination. It was written specially with a court case in mind, to get the best settlement from me when our divorce goes to court. I could never have believed that a girl like you could have such extremity, dual personality.

This was a premeditated plan, expertly executed. I was so mad that I wanted to make you shit a slow and painful grit, although that is against my nature, a blot on my conscious.

I am a firm believer in Om Shanti, not Om Kranti, especially when a girl is the target. But I am not going to be a surrogate apologist. Empire does strike back. It is the age-old principle that if you do the crime, you have to serve the time.

In a way I have learnt in my childhood the ageless principle of self-mastery from my Guru who taught me the finer points of our glorious Hindu dharma.

You accused me of having sex with you against your will, that I forced myself on you, that you were too weak to stop me and denial of sex usually lead to a beating. As you know, I have always treated you with love, kindness and respect that you hardly deserve.

Yes, we had wild sex, especially during our honeymoon. But you were hyperactive, as aggressive as me, even more at times! We both had dyed in the wool attitude as far as sex was concerned. It was you who taught, encouraged me to have cunnilingus sex I knew nothing about.

When I innocently asked how you knew all the finer points, your reply was that a woman has a sixth sense for such details when she is with her sweetheart, some one she loves so passionately and would like him to explore every inch of her body and indeed you let me explore the most vital, inaccessible sexual organs with zest and gusto.

If I ever was over the top, it was just to please you, as you were more assured, a senior partner in our sexual exploits. We both felt ecstasies in our sexual relationship at least that was the picture you pained in my mind, perhaps to let me feel at ease.

You even managed to put fake photographs of injury, to your breast, thighs and other private parts. You enlarged a tiny mark, a spot, a love

251

bite hundred times. After all you are an expert at computer, information technology, adding bits from the phonographic sites on computer to your own photos. This would have been your nostrum, a favourite remedy for a quick divorce, to fool the jury, especially the women jury.

This hurt me so much that I could not even dare to look at you any more. Brevity was the soul of salvation. Some how I managed to keep my sanity intact and wait for the right opportunity to strike; to take my revenge. It would be impossible for you to gauge my pain, my humiliation, my desperation.

Only the support of my friends kept me sane; enabled me to wait for the right time before I strike.

I used the Gladstonian philosophy of simultaneously making love and plotting revenge, like dropping food parcels, toys and bombs on Iraq at the same time, from the same aeroplane? I am sure you did not notice the subtle smiles of enlightenment, perceived satisfaction of dubious nature unfolding across my face, my lips.

One who swallows his pride may be a fool for a while but one who doesn't is a fool for the rest of his life. I let you make a fool of me for a while but in the end I had a glorious revenge. But my victory is tinged with sorrow. One can only be victorious against one's enemy. You are definitely not my enemy, only a misguided person and a tool in the hands of an evil person.

In a strange way, it also made me strong, determined and purposeful, to get rid of you without paying you a dime, without a Green Card and stranded in Mumbai without your passport, visa, return ticket or any documents that may enable you to enter America and pursue me in American court.

I copied every single piece of information you had on your computer, on a disc. I updated the disc regularly and kept it secured in a safe at work, with a copy with two trusted friends who would never betray me, unlike you.

I also kept my own diary, from the day we got married but writing the truth, countering your wild allegations, lies and twisted half truth. If you ever go to court, then I have more than enough ammunition, material to bury you alive, to hurt you, to make you a laughing stock.

It is all in your hands. I am not a vindictive person. I do not want revenge. I just want to be free, to liberate myself from your crutches, your evil intention. I believe in the saying that, "What you sow, so you reap, that truth and justice always triumph over lies and innuendo.

Clouds can not hide sun's rays for ever; that every cloud has a silver lining and there is a light at the end of the tunnel, no matter how long the tunnel may be.

I have already consulted a lawyer, expert in family law, with international connection. They have Associates in every major country. He has advised me to file for divorce as soon as possible. The two year separation close do not apply in this case as the marriage was a sham, entered under false pretext, just to obtain Green Card which is illegal under US law,

The divorce papers will be delivered, served to you in approximately six weeks time, by my lawyer's associates in Mumbai.

If you sign these papers, do not contest the divorce, then no one will ever know or see your sexy, half naked, phonographic photos. If you do not, then it will be out of my hands. I will have to do what my lawyer advice me to do, to act as per his instruction.

I am sending, enclosing a disc that contains the damming evidence, your love letters, diary and photos and email exchanges. You can show them to your lawyer. But I advise you to destroy the disc as soon as possible. If it falls in wrong hands, then you will become a blackmailer's victim who may demand more than mere money!

No matter what you may think of me after reading this letter, I can assure you that I bear no malice, any grudge towards you. I still have a soft corner in my heart for you. Inwardly I do feel bereaved, having lost the reason for living. Your absence will only bring emptiness, loneliness, bewilderment, shock and anguish.

Tina, you impressed practically every one with your indomitable cheerfulness, especially my parents who were so happy with my choice. How can I forget our honeymoon, the haunting excursion, the love in the afternoon in Shivaji Nature Reserve and our coffee breaks at the Shalimar Roof Garden?

You were terrific and I was madly in love with you, my tenacious, charming, beautiful Tina with whom I would have willingly spent the rest of my life, that we may have a family, grow old together gracefully and remain together till death do us part.

I can not but wonder where did I go wrong? I had painted such a romantic image of you but you turned it into the arch-iconoclast. It seems I saw you not as you were but as I wanted you to be. The nail that sticks out gets hammered. I was that nail.

But Tina, it was just a wonderful dream that disappeared when I woke up in the morning. After our divorce, I hope you can get married with your boyfriend, your sweetheart and have a long and happy life together.

But I can't help to think that you are a well-meaning pawn in the wrong hand. Watch your back. Every arrow, every dart that hits the bull's eye is the result of hundred misses. But you thought, to the detriment of your well being that your first arrow will hit the target, make you rich and famous.

From the photos, I can see that he is a very handsome boy indeed; you two make a good couple in every way.

But I can not help wondering what sort of man would let his girlfriend go through such a charade, a bogus marriage, a storming honeymoon in order to go to America! Can you really trust him?

My parents and family members know nothing about your past history. I would not be the one to reveal your secret, not even to my parents, unless it all comes out in court.

I leave it to you what you would like to tell your parents. It is not my concern. You were the apple of their eyes and it will heart them a lot whatever happens from now on.

I have vacated my flat and disconnected the phone, as it contains too many painful memories. The only way you can get in touch with me is through my solicitor or send me a text, as I have not changed my mobile number.

I am not signing this letter, on advice of my lawyer. So this is just a piece of typed paper without any significance. I am also sending this letter by International Registered Mail so that I can trace it on computer and make sure that it does not fall in the wrong hands.

I would also like to thank you for few wonderful months, teaching me so much on love making, on sex front and how to be devious, cruel and heartless when it is absolutely necessary.

I never thought I had this toughness in me but I hope I will go back to my normal self, to be kind, caring and loving person. These qualities are the most essential part of being a doctor. After all medicine is a caring profession meant to save life, mend people, both physically and mentally.

So no matter how heart broken I am now, I will have to learn to trust people again and soon, remove the dehumanization that you have managed to install in me.

From being Lord Rama, I turned into Ravan but I can not and will not remain Ravan for long. How could I be when I am surrounded by so many lovely, caring friends and colleagues? They are my Gandhi, Nehru, Sardar and Bose, Nanak and Mother Teresa.

As I do not want such a repeat experience in my life, I may never get married again, although it is too soon to make any promise. As you know I do have some wonderful friends, they are the gem of humanity. At least in that department, I have the God's blessings.

Friends are angles who would lift us when our wings are clipped and nurse us back to health, to full flight. I could have been such a friend to you. Our resolves are only tested in the time of adversity.

You are the odd one out, an exception to the rule, not the norm. It was my misfortune that we ever met. Even after such heartbreak, I wish you all the best and give you absolution, in true Christian tradition. I feel that a little bit of fragrance always clings to the hand that gives you a rose. You have given me too many roses for you to be rotten to the core.

It seems even you do not understand, gauge or appreciate your own strength, weakness or how to get the best from life in a fair and civilized manner.

This is my final farewell, ***Alvida, goodbye and good luck.***

Nirav

When Nirav finished the letter, he read it couple of times to make sure that he has not written any thing that may be detrimental to his case or help Tina in any way.

Even the disc contained limited materials, mostly her nude photos and explicit love letters that she can show to her lawyer but to no one else. In any case Nirav's lawyer will read every word he had written, before posting.

* * *

Chapter Eighteen
Nirav's Shattered Dream

Now that Nirav had finished the most important matter on hand, he was relieved, in a mood to play with the children. He was not going back to his rented flat. It would be a ghostly place without Tina, her memory lingering on in every corner.

Nirav disconnected the phone and removed his few personal effects still remaining in the flat, before giving the keys back to the letting agent. Nirav was in two minds what to do with Tina's personal effects, mostly her cloths, some jewellery and books.

Nirav packed her cloths in two suitcases and put them in Prem's storage room, that is the huge, well built all purpose room or rather a summer house in his enormous garden.

Nirav also decided to keep Tina's computer intact until the divorce goes through, that Tina becomes a distant dream, no longer capable of harming him in any way.

Nirav consulted the lawyer, gave him all the material he had on Tina and also showed him the letter before posting. The lawyer, a friend of Prem and Priya watched the disc with disbelief and advised Nirav that he should file for a divorce straight away.

Nirav had a strong case and no lawyer would advise Tina to fight it out in court, especially in the US court where immigration scam perpetrators are severely punished. Tina could even go to jail if she ever set foot in USA after the court case.

Nirav would get the absolute absolution from the court, without fail, within three to six months, with or without Tina's cooperation. The lawyer read Nirav's letter to Tina and advised him to post it unsigned.

The most difficult task for Nirav was to talk to his mum and dad. They were upset but understood that Nirav would never hurt any one without a very good reason. Priya had a long chat with his mum and told her that Tina never wanted to marry Nirav; that she regretted the marriage and now Nirav was giving her the freedom she wanted.

Priya also promised them that she and Prem would look after Nirav, who was her younger brother and will stay with them for some time. Nimuben was at least relieved that Nirav was well looked after, as she had heard so much about Prem and Priya since the day Nirav moved to America.

Tina was naturally upset, in fact devastated when she realised that her passport, return ticket and all her papers, documents, photocopies were gone but wisely did not create a scene or upset Nirav's parents in any way. Tina knew that they were as much in the dark as her.

What upset Tina most was that how Nirav came to know about her plan that he behaved so coolly and calmly under such provocation and act normal, outsmart her on all front.

Tina knew straight away that Nirav must have full support from Priya and she must have guided him every step of the way.

Three weeks later Nirav received a letter from Tina, at Priya's address, as Tina knew that Nirav must be staying with them.

"Dear Nirav

I do not know how to begin this letter or what to say or to write. But unlike you, I am able to put the word "Dear" in front of your name and always will be.

Yes, you are right. I under estimated you, your intelligence and your character. Then we were married for a short time only? But I am sure you had full support from Priya. After all she is a psychiatrist. If I underestimated any one, then it is Priya. But she never allowed me to come close to her, to get acquainted and know her better. Now I know why!

As the saying goes, "The tree that bears most fruits is closest to the ground." Priya is such a tree for you. If I had a friend like her, then perhaps I would not have made such a terrible mistake, be dyed-in-the-wool stupid, turned my world upside down, cut the branch I was sitting on, from the wrong end. These painful wounds are entirely self inflicted, due to my naivety, immaturity or even stupidity, whatever you may like to call.

Priya is a wonderful person, at least for you and you are very fortunate to have friends like Prem and Priya. Then we all get what we deserve. I only deserve a friend like Amat, my two penny boyfriend who would not hesitate to sell me short. Why do we, the women behave as if we have no brain? I am sure even God is incapable of gauging the depth of foolishness in a woman, his, God's own creation.

I am very sorry that I hurt you so much. I readily admit that my treatment of you was more like a blasphemy than disrespect. Believe me, if I could turn the clock back, I would choose the different outcome, different ending and we could have lived happily ever after. You would be my number one choice but I know it is all water under the bridge.

It is the wisdom of the widow who had just poisoned her husband for the love of her traitor boyfriend! There is no point in even trying to close the stable door after the horse has bolted. There are no doors to be closed?

Would you believe that it is possible for a girl to fall in love with two men? I was equally in love with you and Amat, my boyfriend of long standing.

In fact Amat, a very handsome boy, is an addiction not love that I find it difficult to give up. You are again right to say what kind of man will let me go through such a bogus marriage, a charade and a honeymoon when I have to give myself to my husband, make love and enjoy sex in every imaginable manner.

Perhaps it will churn your stomach inside out! Then you are a completely different kettle of fish. While Amat is a kestrel, you are a falcon. He is a scavenger who feats on leftovers, you dine in a five star restaurant. He is an ass, you are a thorough breed. That is the difference between two of you.

Now I realised that I had a Kohinoor diamond in my palm, in my possession but I chose a worthless stone. It seems to be the story of my life when it comes to men.

I always choose the wrong one, since my college days. I go for glitter not the gold, try to reach the heaven but end up in hell. I have failed to understand that one can not buy happiness, neither with money nor with sex, with one's body. It has to be attained with sincerity and work ethic.

I do not blame you for what you did to me. I would have done the same if the roles were reversed. But believe me, I would never have used all those notes I made in my diary if we had gone to court. No matter how heartless I may sound, I could never do that to you.

Our life together was a brevity, not a tragedy, at least not until you abandoned me in Mumbai. I am sure you will agree with me that our stormy honeymoon was real, not a put up job. Even I could not act so well. I enjoyed every minute of our time together on our honeymoon.

I have neither slept nor eaten much since we came back from Baroda. It is nice of you not to tell any one about my past. I know your parents were as much in the dark as I was about your plan to leave Mumbai once we were out of the way.

But I had to tell my parents every thing, as looking at me, they knew that you had left me stranded and they wanted to know why. Although they said nothing to me, as looking at me, at my sorrow, they must have felt that what you did was punishment enough for their spoilt but lovable daughter!

I know that I have lost their trust and love, as they have so much respect for you, that you are not to blame. It was all my doing. I cut the branch I was sitting on, from the wrong side and fell to the ground with a thump!

At the moment, I do not even have the desire to live. If the earth opens up, I will willingly jump in, as Lady Sita, wife of Lord Rama said when she was banished to the forest, even though there was not a single bone, a single drop of evil, contaminated blood in her veins.

Lady Sita was paying the price for the over indulgence of Lord Rama for the love of his subjects. What hurt Sitaji most was that she came last in Lord Rama's esteem. Lord Rama forgot that charity begins at home. We never learn from history, do we?

I will sign the divorce papers as soon as I receive them. That is the least I can do for you, as you have not set a foot wrong in our marriage. In any case, as you know, I do not have a leg to stand on. No court would look at me sympathetically if you reveal the facts. I do not mind losing, as I am a sporty person.

But in our case, I have not just lost but I have received a drubbing, the worse kind of drubbing imaginable. The only reassuring thing is that I am at the lowest ebb. From here on I can only go one way and that is up but the summit of Mount Everest from where I fell is out of reach for ever. My life is in ruins, I am in dumps and I can not see a way out. But then it is my problem.

You may have cancelled our joint credit cards but I have not used it here even once and have already destroyed it. Nirav, all I ask you is to forgive me, as even I do not understand why I did what I did. It does not make sense and never will.

In any case, you deserve a much better girl than me. I sincerely hope you will soon find a perfect partner with the help of your friend Prem and Priya. As long as Priya is on your side, you will never go wrong, make a similar mistake again.

Priya is a wonderful person. Please tell her that I do not bear any malice or grudge against her. She did what a true friend should do. Then she is more than a friend to you Nirav. She is your elder sister, your guardian angel.

In a way I used to feel jealous about your closeness with Priya. But I never interfered, knowing well that how much you two love each other.

I wanted to emulate Priya's success by doing PhD and becoming a professor in a San Diego University. But it will always remain a dream. I will always cherish our short time together, the storming honeymoon, the excursion into the unknown and intense but soft love making in the Shivaji Nature Reserve and wonderful lunch time coffee breaks we had at the most prestigious Roof Top Garden in the world. Believe me, it was real, not an act in any way.

Now my enthusiasm is replaced by a deathly sombreness. The flicker of my candle is about to extinguish by a Toofan, the storm that is of my own creation. I am the author of my own misfortune. So it would be futile to blame any one else, not even my boyfriend Amat or Vidhata, the Goddess who writes, charts our future as soon as we are born.

Good luck, goodbye, take care and sincere best wishes.

Yours ever so unfortunate Tina."

Unlike Nirav, Tina had signed her letter, as she had no heart, no desire to face Nirav in court.

After reading the letter a couple of times, Nirav gave it to Priya to read and express her professional opinion. Priya read it slowly, word by word, digesting the content before commenting and then said,

"Bhaiya, I believe her. She is sincere in her regrets. If only she had realised it as soon as you two got married, then you would have a wonderful life together, as good as ours. After all, no one is bad, evil through and through. We all have our good side, a compassion hidden under the tough exterior. However dark the coconut may be from outside, it is always fresh and white from the inside. God is incapable of creating a human being rotten through and through.

Tina is an intelligent girl in many ways. She would have become a professor and reached the top. Unfortunately academia does not denote spiritual intelligence.

Good judgement comes from experience and experience comes from bad judgement. We all have to learn not only from our own mistakes but from the mistakes of others, as we would never live long enough to make all these mistakes.

This is known as the psychology of winning. But Bhaiya, you will have to put Tina out of your mind for good. Do not let her or her memory spoil the bright future you have in front of you.

As I would say to all my patients, do not leave the quality of your life to chance, leave it to choice. Thank All Mighty that now you have a choice. We the humans are mere puppets controlled by twin strings of success and failure, happiness and tragedy, joy and sorrow. Now Nirav, you have, at least the right strings to pull. Bhaiya, we both will be with you all the way. Prem may not say much but bhaiya, he loves you as much as I do. In us, you have a perfect pair of guardian angles.

You will come out of this tragic affair a better, a stronger and a wiser person but perhaps Tina's life is ruined, beyond salvation. Perhaps her fate, her fatalism was predestined by God that no human can change.

I do not believe that her boyfriend will standby her once he knows that Tina could not be his meal ticket, his passport to America. He only wanted to use her and Tina some how fell for it.

It is always the case, the most beautiful and intelligent girls fall for the wrong person. History is full of such examples. But we never learn from history, do we? But Bhaiya, the time for carping is over. Now you will have to move forward, rebuilt your life and turn your dream into a reality, at least on the career front."

Priya turned her head to hide tears in her eyes when Prem entered the room. Looking at sad faces, he said, "Nirav, Priya, what is wrong? We should be smiling, celebrating and happy that Nirav is at last free of evil, conniving Tina. "

Nirav put the letter in his hands and said, "This letter is from Tina. Prem, there are no winners and losers. We both are the losers in this epic tragedy, especially Tina. What a wonderful life we could have together if all had gone according to plan, the life we had charted together in the romantic atmosphere of Shivaji Nature Reserve, our Vrindavan then and for ever.

Perhaps Tina may not be as evil as I first thought. But never the less, I am glad to be free of her." Nirav was clearly feeling the pain and the strain. He was still in love with Tina and felt a bit guilty that Tina will have a tough time in Mumbai. She will have to bear her pain all alone while Nirav had support of wonderful friends like Prem and Priya.

Certainly Nirav's past was a different ball game; more complicated but more exciting and in certain ways, especially on the sexual front more rewarding.

Taking two bottles of Budweiser from the fridge, Prem led Nirav out in the garden where they sat down under the huge sun umbrella, a permanent fixture in their garden and a favourite place to sit down and have a drink, with the view of the vast cactus garden, with some wonderful and precious desert cactus trees, some well over one hundred years old, yet only thirty feet tall.?

Priya soon joined them, overcoming her momentarily grief, with a bottle of fizzy drink, as she would only drink red wine. But it was too early for her to have a glass of wine.

Tina, true to her words, signed the divorce papers and their divorce became final in six months. For Nirav, it was a relief rather than jubilation. He was now free and ready to move forward, thanks to his friends, especially Prem and Priya who were now even closer to him than ever before.

* * *

The End

Woman of Substance

Chapter One
Beginning of a New Era

It was the tenth anniversary of Nirav's divorce from Tina, the day it became final, made Nirav a free man. True to her words, Tina did not put up a single hurdle, any obstacle to make separation any difficult than it already was.

Then Tina was an intelligent person. She knew that any resistance would be futile. It would hurt her more than Nirav and at the end of the day, she would achieve nothing, become a laughing stock, an object of hatred and an object of sexual desire by the perverts, looking at her semi-nude photographs that would raise any one's blood pressure!

At her best, Tina was like Lord Shiva's Menka no one could resist, one of the most beautiful and sensuous woman in Hindu mythology, Goddess Venus of the Greek mythology and at her worse, Tina was a scheming, conniving, conspiring and manipulating beauty without any moral or compassion. In any relations, the sexual attraction is the first shot in love, the rest follows. Perhaps Nirav was first attracted to Tina's bare upper torso at their first encounter, in the hot and humid and steamy atmosphere of an Indian scene.

When two parties cooperate, then divorce becomes straightforward and painless, that is if any divorce can be describe as painless. In the end Nirav and Tina did not have to face each other in the court. It was like a magical slumber after a long and weary day, as if Nirav has come out of an oasis of enlightenment.

Tina's past did not surface, to the relief of Nirav; as such a character assassination is not in Nirav's nature. Nirav's ethos, his cultured up-

264

bringing and etiquette would not allow such a scenario in his real life. It would have hurt them both, especially Tina.

But Nirav's conscious would have taken a long time to heal, to put Tina out of his mind if they had faced each other in court. The emotional upheaval would have like a gushing mountain stream swollen after the monsoon rains.

There is no statute of limitation on hatred, pain and revenge. It may occupy a person's mind infinitely and affect him for the rest of his life if allowed to bubble like lava in one's heart.

Nirav did not want such a scenario in his life, as it would affect his professional judgement, his future happiness. How accurate his assessment proved to be in the long run.

It was a close call but his awareness and enlightenment enabled Nirav to come out of this tragic episode without much outward wounds. But invisible wounds, pain is always more difficult to deal with. Nirav's instinct of self preservation was like the soothing effect of the symphony of nature that enhanced the healing process, especially as Nirav did not allow emotions and fear to become muddled with self-pity, allegiance and anger.

For once, Nirav had all the luck, good fortune and expert guidance from an in-house marriage councillor in Priya, a larger than life Guru with a mantra for any ill, any problem, any situation that life can through at Nirav. Priya was one hell of a councillor, a guru who had a mantra for each and every problem that life can throw at Nirav.

With the departure of Tina, Nirav moved into a flat within hospital compound, reserved for key hospital workers, especially those who are on call so often. But not before spending three months with Prem and Priya, not until his wounds were healing, although a complete recovery would take a long time.

Priya and especially her two lovely children helped Nirav come out of the shell, bring down the wall of isolation that Nirav managed to built around him, a natural defensive mechanism to deal with difficult, painful, heart-rendering situation in life.

It is a nature's way of dealing with pain, in humans as well as in animals, albeit in different ways. It is the pain that produces one of the most beautiful pieces of jewellery the nature could provide us.

Pearls we admire, appreciate and value so much are the result of a very painful process when a grain of sand or such sharp material is engrossed in the soft belly of an oyster or mollusc. To stop the pain, the fish produces liquid white substance, which is calcium carbonate that engulfs the sand particles to stop the pain.

The process continues for at least two years before a commercial size pearl if formed and harvested. There are numerous pearl farms scattered throughout the tropical world, especially on the Mediterranean shores where the climate, the weather condition and sea temperature is perfect.

Tina's betrayal was the most depressing and pernicious episode in Nirav's life. At one point when he was law on esteem, he even thought this depressing episode in his life will handicap him, haunt him for ever.

The crudity of this appalling smear that Tina wanted to throw at Nirav backfired badly for Tina.

Fortunately for Nirav he came out fighting with flying colour. Instead of feeling sorry for himself, keeping aloof and seeking dark corners to hide, developing a beleaguered and bunkered mentality, Nirav looked the world in the face.

Perhaps Nirav had a hidden strength he was not aware of. He was able to explore the realm of extraordinary hidden strength that reside in most of us but only a few are able to muster it in time of need when one may be down and almost out.

Nirav concentrated all his energy on his work and study. Within two years he was made a consultant, performing or rather leading a team of his own, to perform heart-bypass and on the team, as one of the key member of the best heart transplant team in California that operated on the rich and the famous.

California, with Hollywood on its doorstep, has one of the densest concentrations of the rich and famous people on the earth. In true Hindu tradition, it is not difficult for well educated Hindus to assimilate themselves in any culture, any tradition, any civilized society and the West, especially America was no exception. In fact America was a God sent gift for most professional Indians.

Now Nirav was one of the best paid employees, earning some two million dollars per year. He could easily treble his earnings if he go private, became a partner in small private hospital, concentrating solely on illnesses connected with heart problems, treating super rich only, testing prototype equipments for multi billion medical conglomerates.

So often consultants make as much money for being on the payroll of giant pharmaceutical firms, testing new drugs on unsuspecting patients as they do from patients they treat. After all, most heart patients are on drugs for life.

But for Nirav, job satisfaction was more important than financial reward and he receives such accolades by a bucketful from not only the hospital but also from grateful patients whose lives he has saved. Nirav certainly did not have ***Armani-clad*** shoulders that most professionals crave for.

Some how Nirav was able to detach himself from the Western, Abrahamic morality that most professionals fall for. After all America is the land of opportunity, to get rich and famous by any means, fair or foul.

It is worth remembering that the armatures built the ***Ark*** but the professionals built the ***Titanic.*** What benefited humankind most if not even debatable!

Nirav's reward was the job satisfaction, the happiness, relief and sheer tears of joy he observed in patient's and their relation's eyes. Financial reward was a secondary issue which automatically came with fame and success on the operating table. Nirav was accumulating credits that he can use in his next life? He some what believed in rebirth, reincarnation in human form!

Nirav was also fortunate on social front. Priya had introduced him to a lovely girl, a fellow doctor who became his wife some five years ago. Nirav found love and a family life in the most unexpected, unlikely manner.

Priya always used to tell Nirav, drummed into him that, like there is no perfect crime, there is no perfect partner, a perfect wife or husband in real life. But that does not mean we could not have a happy, contented family life, some one we can love and cherish. Happiness is a state of mind, not a bank balance.

It is always the case of give and take, reform and bend with the change, with the wind, with the trend, with changing circumstances. As we say, one man's food is another man's poison! Let the renewing power of heart, the inner strength guide us through life.

Prem and Priya's marriage, family life came as close to perfection as possible, although Prem and Priya were as different as chalk and cheese. Prem was a happy go lucky person who believed in enjoying life to the full but within the bounds of normality, the social structure and the behaviour that one has to observe in such a close-knit Indian community.

When we live in a Samaj (society) we have to observe certain unwritten laws, restraints and restrictions. There is no such thing as free for all in our conservative but well meaning Hindu society.

Then freedom without responsibility is a myth unless one would like to opt out, become a recluse.

Priya did not only earned most but she also managed the family finances, thus leaving Prem to look after children, do all the hard, physical work, the maintenance that such a big house needed, although he had all the help from Pillar, a live-in Mexican nanny cum child minder, a part of Prem-Priya's family.

Then there was Pedro who although employed as gardener, did all the handy work, with Prem joining in now and then to lend a hand when the job may be too much for one person to handle.

No wonder Prem and Priya's house was one of the best maintained and manicured one on the estate. The parties they throw were attended by one and all who may be some one special, important or a close friend of long standing.

That is why Nirav had such a faith in Priya. Their friendship, besides being like brother and sister, was also like friendship between Lord Krishna and pauper Sudama, one a prince and the other a pauper, at least on the family, streetwise experiences, Sudama living hand to mouth, selling firewood cut from a forest to feed the family while Lord Krishna's palace lacked nothing.

Yet Lord Krishna had as much respect and admiration for Sudama, as he had for his friends Kunti putra (sons) Pandav. For Nirav, Priya's words were a gospel, uttered by Lord Krishna when explaining Arjun to do his duty and fire the first shot at his enemies Kaurava on the battlefield of Kurushastra.

These words of wisdom are so ably captured in the Hindu holy book of Bhagwat Gita that the book is widely read and referred by one and all, irrespective of one's religious affiliation. It is a bible for wisdom, kartaviya (duty) and obligation.

The battle of Mahabharat was fought between cousins, with family elders, brothers, friends and relations opposing each other. In the opposite camp, were Bhishma Pita, a grand father like figure for Arjun and his brothers who were as fond of Bhisma as Bhisma was of five Pandav brothers.

Then there were Dronacharya, their teacher, Guru, a father figure who taught them not only every thing they knew about the art of making war, use of weapons of mass destruction but how to be a kind and caring person, a good and honest king would put the welfare of his subjects before his own.

Then there was their elder brother Lord Karna, a warrior of unparallel courage and knowledge who was by any means unconquerable on the battlefield, at least by fair means. He was a human being par excellence!

The character of Lord Karna is the most noble, only second to Lord Krishna and Bhishma.

Karna practically promised Pandav a glorious victory on the battlefield by promising their mother Mata Kunti that he would not harm any of his brothers.

He would rather sacrifice his own life than take the one; slay his own flesh and blood. After all Pandavas were fighting for justice, good governance and honesty, decency. All virtues were with them. He kept his promise and died like a hero on the battlefield. It was a sacrifice beyond the call of duty.

* * *

Chapter Two
Challenge Poised by Priya

When Priya introduced **Richa;** she had come to know Richa very well indeed, as Richa was her patient, had opened her heart and gone through a similar experience like Nirav, having married a fellow doctor in Mumbai, who was like Tina, more interested in Green Card, a cosy life than in Richa, who was not really his type

Like Tina, he wanted to use Richa as a meal ticket. But their divorce, their break-up was a massy affair, needing Richa a lengthy treatment. Who could be better than Priya to consult?

In the end Richa won the case, getting the custody of her little angel Rupa and their martial home and in the process, her cheating, concaving husband was thrown out of USA. It was a difficult case, as Richa's husband Rajesh had a duel personality. He was Doctor Jekyll and Mr. Hyde in real life. He could be very charming when needed, put up a charade that would fool most people.

But like Tina, he underestimated Richa, who was thorough and painstakingly built up a foolproof case with the help of a private detective that enabled Richa to win the case. But it really broke Richa's heart, making it more difficult for Richa to trust any one.

It was a challenge to Nirav, poised by Priya to win over Richa, gain her trust, and make her believe that there are good, honest, decent people in the world, people like Prem and Priya, a shining example right in front of Richa's eyes.

Richa was living at the time, in a small town called Lemon Grove. It was more like a village than a town but it had some excellent medical facilities and a well known hospital.

Lemon Grove is some fifty miles away from San Diego, practically a next door neighbour in American term, a vast country indeed. Richa was working as a Medical Practitioner, but studying to specialize in the medical condition known as Chronic Fatigue Syndrome or M.E.

At one time Myalgic Encephalomyelitis or M.E. in short was a mysterious illness which can occur as a result of an epidemic or as scattered cases not related to an outbreak of infection. It may also occur after a major surgery when a patient's immune system is down.

At one time it was known as Yuppie's flu, as it usually affected young, active, professional people, financial wizards working in a city, who lived a hectic life. But as it took hold, spread, it affected very young and the old, fortunately that myth has been laid to rest.

Now it is certain that it is a virus which enters the body through the respiratory track. It often starts with gastro intestinal symptoms. M.E. may affect the brain but *it is not all in the mind.*

M.E. may suddenly commence with an alarming attack of giddiness but it usually takes the form of influenza like illness, with headache, pain in limbs and joints and loss of appetite.

Even today very little is known about M.E. The condition is mainly characterised by profound, extreme fatigue and muscle weakness, involuntary spasm.

Practically all patients complain of coldness of the extremities and if their temperature is taken, it is most often markedly subnormal with severe sweating. Even the smallest household chore becomes a mammoth task with memory uncertain.

Symptoms may vary from day to day, patient to patient. While on some days patients feel normal, at other times they find it difficult even to get out of bed. Some patients may even end up in wheel-chairs.

With proper management and care in the early stages, many young patients recover completely. But it is difficult for the older patients to get better and it does become progressively worse in this category of patients, as with age, the body's immune system deteriorate, along with all other important organs that sustain life.

There is no cure, no meditation as such but group therapy sessions where some ten to twenty patients are brought together, to talk, to develop positive attitude and to do light exercise works in some patients.

But many patients are even too weak to attend such classes. A couple of hours excursion tires them so much that they may need a month or two to recover. For such patients, recovery is rare. Their only recourse is to come to term with their illness and manage it as best as they could.

Although millions have been spent on research, no cause or cure is in sight. As ME does not kill sufferers like AIDS, it will not get enough funds for research, especially as M.E. is more like an individual disease, cause and symptoms, as well as treatment and remedy varies case by case.

But now M.E. is getting more attention as influential people in sports, finances, TV and film industry suffer from M.E. Special clinics are being opened in countries like America but as usual, Europe some what legs behind, with the exception of Germany.

In recent development, an Oxygen therapy is used whereby patients are put on oxygen for some ten to twenty hours a day. It has some limited success. But as in any meditation, the effect wears off after prolonged use of oxygen, as the body become used to this excess oxygen. But it is the best treatment available for the older patients.

Prem and Priya entertain, held parties at least twice a year in their vast, well manicured garden, to celebrate Diwali, Christmas and Janmastami, Lord Krishna's birth day, inviting close friends and work colleagues.

This routine gave them the opportunity to meet friends, socialize and keep in touch. Priya had made some very good friends, met influential people through her work. But she would only socialize, mix and invite them, her former patients to her home when they are no longer under her treatment, fully recovered and moved on.

Richa was introduced to Nirav at one of her parties. Priya thought they would make a perfect couple. Both had "Once beaten, twice shy" personality, common background, both professionally and socially.

Priya also reassured Richa that Nirav would be the last person to hurt her, to hurt any one. Richa would come and stay with Priya occasionally, on long week-ends, so that her daughter, her little angel Rupa could play with Priya's children.

As Nirav loved children, playing with Nikhil and Nisha, Priya's two children, Rupa soon got friendly with Nirav and that helped to bring Nirav and Richa closer. While in the Western society, it is the dog that so often brings two people together, while in our Indian society, it is the children that do the nature's match making.

* * *

Chapter Three
Beginning of Life Long Friendship

Nirav would also visit and stay with Richa now and then. Nirav knew that Richa was not Tina and never would be. Then Nirav had enough of Tina to last a life time. The sexual relationship with Richa would always be soft, sedate, gentle and dignified, that is if it ever came to having such a close and intimate relationship.

It took more than a year for Nirav and Richa to come close, trust each other and be intimate. Now they were at least able to talk, discuss, analyse and even joke of their past predicament, how two intelligent and well educated people like Nirav and Richa could be fooled, used and exploited by two supposedly naïve and innocent persons. Then are any Mumbaivasi naïve or completely innocent!

But the fact that both had well paid professional career, Green Cards, even American passports and well settled, was a big help, an assurance that no one was cultivating friendship, building a relationship for an ulterior motive, for all the wrong reasons.

It is comforting and reassuring to have a close and loving friendship, companionship and some one to socialize with. But two young and healthy people when in close proximity for some time do need, expect and perhaps desire sexual contact, at least a kiss, cuddle and holding, embrace.

So why Nirav and Richa should be any different? They had not taken vows of celibacy. By now Nirav and Richa have not only become good friends but most importantly they did trust each other. Sexual attraction naturally follows in such a close relationship.

The four of them would also go out together often, leaving the three children with Pillar. One day little Rupa innocently asked, "Mum, why can't I have uncle Nirav as my dad?"

That innocent question made Richa realize that she can not go through life on her own, as a one parent family. Why should she when a perfect life partner is already on her door-step, willing and able to give her and Rupa all the love and affection they would need.

Richa talked at length, opened her heart to Priya, telling her that she was falling in love with Nirav. Although Priya had always encouraged Richa, this was the first opportunity Priya had to press her, encourage her and assured her that she should follow her heart, trust her judgement and go for Nirav, who is one in a million! Nirav was a thorough breed, not a plough horse!

Priya had already told Richa about Tina, how she tried to destroy Nirav and how Priya helped him to escape from the clutches of Tina, bring him back from the jaws of destruction; that how much Priya love, care and admire Nirav who was like her own younger brother.

After Prem and her two children, Nirav was the most important person in her life. Priya even assured Richa that Nirav is incapable of hurting any one, that he could be the best dad Rupa could have.

After a great deal of deliberation and soul searching, Richa felt that it was time to trust Nirav, bring a ray of sunshine in her lonely life and secure her and Rupa's future.

The next rime when Nirav came for the week-end stay, while handing him the bottle of Budweiser, Richa said in a cool, calm voice, "Nirav, I have not prepared the spare bedroom. Would you like to share my bedroom?"

Nirav was taken by complete surprise. He dropped the bottle Richa had just handed him. Fortunately they were in the garden, standing on the patio and not in the tiled kitchen.

"The bottle was shattered. So Richa gave him her bottle, but not before she made him sit down on the chair and put the bottle on the table.

"I am sorry about the bottle but did I hear you right? Did you invite me to share your bedroom or am I hallucinating?" Nirav was still in shock.

"Yes Nirav, I have invited you to share my, our bedroom. Why are you so surprised? I am a woman after all. I do need love, comfort, a shoulder to cry on and a man in my life. Tell me honestly, can I do any better than have you as my husband, Rupa her dad."

"Richa, this is the second surprise you have given me, even before I have finish or rather even touch the bottle. Now you are asking me to marry you. How many bottles did you have before I came?" Nirav could not help but tease Richa.

"Nirav, you know well that I do not drink or even like beer. I just opened it to give you company so that you can not say that we do not have any thing in common. But Nirav, I always feel high in your company. Your voice has such euphony that it is natural, almost obligatory to trust you. I am lucky that you have not been snapped up already, considering how I kept you at an arm's distance for so long.

Nirav was indeed surprised. Richa normally is in serious mood most of the time but recently she has been opening up, occasionally teasing him and pulling his leg. But she rarely joked.

"Richa, I feel like taking you in my arms and give you such a lingering kiss that you would beg me to stop. But I know Rupa is around. So I will wait until tonight."

"Yes Nirav that is a wise suggestion. You can make the night as long and as passionate as you want. I would not stop you in any way." It seemed Richa wanted Nirav as much as he wanted her.

Nirav was patient with Richa. He knew what ordeal she had, as there divorce was not as straight forward as his. Moreover a child was involved that made the divorce more painful.

Fortunately Rupa was very young, almost a nestling who had no recollection of his father or the bitterness generated by the divorce, fought tooth and nail, neither gave an inch. But ultimately truth triumphed over innuendo, lies and deception. After all clouds could not block sun's warmth brightness and sunshine for ever.

Nirav was glad Richa was coming out of her shell. It was time their friendship move forward, takes the next step. After all life is too short to remain standstill, in the limbo or spend the rest of the life in a pond?

"Richa, can I ask you one question?" Nirav was serious.

"Why not? But I can not promise you the answer. It all depends on the question" Richa was still smiling.

"How come you suddenly trust me?"

Nirav was cool, calm but serious, having absorbed the initial shock.

"You know Nirav, time heals most wounds, even the upheaval I encountered, endured in my short married life. But most of all I trust Priya. She assured me that you will never hurt me, not in a million years. You are not capable of hurting any one. We have been going out, seeing each other for some time and you have not set a foot wrong.

Priya not only has a very high opinion of you but she adores you. We are both fortunate to have a friend like Priya. But you are more than a friend. You are her darling little brother."

"Yes Richa, I am indeed very lucky to have Prem and Priya in my life. Without them, Tina would have taken me to cleaners, destroyed me." There was sadness in Nirav's voice.

"Before I forget, Rupa always asks me why she can not call you dad. Would you like to tell her that now she can?"

"Yes, that is one task I would love to perform. You know how fond I am of Rupa." Whenever Nirav visited Richa, it was his duty to put Rupa to bed, reading her a story or just playing with her until she falls a sleep.

Today when Nirav took Rupa upstairs, putting her to bed, he said, "Rupa, today I would not read you a story but I would very much like to talk. Is it ok?"

"Yes uncle. But what should we talk about?" Rupa was, like any child of her age, inquisitive.

"Well Rupa, I would like to tell you a secret. Can you keep it a secret, not to tell even your mum until I say so?"

"OK uncle. I will not tell any one."

"Rupa, would you like to call me dad?"

"Yes uncle, sorry, yes dad" Rupa said with a giggle. She was too young to understand the difference between uncle and a dad.

"Rupa, you can now call me dad but only when we are alone, you, me and your mum. Do you understand?"

"Yes dad, thank you" Rupa went to sleep feeling happy.

When Nirav left the room, he went to guest room out of habit. But it was locked. He soon realised that he would be sharing the bed with Richa tonight. In a way he felt nervous, as he had not been with any woman since the break-up of his marriage.

Even when he changed into pyjama and joined Richa in bed, stroking her hair, Nirav said, "Richa, are you sure this is what you want? I value our friendship more than having sex. I am willing to wait as long as it takes, until we get married."

"I know that Nirav. But I have complete trust, faith in you. In any case, we are not getting any younger and I do not believe in fiddle-faddle nonsense, no sex before marriage.

Moreover I would like to enjoy us as a family while we are still young and perhaps have more children; that is if you wish."

After a long pause Richa continued, "I hope I am not jumping the gun."

"No Richa, I think you understand me well. But you will have to agree to my one condition and that is we should sign a prenuptial agreement, not that we are ever going to end up in court."

Richa thought Nirav was getting too serious. So to lighten the atmosphere, she joked, "I know Nirav that as a prominent heart surgeon, you will be earning much more than me" That brought a smile on Nirav's face.

Now it was Nirav's turn to pull Richa's leg. "Richa, you misunderstood me. I am not talking about money. I am talking about Rupa. I just want her and nothing else. You know we had a heart to heart talk and she is going to call me dad but only when we three are alone"

"Well Nirav, I am sorry to disappoint you. But we two come as a package; you may not have one without the other. But you can become Rupa's fiduciary any day." Richa had a ready answer.

"Well, I will have you both, a ready made family. You know Richa that there is a saying, perhaps by Socrates that if you get a good wife, you will be happy, if not you become a philosopher. Husband and wife are two sides of a coin. They can not face each other but still they stay together."

"Nirav, we are not yet married and you have already become a philosopher. I would prefer a husband, a heart specialist, not a philosopher. After all they do not earn much. Do they? How would a philosopher support an expensive wife like me?" For the first time there was a naughty smile on Richa's lips. She was coming out of her shell.

* * *

Chapter Four

The Ever Lasting Dream

They talked and talked well into the night, while making love intermittently. So often Richa had to arouse Nirav to make him act, give her what she wanted. But once Nirav got going, Richa found it difficult to dislodge him; her tiny body lacked both the strength and the desire to escape from his intense love making. Nirav wanted to embrace every moment of this first time in this exotic land or rather an exotic four poster bed of Richa.

Richa had her own beautiful house without mortgage. She was an equal partner in the private clinic with nine other doctors. It was like a G.P surgery but on a grand scale, with x-rays, blood tests, dental care, pharmacy and performing minor surgeries. It was a state of the art Medical Centre, popular and well attended.

Richa had wise head on young shoulders. She had wisely taken out legal protection, along with medical insurance. It included family break-up, divorce and a third party liability, to the tune of a $5 million dollars. So the divorce court case cost Richa nothing.

It seemed the God was smiling on Nirav and Richa. At last their luck had changed. Whatever they did or touched turned into gold. Their every plan materialised to perfection.

Mount Sinai Residential Complex where Prem and Priya had their house was being extended by the developer, adding another thirty homes. Nirav and Richa put down the deposit as soon as the plans were published.

Being an exclusive, top of the range development for professional people, houses were expensive, out of reach for most but the highest earning professionals. But with the planning of the fast, Bullet Express train, joining San Diego with Los Angeles, thus making San Diego just a suburb of LA, it was inevitable for San Diego to become a golden city, the El Dorado of the State of California.

It was one of the most desirable, sought after development in the region, known as **Mt. Helix** elevated plateau, with underground water that could be brought to surface by artesian wells. There was a big lake in the middle, fed by underground water, a state of the art gym, a child nursery and a well stocked library.

The house Nirav and Richa bought was even more luxurious, as it was a later development that incorporated all the latest gadgets, including a huge basement, with a launderette, a sound-proof music room and state of the art gym, with five double bedrooms.

But there garden was much smaller but with three acres, it was more than enough to enjoy the outdoor life, have a pool and a large, well furnished summer house at the rear.

Next to the complex but in an enclosed, secured area, there was a Medical Centre, a café, a pizzeria, a pharmacy and an entertainment centre that served four such complexes. The price of their home will more than double in less than ten years.

Medicare Excellence, the company that builds and runs top of the range hospitals, were building or rather adding a new wing to their existing hospital in the San Diego area and that included a M.E. or Chronic Fatigue Syndrome treatment centre, with ten beds for long term sick who may needed hospitalization.

It was not difficult for Richa to get a consultant's post, as there are very few physicians with special qualification to treat M.E. patients. On getting married, Richa sold her home and her share in the Medical Centre where she was a partner.

Six months after paying the deposit, they moved into their luxurious home, the huge deposit provided by Richa, from the capital generated by the sale of her home and the practice.

Even though Nirav was prepared, willing and ready to sign the prenuptial agreement, Richa refused to do so. But they bought their matrimonial house in the sole name of Richa, at least for the time being, as she had invested a big chunk of her life savings in their first and hopefully the only matrimonial home. The balance was invested in a trust for Rupa.

Prem and Priya were ecstatic to welcome Nirav and Richa to the complex, their homes being only a ten minutes walk, where their children can play together in complete safety. Now they can meet at week-ends, go out together and have a barbecue at regular interval.

Their happiness, their family was complete when Richa gave birth to a baby boy. Nirav's parents came to stay with them for six months during Richa's pregnancy and child birth. Rupa was by now six year old, a charming little girl, spoil rotten by her dad Nirav but always kept in check by mum Richa.

What Richa appreciated most and thanked God and Priya was that she had married Nirav who loved Rupa even more than their own son. Rupa will never know that Nirav was not her biological father, although it would make no difference to her. Nirav was and always will be her one and only father.

Real parents are those who love and bring up there children, who are there in good times as well as bad, in sickness and health, not the ones whose genes they carry or give birth and then abandon them.

Nirav and Richa even went to Mumbai for a short holiday and to meet their parents, brothers and sisters, friends and relations.

While in Mumbai Nirav learnt that Tina was abandoned by her boyfriend as soon as he realised that Tina would not be his meal ticket, some one who could take him to Europe or America. Even her parents kept a distance from Tina. She soon left Mumbai and no one knew or cared where she was. In a way it was sad for Nirav. Even after their divorce, Nirav wanted Tina to be happy, as they say, to err is human but to forgive is divine. Tina paid a heavy penalty for her momentary madness, her love for some one who did not deserve her.

Nirav learnt through bitter experience that when you let your heart rule your brain, then such tragedies happen. It is a human frailty that differentiates us from the rest of the animal kingdom.

Today Nirav and Richa's garden was full of sweet smelling roses. Both knew that only death can part them, that they will grow old gracefully in each other's company. All's well that ends well and the one who laughs last, laughs loudest, longest.

Nirav and Richa lived happily till the end, thanks to Prem and Priya who had been all very good friends, helping each other in their hour of need. This friendship is still in evidence in their grown up and well settled children who still lives in the same houses, the same but much extended complex.

They have followed in their parents' footsteps and continued this special relationship, a rare, precious jewel in the sea of human frailty. Perhaps Prem and Priya, Nirav and Richa are keeping an eye on their offspring from above, their new abode in heaven with a sigh of satisfaction, a job well done!

* * *

The End

CHANDA
(Village Anarkali)

Chapter One
Fruits of Political Posturing

The village of Tulsipur had a tiny surgery but was manned by a sort of herbal pharmacist with some knowledge of Western medicine, a sort of Ayurvedic doctor, a traditional Indian herbalist, man Friday of medicine, a jack of all trade and all illnesses. One may call him a quack, who dispenses a mixture of herbal and Western medication, a Vaid, a traditional title for herbalist, a semi doctor but not capable of handling a real, a serious illness that require a qualified doctor.

Such a doctor was only available in the nearby village of Kathipur, where there was a well stocked surgery or rather a small, a tiny hospital, as Kathipur, although not much larger than Tulsipur, was the administrative centre for the region where there was a police station, office of the tax collector and a school that gave the village a preferential treatment, an unseen superiority when it came to distributing government resources.

In a country like Bharat, (India) more like a continent than a single entity, with thirty major languages and some three hundred dialects, it is not that uncommon for a village of the size of Tulsipur not to have a surgery, a school, a library and a police station, unless villagers are willing and able to contribute financially for building such an infra structure themselves. But a village is never deprived of a place of worship, may it be a temple, a mosque or a gurudwar.

After a long wait, the villagers were rewarded with the surgery, more out of political infighting, when two candidates standing for the Lock Sabah (Parliamentary) election, promised a school and a surgery for the village. Each was outbidding the other. Opening a surgery was the first part of the promise the winning candidate was fulfilling. It was nothing more than a marriage of opportunity with political posturing. The winning candidate wanted to ignite the flames of personal potential, to produce startling results in future elections.

Bharat (India) is a beacon of democracy in this part of the world, where military dictatorship is the norm. So no matter how inadequate, corrupt and mollifying, self-accommodating the Indian democracy may be, it is still a great achievement against all odds. The credit goes to the majority Hindu population, who are, on most part considerate and accommodating, even docile to change.

There are very few thorough breed politicians in a democracy. Most are plough horses, useful at certain times and a drain for the rest of the time, go on babbling, talking double Dutch that most voters could not understand. Then politics is and always have been a complex, shifting, intricate and energy draining profession, not for the faint heart or for those who would like to upheld high moral standard and integrity in public life.

In India most politicians are obsessed with trappings of the office and taking backhanders to enable them to spend a fortune on election propaganda and get elected. No wonder most people see ministers consumed by a risible "foil de grandeur" and in the pockets of the moneylenders who financed their political adventure.

They are, on most part ballerinas who dance to the tunes of whoever that pour the money in political propaganda black hole. It is a worrying concept, a thought like an embryo. It starts small but grows and grows until it takes over most functions, makes the politician a puppet on a string.

In India most politicians come from families and background intoxicated with arrogant certainties. But they all know how to smile, that the smile is an inexpensive way to improve their looks, that every one they meet deserve to be greeted with a smile and a hand-shake, especially on television. That is why a leader is chosen, not on how good he may be but how well he performs on TV?

In India people knows well that democracy is not merely a right to vote but a right of choice, a right to opt for an alternative government, an alternate medicine if the traditional one does not work. The fact that it was a hung parliament meant that every Member of the Parliament was as good as gold for the survival of the government, where fear and emotions become as muddled as allegiance.

Rajesh, the local MP was able to deliver, fulfil his promise when all such pledges were quickly forgotten in the past, after the election, with one party gaining a huge majority. But it was different this time. People were not taken in by hollow promises.

The villagers had formed a vote bank that would support any one willing to keep his or her promise. Moreover Rajesh had the magnetic power of the mind to attract spiritual and material abundance.

Rajesh believed in exploring the museum of the past politicians and came to the conclusion that the one who serves the people, fulfil their aspiration reaps the political harvest. The art of staying in power was to be in the heart and mind of the people all the time. Some politicians are wise but those who study themselves, analyse their actions are enlightened. Self knowledge is the DNA of self-enlightenment, self-advancement and self-satisfaction. Ignore it at your peril.

In Rajesh, they had a good, caring, patriotic MP with village background who would fight tooth and nail on their behalf, indeed a rare political breed in the murky world of Indian politics.

Rajesh was a fountain of hope, inspiration, human civilisation and superior cultural values. He was not a surrogate apologist; neither for his party nor for his government. Rajesh was proud of his Hindu roots and was willing to wear bandana, a bhagwa orange scarf that most phoney secular politicians would like to avoid like a plague. It may dent their phoney secular credentials.

There is something wonderfully Gastonia about simultaneously promising the voters heaven and earth and delivering hell or high water! But now voters, even village voters were getting wiser by each election.

They were not prepared to accept the same old sound-bite slogans, polished, twisted and spun by the seasoned politicians who had taken voters for a ride for so long. They can fool some of the people all of the time but not all of the people all the time.

Now a day politician has to pay with a loss of seat, the seat of power if they take voters for granted, for fools. The constituencies and voters are no more hens that lay golden eggs. Politicians have to work hard for their rewards.

In deed Rajesh was a ray of sunshine in a far outpost rarely visited by politicians except during the election time. Rajesh was also a firm believer in ancient religion of Hinduism and the Hindu doctrine of Karma, one reaps what one sows. Being immensely patriotic, singing patriotic hymns was not good enough for him.

Rajesh wanted to turn villagers into true patriots, who are eager and willing to serve Mother Bharat or Bharatmata with all their will, energy and ability, not just to pay a lip service the politicians normally do. He would say, "Don't race against others, race against your-self. Freedom, trust and loyalty is like a house, you built it brick by brick and furnish it with your life savings, life blood. There is no short cut to serving people, gaining their trust and loyalty. His beliefs were in sharp contrast to those of other politicians who were "Here today, gone tomorrow."

For Rajesh, an ounce of practice was better than a ton of theory. How can he turn his back on his constituents who were all God's children? He also knew that the taller a tree grows, it would need more roots, deeper roots to steady it self, to stand tall and remain erect, standing in a storm. Rajesh did not intend to be a one term wonder but go on serving, stay in politics as long as he could do, as long as his constituents want.

Rajesh was a man of action. Sitting pretty at one's desk and dashing off letters, pamphlets drafted by an expert in political propaganda was not his cup of tea. His place was amongst people with true grit. He was a career politician, not a one day or rather one term wonder who comes in like a hurricane and leaves like a monsoon, bearing a rich harvest after a good downpour, for himself rather than his constituents.

* * *

Chapter Two

Dr. Samir Shah

When the town folks heard the good news that Dr. Shah has been posted to their village, to be the first doctor to work in their newly built and well furnished village surgery, they were more than happy, indeed elated to welcome him, as Dr Samir Shah was not a complete stranger.

He was indeed well known in Tulsipur and surrounding villages, as he had spent a couple of years in Kathipur some time back. So the villagers were familiar with the doctor. They knew how good, experienced, caring and capable doctor Samir was. He was well trained, able to carry out minor surgeries, such as removal of tonsils, appendix, varicose veins and such minor elements.

Dr. Shah was veracious, vernacularist and no one's ventriloquist, rare qualities in some one employed by the government, a civil servant in more ways than meet the eye. Medical profession is like a mind that could be compared to a fertile garden and for any garden to flourish, one has to nurture it daily. Dr. Shah had such relations with his patients, cultivating a lifelong contentment with his profession and all those who use his services. He believed that the secret of success is the constancy of purpose, as Benjamin Disraeli once said.

Dr Shah was known and respected for his good manner and helpful personality. But he was not exclusive for the village of Tulsipur. He was responsible for three other villages within the radius of thirty miles, that he would have to visit once a fortnight or as and when it was necessary, if there was an emergency, outbreak of cholera and malaria in the rainy season, the monsoon that strikes India like a tornado, water pouring from the dark, water laden sky as if some one had opened the shower with full force.

According to Hindu doctrine of karma, one reaps what one sows. Dr Shah had done a lot of sowing during the last twenty years of unselfish service and now he was rewarded with trust, respect, esteem and honour if not financial bonanza that he could have accumulated in a private practice but a practice without a soul, without a heart and certainly without conscious but full of hype and big sell that keeps the bank manager happy, enabling him, the doctor to live in the lap of luxury.

The logic of easy, luxurious life can be so compelling, so often leading to a demeaning and presumptuous charade of medical profession, one of the noblest professions that could serve humanity.

So being a doctor is a kind privilege, a gift of talent from God, not a licence to print money or to heap misery on your fellow human beings.

That is what they are taught in medical school. But they soon forget it once they enter the materialistic world. Some in medical profession go out of their ways to sell make-money-fast manuals like snake-oil salesmen preying on the weak, sick and the disable person, mounting misery on already luckless and sick human beings.

Dr. Shah was provided with a converted Volkswagen twelve sitter, seats removed and the space filled with all the latest gadgets that include a refrigerator, mini oven, a powerful fan and a comfortable folding bed that would be handy if stranded in a remote place. Doctor, a bit of a handy man, added a couple of large batteries to accommodate a large fridge freezer to add to his comfort, the most essential item during these scorching summer heat that may become unbearable without such small luxuries.

Dr. Shah added stock of tinned food, baked beans, craft cheese, butter, baby potatoes, carrots, frankfurters and variety of fruit tins, mostly imported from Europe where tinned food was a staple diet but in Bharat where fresh vegetables and fruits are available in plenty, tined food is a luxury not many could afford.

This food would be supplemented, go well with his favourite drinks that include some aperitif in more ways than one, to satisfy his gastronomic needs. He also carried on the roof some folding chairs and a table, so as not to take up any space in his tastefully decorated mobile home, a four star hotel room on wheels.

Dr. Shah did not forget the importance of living with unbridled exhilaration. He was a medical gunslinger in a literary sense with a romantic heart of gold and compassion. His thinking, his philosophy that never be a prisoner of your past but be an architect of your future served him well in his some what nomadic life style. The quality of life will ultimately come down to quantity of your contribution. More you sow, more you reap. But one must have a capacity to store and utilize what one may reap.

These small luxuries would turn an unscheduled stop in the middle of no where into an enjoyable picnic fitting for a prince. Dr Shah had invested his expertise and experience, backed up by his own cash to make his life as enjoyable, relaxing and comfortable as possible under the circumstances. He had succeeded in bringing a bit of his city life, a tiny lap of luxury to his village posting. It was his habit, his training to make the best of a bad situation, a remote posting.

Dr. Shah firmly believed that necessity is the mother of all inventions, all compromises. For doctor Shah, a comfortable living was not a matter of chance but a matter of choice, the choice we all make in our every day life, some choices are intentional, others made subconsciously, even without realising it but out of sheer necessity.

His belief, habit and easy go lucky attitude enabled him to be a civil servant, a government doctor earning a peanut of a salary, without bitterness or recrimination.

But worldly possessions and goodies in life did not drive Dr. Shah to the medical school. He was aiming for a higher reward, the spiritual attainment most of us do not even understand, let alone aim for. Dr. Shah was immune of the city loot mentality that drives the wheels of the modern day Bharat. No wonder so many of us ended up in the bunker of despair without an escape route to sanity.

Ramji, a local resident of long standing, was his assistant, his driver and his right hand man, indeed his Man Friday who would accompany him wherever he goes, taking care of his every need.

Ramji was not only familiar with the area but knew most of the patients by name, as he was looking after the surgery well before the arrival of Dr Shah who was like an elder brother to Ramji.

So Ramji was more or less indispensable part of the team without whom it would be difficult if not impossible for Dr Shah to function, to manage the surgery smoothly and efficiently.

After all two pairs of hands are better than one, especially when our resolves are being tested in the time of adversity, in the wilderness when the help is not readily available at the end of a telephone line.

As Tulsipur was a tiny village without educational or any other facilities, it was not possible for Dr. Shah to bring his family with him.

So doctor came alone here, leaving his family in Baroda where he had a comfortable three bed room flat, with all the modern facilities that well off city dwellers expect and get.

The flat was occupied by his wife Shruti and two teenage or rather young lads who were on the verge of entering Uni, with the intention of following into their father's footsteps, to qualify as doctors but perhaps not to join the Government service, to be a roving ambassador for medical profession on the cheap.

Unlike their father, they were a bit less sentimental, less patriotic and more practical, as they were exposed to the city atmosphere that is more geared to self preservation, self advancement rather than being a surrogate apologist for being born and fed with a silver spoon. We see the world not as it is but as we are.

In reality, their silver spoon was neither that big nor shining brightly, as both their parents had made huge personal sacrifices. They had given back to the society more than they had taken out and these children who only saw their father now and then knew it.

When they were young and missed their father, they were right to think that he was an elusive figure, a kind of Santa Claude who visited them only on special occasions, at Dipawali, Christmas and occasionally during their school holidays.

This was the routine on most part, Shruti unable to accompany her husband on majority of postings, especially after their children were born; as such postings inevitably involved villages where no private doctor would like to establish his practice, as there was more hassle and less comfort, more inconvenience and less financial reward.

It was like the difference between well being and being well off. No one can achieve the status of being well of as a doctor employed by the government, unless he is bent and without any moral, any principle.

As Dr Shah was alone; he elected to stay with the village elder, **Pitamber Patel**, who was a kind of unelected leader, a village Mukhi. (Chief) He was popular and every one trusted and respected him. His word was the holy mantra, a word from the Bible, the Gita, the utterance of Lord Rama and Lord Krishna.

Mukhi is like a tree that bears most heavy fruits, thus closer to the ground and in reach of every one, rich and poor, Krishna and Sudama, one a king and the other a pauper.

This was indeed a necessary quality, as there was no court, no solicitor and very few crimes or disputes. It was part of Mukhi's job, his duty, his obligation to the community to settle such disputes fairly and honestly, without fear or favour. Most disputes involved minor family differences that could be settled amicably, over a cup of tea, sitting in the village square or the temple compound.

By tradition, Mukhi is one of the wealthiest and most educated person, at least on most part.

So Pitamber Patel was no exception, that he was a savvy person of the calibre of a shrewd politician. He had a vary large, four hundred acre field and a well built house on one corner of his field, away from the village and with a luxurious annex, built for the visit of his children who all now live in the city.

Even for doctor Samir who lives in the lap of luxury, at least when he is in his own well furnished flat in the city, this annex was more like a penthouse than a pavement, comparable to his city amenities.

It was a perfect place, a desirable retreat to contemplate in solitude, willingly set aside by the Mukhi for Dr Shah, as doctor is a semi God in a village community where most people can hardly read or write. Education, literacy is for the city dwellers, not villagers who are, on part, hard working labourers.

This in-house residency was a perfect arrangement for the doctor, as his every need, especially his evening meal was taken care of. It would be inconvenient at best to cook an evening meal just for one person, after a hard day's work in the hospital, especially when the working hours uncertain, flexible to suit a patient's need.

Dr Shah has to be practical and butter would not melt in his mouth personality and underneath the young, almost boyish outward appearance was a steely determination to make the best of any opportunity that came in his way and why not? For Dr. Shah, every dawn is a new day, a new beginning to the one who is enlightened and liberated, in a manner most city dwellers are accustomed to.

Dr. Shah was already performing a public service by accepting a job that not many, so highly qualified doctors would accept, on a peanut of a salary but some good perks, that include long holidays, generous travel and relocation allowance and use of a car, a combie or a converted van, even a four wheel drive vehicle, so often the use of more than one vehicle did compensate for the lack of financial bonanza.

Then not every one prays to Goddess Laxmi, the Goddess of wealth. For some Goddess Saraswati, the Goddess of learning, knowledge and education is supreme, who charts their path and lays the foundation of their adult life. Academia does denote their spiritual and material intelligence.

It was a public service where a little bit of a fragrance will always cling to the hand that distributes roses and some of these roses do have thorns that may sting from time to time. But the reward was worth the pricking, the pain and the sacrifice on all fronts.

The smiling Buddha on his favourite disciple is worth every sacrifice to these dedicated professionals. Like five fingers, no two human beings are the same.

Mukhi and his wife Parvati were the sole occupants of this specious, well furnished accommodation, as Mukhi's children left the village to pursue their carriers in the city where they went for further education, a normal practice for leading and wealthy village families, got married and settled down, preferring city life to a village existence.

This isolation, some five miles away from the village gave doctor a perfect dwelling, with much needed privacy, solitude, a clean break once he leaves the surgery, clean, fresh, crispy, pollution free air, noise free atmosphere, waking up to birds' singing, cooing and cows' mooing, in sharp contrast to car horns, city traffic and human indifference.

Mukhi had built an annex, even better furnished than the main dwelling, for the occasional visit from their children, with all the city mod cons, modern conveniences, such as running hot and cold water, shower, well equipped kitchen and fridge-freezer, an absolute necessity during the hot summer months when heat become practically unbearable.

* * *

Chapter Three
Doctor's Philosophy
(Fruits of Positive Thinking)

Although doctor was a kind, caring, friendly and obliging person, he has learnt over the years, through experience, that it was absolutely necessary to keep a distance, not to be over friendly with villagers, to maintain his professional aloofness, the necessary courtesy. Otherwise he would be overwhelmed, consumed by the ailing villagers, become a part of their every day life without having any private life of his own.

The slogan "One for all and all for one" may sound appealing on paper but not in real life, especially for people who are the servants of the people in real sense and these include doctors, politicians, priests, social workers and every one who deal directly with the public. Such kindness is like opium, a drug habit that makes people dependent on others, even for minor ailments.

Doctor would be on call twenty four hours a day and in the absence of a Veterinary Surgeon, villagers would so often bring their animals for treatment? Although adulation is swansong Gaulism, there are times Samir has to be cruel to be kind, lay down rules and draw a line, a Laxman Rekha he would not cross. He would never treat an animal, no matter what emergency it may be. In any case, he is only allowed to treat humans under the rules and regulations that govern his contract of employment, although no one adheres to this written mumbo jumbo that only forms a guideline, not the bible.

So doctor Shah, although a kind, considerate and helpful to his patients, he never the less was firm but fair, laid down rules and followed routine in order to retain some privacy, dignity and private life outside his work. After all he has opted out of the hectic pace of life that personifies a city practice, in places like Mumbai, New Delhi and Calcutta.

Besides his work, doctor had many hobbies that include cooking, reading, listening to music, walking, yoga, wild life, bird watching of feathered type and water colour painting. Indeed Samir had a vast and varied interest that would keep him going even in the remotest of postings where most doctors get bored outside work. Then it is an art to live fulfilling and austere life without prominence and privileges that most isolated and remote places are devoid of.

Doctor soon settled down in this pleasant village environment. Even his work load was not that heavy, as these villagers were, on most part healthy. Drinks, drugs and obesity were not yet on the horizon and no one was a crouch potato, preferring outdoor life in the absence of over bearing TV and Bollywood domination.

Some villagers even preferred ayurvedic, herbal medicine which was effective on most common illnesses and even faith healing was not out of question, out of place in village life.

It is a common knowledge that half of the not so obvious illnesses have their roots in mind, a matter of mind over body and in such circumstances, faith healing works wonder, a kind of anti depressant treatment but without the use of drugs. What a sharp contrast from the present day environment when we have a pill for each and every illness.

Dr Shah was not an exception. He was a health fanatic, preferring to walk whenever possible. He loved long walks, through forests and vast, open semi forested areas, observing wild life at close hand. It seems city dwellers are more interested in preservation, nature and wildlife than village folks. It seems scarcity is the mother of attractions, necessity the mother of all inventions and familiarity breed contempt.

At one time Dr Samir Shah was in two minds, whether to take up medicine or to study zoology, marine biology or even astrology, how stars, planets, sun and moon affects human being. It is interesting, almost fascinating; but not many believe in such a science, especially for a career.

As a child, Samir was brought up in a sort of religious environment, as his parents were the devotee of Lord Krishna. So Samir was taught, brought up on Lord Krishna's thoughts as laid down in the holy book of

Gita. The book is considered to be the most amazing, spiritual and full of wisdom among all the religious books. Every word or rather every sentence in Gita has a purpose, a meaning and a word of wisdom.

Being a clever, well read and logical person, Samir was able not only to digest but expand on what he learnt from Gita and other holy books he read, the meditation and yoga he learnt, performed and even taught at various times in his life.

Samir's philosophy was, healthy mind leads to healthy body. Mind is like a big lake, a reservoir of positive energy, an ocean of untapped wealth. While each and every positive idea, thinking, notion brings wealth to a body and soul, in a similar way, each and every negative thought hinders progress, harms the body and soul that leads to ill health and early grave.

Early to bed, early to rise, positive mind and worry free life, makes a man, healthy, wealthy and wise, wealthy is a spiritual sense if not financially.

Power of mind, the mental mastery is the most essential ingredient to attract spiritual attainment, the Mox, the Nirvana and material wealth in abundance. No wonder Samir so often thought of specializing in psychology, become a psychologist. But in a country like India, psychologists are not in great demand, unlike America where every one has a personal lawyer, an accountant and a psychologist who they visit on a regular basis.

In the end Samir opted for medicine, to become a doctor, a physician or a surgeon, rather than a zoologist, environmentist, as medicine is an old and trusted profession where no one is out of a job for too long. Zoology can be interesting, even glamorous but job prospects are not that high, unless one is David Bellamy or David Attenborough who now brings wild life in our lounge and bedroom. Such success is rare, more by chance, luck than hard work, dedication and qualification.

Dr Shah was war returning to Tulsipur after a visit to a nearby village of Gadhli, no more than an hour's drive. Now and again doctor would give Ramji a day off, as he was on duty, on call practically seven days a week, as he has lived all his life in the village, among the people he knew.

So if villagers can not get hold of doctor Shah, they would not hesitate to turn to Ramji who had indeed looked after them for a long time. For treatment of minor illnesses, he was as good as doctor Shah himself. So today doctor was alone in his Volkswagen, as it was supposed to be a short, routine visit, more like a pleasure drive, an outing than an arduous medical task.

* * *

295

Chapter Four

Renewal of old Friendship

While in Gadhli, doctor Samir met an old friend, a fellow doctor who was passing through, on the way to taking up another appointment. Like doctor Samir Shah, doctor Raj was also on the move all the time and being alone, a confirmed bachelor, he was posted to even more remote of places where it would be difficult for a family men to settle down, even for a short while.

They met after a long time. Knowing their routine, their work load, they knew it would be a few more years before they will meet again. So why not make the most of this chance encounter? It was an unexpected opportunity to role back the years, go back to their carefree college days.

It would be wonderful, soul lifting to go down memory lane. It was the time when, as junior doctors in the hospital where they did their internship, laid the foundation of their future career, when they had to work so hard, some seventy hours a week. But in so many ways it was a fun, appreciating all the attention they received from student nurses. Some even had inappropriate liaison with these ambitious and beautiful femme fatale Joan of Arc of the medical profession. Then India is blessed with beautiful women from the time immemorial.

Raj, in line with most Punjabis, was a tall, handsome, very good looking young and ambitious person. He received most female attention. Perhaps he was good at socializing, making the most of very few opportunities young doctors would get, as their work load was so heavy and outside interests take second place over their commitment to their patients, hospital and their careers.

But that does not mean that they did not have a good time, a friend circle or lacked partying, enjoying themselves. It only meant that their lives, both private and professional, were confined within the hospital compound and their friend circle, on most part came from the same background, from a narrow social environment. In a way it was a close knit community which has some disadvantages but many blessings as well, as every event has a purpose and every setback has its lesson, an opportunity to refine one's social skill!

Raj had a series of girlfriends, not only among nurses but among his fellow junior doctors as well. In fact he was very close and perhaps in an intimate relationship with a beautiful girl by the name of Anjali, a daughter of a wealthy Sindhi businessman.

We all thought they were a very handsome couple, as Sindhi girls are among the most beautiful Indian girls, with milky complexion and tall, slim figure. Sindhi community is also in the forefront when it comes to education, ambition and financial management, advancement on the field of social and wealth creation.

But such romances generated out of necessity rather than true love is more often than not fails to last the distance. They have, on most part not much in common except their work, that may, in the long run become more of a hindrance than a help, as they live in each other's pocket all the time, in a pond like atmosphere than the freedom of the ocean, without having a break from each other. They lack the variety which is the spice of life, the oil that keeps the wheel of life turning.

Raj and Anjali's romance lasted two long years, was more secured than most but in the end the pressure of expectation on Raj from Anjali and her parents was too much for Raj to bear, to endure. Anjali was much smarter, more sophisticated and much more ambitious than Raj, who was more relaxed, easy going, kind and considerate person.

Anjali would like to become a consultant even before the ink on her medical qualification has dried and she was willing to make any sacrifice to further her career that Raj found it difficult to handle, to comprehend.

Anjali soon found a young and up-coming hospital consultant by the name of Sachin, a better bet than Raj in most ways and got married within a year of breaking up with Raj. Although Sachin was some ten years older than Anjali, they were a perfect match; both were very ambitious, money minded and social climbers. Perhaps that was the last time Raj was serious about any girl. Whether Anjali is happy in her present life is a question difficult to answer! Then who can define happiness?

If Raj was heart broken, he did not show it at the time, still having good time and fun with other girls, mostly with trainee nurses, as it was much easier to remain close but aloof at the same time with these girls who were, on most part, not in the same league with these high flying trainee doctors.

That was Samir's impression about Raj at the time and it seems he was right. Once bitten, twice shy and Raj did not want to engage into a serious relationship after his bitter experience with Anjali whom he loved to bits, wanted to spend the rest of his life in her company and who can blame Raj?

Anjali was such a beautiful, charming girl, full of fun and tender mischief. She was an obviously the most desirable girl but without being too obvious?

Reminiscing the past is always a bitter sweet experience. While it was a sweet experience all the way for Samir, it could not be the same for Raj, although he never allowed his bitterness to surface in the conversation. But he could not hide his disappointment, if not pain from Samir, a friend, a good listener and a trained observer.

By the time Samir and Raj parted company, after a good dinner, a few bottles of ice cold Kingfisher beer, thanks to the excellent fridge-freezer doctor had installed in his mobile dispensary cum home, it was already late and Samir was a tinny bit tipsy, was in the Tin Pan Alley, over the moon.

But as his home, his abode was only an hour's drive away, Samir chose to drive back to the farm rather than spend the night in Gadhli, which he often did if it was a long, tiring drive, especially if Samir was alone, without his assistant Ramji who did most of the driving.

Although it was late and Samir was alone, he had a relaxing day and the night was still young, shining bright under the full moon, the moonlight gave the countryside a pleasant, romantic, charming and appealing atmosphere. Not many city dwellers would get such an opportunity to be one with nature, that also at night, under the full moon, watching stars dancing in the moonlit sky, moon being the chaperon?

No wonder Samir was more interested in watching the sky, the moon lit countryside, the romantic forest littered with an oasis of trees and occasional shooting star falling out of the sky, so often easily visible in a sky not polluted with city lights.

* * *

Chapter Five

The Mystery of Universe

It is estimated that some ten thousand shooting stars enter the earth's atmosphere every week, most no more than the size of a golf ball and will burn out in the atmosphere even before reaching the earth. Those few that reach the earth, 99% fell in the sea or uninhabited land like Siberia, central Australia and the Brazilian forest.

It is indeed rare for a shooting star, however small, to fall on a populated area, unless the earth is passing through a tail of a comet that may be a few million miles long, containing several million billions of particles, tiny rocks and cosmic dust. The universe is littered with such comets.

One such famous comet is Halley's Comet that orbits the Sun every seventy six years. It is the brightest of the periodic comets that orbit the Sun, although it reflects only 4% of the sunlight it receives and is also the one that comes closest to earth, the only comet visible through naked eyes and stays on the horizon for nearly a month before disappearing, bidding farewell to earth.

It is named after Edward Halley who was the first astronomer, cosmologist to calculate the time that the comet would take to orbit the sun, thus giving the exact date for the stargazer. The comet has a long tale, composed of jets of gases from fissures in the outer dust layer. The tale, although long, stretching ten thousand miles, yet in astronomical term, it is only a few inches long.

One may only get one opportunity in a life time to watch, to observe this comet which has a chequered history. It last visited the earth in 1986, so the next sighting will not be before the year 2061. The first recorded sighting goes back some two thousand years, coinciding with the birth of Lord Jesus Christ. Perhaps this is the star the three wise men saw, prophesying the birth of baby Jesus, the noble son of God.

When the earth is passing through such a tail, the gravity of the earth sucks in millions of tiny particles, a few as big as cricket ball or even football. But the sky is lit up and the firework display is so spectacular that those who are lucky enough to watch it; will remember it as long as they live. The firework on display is a million times more spectacular than any thing a human being can manage to create, going on night after night until the earth passes through such a tale.

Occasionally, once in hundred million years, a meteorite the size of a ten story building and weighing millions of tons do fall on earth, creating unimaginable destruction that would wipe out most life on earth, as the sky is covered with the debris that blocks sunlight for months, even years, killing all plant and animal life.

Such an occurrence is blamed for the destruction of dinosaurs some one hundred million years ago. Craters created by such an impact are still visible in Mexico and Siberia, although the long time span has all but destroyed the scientific evidence needed to study and confirm the theory of the demise of dinosaurs.

Such an occurrence, the earth passing through the tale of a comet, is vividly described in Hindu mythology, in the books of vedas, written some twenty thousand years ago, when the human civilization was supposed to be entering the stone age, is fascinating, to say the least.

Such meteors' pyrotechnics and collusions have been described in varying details in our Hindu culture and various books of knowledge and records. Hindu scripts have vivified and graphically narrated the Tandav Nritya of Lord Shiva, the last dance by the God Shiva, the God who will bring the human existence on this earth to an end when he could no longer tolerate the sins of humanity. His icon is popularly known as Natraj, with multitude of hands carrying fire in each palm, can be seen not only in most temples but also in most Hindu and some Western homes.

This is the symbolic image of galactic pyrotechnics as understood by learned Hindu Sages and Rishis who had the knowledge of our universe, much deeper and in more detail than the modern day scientists, astronomers, cosmologists and space experts from NASA and the Western world. It is indeed a matter of great pride for the people of Bharat, the ancient name for India that they possessed such scientific knowledge at a time when the rest of the world was still emerging from the Stone Age.

Many Bhramastras showering fire on earthlings may be as symbolic as an acknowledgement of the meteors showering the earth. Rumbling caused by the elephant of Lord Indra, may be Sage's interpenetration, explanation of astral hullabaloo.

The earlier stages of Dashvatar clearly describe such collusion and how Mother Earth was saved, rescued from the destructive extra terrestrial fires unleashed by nature. The rescue, the cleansing came in the form of continuous rainfall lasting thousand years, submerging the entire earth under water.

The early life, the evolution of living organism and later the more advanced marine and amphibious life depicts refinement into human being, through a long process of evolution. The Lord Hanuman, half human, half monkey, the devoted servant of Lord Rama may be part of such a chain of evolution.

It injected the Devine ethics, the emergence of Hinduism, the oldest, richest and most cultured and vastly knowledgeable of all religions. It seems there is no comparison when it comes to knowledge about medicine (Ayurvedic) earthsastra (Economics) Yoga and the ancient art of Youdhsastra, the knowledge about the weapons of mass destruction. Hinduism reigns supreme.

Meteorite showers are also described in the later day religion of Judaism, Buddhism and Christian parable in their holy books of Bible and the Old and the New Testaments with stories similar to our own.

Although today the earth was not passing through the tail of a comet, for doctor Samir, it was as romantic a night as any he has ever experienced. Some how he was totally oblivious to the surrounding, that is until he came down to earth with a bump, shattering his romantic dreams that had taken over his rational thinking.

He hit a boulder that was right in the middle of the road or rather a dirt track that he had navigated numerous times before. But today his mind was not on the job on hand. He was not concentrating. Samir came to reality, his dreams were over or rather rudely shattered, made him wide awake when the vehicle stalled and came to rest with a moan. Samir came out and inspected his combie that had a big dent in the front. But otherwise the vehicle was not that badly damaged.

When he tried to restart the engine, Samir could not get any response. It was as dead as dodo. After struggling for half an hour, he realized that he needed Ramji or even some one more qualified to put life back in the engine.

Chapter Six
Moonlight Walk

Now Samir had two choices, either to sleep in the vehicle which would be not only a bit crampy but without the engine, he could not even operate the fan. So it would be a long, hot and very uncomfortable, lonely night, as it was nearing the end of summer, yet it is the hottest part of summer, with midnight temperature rarely below 30*C. It is like the last rays of the extinguishing devo, the candle burning the last drop of the oil, yet shines the brightest before finally bowing out to the inevitable.

Other option was to walk, not more than an hour's walk, as he was almost home. This was his daily patch, his routine with every track known to him. With full moon giving company, lighting the path, leading the way, it would be a joy to walk through this vast, open, lightly forested land with a cluster of trees here and there, to give it a some what undeserved name of wild jungle. The cool breeze was more pleasant in the open than in the confine of his vehicle.

At the end of the walk, there would be his home, sweet home, with a soft bed, a fast and furious fan and a cold shower to get the stanch out of his sweating body. It was no contest when he decided to walk. Was it a wise decision? Well who can tell, perhaps yes, as he may have seen the most beautiful girl who ever lived. What he saw, experienced, will live with him; in his heart till the death do us part.

Samir was walking through the jungle, occasionally passing through the cluster of trees, that include fruit bearing trees, such as black plum, almond, custard apple and others like whistling pine, banyan, pippal, birch, acacia and wild fruit bearing olive trees, fruits not fit for human consumption in any form but a real treat for birds, wild life and babul, bawad or a toothbrush tree, as the thin, new growth branches are used by the villagers to clean their teeth, in place of nylon tooth brush we are more accustomed using in the city. But then we have no choice. Bawad is no longer available in cities any more.

The Bunyan trees were most prominent and noticeable and they gave the forest a distinct identity, as they spread by spouting roots from branches that so often resulted in mother tree having several off springs, forming a cluster of dense trees that provide a wonderful habitat for not only birds but for ground hugging animals and flightless birds as well. Bunyan trees were typical to these forests that gave them a special attraction and superior aroma.

The juicy stick of bawad tree is so full of medicinal nutrition that protects teeth well into the old age. No wonder there are no dentists in villages, not yet at least. This is a wonderful advert for ayurvedic medicine researched and developed well over five thousand years ago and still going strong.

Occasionally there were dense scrublands with desert type thorny, ground covering plants, cacti and the likes that provided a heavenly habitat for flightless birds and those birds who would like to lay their eggs on the ground rather than high up in trees.

This light forest was a perfect place to take a walk, pass through with a full moon hanging so low with moonlight filtering through tall trees or blazing the ground with direct, unhindered brightness that gave the forest a romantic atmosphere, a perfect abode for lonely hearts in search of soul mates.

As Samir had taken many a walk through this forest, he was familiar with the area, the surroundings and kept away from the thickets so as not to disturb, startle birds and start a panic, disturbing the heavenly peace.

Samir kept to the tiny path, known as Kedi, carefully mapped by the villagers and formed by the daily human usage. So it was an easy, pleasant, scenic loop and enjoyable walk for Samir, a perfect antidote for his tipsiness, his over indulgence in food and drink that may have led to this situation.

For once responsibility was out of fashion for Samir. Then again, he may be a doctor but first and foremost he is a human being, with feelings, need and aspiration. Samir could no more shed his inhibitions than any one else and why should he?

There were no wild mammals as such; especially carnivorous animals like wolves, hyenas, leopards, mountain lions and the likes, although there were a few fox's dens with cubs. But they are harmless to humans and no more than a small dog in size. They would avoid human company at any cost and only seen at night.

There were other animals like tiny Nilgiri deer, wild goats, rabbits, hares, squirrels, wild hogs, boars, guinea fouls, bandicoot rats that dug burrows in the ground to use as nest, thus making the ground porous, amiable to rain water and the likes of animals but it was the bird life that gave this place some importance and uniqueness that made it so enduring to the villagers and visitors alike.

The birds, those include the local, permanent residents as well as the migrating ones were eagles, barn owls, tiny woodpeckers, bulbul, magpie, cockatoo, falcon, lark, parrots, swallows, weaver-birds, quail, thrush, martins, wood pigeons, skylark, starlings, imperial eagle, pale harrier, laggar falcon and nightingale, a few among many local, popular and common verities.

All together there were some four hundred varieties of birds seen in this part of Bharat with Nilgiri and Palani Hills almost on the horizon, a real heaven for mountain birds, as such a habitat is not that common or plentiful.

The vast stretch of fertile and forested land was converted into a national park, a game reserve, a bird sanctuary, under the influence of the great Indian anthologist, the one and only Shri Salman Ali whose books on Indian birds are so popular and widely read amongst all enthusiasts, a novice like Dr. Shah and Mukhi, eco tourists and professionals, college professors, with equal zeal and fascination.

All these separated forest areas and the National Park formed a one big bird sanctuary. There were also other birds seen occasionally, mostly migratory varieties that were popular and raise, create intense interest, curiosity among the knowledgeable bird watchers and Ornithologist. Such birds include Purple Sunbird, Streaked Spider Hunter, Forest Wagtail, Thick billed Flowerpeckers, Indian Tree Pipet, Isabelline Chat, Black Capped Sibia, Red Munia and many more.

There were also a few flocks of peacocks, pride and joy of the villagers, fed and pampered by one and all, as peacock is the national symbol, a protected bird with much reverence in the Hindu mythology, culture and religion. It is the symbol of Goddess Saraswati, the goddess of learning, knowledge, culture and elegance. So how can any one harm such a beauty, an elegant bird and pride of a nation!

The local royal family members, who were the decedent of the great Maratha king Shivaji, were conservationists at heart with special love for bird-life. Some of the princes were educated in England and as usual, they bring with them some of the British habits, culture and traditions. Their hobbies include hunting wild and dangerous animals like lions, tigers and leopards, often using elephants.

But with the decline of these wild animals, conservationists gained an upper hand. It soon became as fashionable to observe, draw and photograph these animals and colourful birds as hunting was in its heydays. The creation of the bird sanctuary increased the bird population ten fold, as many fruit bearing trees were planted and artificial nests of different shape and size were constructed, hung on most trees. It provided a safe heaven for these birds with no enemies, only admirers.

The birdlife was thriving here, as there were six separate forested areas in the region, separated by only tiny human settlements, in villages with no more than a thousand people or so, living a simple life, making very little demand on the vacant, forested area or the environment, thus giving birds and wild life all the freedom they need to sustain and even thrive, multiply.

But with fast expanding human population, the land being needed for agriculture as well as for dwellings, it is only a question of when rather than if humans will encroach on this beauty, a Vrindavan, Lord Krishna's abode; a gem of a forest with perfect eco balance, a pictures postcard image where wild life coexisted with humans without conflict of interest.

The conflict between humans and wild life is the trend worldwide but especially in India and China, with one third of the world human population, where the land is needed for agriculture to feed the billions. When there is a conflict of interest between humans and wildlife, humans are the winners on most part.

It is time to rebuild the partnership between all creatures, great and small, that occupy this wonderful, green green planet we call Mother Earth, as this is an unique planet, the like of which do not exist, at least not known to us, although we are now able to watch, observe and analyse all stars and planets within a distance of twenty light years?

One unpleasant aspect of the forest management was the occasional cull of the wild goats and perhaps wild pigs as well which are the most destructive animals, can survive in the most inhospitable habitat and without a natural enemy, carnivorous animals to keep them under control, they would soon over run this beauty spot if allowed to multiply uninhibited. Mercifully, they were gathered, herded and taken away rather than killed on the spot.

Villagers never enquire what happens to them once removed from the forest. Ignorance was the bliss as far as villagers were concerned, although Samir knew what happens to such surplus animals. They were too wild to be domesticated. So selling them was not an option, except to butchers for meat.

The best fate they can expect was letting them loose in forests like Gir with a thriving lion population, a lamb led to a slaughter house! Then all animals are in a food chain, some high up in the order.

Samir, walking at a brisk pace, soon passed the waterhole, the favourite place for the wildlife. The villagers had dug a small pond or rather a trough to let the water overflow into and used by all the forest wildlife.

The water was semi sweet with high mineral content, a blessing in disguise, as it was unsuitable for human consumption but perfect for the animals. So there was no conflict of interest as far as the water usage was concerned, reserved exclusively for the wild life.

* * *

Chapter Seven
Romance Under Full Moon

Samir was lost in his thoughts, sailing smoothly in his own world, unaware, oblivious of the surrounding, enjoying this rare opportunity of a midnight walk when his concentration was broken, his attention drawn by a sound of laughter, a human laughter of a girl, at midnight, deep in the forest.

No wonder Samir was taken back, his curiosity aroused, as he could not imagine any one from the village could venture so far away into the forest, however safe, romantic and enjoyable it could be, especially under such a romantic full moon night. Even during day time, the place is more or less deserted, devoid of any human activity, human encroachment except occasional wood gathering, the dead wood that may litter the forest, as cutting trees was against the law, laid by the Forest Commission who managed the forest with diligent and perseverance.

The laughter especially that of a girl, was sweet, sensual, romantic and pleasing to ears. Samir could not hold back his curiosity. He unintentionally moved towards the source of the sound. It was a conflict between his heart and his legs which wanted to move in the different directions.

But in the end his heart was victorious. His curiosity obviously triumphed over his common sense, his dignity even that of a doctor, a well respected person, over his urgent need to reach the comfort of his comfortable flat and the soft, inviting bed. Samir did not have to walk long before he saw a young couple, an eighteen year old girl, perhaps much younger, as so often these village girls are well built, looking much older than their age, physically well developed with all the outward sign of sexual maturity, yet on most part, as innocent as a newly born lamb. But certainly not Chanda, not this girl. She was the incarnation of Menka, the most sensual, provocative girl in Hindu mythology.

She was romantically involved, tightly held by the youth a couple of years older than her. The faces were only partly visible until the moon came out from behind the cloud, throwing full light on the couple, revealing their faces who were only a few yards away from Samir, who was careful not to disturb them in any way.

After all he was young once and remembered his wild, love making nights with Shruti, his first and only girlfriend, now his charming, sexy wife and mother of his two beautiful children.

So often we all go through these stages, phases in life. Yet when we become parents, we are quick to judge, even condemn such behaviour with the same old sound bite slogans, adopted, polished, twisted and spun by the society when two young, innocent souls are involved.

Then perhaps parents, who would have gone through such a phase, may realise how easy it is to lose control, for the girl to get pregnant, a moment's madness that may ruin her life for ever.

Although Samir was here for the past few months and had met most of the villagers, the couple did not sound familiar; their faces did not register with him.

How could he fail to notice such a young, beautiful and sensuous gem of a girl if he had met her, seen her in flesh before. There was some sort of strange attraction, a tantalising beauty, sexiness that puzzled Samir, made him envious of the young man who was making love to her but a bit apprehensive at the same time.

The couple were engrossed in each other, making love, unrestrained love, sex in many ways, as if they were in the garden of Adam and Eve, the Ashok Vatika, the most beautiful garden in Hindu mythology, where Lady Sita was kept prisoner by the not so evil Ravan.

As they knew they were alone, in complete isolation, as far as possible from the meddling crowd, there was no need for caution or any restrain, as they may not get such an opportunity that often. The girl was practically naked, her turgid, smooth body reflecting the moonlight with ease. Her cloths were lying on one side, thrown away with contempt, as if surplus to requirement.

The youth was trying to undress, to remove the couple of under garments that were barely covering her most private parts, her well developed thighs and the bulging buttocks that invited love bites through her flimsy clothes.

The girl was holding tightly, perhaps teasing and daring him to try, to succeed at his misdemeanour. As the girl was strong and well built, it was not easy for the boy to carry out his sweet but naughty raids on her most obvious attractions they both clearly wanted.

Even Samir, from such a distance can feel that the girl's resistance was superfluous; a part of teasing ritual to make him more excitable, want her badly that may lead to a fantasy sex.

After a few minutes, the boy gave up his attempt to remove her panties and concentrated his attention on her already bare, bulging and sexy breasts and sweet, broad lips.

She allowed him, even encouraged the boy to give her love bites, massage her breasts, occasionally screaming with pain associated with laughter and grunts of sexual satisfaction.

For Samir, it was like watching the most explicit sex video especially shot for a honeymooning couple. There was no need for this couple to watch any such video or to read Kamasutra, the most famous and ancient book on sex, as they instantly knew how to maximise their pleasure, their sexual fantasies without going overboard.

It was obvious to Samir that they were not a married couple but madly in love. As they may not get such a privacy and opportunity that often, in complete seclusion, they were determined to enjoy this solitude, moonlight romance but stopped short of the final act that may make the girl pregnant. It was only a question of touch and goes that made even Samir excited and wondering how far they will go.

Although Samir felt uncomfortable watching them secretly from behind the trunk of a large Bunyan tree that littered the forest, he was aroused at the muted, suppressed, grunts of kissing, love making and biting, at times painful but must be extremely pleasant, as the girl was giving as much as she received, perhaps her bites were more aggressive than his. His cries were certainly much louder than hers, the sound it self was enough to paint the picture of what was happening. Samir was curious and could not help being a peeping Tom. But he was careful not to disturb the couple in any way.

In a way Samir was trapped. If he tried to leave, make a movement, he was bound to attract attention which would be detrimental to his reputation and may upset the couple. So Samir was relived when the couple at last decided to get up, adjusted, put on the few cloths they were wearing in this heat and started walking towards the village, still not leaving each other alone, specially the boy tagging at her big, bulging breasts at every opportunity.

The girl had calmed down some what, trying to keep the boy at bay, telling him that he had more than enough of her for the night. Then love, sex ever enough when one is in his or her prime?

Samir was surprised that such intense sexual encounter can be a part of village youth, as sexual contacts outside marriage were still a taboo on most part. But then there is always an exception to the rule.

Then again why should these youngsters be different from their city counterparts or any other humans, living any where in the world!

We all have feelings, sense of adventure, sexual appetite and passion. Moreover we all fell in love and when that happens, nature takes its course that no amount of social taboo, threat or even punishment can make any difference. It is the heart, the feelings that rules the mind and body and not the social environment, at least not when madly in love.

Social environment, hierarchy and standing, unwritten community rules make no difference. Love, sexual desire is more addicting than smoking, drinking or even drug taking. So often these youngsters would willingly give up their lives, jumping off the high cliffs, rather than be separated. On every island, there is a high cliff from where these youngsters jump to their death rather than give in to pressure from their elders. These suicide points are well known and famous in many places, especially islands.

Samir followed them from a safe distance, as they all were going in the same direction. When they came to the edge of the forest, where there is a beautiful temple of Lord Shiva, the couple disappeared behind the temple perimeter wall, in the mango groves that provided the villagers an unlimited harvest of mango fruits during the season.

* * *

Chapter Eight

Restless Night

Having lost them, Samir took the short cut to his abode and was in his bed within half an hour of parting. But it was a struggle to go to sleep, although the cold shower helped him to douse down his excitement, wash away his day long sweating in this unbearable heat that most would like to escape from.

No wonder those who could afford, would move out, retreat for a month or two, to the surrounding hills where places like Rajpar, Panipat and Sagarpur were fast developing into a summer resort, summer retreat, as these villages were situated at the height of three to five thousand feet, with cool, bearable climate, surrounded by trees, forests and dense bush that made them ideal places to cool down during the summer excesses.

In the absence of sleep he could not help but remember, visualize the young, turgid beauty with excitable bulges, all in the right places and her intense, almost barbaric love making that even a six footer, strong, young man find it hard to handle. How Samir wished his wife Shruti was by his side, in his bed and what he would do to her.

Was it Shakespeare or the Bronte Sisters who wrote that body may grow old, may lose the spark but a bright, active and inquisitive mind will always remain young and imaginative. There may be a Viagra pill for the body but not for the brain!

Tonight Samir was as excitable, energetic and young at heart as he was on his honeymoon night. Perhaps he was in the arms of his beautiful and sensuous wife Shruti whom he married when she was just twenty two, with mind and body to arouse any one, beguiling beauty. Samir's mind was going back to the days when he first met Shruti, in those distant days when they were entering into adulthood, setting foot in the real world, charting a life, making plans for the future together.

This was not the first time Samir had missed Shruti. When he was an intern, then a junior doctor living in the hospital hostel, he was similarly aroused and missed Shruti when his friends like Raj had a wonderful love life with young, turgid and so often very beautiful nurses. But Samir, although in demand, would not waver from his resolve to remain faithful to his girlfriend, his fiancée Shruti.

So when Samir and Shruti met briefly while on vacation, they made love in some what similar manner, perhaps even exceeding this encounter Samir had just witnessed.

Like any true Hindu girl, Shruti would not have a sexual relationship with Samir, although they were engaged to be married. To resolve their dilemma and to enjoy their relationship to the full, they got married, albeit only in front of a registrar and two witnesses, that made them husband and wife in the eyes of the law but without informing their relations who would never have accepted such a marriage as a licence to go on a honeymoon, having a sexual relationship.

But for Samir and Shruti, it was more than enough to enjoy the fruits of a married life. Each meeting, after a long separation, was a honeymoon indeed. This step, arrangement made their relationship strong and binding, to enable them to survive long separation and kept Samir out of the clutches of female predators, kept him loyal to Shruti, as he could always look forward to their next meeting, next encounter, perhaps in a hotel while on holidays, with anticipation and eagerness.

The next day Samir did not get up until late, when it was nearly midday. Being Sunday, it was his day off. Samir would normally have his breakfast with Mukhi and his wife during week days but at week-ends, Samir would get up as and when he liked. He had the freedom of the kitchen in the annex to prepare, to cook what he may fancy, including a hot, masala omelette with slices of chillies and spring onion fresh from the field, his favourite Sunday morning breakfast.

Having lived on his own now and then, so often for a long period at a stretch, in remotest of the places, made him self reliant. His cooking skill developed more out of necessity than love for the art of cooking, as per saying "Necessity is the mother of all inventions" which was absolutely true in this case.

At home Shruti would bar him from the kitchen, as he would make more mess, like a bull in a China Shop? Moreover Shruti could not eat, stomach his cooking. Samir did not mind and why should he? It was a change to be pampered by a beautiful and sensuous girl like Shruti whom he loved to bits.

In fact Shruti so often dreaded his home-coming, perhaps a bit apprehensive, especially after a long separation, as Samir would not let her out of his sight, making love like a gladiator the night before he is sent into a battle to death. He could do what he like with the girl who has no say, who was there to satisfy his every fantasy before dying in the vast arena, teaming with humanity, who all had come to see him kill or be killed.

So often Shruti had to wear a heavy makeup to hide all those love bites openly visible, not to mention the numerous ones on her private parts covered by undergarments and loose cloths. With teenage children in the house, she had to walk a tight rope but she would not have it any other way.

Secretly she thanked God for giving her such a romantic, wonderful, kind and caring husband who loved her so much, want every bit of her no matter how much she has to struggle to avoid some of his excesses, even after twenty years of married life.

Then again it is true that the older is the bull, tougher are his horns, older one may get, there is less time, less years left for romancing. Could that be the reason for the famous quote that there are no fools like an old fool, especially when it comes to love, sex and enjoyment?

So often Shruti would send the children to her sister's house for the weekend. Even for a week or two if Samir's home coming coincided with school holidays. When unshackled, Shruti would not mind going wild for a night or two, giving a hell of a time to Samir who would not mind in the least when Shruti had an upper hand in the love making, climbed all over him and gave him more bites than she received.

Why should he? If only there was such love, such passion in every married couple's life? Last night's scenes made Samir remember his wild days and missed Shruti so much. It is only the body that grows old. Love and imagination always remain as fresh, as tantalising, teasing, exciting as ever, the day love and sexiness was born.

* * *

Chapter Nine
Rama's Retreat

As Samir was not hungry, he only had a cup of a strong masala tea before he left home in search of Mukhi, who would be in the hut or rather a small outdoor building he called **"Rama's Retreat".** It was near the pump that drew water from the artesian well which was located in the centre of the field and provided all the water that this vast and extensive field needed in order to survive the summer heat, especially just before the start of the monsoon season.

Mukhi built this retreat when he took over the management after the sudden and unexpected death of his father. As he had a young and noisy family, with four hyper active children, he needed this retreat to recharge his batteries, plan ahead and to become a man of substance.

Although Mukhi Pitamber Patel gave up his city life, his ambition to settle down in the city and give his children the modern, scientific and contemporary atmosphere, opportunity, he was not willing to give up his city comfort of hot and cold running water, shower, electricity and gas, fully fitted kitchen with gas hob and fridge-freezer that he installed in his Rama's Retreat where he spent more time than in his main residence.

The Mukhi introduced the modern way of farming and the field yielded a variety of crops, the chief being millet, wheat, cotton, maize, chick peas, sugar cane, onion, chillies and potato, in a five year rotation to get the best yield and to keep the soil fertile.

The chemical fertilizers were beginning to hit the market but the Mukhi wisely kept them out, his field free of chemicals. Even in those distant days when no one was talking about organic produce, Mukhi some how realised that the old age method, the tradition of using cow dung, horse manure and goat droppings, mixed with freshly cut straws, leaves and wheat and maize plants, allowed to rot in big silos, trenches or wooden containers.

In this tropical climate with year round heat and temperature routinely touching 45*C in summer months, it is easy, cheap and effortless to produce one's own organic fertilizer, especially when there is no shortage of cheap and efficient labour force. This indeed gave Mukhi an advantage in cost and quality of the yield over his rivals who were bamboozled in using expensive, so often imported chemical fertilizers that gave them a temporary edge in the yield but for a short time only, so often polluting their wells, streams and water supply.

Mukhi, with his education, his college degree behind him, exploited the land, made the best use of it, getting three crops a year, made possible by the availability of plentiful water all year round, from the artesian well that was sunk a long time ago, even when most farmers depended on rain and the river Gomti for water. It was a wise decision on the part of his grand father to sink the well.

Mukhi Pitamber Patel was the first farmer to plant what is now known as cash crop that is to grow sugarcane, tobacco and cotton which were in great demand in Britain, to keep the wheels of the Lancashire cotton mills turning and to keep their tea, also imported from India, sweet and pleasant.

Mukhi had set aside, turned a ten acres of his land into an orchard, planting fruit bearing trees, prominent trees being mango, guava, black plum (Jambu) Chania bor (sweet berries) pomegranate, oranges, lemons, grape fruits, Indian variety of peaches, two type of custard apple, known as Ramfal and Sitafal, named after Lord Rama and his wife Lady Sita. Mukhi had even managed to create a coconut grove of some twenty tall, elegant coconut trees laden with fruits all year round, as like sugarcane and banana, coconut has no fruit bearing season. Trees provide fruits all year round but more so in summer.

Normally coconut trees do not grow well so far away from the sea. Mukhi had built a ten feet of artificial layer of soil, matching the one found near the sea, with salt and other mineral contains that imitated the condition in which coconut trees grow well.

Mukhi, a great admirer and consumer of cool coconut water to drink and soft inner layer of copra that taste wonderful when only half ripe, had put in enormous work and great expense just for pleasure, so that he can enjoy a cool drink during hot summer months.

Coconut tree is also known as a refrigerator plant, as the coconut fruits, hanging in a 50*c temperature, a boiling temperature, will have almost ice cold water when split open and freshly drunk. The thick, wet outer layer of husk acts as insulation, protecting the fruit from the extreme heat. What a wonderful evolution, the fruit, the nature at its best. No scientific advancement can recreate such a fruit.

Mukhi, at the age of seventy, was only taking a superfluous interest. The farm was managed by his nephew Dhanji, as Mukhi's own children were not interested in a village life, preferring to settle in Baroda where they were educated.

They were all professional people, in well paid jobs for whom farming was a hard labour, even though they only have to supervise and not to do hard, break breaking labour. It was and still is done by the hired men, as there is no shortage of labour in a village.

Mukhi, by any stretch of imagination, was a rich man indeed, deriving a very good income from his field, a well managed, well run, high yielding enterprise and without any responsibility except to act as a Mukhi, to look after the welfare of the village and villagers. That was his main job and he enjoyed it, as villagers were appreciative, grateful and on most part good citizens with few problems.

In the field, he concentrated his energy looking after the orchard with some one hundred fruit trees yielding a variety of fruits for the personal use of Mukhi. His crop was in great demand in the neighbouring cities but now he distributed the surplus to various temples, schools, orphanages and to old people in the village, as he no longer needed the income from the orchard to maintain his lifestyle.

His orchard yielded such fruits, besides coconuts and mangos, custard apple, oranges, lemons, guava, Ramfal and Sitafal, a type of Indian pears but with plenty of black seeds, named after Lord Rama and Lady Sita, as they were their favourites fruits, black plums known as Jambu, a favourite fruit of many but it can only be eaten within a few hours of plucking, thus only available where it is grown, pomegranates, Chania boars or sweet berries and many more.

* * *

Chapter Ten

Game Reserve with Difference

One occasional hazard to Mukhi's orchard is from the band of langoor monkeys that may descend on his orchard when these monkeys leave their natural habitat, in the Vrindavan Nature Reserve that is situated at the foothill of the Palani Hills.

This game reserve was created at the turn of the 20th Century, more of a bird sanctuary than a big game reserve, as this part of Bharat has one of the best concentration of wild birds in the whole of Asia. These hills, Nilgiri and Palani with the highest peak no more than ten thousand feet, are densely covered with vegetation, open grassland at the foothills, forest in the middle and thick scrubs in-between with Alpine vegetation near the summit that provide a natural home to well over four hundred species, some permanent resident while many others migratory birds.

Vrindavan Nature Reserve or the Park is a jungle book like wildlife paradise, carved out of the area of natural beauty, some farm land and grazing area at the foot of the mountain range, natural forest and some scrubland, all merged with a beautiful lake, fed constantly from the mountain springs and melting snow to create a heavenly sanctuary.

The wild life consist of variety of deers but mainly tiny but swift Nilgiri deer, Palani gazelles, wild hogs and piglets, mighty wild Indian buffalos, various types of monkeys and predators like wolves, big wild cats not too dissimilar to cheetahs and mountain leopards, an elusive creature difficult to track down, let alone hunt.

However the main attraction is the vast and varied bird life that formed the part of the forests that surrounded Tulsipur and other four villages that provided a vast and varied forested area with plenty of water, fish and berries, a standard, staple diet for most birds with the exception of hunting birds that depend on rabbits, hares, burrowing mouse, pigeons and sparrows to hunt and feed their young ones.

The Bandhavgarth Game Reserve and Bird Sanctuary was very well managed by the Forestry Commission, under the direct management of the British Raj but in reality financed and administered by the local principality with the crown prince Youvraj Singh in charge, an Oxford educated naturalist who loved wild life.

The Prince was responsible for digging or expanding many natural ponds and water reservoirs, planting many trees and putting up artificial nests out of reach from the permanent, noisy and some what destructive monkeys.

He would not hesitate to carry out the orderly pest control exercise if these monkeys become too destructive, threat to bird life. It seems animals soon learn to live side by side with humans and other animals given the opportunity.

The best time to visit and enjoy this park, natural beauty spot is just after the rainy season when the land is carpeted with green, green grass, meadows covered with wild flowers that include orchids, periwinkles, variety of wild roses, especially on the cooler part of the park, wild magnolia, daisy and pink rose, a few among many varieties that carpet the land after a good downpour. It was a mixture of wild flowers and artistically planted flowering bushes at the right, strategic junctions. It was like a beauty of a maiden and the beauty of a sophisticated city girl, living in perfect harmony!

After a long, hard and savage summer, the arrival of monsoon, even a destructive monsoon from time to time, when the sky opens up and water pour down by a bucketful, comes as a breath of fresh air.

The merciless clear blue sky breathing down fire turns dark overnight, laden with water bearing clouds, pouring down water as if coming out of a bust water pipe. The parched land, a feature for a long time, turns into an eye pleasing, mind soothing green pasture land, covered with a carpet of flowers.

This transformation takes place almost overnight. Every hole, every pond, lake and depression in the landscape becomes a temporary or even a permanent waterhole, attracting birds, insects and wild animals of all size and shape. Jungle truly comes to life with mawa trees in full blossom, the delicate flowers and tender new growth providing a feast for languor monkeys, birds and human alike.

The abounding pale blue lantana flowers stippled the grass; jasmine like blooms perfumes the warm air. In the distance, the foothills of Nilgiri Ridge, a dream like vision, were sharply and clearly etched against the slightly pale ocean blue sky. The band of white cap monkeys, normally the resident of the upper reaches of the mountain range become the uninvited guests of the languor monkeys who would watch them from a safe distance.

This is the time for romancing, mating, building nests for the arrival of the young. The sight of peacock dancing in all his glory, majestic charm, sweet smell of scented wild flowers and sweet tunes flowing freely from love birds soon turn Bandhavgarth National Park into Lord Krishna paradise.

It would rival Vrindavan, albeit for a short span of time only, just a flicker of the eye in the span of this great universe where a million years is just but a second in human life.

This is the time when the park gets over crowded, so often the hunting birds forcing the languor monkeys to seek the pasture new. It is akin to poacher turned game-keeper. They spread out to the forests bordering the villages and as Mukhi's farm is not too far away from the forest; his orchard becomes a magnet for these roaming monkeys where they find the fresh, juicy fruits easy picking, to their taste.

Mercifully this happens only on rare occasion, as monkeys have to cross the open field between the forest and Mukhi's farm to reach the orchid, a hazardous journey at most times, especially in day light, the only time these monkeys are on the move. Monkeys are unable or unwilling to travel at night, preferring to stay high up in these, out of their natural predators.

Mukhi do not mind losing his harvest of fruits. But the havoc they cause to bird nests was unacceptable. Normally a gang of drum beaters would drive away these monkeys. But if every thing else fails, then Mukhi has to use his ultimate weapon, developed through experience, the firecrackers tied to an arrow and fired at the trees.

The noise is deafening but very effective indeed. No monkey worth his salt would stay a moment longer but it may also affect the birds that may leave their nests and some may not return. But mercifully this occurrence, monkeys raiding the orchard was rare indeed, out of desperation on the part of monkeys.

Chapter Eleven

Mukhi's Age Old Wisdom

Giving away the fruits from his orchard, fruits of his hard labour was Mukhi's contribution to the community, to put some thing back into the community's coffers that gave him so much respect, riches and mould him into a man of substance.

What more one can expect, may want in this life where we are but transit passengers, on the way to Mox, (Liberation) Nirvana (Salvation) and ultimate freedom from the cycle of birth and death.

This is the Hindu philosophy, cool, calm, law abiding, well rooted in Hindu belief, Hindu tradition, Hindu thought and meaning of life. Hinduism, besides being the oldest religion, is also the most noble, knowledgeable and culturally rich religion in the world.

Hinduism is the only religion which recommends the cremation and not the burial of a human body, the most hygienic, practical and scientific way imaginable. Now even most other religions are recommending such a practice that Hinduism invented and practiced for more than ten thousand years. It was based on scientific belief and research.

Mukhi, although living in a village, was an educated person with a BA degree in literature, obtained in the thirties when higher education was the privilege of the few, when university degree meant so much. Like his children, he could have stayed behind in the city.

But it was an era when children respect their parent's wishes. Mukhi was already engaged to a village girl, a gem of a person whom he would not let down under any circumstances and in a city, she would feel like a fish out of water, a lion in a zoo, a parrot in a cage, even a gold cage is after all a cage, an instrument to suppress, to curtail one's liberty.

Mukhi and his wife Rukhi had four young, hyper active children. So Mukhi had a tiny retreat, a beautiful summer house built in the middle of the field, neat the well, a part of the field covered with trees, well shielded from the sun, almost as good as a place on the mountain, in a hill station but on this own doorstep.

Although there were two rooms, one large room and a small bedroom, with a kitchen and shower, it was well furnished, almost luxuriously furnished with all the comfort, mod cons that would let Mukhi spend a considerable time away from the main residence.

Mukhi loved the Rama's Retreat that provided him with tranquillity, piece and quality time to recharge his batteries when he had a demanding, growing family and the field to manage, to make it a financial success.

Mukhi did not have such healthy finances, a bank balance to be proud of when he first started out. In fact when he inherited the farm, it was in debt and without proper management he would have lost the family inheritance, family heirloom, that was in the family for the last two hundred years. This financial security was the result of his hard work and prudent management. Now he can relax, put up his fit and let others do the work, take the strain!

At one time, this summer house was his remote outpost, his last retreat, his Fort Alamo from where he executed his plans, carried out his ambitious project of making his farm, his field the most profitable and well run farm in the village.

It was no surprise to Samir that Mukhi still spent so much of his time, even spare time in this summer retreat. It was certainly much comfortable, cooler than the main residence during the summer months.

Samir knew where he could find Mukhi on a Sunday afternoon when the temperature was touching 40*c. So Samir took the shortest route to Mukhi's retreat, as he knew that if any one in the village knew any thing about this mysterious couple, then Mukhi would be his man, his source of information, as Mukhi was a walking encyclopaedia when it came to village affairs, village gossips, village past, present and the future.

Mukhi knew all, done every thing and blessed every one, attended all functions, whether they were marriages, child birth or tragedies. He was like a bright, shining star in the vast, open sky. One may not see it all the times but knows that it is there, giving away light, shining bright and sustaining life.

When Samir reached the out building, Mukhi was about to have his lunch break, with a glass of sweet cool lassie, liquidised yoghurt, a popular and beneficial drink served especially during summer months. It can be sweet or salty but both Mukhi and Samir preferred the sweet variety.

Mukhi was a fruit and nut case, as his lunch consists of fresh fruits plucked from his orchid and lassie made from goat's milk, half a dozen or so goats he kept on the farm, especially for their milk yield.

Like Gandhiji who made goat's milk famous and desirable, set the trend, Mukhi loved goat's milk and all dairy products made fresh from the milk.

Moreover it is easy to milk a goat as and when the milk is needed, thus one can always have a fresh supply of milk, more or less on demand. Goat milk is also free of lactose. So it can be taken by those who are allergic to this white crystalline sugar occurring in milk, especially in cow milk.

Height of summer is also a fruit season, with mangos, sugarcane, custard apple, oranges, bananas, pineapple, peaches and numerous other fruits widely available, along with fresh vegetables such as muli, (Indian reddish), green, white and red cabbage and onions, chillies, aubergine, baby cucumber, French beans, Chinese leaf salad, celery and many more.

A goat cheese salad was a speciality in Mukhi's family, readily picked up by Samir, as a lunch time snack, in hot season. Mukhi's dining table was always well arranged with these fruits, freshly plucked from the orchard, early in the morning when they are at their best.

Mukhi was a bit surprised but pleased to see doctor, as they loved their occasional chat, meaningful discussion on religion, culture, politics, film, family and any subject that may be making headlines in the local papers. They also shared the interest in music.

Both liked country and classic music, including bhagans, the devotional songs in praise of Lord Rama and Krishna, written by their favourite devotees, Meerabai, Narsi Mehta, Sant Kabir and their likes.

The old film music based on the classical tunes, being played on famous musical instruments like Sitar, Sarod, flute, tabla and many more, the music they both loved was now taking a back seat to the Western tunes of Jazz, Rock and Role and the Brazilian Samba that go hand in hand with the musical romantic films, so often a comedy that the Bollywood production line was churning out in abundance, aimed at the young audience, the up-coming generation and to provide the romantic escapism to the middle and poor class Indians who throng cinema halls in search of cheap entertainment.

But it was not the cup of tea for either Mukhi or Samir, as there was nothing in their life they would like to escape from. They were well passed that craze, now living in a real world, not in need of cheap entertainment, artificial uplifting or any form of aphrodisiac or even the Viagra pills that is today's craze in the West.

There was hardly any one in the village educated to Mukhi's standard, with whom he can have a meaningful, intellectual conversation. So despite their age difference, Mukhi and Samir enjoyed each other's company. Both were street wise, family oriented people who loved stimulating human company and intellectual discussion.

The conversation between them was always polite, meaningful but none the less with imparting vigour, although without the autocratic determination to ram down the throat their own ideological belief, agenda that most politicians possess.

In a way Mukhi was a politician. If Mukhi had a political ambition, he could have got the party ticker, as he was so often touted by various political parties, as a popular, clean and decent person who would give any one a tough fight in an election, even to a sitting Member of Parliament, who, on the whole were a one term wonder, as they never carried out the promises made during election time, indulging in their secular sainthood, gradually losing touch with the people who elected them.

But Mukhi knew that there was not a drop of political blood flowing in his veins. He was simply too honest, decent and caring person to change overnight, to become a political stooge, a yes man, obey party line and betray his constituents, even his friends. That is the requirement in the modern day Bharat, the dharti (earth) of Mahatma, Sardar, Bose, Rama and Krishna was but a distant dream.

Mukhi, like Samir, was a devoted, a proud Hindu and a patriot. He was not affected, consumed by centuries of adversity, foreign rule and so often outright slavery which meant that we often keep our innermost thoughts, pain and sufferings to ourselves, a stiff upper lip to survive in a hostile environment. So often we behave like a sheep in wolves' cloths, betraying both our Hindu culture and our motherland Bharat. Fortunately for Samir, they both shared these patriotic intense views.

After all Samir was not only living in Mukhi's house, as his guest but Mukhi was also much older than him, almost like a father. In a Hindu society, silver hair is respected, as wisdom comes as much with age and experience as through education, reading and by any other means.

On Mukhi's part, he appreciated that although Samir was so much more educated than himself, indeed a doctor, he did not show any sign of superior complex, the metropolitan elite, aloofness that is so common in the medical profession, the *"I know all" attitude*. In Mukhi's book, it was a sign of good upbringing.

Samir sat down opposite Mukhi and filled himself a glass of lassie and some fruits, mainly mango, banana and his favourite custard apple. It was indeed cool here, under the shade of the trees that blocked most of the sun light. The cool, clean, clear and running water some how a cooling, soothing had effect on the place.

It was like a small stream, running through a private stretch of land that provided this heaven in otherwise a wilderness. Only a fishing rod was missing?

By the time they finished light lunch, it was the hottest part of the day, with temperature hovering near 50*c even in the shade. This was the time to take a dip in the big trough where the water was stored after being drawn from the well, before being released to the field through the shallow canals dug throughout the field.

The water was waist deep but so soothing to sit and talk. Mukhi was a good judge of human being. He can almost read one's mind, thoughts by just looking at the face. He could see through lies, half truths and an attempt to hide real feelings.

Mukhi instantly knew that Samir was not here to share his lunch or even to cool down in this big, luxurious bath tub, indeed a small swimming pool. But he did not have to wait long before Samir opened his heart and narrated last night's experience, trying hard not to get excited, leaving out the juicy beats that he thought Mukhi would not be interested at his age but without much success. His tone, his inquisitiveness and excitement was too much to hide, too obvious to be ignored.

Mukhi was an experienced hand; no one can fool him or hide any thing from him, however hard one may try. When Samir finished talking, Mukhi said with a smile on his face, "Samir, you have left out the most interesting part of your story. Surely you must have noticed how beautiful the girl was and so scantly dressed, wasn't she?

I also know that you have hardly slept last night. She could raise any one's blood pressure, at any age, even when fully dressed while what you saw was more or less a naked pose, an erotic pose, a Mona Lisa, Anarkali posing for an artist in the scantiest of attire, only a lucky few have managed to catch her in such a pose? So count your blessings and be grateful to the All Mighty.

* * *

Chapter Twelve
Chanda: The Village Anarkali

Noticing that the doctor was feeling a bit embarrassed, Mukhi, an old hand, gave Samir a mischievous smile and continued, "There is no need to feel guilty in any way. The girl you saw is or rather was a village beauty by the name of Chanda (Moon) but we affectionately called her ***Anarkali,*** a rose bud, the beautiful one.

What you saw Samir was not real, at least not now. They are not living persons but two souls lost in the maze of unreality, in the world beyond our comprehension, our imagination and our understanding, that is if you believe in a world after death, in heaven and hell.

They were what we may call ghosts, spirits, lost souls, the images of two people who lived in the village a long time ago and died a terrible death, all because of our rigid class system and social hierarchy and the so called family honour that is worth more than the lives of our children. What a twisted world we live in!

This was the equivalent of present day honour killing when a father kills his own flesh and blood to protect the twisted belief of family honour. It would be difficult for a rational person to understand how a mother who gave birth after bearing the bulge for nine months and a father who had brought up his unique child, a defenceless daughter, to kill her, murder her in cold blood. I will never understand it even if I live for s thousand years and beyond?

The tragic love story between the son of a village tin pot Mukhi and a lowly but lovely Chanda, the moon like daughter of the village blacksmith, who was as beautiful as the legendary Anarkali is famous, well known not only in our village but in all surrounding villages as well. Yesterday night was the anniversary of this tragic incident that took place more than fifty years ago.

No one would have let you walk through that forest, on a full moon night if they had known. But yours was an unplanned incident no one could foresee. Perhaps you were destined to see this beauty that once captivated the whole village, before she permanently disappears from the scene, their favourite place, the forest, as their sightings are becoming indeed rare with the passage of time. Let us hope that they will soon take their rightful place in heaven and stop being a wondering, unfulfilled spirit in search of worldly, bodily pleasure.

In a way you are fortunate to see this girl, one of the most beautiful, charming, sexy female ever to born in our village and mind you, our village is not short of beautiful girls either" Even Mukhi's eyes sparkled at the mention of this girl.

No wonder Samir had to twist and turn whole night, he could not go to sleep and every time he closed his eyes, he saw Chanda, the dream girl, half naked beauty even a God could not resist. Samir felt at the time that she was too good, too beautiful and too sexy to be real even while he was watching her.

But how could he doubt her existence when she was in front of her, only a stone throw away? So near, yet so far, like a child watching the reflection of a full moon in water, he would like to touch, to catch. When he was in bed, he did wonder, was it a delusion, his fertile imagination on a beautiful, romantic moon lit night?

Did he miss Shruti too much? Such remote postings are in a way exile. Was it a dream of glorious return to his beautiful and charming wife? His anxious, excited heart raised many questions but his mind could not provide a single answer. Samir was lost, did not know what to think, what to believe, what to make of this chance encounter.

It seemed fair for the girl to be compared, called the village Anarkali. But no one knows how beautiful the legendary Anarkali really was. She captured the heart of the Mogul Crown Prince Salim, heir to the throne of one of the most dynamic dynasty in the Indian history.

Anarkali was a courtesan, a classical dancer of great skill, elegance and a rare beauty who entertained the royalty and their guests. No one was much aware of this story, a tale more or less shrouded in mystery, in secrecy; that is until the Bollywood industry turned it into an all time great, a box office hit, the first coloured movie, starring Madhubala, the most beautiful actress of the time who portrayed Anarkali to perfection. Madhubala herself was a rare beauty, with haunting, teasing eyes and captivating, mischievous smile that forced educated people like Samir and Mukhi to go and watch the movie, just to watch, observe Madhubala, in her body hugging dresses, exotic dances in the Mogul court, in front of the Emperor and Prince Salim.

This is the only Indian movie Samir had watched more than once on the big screen. In fact he saw it five times in one year, at every available opportunity.

With enchanting music, heart penetrating lyrics and haunting tunes, classical dances performed on most part by Madhubala her self, this film, a four hour epic "Mogul A Azam" will always remain one of top ten Indian films ever produced, in line with Samir's other favourites, Awara with Raj Kapoor and Nargis, a true life romantic pair entangled in a love triangle, Mother India, Guide, Madhumati, Azad and many more.

There is no need to say that Anarkali met a tragic end, buried alive by the raging Mogul Emperor, played with panache and style by Prithviraj Kapoor, another legendary actor, for daring to trap Emperor's son, heir to the throne, falling in love and winning over his Prince Salim who was willing to go to war against his own father?

After a short pause to regain his composure, which gave time to Samir to contemplate on the last night's event, remember his wife Shruti and indulge in the nostalgic past, Mukhi continued with a bit of a sorrow and sadness on his wrinkled face. "The name of the girl was Chanda, the moon but was better known as Bijli (Lightening) or Anarkali.

She would light up any sky, even the darkest of the night, a black, dark moonless night but only for a while. She was too good, too beautiful to be true, the real Mona Lisa of the village. The pre and post independent period was a romantic era, romantic age for the people as well as the Indian film industry when such great hits were produced.

Chanda was a daughter of a local blacksmith, one of his four children. Chanda was the youngest child, as she was born well after the rest of his children were grown up and well settled.

She was born at a time when her parents were near the retiring age, although no one completely retires in villages. They merely slow down or take a back seat.

So even the birth of Chanda was a novelty, an unique occasion, a topic of conversation, gossip and chit chat. Chanda was born when her mother was in her late forties or even early fifties, well past child bearing age that raised many eye brows. Her birth was neither planned nor wanted or welcomed by her parents. But once she was born their attitude changed.

All children cry when they are born but there was a smile on Chanda's face, at least most who witnessed the birth thought at the time. Chanda was a big, healthy girl at birth. As she grew up, it was apparent that there was nothing in common between Chanda and her parents.

While her parents were like any other villagers, well built with medium height, semi dark skin and jet black hair, Chanda was just the opposite

Chanda had a light, fair, milky skin with long, light brown hair and very light brown eyes of unusual colour that shined in the darkness, just like eyes of a cat!

She was tall, even taller than most of the boys of the same age. Moreover she was clever, inquisitive and smart, a real gem of a lovely little girl every villager wanted to play with and take her to their home, wished they had a daughter like her.

She was the talk of the town in many ways. No one could believe she could be a daughter of a simple village blacksmith. She was so different in so many ways, a chalk and cheese combination. Soon she was hailed as a miracle child, a virgin birth and perhaps she was conceived outside the norm of the sexual relationship! When village gossip gets hold of a story, then there is no limit to one's imagination!

* * *

Chapter Thirteen

Virgin Birth

In Hindu mythology, in the holy book of Mahabharat, there is a very interesting story, an incident of the virgin birth of Kunti Putra Karna, the elder brother of five Pandavs. For those who may not be familiar with this story, it is worth mentioning here.

When Princess Kunti was young, a real beauty, she was also a great devotee of Lord Surya (Sun God). She would stand in her palace balcony facing, looking over the mighty river Jamuna, at sunrise and pray to Suryadev for an hour or so, every day without fail, come hell or high water.

When she was sweet sixteen, the God was so pleased with her devotion that he appeared in person, stood in front of her just before she opened her eyes. When Kunti saw the God, she was speechless, in awe, could not believe her eyes for a moment.

But when she bent down and touched the feet, a tradition among Hindus to show respect for the God and the worthy, that could be a Guru, (Teacher), a Vaid, a kind of doctor, a herbalogist blessed with healing power, a learned, elderly person, priest, parents and any noble person that is held in high esteem, a ritual that is still part of Hindu culture. Kunti soon realized that she was in the presence of God, Suryadev.

Suryadev blessed Kunti and requested her to make a wish, any wish and it will come true, will be honoured. Kunti always wanted her first child to be a boy, a prince, that is when she get married and settle down.

The first sentence she uttered, that came out from her mouth, from overwhelmed Kunti was, "My Lord, I want a child, a prince" and she paused for a while to regain her composure. She forgot to mention that she would like this wish, this blessings to be fulfilled when she get married. Kunti was on the precipice of being naïve.

The God blessed her and disappeared in a flesh, like a lightening. Kunti did not realize her mistake, the confusion until she got pregnant a few days after she received the blessing. By now it was too late for the God to intervene, rectify her mistake.

After nine months, Kunti gave birth, a virgin birth to a baby boy, a prince when she was just seventeen. She was unmarried and she knew that no one would believe her story, this amazing incident.

Kunti had no choice but to let the baby go. She put him in a wooden box and let it float away in the river. The boy was rescued by a fisherman who named him **Karna** and raised him as his own. He was an extremely bright, clever and ambitious person. But he was also kind, considerate, loyal, dedicated and a man of principle.

Karna joined the army and soon rose to command one of the greatest army, even though he came from a lowly family background, a son of a poor fisherman. He was spotted by the Kaurave Crown Prince Duryodhan who took him under his wing.

Duryodhan, although an extremely ambitious, cunning and ruthless person, he was also a good judge of character and in Karna, he saw an ally who would stand by him through thick and thin, in good time as well as bad. How right he was?

He immediately realised the noble qualities of Karna, took him under his wing, declared him as his friend, his adviser, his right hand man. He gave Karna a small kingdom and bestowed him the honour, the all important title of a king, thus making him a noble person, equal in status with Pandav and other kings that Karna was lacking.

Karna had unique qualities, unrivalled skill on the battlefield where no one could defeat him. Duryodhan knew that Karna at his side, no one can defeat him on the battle field, his victory is assured.

In this unique mythological tale of Mahabharat, the character of noble Karna stands towering above the rest, as a kind, caring, loyal and noble person and a warrior of utmost ability.

After all he was the offspring of Sun God Suryadev. Only one other person, Bhishma Pita has more standing, nobility than Karna, although Lord Krishna towers them all. But then Krishna was God, a unique personality in the same league as Lord Rama but also different in many ways.

Princess Kunti went on to marry Pandav king and gave birth to five unique princes. In the great war between the evil Kaurave Prince Duryodhan and noble Pandav king Yudhister, Karna remained loyal to his friend Duryodhan, although by now he knew who he was, the eldest son of Rani Kunti, that he would be fighting against his five brothers who were the virtuous, noble, caring princes, fighting for justice while his friend Duryodhan was in the wrong, was an evil person, who was fighting for his personal glory, to subjugate and rule others without mercy or favour.

When Karna's biological, real mother Kunti begged him to change sides, take his rightful place as the eldest son of Pandav clan and be crowned as an emperor if they win, noble Karna refused to abandon his friend Duryodhan who gave him a kingdom, made him king and stood by him at all times, even when no one else was willing to recognize him as a noble person, due to his poor background, a son of a lowly fisherman.

Karna had a troubled life as a child. He was clever, intelligent and full of ambition. But his position in the society and the social and financial standing in the community was a restrain that restricted his progress.

After a great deliberation, heart searching, he had to tell Kunti that he could not desert, could not bite the hand that fed him, looked after him all these years. But he promised his mother Kunti that he would not kill his five brothers on the battlefield, thus promising them a victory they deserved.

He even let his brother Arjun kill him on the battlefield, thus letting truth, honesty and noble cause triumph over evil, greed and wickedness, let right triumph over wrong, virtues over evil intention, even at the expense of his life but remaining loyal to his friend Duryodhan till the end.

There are very few examples of such sacrifice, nobility, friendship, even in rich Hindu mythological tales. Karna, a virgin child, a gift from God to Kunti, to humanity was unique.

Even Gandhiji who had all the virtues, all the good qualities, designated, regarded Karna as his role model, to follow in his path and ultimately became a symbol of hope to millions of Indians and led Bharat to freedom without a single shot being fired in anger.

No wonder Gandhiji was declared the personality of the 20th Century. But those times were different. We were living in a different world. Today it would be difficult for a nation to give us Karna, Rama, Krishna, Gandhi or even Martin Luther King. Perhaps Nelson Mandela is the last in line of these great souls. No wonder Mandela rules every one's heart and soul.

No wonder the name of Karna has become a byword for nobility, devotion, sacrifice and fair play. Then a virgin birth, a gift from God can never be any thing less. So a virgin birth is associated with such character in the Hindu mythology, willingly taken up by other civilizations that followed Hinduism.

* * *

Chapter Fourteen

Chanda and Machu: Beauty and the Beast

Even at school Chanda was a bright pupil, a clever, inquisitive and smart girl. She was a real gem that the villagers took to their heart; that is until she started developing into a real beauty, a sex symbol in Bollywood style, with big, bulging, over bearing breasts and curves no other girls had.

Chanda's physical attractions were supplemented by her kind and caring nature, her sharp and inquisitive mind and the way she dressed, walk, talk and approach people. No one is perfect, that unique, that is until one may fall in love with such a person and every villager was in love with Chanda, in one way or another. She became a perfect life partner, from pauper to prince and beyond!

In villages where most ladies do not wear under garments and even clothes were loose and few, more revelling than concealing, especially during hot summer months, it was difficult for an innocent, naïve girl like Chanda to hide her big, bulging breasts, thighs and buttocks which were still developing, physically, mentally and morally, learning how to hide her vital parts, not to offend any one, at the age of just fourteen.

The village folks who once adored this little girl, who resembled an angel, were quick to turn against her, especially women who could not help but notice the keen interest their men folk were taking in Chanda. By the age of sixteen she was a raving beauty, a sex symbol, well known throughout the neighbouring villagers as well. Chanda was a dream girl, adored and secretly wanted by all, as a lover if not as a wife, a life partner."

Mukhi paused for a while to refill their glasses and catch his breath, as even Mukhi, at his age, was clearly getting excited, remembering Chanda as she was all those years ago. Moreover they were, although in a cool, fresh water, were directly under the sun but not for too long, with the sun moving towards the horizon, vacating the prime, overhead site that makes the heat so unbearable.

Samir was not surprised a bit, as he had witnessed at first hand how beautiful, sexy Chanda was, now a bit naughty, teasing and wise as well. She had all the charm, attraction and sexiness of Anarkali, capable of captivating a prince!

Most young, eligible village youngsters or rather young men would have willingly married Chanda, to contemplate in solitude, made her a bride, a life partner, even though she was attracting notoriety.

Chanda's reputation and eminence were attributed for all the wrong reasons she neither desired, sought nor deserved. Then, in a village, gossip is a big business, a kind of entertainment that villagers loved, as long as they are not at the end of it,

But no parents would like such a girl as their daughter in law who would always be a centre of attraction, subject for gossip and object of desire for all the male villagers.

Moreover the rigid class system would bar most youths from marrying a girl from a lower caste. She was a sweet, bitter fruit, a wild apple in Adam and Eve's garden. She was a tasty meal that would give a stomach ache. Samir, it would be difficult for you to understand, even to imagine what a dilemma she imposed on the village elders.

A few strong headed young men and perhaps a few not so young would have defied the will of their elders and married Chanda if only she had encouraged them.

But Chanda was a decent girl, perhaps too decent for her own good. The village elders knew that Chanda was a kind, caring and extremely beautiful girl who would not set a foot wrong but that would not solve their problem until Chanda gets married to some one from her own background, her own community. Chanda has just to talk to some one of her own age to set the tongue waging.

In any society there is always a rotten apple in the barrel. One day when Chanda was returning from an out of the way farm, having delivered the lunch, a task she often performed for neighbours, as a favour or perhaps to repay their kindness, she was attacked by a well known vagabond, a trouble maker from a neighbouring village of Suryapur.

Perhaps Machu was following her, keeping a tab on her moment or perhaps it may be a pure coincident that Chanda encountered Machu on a lonely path, at midday when there is no one around.

Although Chanda was herself a strong, well built girl, she was no match to a six feet tall trouble muscle with bad temper and no regards for any one, accustomed to taking what he want by any mean, fair or foul.

Machu grabbed Chanda from behind, tearing her blouse, exposing her chest and upper torso, her big, over bearing breasts. Perhaps under the influence of drugs he attacked Chanda like a starving wolf who had just found a defenceless lamb at his mercy, to be mauled and eaten at his leisure.

Although Chanda fought back bravely, giving Machu some nasty blows, she could not stop him from giving her painful bites all over, particularly on her breasts, leaving them bleeding and badly bitten.

Fortunately for Chanda, Mukhi's son Kanu was watering the nearby field who came running to her aid, on hearing her cries for help. Kanu floored Machu with one blow while he was still struggling to undress Chanda below her waist line.

A nasty piece of human being like Machu is coward at heart. They get their strength, their courage when operating in a gang, attacking defenceless women and old people. Machu soon realized it was time to make a hasty retreat before he sustains a real, serious injury.

Even one blow had already loosened a couple of his teeth and his mouth was already bleeding badly. He was no match to Kanu, a healthy, well built young man in his prime, shaking with rage and anger, looking at the injury, bites sustained by Chanda who collapsed in his arms, sobbing uncontrollably.

"I will show you what happens to any one who dares to raise his hand on me. From now on, you are a marked man, so watch your back." These were the parting words of Machu who made a hasty retreat.

Kanu instinctly hold Chanda tightly in his arms, letting her cry, patting her bare back and long, silky, fair hair gently without much thought, trying to calm her down, telling her again and again that she was safe, reassuring badly shaken Chanda that no one can now harm her, that she was in no danger.

It took a while before he realised that Chanda's bleeding bare breasts were pressing hard against his open chest, as he was wearing an open sleeveless shirt, a common dress for a working farmer during scorching summer months.

When he realised that, he took off his shirt and wrapped it round her shoulders, gently holding her hand and escorting her to the farm, the hut that provide the shade. It was a five minute walk before they reached the safety of the hut where Kanu provided Chanda with fresh cold, clean water and antiseptic to wash and clean her superfluous wounds with cotton and a clean towel.

While Chanda attended to her wounds, frantically trying to remove the visible love bites from her neck and arms, Kanu stood outside the hut until she was ready to call him, let him in the hut.

They had a cup of tea and some Nan bread. It took some time for Chanda to recover her pose, her composure, her self confidence and her trust but Kanu was a perfect example of how a gentleman should behave.

Kanu was an articulate person who knew how to treat a young girl in distress, never starring at her bare breasts or making Chanda uncomfortable in any way.

Chanda was soon at ease in Kanu's company having washed herself, having a hot cup of tea with plenty of sugar. Such a drink is so often more soothing in a midday heat than a cold drink.

They spend an hour before they were ready to return to the village. Kanu walked Chanda to her parent's home who were worried sick, as Chanda, a punctual girl was at least two hours late and were about to go out in search of her when she entered her home and collapsed in the arms of her mother, sobbing uncontrollably.

Chanda's parents could not thank Kanu enough for saving the honour of their beautiful, innocent but charming girl. Within hours, the village was buzzing with rumours, innuendo and allegations.

While most villagers were sympathetic to Chanda's plight, as Machu had a nasty reputation, there were some who would like to take this opportunity to pour oil over the fire, kick Chanda when she was down and trying to blacken her name, who was a much desired forbidden fruit they can not have. Chanda was village **Anarkali, a femme fatale.**

Chanda must have encouraged Machu or was it a clever plan to draw the attention of Kanu, the most eligible bachelor in the village? Well, in some ways, it was a legitimate question but only if some one else and not Machu was involved. It would be like asking a tiger to look after a lamb, a Sharabi (drink addict) to look after a pub?

This incident indeed brought Kanu and Chanda closer. Perhaps Kanu may be the only male who was not madly in love with Chanda, wanted her, desired her and marry her as well. Yet he was the only one to see Chanda practically naked, hold her in his arms, feel her overbearing breasts pressed against his chest, patted her bare back and spend an hour or two alone in her company.

* * *

Chapter Fifteen

Smitten Kanu

Perhaps, not unnaturally, Kanu found it difficult to put Chanda out of his mind, to forget her and her turgid, inviting, well developed and overbearing body. It was worse at night, as when he closed his eyes, Chanda was there, teasing, inviting him, like Anarkali daring his prince Salim to come and get her.

Kanu visited Chanda a couple of times, at her home, on the pretext of inquiring about her health and Chanda more than welcomed him with open arms, showing her genuine gratitude. She could not imagine what would have happened to her if Kanu had not intervened at the right, most appropriate moment.

Even Chanda's parents did not see any thing inappropriate in Kanu visiting Chanda in her home, who were naturally worried about their daughter, as there was no suitable suitor for their princess, either in their own village community or beyond and they were getting old and infirm.

Like Kanu, Chanda was mesmerised. She could not put Kanu out of her mind, however hard she tried, knowing full well that Kanu was untouchable, out of her reach under any circumstances.

But Chanda was besotted on Kanu, even though it would only bring tears and misery for her and her family if she encourages Kanu in any way. She would be the black sheep that would blight not only her family but the whole village.

In a way, it would be a fate worse than death, especially for Chanda's family who were the innocent victims, bystanders in a drama that was unfolding in front of their eyes, yet did not realise the utmost seriousness of the situation. It was like a horse wearing blinkers that prevented him from looking side ways.

But Kanu did not need any encouragement or an invitation. He was already smitten, secretly in love and took every opportunity to meet Chanda whenever and wherever he possibly could. Chanda was in his mind, in his body and in his sleep, no matter how hard he tried to control his thought, his emotion and his desire that were becoming obvious to every one by the day.

Kanu was being consumed by the hunger of love, sex and sensuality that was increasing by leaps and bound every day, even when the sign of impending doom were looming on the horizon.

Kanu was like a helpless deer caught in the glare of a hunter's headlights, even with the burden of overbearing sexiness.

Kanu, a sensible person under most circumstances, was already dreaming, planning a life with Chanda, charting his, their future together. Chanda was his dream girl in more ways than one. Some times one may wonder why a sexual attraction, a big sexy breasts and curving body takes precedent over all other qualities. That does not mean Chanda's sexual attraction was her only asset.

Far from it, she was kind, considerate, obliging and a very clever person indeed. She was reasonably educated as well. There was absolutely no reason why she would not make a good wife, a caring partner in a marriage.

Love is like an addiction. Once it enters the blood stream, it infects every part of the body. Kanu and Chanda tried their best to keep their feelings in check. But it was Chanda who gave in first, succumbed to her physical need, her desire for love and being loved overcame her shyness.

After all she was a woman, a rose bud in full bloom. Every part of her body was well developed and in need of a bee who would extract her nectar, her honey.

One afternoon Chanda visited Kanu in the field, in the afternoon knowing full well that Kanu will be on his own. As it was a very hot afternoon, Kanu was cooling off in the big water trough, with oxen drawing the water from the well and filling the trough with cool, fresh water every five minutes, as the well was shallow with water practically overflowing the well.

Looking at the big, bulging and healthy body of Kanu, covered with only a short swimming trunk, Chanda did not need an invitation to join him in the water, after removing all her cloths except the flimsy underpants.

For two young, healthy, physically and sexually at peak youngsters, brought together by a freak incident, the small water tank was the perfect place to bring them together, soul and body, love and sex, in each and every way. It was impossible to show any restraint.

The good manner, respect, responsible attitude and social taboo all went absent, thrown out with the bath water. To preach restrain to two sexually overflowing hearts was like preaching the advantage of fasting to an audience who did not had a one square meal in days. It would be a mockery of holy concept.

The lust, repressed feelings and sexual desire had an upper hand. They made love without any restraint, Kanu almost attacking Chanda as brutally as Machu did but this time without a murmur, any protest from Chanda.

In fact Chand encouraged Kanu every bit, letting him bit every inch of her body that would be covered by cloths, her breasts, upper thighs and buttocks, even the most private parts that Kanu would not let go of once exposed to his uncontrollable urge until sheer exhaustion sets on.

Chanda gave back as much as she received, kissing, bitting the most private parts of Kanu, even making Kanu suffer the pain that he never knew. So often he was in agony, pushing away Chanda or pulling her head under water that would made Chanda to let Kanu go.

This was the first time, the first sexual encounter for both of them. Yet they knew every trick of the trade, making love, having sex like an experienced married couple. Even Machu could not have hurt Chanda more than Kanu, with his bites all over her soft, private parts but this time it was at her invitation, the pain she loved, needed, enjoyed, encouraged and desired. She was in seventh heaven when making love

In just two hour, they put in more effort, had more sex, inflected more sweet and sour wounds, leaked every inch of their body than a honeymoon couple would manage in a week? This is known as the psychology of sexual climax, sexual satisfaction, psychology of making the most out of an unexpected opportunity, making the best use of the bad situation.

It was obvious for both Kanu and Chanda that they were meant for each other, a perfect couple in every way, could not keep away from each other however hard they may try. In the end they gave up pretending, taking every available opportunity to enjoy each other.

It would be follies to preach restrain, dharma or obligations to Kanu and Chanda, akin to preaching dharma, honesty and integrity to starving people by a Pundit or a Guru with a beer belly, a result of over indulgence, extravagance with food and drinks. Even Kanu's academia did not denote his spiritual intelligence.

* * *

Chapter Sixteen

Village Gossip

In a small village, it was difficult to keep such an affair secret. Soon every one knew, heard through the grapevine what was going on. The gossip mongers had a field day but for once they were right. They hit the gossip jackpot. Nothing like this had happened in the village as far as they can remember. These extra-curricular activities were the juiciest gossiping tales the village had ever endured. This was the mother of all affairs, all gossips and all sins.

But Kanu, being a Mukhi's son, was beyond reproach, beyond criticism. Kanu was the rainmaker in waiting with blue blood running through the family. He could do nothing wrong, however hard he may try. So Chanda became the target, the object of desire became an object of hate, more out of jealousy, envy and lust than any other reason.

What troubled Kanu and Chanda was that it was only a question of time, weeks rather than months before Chanda would become pregnant, as the word contraception was not yet even invented, let alone the pills.

In an ultra conservative village atmosphere, for a girl to become pregnant outside marriage was the ultimate sin, treason punishable by banishment at best and death at worse, under moral obligation if not under law and no one would raise a finger to protect Chanda if she became pregnant.

No one would intervene, not even local police or court when it was a question of honour, morality and good name of not only the family involved but for the entire community. Murders have been committed and feuds have lasted generation after generation for even lesser sexual indiscretion than being pregnant.

Kanu had spent two years in a city where he went for further education. His time in the city was the personal odyssey of the self discovery, a time well spent in gathering, creating a pool of self belief, ancient wisdom. But for a lad born and brought up in a clean, pollution free atmosphere, traffic free lanes and the only noise that may disturb one's sleep came from early morning temple bells, wild birds, crowing of cock and mooing of cows and other animals rather than road traffic and wake up calls from the cotton mills, it was difficult to adjust.

In the end Kanu, known as Kamal (Lotus) to his city friends, gave up his dream of becoming a teacher, the job he admired most but needed a degree to teach at secondary level, as he loved children, was at ease with them from babies to teenagers and decided that his future was in the village where his heart was.

City personifies the hectic pace of life that may so often be an obstacle for a village boy if he would like to settle down in a bustling city like Ahmedabad. Village life may be austere and puritanical, may lack prominence and privileges in some ways but it is more fulfilling in many other ways, especially for those who love nature, fresh air and wide, open countryside.

He knew every one and every one knew him. No one was a stranger, alone or lonely. In the old days, a village life was like living in a kibbutz, a communal living during the day and utmost peace, solitude and privacy once you shut your front door.

His father, the Mukhi was over the moon when his eldest son, a future Mukhi put village life ahead of city attractions. Not many village children who went to the city, ever came back to settle down in the village. Now Mukhi knew that the family tradition, the prosperity and the tradition of being the most respected family, will continue, at least for one generation more.

Kanu had all the qualities, cool, calm and matured head over his young, broad shoulders, respected by one and all. No one had a reason to say an unkind word for Kanu, not even when his liaison with Chanda became a public knowledge. Yes, many envied him but did not blame him. After all he was just a lad, a village lad who had the luck, the fortune and the good look to get a sex symbol, the village Anarkali mad after him.

But in a flesh, or rather in the arms of Chanda, all his qualities, calmness, cool head, duty to his family and the village community sound so hollow, so unimportant, artificial and meaningless. Just like King Edward who gave up his throne to the greatest empire the world has ever seen, for the love of not so beautiful or sexy married woman Mrs. Simpson. Then again, love is in beholders' eyes, one man's food is another man's poison, a lump of sugar for a diabetic or a piece of a meat for a vegetarian.

The history is full of such examples. Salim took up the challenge of the mighty Mogul army, Cleopatra brought down the great Mark Anthony and Helen of Troy, the daughter of Zeus and Leda, the most beautiful woman of the ancient world, who married the king of Sparta and was abducted by Prince of Troy which precipitated the Trojan war, inspired the Trojan Horse war tactics and became immortal.

For Kanu, Chanda was now his world, his life, his love and for that matter, sex or sexual attraction is part of love, part of life. Kanu could not imagine, envisage or conceptualize life without Chanda. He wanted Chanda by his side, in his bed, to make love to his heart's content, pleasure and gratification, each night and every night and to look at her beautiful face when he wakes up in the morning.

Perhaps Kanu was consumed by the hunger of sex, beauty and prestige of having such a beauty by his side. Perhaps his cluttered conscience would not let him think as freely as he would like, as impartially or in an equitable manner that would make sense.

Love for a woman, especially when she is a forbidden fruit, is the most inflecting, attractive, mesmerising, enslaving aphrodisiac known to human being, even if it may lead to personal tragedy of the apocalypse proportion. Kanu, for the privilege of marrying Chanda, sharing a bed with her, was ready and willing to sacrifice every thing he once held dear, including the love of his family and respect of the villagers, his opportunity to become a Mukhi when his father retires.

Then Chanda was tantalizingly beautiful, unimaginably sexy while Kanu was a mere mortal, a flesh and blood who would succumb to some one half as desirable as Chanda. Perhaps this was the psychology of sexual confusion, heart over-ruling head.

Chanda, a virgin child, was as beautiful, as charming as any woman, as mesmerising as Menka, a woman especially created by God to distract Lord Shiva, the indestructible, supreme God that no one can influence or distract but Menka did?

To confuse, to compound, to muddy the water, Kanu's father Mukhi Shambo Patel had received a marriage proposal from the Mukhi of the neighbouring village who had a petit, shy, pretty daughter called Rukhi, a perfect match not only for Kanu but for both the families that will unite two leading families for the common good. In a village life, building such close relationship is as important as having a close ally, who would stand by you in your hour of need.

Kanu had even met Rukhi a couple of times, in the presence of other family members, family elders while Kanu was trying to make up his mind when he was struck by the lightening in the form of Chanda. No matter how charming, shy and attractive Rukhi may be, she was no match, not in the same league as Chanda.

If Kanu was an enchanting cupid, than Chanda was definitely the Goddess Venus, the Roman Goddess of love, beauty and charm.

No other girl in any surrounding villages can come even close to Chanda in beauty, appearance and sexiness. Chanda was unique, a one off creation of God, a virgin child, a God's gift or a curse to the village, depending on how she effected you, the villager, the family. She was fit to be the bride for King Karna, another virgin birth child, a hero of Mahabharat, let alone the village lad like Kanu.

Mukhi Shambo was at a loss how to handle his eldest son Kanu. He knew no amount of threats, bullying will influence Kanu, as he himself was once young, ambitious and with a streak of rebellious spirit. Perhaps Kanu had inherited his genes, his stubbornness. Would he have backed down, let go the opportunity of marrying Chanda?

Mukhi even considered, although for a moment only, to let Kanu and Chanda get married, as observing Chanda at close range, in full flight, he could not help admiring her charm and beauty, her grace and elegance.

* * *

Chapter Seventeen

The Age Old Dilemma

It was not difficult for Mukhi to understand why Kanu had fallen head over heel for Chanda, why was he under her spell. But Chanda or rather her family background poised several problems, raised many awkward questions which had no answers.

Could such a beauty, a sex symbol, an object of desire for every young and not so young male could be pride and joy of a well respected family? Could he really depend on Chanda to be a faithful wife to Kanu as long as she lives? How could a village girl of just seventeen dare to have a sexual relationship outside marriage?

This destroyed all her credibility even if Mukhi was willing to forget her caste and lowly background. Mukhi or to that extent every one knew that Chanda's family pedigree reflected no blue blood of any sort, no matter how back one may go. But then there were no skeletons in the cupboard either, that is until Chanda's liaison with Kanu.

Chanda may be a little, charming girl in the silent theatre of mind, at least for the time being but in reality Chanda was like a smouldering ember burning quietly, slowly gathering pace and energy before revealing the full extent of her destructive power that may ruin many lives.

Moreover if Mukhi let Kanu to break up his impeding engagement to Rukhi, he would make a powerful enemy that may one day cost him dearly. He may even lose his pride of position as the leading family in the village, even his Mukhiship may be challenged, he will lose his righteous self-certainty and it would certainly ruin the chances, the opportunities for his other children to get married in a respected family.

Among his children, there were two young girls who were fast approaching the marriageable age and they were a prime concern for the Mukhi. After all, parents are only a short term guardian of their daughters. In reality they belong to the families of their husbands where they would spend most of their adult lives.

Mukhi knew that good judgement comes from experience and experience comes from bad judgement and God knows how many mistakes Mukhi had committed in the past that had come back to haunt him. But nothing came remotely close to what a good judgement or a monumental blunder Mukhi was about to make.

Could Mukhi let down his other children; betray his other offspring just to let Kanu have his sexual fantasies fulfilled? Was all these hassle worth it? After all, in few years time, after raising a few children, breast feeding them, Chanda would be no longer, no more special, attractive or a raging beauty that would turn heads, no more sexy than most women of her age and background.

Mukhi Shambo, a keen observer had noticed how so many young and beautiful village girls a few years back, now have sagging breasts, bulging waistline, protruding stomach, fat and curves in all the wrong places, overbearing buttocks, attracting no attention, turning a few heads and that also for all the wrong reasons. Chanda would fall in the same category. In time Chanda would be no more special than any woman in her age group. How would Kanu or Mukhi feel then? Was this sacrifice worth for a momentary beauty? It hardly mattered with whom one may be having sex behind closed doors, in the darkness of a bedroom!

Once Mukhi weighed his pros and cons, he realized that his family name, honour and future of his other children should take priority, take precedent above Knau's desire, his love or rather obsession for Chanda. But he failed to realize that family, children are not a possession. It is a responsibility where so often parents have to make a huge sacrifice and at the end of the day, the reward is small. But then that is parenthood and it is neither easy nor always rewarding. Then parents' love is never conditional.

A couple have children for love, not out of duty or obligation. A family is more complicated and less absolute but more immediate, lovable and tangible. Could this, the bad blood between a father and his son be fool's feud? If so, Mukhi did not know how to avoid it. Perhaps it was the satanic pride that over ruled all other considerations.

347

So when Mukhi had yet another opportunity to talk to his eldest son, he did not mince his words. He forbid Kanu to see, meet or even talk to Chanda and he set a date to announce Kanu's engagement to Rukhi who was the right girl, a good choice and a perfect partner for his son.

This union will increase Mukhi's prestige and above all, the marriage prospects of his children, especially his two daughters, as Rukhi had two brothers who, like Mukhi's two daughters, would soon enter the group of eligible bachelors, much in demand, a good catch for any girl.

Mukhi thought that within days of marrying Rukhi, Kanu will forget all about Chanda, who was more like an addiction, a bottle of sharab (alcoholic drink) to a Sharabi, more an edict than any thing else.

One can not surrender to such an addiction, let it have the upper hand and ruin so many young, inspiring and promising lives. Addiction has to be overcome, conquered and sanity, calmness restored.

Kanu was in a dilemma. He had to choose between a devil and deep blue sea, a problem that had no solution. No matter what he did, he will end up hurting some one close to him, so dear, so important in his life.

Kanu will not obtain approbation, seal of approval, not even blessing in disguise from any member of his family, any community member, even from a friend or a foe. In this situation, his dilemma, he was all alone, sink or swim, it has to be his decision, his nightmare or a paradise, depending on his luck, what number the dice may come up with. Deep inside his heart, Kanu knew that he should treasure every moment of his time spent with Chanda, in his exotic world, as the end may come sooner than he would expect.

But Kanu passionately believed that every event in life has a purpose and every setback has its lesson. Kanu was a disciple of Lord Krishna, his favourite God and perhaps in Lord Krishna, Kanu found the mentor he was searching for.

For a moment Kanu thought of giving in to his father's demand. But then he realised that by marrying Rukhi, he would not destroy his own life but that of an innocent girl like Rukhi whom he will never be able to love, appreciate or even have sex with her.

Making love to Rukhi, in a dark, behind closed doors would be like making love, having sex with necrophilia? She would be his wife in name only. He would be marrying her, not to please himself but to please others. Does Rukhi deserve this insult? After all Rukhi was a young, ambitious, kind and caring soul who deserved the best, the whole hearted attention he could not give.

The concept of marrying Rukhi was too heart-rending even to contemplate, for all three of them involved in this love triangle. In a strange way, Kanu was fond of Rukhi, although not in a romantic sense. That was a good reason not to ruin Rukhi's life.

Then what about Chanda? After the way they fell in love, made love that was beyond their wildest dream, without any restraint, constraint that hurt and pleased them both at the same time, was beyond their control.

It would be assiduous, sedulous for Kanu to make love to any one else. After all, there is only one Menka, one Mona Lisa, one Anarkali and certainly one and only Chanda, a beauty that would melt even the heart of Lord Shiva, the God most difficult to please!

Yes, by choosing Chanda as his life partner, he would enter the zone of the unknown. But it is nothing more than a negative stream of consciousness that one has to face from time to time, while charting one's life, moving away from the norm. It is part of the ageless principle of self-mastery. Was Kanu up to it?

Could Kanu ever make love in a similar manner to Rukhi? Perhaps she would run a mile even if he tried. Moreover Chanda was not fit to be the wife of any one else. Even if some one marries Chanda, it would be not for love but for her beautiful and sexy body, the body her husband would mercilessly tear a part, limb by limb every night, in the darkness. She would be a pride possession to show off, a mere chattel, not a life partner.

Does Chanda deserve such humiliation? After all what has she done wrong? Why she should be punished who had not set a foot wrong until she was so brutally attacked by Machu, rescued by Kanu and falling in love with some one who was her Knight in shinning armour that produce subtle smiles of enlightenment unfolding not only across her lips but in her heart as well.

Yes, they should not have sex before marriage. But then we all do so many things we are not supposed to do. It was out of their hand, beyond their control. The fate led them to such an uncompromising situation and may destroy their young and ambitious lives.

Perhaps love and time would heal all wounds but anger, envy and surrender may open and even infect them. Chanda, the virgin oil had lost her virginity, after many a tasty fry-ups enjoyed solely by Kanu. It would be wrong to pretend otherwise.

It was time to take stock, appraisal the situation with cool heart and astute mind. Would Kanu's cluttered conscience let him abandon Chanda?

349

Pain is a powerful teacher and to transcend the pain of separation from someone whom you loved, it had to be experienced at first hand.

Kanu was incapable of going through that pain barrier, not for his father or any one else. When Kanu realized that, he was a different person; he was inspired, disciplined and energized beyond his capability. No one could now sell him a snake-oil in the guise of a perfume.

* * *

Chapter Eighteen
Kanu's Last Stand at Harvest Festival

It would be Navratri, the harvest festival in a week's time. That was the time Kanu and Chanda decided to elope, leave the village for good and start a new life in the city where Kanu still had a few friends on whom he can depend. Kanu knew that a faint heart can never won a fair lady and Chanda was more than a fair lady! Chanda was a reality bigger and better than make-believe.

No amount of mud slinging could ever blur the brightness of Chanda. She was a classical music, classical literature, not a graffiti or Rock and Role music. Moreover both Kanu and Chanda would easily assimilate in a city teaming with humanity, yet anonymity, the incognito existence is more or less guaranteed.

On that fateful evening, when the sun had just set behind the distant hills and the full moon was beginning to appear in the clear blue sky, Chanda was eagerly waiting for Kanu outside Lord Shiva's temple, on the bank of river Gomti that was flowing fast and furious after a good monsoon that will provide fresh water to surrounding farms well into summer months.

Right at the appointed time, Kanu came riding his favourite horse Chatak, named after another famous horse and even more famous rider, Maha Rana Pratap, the king of Mewad in Rajasthan who gave the Mogul emperor a touch time on the battlefield, so often fighting a hopeless, losing battle with his fellow Rajput kings in the pay of the Mogul Emperor, a foreign invader, aggressor who was bent upon destroying the Indian culture, Hindu way of life.

On the other side of the river Gomti, on the opposite river bank, there was an open road leading to the city, freedom and married life with for Chanda and Kanu. Chanda climbed, behind the horse behind Kanu, hold him tightly

351

and slowly rode down the hill towards the river which was flowing fast but at this point, it was wide and only three to four feet deep, easy to cross, especially on a horseback.

But before they could cross the river, they saw Mukhi Shambo Patel standing in the middle, with a loaded shotgun and his cheeks painted red, a tradition among noble, ruling class when they want to show their anger, their disapproval and would like to take revenge. In the olden time, the bygone era, it was the sign to start a war that so often led to a massacre.

Mukhi ordered Kanu to dismount and walk back to the village while he dealt with Chanda, in his own way. It was Mukhi's right to punish Chanda in any way he likes. It was a one man Kangaroo court, Mukhi being the judge, jury and the executioner, all rolled into one.

Kanu tried to reason with Mukhi, his father, to make him understand that he was leaving for good and will not be coming back so that no one can blame him or any one associated with his family. But Mukhi was in no mood to listen, try to be rational. Mukhi was consumed by the hunger for revenge, anger, envy and frustration. For Kanu, it was an exercise in frustration, in lost cause to try to make his father listen to him, to reason with him.

Mukhi was boiling with rage, perhaps high on afin, a kind of drug smoked by village elders, using a long pipe that gave Mukhi the courage to masquerade as the saviour of family honour, to murder his own son and his bride to be, in cold blood, without remorse, without conscious and without any kind or retribution from the village community or the law. Mukhi was the law.

When Kanu tried to ride away, having realised that there was no point in having a dialogue or rather a slanging match with his father who would not listen to reason; Mukhi fired the gun at Kanu, from a short distance, too drunk with hatred to realise the impending doom. Kanu and Chanda were like two deer caught in the glare of a powerful but intruding pair of headlights.

Kanu took the full blast on his chest. The horse bolted, throwing both Kanu and Chanda to the ground. Kanu was badly hurt but still alive while Chanda had superfluous wounds. Mukhi, still bursting with rage, moved forward to empty the second barrel into Kanu, to put him out of his misery.

Instead, Chanda, standing between Mukhi and Kanu, took the full blast, she fell black, bleeding profoundly, her big, beautiful breasts torn to pieces with the numerous pallets of the shot gun. She fell, stumbled back into the arms of Kanu and died within minutes: while it took Kanu long, painful fifteen minutes to lose consciousness when Mukhi left him to his fate, die a long and lingering death.

The blood from the two, young and healthy bodies was flowing into the river, polluting the water. When Mukhi realised what he had done, it was too late to repent. "

Samir realised that Mukhi Pitamber was talking for a long time and they should have a refreshing drink before he should let Mukhi continue.

Mukhi badly needed this break. His voice was breaking up and was full of emotion, clearly in distress. Samir could not help but wonder why an event that happened more than fifty years ago was troubling, upsetting Mukhi Pitamber so much. But he did not have to wait long. When Mukhi regained his composure, he continued. "This is what may happen when we ignore morality, customs and one's obligation to the family and society at large, when power becomes our touchstone, our benchmark, our fiducial line.

At the time I was a couple of years younger than Chanda. But in common with every boy of my age, I was mesmerised by Chanda. But I was glad that Kanu was going to marry her and bring Chanda into our family. Kanu was my cousin, the son of my eldest uncle.

Chanda will at least be part of our extended family. We will be able to see her, feel her presence and observe her sweet smile every day. But in a moment of madness, an act of thuggery, our family fell apart, the heart was ripped from our family members and the village was cursed, perhaps by Chanda who was an innocent victim, so brutally murdered, who had not set a foot wrong until she was brutalised, rescued, fell in love with the Prince Charming, wanted to marry him and live happily ever after. One may ask what is wrong in that.

This happens all the time, in the lives of millions of young people madly in love, even when they have family millstone hanging around their necks. Basking in borrowed, corrupt and hollow ideals is a "cuckoo land" syndrome not in line with traditional Hindu custom and liberal religious optimism.

Why should an accident of birth be a wall, a thorn on the road to happiness? Could girls or even boys born in different families have different armans, measure happiness with different tape, have different criteria for ultimate happiness?

* * *

Chapter Nineteen

Revival of River Gomti

River Gomti which was in full flow at Navratri, the harvest festival, after one of the best monsoon in living memory, whose water was polluted with the blood of two innocent victims, so brutally murdered in their prime, soon dried up, depriving the village of a valuable source of fresh water.

In the past, even during the worse summer months, before the arrival of monsoon, when there was only a trickle of water flowing, the villagers only had to dig two to five feet on the apparently dry river bed before the water would start flowing freely, filling the surrounding area, the depression on the river bed, creating a shallow pool full of sweet water that would keep the village folks in water until the arrival of monsoon. The river had never let the villagers down, deprived them of sweet drinking water and for the farms on the bank, water to cultivate the land, raising crops up to three times a year.

Now the river Gomti did not have running water nor do any underground water either, no matter how deep the villagers may dig. Soon the villagers faced financial ruin without water and turned against the Mukhi Shambo for killing, murdering two innocent souls who were madly in love with each other and the world. This was a group, communal punishment for all, guilty as well as innocent. Then was there any one who would not have criticised, find fault in the couple, especially Chanda, the raving beauty and a sex symbol that every one loved to hate, want her but not admit it openly?

It was too painful, too humiliating for Mukhi Shambo to remain in the village. He soon left the village for good and settled down in the city where no one knew him, recognize him. Moreover in a city no one cares. Everyone minds his or her own business. They are too busy, too preoccupied earning a living, providing a roof over their heads or accumulating wealth beyond their need or necessity.

This is when my father was elected the leader, the new Mukhi for our village. He was the natural heir and moreover he was not involved in this tragedy, in this tragic episode in any way. He was as clean as a whistle with a reputation of Lord Rama, the patron saint or rather the favourite God of the village people.

As the eldest son, I took over his duty, his responsibility when he passed away. But I do not know who will succeed me; take over from me when I am gone.

All my children are living in the city where they have built up a new life, where they would like to stay except when they come here for a short break, to be with us during school holidays.

The job of Mukhi is hard, difficult. He has to be a diplomat, honest and possess good manner and friendly disposition. Work is demanding but reward is small, minimal on the financial front, at least for an honest Mukhi. But that would not be my problem when I am gone.

The time is changing fast. Perhaps by the time I am gone, the village may not need a Mukhi. They may have a court and a Vakilsahib (solicitor) to resolve their differences, solve their problems. But I can not help wondering whether such a development would serve the interest of the villagers, as it will inevitably bring corruption, dishonesty and political immorality in the village life.

So doctor Samir Shah, what you saw last night, Prince Salim and Anarkali, what you witnessed is rare. At one time Kanu and Chanda were regularly seen in the forest, especially when there is a full moon. But no one has seen them recently. So I was a bit surprised when you mentioned your experience.

The river has also started flowing again during the last five years, the flow lasting few more weeks every year. It seems the curse has been lifted. Hopefully within the next five to ten years river Gomti will be back to its best, full of sweet water, will regain its past glory it enjoyed before the tragedy and flow all year round, as in the past, enriching the lives of every villager.

The experts, the geologists have always told us that the ground water level is so high that there is no reason for the river to dry up in the first place, that is within weeks of the end of the monsoon acting only as drainage to carry the water away from the village, to the sea. There is no reason why should it not flow again all year round. No one could understand this mass punishment for not only this village but the surrounding villages that were on the bank of the river.

Then perhaps we all could have played some part in the downfall of Chanda and Kanu, even unknowingly. Now some one, in a similar manner may have participated in the redemption of these villages, in the same way like Christianity's deliverance from the sin through the incarnation and death of Lord Jesus Christ, the Son of God and Lord Rama spending fourteen long years in a forest, away from his beloved capital city Ayodhia and his mother and brothers, his beloved family members.

It is difficult to understand the mystery of the Creator, how His mind works or how to redeem one's past mistake, misdeed and to reinstate one self in God's good book. That is a perpetual mystery and will always remain so, no matter how far the science may advance.

Most villagers, that is those who could afford it financially, installed deep water wells that kept their farms, fields and orchards in the business. As the ground water was so high, hardly any well failed to deliver an all year round flow of water. A few who could not afford it or failed to find water on their land lost every thing but most managed to stay solvent. Now the prosperity is on the way back and farm prices are rising rapidly, have already doubled during the last five years since the river Gomti started flowing again.

Well Samir, now you know the full history of our village and every detail of my family. Now I will have to show you some very old photographs and a painting of Kanu and Chanda, our own Mona Lisa, our Anarkali and our Prince Salim.

At one time the villagers wanted to build a deri, a small temple that we so often see on the roadside and on the outskirt of many villages, in memory of Kanu and Chanda but the plan never got off the ground, as villagers were too busy apportioning blame and now no one cares about what happened such a long time ago. Today Kanu and Chanda are nothing more than a series of fading memory pegs, even in our minds, those who witnessed this tragedy first hand. Who would like to be the prisoner of the past? I would rather enjoy today than look at tomorrow, the future that may never materialize. As Oscar Wilde wrote, every saint has a past and every sinner has future.

However there is a small headstone, marking the place in the temple background, where Kanu and Chanda were cremated. As for me, this episode is a lake of memory, sea of souls and ocean of emotions. How could I or any one else who saw Chanda at her best can ever forget her charm, beauty and captivating, mesmerising power, influence. As we say, it is better to live like a lion for a week than like a lamb for a year. In their short life, Kanu and Chanda packed more punch; enjoyed each other more than most of us could do in our entire married life.

Surely the world has changed beyond reorganisation since then and not for the better, no matter what young people like you may say. Yes, we had our faults but it was a caring society where every one had a roof over their heads and no one went to sleep on an empty stomach, on a glass of water.

The saying that God may wake you up hungry but would never let you go to sleep hungry was absolutely true at the time."

Mukhi finished this wonderful, unbelievable love story with a sigh, perhaps remembering Kanu and Chanda after a long time. The time may heal wounds, dim the memory but such events always stay buried deep in our subconscious mind that will surface, re-emerge as we grow old and take a refuge in the past, as the present age, era has nothing similar to dwell in.

The sun was already behind the trees and without the direct sunlight; the water was feeling really cold. Samir and Mukhi hurriedly came out of the water, dried their bodies and went into the summer house to have a cup of hot tea, to replenish the body heat lost being in the cold water for a long time without realising it and before they walk back to the home, where a hot, tasty evening meal was awaiting them.

But for Samir, this experience, this tale of love, duty and sacrifice will remain with him for ever. It was as good a tale as that of Salim and Anarkali. Samir could not help but wonder when some one from Bollywood will get hold of this wonderful tale and turn it into an all time great movie, in line with Mogul a Azam, the life story of Prince Salim and courtesan Anarkali, a beauty par excellence.

* * *

The End

LETTER OF DESTINY

Chapter One

Our Wonderful Winter Retreat

In common with most writers, I get my inspiration, urge and the ability to devise the plot for my novel when I am on holidays. Our favourite destination is one of the seven Canary Islands, although we are, on most part only able to visit one of the four big ones that are on the tourist map and easier to reach from our favourite and local Luton airport.

It seems relaxing in the sun, relaxing on a sun-bed in our own balcony facing the sea, on most part the sea being not more than a couple of hundred feet away, listening to the murmur of the waves and the shrikes of the seagulls, with a bottle of cold drink nearby, brings out best in me, at least on the literary front if not on the physical front.

This is also the time when I do most of my serious reading as well, the books written by my favourite authors, serious, philosophical authors like Herman Hess, Rabindranath Tagore, Tolstoy and Robin Sharma, a few amongst many authors whose books I consider a treasure trove, at least for me, as I know these books are not for the masses who prefer romantic or detective novels, the ones I used to read when I was in my teens, like Agatha Christie, Earl Stanley Gardiner and their likes. How taste change with age, education and maturity.

These books, novels were like virgin olive oil but now they appear to have lost their virginity after many fry-ups, in greasy-spoon cafes and retail park restaurants that cater for the masses.

It is difficult to do such serious reading at home when we are constantly on the go, in one way or another, all the time. Even reading a newspaper in

359

its entirety is a rare achievement for me. That is why I only buy week-end papers that last me the whole week.

Being a journalist, I have an inquisitive mind and nostalgic outlook. I have also been told, especially by my wife Kumudini that I am a chatter-box, as I like to chat, talk and make friends with my fellow guests who so often provide me with a plot, an idea, and an inspiration for my next novel. After all print industry, like film industry is depending, prospering on nostalgia that turns the wheel of our social life.

Certainly I do not behave as if I was embalmed when I am on holidays. To be a writer is a privilege, the opportunity to shape a young mind that would make a difference. There is no difference between a teacher and a writer except that a writer can reach a much larger audience than a teacher. I feel the saying *"Pen is mightier than sward"* is more true, appropriate and make sense in our present day media mad society that at any time in history.

I feel it is a privilege that we are able to let our mind drink deeply from the works of great philosophers in the mould of Confucius, Epicetus, read the wisdom that drips like honey from the writings of Mahatma Gandhi, Chanakiya, Mother Teresa and Nelson Mandela and pass them on through our writings so that these written gems never go out of print, out of sight, out of mind, stop influencing young people and older mind.

It seems tranquil, worry free environment brings out the best in us. We are courteous, friendly and hospitable to each other when it is difficult to be even civil back at home. So my latest holiday to Tenerife, the largest and most fascinating of all the Canary Islands, with snow covered Mount Teide towering over the Atlantic Ocean, stealing our hearts was no exception. Yet the island is only a stone throw away from Europe.

Canary Islands are our winter destination. It is in fact a second home for us during our wet and gloomy winter months with bone chilling dampness when our aching bones and tired bodies are in need of sunshine and warmth. After all we are not spring chicken any more, not even when we arrived on these shores some five decades ago.

Our age and delicate state of our health rules out exotic destinations like Goa, Kerala, Kenya and Florida. These are the places we used to frequent just after retirement when we were comparatively in good health. As we say, youth, health and wealth is never steady, permanent or should be taken for granted. It is liable to change at any time, without notice, without cause or without rational explanation.

I distinctly remember the words of wisdom, in form of a joke when I was a young boy. An old women who had a badly deformed back, was stooping low, walking with a stick. A young boy could not help but ask a mischievous question. "Grandma, what are you looking for?"

The woman with considerable wisdom that comes through age and experience, answered, "Beta (son) I have misplaced my youth. Please help me find it." The boy got the message. The old age and poor health are not fantasies of diseased mind and over imagination.

It is a reality that touches our lives sooner or later. But when we are in our prime, nothing is further from our thought than old age and infirm body. We all feel that we have eaten *amarfal,* the fruit of eternal youth and longevity.

When booking a holiday, I always request a high floor and a room with a sea view or rather facing the sea. So often we have to pay a hefty supplement for this privilege. But for me it is worth every penny.

Showing my membership card of ***Charted Institute of Journalists*** and presenting a copy of my latest book ***Ivory Tower*** to a manager at our next meeting that I always request, works wonder for me. It certainly brings quantum improvement in my satisfaction and motivation level. What you sow, so you reap work wonders for me when we are on holidays.

It is also wise and prudent to give tips to all the important staffs, especially to the chambermaid, head chef and the receptionist, at the beginning of your holiday rather than at the end.

From then on, we are privileged clients, even provided with sun beds in our own balcony, thus able to avoid the morning rush to reserve a sun bed by the pool that is the norm for most sun hungry Europeans, especially the over confident and demanding Germans who have the highest spending power and now Germans control most of our holiday firms. No wonder German holidaymakers are stereotyped as blonds with a hyper-nationalistic pride who came from a country intoxicated with arrogant certainties.

On our second day when we were having a breakfast, occupying rather a large, round table meant for six, as we were expecting our friends to join us, we met a lovely but some what shy, cautious lady.

I can not pinpoint but some how I felt she is a special one, a rainmaker in the waiting who would be a goldmine for me on the literary front. Perhaps my instinct came through a grapevine, as they often do.

But on most part my first impression, my instinct; my observations are on spot most of the times. They rarely let me down, prove me wrong.

Well, we all have some gifts if only we are aware of it and utilise it at the right time.

She must be in her early sixties but as she had taken a great care of her body, she was in her prime, for her age. She was slim with smooth skin and bulge in all the right places, highlighted by wearing the right cloths. When on holidays, especially in a warm climate, every one wears as few clothes as possible.

It is a fine art what to wear and what not to, which part of the body to cover and which part of the upper torso to expose to the staring and lusty, hungry eyes. It is no secret that even some older ladies have wonderful figures, bulging breasts and slim figures that put youngsters to shame. Joan Collins and Johanna Lumley are the two prime examples who would put us all to shame.

This style of dressing may tell us more about the person than any conversation. Then I have always been hopeless at guessing some one's age, especially when it comes to a fairer sex. Perhaps it is a blessing to admire and appreciate older generation for whatever reason it may be. But on the whole my first impression is right on most parts.

It may be hilarious, even cruel and pretentious but entirely true to say that on most parts these ladies, well into their retiring age are like virgin olive oil which would appear to have lost its' virginity many fry-ups ago, in many restaurants, cafes or could be cheap motel bed-rooms in a one night stand!

She was on her own, standing in the middle of the dinning room, searching for a vacant table, with a plate full of usual breakfast goodies. It was the busy time and an empty table was at a premium, as good as a gold, especially for a single person.

When our eyes met, I unintentionally gave her a smile, like a smiling Buddha looking upon a favoured pupil and as a matter of courtesy invited her to join us at our table, as there was plenty of space in the absence of our two friends who must have decided to stay in bed a bit longer. After all we had a late night as the floor show was more than interesting and the drinks, mostly local wines were included in the price!

We, the English are on most part too reserved and shy people, unable or unwilling to mix with others. But this rule, tradition or habit is on most part confined to dustbin when we are on holidays. Perhaps the unfamiliarity gives us the courage to talk to people, even make friends and trust them with our innermost secrets in the belief that we are not going to meet again. Our secrets are safe with these strangers and on most part they are.

As ours was a some what long stay holiday, three weeks in the sun and warmth of a sub-tropical island, we had plenty of time to know her, gain her trust and develop the friendship, even taking it to a higher level than the holiday romance which ends when we catch the plane home, out of sight, out of mind type of a romance.

But I soon realized that although she was kind, friendly and polite with raspy honey smooth voice, it was difficult to find out or rather pry in her private life, to get close to her. Even normal holiday chat, shallow, unintrusive information was hard to come-by. She was on her guard all the time. Indeed it was her second nature of this weary visitor from the cold climate, perhaps with a cold heart as well. But it was too early, too draconian to confine her to a dustbin of having met once!

It was more than obvious to a trained eye or perhaps a prying eye of a journalist that she has gone through a difficult patch in her life. Once bitten twice shy was her approach to life. Perhaps it is better to be safe than sorry was her motto and there may be a good reason behind her aloofness, although her mind had not lost any of its lustre.

My experience tells me that when people become withdrawn to such an extent, there is normally a life shattering experience, on most part associated with either love or a loss of a dear one. Perhaps Janice, that was her name, was such a person who may fall in love but once in a life-time.

* * *

Chapter Two

Janice, Our Constant Companion

We spent two wonderful weeks together, riding the ocean waves when we visited the tiny island of La Gomera, just a stone throw away from Tenerife but completely unspoilt or rather untouched by the modern day tourism, at least so far, as it had no airport or a hotel to take care of us, the pampered modern day Vasco da Gama! It is only a question of time before La Gomera will join the rat race of cheap, mass tourism, as the island is too pretty to be ignored for too long.

It takes less than an hour's sailing if one takes hovercraft or a fast ferry. But we prefer a sailing vessel, the slow boat to China, a Viking type wooden boat that becomes part of nature, be one with mighty Ocean without making waves, depending on the wind power rather than a diesel engine to reach the destination.

No wonder we are, on most part, able to observe marine life, dolphins and whales on our sea adventure when most of our friends fail to spot any wild life on the ocean waves. They are driven away by the engine noise and oil pollution that is the down side of the modern day tourism.

We also visited many places of interest, nature reserves and beauty spots, not forgetting Mount Teide, the heart and soul of the island and the highest mountain in Spain.

The Mount Teide excursion through Esperanza Forest led us to National Park of Las Canadas. The coach took us to 2700 meters high but the last 1000 meters we had to sail, go up in a ski-lift, passing or rather gliding over a lunar like rocky, barren landmass that reminded me of the famous movie, A Million Year BC with sexy Rachel Welsh in her animal skin bikini that made her a sex symbol of her time and sold a million posters which are a collectors' item today.

As we had travelled, traded this route before, having been to Tenerife, our winter watering hole, many times, we were naturally not in owe as Janice was. But for Janice, who had never been beyond Lake District, this simple holiday was a real treat, a highlight of her life.

For her, each excursion was an adventure into the unknown. It brought out her girlish charm and for a moment or two she would lower her guards and be talkative, relish our company and would even let slip a word or two about her private life.

Janice was extremely grateful of our company, enjoying every minute, embraced every movement of her time on this fascinating, exotic and contrasting island full of charm, rugged beauty and kind and helpful people who radiated a refreshing perspective on the true meaning of happiness.

We could not explain or put a finger as to why we felt such affinity towards Janice, as if we have known her for a long time. Perhaps it was Kismat (destiny, fate) that was meant to happen. Then life is full of such incidences that have no reasonable explanation. Perhaps it was the personal odyssey of the self.

It was a chance meeting that certainly changed Janice's life beyond her or any one's realm of reality and in the process we became not her best friends but as good as her family members. We certainly put to good use our pool of ancient wisdom.

We were responsible for bringing so much happiness in her life, in her twilight years. It is needless to say that during her stay of two weeks, we were inseparable. Her kind, caring nature and easy going manner won us over. But I could not help noting that behind her pleasant nature, sweet smile there was pain, disappointment and perhaps letdown, a tiny mistrust, may be not towards us but towards the world, the humanity at large.

No matter how hard I tried, in line with my journalistic nature, curiosity and desire to come close to her, gain her trust, Janice did not open her heart, not in a way that I would have liked.

I only learnt that she was a retired nurse, living in an upmarket Retirement Home. She has one daughter called Rebecca who was her heart and soul. Rebecca was married with two wonderful daughters, Willow and Maple. These names were certainly different, artistic and some what romantic as well, some one who may be nature enthusiast.

Janice did not give us her telephone number, nor the address until the day of her departure when I gave a hug, hold her tightly for a minute or two, put my card in her hand and requested her to keep in touch, that she was most welcome to visit us in London and stay with us, in our spacious and comfortable home.

When Janice realised how sincere and caring we were, she could not hide her tears, feeling guilty that she did not trust us the way we trusted her, told her all about us and treated her like a true and close friend, even though we had known her for only two weeks.

Having in this situation before, perhaps we had learnt the art of mind control and spiritual awareness, lifetime spent in quiet contemplation on the loftier issues, mystical landscapes of paradise islands.

No wonder her hug was strong and her tears of joy and sorrow were genuine. This was the first time I saw Janice become emotional, willing to trust us. Perhaps we broke the ice, the baggage of the past was shed and perhaps it would be plain sailing from now on. But I always live within the realm of reality, nothing taken for granted.

Janice was here for two weeks while we had three weeks. Our third week without Janice was a bit lonely, a climb-down. So I spent this spare week reading and writing, letting my mind, my imagination drink deeply from the wells of great philosophers, such as Confucius, Epictetus, read the writings of Mahatma Gandhi, Albert Einstein and Nelson Mandela.

These activities supplemented by taking in the sun, observing sunrise and sunset, watching the stars dancing in a moonlit sky, my soul expands in the worship of the creator, replenishing my old and tired body with sun, heat and energy, physical as well as spiritual uplift that keeps me going for the rest of the winter months, until the sun shines on my wonderful homeland, the green, green garden we call England!

This was the summit of serenity for the leisure, the relaxing time. Most of us live as if we have an infinite amount of time to do what we please. But even a lifespan of eighty is just a drop in the ocean, a tiny particle on this enormous earth, the universe where a million years but an hour in our life.

That is the purpose of our frequent breaks in hot, humid and stimulating lands or rather islands floating in the vast span of the ocean. It personifies the modern thinking into retirement, having an austere, ascetic but fulfilling life.

* * *

Chapter Three
God Works in Mysterious Manner!

A few days before Janice left, she gave me a book to read. It was her favourite book that she had read again and again. Perhaps it was a gift from some one special. The book was ***"Town like Alice."***

By pure coincidence, it was also one of my favourite books, along with Lost Horizon, Dr. Zhivago, Snows of Kilimanjaro, A bend in the Ganges, The House of Mr. Biswas and Farewell to Arms, a few among many of my favourite books that captured my heart when I was at the college and led me to journalism, become a writer and an author. These books taught me the distinction between simply surviving intellectually and really thriving, as we are all endowed with the intellectual capacity for being genius. It is how we use this gift that determines our life, charts our future; make us what we are in our adulthood.

Although I had read the book "A Town like Alice" a couple of times but long time ago, I decided to read it again, as Janice's insistence aroused my curiosity. I felt and rightly so that reading the book word and chapter may perhaps help me to understand Janice better and with a bit of luck, I may even unveil, solve the mystery about her past, the reason behind her mistrust of every one that basically went against her caring nature, even though it was cleverly concealed.

In my experience one may develop such personality, such mistrust when one is betrayed in love, especially in her young age when the heart is tender, nature idealistic and it becomes a barrier for all future romances which are rightly or wrongly judged against first love. It would be difficult for any one to understand such a scenario unless one has gone through such an experience. As I had gone through such a scenario, I understood Janice perfectly well. It is supposed to be a holistic integrated set of ageless principles. I had come out of it and my philosophy was *"Let us judge not, that we may not be judged."*

I was supposed to give the book back to her before her departure. But in the hustle and bustle of saying farewell, the unseen pain of separation, the book was completely forgotten. Perhaps it was Kismat, the destiny that made Janice, a very particular and organized person to forget such an important and sentimental item that she had carried with her almost all her adult life.

It seems God works in a mysterious ways. Janice had kept this old book in a tip top condition, wrapped in a plastic cover.

When we were packing, Kumudini dropped the book to my annoyance, the plastic cover came off and out came a hand written envelop, fell to the floor.

My curiosity got the better of me. I could not resist reading this very private and personal but touching letter. Although I felt bad at the time, my curiosity was fully vindicated with the unfolding of events that united two lost souls, gave the love story a fitting and happy end, a love story with a difference.

I could not have even imagined such an ending for one of my novels. So often truth comes out of oasis of enlightenment. It is more unbelievable than fiction.

The letter was from a young boy hardly out of his teens. The boy whom I would like to call Julian was Janice's neighbour and they were childhood friends, indeed sweethearts. The post war life in a tiny English village was completely different from what our teenagers experience today.

The friendship between a boy and a girl was real, sincere and honest in so many ways. No one had even heard of one night stand, let alone preach and practice it.

The friendship was like part of nature, oneness with the surroundings, tribute to the symphony of nature, music of mankind. It was not only common but it was the norm, although when these young souls become adult, most get separated and make their own way in the fast changing world.

It was a pleasure and a privilege to watch the sun dance along the colourful horizon. Every human being has a wondering spirit, a gypsy nature and Englishmen have turned this inner desire to a fine art, discovering and conquering half the world. At its best British Empire covered one third of the world, some forty million people ruling, lording over one billion people worldwide.

But Julian and Janice's friendship was an exception to the rule. They were known as an odd couple among youngsters of their age. While most boys and girls from their group moved on after school, Julian and Janice cling to each other, remain faithful to their childhood promises and aspirations that is until the events, the fate turned against them. Their desire of life together until death parts them was shattered as if it was no more than a pleasant dream.

The letter was in remarkable condition considering its age and the fact that it was read again and again until Janice could recite each and every word by heart. I did the same, read the letter a few times to grasp the hidden meaning, love and sacrifice. I read it once more.

"Dear Janice

I do not know how to break this news. I feel I am a coward, a worthless human being to let you down, to trample on your, on our dreams.

I am sacrificing our happiness and aspirations, to desert you when we promised each other to remain together, get married, have children and get old gracefully in each other's company.

I know no amount of apology, excuses and reasons will ease your pain, your disappointment. My father is being transferred to Liverpool and we all have to move. At 17, I feel I am too young to break away from my family and get married, as we can not be together unless we get married.

You are even younger than me and most probably we will need the permission of our families to tie the knot which I know will never be forthcoming. You are an excellent student with bright future in front of you, with Uni and a degree beckoning you. How can I be selfish and ruin your future even before it has the chance to blossom, materialize.

I am sure in time we will forget each other and settle down in our new life, amongst new friends. But I am sure one tiny corner of our hearts will always be devoted to each other for ever. How I wish my father was given the opportunity to live in our village for a few more years, until we have completed our education and had the opportunity to put our plans into practices, turn our dream into reality.

Perhaps God has already charted our destiny the day we were born, the future that is different to what we want, we deserve.

Please forgive me and I hope in time you may even understand my sacrifice. I love you so much that this separation will hurt me for a long time; perhaps these wounds may never heal. Good bye and GOD bless you. If you believe in reincarnation, then perhaps we will be reunited in the next world.

Always yours Julian

On reading the letter, I realized the reason behind Janice's well concealed sorrow and mistrust in general. But this was only half the story. It only scratched the surface. But so often life's worse setbacks revel the greatest opportunities. I hoped this may be so in Janice's case that she bears no grudge at this boy, as when you bear a grudge against some one, it becomes a milestone around one's neck and you may carry that person around on your back for ever.

Forgiveness is not only divine but it is also the fragrance that the beautiful and sweet smelling flowers like violet, gardenia and roses shed on the heals, the hands that crush them. As the letter was in original envelop, I was able to learn Julian's full name and his and Janice's old address in the village as well.

While we were still on holidays, I received a couple of telephone calls from Janice, reminding me that she would like to get her book back as soon as possible.

The anxiety in her voice led me to give her assurance that I would personally return the book to her, as we were not that far from her. In fact the time would tell us that we had never been so close.

As far as Janice was concerned, the letter was safe and untouched, well hidden in the book cover, from prying eyes of a nosy parker like me.

On returning home my first task was to find out, trace Julian, where he was and what his life was like. We, the investigative journalists are a hardened lot, capable of extracting blood from a stone, although I would not put myself in that category. But my fellow journalist and a very dear friend of mine by the name of **Chantal** is just the opposite.

Chantal is smart, cool and being half French, is beautiful, sophisticated and extremely good at her job of being an investigative journalist. We always joke that Chantal can easily charm the Fort Knox guards and steal the gold!

Even some politicians, especially male ones would think twice before coming too close to her, feeling uncomfortable under the combined weight of her irresistible beauty and overwhelming charm and personality. They would think twice before offending her in any way! Sometimes being a female is a great asset in journalism.

As I wanted to trace Julian before I return the book to Janice, I thought it prudent to enlist the help of Chantal. I am blessed with friends in the high places. I believe that one is bound to reap a rich harvest of loyal friends if I plant the seeds of friendship at the right time.

It would be a child's play for Chantal to find Julian, as I had his full name, his old address in the village which was his birth place.

In just 48 hours, Chantal gave me a file not only on Julian but on Janice as well. It contained more details on both of them than even they knew themselves. The first step is to obtain their birth certificate and then their National Insurance number, passport details and marriage certificate that lays the foundation to strip some one bare of any privacy, put one's entire life in public domain.

It is frightening how these investigative journalists and private eyes can find out tiny details, utmost secrets, any skeleton in their cupboards and even Prime Ministers and Presidents are not immune from their prying eyes, as President Nixon and many aspiring presidential candidates found out to their cost.

No wonder most politicians would like to turn their lives into an open book, laid family secrets bare and even minor misdeeds as a child are told to the press before they run for a high office.

Barak Obama wrote two books about his past, one about his childhood and the second about his political achievement even before he dreamed of becoming a presidential candidate. He closed the door before the horse had the opportunity to bolt, to escape.

Unanimity in politics is not always a blessing in disguise! No doubt writing these books served Obama in good stead, as any mud thrown at him was an old affair, already in public domain. He did not have to bend to the demands of social or political pressure.

* * *

Chapter Four

The Reunion of Two Lost Souls

I first picked Julian's file which contained twenty pages, full of information that was a goldmine for me. When Julian moved to Liverpool, he was expecting to forget Janice and move on. He tried to make new friends. He even went to a Uni and came out with a degree in social science, specializing in food science and developing vitamin and mineral content of the food, cooking and inventing new dishes with high nutrition value, especially for the young, the old and the army on the ration when on the battle field or confined to a naval ship, a submarine for a long time.

Janice was like a breath of fresh air, a bunch of roses he would rather have in his room than a diamond necklace on his neck. Lost opportunity is like running water. It will rarely come again. He realized that Janice was gone for good.

Although Julian succeeded on many fronts, he could not forget Janice. He found it difficult to get close to any girl. When he realized that Janice was the only girl for him, he tried to get in touch with her. But it was too late, all to no avail. Diamonds are formed by relentless pressure over a long period of time. Janice was such a diamond for Julian.

Janice has already moved away from the village and no one was prepared to give him her address, tell him how to get in touch with her. Julian was disappointed and disheartened. He was restless and believed that he was the author of his own misfortune.

Too many of us die at twenty but get cremated at eighty. In the end Julian did what many boys do when they fail in love, separated from their sweethearts by misfortune. He joined the Navy, in charge of the kitchen, as he had a degree and the Navy was short of such skills. Not many boys would study Social Science and cooking in those post war days when machoism was the order of the day.

Julian served in the Navy for thirty years before retiring. He visited all four corners of the world but he certainly did not have a girl in every port! In fact he never got married. He was a recluse on the marital front. In fact he made the Navy as his oasis in the world of stress, ignorance, selfishness and stupidity.

Like Janice, Julian was now living in a retirement home for the naval personal. To my great surprise this home was only half an hour's drive from where Janice was living.

They were at each other's door-steps without realizing it and without my intervention, our holiday friendship with Janice, they would have never met, rekindle their romance and lived happily ever after!

As soon as I finished Julian's file, I picked Janice's file as I was so eager to learn about her past. I sincerely believed that there is a twist in the tale, that Janice was hiding some secret. I was not disappointed. Her life was a bitter sweet tragedy.

Janice realized after Julian had left that she was pregnant. In those claustrophobic, righteous days with holier than thou attitude, getting pregnant outside marriage, especially for a Roman Catholic girl, was a life sentence, not only for the girl but for the whole family.

They would be shunned, barred from even their local church, the God's house where every one should be welcome with open arms, even though Janice's family pedigree reflected blue blood that would be a blessing in most situations, save the family from the social ghettos.

By the time Janice had the courage to tell her mum that she was pregnant, it was too late for the abortion. In any case abortion was not an option for a Catholic girl. It would be a cardinal sin. Can a monotheist religion bring fascism and deprive their followers the spiritual democracy? Janice was thrown between the devil and the deep blue sea. So often life's greatest setbacks revel life's biggest opportunities.

As Janice had just completed her secondary education with flying colours, obtaining nine good O Level Grades, it was a perfect opportunity for her family to send her away to London under the pretext of further education, going to a university. Her family was one of the leading one with financial status to match their social standing.

This was a lesson in the psychology of winning, an exercise in frustration being consumed by hunger for preserving the family prestige, good name. As we all know many situations, positions and prestige are not as idyllic as they appear to be at first glance. Janice was a strong character with the reservoir of inner mental and physical reserve. Youth was not the time of life for her but it was the state of mind that she had to overcome, conquer.

Janice had an unmarried aunt living in London who was willing to take Janice under her wing, give her shelter until the child was born. Her aunt Martha was a nurse, indeed a matron who was married to her profession, in true *"Florence Nightingale"* tradition. Martha was a real angel who would nurse Janice when her wings were clipped; she had forgotten how to fly. Our resolves are only tested in time of adversity.

She realized that Janice was like a helpless deer caught in the glare of an intruding pair of headlights without her help and support. They will have to shed the shackles of complacency and come to terms with reality but without giving up enthusiasm that would wrinkle the soul.

By moving away from the village, Janice had avoided psychopathic bullying under the guise of religion, as Christianity was alive and active in its historic citadel of Europe. The healing harmony of Christianity would not reach a single teenage mother, no matter what the circumstances may be.

Martha encouraged Janice to join nursing after the child was born, a lovely little girl she named *Rebecca,* after Julian's younger sister. Martha was as free to help Janice as her cluttered conscious would let her. She did not have any Armani-clad shoulders to impede her in any way.

Janice, although young, was a clever and a sensible person. She knew that no decent and well to do person from a respectable family would marry a girl with a little baby to be brought-up. Those were different times when most husbands would not like to raise children not fathered by them.

Janice was determined to raise Rebecca her-self rather than put her up for adoption or let some children's home, so often run by a church get their hands on Rebecca. In any case she was still in love with Julian and was determined to bring up their daughter in a loving, caring family atmosphere they would have given to her if they were married.

Devoting her life to nursing, looking after the sick and elderly was the best solution for Janice, especially as Martha promised to stand by her, through good as well as not so good times that Janice was bound to encounter. Martha was smitten by Janice and little Rebecca, as they were now her family, daughter and grand daughter she never had.

There was a time, a moment when Martha regretted devoting her life to nursing at the expense of getting married and having a family of her own. These two young, charming and beautiful girls brought laughter, happiness and fulfilment in Martha's some what lonely and mundane life.

Within seven years Janice became from a trainee nurse to a ward sister in charge of a busy ward and ultimately the Matron when Martha had to retire due to poor health, having lost the use of her limbs due to severe arthritis. Martha was glad that she took Janice under her wing who was now her daughter, taking care of her in her hour of need. Janice would never forget that it was her aunt Martha who gave her shelter, stood by her in her hour of need. Now it was her turn to return the favour, to look after her ailing aunt.

Today Martha was no longer with them, who left her spacious house to Janice, her daughter rather than her niece. When Rebecca got married, she would not leave her mum, as she knew what sacrifice Janice had made to raise her, what tough time she had while bringing her up with a demanding career at the same time. But after Rebecca had two lovely daughters and a family of her own, Janice thought it prudent; that it was time to let Rebecca had her space, time to move out.

Moreover the Retirement Home Janice moved in was only a stone throw away from her home and as a couple of her nursing colleagues had also moved there, she was in a good company. She was free, independent yet well looked after in the sheltered accommodation with some eighty one and two bedroom apartments, in six floors of steel and glass monolith, twenty four hour warden, in-house GP, canteen that serve the resident community well.

In fact the home was a hub of activities, all arranged and supervised by professionals, with frequent trips to seaside, beauty spots and other places of interest during summer time. Janice was indeed enjoying her well earned retirement.

After reading two files and using my journalistic licence, I knew I had more than enough material for my next novel which was eagerly awaited not only by readers but my publisher as well. But having a happy ending is a must, a prerequisite before I even start writing.

When I was ready, I rang Janice and made an appointment to visit her and return her book she was missing so much. By sheer co-incidence, it was her birthday as well. She was having a small party, a gathering of family and a few close friends from her nursing days.

Janice was really pleased to have us as her special guests, as by now we had gained her full confidence and she very much wanted to introduce me as a famous journalist, a writer, to her family and friends.

Now my dilemma was how to take Julian with us to Janice's party. But as usual, Chantal, my soul mate, my trouble shooter had the perfect solution. Chantal arranged with the warden to take Julian to a surprise birthday party of a mate of Julian who had served with him on HMS Wellington and a couple of other naval ships but was out of touch with Julian for the last few years.

I was Julian's driver cum minder for the night, responsible for his safe return to the home. Chantal accompanied my wife so that we four can make a joint entrance.

We took the elevator together to the 4th Floor where there was a day room or a medium size lounge where residence can celebrate their birthdays, have such parties for up to twenty people or so.

The main hall was on the ground floor that could accommodate up to two hundred people, mainly used for Xmas parties, marriage celebrations between two inmates that often take place, as love knows no age or any restriction, impediment or hindrance. The union of two old souls who have not long to go is always a joyous occasion.

Where there is a gathering of such people, enjoying their twilight years, the tragic event, departure of an old soul, an old soldier is always a possibility, as most have already passed their sell by date. So this hall is more often used to say, to bid final farewell to an inmate than for any other event. As day is followed by night, so is birth followed by death.

The world is it self a guest house where we are guests for few days, before proceeding to our final destination and Mox or salvation from the circle of birth and death; that is for those who believe in reincarnation.

When we entered the room, Janice was eagerly waiting for us. She came running or rather stumbling to us and gave us a hug that said a thousand words. Putting the book in her hands, I said in a soft but mischievous voice, "Janice, let me introduce you to a dear friends of yours whom you have not seen for a very long time."

Then dragging the reluctant Julian forward I said, "Janice, do you remember Julian? He comes from your village and you were together at school before he moved to Liverpool with his family."

Janice was speechless. When she steadied herself, gathered her thoughts, regained her composure, She stared at me in disbelief and said, "Ben, you have read my letter which was in the book cover."

I smiled and said, "Janice, I am guilty as charged. It is my journalistic background, my inquisitive nature, my instinct that puts me in hot water now and then. But I hope this time I have achieved my goal, put my curiosity to good use and I hope I am going to unite two lost souls and it will end in lifelong happiness for both of you."

I pushed Julian forward who was dumb struck, did not know how to react, what to say. But he instinctly grabbed Janice, hugged her for a long time.

When he regained his composure, he said, "Janice, please forgive me. I have wronged you, let you down and paid a very heavy price for my mistake, my cowardice. I could never forget you, I never even got married and today I am all alone. There is no one I could call mine, no blood relations."

Julian was really shaken with tears running down his cheeks, like a gushing mountain stream after the rains. Janice let him calm down before leading him to Rebecca and said, "Julian, this is Rebecca, our daughter" and pointing to two young beautiful girls, she continued, "These are **Willow and Maple**, your granddaughters. You are not alone any more. You have plenty of blood relatives."

This was too much for Julian. It was beyond the realm of reality. His shaky legs gave way and we had to hold him and let him down gently on the sofa.

We spent three wonderful hours in an emotionally charged but very happy atmosphere before we left. Julian's spark of life that had begun to flicker and on the way to be extinguish, now found a new wick, a wax of life to burn it bright again. Perhaps this was the moment when Julian regained his serenity, enlightened in substance and real inner peace that may be lacking since he was separated from Janice.

When we dropped Julian at his flat in **Marina Court**, a retirement home for ex sailors, I requested the warden to keep an eye on Julian, before he go into a magical slumber after a long, weary but fulfilling day, although after the initial shock, Julian completely regained his composure. After all he was a marine, the toughest profession one can earn a living from.

Since that wonderful reunion of two lost souls, Janice rang me a couple of times. But she left it to her warden to invite us and Chantal to attend her wedding, with an invitation in the post.

The marriage of Julian and Janice was on Saturday, 18th May which was incidentally my birthday as well. I was bestowed the honour to be the best man and sign the register as a witness, a final and natural tribute to this enchanting fantasyland, my final and most important duty in this wonderful tale of reuniting two lonely hearts who should never have been parted in the first place. But today we were rejoicing in the beauty and splendour of this tiny slice of luck, a peace of heaven, a dream like atmosphere.

But we live in a cruel, unpredictable world. Our childhood plans, dreams only materialize for a favourable few, the chosen ones.

I was happy that I was an instrument in bringing Romeo and Juliet together; unite two souls so cruelly separated by circumstances beyond their control. This was indeed a match made in heaven that only death would part.

If you ever see two elderly geriatrics behaving like teenagers in love, like Romeo and Juliet, then you should know that they are Julian and Janice.

Alls' well that ends' well. This was certainly a happy ending beyond my or any one's imagination. Who said that truth is so often stranger, more unbelievable than fiction! It certainly was in this case, an unusual, unique love story but with a happy ending!

* * *

The End

Epilogue:

It took me some six months to turn this touching, thought provoking, bitter sweet love story into a 400 page novel. I gave the book the title of **Nasib** which means fate or destiny. It was a triumph of love over adversity and the book was enjoyed by all, especially by Julian and Janice.

I always take great care not to identify the real characters on whom the book, the short story may be based, although Julian and Janice could not care less, as they are already in their twilight years and would not mind any publicity, good or bad. But I believe that one's creditability decreases as one become or come to be known as *"A loose cannon"* I would certainly not like to fall in that trap.

They feel that without my curiosity, intervention and hard work, they would not have found each other, given the opportunity to spend the rest of their lives together as husband and wife, as teenage sweethearts.

Most of my novels are based on true life experiences. But the identities are cleverly concealed. Writing such novels is an art, a gift from God. That is why writers, authors and painters are born artists.

They can not be churn out from our modern educational establishments like accountants, lawyers and doctors. For me it is a gift from Goddess Saraswati, the Goddess of learning, education, knowledge and sophistication. That is why I feel that it is my duty to use this gift wisely for the benefits of mankind, to create love and understanding rather than conflict and hate.

After all our present day world is not the heaven we experienced just after the end of the war that mellowed humans and nostalgia industry prospered even if only for a short time.

* * *

SISTER USHA

Chapter One
Hospital Stay with Difference

Mayur was staring at the big clock on the wall of his room, as it was approaching nine, the time the *Ward Sister Usha* would come in his private room to say Good Night, a routine visit before she goes off-duty. It was her daily routine since Mayur was admitted to the private wing of *Tata Memorial Hospital,* ten days ago.

First it was to carry out some tests, as his Ulcerative Colitis was playing up again and he could not get it under control with drugs, not even with steroids that usually help him at most times. But steroids are notorious drugs with complications and side effects. So the long term use of steroid is neither beneficial nor incorrigible.

Chronic Ulcerative Colitis is a tedious, long term inflammatory disease that affects the lining of the rectum, the back passage. So often it spreads to the lower part of colon and may even result in patient having a prolapsus problem, the slipping down of the muscles surrounding the bowl, especially when the patient is having severe diarrhoea.

This is an uncomfortable problem and on occasion the patient has to rush to hospital for emergency treatment, to push the muscles back in the right position, as prolong exposure may damage the muscle, leading to a serious condition and instant operation that result in the loss of control on bowl movement.

The symptoms for Colitis are vast and varied but most common symptoms are bleeding, diarrhoea with mucus, loss of appetite, weight loss, fatigue and dehydration. It also brings on depression, mood change, anxiety and loss of concentration.

Normally it is a young person's disease, more common in men than in women. People over fifty rarely suffer from Colitis. But there is always an exception to the rule. No one knows the exact cause, as they are vast and varied but mostly associated with work related stress, disharmony in the family life; break up of marriage, loss of a family member and even unknown bacterial infection.

With advancement in medical care and new drugs, surgery is the last resort, as it is serious and complicated. But so often it is unavoidable, inevitable and perhaps the best long term solution if medication does not have desired effect.

Mayur had to undergo numerous tests, that of Barium Meal was one of the most unpleasant meal one may ever have to take and painful and some what risky colonoscopy, sigmoidoscopy and numerous blood tests as well as the biopsy of the inner lining of the large intestine.

After all these tests, it was decided by his surgeon that the best solution for Mayur was a surgery, especially in his case it would be a straight forward surgery, as only one part of the large intestine was badly diseased. It was the best option to stop the disease from spreading to other parts of the digestive system.

However hard Mayur tried, he could not go to sleep, as the discomfort and the pain he felt from the fresh wound of the operation that he had to undergo, to remove the part of his large intestine made it difficult to sleep, without some kind of medical help, or perhaps divine intervention! Then in a way Sister Usha was a divine gift, a divine intervention, as Mayur was getting more than his share of attention and Sister Usha was more than just a nurse who was looking after him!

Well, it is absolutely true that the God works in a mysterious way. No one can second guess God or his work, his blessings! Then we see the God not as he is but as we are. We create God in our imagination rather than the other way round. That is why our resolves are only tested in time of adversity. Do we really think, sincerely believe that we are all children of Almighty God!

As Mayur was suffering from a severe attack of **Chronic Ulcerative Colitis,** that needed a major surgery, resulting in removing a part of his intestine, he was not allowed to take any medication, food or even water by mouth. All nourishment, along with drugs were provided through interventions feeding, a safe and quick way to help the body and mind to recover.

Mayur was banking on ward sister Usha to give him a liquid Valium or a Morphine injection to enable him to go to sleep, that would give him at least a temporary relief for few hours, especially during the night, the time most difficult to pass in a hospital ward, as it is so quiet, almost frighteningly quiet, the atmosphere not akin to a cemetery, at least for those with a vivid imagination?

Mayur would not like to let the renewing power of solitude to take hold of his mental faculty that would create an additional problem where there may be none! After all human mind is as fertile as the plains of river Nile and river Ganga!

Surely as the clock struck nine, Usha entered the room to see that Mayur is comfortable and perhaps soundly a sleep. But on entering the room Usha saw his favourite patient wide awake, some what in pain, in discomfort, not unusual after such a major operation. It is also a state of mind when one is confined in the realm of hospital ward where one may be nervous, even at best of time, especially if one is in an ICU where less than half the patients survive, recover and go home.

Mayur had a significant part of his badly bleeding and diseased large intestine removed, as Chronic Ulcerative Colitis is a tedious disease which on most part fails to heal, although it may go in remission from time to time. But cure or rather healing is, on most part unachievable, at least not without an operation.

No one knows the cause, why some one may get this tedious disease. But it is widely associated with stress that triggers the failure of the defensive mechanism so necessary for the proper function of the digestive system. It may also follow after food poising and a severe attack of dysentery.

In the case of Mayur, the tragic death of his lovely, beautiful baby sister Nikita may be partly responsible; the cause for Mayur developing this illness, as he normally lives a clean, healthy and stress free life as far as humanly possible when one is in a pressurised job, profession.

With a vast leap and advancement in medical science, especially in surgery technique, this operation is now much safer and less debilitating than before. Now the operation is carried out in two stages. During the first stage, the diseased part of the large intestine is removed and the end of the intestine is attached to a bag outside that collects the stool, the stomach waste.

But it is uncomfortable, unhygienic and debilitating for many, as the bag needs emptying and the opening so often gets infected, requiring a great care and attention all the time.

But now, after a period of some three months when the wounds have healed, a second operation is performed that reconnects the two parts of large intestine, thus removing the need of having a bag outside.

Since this advancement, more patients are opting for an operation that was shunned by most sufferers before. Mayur had successfully undergone the first part of the operation.

During his stay in the hospital, Mayur had developed a close, friendly and some what intimate relationship with Usha, who saw him as her elder brother, when she came to know that Mayur comes from a family of two brothers but lacks a sister whose love, the feminism makes the family perfect.

According to unique Hindu tradition, Hindu culture, a family is not complete if a brother does not have a sister or vice versa. Some how Usha had an inclination, she felt that Mayur was taking a keen interest in her, a brotherly concern that is not so uncommon when a brother lacks a sister. It was in a way kind and touching, especially for Usha who had lacked such attention, such pampering since her pre marriage days. To give up hope, enthusiasm wrinkles the soul.

After Dipawali and New Year, similar to Christmas and Janmastami, Lord Krishna's birthday, *Raksha Bandhan* is the most important occasion, a day of celebration when a sister invites her brother for a dinner, to her home, that is if she is married and ties a piece of holy string around the right wrist of her brother.

This ties, binds, cements their relationship, their love and affection for ever. This is a unique Hindu tradition not found in any other religion. Then no other religion is ten thousand years old.

In return she is allowed to make a wish, ask for any favour from her brother. But being a kind, loving, caring sister, she only asks for brother's love and a promise to come to her aid in her hour of need. Both Usha and Mayur were lost in their thoughts when Mayur realised that he better ask her for the medication before she leaves.

"Can you please give me a Valium, Diazepam or Morphine injection?"

Pain on Mayur's face was evidence enough to convenience Usha that he really needed some medication to go to sleep, have a restful night and wake up fresh in the morning, a pre-requisite to quick, rapid recovery.

"Bhaiya, (brother) you know that I can not prescribe you the injection without the permission of the Registrar. Let me go and speak to him, ask him what he would like to prescribe." With a smile on her face and an energetic walk, Usha left the room.

After some twenty minutes, a life time for a patient when he is in pain, Usha came back with a smile and gave Mayur a small dose of pain relief, in the form of a morphine injection through the tube inserted to give Mayur intravenous medication.

* * *

Chapter Two

Sister Usha

As Usha was now off duty, Mayur half expected her to draw the chair and sit down for a chat. Surely Mayur was not disappointed.

"Ushabahen, (Sister Usha) Can I ask you one question?" Mayur said some what hesitantly, not sure how Usha would react to his unusual request.

"Bhaiya, (brother) I know your one question will be the thin edge of the wedge. But go on, ask me what you like and I promise you that I will answer your question truthfully and to the best of my ability, albeit with constrain, tact and diplomacy. After all I do not want to upset my patient in any way and retard, set back your recovery with my answer?" There was a mischievous smile on her face.

"Usha, how long you have been working as a nurse?"

"Some four years and before you ask, yes would like to tell you that I have been to Uni and have a degree in biology and chemistry." Usha rightly anticipated Mayur's next question.

"Usha, it seems you can read my mind. So what I am going to ask you next will not come as a surprise to you. I do not have to tell you that you are a clever, kind, caring, charming and a good looking girl. But I can not help feeling that you are lonely, there is no one special in your life.

You are not wearing the engagement ring and you are always on duty, even when you are off duty. It seems this work is your life. It is your escape from the world that you do not want to be a part of. Perhaps some one has hurt you, treated you badly and you have lost faith in humanity."

386

Mayur's simple, straight forward question took Usha by surprise. For a moment she was speechless, at a loss how to answer this extremely personal question. So Usha kept quite, silence is golden, she thought, until she regained her composure.

Mayur was right. He touched the sore point in her life, analysed her life as if he had known her for a long time and knew all her inner most thoughts.

After a long pause, Usha replied, some what mischievously, "Bhaiya, I did not know that you take such a keen interest in my personal life. Do Mayabhabhi (brother's wife, a sister- in-law) know this, your inquisitiveness about my private and personal life?"

There was a mischievous smile on Usha's face, demonstrating a truly brother and sister relationship. But it made Mayur some what uncomfortable

It was a sweet revenge on Usha's part to see Mayur uncomfortable and a bit embarrassed.

"You know Usha that my inquisitiveness, my concern is purely brotherly, paternal, but you like to tease me, don't you Usha?"

In reply, Usha nodded her head and said, "Yes Bhaiya, I know that and I am grateful that you take such a keen interest in my welfare, considering me as your little sister. Believe me, it means so much to me, as I do not have a brother and as you know, a girl's life is never complete, fulfilling without a brother and a husband. I have neither. I have been unlucky on that front. But some how I feel my luck is about to change."

Usha's voice was cracking up, filled with emotion. Perhaps no one had shown such kindness, bestowed upon her a brotherly, selfless love for a long time. Now Usha was prepared to open her heart, tell Mayur her life story, as she knew that in Mayur and Maya, she may have found a brother and Bhabhi on whom she could depend, be friendly and even be a loving part of the family.

Usha was indeed leading a lonely life since she was separated from her husband Tilak. Her life was like that of a frog who lives in a small pond, that is its whole world, nothing outside exist, that it may be aware of.

Although both Mayur and Usha were eager to carry on their conversation, Usha realised that the injection was taking effect. It would be prudent to let Mayur go to sleep. So she bode good night, wishing him a sound, painless sleep, the most important ingredient in a rapid recovery.

After spending some fifteen days in hospital, Mayur was being discharge the next day. The first phase of his operation was a total success.

Although it was Usha's day off, she came in early to say goodbye to Mayur, her new found love, a brother.

By now they were close, at ease in each other's company and now she knew why Mayur was taking such an interest in her, treating her as his little sister. Usha was indeed his baby sister Karishma who was the apple of his eyes.

Mayur was the eldest son in a well to do Kapoor family, with a younger brother and a lovely, charming, beautiful baby sister **Karishma** who passed away in a tragic accident, at the tender age of just nineteen, a flower that was still in bud, struggling to be in full bloom, with beauty and glory that would captivate the world when it was plucked and thrown away.

She was the darling of every member of the Kapoor family. Mayur took her death very badly indeed, blaming himself for the tragedy, as he was late in collecting Karishma from the Uni. The bus Karishma was travelling in, with her college friends, was involved in an accident with a tanker carrying an inflammable liquid that caught fire on impact, killing some thirty five passengers on the spot, a gruesome, tragic and bizarre, freak accident that ruined every one's life, especially that of Mayur, a kind, caring and sensitive person who loved Karishma to bits.

Mayur could not forget or forgive himself, for being late. If only he had been on time to collect her, if only Karishma had waited for him, is she was not on that particular bus, if... if ... if. There were million and one questions in his troubled mind but not a single answer.

No one blamed Mayur. How could they? It was not his fault. The traffic in the city is unbelievably chaotic, with poor roads, scooters, rickshaws, buses, taxis, lorries fighting for space, against each other and with careless, daring pedestrians and cows, dogs and pigs, obstructing, monopolizing roads.

Accidents are common place, adding chaos to an already cooking pot. Even ambulances are struck in the traffic for hours and many patients die even before the ambulance could reach the safety of the hospital. To add salt to the wound, his mother passed away within a year of the accident, perhaps died of broken heart, as she was as good as gold, at least on the health front, before this tragedy struck the family, now leaving two brothers alone, on their own, as Mayur had lost his father when he was still in a college.

Although Mayur was well settled today, with a charming wife in Maya and two beautiful children, he could neither forget the accident nor stop blaming himself, even after ten long years, as there was no one, no sister to tie a Rakhi on his wrist, on the auspicious day of Raksha Bandhan.

Karishma, as Mayur remembered her, was in many ways resembled Usha, in her good looks, the way she talked, smiled, joked and even pulled his leg. Mayur some how felt that God has given him another chance, opportunity to redeem his past mistake, keep a promise he made to his parents.

Usha was as beautiful as Karishma, even more in her Nursing Uniform that some how gave her an authentic look, a perfect fit for her tall, slim body with curves shining through the tight uniform.

The long hair systematically, artistically hidden under a cap, twinkling eyes and some what shy, appealing smile, a beauty that may not be apparent at first sight but will grow on you as you come to know her more, better. Although for Mayur, it was love at first sight.

So now Usha understood and even encouraged Mayur to treat her as her long, lost sister, as she knew that this will help, would speed up his recovery.

There is no medicine, medical substitute for true love, care and affection, even for a love between a brother and a sister.

If Usha knew all about Mayur, than Mayur knew even more about Usha. Her young, ambitious life, her dreams, her armans were shattered by the person she loved and trusted most. No wonder she was reluctant, a bit weary of life, unable or unwilling of trusting any one after the way Tilak, her husband, her love, her joy turned against her, divorced her for no apparent reason at all, at least for Usha.

Tilak was following his mother's wishes rather than his own heart. Usha and Tilak met at Uni. Like all collegians, they used to go out in a group of four. Nature took its course. Both Usha and Urmi got married to Tilak and his friend Manish.

While Urmi and Manish's married life evolved smoothly, Usha ran into a storm, faced a brick wall in the form of Shanta Devi, her mother in law. The name Shanta means peace, harmony, calm and cool but she was more like a storm, a monsoon, a hurricane, a one person demolition team.

She felt that Usha was not in the same league as her son Tilak. She was a fraud, a gate crasher, an uninvited guest, a party spoiler who came from a poor family, a simple background, a family that lived from hand to mouth which was only true if you take it to the extreme.

Usha and her sister Shammi were the only children. When their father had a stroke, he was paralysed on the right side, unable to work. Their mother Mamta, the name means love, affection, was a wonderful, highly educated lady, a senior school teacher who now became the main, the only bread winner in the family.

Naturally Mamta could not give her lovely daughter Usha a marriage to remember, a send off that could be the talk of the town. They were not in that league, at least not without borrowing, incurring debt burden that could ruin the family. Usha could never allow such a situation, nor would Tilak. They knew what happens to a family that is heavily in debt.

In an ultra conservative Hindu society, it is the girl's family who bear the burden, pay all the expenses, although this is a dying tradition, especially in a love marriage where cost is shared or the wealthy family may offer to pay all the bills.

This was the point of contention with Shanta Devi; Tilak's mum, as she could not boast what a great catch Usha was for her only son. These ladies, with more free time than brain, get together for supposedly charity work but spend most of their time gossiping and their topic of conversation is their children, especially sons and daughter in laws who bear the blunt of the jokes and insults.

As long as there was love, understanding and harmony between Usha and Tilak, Shanta was unable to interfere, to influence Tilak or turn him against Usha. But as it happens in the lives of all married couples, especially those who live with their parents, in-laws, occasional argument, disagreement and misunderstanding may happen between newly wed couples.

Shanta took full advantage of such occasions. Ultimately, with great cunningness and mischief making, she succeeded in splitting up Usha and Tilak, her intention all along, since the day they got married.

Usha, a kind, caring, considerate and sensitive girl, who bent backward to keep her marriage intact, was badly shaken at Tilak's indifference to his mother's attitude towards her and her constant criticism , putting Usha down at every available opportunity.

* * *

Chapter Three
End of Marriage

In the end, Usha snapped, could not take this bullying any more and moved out. But she knew that if she goes back to her family, it may ruin family name and dent the opportunity, diminish the marriage prospect for her younger sister to get married in a respectable family. In such separations, girls are always branded as mischief makers who can not and will not live in a joint family. They are too demanding.

So Usha, instead of returning, moving back with her mother, decided to take up nursing, as it provided her with the accommodation, a powerful incentive in an over crowded city like Bombay, where even a pavement space requires a premium?

Moreover, as Usha was a science graduate, with biology and chemistry as her main subjects, it was not difficult for her to secure a sought after placement for a trainee nurse, as nursing career was and still is a second choice among Hindu girls. Perhaps the unsocial hours and living in a nursing home may be a deterrent in climbing a social ladder that is becoming more and more a trademark for success.

With exemptions for science graduates and hard work, Usha completed her nursing training within two years, becoming a Qualified Registered Nurse (QRN) a much sought after qualification in the medical profession.

No wonder Usha became a Ward Sister in charge of a busy ward with twenty beds and a team of fifteen nurses, many a training nurses, responsible only to Matron, all these achievement by the time she was only twenty five. Nursing is a hard work but if there is a wish, a burning desire than nothing is out of reaches, impossible to achieve, even under the most unfavourable and difficult circumstances.

Mayur was eagerly waiting for Usha, as it would be unthinkable, out of question to leave the hospital without thanking, saying goodbye to Usha who was as much responsible for his speedy recovery as the doctors, medical care and medication put together.

Mayur was going home in better health, better spirit than when he was admitted. Not only his Ulcerative Colitis but his mental wounds, his anguish, were his unseen, suppressed depression definitely better and on the way out. How could he not feel better when he found Karishma, his lovely baby sister, a bit grown up but more lovely, witty and affectionate than when he lost her all those years ago.

Mayur was sure that her mum must be watching them from above and perhaps engineered this situation for him, to redeem his assumed guilt.

When Usha entered the room at the stroke of mid-day, both Mayur and Maya were eagerly waiting for her, as Mayur had to vacate the room after the lunch was over but only after a visit from the hospital Registrar and the Matron who would dispense the medication, to last until the next outpatient visit to the hospital in two weeks time.

Although it is a daily routine for doctors and nurses to see the patients come and go without forming, developing any sort of personal attachment, Usha's eyes were wet and her heart in turmoil when Mayur gave her a kind of strong brotherly hug, a brother, sister ritual.

Maya, standing on one side watch this episode with satisfaction and some anticipation, as she had not seen Mayur so relaxed and happy for a long time. Perhaps this illness, hospital admission was a predestined encounter, a blessing in disguise, arranged by God, by Mayur's mother from above who could not see her elder, favourite son unhappy, blaming himself for a tragic but freak accident that has nothing to do with her son.

On the spur of the moment and before Usha could leave the room, Maya requested Usha to accompany them to their flat, that is if she is free and would like to help Mayur. Maya, a born diplomat, put her request in such a way that it was practically impossible for Usha to say no without sounding uncaring. But Usha was more than happy to oblige, to accompany them to their comfortable flat in the suburb of Valsad, only a stone throw away from the hospital.

As both Maya and Mayur were professional people, Maya a University professor in Social Science and Mayur, a Bank Executive, they were living in a much desired area of Bombay, in a 15th storey three bed room apartment that not many could afford.

Mayur was only able to buy this flat in a luxurious, a special development, as this complex was part of the bank's asset, in their investment portfolio. Yet it was a tied flat in some ways, as he could not sell it in the open market if he changed the job. This was a clever ploy by the bank to tie down their best executives on a long term contract.

Although Usha had not visited the flat, she was already like a part of the family, a favourite aunty for Mayur's children Nina and Nihil.

As the time went, Usha became an integral part of Mayur's family. For Maya, Usha was a God sent gift, with her culinary skill and her love for children, a unique combination in a modern girl like Usha.

Mayur was often away on bank business that gave Maya and Usha a quality time together, to lay the foundation of a life long friendship that is unique to Indian culture.

Although Mayur was happy, over the moon at finding, discovering, knowing Usha who was by now an integral part of the family, as precious to him as his little sister Karishma was, he knew deep down inside his heart that Usha, at the age of 26, was too young to remain single, on her own, a spinster for the rest of her life. She does not deserve such a lonely, solitary life. She was neither a nun nor a Sister Nightingale, without dream, without ambition, without desire, although it may be suppressed temporarily in light of her past bad experience at married life.

It was always Mayur's wish, his ambition to give his sister Karishma a grand wedding, when she was ready, after gaining a couple of degrees that she always wanted, dreamed about. Karishma's life ambition was to follow into the footsteps of their father who was well respected professor of political science at a prestigious university, while Karishma's preferred subjects were economics and business administration, as she could neither stand politicians nor the democracy in India which was corrupt to the core.

Mayur's dream of giving Karishma a wedding to remember was shattered by her untimely death. But this chance meeting with Usha revived this dreams to some extent, as Usha who was already married once may not want too much fuss second time around, that is if Usha even consider marrying again.

However hard Mayur and Maya tried at match making, taking Usha with them to various parties and gatherings, they felt it was a lost cause, as Usha was not interested in marriage, not even getting closer to any one, any male company with the one exception of Umesh, who was Mayur's PRO, his assistant, his Man Friday, a trouble shooter who had to do Mayur's dirty work or rather gauge the depth and murkiness of the water where Mayur had to go on a fishing expedition.

The multinationals and information technology has turned the world into a one, big village. Some of these conglomerates are so big, so powerful and budget, turnover even bigger than most Asian and African countries, that they are the real power, with corrupt politicians in their pocket. This was the environment Mayur had to work, to negotiate the contracts and deliver the goods.

He indeed needed some one like Umesh, a Charted Accountant and a Member of the Charted Institute of Bankers, was more qualified than Mayur who had a mere masters degree in finance and PhD in International Banking behind his name?

Mayur and Umesh were a great team. They trust each other, loved working together as a team. Umesh even turned down a promotion, to head his own team, as he knew Mayur needed him, who was a kind of elder brother for him. Mayur knew how loyal Umesh was and he would trust him with his life. This was indeed Ram Laxman combination unique in this cut throat business environment.

Umesh was a regular visitor to Mayur's flat. So often his visits were work related but Maya started inviting him more often for dinner, on any pretext, hoping to bring Usha and Umesh closer. Yet Usha's interest in Umesh was superfluous, some what de trop but none the less polite. Usha knew how important Umesh was to Mayur. Indeed if Usha was his younger sister, Umesh was his younger brother.

It was difficult to gauge who were more fortunate, Usha and Umesh or Mayur and Maya?

Perhaps the saying, what you sow, so you reap was true in this case. Mayur had invested so much love, energy and trust in these two and now he was getting a handsome harvest, a big dividend from his investment.

Umesh admired and liked Usha and who wouldn't, as she was charming, articulate and beautiful, full of self esteem, self confidence and proud of her achievement in most difficult circumstances. Umesh would like to know Usha even better, come closer to her. But Usha did not reciprocate his enthusiasm, his attention in any way. Umesh, being a polite person who knew Usha's background, kept his faith and knew that one day his patience, his endurance and his trust in Usha and God will be rewarded. After all Usha was worth waiting a life time.

Chapter Four

The Happy Ending

For Umesh Usha was a self made person who deserves his utmost respect. She was one in a million, as Umesh has seen many good looking gold digger who always hover around a high flying executive like him.

The fact that Usha was not interested in his money, position or his social standing, made Umesh more determined to get accepted by Usha. It seems it is human nature that we are more interested to acquire some thing, some one which may be out of bound for us.

Perhaps Usha was a forbidden fruit that made her more desirable an apple to be picked from the Garden of Eden! She was a challenge to Umesh who would never walk away from an opportunity that would test his mental faculty to the limit.

Usha knew about Umesh's interest in her. She appreciated his gentlemanly conduct. Perhaps she may even had a sneaking admiration for Umesh, a silver lining, a ray of hope but she was not yet over her nightmarish experience, once bitten twice shy. But given time, she may change her mind and Umesh knew that patience is virtue, at least in the case of Usha. She was worth the wait.

Fortunately Umesh had a patience of a saint, the one quality that was an asset, most needed virtue in his job when negotiating difficult and complicated contracts with clients, governments which may drag on for days, even weeks.

Umesh also knew Usha's tragic past and was willing to wait as long as it takes, give Usha time, to let her wounds heal, give her space and opportunity to make up her mind in her own time, without exerting any undue pressure.

But Umesh did not have to wait for long. An incident in their lives changed every thing, Usha's inhibition about relationship, her attitude, her bitterness and mistrust of men, relationship and ultimately marriage. It all evaporated in the maze of hope, kindness and anticipation. After all Usha was a woman, a well educated, sensible and sensitive woman with all the armans, ambitions and inspirations.

So often Mayur and Maya went away for a short break. When Mayur go on a short business trip, Maya would accompany him if there was a school holiday and Usha was free to stay in the flat and look after the children.

Even children loved this break, to be with aunty Usha who would spoil them rotten. It was also a perfect break for Usha, from her hospital routine, associated with pain, illness and occasionally death that would affect her, affect any one, no matter how well trained one may be to handle such a situation.

On one such occasion, when Mayur and Maya were on such a break, the little girl Ani, short for Anita, had a severe stomach pain. Although Usha was a nurse, she was at a loss what to do, except rush her to hospital.

But to call ambulance would take hours, as it was a rush hour with a very heavy traffic. Ani was in too much pain to wait that long. Usha suspected appendicitis. But Ani was too young to develop such a problem. Then again, any one can develop any medical problem at any age and that also without reason. It is not that uncommon for a healthy, young and active person to get a heart attack or a teetotaller to develop liver complications.

In desperation, Usha rang Umesh on his mobile and he was at her side within minutes, on his motorbike, the only mode of transport that can dodge the traffic and travel fast. They took Ani to hospital where she was admitted, taken into the theatre and operated on within an hour, to remove the appendix that was on the point of bursting and would have if they had waited for an ambulance.

So Usha and Umesh saved the life of little angel Ani, the apple of Mayur's eyes. By the time Usha managed to get in touch with Mayur and Maya, the operation was a total success, the emergency was well and truly over.

But Usha was badly shaken. She was a nervous wreck who could not even help in the operating theatre. Dr. Shah, a noted surgeon realized that

Usha was too near, too involved with the patient and would be more of a hindrance than help in such a situation.

That is why a relative, who may be a brilliant surgeon, is not allowed to operate on a close relative, although they can be present in the operating theatre as an observer. But Usha was not fit even to be in the theatre. During this crisis, Umesh kept his cool was a tower of strength to all, especially to Usha.

While Ani was in the operating theatre, Usha was a nervous wreck, shivering like an autumn leaf, comforted by Umesh, who did not leave her side, even for a minute. The thought of losing Ani, after the tragic loss of Karishma, will surely ruin Mayur's life; that is if he survives the initial shock that would not kill him first.

There is nothing as effective as a tragedy, a tragic situation to bring two people together, especially those who keep themselves artificially apart. Usha spent the entire three hours, the time Ani was in the operating theatre, in the arms of Umesh, who comforted and assured her, gave her moral support, mental and physical strength, wiping her tears now and then and uttering a few words of comfort.

When the surgeon gave the good news that the operation was a total success, that little Ani was not in any danger, Umesh could not hide his relief, his joy and his jubilation while Usha collapsed in the arms of Umesh, in sheer relief. Umesh unintentionally squished Usha hard against his chest, raised her head and kissed her on the forehead.

Seeing a smile on the face of Usha, he was about to kiss her on the lips, to give her a passionate kiss that would tell Usha how much he loves her, when he realised that this is not the right moment, that he should not take advantage of Usha when she is in a delicate, venerable state.

Umesh immediately realised his mistake and withdrew his lips which were on the verge of touching Usha's and apologised unreservedly, expecting an angry reaction from Usha. But to his surprise and immense joy, there was a smile on Usha's face. She made no effort to move away from his grip, instead holding on tightly to Umesh, mustering all her strength.

Raising her head again, Umesh said, "Sorry Usha. Please forgive me for lack of control, my moment of madness. I do not know what overcame me?"

There was sincerity in his voice but he was not ready for the response he received from Usha, a sweet response worth the entire wait.

"Umesh, don't be silly. I know you like me, fancy me, and even want me. Don't you?" and looking around the empty waiting room, she said,

"Umesh, this is your opportunity to kiss me passionately to your heart's content, to your heart's desire. I know you have spent a lot of sleepless nights on my account. So don't be shy. I am in a mood to give you any thing you want. But I know that you are too much of a gentleman to take advantage of me when I am venerable. Aren't you?"

By now Umesh was over the initial shock, his disbelief. He was more than willing to seize this golden, God send opportunity and give Usha what she wanted. Even before Usha could complete the sentence, Umesh grabbed her and gave her a long, hard and a lingering kiss that almost choked Usha.

When it was over, he added, "Usha, yes I am a gentleman but a bit of a romantic rogue as well. Yes, I fancy you the day we met and wanted to kiss you for a long time.

But I was willing to wait until you are ready. I love you and want you more than any thing else in the world. Let us admit our true feelings for each other and stop pretending that we are just friends." Umesh was holding Usha so tight that her well developed, turgid breasts were pressing hard against his chest, almost hurting her.

The smile on Usha's face said it all. By the time Mayur and Maya managed to fly back to Bombay, Ani was, more or less as good as gold. They came straight to the hospital from the airport. By now Mayur was aware, knew exactly how Usha saved the life of his little angel.

On entering the hospital, Mayur grabbed Usha, holding her in his arms with tears running down his cheeks.

"Usha, this is the second time you have come to the rescue of my family. Without you, I would not have made such a quick and complete recovery. Now you saved the life of Ani. I do not know how I am going to repay my debt to you." Umesh was emotional.

"Bhaiya, God and Umesh came to our aid. Without Umesh, I don't think I could have brought Ani to hospital in time. You know how long it takes for an ambulance to navigate the traffic. Moreover he was the tower of strength when I was in panic, as cool and calm as any one could be in such a difficult circumstances. Usha was eager to give credit to Umesh who was standing on one side, with Maya.

Then remembering how much Mayur hate motorbike, as it is the main cause of death in young people, in a city like Bombay, she added, some what mischievously, "Bhaiya, you are always telling Umesh to get rid of his scooter. Now you know why Umesh prefers motorbike than a car. We could have never reached hospital in time in a car!"

Within three days Ani was back home, in the homely comfort and the familiar surrounding, with all her favourite people making such a fuss, as Usha had taken a week off to look after Ani who wanted her favourite Usha aunty to be with her more than her mum and dad.?

It soon downed upon Mayur that even if he was at home, the result could not have been better. In fact Mayur would have called the family doctor who might have or have not diagnosed correctly, taken in the seriousness, the urgency of the situation.

Even if he had judged the seriousness, he would have rang for the ambulance, the normal procedure in such a case, such a scenario. It would have taken from a minimum of two hours, if some one is extremely lucky.

The norm was four hours to cut through the city traffic and reach hospital, before Ani would have been operated on, perhaps too late to save her life. It was the scooter, the motorbike that made the difference and of course Usha's judgement, quickness and dedication that won the day for the Kapoor family.

It took some three months for Usha and Umesh to turn their first passionate kiss into a true love, a permanent relationship both wanted and cemented. They were eager to tie the knot, as it was difficult for them to remain apart but neither would like to get involved sexually before marriage. That is the cultural influence among the Hindu community, even though Usha was not a virgin, having already married once.

So when Usha announced the date and requested Mayur to give her away, as her father had already passed away, with her sister and little Ani as bridesmaid and Maya a Matron of Honour, this was the happiest day in their families, especially Kapoor family. But the course of true love never runs smoothly. God always like to test one's belief, faith trust and conviction. Then fruits of hard labour are always much sweeter than some thing handed on a silver plate!

Usha suddenly, out of a blue received a letter from Tilak, her last husband. Although it was simple and not in any way suspicious or inauspicious, Usha was at a loss how to handle the situation. Should she confine in Umesh and show him the letter or just destroy it and forget all about it? In the end Usha thought it best to let Umesh read the letter, since he was such a calm and calculating person who can handle any situation.

The letter, which Usha read again and again, was:

"Dear Usha

I know this letter will come to you as a surprise if not a shock, as I my self find it difficult to write. But I feel after the way I treated you, it is my duty to apologise and let you know that you were not at fault in any way for the break-up of our marriage.

After the divorce, I got married with Trupti, a girl chosen by my mother. She was not even half as beautiful or as educated as you are. But she came from a rich, respected and well known family.

But the marriage did not last even one year, as she was head strong girl who would not put up with my mother's interference. Just like you, she left me and made me realise that as long as my mother interferes, I will not be able to hold on to any girl, I would not have a life of my own.

That was the decision making time. I moved out, bought my own flat and now I live on my own. My life is not bad but it is lonely. This painful experience made me realise how much I loved you once and what a wonderful person you are.

I don't know much about you since we got divorced except that you took up nursing and made a carrier for your self. I would like to meet you and perhaps take you out for a dinner. That is if you still feel the same way about me as I do about you.

Perhaps you may have moved on and may not want to have any contact with me. But please do let me know one way or the other. It goes without saying that I would respect your wishes.

Yours ever Tilak."

When Umesh read the letter he smiled and said, "So this is the cause of your sadness for the last couple of days. Don't worry. Tilak will not cause any problem for us. But let me deal with it in my own way."

This brought a sigh of relief and satisfaction on Usha's face, knowing well that Umesh will deal with it in a fair, firm but sensitive manner. Usha's dilemma, her problem, her worries were over. Her conscious was clear and now she can get married without any last minute hitch.

On the other front, some how Mayur felt that God had given him a second opportunity to fulfil the promise he gave to his mum and dad that he would find a good boy from a respectable family and give his little sister Karishma a wedding that would be the talk of the town, the envy of every young bride.

Usha and Umesh did not want a grand wedding. They wanted it a family affair, with the ceremony taking place in a Hare Krishna temple nearby, with only close family members present. But they had to arrange the reception in a five star hotel with friends from the work, both from the hospital where Usha was working and the bank where both Umesh and Mayur had so many friends and acquaintances.

As Usha was marrying Umesh, Mayur's assistant, although not for too long, as he was offered his own team, his own section and this time Mayur would not allow him to turn down this golden opportunity, as this would lead to Umesh able to buy a flat in the Sandy Beach Complex, the bank's latest acquisition, Mayur was not losing his sister Usha but gaining, adding a new member to his family.

Another surprise Usha and Umesh received was when they were opening presents, in Umesh's rented flat where Usha had moved, after the marriage.

According to the latest trend, a new tradition, every one gives the newly wed a present in the form of card and a cheque, not the unwanted gifts that are passed from one wedding to the next.

What drew their attention was an unusual but beautifully decorated gift box, as it was the only boxed present. When they opened it, they found a card from Tilak with his best wishes for the future and all the gold jewellery that Usha's parents had given to her on her wedding day but not returned to Usha when they got separated, as they were in charge of Tilak's mum.

This was indeed a kind and noble gesture on part of Tilak appreciated by both, Usha and Umesh. That was Usha's last link with her past, with Tilak and now both Usha and Tilak knew that they have moved on in life for good.

It was indeed a happy ending; the end justified the means, alls well that ends well. Could he dare to say they lived happily ever after? Why not!

Usha, a great fan of Indian films who loved the romantic escapism after her own life turned from a fairy tale to a tragedy and again she was standing at the gate of heaven, could not help but murmur her favourite song.

Khoya khoya Chand
Suna asman
Bato me sari rat jaya gee
Hum ko bhe kaisa nind ayagi
Khoya khoya chand.

* * *

This is one verse difficult to translate in English. So I will leave it as it is. But fans of Bollywood do not need a translation.

* * *

KISMAT
(FATE)

Chapter One
Everest Tea Estate

Rakesh has just completed six months in his new job as a manager of the **Everest Tea Estate**. It was one of the biggest tea estates in the area with a workforce of some one thousand people in total, mostly Assamis but few Bengalis and some tribal people as well.

The estate was some three hundred kilometres from **Cherrapunji,** the nearest town in this green, wet and solitary wilderness of Assam. The hills around Cherrapunji are world famous as the place that receives the highest rainfall, some six hundred inches of rain every year. It does not rain, it literally pours. So often the rain can deposit ten inches of water in just a couple of hours. Those who live in a moderate climate with normal rainfall of sixty inches a year, it is even difficult to imagine what a havoc such a downpour will cause.

Rakesh has a BSc in agriculture and forest management from the famous Wadia College in Pune and a Master's degree from Durham University, England, where he had spend two years studying agriculture and Estate Management, just after Bharat gained independence in 1947.

It was the time, the era when an English degree was at a premium, the qualification that would open most doors in India, as British were in a hurry to leave and there were not enough Indians, especially with a British degree to replace them, although it is too simplistic to equate such a degree alone with efficiency, hard work and business acumen. Then again Britain did rule the world for some one hundred and fifty years, establishing the greatest empire in human history.

Rakesh's stay in England inspired, disciplined and energized him for the stern challenges which will confront him when he returns to his motherland Bharat which was still finding its feet, to stand upright and steady after the turmoil of partition that left millions dead and homeless. Bharat which was once the oasis of tranquillity was today the eye of the storm, the hurricane that would leave a wasteland in its path.

Since returning from England, Rakesh had worked at various tea estates, mainly in Kerala, on the slopes of Western Ghats, the green, fertile and most beautiful land in Southern India, the land where the God resides or at least takes winter holidays, coming down from Mount Kailash in Tibet. Then Hindu holy literature if full of mind boggling stories. It is an oasis of enlightenment and her holy literature is mostly based on some sort of truths that have and will turn into reality in the near future.

The tea estates on the slopes of these mountain range were much smaller in size and less productive than those in Assam, at the foot of the mighty Himalayas where climatic conditions for growing tea are most favourable in the world, producing the best type of tea that include Darjeeling and Dehra Dun tea, widely drunk amongst the aristocrats in India and England.

The last tea estate where Rakesh worked as a deputy manager was a Rani Tea Estate, near the beautiful hill station of Munar in Kerala. Today Munar is a world renowned place, a centre of tourist trade, due to local beauty spots like beautiful village of Thakadi on the shores of Lake Periyar.

The focal point for nature loving tourists is the nature reserve, the wild game safari park where lions from the forest of Gir in Gujarat are introduced and allowed to roam in relative freedom in this vast and well managed natural cum man made safari park that has become the magnet, the honey-pot that draws tourists in their thousands.

This place Munar is a favourite holiday destination for the people of Indian origin now residing in the West, especially in America, Canada, Britain and Europe as well as most Commonwealth countries, all ex-British colonies with significant Indian expatriates population, that include Singapore, Hong Kong, Fiji, Guyana, Surinam and Mauritius.

But during early fifties it was an unknown place outside Kerala. All big tea estates were concentrated in Assam and Ceylon, now known under its new name of Sri Lanka.

When Mr. John Smith who was managing *"Everest Tea Estate"* took an early retirement, perhaps due to the changing political climate that many colonial minded British expatriates found it difficult to stomach, to adjust, the holding company in Britain *"The Windsor India Company"* found it prudent and wise to appoint an Indian as a manager to replace an ageing British expatriate who was eager to retire to the green and beautiful land of England.

The Company Directors knew that it was only a matter of time before Indians will be in a prime position, capable of taking over, managing most businesses, as they are hard working, well educated and capable people.

So why not jump the queue and be the first on the ladder of change that was blowing throughout the world, especially in South East Asia. After all a branch has to bend with the wind or it snaps, breaks and gets destroyed. If nothing else, the change will come like a magical slumber after a long and weary day, a natural tribute to this enchanting fantasyland that was the pivot of the British Empire.

Rakesh had all the qualification to manage such a tea estate. In fact he was more qualified than the retiring Mr John Smith who was purely appointed for his Englishness, his upper stiff lip and colonial mentality, his aristocratic background. But now in these changing circumstances, Mr Smith was the prisoner of his past which was more of a liability than an asset in an independent India.

Rakesh had a degree in Agriculture and Estate Management from a famous British University. He had also lived in England as well. So he was familiar with the English etiquette, code of behaviour, the all important British protocol to deal with the directors who sit in their comfortable London office but may occasionally visit the estate to make sure that every thing was quiet on the Western Front?

Profitability and the aptitude to be part of emerging Bharat was the sole concern of the Board of Directors but the knowledge of English social life was a distinct advantage when entertaining the Managing Director and his associates who may visit Bharat from time to time, so often accompanied by their wives, as the ships, the passenger liners were becoming luxurious and being on such a cruse liner was more of a holiday than a mere means of transportation.

Rakesh, being a Punjabi, was a tall, well built and adventurous person with a taste for hunting which would be an asset on such a lonely posting, far removed from civilization. In such remote places, life would soon come down to the quality of one's contribution, awareness and enlightenment in matters other than work.

Rakesh had also worked as a Forest Officer, as a Chief Game Warden and involved in tracking down and killing men eating tigers and rogue bull elephants that would go berserk when ousted from a herd, after losing a leadership challenge.

Such wild animals are the most dangerous preys and it takes the nerves of steel to go after these animals once they have tasted human blood, human frailties and the human weaknesses. Rakesh knew, believed that fear is nothing more than a negative stream of thoughts, consciousness.

Assam was at the time Garden of Eden, the most fertile land outside the Ganges river basin and attracted more foreign agricultural investment than any other sector and other states in the Indian Union.

* * *

Chapter Two

The Beginning of the end of British Empire

These were still early days for industrialization for an agricultural country like Bharat, although the Communist countries, especially Soviet Union was trying to help India to lay the foundation for the heavy industries, such as steel making and manufacturing armaments.

Although the Soviet Union could not compete with the West when it comes to manufacturing consumer goods and the agriculture products, it was par excellence in some fields, notably manufacturing of steel, heavy industry and sophisticated armament, including rockets and exploring space.

After all it was the Soviet Union who put the first sputnik, first man and a woman in space, orbiting the earth that shook the foundation of the West and forced President Kennedy to divert the enormous might of USA in defeating Soviet Union in the race to put a man on the moon.

Unfortunately India made the mistake of choosing Soviet Union as a role model on the economic front, a system now being discarded by every country, including Russia, in favour of free market economy once described as a capitalist imperialism but now recognized as the system that makes quantum improvement in one's satisfaction and motivation level. How times have changed?

But we all know now that it is not the system that succeeds or fails but the persons, the autocrats running it, managing it. While Communism has failed economically in the Soviet Union and other East European countries, it is a blessing in disguise for Communist China, the most dynamic economic power in the world today, fast overtaking Japan and even mighty United States. It is the super power of the 21ˢᵗ century.

In a way Assam was neglected, a far flung province, corner of British Raj where people were kept poor, uneducated and ill-informed so as to provide a cheap, so often a bonded labour on such vast, profitable tea estates which required an enormous number of farm workers, cheap farm labourers to pluck the tea leaves as soon as they open, before these leaves mature, lose flavour and produce lower quality of tea. India and China are the only two countries blessed with such a vast reservoir of human resources.

It was not luck or coincidence for such a tiny country like Britain to establish the greatest empire in the history of the world, far bigger and more prosperous than the one established by Alexander the Great, The Roman, the Greek or the Mongol Emperor Kublai Khan, the greatest warrior king ever to rule the world.

It was said that the sun never sets on the British Empire which stretched from Hong Kong in the East to British Guyana in the West, from Ireland in the North to Falkland islands in the South, a distance of some twenty thousand miles, covering one third of the land mass, with countries like Canada, India, South Africa, Central and East Africa, New Zealand and Australia being the mainstay of the Empire in its hay days. Even USA was a British colony once?

It was like a dog keeping an elephant as a servant. It was the loss of the American colonies that forced this great sea faring nation to look East and colonize India and South East Asia.

Japan entered the Second World War to drive out America and European countries from the Pacific Rim which Japan rightly considered as their backyard, the spear of influence.

Missionaries were very active in this part of the Raj but they were more interested in converting the locals, who as Christians would be more loyal to the Raj than to their own kith and kin, to their motherland. They were trying to create a privileged class based on their religion and political thinking, political affiliation and not on their ability, their achievement. It was a caste system within a caste system.

But missionaries did provide education, health clinics and tried hard to break down the caste system based on Indian tradition that had divided the people of India for centuries. Even Gandhiji, the saintly figure and father of the nation failed in his attempt to eradicate the caste system because he was and still is so deep rooted.

Now even the so called lower caste do not want to change, to integrate, as they are, in so many ways a privileged class who are given preferences in education, employment and even in politics! Why kill the hen that lays golden eggs!

Even after independence, the people of Assam were underprivileged class, the majority tea estates remaining in the hands of British companies and expatriates holding the high post but doing little work. But in a country like Bharat, changes take a long time.

Their resolves are only tested in the time of adversity and on most part these people leave the quality of their life to chance, to opportunity rather than fight, take the bull by the horn.

If any thing, Bharatwasis are too timid, too laid back to raise a ripple. That is the reason Bharat was ruled for over one thousand years by foreigners, by every Tom, Dick and Harry.

It was beginning to change, slowly but surely, as Indians began to believe in them-selves and realized that all that glitter is not gold and all that is white is not milk, a sweet, a smooth, heavenly drink. But it would take a long time to wipe out the slave, the inferior mentality the British had planted in the minds and hearts of the Indian people, imposed their warped politically correct views and social attitude on the Indian ruling class.

That was the trend, the survival game, change or perish atmosphere in the aftermath of the independence hysteria throughout the British colonies in Asia and Africa. India gave the lead that others followed.

In a way losing India, the jewel in the British Crown broke camel's back and its desire to hang on to other colonies. From then on, Britain was on a downward slope of influence, prosperity and above all, the military and industrial might.

* * *

Chapter Three

Rakesh: The Manager of Everest Tea Estate

The owners of the Everest Tea Estate were a few English aristocrats, who controlled the estate through a private limited company. MD may visit the estate, a kind of social visit, to show the face if not the flag but they would leave the day to day running to the staffs, especially the manager.

They were satisfied as long as the estate makes a good profit for their share holders, a good return on their investment, their capital, in true British tradition. Quality of their thinking determined the quality of their life, their financial prosperity. DNA is the basis of British self-enlightenment.

Rakesh was as capable as any Englishman who fervently believed in the ageless principle of self-mastery. If you do not respect your-self, no one will. Self belief is the nectar of life, of success. Ignite the flames of your personal potential which will produce startling results, tumescent as a young stallion. Rakesh fervently believed that lost opportunity is like a lost love, like running water. If ignored, it is gone for ever. So grabbed the opportunity, be part of the festival before it moves away, before others can grab it. Make the quality of life a choice, not a chance.

Rakesh had some twenty people working directly under him in the office, to administer the estate. That included office secretary, office junior, accounts clerks, a welfare officer and financial overseer to run such a vast state efficiently, with some one thousand labourers, tea leaves pickers and general maintenance men.

These were mainly Assami and Bangladeshis who all lived on the land owned by the estate, most with their families. Half the workforce was made up of women who were more efficient pickers than their male counterparts. Besides picking leaves, they would keep the estate tidy, clear the undergrowth and work in the factory where leaves were dried, graded and packed in wooden boxes.

The accommodations provided by the company were basic but most were given a piece of land, an allotment where hardworking families would grow their own vegetables and keep few goats or an occasional cow to keep them supplied with milk.

For these poor people earning a subsistence living, milk was the nectar of life, especially for the young children, as so often a mother would have more than one breast sucking children that would need replenishing her breast milk supply.

There was a school and a health clinic run by a couple of English nuns in association with the local Church, with the help of local Indian converts. These Christian missionaries fervently believed that lifelong contentment will come from fulfilment of Dharma.

An Indian doctor would visit the clinic a couple of times a month or whenever he was badly needed in an emergency. These institutions who served the poor created a sense of inner harmony, in the lush Garden of Eden but without Adam and Eve who may rupture the innocence of the inner core. But it was only a question of time before such innocence is lost for good, as the world is changing at a breath taking speed.

There were two Englishmen working directly under Rakesh, an accountant and an engineer who was also responsible for other tea estates. So his presence on the estate was intermittent but the accountant, financial expert was ever present, to keep an eye if nothing else! Even under these changing circumstances, an Indian manager was not entirely trusted! Then old habits die hard.

These Englishmen were there as a token presence, the legacy of the Raj. They were no match to Rakesh when it came to management skill, hard work and dedication.

They knew it and respected Rakesh's overall authority and management skill. Rakesh had a large, well furnished office in a building which was situated in the middle of the estate, making it easy and quick to reach any part of the estate. Today before entering his office, Rakesh stopped for a moment, looking proudly at the board on his office door, *"Rakesh Sharma MSc. Estate Manager."*

Rakesh was not a glory hunter but he wanted to prove his ability, that he was as good as any English manager still working, managing a tea estate in independent Bharat. He wanted to prove his worth and that is a wonderful Mantra! Rakesh wanted to mix his academia excellence with his spiritual intelligence.

After all Bharat, an ancient land of Rishis and sages is renounced as a land of Mox, Attainment, Karma and Deliverance. Rakesh may be outwardly westernised but his soul was till residing in the ancient land, the wisdom and tradition based on centuries old teachings and prayers.

Rakesh had invested all his hopes and hard earned money in his dream, his profession. He was not afraid to build his future, his career brick by brick till he sits on the podium.

He was also aware that in pre independent Bharat, such estates were so often managed by sanctimonious dimwits who were simply there for being British, pretending to be Einstein.

Rakesh could not help thinking how proud his late father would be if he was alive today. Rakesh lost his father when he was barely in his teens. His mother Motibai brought him up, working all God send hours with peanuts of a pay.

Rakesh was her only son, her sole reason for living after her husband died of a heart attack at a relatively young age of forty. Rakesh, in return worked hard, gaining scholarship and was now at the height of his career.

His first action, his first good deed for the family when he was financially independent was to buy a small but comfortable and well furnished one bedroom flat for her mother in their village, with a live-in girl, what we call au-pair to look after her aging mother, as he could not be with her all the time. His one aim, his duty and obligation was to make his mother as comfortable as humanly possible in her old age.

For Rakesh, charity certainly begins at home and no one was more important to him than his mother. He would visit her as often as possible, at least four to six times a year, even if some of these visits may be just a flying visit for a day or two, a weekend visit. Rakesh could see how excited his mother gets every time she sets her eyes on her son, her Lord Rama. On Rakesh's part, his enthusiasm for home visit was as desirable as his first visit after he returned from England and had not seen his mother for three years.

Rakesh was a conscious and energetic worker who would prefer to perform as much work and carry out his duty, his responsibility personally as humanly possible.

But on such a large estate, delegation of work, duty was the name of the game. Clever supervision was more important, more productive than sheer hard work on the part of the manager. Rakesh did not believe in politically correct obsession with nobility, privileges or aloofness. After all even Lord Rama needed an army of half human labourers to build the bridge that enabled him to free Lady Sita from the clutches of evil king Ravan.

This is where management skill would come in, be helpful in running the estate smoothly and efficiently. His learning curve was never ending, even when he was at the height of his career.

Social skill was as important as work expertise to get along with the aristocratic directors and share holders. Rakesh believed in learning not only from his own mistakes but from the mistakes of others as well, as he knew that one can not live long enough to make all these mistakes by one self.

He learnt this sense of inner harmony while socializing with his English friends in Durham. He learnt never to forget the importance of living with unbridled exhilaration.

Further more when he was young, he was taken under the wings of a local sage, a learned holy man who installed magnetic power of the mind that would attract spiritual and material wellbeing in abundance, made Rakesh a spiritual gunslinger. Guruji's mantra was, "Some are indeed wise people but those who study themselves are indeed enlightened souls and vision without action was a waste but an action without vision was a disaster. That is how most wars start."

These wise words still ring bells in Rakesh's mind, although Guruji had departed a long time ago. Rakesh's life philosophy was based on his childhood upbringing and wise words of a sage played a major part who often said that every saint, including himself has a past and every sinner has a future. It is human for Rakesh to make a mistake some time in life.

Rakesh's constant presence on the estate, among the workers, his readiness to get his hand dirty and mix and mingle with the workers made him not only popular but easily accessible as well.

The previous managers, especially the English ones, hardly used to leave their comfortable, air conditioned offices, rarely seen by the workers on the ground, at the bottom of the ladder who produced the goods, were responsible for the success or failure of the company, its profitability but ignored by the management. This was the tyranny of the impoverished thinking.

Unlike these captive souls, Rakesh's philosophy was "Mind is like a fertile garden and for it to flourish; one has to nurture it daily, in the form of hard work and intellectual engagement." This was one of the fundamental gems of worldly wisdom Rakesh has accumulated through his wandering in some of the loneliest places one may have to work and stay.

No wonder the production was on the increase, absenteeism due to illness, drunkenness and laziness was also down. The disputes among the workers were settled fairly and quickly before they get out of hand and the production could be affected.

Although Rakesh was well acquainted with managing an estate, this one was a large estate, even among Assam standard where most tea estates were large, even enormous.

This Everest Tea Estate was also one of the most modern tea estates in the country. Except picking tea leaves, the young and tender foliage, most other tasks involved use of some machinery.

The tea bushes were restricted in height but allowed to spread, thus making it easy to pick leaves. The undergrowth was kept clear of weeds and long grass with the use of straws, gravels and ground hugging plants, so as to keep the snakes, the main danger to workers, out of the estate.

Snake bites, mainly from the most poisonous King Cobra snakes were the main cause of deaths in the past, with one in fifty workers regularly bitten by these snakes. It was now a rare cause of death since Rakesh took up the management and introduced these measures, to remove the habitat where snakes can live, breed and multiply.

Now pickers could work in peace without the fear of snake bites thus raising the productivity and the quality, as more and younger, tender leaves were picked as soon as they open, grows to the right size.

These leaves were left in hot and damp air for twenty four hours, in a specially constructed storage places. Then the leaves were moved on a conveyer belt, to a drying place.

When dried to the right standard, they would come under a light roller, then sheaved, graded and packed with most work done with minimum human involvement, a rarity in those early days of mechanization.

In a short time, Rakesh came to know the estate well. Using his powerful, spacious and well equipped 4 by 4 military Jeep, the vehicle he demanded as part of his employment package, he would tour all four corners of this vast estate, working long hours.

But this was as much a labour of love as his duty, his obligation and his desire to prove his worth. Rakesh would also send a detailed regular three monthly reports to the head office in England, a vast improvement on the previous management when an annual report was the norm.

But now, with the beginning of the rainy season, the estate roads became impassable, some areas impenetrable, even for a four wheel drive vehicles. Most of the work on tea estates in Assam comes to an abrupt holt for two to three months during a monsoon season when up to 500" of rain fell in a short period.

It so often washing away part of the estate, especially on the steep mountain sides where steps were created by hard work, digging the mountain sides and creating a narrow, strip field where tea shrubs thrive and produce the best tea.

But as they were difficult to harvest, only a tiny proportion of tea leaves came from these narrow stripes of land. The rest were given to workers to grow their own vegetables.

The land management was as important as the estate management, to make sure that the land does not lose its fertility, do not lose the fertile layer of top soil, as without top soil the land would become unfertile scrub land. It was important to plant trees, create a forest at regular distant to avoid land erosion.

This is where Rakesh's experience as a forest officer and his education in England became his great asset, gave him the edge over other managers in the region. He put the theory he learnt in college in Durham into practice and came up with a winning formula, a winning solution.

* * *

Chapter Four
The Mistry of the Castle Ruins

As a manager, Rakesh had the best accommodation, a three bedroom bungalow, built in the colonial style, but on an artificially raised land, a plateau created by the use of bricks, sand, stones and cement, with a raised veranda and an open, large patio in the front.

It would be difficult to imagine that this was not a real plateau but an artificial one, some one hundred feet higher than the surrounding land. Rakesh envisaged that this must be a natural plateau but the height has been raised artificially, as it would be a mammoth task to create such an enormous plateau from a scratch, especially in such a wilderness, without modern machinery.

The bungalow was fitted with all the modern facilities that an English expatriate would expect and demand when living and working such a long way from home, in a complete alien environment and isolation.

Even though Rakesh was amongst his fellow Indians, he was as isolated as the Englishmen. He could neither speak their language, Assami and Bengali nor could he mix with any one socially. He was more at ease with the expatriate English than with his fellow citizens.

Rakesh had the wonderful magnetic power of the mind to attract social, spiritual and material advantage in abundance. Although Rakesh was not particularly religious, he always wore a locket round his neck with the photo of his mother on one side and that of Guru Nanak on the other.

Some how that made Rakesh feel close to both and a comfort when he may be down and lonely that we all feel from time to time, especially when

417

we live alone, on our own, without a company, although it was Rakesh's mantra to live with unbridled exhilaration and to master the principle of self-mastery.

Besides being well furnished, all doors and windows had mosquito proof wire-nets, iron grills, ceiling fans in all rooms and primitive but effective air-conditioning in the main lounge, the best available at the time.

The location of the bungalow gave it a panoramic view, being on an open, elevated land, overlooking the estate and the surrounding area, the distant hills adding to the beauty and charm of the location. Living in such a panoramic beauty spot made Rakesh full of serenity and inner peace that made him appear angelic in nature.

Rakesh had a perfect view of the ruins of the castle from his main bedroom as well as from the veranda, as the ruins were on a hill some three miles away. He was eager to visit this place but until now he was too occupied with his work so that such personal interest, activities not connected directly with his work took a back seat for the time being. But now, as every activity was at a standstill, Rakesh's mind was like an uncaged monkey, rushing from one place to another, on most part without any purpose or direction.

Today it was Saturday, the beginning of the weekend for rest and recuperation for all estate workers. The rain had also failed to materialize, a break of three days, a dry spell that occasionally punctures the rainy season and gives every one a relief from the storms and lightening that keep them confined indoors for days.

It was a perfect day for walking. So after early lunch, Rakesh put on his knee high rubber and lather walking shoes, put a loaded revolver in his holster, a must for Rakesh, along with a strong sesame walking stick embodied with cast-iron beadings and knobs. The stick was a formidable weapon in itself, especially if attacked by fellow human beings, capable of doing serious harm if used as a weapon, used in anger.

After walking for a couple of hours at a leisurely pace, observing the surrounding area which was more of an open ground then a dense forest, Rakesh was some three quarters way to the ruins which he wanted to visit.

But as usual in this part of Assam, during rainy season, it suddenly got dark with lightening and thunder on the distant horizon. It was a sign, a signal every one would head who is familiar with the monsoon season in Assam.

Rakesh knew that in less than an hour, the rain would be upon this area, with dark, heavy clouds that would turn the day into the night, making it dangerous to walk, to be out and about in the forest.

So Rakesh decided to turn back, to put on hold his desire to view the ruins and with brisk walking, he just managed to reach his bungalow before the sky opened up, the nature went berserk and the thunder and lightening had a field day.

From the safety of his living room window, Rakesh was looking outside, at the distant hill with the castle ruins which soon disappeared behind the mist, clouds and the lashing rain, in the doom and gloom of the rain soaked day.

Breaking his chain of thoughts, Rakesh heard the worried voice of his servant Motilal but every one including Rakesh called him Dada (grand father) as he was considerably older than every one on the estate, with silver- grey hair but remarkably fit for his age.

Dada and his wife Jamuna who was considerably younger than him, perhaps his second or third wife, took care of Rakesh's every need. It was unfortunate but common occurrence to lose a wife, especially in child-birth and subsequent wives may be much younger.

It was a common practice among the hill tribe girls to get married as soon as they reach the age of puberty, that is at the young age of fourteen and even younger.

As these hill tribe girls were well built, even at the tender age of fourteen they look strong, mature and more of a woman than a child, unlike their city counterparts.

Jamuna, who was in her late thirties or perhaps early forties, was not only a kind and a caring person but a wonderful cook who treated Rakesh as a kind of a younger brother, called him Bhaiya (brother) rather than Sahib (boss) and she loved taking care of him.

Although it was unusual for lowly servants to call their boss a beta (son) or bhaiya (brother) it did not matter to Rakesh, as both Dada and Jamuna took good care of him. They called him these names, beta and bhaiya out of love and respect, not to gain familiarity or any advantage. But they were careful to address Rakesh as Sahib, Sir or the boss in the presence of guests and other estate employees. After all Dada was too wise and experienced to offend Rakesh in any way. Dada knew his place, his position in the household.

Rakesh himself was not a bad cook either. Having lived a bachelor life, so often in far flung, remote places, away from cities and civilization, he had no choice but to learn cooking which he took to like a duck to water, as most Punjabis love their food.

Jamuna soon picked up all the tips, mastered cooking Rakesh's favourite dishes and with fresh vegetables and spices widely grown on the allotments, Rakesh lived a life of luxury, at least as far as food, gourmet dishes were concerned.

Rakesh's favourite dishes, cooked with enthusiasm and expertise, were chicken tikka masala, chicken corma, vindaloo and Madras curry, lamb special, bhuna and balti lamb, Karai dishes (dry) and some Chinese dishes such as aromatic crispy duck, chow mein and noodles along with vegetable curries of potatoes, peas, bhindi bhaji marinated in vinegar and stuffed with mixed curry powder, spinach, aubergine sliced and grilled with cheese, green peppers, crushed garlic and fresh tomato slices were indeed appetizing and mouth watering.

These dishes went well with egg; mushroom and jeera fried rice and freshly baked tandori chilli or garlic naan over an open fire. Jamuna was good at making pickles, from lemon, mango and ginger, along with yogurt mix and green salad using garden grown fresh ingredients.

No wonder Rakesh thought she was a better cook then her mother? Then again his mother had to do without half the ingredients, spices and fresh vegetables, as money was tight and whatever she earned went on educating Rakesh, not on food or clothes.

Breaking Rakesh's concentration, his chain of thoughts, Dada said in a soft, kind but concerned voice, "Beta, did you visit the ruins on the Anupama hill?" This was the first time for a while Dada had addressed Rakesh as beta rather than Sahib. Normally Dada would address Rakesh as Sahib in presence of other estate workers but when alone, he may call him beta from time to time.

"Yes Dada, it was my intention to visit the ruins. But the sudden darkness and the rain made me turn back before I could reach the ruins." Rakesh said it in a calm, calculated voice.

"Beta, thank God for his mercy, his timely intervention. Any young man who visits these ruins a few times normally dies within a month or two. Please beta, promise me that you will not go any where near that fateful ruins." There were virtually tears in Dada's eyes.

Rakesh could only smile as he had heard such stories about ghosts, witches and even angles on most of his postings, especially among the hill tribesmen.

But as dada was like a grandfather for Rakesh, a kind and caring person, Rakesh could only oblige.

"Well Dada, I would not go there but please tell me how any one can die after visiting these ruins?"

"Beta, what can I say to an intelligent and educated person like you! I am sure you would not believe me but this is my own personal and true experience with two young men of this estate.

There is a witch who lives there, among the ruins. She is indeed very beautiful and young men like you are easily attracted to her, like a bee to a honey, a fish to an angler's bait and dance to her tune, like a snake to a snake charmer's flute.

Life here for a single man is indeed lonely, isolated and unfulfilled in many ways. But Sahib, can I give you one good advice! Why don't you get married? I understand she does not trap, snare or lure married men. She leaves them alone." Dada was suddenly relived, with a smile on his wrinkled face which was only a few minutes ago, full of fear and apprehension.

"Well Dada, I will have to meet this angel of death one day but not before I get married." Rakesh said it with a smile, half expecting Dada to say that he had already selected a girl, a bride for him!

Dada said nothing but retreated to go back to his hut not too far away. Perhaps dada felt he may have gone too far, crossed the line, spoken out of turn to a Sahib.

But Rakesh knew there was nothing but love and concern for his wellbeing in Dada's heart. He was not offended in any way but amused certainly he was and perhaps his curiosity, his interest and inquisitiveness made him determined to meet this girl that is if she really exist, was not a fabrication or an extension of fertile imagination on the part of dada and other estate workers. But then Dada was a wise man, not easily fooled or who may believe in fairy tales.

Next day being Sunday, a bright and beautiful day, Rakesh could not resist but go out for a walk to the ruins. Today he was in a hurry to reach the ruins. Dada had wetted his appetite rather than put him off visiting these ruins, with the tale of a beautiful, charming young witch, a princess or perhaps a local village beauty. Such local beauties were not rare among the hill tribesmen. Rakesh may not admit but he would not be averse to meeting this mysterious beauty. It will be at least a pleasant distraction from his daily routine of work, work and more work, as the bungalow was too lonely to come back to.

But Rakesh was street wise, experienced and full of self belief, self knowledge, the DNA of self-enlightenment to be trapped by a village beauty. After all he had seen, met and experienced real English Rose during his stay in England.

Rakesh remembered the history he had learnt as a child, the love triangle, the love storey between Siddhraj Jaisinh, the emperor of Gujarat and Ranakdevi, a low caste woman who was working as a labourer on the fort he was building on the slopes of mount Girnar.

The king was so obsessed with this tiny but very beautiful girl, who looked stunning even when covered with dust and mud, who was in fact a married woman that the king kidnapped the girl and kept her a prisoner, tried to add her to his harem. But the girl killed herself rather than live a dishonourable life but not before she cursed the king and ultimately brought his downfall and death.

This was a tragic storey that made Ranakdevi a Goddess, a patron saint of married women and the king a villain and a dishonourable royal person. without honour or character. It was a cardinal sin, a royal tradition among Hindu kings to kidnap a married woman. According to Hindu custom and tradition, a married woman is honoured and respected, not abducted and turned into a sex slave.

* * *

Chapter Five
The Encounter of the Third Kind

Today Rakesh was even better equipped, adding a powerful torch and a light raincoat with a plastic hood to his normal accessories of a walking stick and a revolver, to give him a complete protection against the rain, in case he is caught in a storm.

Avoiding Dada and Jamuna, Rakesh slipped out unnoticed. Yesterday he had spent some time in observing the surrounding area but today he took the short cut, the direct route to the ruins, passing through some long grass, a passage made by occasional human activity but almost hidden under the weight of long, tall grass. Perhaps Rakesh was eager to keep an appointment with his destiny!

Rakesh was walking at a brisk pace, whistling his favourite tune from the Swan Lake Opera and keeping a watchful eye on the surrounding area, the long grass and thick bushes through which he was passing.

Although there were no dangerous wild animals like tigers and elephants in this part of Assam, there were wild pigs, large monkeys and occasional sighting of leopards but the most danger was poised by huge king cobra snakes whose bite would kill a man in minutes.

Moreover these snakes can spit the poison, the venom at human beings from a distance of twenty feet, aiming at eyes that would render a man blind if not treated quickly.

The best protection against spitting cobra is to wear tight fitting glasses to protect eyes and long boots to protect against snake bites. Rakesh would never go out without this simple but effective protection, always ready for any eventualities. After all he can not call an ambulance in an emergency?

This is the name of the survival game, learnt over a long apprenticeship, first as a Game Warden and later as a Forest Officer.

His first aid training and the generous use of his own money provided such essential items to many estate workers who may be too poor to take such precautions themselves.

The footpath was made by the constant use of the track by the local villagers who used it to visit far flung and isolated settlements. Rakesh was enjoying the walk.

He was an avid walker. He loved walking on the soft soil, changing pace, running, jumping or just loitering, drinking water from a spring that may be just spouting, water being as fresh as rainwater.

It was an ultimate pleasure picking wild berries and fruits, stopping at every vantage point to observe the scenery, be part of nature.

It would be difficult for a city dweller even to imagine the forest life until one has tasted it, although to be honest, it is not every one's cup of tea, especially with snakes and other wildlife in abundance. But for Rakesh, forest lead to the elevation of the soul, a fountain of peace and tranquillity where he is the king of his own domain.

One reaps what one sows and Rakesh was a firm believer in sowing the seeds of trust and friendship with his workers who would love a boss who is not too big for his boots, who may occasionally visit them in their huts, especially when some one is sick or celebrating a social event, like marriage or a birth of a child. How can Rakesh renounce these poor but devoted souls who were after all God's children, God's creation!

Rakesh loved hunting but not just for the sake of thrills. He would only kill wild animals if they become a danger to villagers. He would shoot wild pigs, deer and antelope so as to provide fresh meat to plantation workers who are on most part under nourished. Game meat is a luxury they appreciate. Such a gesture on part of Rakesh would go a long way in establishing harmonious relations with the estate workers. Rakesh firmly believed, perhaps gained through experience that an ounce of practice is better than a ton of theory.

This was the life Rakesh loved and yearned for, rather than living in a city with pollution, traffic and overflowing with humanity. Some city dwellers are super rich living in the lap of luxury while others live on the street who may not get even a single square meal a day, reducing their lifespan to less than forty years. Yet the hearts of these super rich are empty, devoid of any feelings. There is not even an ounce of compassion in their entire body unless they would like to cash in on the popularity of certain ethos.

One may never find such disparity in villages or on plantations, tea estates and remote settlements where every one has a roof over one's head and no one goes completely hungry. They believe that God may wake you up hungry but would not let you go to sleep on empty stomach.

As Rakesh neared the ruins, he found a lovely mixture of nature and human endurance, with bamboo bushes, occasional hardwood trees and even some rogue tea bushes hidden among the long grass, huge boulders and rolling hills.

The trees and occasional tiny patches of forests were hidden in the valleys and lower ground at the foot of the hills, like a neglected Garden of Eden. The whole area was sparsely populated, almost devoid of human presence, human activities. As a result, it was immersed in peace, calm and beauty that gave the place a unique, captivating, bewitching atmosphere difficult to describe, to put pen to paper.

It was like a glass of nectar, an expensive wine that we would not like to stop drinking once put to lips but difficult to get hold of in the first place. Rakesh was so engrossed in his thoughts that he arrived at the ruins without even realising it.

Rakesh started viewing, examining these ruins of an ancient castle which were like exploring the museum of the past. He who is most attentive reaps the most benefits, emotionally, physically, mentally, spiritually and materialistically. One may be wise but the one who studies and psychoanalysis one self can extract most out of one's life. This is the ancient wisdom of the sages that Rakesh learnt in childhood from his Guru. No wonder Rakesh was so attentive to these ruins that most would ignore.

The building may not be artistic from the outside but was well built, with security uppermost in mind. The fort was in ruins, a sleeping beauty castle, covered with wild vegetation, thick stone walls crumbling with age, neglect and some vandalism.

The interior was well planned with all the necessities taken care of. Janankhana or ladies quarters were isolated. There were plenty of storage space for water and grain and stables for horses. Bedrooms must have been spacious and well decorated, bathing areas tiled with marble and granite.

This was Rakesh's impression, accompanied by his experience, as he had seen, visited and studied many such ruins in various places, forests and hills, including many castles in Wales and Scotland. This is the world Rakesh could not renounce. Rakesh also had a vivid imagination that went hand in hand with his experience, familiarity and reality.

After browsing through the courtyard for half an hour, soaking the silent atmosphere, akin to Shah Jahan's tomb, spirit wondering in search of one of the most beautiful women, Noor Jehan, the Aphrodite of Indian history, sad silent yet some how fulfilling, the atmosphere that would completely drain the admirer of his emotion, sentiment and ardour.

The whole of Bharat is an ancient museum, every state, city and forest is littered with thousands of years of history with monuments, castles, battle grounds, mausoleums, tombs and palaces fit for kings and emperors.

Then there are temples and places of worships, such as mosques, gurudwar and churches. Bharat is the crossroad and cradle of civilization of Asia, if not the world.

There was an outer wall, a perimeter fortification some fifty feet high, still standing intermittently, with occasional soaring watch towers, deep moat now all but filled with mud, rubbles and vegetation and stone parapet but these outer ruins were plundered by the locals for their stones and building material value but no one would touch the palace ruins as they were supposed to be cursed. In a way such a superstition helps to preserve the ruins and historical buildings in many parts of Bharat.

The roof was missing from all the rooms and most of the walls were covered with vegetation, with wide cracks and the floor was covered with rubbles and overgrown with weeds, a perfect place for snakes to monopolize. So Rakesh was extra careful, avoiding all places where snakes may hide, make a nest to mate, using his long and sturdy stick to make a way, to study the place before venturing in, putting a foot in a lion's den.

Within an hour Rakesh inspected the ruins from top to bottom, from room to room, having a very good idea of how it would have looked when it was first built, in its heydays or how it could be restored. He would have become an architect if he was not so much interested in outdoor life, living away from cities, so often out of a suitcase that would be a symptomatic malaise for most city dwellers.

Rakesh sat down at a vantage point, on a big boulder or some sort of structure, clear of all debris and weeds. The sun, a ball of red fire, was fast sinking behind the distant hills, covering these ruins in perpetual darkness which was some how intellectually stimulating for Rakesh.

Suddenly Rakesh felt unusual loneliness. Perhaps he was sitting on a tomb, not a boulder. He may have realized that he was all alone in this wilderness which may be dangerous if it becomes too dark.

He remembered the lines he read on a tombstone when visiting a castle in the far flung corner of Scotland.

> "I rest here, in a sombre isolated place
> Put to rest, well over thousand years ago
> Now covered with pest, overgrown with weeds
> Yet I lived a life, full of zest and valour
> But it all came to an abrupt end
> As suddenly as I came and went
> Remember me as you pass by my grave
> That I was once what you are today
> A healthy, wealthy, wise and cheery
> A soul respected, in essence a pillar of society
> A VIP in making, a bud about to blossom
> A man of substance and influence
> But do not forget, you will be one day
> What I am today, a soul lost in a maze
> Entombed in a coffin, forgotten by all
> For this is the way of nature
> Here today, gone tomorrow
> Sunk like Titanic, without a trace
> So make the hay while the sun shines
> Before you change from a man of substance
> To a man of mere straws
> Good deeds never go unrewarded
> Before the sky laden with dark clouds
> Gloom and doom, all too familiar
> Descent upon you from the thundering grey sky
> To reunite in death, with Mother Nature.

* * *

Rakesh started going down the hill, an easy descant, a pleasing, effortless walk, hoping to reach the safety of his comfortable and inviting bungalow before the sun completely disappears behind the distant hills and plunges these hills in perpetual darkness. These hills, wilderness is a completely different ball game at night, in the darkness.

427

Somehow Rakesh felt nervous, as if he was watched, being followed but he knew that it was just his fertile imagination. Moreover he was well armed with a lethal walking stick and a revolver, more than enough to deal with any small wild animals that inhibit this part of Assam.

Rakesh was glad that no wild animals like tigers and elephants were seen here for well over thirty years. But somehow Rakesh started remembering his encounter with a man eater, a tiger known as Devi's tiger, the one he had to track down and shot dead when he was a forest office in the state of Madhya Pradesh, a vast state in central India, with world renowned game reserves and forests especially reserved for hunting during the British Raj.

The tiger had already killed, devoured well over two hundred villagers before Rakesh was called upon to track down and shoot the tiger.

One of tiger's preys was a white forest officer by the name of Peter Kenyon who was a well known hunter. Having shot dead, hunted some fifty such tigers, he took the challenge lightly and paid with his life.

Normally a tiger becomes a man eater due to old age or injury sustained in a fight with another tiger or loses a paw due to thorn penetration, becomes lame when caught in a trap laid by poachers. Such injuries prevent tigers from going after their natural preys. Humans are easy preys as they could neither run nor fight back.

Once a tiger tastes a human blood, he would rarely go back to his normal preys, even after recovering from such injuries. With each killing, the tiger becomes more dangerous, more difficult to track down and to shoot. Tiger is a quick learner and so often out-smarts, out-thinks the hunter.

The tiger soon learns how human mind works and would never return to the kill, even if he may have eaten only half the kill, that he normally does in the forest where no kill is allowed to go to waste.

The tiger, an experienced man eater would also not fall in the trap of attacking a goat, tied to a tree. He almost senses human presence that may be detrimental to his survival and would stay one step ahead of their pursuers. It is not an easy task to kill such a tiger and before they lose their lives, they normally devour a few dozen helpless villagers.

Perhaps one has to be an eccentric, a foolhardy with a heart and nerve of steel and of course a very brave person indeed to go after such a wild and dangerous animal.

Then all forest officers, game wardens are a different breed of people, not our every day city dwellers, office workers. They live dangerously, enjoy flirting with death. It was the thrill and not the money that attract such breed of men to become Game Rangers, Forest Officers.

This young, strong and fierce man eater tiger had an interesting history, an unusual tale. The reason behind his injury was that it foolishly tried to provoke a porcupine with its sharp, defensive spines and quills. The tiger ended up with its sharp quills being lodged in the tiger's paw. This made him lame and unable to chase deer, pigs and other wild, hoofed, grazing animals, natural preys of tigers, lions and leopards.

This man eater, known as Devi's tiger had already killed well over two hundred villagers. The superstitious mountain tribesmen were unwilling to help Rakesh in tracking down this man eater and to provide drum beaters to force the tiger into a corner. They believed that the tiger was protected by the Goddess. So no human, no hunter can kill it. Those who assist the game ranger will be cursed and will be killed by the tiger.

Rakesh had to enlist the help of the trackers and drum beaters, torch bearers from other areas, other tribes to pin down and kill the tiger. Rakes nearly lost his life, became another victim of this cunning animal. But he did lose two of his trackers and drum beaters before the tiger finally succumbed, became the victim of Rakesh's super determination to kill any and every man eater.

Thinking about this encounter, his worst nightmare, brought fear and sweating even on this cold and damp evening, with sun fast disappearing on the horizon.

When Rakesh negotiated a sharp bend on this narrow track, he suddenly observed a person some hundred feet in front of him. This startled Rakesh for a moment, as he was lost in his thoughts, least expecting to see another human being.

Rakesh had no inclination that any one else could be so near, let alone just in front of him. He was even more astonished when he realized that the person in front of him was a shapely girl.

She was tall, at least five feet eight, a really good height for an Indian girl, although mountain girls are normally much taller than city girls. She was wearing a long leather jacket with a thick fox tail fur scarf round her slim and elegant neck.

Her long, thick jet black hair were artistically arranged, so that it covered most of her back from the neck to her hips which were moving rhythmically and artistically. Her slow walk and easy going manner were more akin to walking in a park rather than in a wilderness where a danger could be lurking at any corner.

Rakesh could not take his eyes off her. The path or just a narrow trail was so narrow that there was no way Rakesh could pass her without bumping into her. Within few minutes Rakesh was right behind her and to draw her attention, he said, "Excuse me. Can I pass?"

The girl looked back and gave Rakesh a broad smile, a smile that would melt any heart. For a second, Rakesh was speechless. He had never seen such a beautiful face, a perfect match for her equally gorgeous figure, a lean, slim line body but well developed features trying hard to be visible from behind her cloths. Rakesh could see, imagine all the curves, although most of her body was covered with her black, knee length leather jacket.

"Sorry for blocking your path. I did not know you were walking behind me." She said apolitically, in a sweet, sensuous, honey smooth voice, to go with her equally good manner, a sign of good upbringing.

"Thank you" and after a long pause Rakesh continued. "Are you alone?" Thinking how could any girl risk her safety wandering in such a desolate and lonely place?

"Not any more! I am in good company." Said the girl with a mischievous smile that she knew no one could ignore. She seemed to have a permanent smile, a God given gift, a feature on her pretty, smooth and radiant face, with pale complexion that is normally the result of lack of sunshine but very much appreciated by Indian girls. Scandinavian people in Europe have such pale complexion as they more or less live in perpetual darkness for six months in a year.

Not knowing what to say, Rakesh restricted his response to a mere smile. Then smile is the best weapon, both defensive and offensive. But the young lassie was not ready to give up or let Rakesh walk away in a hurry.

"Your face does not look familiar. Have you moved here recently?" She said without letting the smile dwindle in any way.

"Yes, I moved here some six months ago. I am the new manager of the Everest Tea Estate." Rakesh said, putting emphasis on the word manager.

"Oh. So Mr. Smith has retired. Has he gone back to England?"

"Yes. He retired a month before I came here. So I have not met him." Rakesh was surprised. How did she know Mr. Smith? Rakesh had never seen this girl before.

As the footpath was narrow, walking side by side obviously involved physical contact. So often Rakesh had to fall behind when it was impossible to walk side by side without being too close for comfort. But it seemed she was not averse to physical contact.

She was dignified, accepting that such a contact was impossible to avoid if they were to walk together, appreciating Rakesh's willingness to fall back as and when it was unavoidable.

"May I know your name?"

"Why not? I am Rakesh and as you know, I work on the estate."

It seemed she was more forward, friendly than Rakesh had expected. But it was too early to read anything from such a short conversation. But the first impression that one may make is more or less right, as it is made without any prejudice, before one knows too much about the person.

"My name is Rajshree but all my friends call me Raju, short and sweet." The customary smile accompanied her all the way.

Then she continued. "I come here for a walk whenever the weather is nice. So I expect we will meet again." Raju said it casually, perhaps teasingly. Perhaps trying to gauge Rakesh's reaction.

Half a mile from the estate bungalow, the footpath divided. One was leading to the bungalow while the other was going downhill towards the settlement where there were few bungalows.

"Would you like to come to my place for a cup of tea?" It was now Rakesh's turn to be forward, not to miss a golden opportunity to know a girl that may be a God send gift in this wilderness. Rakesh was eager for a female company. But he had neither time nor the inclination to look for a suitable female company, as Rakesh knew that he would be like a fish out of water amongst the local people.

"Can I take a blank cheque? It is getting late. I would better reach the safety of my abode before it is too late." With these words, they parted company.

Rakesh wondered why she said abode and not home? Her language, some of the words she spoke were, how to put it, Shakespearian or Valmakian, the sage who wrote the holy book of Ramayana. But her language was very sweet and polite, civilized and refreshingly assuring.

"Good night, sleep well and hope we will meet again soon." Said Raju before she disappeared down the tall grass. The bending, twisting, tiny, narrow footpath was the perfect cover to hide, to disappear, making sure that Rakesh was watching her elegance, her natural but captivating hip movement as long as visible. What a girl! Rakesh could not help but wonder whether it was a dream or a reality!

* * *

Chapter Six
Tea for Two

While serving dinner, Dada was quiet, in apprehensive and anxious mood with almost tears in his sad, old eyes and wrinkled face, looking even older than normal, as if his personal odyssey was coming to an end.

Rakesh realized that Dada, some how knew about his visit to ruins and perhaps his chance meeting with Raju. But Rakesh was in such a happy, jolly mood that it would have been obvious to Dada that the reason for this euphoria, elation and exhilaration must be a girl, a beautiful and charming girl that could elevate even Rakesh, a kind but sophisticated person who had met many girls.

Dada was an old, wise man from whom one can not hide any thing, difficult to keep any secret. He can read the face and the mind like an open book. So it would be useless to pretend otherwise.

But Rakesh did not bring up the subject, although he was tempted to tell Dada about Raju. If any one knew Raju, Dada would. But he thought it prudent to keep quiet, at least for the time being, in case he may never see Raju again!

After their fifth meeting in the ruins and around, Raju at last agreed to come for a late lunch or rather an afternoon tea. On Saturday, Rakesh was eagerly waiting to greet Raju. The clock struck three and at the same time Rakesh heard the bell.

Rakesh rushed to the door. There she was, in a stunning pale blue sari, the traditional Indian dress, with slightly darker blue, sleeveless, low cut blouse that showed her long, pale arms right up to her armpits, with her firm and bulging breasts giving only a glimpse of her under

432

garments. She was teasingly dressed, as if to attract Rakesh's attention and to raise his blood pressure. If so, she indeed succeeded beyond her wildest imagination.

During all these meetings, she wore a kind of Punjabi, Rajasthani dress; that is a top, a loose trouser with a dupatta or scarf like long, thin and silky piece thrown across her well developed bosom. But in the windy condition, on a hillside it was always difficult to keep the dupatta in place.

So often she would just wrap it around her neck, leaving her low cut top to revel her beautiful bosom, her upper chest with consuming ease and without embarrassment. It was so natural for her to dress in such a sensual manner without even noticing it. Then again no girl would dress in such a provocative manner unless she would like to be noticed, especially by the opposite sex, some one she may have feelings for.

Well, if you have got them, why not flaunt them? That is the motto, the norm in so called higher society, the fashion world. That surprised Rakesh but he was not in a position to comment or judge and why should he?

She hardly used any makeup but then she was so beautiful she hardly needed any makeup. However she never forgets to put a bindi, normally a red spot on the forehead.

But her bindi always matched the colour of her dress. She also had some very beautiful pattern on her hand, her palm made up, painted with henna or what we call mehendi, normally used by the bride and the bridesmaids during a wedding.

This was a permanent fixture on her soft hands that Rakesh had examined whenever they set down at a lonely place. Today she was wearing beautiful and very expensive gold bangles, eight in each hand.

In her neck was a long gold chain with an oblong diamond pendant with at least a dozen good-sized diamonds. She looked even more beautiful than usual in this traditional Indian Sari and very expensive gold jewellery. In a way Rakesh was stunned and a bit nervous. She indeed looked like a princess, a very desirable young lady.

She had a full head of jet dark but smooth hair that constantly covered her face in the wind, enabling Rakesh to sweep them back with dignity.

Rakesh had fallen head over heels in love with Raju, although he was careful not to make his feelings too obvious or be too forward, in case he may startle her, driving her away. He knew the difference between an Indian girl and an English girl and how not to offend by being too explicit.

Today was again a bright and sunny day. It seemed whenever Rakesh met Raju, they always enjoyed a perfect day, as if Raju knew what the weather would be like and come prepared for the eventuality that is lightly dressed, never carrying an umbrella as if she knew it was not going to rain, even in the middle of a rainy season?

As it was warm, they sat down in the front veranda, right in front of the sitting room and the front entrance. It was thatched for comfort and coolness in this hot and humid climate. But so often such a roof also attracts snakes.

One has to be careful, be vigilant when one had a thatched roof. However this veranda was equipped with a wire netting underneath the entire roof which would stop the snake falling on the people below. However snakes do get trapped here and had to be removed by expert snake catchers who would catch them and release them in the wild, far away from the bungalow, from the human presence.

When they sat down, Dada brought the teapot, milk, sugar and some biting, followed by China cups and plates, the ones Mr. Smith had specially brought all the way from England but left behind for the new manager. It was clear from Dada's manner and his face that he was worried but could not speak out of term, insult a guest, a special guest that his boss had invited.

Rakesh preferred biscuits, goat cheese and scones. But today it was supplemented by traditional Indian savoury, Bombay mix and methi bhaji specially prepared by Jamuna.

She was more amiable and less worried about these stories associated with a beautiful girl, the ghost of a young, beautiful princess who was some how responsible for the death of two young estate employees. But this was the time when Jamuna's resolves would be tested to the limit.

When the tea was over and table cleared, Rakesh excused Dada and Jamuna, as Rakesh was aware that Raju was not at ease with Dada around. How could Rakesh blame her? Dada's manner made it clear that she was not a welcome guest in this bungalow.

They listened to the Indian and English music, as Rakesh had a vast collection of records, the only entertainment available in such an isolated place.

Rakesh had now known Raju for well over two months but knew next to nothing about her, except that her father was Diliprai and mother Sitaradevi. They live in one of the bungalows scattered on the slopes, a couple of miles from the estate.

From their names, Rakesh gathered they may be Rajputs, once a ruling class but their kingdoms were merged into the Indian Union by the dynamic politician Sardar Vallabbhai Patel who was the man of action whose motto was that a lost opportunity is like lost love, gone for ever.

After enjoying each other's company for few hours, it was time for Raju to leave. Raju would always leave before the sun went down. Perhaps it was a sensible, a wise precaution for a single girl walking alone.

Today, as she was wearing such expensive jewellery, Rakesh insisted that he should accompany her to her front door. She was looking so beautiful, sexy and desirable; it was difficult for Rakesh to take his eyes of her, let her go. But how could he detain her against her will? Rakesh was too much of a gentleman to behave in any improper way, especially with such a charming and sophisticated young woman.

Today, instead of separating at their usual junction, Raju let Rakesh walk with her for another half an hour, until they were some two hundred meters away from those bungalows.

"Rakesh, my home is just over there. You will have to let me go alone, as my parents do not know about us, at least not yet." Raju pleaded.

Rakesh had held her hand all the way and was reluctant to let her go. In one swift move, he grabbed Raju and gave her a passionate kiss, a long lingering, full blooded kiss. Raju did not oppose or showed any sign of resistance but let Rakesh feel at ease; let his emotions flow for a while before gently sliding away from his grip and said,

"Rakesh please let me go" and she disappeared among those bungalows.

Rakesh always came second best in front of her charm, beauty and persistence. Could any one conquer Cleopatra?

* * *

Chapter Seven
Gaurita: The English Rose

When Rakesh came home, the evening was young but it was a beginning to get dark and a bit late to sit in the veranda, as mosquitoes were a major health hazard, especially during rainy season.

So Rakesh moved to the lounge but kept the mosquito proof door leading to the veranda open, letting in the fresh air and the rays of the setting sun without being troubled by mosquitoes. Rakesh, a romantic at heart, enjoyed watching the sun dance along the colourful horizon, a kind of Lord Shiva's Tandav Nutria, a kind of ultimate dance, the final dance, a tribute to the symphony of nature, to this enchanting fantasyland.

Rakesh stood at the window, with double peg of single malt whisky, poured over crushed ice, shaken but not stirred. This was his favourite drink, a habit he picked up in Scotland when he used to visit Scottish highlands while in Durham.

Today he even lighted a Havana cigar to go with his drink. He rarely smokes, on special occasion and that also Havana cigars only. He was looking at the setting sun, fast disappearing behind the hills, restoring serenity and peace, isolation and solitude. He could not help but murmur his favourite song from the film Kismat, starring his and every one else's favourite actor Ashok Kumar.

"Dhira dhira, badal dhira dhira ja
Mera bulbul sow ra ha hai
Shore tu na macha!"

436

In the film, Ashok Kumar sings the song, standing on the balcony, adjourning the bedroom of his sweetheart, looking at the sky, the clouds and the moon, pleading with the clouds.

> "Slowly slowly, the clouds go slowly
> Without a noise or a murmur
> For my sweetheart is sleeping soundly
> Do not disturb her, wake her up
> With the sound of your movement
> Your wondering habit."

It was difficult for Rakesh to go to sleep after seeing Rajshree today. She was looking so stunning and beautiful that Rakesh was bowled over. It was a dream, not a reality. He would not have believed it if Dada and Jamuna were not the witness.

Slowly but surely their friendship blossomed in the ruins of the castle where they would meet once or twice a week. Raju had a mesmerizing effect on Rakesh. But then who could resist her charm, her permanent smile and her near perfect figure, well developed body, almond shaped innocent eyes and her long silky free flowing hair, along with her sense of humour, her intelligence and her ability to converse on almost any subject.

She was Rakesh's equal on intelligence and intellectual level. She was beyond human endurance, too good to be true. In a way Rakesh was getting impatience, as if he believed, feared that he did not have infinite amount of time with Raju. Even Rakesh could not make out what it meant or why he felt that way. So often our inner most thoughts do not match, fit with our outward thinking, the events that take place on the ground.

For the last few days, Rakesh was having a strange experience at night. For some one who would go to sleep as soon as he hits the pillow, he was finding it difficult to go to sleep.

So often he would wake up in the middle of the night, perspiring so much that he wound need a change of clothing. Windows of his bedroom would fly open even when there was no wind.

His mind wound wonder, thinking unthinkable, having a strange feeling that some one, Raju was sleeping next to him, urging him to make love to her. He was feeling nervous, irritated, disgruntled and enraged, without reason, without justification or cause.

Even Dada, Jamuna and those who work closely with him noticed these mood change and deviation from his normal behaviour. But even though Rakesh was aware of this change of personality, he could not put a finger on the cause, the reason for his irritation except that he was not getting enough sleep.

There was no change in his lifestyle, diet or work pattern except his closeness, his involvement with Raju. Some how he felt Raju may be the cause of his problems, his change of mood. That is if he could call it a problem which could be just his imagination.

Rakesh could not help but wonder Dada's warning and occasional comments by those who work closely with Rakesh. But how could an intelligent, England return person with modern outlook, who could compete on equal terms with any Westerner, could believe in such superstitious nonsense. He even refused to entertain such a thought, lower his intelligence threshold.

Rakesh was head over hill in love with Raju, although he was too proud to admit it. Then who wouldn't be in love with her, a princess, a beauty queen and a nice, articulate, well bred person with immaculate manner and ever increasing charm. She was almost a perfect girl, a perfect life partner, too good to be true.

Exploring the museum of his past, Rakesh had to acknowledge that he had already lost one such girl by being too cautious. He would not like to lose another such girl, a beauty par excellence. He was indeed fortunate that such an opportunity has knocked on his door not once but twice, a rarity in real life.

Rakesh should examine the DNA of self-enlightenment. Rakesh remembered the words of his Guru who told him time and again that one should not hesitate to take a bold decision, to grab the opportunity, as time and running water never returns. Once gone, it is lost for ever. Hesitancy is nothing more than a negative stream of consciousness that would not water the lush garden of your mind. An ounce of determination is better than a ton of hesitancy.

Rakesh could not help comparing Raju with his first girlfriend. When he went to England, he met a lovely girl at the University, with an unusual name of **Gaurita.**

There was an interesting storey behind her name. Her parents were posted to India before the Second World War. They were stationed at Simla, a very beautiful hill station, not too far from Himalayas. In fact on a clear summer day, Mount Everest could be visible on the horizon.

Simla was more like English or rather a Scottish town with similar weather, fauna and flora. Simla was the summer capital of British Raj where all high ranking British officers retreated during the height of oppressive Indian summer months of May to September.

Gaurita's father was an administrative officer in charge of looking after the high flyers and VIPs when they come to Simla. Her parents, Graham and Genevieve had an Indian couple who looked after all their needs.

This couple had a lovely, cute four year old daughter called Gauri, the name of a Hindu Goddess Parvati, consort of Lord Shiva. Graham and Genevieve were so fond of this tiny little girl that they treated her like their own daughter, as they had no children of their own, even after ten years of marriage. When they had to return to England after India gained independence, they wanted to adopt Gauri and bring her to England with them.

But Gauri was their parent's only child and an apple of their eyes. How could they allow her daughter to be whisked away to an unknown land, so far away that they would never be able to visit her, see her again, although they knew that Gauri would be treated like a princess in England?

Poverty does not mean lack of devotion, dedication and diminishing of parental love for their children. It was a very difficult decision for them not to oblige, to let Graham and Genevieve take Gauri to England.

If they had more than one child, as is the norm with Indian families, they would have willing allowed Graham and Genevieve to adopt Gauri, as they would give her more love and attention than they ever could.

So when Graham and Genevieve had their own child, a lovely daughter, Graham wanted to name her Gauri while Genevieve preferred the name Rita, after her baby sister who died so tragically, at the age of twelve, from a brain tumour.

In the end they compromised and named their daughter Gaurita, a sweet name, although a bit unusual name for an English girl, with a milky white complexion and blonde, golden hair, accompanied by well built and fully developed body, a hallmark of the European race.

Gaurita had all these essential statistics in addition to being tall, slim and lovely shoulder length hair with natural curves, which she let grow to waist length, to please Rakesh who liked long hair in true Indian tradition and the style.

Rakesh and Gaurita was a perfect match physically with many common interests, including mountaineering, walking and tracking for which Scotland and Wales are an ideal destination. But so often we do not appreciate a jewel that is right on our door-step.

In those days racism in England was widespread. Many houses, establishments that lent out rooms used to have a sign "NO dogs, No black and No Irish need apply." But mercifully the word Paki was not yet invented.

Even in this harsh racial environment, Gaurita's parents were willing to bless her only daughter's marriage to Rakesh, as they were fond of him. They found Rakesh as clever, charming and with good manner who would treat their daughter with love, respect and will definitely make her happy. What more parents could wish for their children?

But there was one serious obstacle. Rakesh found the English weather, especially long and dark English winters damp, cold and some what depressing, especially in the North.

Rakesh loved sunshine, warmth and vast open spaces of India. He could never settle down in England, even for the love of Gaurita, who loved this climate, where she was born and brought up.

Gaurita was not willing to leave her native Durham where her parents and most of her friends were, not even for the love of Rakesh, the sunshine and wide open spaces of the distant land of Bharat.

India was only a name, a distant place that held no attraction for her. It was not the age of mass travel, package holidays or even adventure travel. People were happy and content to remain where they were born.

They preferred familiarity of their country and their loved ones than the charm, beauty and wonderful climate of a distant land. If Gaurita wanted such an outdoor life, she would rather emigrate to the familiarity of Australia than the unknown charm of India.

So after a close and a loving friendship, Rakesh and Gaurita parted company, much to the sadness and regret of her parents who were even willing to let their only daughter settle down in India, the country they loved, where they had spend some ten happy years. India was a magic land, full of beauty, palaces, mountains, rivers, forests and above all thousands of years of cultural heritage that had influenced people, taken them to a spiritual height difficult to find in any single country.

They still regard India as their second home, a country where they learnt a great deal, about love, human brotherhood, sacrifice, the richness of Hindu culture and religion.

They admired enormously the way India fought and won independence, under the leadership of Mahatma Gandhi, who single handedly brought the British Empire to its knees, without firing a single bullet in anger. When Gandhi was sent to prison, the prison doors were never locked, as Gandhi would never leave the prison until he completes his sentence, however unjust, unwarranted it may be.

They love Bharat as a land of Mox, deliverance and enlightenment, the land that gave the world Lord Rama, Krishna, Buddha, Guru Nanak and Gandhi, a few among many noble citizens of the world, the contribution unmatched by any other country, singularly or united.

They knew that their daughter will be treated like a royalty by every one, including Rakesh's family. The day they split up, albeit on a friendly term, was a sad day for every one, especially for Gaurita's parents.

Their dream of visiting their only child in Bharat was shattered. But they were pragmatic. They knew that Gaurita, who had never been outside England and Scotland would find it difficult to understand, love or admire India the way they did. After all it was not the Raj any more.

Rakesh believed in fate, Kismat, destiny. Although he was heart broken at losing Gaurita, a charming and beautiful girl, he consoled himself that every cloud has a silver lining.

Some good may yet come out of this tragedy, the heartbreak. At least he met an English couple who were more Indian, Hindu at heart than most indigenous Indians. It was indeed a rarity at the time when every thing British was the best, including the Christian religion, Western culture and above all an English Rose!

* * *

Chapter Eight

Rajshree: The Angel Delight

The uneasiness with his friendship with Raju brought back Gaurita's memory. He wondered what she would be doing, whether she was alone or got married, as he had lost all contact with her. But first love never goes away. It is always there in our subconscious mind and will surface from time to time when least expected, when we are confronted with a similar situation.

It was indeed his good fortune that he met a girl like Gaurita and still wonders whether he made the right decision in not marrying Gaurita and staying in England, making England his home.

But he could never leave his mother alone in India. Perhaps she was the deciding factor in coming back to India. It was Rakesh's doctrine of Karma, (fate) Dharma (religion) and Kartavya (duty) based on the Hindu holy books of Vedas that guided him in time of stress and uncertainty, when he is caught between the devil and the deep blue sea. His decision was practical, not merely rhetorical.

It was Sunday. As Rakesh had not met Raju for nearly a week, he some how knew that she would call, pay him a visit, especially as the weather was also accommodating. Rakesh was not disappointed.

Sharp at three in the afternoon, Raju knocked on his door. She was wearing her usual walking cloths with knee high leather boots, a must when visiting the ruins.

Raju was an expert in martial art, quite capable of defending herself if ever attacked by another human being. But it was an age of chivalry when women were accorded respect they deserve. No one wound insult them

442

in any way, let alone attack them physically. Moreover Raju had a divine personality. She looked every inch a royal princess that would put most men ill at ease in her presence, unless they were of equal social, cultural and financial standing.

Soon Rakesh and Raju were at the top of the hill, among the ruins, Raju's favourite place, perhaps her abode in her previous life or could it be this life?

Rakesh was determined to solve the mystery of Raju, the reason behind his sleepless nights, his strange, nervous and sensuous feelings that was draining his strength, damaging his health and above all interfering with his work routine. He could not and would not allow such a situation to drag on.

It would be like neglecting, renouncing his work ethic, every thing he stands for. Rakesh was not the person, the manager who would sit in an office, behind a desk and delegate the work. He was a man of action who would like to be in the thick of things, where action is.

The estate was so large that it would take some four hours to travel from one end to another, requiring Rakesh to put an occasional twelve hour shift. He could only do such an arduous task with a good night sleep, clear mind and total dedication.

Rakesh and Raju had by now known each other for four months. They were meeting, on average twice a week, enjoying each other's company and occasional picnic. But Rakesh was none the wiser about Raju's background, her family members whom he had not met so far. Raju was very clever at avoiding such a talk, using her considerable charm that would be difficult to resist for any one, let alone for lonely Rakesh.

Rakesh and Raju sat on a large boulder, their favourite seat, hand in hand, watching the red hot sun casting a long shadow, dancing on the red sky, the stage specially constructed by nature to amplify the glory of the setting sun.

Raju was looking even more beautiful, in a sleeveless, almost transparent top but modestly covered with a dupatta and her dark, soft and silky hair, flowing gently over her face obliging Raju to flick them back when they covered her eyes, the action, the coordinated movement of the face and hand Rakesh found so delicate, pretty and sexy! Then for Rakesh, Raju was the Menka, the expert dancer whose every move was coordinated to perfection. Then again who else but Menka could steal Lord Shiva's heart?

Without the cover of dupatta and her hair, Raju looked really sexy with her breast half revealed. Rakesh could not help but gently grabbing her, holding her tight in his arms, barely able to restrain his feelings.

Looking in her eyes and playing with her hair, kissing her gently on her forehead at first, then on her rosy lips, Rakesh said, "Raju, you know that I love you very much and I would like to marry you. But can I ask you one question?"

Raju was startled. She could not believe her ears. She kept quiet for a long time and then said in a soft and shivering voice. "Rakesh, I love you too, more than you will ever know.

I had an inclination that you are eager to ask me a question, in fact more than one question. Go ahead. Ask me any question you wish that would put your mind, your anxiety at rest.

But let me be frank, warn you that the answers may not be to your liking, what you want to hear and be prepared for the unexpected. Raju was serious but calm and dignified.

Rakesh told her what he had heard from Dada and a few other estate employees. But Rakesh empathised that he did not believe in these tales, chit chat and gossips, so as not to offend Raju.

Hiding her face in the broad chest of Rakesh, Raju kept quiet for a long time. Getting no response, Rakesh gently lifted her face by her chin. Seeing tears in her wide, almond shaped eyes, Rakesh said, "Sorry Raju. I did not mean to upset you or hurt your feelings in any way. But there are a lot of questions that need answers" and to lighten the atmosphere, he added, "before we get married and go on our honeymoon.

But right now, I am in a quandary, predicament and perplexity. I have never met your parents. I do not know where you live, that is after we have gone out more than thirty times, while you know every details about me, even about my first girlfriend, Gaurita. You are the only one who knows about my first girl friend, my first love Gaurita. We so often choose to be Indians when it suits us. But I have been open, honest and sincere with you from the beginning.

But if my questions upset you so much, then please forgive me. You do not have to answer them. I love you unconditionally, regardless of what or who you are, your family background, caste, creed, culture or religion.

"Rakesh I want to tell you every thing, to come clean, even if that mean losing you." Raju was equally determined to answer Rakesh's questions.

Freeing herself from the grip of Rakesh, standing up and moving away from him, Raju said, "Rakesh, I do not know how to begin. I guess the best way is to tell you the truth. But as you know, truth is so often stranger than fiction, more unbelievable than a made up storey. It will be difficult for you to believe that I am telling the truth, at least in the beginning. But it will soon dwell on you as my story unfolds.

Be prepared to get the shock of your life. But please believe me when I say I love you and that you are absolutely safe with me. No harm will come to you as I love you so much."

Rakesh was confused, puzzled but he realized that Raju's answer would not be what he wants to hear. Raju was preparing him for the worse, fattening him up before sending him to a slaughter house, giving him a kiss of Dracula. Is he in for another Gaurita type experience or even worse? But Raju soon put his anxiety, his mind to rest, in a sort of way.

"Rakesh, what Dada told you is the truth? I am not an ordinary girl but I am indeed a lost soul, what you may call a ghost but that is not a right word to describe me, not a proper definition. Ghost is a blanket term that covers each and every supernatural event. I am perhaps an angel."

"R A J U .... This is not the time or the occasion to make jokes." Screamed Rakesh. There was a shiver in his voice and in spite of the cold wind going through his spine; his forehead was covered with perspiration.

"Rakesh, I know how serious you are. Believe me I could never joke with you when it comes to a matter of life and death and this is as serious as that for me but especially for you."

After a long pause, Raju continued, "Rakesh, you must have heard that ghost, angel and god do not cast a shadow. Look at your long and clear shadow. Every tree, every object casts a shadow in the setting sun. Now look at me. Could you see my shadow at all?"

Raju was absolutely right. She had no shadow at all, as if she was transparent like a glass, the light going through her without any resistance."

She continued, "Do you remember you took a couple of my photos, against my wish, ignoring my protest? The film was spoilt. You could not capture me on the film. That is why I gave you my drawing which you keep near your bedside table."

Rakesh was dumb struck. Raju was absolutely right. She cast no shadow. Rakesh remembered dada's words, his warning but looking at Raju's kind and smiling face, her light make up spoiled by her tears, Rakesh knew that he was not in any sort of danger, not from her. Raju could never harm him, as she loved him so much and he was absolutely right.

Sitting beside Rakesh, she continued. "So now you know that I am not an ordinary girl. I am a wondering, a free spirit with no home, no parents that I could introduce you to. But my love for you is real and I will never let any one harm you. In fact I will always keep an eye on you, become your guardian angel so that no one can harm you. I owe you that much."

Then with a smile, the innocent smile that had captivated Rakesh, she continued. "My life storey goes back a very long time in history. My father, as you know was Diliprai and mother Sitaradevi. We were Suryavansi, the descendent from Sun dynasty, originally from Rajputana or Rajasthan.

My father was a ruler of a small kingdom, with Suryapur (Sun City) as the capital. It was some one hundred miles from these ruins. The city is now buried under hundreds of feet of earth, after a severe earthquake.

I was the only child. As you know my name was Rajshree." Then she added with a mischievous smile. "I was considered the most beautiful princess and an object of desire for many a prince and kings."

"Well Raju, I can certainly vouch for that. You are definitely the object of my desire and now I know why I am unable to sleep soundly at night."

Rakesh could not resist this opportunity to lighten the atmosphere, to grab Raju, hold her in his arms. But some how he could not kiss a princess, not without her permission!

"Rakesh, remember I am a princess, not an ordinary girl." Joked Raju and then continued.

"Just west of Calcutta, there was another small kingdom, ruled by Arjansinh. My father and Arjansinh were great friends. His son, crown prince Pratapsinh used to visit us, along with his father. We were brought up together. We knew sooner or later we will get married and bind the two families, cement the friendship for ever.

It was the happiest day of my life when our engagement and then marriage were confirmed. I was over the moon. He was indeed a handsome, charming, dashing and a caring person, a rare quality among princes in those days.

At the time there was a tradition among Rajput kings to have many wives. But both our families believed in the tradition set by Lord Rama, one man, one wife.

My father even had the famous quote from our holy book framed and hung in his bedroom.

"Paranu hu eak, age manave ta no tek
Ghani Rani nu shu cha cam
Eak Sita ya santoshya Ram."

Translated in English, it means:

"I marry but once, that should be the tradition
The custom, the belief, the convention and the ritual
Why do I need so many queens, concubines
When one queen Sita was all that Lord Rama needed
To satisfy all his wishes, his desire."

* * *

Chapter Eight
The Unfulfilled Desire

As my beauty was well known and as I was the only child, naturally many princes were eager to request my hand in marriage, with the hope that one day they will inherit the kingdom on the death of my father. But most of these suitors were already married with a wife or two and many more concubines.

After our marriage, we came here, to these ruins for our honeymoon. It was a beautiful, comfortable and above all a safe place to relax and enjoy, starting our married life, consuming our marriage.

This fort was in the middle of no where, in joint ownership of our two families. It had high walls all round, with watch towers at the interval of five hundred feet, with a clear view stretching on all sides. It was impossible to attack without being seen.

Moreover with a deep well, we had our own water supply and huge silos were full of grains. The palace was lavishly decorated with sandalwood furniture, Kashmiri silk furnishings and every kind of tropical flowers growing within the fort.

Every inch of our honeymoon suit, floor space was covered with petals, mainly marigold, sunflower, periwinkle, Champo or Indian magnolia, sweet smelling gardenia, jasmine and ratrani (night queen) Fresh petals were spread daily early in the morning before sunrise.

We arrived on the day of our honeymoon. As soon as our guests who were mainly family members left, we retreated to our honeymoon suite. We talked, kissed and cuddled until midnight.

It was time for us to retreat to our four poster bed, covered with rose petals and smelling like perfumery. This could have and should have been the happiest day in our life, a day or rather a night to remember. Instead it turned into a nightmare.

Before we could consummate our marriage, become one, lost in each other for ever, there was a knock on our door. A messenger from my father had delivered a message that shattered our lives that would make me a widow even before we could have our honeymoon, spend a night together and consume our union of body and soul.

Some where near our present day Calcutta, there was a town called Kanakpur, the capital city of the Mayur (peacock) kingdom, a powerful kingdom ten times the size of our two kingdoms put together.

Mayur Naresh (king) Virendra had a son, his crown prince Vanraj, a real playboy but a good general and an apple of his father's eye.

Vanraj was not only married with two beautiful wives who would be future queens but he also had a harem of young, beautiful and innocent girls with an addition of one or two every few months.

Naresh Virendra had frequently expressed his wish, asked my hand in marriage for his Crown Prince Vanraj, as his third wife. He was bewitched by my beauty, charm and personality. Like a spoilt child, he would not rest until he gets his favourite toy, what he wants.

But my father knew that I would never be happy or be treated with respect and dignity I deserve. I will be no more than a trophy to be hung on his bedroom wall, for every one to see and admire. Moreover my father knew that I was in love with Pratapsinh who was like a son to my father.

So he tactfully turned down the marriage proposals of Prince Vanraj. But when I got married to Youvraj Pratapsinh, all hell broke lose. Both Naresh Virendra and Prince Vanraj took it as a personal affront, a snub and provocation.

There was no reason to hold back their anger or not to take this opportunity to conquer our tiny domain and merge with his vast kingdom. Vanraj himself led an army of 20,000 soldiers to attack Suryapur, the capital of our kingdom known as Devital. My father had an army of some five thousand soldiers, mostly part-timers.

My father was a kind, trusting and caring person who considered Naresh Virendra as a friend. He did not imagined, even entertained the thought that my marriage will result in a war. As far as he was concerned, he had done nothing wrong. It was his big mistake.

My father had emptied his treasury of money and his silos of grain by distributing these commodities to the poor people of his kingdom. Our marriage was the most important occasion in his life since he himself got married to my mother Sitaradevi over thirty years ago.

He was caught unprepared, caught napping. He only had few weeks before he had to surrender or die. The message from my father was that we should leave at once and take shelter with Samrat (Emperor) Ranjitsinh, the ruler of the kingdom of Mahapradesh and a family friend. His kingdom was vast that include the present day Orissa and most of Madhya Pradesh. He would not be intimidated by Naresh Virendra and his cronies.

But on hearing this tragic news, my husband, my life partner, my soul mate was eager to join my father and his family to fight the tyrant Vanraj. I was tempted to urge him, even beg him to heed the advice of my father and seek shelter with Samrat Ranjitsinh.

But my husband was a born warrior, a full blooded Rajput. How could I try to stop him from doing his duty, rushing to help his, our families? Vanraj surrounded the castle. My husband was not able to enter the castle. But he camped some thirty miles away with his just five hundred soldiers and harassed Vanraj every night.

After six weeks, food and water ran out forcing my father to attack Vanraj one day at midnight. It was a sudden and a coordinated attack in true Rajput tradition, known as kesaria or do or die attack. In the ensuing battle both my father and my husband died a heroic death. But not before they destroyed more than half of Vanraj's army.

After destroying, ransacking Suryapur, Vanraj came for me. We had some four hundred loyal and well trained soldiers guarding this place, this castle which was like a Fort Knox that we could defend with minimum effort, few soldiers. At the interval of just five hundred feet, there was a tall watch tower which can be manned, defended by just two soldiers.

We held Vanraj back for six long months. As you know, these hills are so often immersed, hidden in thick mist. During such a time, we would lower rope ladders and send a team of five to ten soldiers, with bows and arrows and bucket of oil, kerosene to attack Vanraj's camp and set fire tents housing his soldiers.

These soldiers would then disappear in the nearby forest if not killed or captured. At one time Vanraj even thought of abandoning the siege and go home. But my attraction, making me his queen, the temptation, the greed, the lust was too great for him. It was also a matter of pride for him. In the end we ran out of food and water.

I led the suicide attack with just three hundred soldiers. It is needless to say that we all died a heroic death. This patriotic action led to the elevation of our souls, the ultimate sacrifice that gave our enemy a bloody nose.

During the six months siege, Vanraj again lost half of his army. By the time he went back to his capital Kanakpur, he had just four thousand soldiers left, out of the original army of some twenty thousands.

Vanraj was so weakened and demoralized that he could not dare attack my husband's kingdom. Moreover he was a figure of hatred, loathed by all the small kingdoms, as our families were popular, peace loving and progressive.

But I lost every thing that was dear to me, all my family members and above all my husband even before we had an opportunity to consummate our marriage. I died a virgin bridge with all my armans (desire, ambition) unfulfilled.

There may be honour among thieves but certainly there was no honour among Rajput kings. I hate to say that we are our own worse enemies. It is sadly true. Rajputs are responsible for keeping Bharat desh a slave nation for the last three thousand years, if not more. Rajputs are a brave people who should be a boon, a blessing to any nation. Instead we are a curse, a burden on our beloved motherland Bharat.

Our kings hate each other more than they hate our real enemies who invade our motherland, rape and plunder the rich and holy land of Bharat. They were responsible for Bharat being occupied by Alexander the Great, Moguls, French, Portuguese and the British.

Greed and hatred knows no bounds. Most Rajput kings were cursed with these two shortfalls that led to constant wars between them. Moguls and Marathas were able to establish great kingdoms but not Rajputs who preferred to fight amongst themselves and betray their brothers to a third party without blinking an eye.

Although my father in law Rana Arjansinh survived, he lost his son Pratapsinh, his crown prince and the apple of his eyes, not forgetting his best friend, my father and our entire family. He was determined to get rid of tin pot Naresh Virendra and his playboy prince Vanraj.

Arjansinh send an envoy to Emperor Ranjitsinh, inviting him to attack Naresh Virendra, promising him to provide a well trained army of at least ten thousand soldiers, raised by various small kingdoms who were enraged with Vanraj, for his attack on our tiny kingdom and being responsible for my death, as I was a popular princess.

Ranjitsinh accepted this invitation, sent a huge army, led by his popular and battle hardened commander Mansinh. Within two years of our deaths, kingdom of Mayur was conquered and all the members of the Naresh Virendra's family were killed. Rana Arjansinh took a leading part in the downfall of the Naresh. It was the happiest day throughout small kingdoms. At last our deaths were avenged, justice delivered and the tyrant removed for good.

Soon afterward Rana Arjansinh died of a broken heart, as if he was just hanging on to take revenge for the loss of his Crown Prince, his only son Pratapsinh. No one was the winner in this tragedy of Herculean proportion.

This is my tragic story, the kahani (life history) of my unfulfilled life, so brutally ended before it even began; the end of my arman, my ambition and attainment.

My Kismat, my Karma, my fate was against me, against us. We say one reaps what one sows. But our families had only sowed love, friendship, dignity and respect for all. Yet we were the losers.

This unfulfilled lechery, lust and the desire of the flesh denied on the verge of consummating the marriage made my soul a gypsy, a wonderer and an outcast, denying me the Salvation, the Mox, the ultimate release from the cycle of birth, death and punishment, turned me into a ghost, what I am today.

Raju's voice was cracking up. It was choked with emotion and her eyes were shedding tears by a bucketful. She was hanging on to Rakesh tightly, as if afraid of losing him?

* * *

Chapter Ten

Mox: The Liberation of Trapped Soul

"Raju, what is the difference between you and a real human being like me? I know you will remain young and beautiful for ever and you can not die, as you are already dead. Aren't you?

So in a way I am lucky. I will always have a young and a beautiful wife that every one would envy, even when I may be using a Zimmer frame? But Raju, I do not want to live so long that people may think you are my daughter, even grand daughter!" Rakesh tried to introduce some humour to lighten the atmosphere. That joke certainly brought a smile on the face of Raju, covered with tears that Rakesh was trying so hard to wipe with his bare hands.

"Well Rakesh, I can never give you children nor can I mix with your society. I am not human. I am not real. There is a side of me that no one would understand, not even you." Then added with a mischievous smile, "By the way, I can't cook either but I do love you to bits."

Rakesh tightened his grip on Raju and kissing her on the lips, said, "Raju, I love you and I would like to marry you and by the way, I am a good cook. So it does not matter whether you can cook or not. All you have to do is keep smiling, keep looking so beautiful and give me your undivided love, attention and be an apple of my eye.

I know this does not sound right. I may be crazy but I have been a sane, mature and sensible person for too long. I do not want to lose you, even if that means I may have to live in a different world, the world I know nothing about. I lost a wonderful girl Gaurita once but not again. It is time for me to misbehave, be an idiot, enjoy now and pay later." There was a mischievous smile on Rakesh's face.

"Raju, I love you so much. You are one in a million, Please marry me." Repeated Rakesh with even more sincerity second time round.

Raju stood up, moved away from Rakesh and said, "Rakesh, you have liberated me from this hell. Now my wandering spirit will attain Mox, Nirvana and eternal freedom. I will be able to join my husband, my soul mate in heaven. We have been kept apart for too long but not any more.

My burning desire to spend my honeymoon, to enjoy the fruits of marriage, to satisfy my sexual fantasies which remained unfulfilled when my husband was so brutally taken away from me on our honeymoon night made my spirit wonder, turned it into a ghost, a wondering soul.

I do not know why I was punished not once but twice, without reason, without any fault on my part.

My liberation, my escape from this hell, my curse would only end, lifted if a human being, knowing that I am a ghost, a wandering spirit and not human, is willing to marry me, proposes marriage, then and then only my curse will come to an end and I will be a free, a liberated spirit, attain Mox.

I can not explain why, how or for what reason I was burdened with this curse but I know that you, your selfless love for me have liberated me from this hell.

Dear Rakesh, you are a carbon copy of my husband. I fell in love the day I saw you, set my eyes on you. In fact it was so difficult for me to keep away from you that I was sleeping with you in your bed, in my invisible, suspended state. That is why you were unable to sleep soundly at night lately.

My regret is that now I have to leave you. We will never meet again. Please forgive me for playing with your emotion, your love and your kind and caring nature. Forget your beloved Rajshree, your Raju. Consider it as a dream and not a reality.

Please believe me when I say that you are not destined to be alone for long. You will soon find a wonderful girl by the name of Amisha, who will be your wife, give you wonderful children and you will have a long and a happy married life.

I have left a leather pouch where I was sitting. It contains a gold chain with a diamond Pendant. On one side there is our Coat of Arms and on the other side an image of our Kuldevi. (Family deity) This piece of jewellery is thousands of years old and priceless.

Wear it round your neck and you will be protected, no one can harm you. I know you will not sell or misuse my parting gift. That is why I am giving it to you. That is my final, ultimate, farewell present to you, my liberator, my hero and my darling as well. Alvida, goodbye and God bless you."

The figure of Raju started melting away in the evening mist of the setting sun, rising high in the misty red sky of the setting sun. The ground where Raju was standing was soon covered with white rose petals, falling from the sky. Soon there was no more Raju.

Rakesh could not believe either his eyes or his ears.

"RAJU .... RAJU .... Please do not leave me alone, do not desert me. I love you. I want to be with you." Shouted Rakesh but his voice was lost in the wilderness.

Rakesh could not control his anguish, his pain and his extreme distress. For the first time since he was a little boy, he cried uncontrollably. But there was no one to consol him, wipe his tears or say a few kind words.

At last he got up, put the chain that Raju had left behind, round his neck, gathered some rose petals in his handkerchief and started the long, dangerous and lonely descent to his bungalow, a few miles down.

Rakesh could understand losing Gaurita but not losing Raju. It was bizarre to say the least. He remembered an Urdu ghazal he liked so much when he was at the college. Today this piece of poetry made a perfect sense.

**"Muze ye baat ka gum nahi
Ke meri kesti, naya dub gai
Magar gum ya baat ka hay
Ke jaha meri kesti dubi
Waha pani bhe both com tha!"**

Translated into English, it comes out like this.

**"I am not perturbed
That my boat has sunk
But my misfortune is that,
Where my boat sank
There was hardly any water
Even to immerse my tiny boat
To justify the sinking**

In such a shallow water
That is my misfortune, my Kismat
My bad luck, my downfall.

How true the situation was for Rakesh. No one would believe this storey if he was mad enough to tell any one, perhaps with the exception of Dada who always suspected that Raju was not real. She was too good to be true, to be a mere human being! How right Dada was!

The sun had already gone down some time ago. It was getting darker by the minute, making the descent dangerous. It was lunacy, insane to be out at this time of the evening.

But today Rakesh was not worried about any danger, any wild animal, not even the man-eater Devi's tiger or a spitting cobra.

In a way Rakesh was glad that the God gave him this opportunity to be an instrument in liberating Rajshree, her wondering spirit and send her back to her husband whom she loved so much, a reunion of two lost souls.

The few months he spent with Raju were wonderful time. Raju was indeed a very beautiful, charming and sensuous girl, one in a million. Could it be Kismat, nasib, destination that he got this manager's job against all odds, in order to meet Rajshree, help her and liberate her spirit?

At last he felt a little relief. His pain, his sacrifice was not in vain. When Rakesh reached his bungalow, he was already calm and reconciled with the evening's event which was stranger than fiction, unbelievable in the extreme.

Rakesh never believed in ghosts, in supernatural happenings. But he had the gold chain and the diamond studded locket that would worth a fortune to prove that it was not a dream. But Rakesh could not help wondering about Raju's prophecy of meeting a wonderful girl by the name of Amisha and his future happiness. Well, only the time will tell whether Raju's prophesy will come true or not!

* * *

The End

Chance Encounter

Chapter One

Our Caring, Sharing Family

Life is full of mysteries, incidents and strange encounters that we may experience from time to time when least expected and without realising how important, life changing these events may be. Then rarely any one has a sixth sense! We may acknowledge once in a while that God works in a mysterious way.

No wonder on most part we fail to embrace the moment, fail to understand the significance of such occurrences and so often even God send opportunities we neglect, fail to realise that we have been placed on an oasis of enlightenment, take advantage of such unexpected gifts that come our way but once in a life time.

We fail to come out of comfort zone and take the bull by the horn. Our attitudes are cemented in safety first mentality. We fear corrosion more than failure. We prefer to bend to the demands of social pressure.

As soon as we are out, unengaged, walked away, disassociate ourselves with these circumstances without realising the God's gift, we forget, put them out of our mind. We fail to be a catalyst of our own destiny.

So often this is a gift from the Supreme Power that we ignore and perhaps regret later on; that is if one is enlightened enough to realise what the opportunity was all about in the first place. Some of us even sleep walk through life, remain in magical slumber until an event that may take us to a rude awakening!

Then life is a complicated existence. Not every one possesses awareness and enlightenment, climb the submit of serenity, live in the oasis of enlightenment. Every one can not be Gandhi, Mandela or Martin Luther King, the enlightened ones who personifies the human values.

Every one in his or her life worships another human being, madly in love with a boy or a girl of their dream, Ashwaria Rai and Shilpa Shethi of this world, at some time in our lives.

But how many of us have shown the courage and confidence to confront such a person, admit our love, even if they know that at worse the person may say a polite no.

But at most times, the answer will be affirmative and would fill our lives with love and happiness beyond our wildest dreams if we show moral courage, strike while the iron is hot.

What I am saying, preaching is pertaining to modern world, the present era. It was completely different back in Africa, in post World War Two era, where most of us spent our childhood, our early life.

The only friendship that existed between a boy and a girl was, on most part pure, simple and uncomplicated. But on few occasions, elopements did occur, especially when caste and religious differences were an obstacle to tying the note but ultimately lead to a fulfilling life.

Our resolves are only tested in time of adversity. It is a wonderful mantra when we say do not leave the happiness, quality of your life to chance but leave it to choice. Be a catalyst of your own dreams, ambitions and expectations.

But on most part, by the time we gather the courage and approach the person, it is already too late, as some one else may have jumped the queue, make most of the opportunity that may have come their way and snatched Eve from Adam, Anarkali from Prince Salim and Laila from her Majnu and in Hollywood sense, Scarlet from her Rhett, *"Gone With The Wind"* fame.

I can say that I was a lucky one, born with a silver spoon in my mouth. Perhaps our family pedigree reflected true blue blood down the line, as education was and still is the hallmark of our family tradition.

Most of our family members going back generations were professionals and our younger generation is following in our footsteps, climbing the educational ladder with ease and determination.

In a way I was fortunate, as I was the only son, with two adorable, gorgeous elder sisters, with a ten year gap between me and my second, the younger sister, a serine and peace at its best.

As such, I was, in a nice way, spoilt rotten by all family members, especially by my two lovely, kind and caring sisters who were ambassadors of love, angles in disguise, specially dispatched from heaven to spoil me rotten. Then my sisters made many sacrifices, gone to temple and bagged God to bless them with a brother.

I was like a teddy bear that they would like to cuddle, play with and heap all their love and affection that only sisters are capable of showing, especially to some one much younger then them.

Perhaps I was looked upon by my sisters much as the smiling Buddha would look upon his favourite pupil, his disciple, except that my sisters had only one brother while Lord Buddha had thousands of pupils to choose from.

No matter how naughty, mischief making I may be, my sisters would never get annoyed with me nor showed any anger, as they used to say *"Anger is one letter short of Danger."*

No wonder I got away with murder on some but fortunately rare occasions. But as soon as I grew up, began to understand the love, the bond between me and my sisters, I loved them to bits, reciprocating their love and affection ten times over.

Back then, we lived in a different atmosphere; different environment and our values were as different as chalk and cheese. There was respect, unity and brotherhood. It was in a way communal living, a Kibbutz with attitude, one for all and all for one. No one would go hungry or sleep rough.

We used to share every materialistic possession, take care of each other. Naturally, even in our Hindu society, it is difficult to find such bond between a brother and a sister in today's world where wealth and prestige rules the roots.

There is a saying in Gujarati, *"Jar, (wealth) Jamin (land, kingdom) and Joru (woman) Kajyana (disagreement, quarrel) na choru (cause, reason) which literally means that all disagreements, quarrels and even wars have their roots in three possessions that others want from you and they are, your wealth, your land and your beautiful woman, may she be your wife, daughter or a sister.*

Our prime object, ambition is to build a financial empire, climb the social ladder and sit on the podium by any means, fair of foul but so often neglecting our children, the weak and the older members of the family. We no longer give them respect they deserve nor consult them in our hour of need. This is our loss, our misfortune, as separation, divorce and family break-up is fast gaining ground in our once solid and proud society, community. Our family life is no longer the **Rock of Gibraltar**!

In many respect, our family was a special one, a blessed one. It was a close knit family. It was an oasis of enlightenment, a tribute to the symphony of love, devotion and cultural, family values that we have inherited through generations.

Our parents radiated warmth, kindness and a refreshing perspective on the true meaning of family life. None of my parents were after grandeur in any materialistic field except family love.

They had installed discipline, drilled in our unique cultural heritage and taught us the riches of our noble Hindu religion, the best religion in the world, as they believed that such activities, togetherness make quantum improvement in our satisfaction and motivation level and increase awareness and enlightenment in our lives.

They believed that in every Hindu, there is a pool of ancient wisdom, derived from our deities like Lord Rama, Krishna, Buddha, Mahavir, Guru Nanak and last but not least saintly Mahatma Gandhi, the noblest person to be born since Lord Jesus Christ.

But unfortunately a few of us would harvest this ancient pool of wisdom for the benefits of mankind at large. With such wealth, richness, cultural heritage and numerous books of wisdom, Hinduism should dominate the world, not play a second fiddle and be an auxiliary to Christianity and Islam.

But Hindus, brilliant at most activities, are too shy, too modest and some what ignorant of our own noble religion to push it in the forefront, shout from the rooftop about the nobility of Hinduism, our rich cultural heritage and our unique achievement. Perhaps the time is changing, as Hindus are considered as the axis of good, progress, advancement and most law abiding people in the West.

With so much bloodshed, violence and terrorism, the world is slowly but surely learning about the greatness of our ten thousand years' old culture and noble religion.

We would always sit down together for evening meal and had satsang, the prayer meeting once a week when we would recite Bhagwat Gita, our holy book that contains the words of wisdom uttered by Lord Krishna while guiding Arjun on the battlefield of ***Kurushatra.***

We used to discuss many subjects, many topics after the prayer was over. We were allowed to ask any question on any subject to our parents and they would answer them truthfully and honestly, to the best of their ability.

Some times even our priest would join us, as he appreciated the wisdom and knowledge our parents had and regularly join us for dinner, especially on auspicious occasions like Dipawali and Janmastami, Lord Krishna's birthday.

In a way, all our family members were blessed with the psychology of winning, especially on the educational, literary front. But we were never consumed by the hunger for success, making money, become famous and create wealth, except spiritual wealth.

Our parents were like a gushing mountain stream after a heavy rain, always full of fresh water that would enrich the soil and produce food in abundance. They certainly enriched our lives. We were led to believe that we should act as a catalyst of our own dreams and ambitions. Our destiny is in our hands, as we are all endowed with the capacity of being great, successful in one way or another.

As a young boy, I did not understand the wisdom, the knowledge and sheer enormity of **Bhagavad-Gita** which is Holy Bible, Vedas and Ramayana all rolled into one. The Hindu doctrine is known as Karma, one reaps what one sow, that heaven and hell is on earth, in our mildest.

The greatness of Hinduism is the freedom to believe, to choose and not to be dictated to. Every human being is a free soul, free to follow the path that his inner voice may dictate, urge. We believe that if we start judging other people, then we will not have the time to understand and love them.

No other religion gives such freedom to their followers who are lead on a narrow path from which they can not deviate, so often under mental and physical threat, punishment.

Hinduism is like a huge river with many tributaries that constantly feed the main stream, thus enriching itself from the flow, wisdom of others. Hinduism is a practical religion and we believe that an ounce of practice is better than a ton of theory.

After all it is easy to read one hundred pages of a good fiction book but it is difficult to read just a few pages of any religious book, especially Bhagwad Gita, a complex book where every word, every sentence has a hidden meaning.

According to our Hindu tradition, a sister's life is unfulfilled if she does not have a brother to whom she can tie a **Rakhi.** For a long time, my sisters must have thought that the Vidhata, the Goddess that charts a child's life, his or her destiny, on the sixth day after birth, the occasion when we name the child, the ceremony we perform, must have decided not to bless my loving sisters with a younger brother to share their joy, their hope, their success and sorrow with a brother, be their guardian angle in their hour of need.

In today's progressive society, most families are contended, even happy to have all their children female. But priorities were different, social structure was different and the family would not be complete without a male child who would inherit the throne, take the family forward, keep the family tree in fruits in the new age.

So it was indeed an extremely joyous occasion when I was born, when least expected, as my mother was in her early forties, well pass child bearing age. So I was, in a way a gift from God, a special child. My parents distributed penda, a kind of sweet made from milk and normally distributed on a holy, joyous occasion.

There is no better, more fulfilling occasion than the birth of a first male child, especially so late in a woman's life when she must have given up all hope of being a mother once more.

Although this may sound sexist, anti feminist, but old traditions die hard, especially in our ultra conservative Hindu society where a male child is a must to complete the family.

For those who are not Hindus may not understand the meaning of Rakhi, a piece of holy string, usually red or green in colour, decorated with beads or any appropriate piece to make it look ornamental.

The sister ties this string, Rakhi on the right hand wrist of her brother. If the sister is married, then she invites her brother for a lunch or dinner. After tying Rakhi, the sister is allowed; it is indeed her privilege to ask for any thing, any gift from her brother who has to oblige.

But she usually only asks for his love, his blessings and to come to her aid in her hour of need, although that goes without saying. Materialistic consideration does not come into equation.

The love between a brother and a sister is pure, holy, unique and ever lasting, like a bond between a mother and a son, a daughter and a father, as pure as water from river Ganges when it emerges from the hidden depth of Himalayas, cool, fresh and fit to quench any thrust, a pure nectar, amber liquid.

This ceremony ties, cements the bond between a brother and a sister. This is one of the better traditions of Hinduism not yet commercialized.

It was widely adopted by the followers of other faiths in East Africa, mainly Jains, Sikhs, Ismaili and Daudi Bhora Muslims.

It was the time, the era when we, the people of different faiths used to live together in peace and harmony, love and brotherhood. How the time has changed!

In a way, our family, my parents were liberal, well educated and well ahead of their time. They were both graduates and teachers. My mum Shakuntala was a Deputy Head Teacher.

My dad Shyam, a name that refers to Lord Krishna, was a Head Language Teacher in a secondary school, teaching English and Gujarati, as well as French in evening classes to University students and aspiring young businessmen who were eager to do business with France, the country that was trying to penetrate this bastion of British influence on the commercial front.

This was the time, the cultural atmosphere as well as financial constrain that put restrictions on educating girls. But our parents were broad minded, ahead of their time and indeed hard working, in better paid jobs that enabled them to educate my two sisters, Priti and Priya to the highest level.

Priti became a doctor, a gynaecologist, married a fellow doctor and settled in San Francisco, in Northern California. Priya became a lawyer and after marriage, went to Vancouver in Canada. The distance did not weaken our ties, nor our love and affection. If any thing, the distance, the absence, the lack of daily contacts made our hearts grow fonder.

When we met, which was often, at least in the beginning, it was a reunion of souls, a joyous occasion. There is not that much a distance between San Francisco and Vancouver.

So my sisters were in a way neighbours who met regularly, especially when my parents went to stay there during winter months, although it is not that much warmer in San Francisco during the months of November to March.

As the only son, I was obliged, it was indeed my duty to stay with my parents in London and take care of them in their old age. But this is an old assumption, an out dated concept that has no relevance in today's liberal atmosphere. It was an old stallion with tumescent past.

Moreover now a day the government has taken over the responsibilities of looking after our elders and they are doing a better job of it than we could ever do, as we are a creature of habits, stuck in the past and above all we are selfish, our needs take a priority, precedent over the needs of our fragile and ageing parents who could never say no to their off-springs, especially when it comes to baby-sitting! After all, they are their grand children.

So often we use our elderly parents as free baby minders, so that we can go out and work; improve our financial and social standing at the detriment of our parents who should be enjoying their lives in their twilight years. Our hectic pace of life personifies our neglect of our elderly parents.

But our elders have now discovered retirement homes. Most such homes have some thirty to fifty one bed room flats and a resident warden who would look after the elderly, living an independent life in their own flat but having all the advantages of a joint, extended family, as most would attend morning tea sessions where they meet and play games, such as darts, bridge and chess.

They would celebrate various religious and social events, such as birthdays, Diwali, Christmas and such multicultural festivals. During summer months, picnics in a beauty spot and organized holidays to warmer climates are other activities residents love and participate eagerly. Above all, medical help is just a pull string or an emergency press button away.

So they are not cut off from the rest of the world, especially during the dark, cold and damp winter months which make their lives miserable, even intolerable.

Those who can afford, spend winter months in the warm climate of India, Africa, Florida, California and Canary Islands, a tiny piece of heaven on our doorsteps, just four hour's flying time.

As usual, we are a light year behind America when it comes to providing or even exploiting the spending power of the senior citizens. In USA, they have purpose built villages, so often with more than one thousand flats, town houses and bungalows, an ultimate word in luxurious living.

The whole complex is surrounded by a ten feet wall with razor sharp nettings to discourage intruders, uninvited guests and down right crooks, thieves who thrive on the old and the infirm with only a main entrance gate, guarded twenty four hours a day.

One can only enter with a special, tamper-proof pass. Such homes are as safe as Fort Knox and no residents have to lock their front doors! In a way, it is living like in Ram Rajya, under the domain, protection of Lord Rama, the golden era in Hindu mythology!

Such retirement villages have a social club, a medical centre, a gym, a lake, a well stocked, beautiful garden, a picnic spot, a café, a restaurant. Even churches, and a synagogue or such worshipping places have its place, with a large hall which acts as a place for social gathering and celebrating special events, the American Independence Day being the main event.

Such retirement homes are usually built on the outskirts of the towns with greeneries and forests the main attraction. It provides fresh, crispy air, far away from the city pollution.

Americans are well known for planning ahead. Some buy or reserve such a place well in advance, while they are in their prime and afford to pay the mortgage on two properties.

I was, in a way, a black sheep of the family, at least on the literary front. As usual, my parents wanted me to choose science, law or accountancy, become a doctor, a dentist, a Charted Accountant or even a pharmacist. But I never had inclination for science or maths and accountancy was never in our blood.

In a way, I had inherited my father's genes. I was very good at languages, history and geography. I may have even followed into my father's footsteps and became a teacher or rather a professor in a college or a Uni if I had failed in my chosen field.

Some how, I knew, I mastered the art of mind control and spiritual awareness that I am destined to succeed in journalism. I wanted to live a life with unbridled exhilaration that only my chosen profession would provide.

It was only a matter of time before I shine, live a life of prominence and privileges that goes with journalism, the best of them at least.

I had a vision and a vision without action, without determination is a waste. If I had not followed my heart, my mind would have become like an uncaged monkey, rushing from one place to another, from one job to another without any purpose.

But on the other hand action without vision is a disaster. So there was a thin blue line that divided my dream from becoming a reality. Every saint has a past and every sinner has a future. Does this sound confusing? Well, life is never a bed of roses!

My ambition was some what different. Perhaps I had read too many novels written by my favourite authors like Sir Arthur Cannon Doyle, Earnest Hemmingway, James Hilton, Agatha Christie, H. Ryder Haggard, Bronte sisters, Jules Verne, Rudyard Kipling and such authors who wrote adventurous novels.

The books that had most effect on me, perhaps moulded my thinking and ultimately guided me to my present profession of being a journalist, travel writer and author were "A Town like Alice, King Solomon's Mine,

Lost Horizon, Jungle Book, Hound of Baskerville, For Whom the Bells Toll, Doctor Zhivago, Snows of Kilimanjaro and their likes.

I also read many Gujarati books. In fact Gujarati being my mother tongue, it was but natural to start reading Gujarati books first, the natural step to take, master the mother tongue before embarking on English.

The English sounded a foreign and difficult language to master, at least in the beginning that is until we had English teachers when it became a matter of pride to be able to communicate with him, show him our command of his mother tongue.

We had some very good authors. The names I remember with fond affection are, Ramanlal Vasantlal Desai, Kaka Kalalkar, Panalal Patel and Vaju Kotak, a few among many whose books gave me hours of satisfaction before I became proficient enough in English to enable me to read all those wonderful authors' work.

I am so often asked which one is my favourite book, the book I enjoyed most and the book which had most effect on me, the one that perhaps changed my life, steered me to my present profession of journalism, created the ambition in my heart to become author, follow into the footsteps of Noble Prize winner author Sir V. S. Naipaul.

I feel *A Town like Alice* tops the chart, followed closely by *The Lost Horizon*. I even enjoyed the book "*Kon-Tiki Expedition*" by Thor Heyerdahl, the book I chose for my GCE English Literature subject.

But then there was not much choice. Two other books were Shakespearian work, Julius Cesar and Hamlet, not my cup of tea! I like simple, straight forward novel, albeit with a sting in the tale!

But I love sea and each and every activity associated with water. Then I was born in Dar es Salaam, one of the most beautiful seaside towns in Africa.

Fortunately for me, my parents were liberal, financially in comfort zone. They believe in giving us, their children the freedom to study what we like, what we were good at.

They knew that I will struggle to make a decent living, at least in the beginning if I go into journalism. So they encouraged me to continue my studies after I gained my Masters or rather MBA in English.

My parents' motto, their philosophy and advice to us was that concentrate on your chosen path, mission in life, as concentration is at the root of success, mental mastery.

These were words of wisdom that guided me throughout my life and helped me to achieve my goal, albeit to a limited extent so far.

But I am sure I will sit on the podium one day and that day is not too far away, especially if I cash in on the popularity of Hindu ethos that is gaining momentum in our profession and throughout the western world.

I feel my resolves were tested in time of adversity, albeit on few occasions, as my family support negated such shortfalls in our lives.

I took a part time, a low paid job, a professorship with the University where I obtained my Master's degree, teaching English literature and studying for my PhD at the same time.

Our family motto, not to leave the quality of our lives to chance but to leave it choice, served us well in time of adversity. In any case life's greatest setbacks revel life's biggest opportunities.

Perhaps my parents were hoping that I may take up teaching which may provide me with a higher living standard and better job security. But I was never interested in chasing that elusive pot of gold that so many of us consider our ultimate goal.

With PhD behind my name, it would not be too difficult to find such a post. But I was determined to make my mark, my name on the literary front. Any thing else would be an exercise in frustration. My mind would have lost its lustre.

I feel I had the psychology of winning. I owed it to myself to give it a try and using my PhD, a teaching post was a secondary choice if I fail in my mission, my parents sometimes jokingly called it mission impossible. Perhaps we are all watching too many serials on TV!

I feel these two years were not only most productive but most enjoyable time in my life, mixing, flirting with my fellow female students and of course occasional parties. But I was never into drinks or drugs.

Writing gave me most pleasure. It was a pleasant hobby rather than a job I had to do in order to earn a living. Every minute I spent writing was a time spent in an exotic land, a personal odyssey of the self. Perhaps I was drawing from the pool of the ancient wisdom!

I wrote my first and second book *"Ivory Tower" and "Kismat"* while I was doing my PhD. In fact part of these books formed the basis of my thesis on Hindu religion, its origin and its effect on our every day lives. The subject I chose was and still is as vast as ocean. I could have written a million words if I was allowed to.

It was a complex subject, incorporating Hare Krishan Movement, Swaminarayan Hindu Mission and Arya Samaj, the Hindu philosophy on economics, family life, why Hindus are so law abiding and successful on academic, financial and business front. But fail so badly on political front when it comes to influencing people of other religion and faith.

The malaise is symptomatic of the Hindu "flock" every where. In India, we have Aunty Sonia, a foreigner who rules the roots and in the West, we still suffer from inferior complex, the legacy of our colonial past that we are unable or unwilling to shed, even after a thousand years of colonialism.

Writing is a lonely profession, spending hours and days in front of a computer.

But I possess the renewing power of solitude and let it take hold of me. In many ways it is a rewarding profession as well, to see one's name in print.

Every one, especially on the political front, is a friend, in deed a bosom buddy if you write, praise the politician, especially at the election time. Then it is easy to displease, make an enemy as well. One has to trade a fine line between being into a politician's pocket and be fair and constructive.

I was fortunate to find a job, more like an apprenticeship with a prestigious national newspaper, although my parents would say it was my hard work, sincerity, work ethic and mixing nature that enabled me to a fast track promotion in my chosen profession.

Perhaps my Hindu identity may have helped me indirectly. We the Hindus wear our ethnicity or faith very lightly and thus enjoy good relations with all, especially with the English people who are the natives of the land, although there is a very thin dividing line between a Hindu and a member of other faith, as we all look alike.

There is also ignorance and that may be one of the reason we are all called Asians. But fortunately British politicians are beginning to understand the difference and many call us British Indians or British Hindus, the label most Hindus prefer.

I must not forget the contribution my parents made in my success, as living at home, means I had no financial worries. So often my father, who had a wonderful command of English, would read, correct and enhance my piece, especially when I may be working with a tight schedule, a deadline that is the norm in my profession.

In print business, yesterday's news is a history, tomorrow is a mystery and today's news catches headlines, makes news on TV and radio.

The exclusivity is the name of the game and to succeed, one may need a pool of influential friends in the right places.

Fortunately I had many, amongst politicians, academics, businessmen and above all among my fellow professionals with whom I got on very well, even in such a cut-throat business.

After five years, at a relatively young age of twenty eight, I was well settled in my chosen profession. I had my two books which I wrote while doing my PhD, were published, thanks to the enormous input by my father, who edited and spell-checked my manuscripts, found me an agent.

It is indeed very difficult if not impossible to find a well established agent as they are reluctant to take on unknown authors. Perhaps being a journalist and PhD behind my name, helped me, impressed the agent who gauged me as a future celebrity!

So this was a lucky break but through hard work. My father, by now was my best supporter, admirer and as proud of my achievement as he was of my two sisters who were both high flying professionals.

I may not be in their league when it came to earning, gathering wealth. But it was only a question of time before my books; a collection of short stories would go on the small screen and hopefully earn me a fortune, as I have already started writing TV scripts.

Slowly but surely, I was making some inroads, good influential friends in the field of TV journalism. So often whom you know is more important than what you know.

* * *

Chapter Two

An Unforgettable Plane Journey

Journalists have no fixed working hours. Like some professionals, we are on call twenty four hours a day. We have to follow the events, tragedies and late night sittings, even all night parties!

But what we get is generous holidays, some six to eight weeks paid holidays depending upon the seniority and the length of the service, as well as one's ability.

Good writers who can penetrate readers' hearts and minds are as good, as precious as gold dust. But it requires a steely determination to succeed where too many applicants are chasing too few jobs. So how good you are is only one factor. Whom you know is as important as what you know. Then this scenario is not that uncommon in other fields, especially politics!

Perhaps one's determination to be a German shepherd dog will give an edge over one's ambition to be an American poodle. One has to come from the right side of the social and political divide to make a rapid progress in this toughest of the though profession. But in the end one's ability and determination do shine, come out from the clouded sky that can never hide the sun for ever. When a true star is born, it soon gains momentum.

Unfortunately I do not have the killing instinct. I find it difficult to stab some one in the back, betray the confidence, no matter what the final prize may be. I believe in addressing my co-writers with relevant civility if not giving them the red carpet treatment.

Basking in borrowed plums is a *"cuckoo land"* syndrome, at least for me. No wonder my parents have so often doubted my ability, how I

471

would fit in this cut throat profession with Hindu ethos and believing in
"Honesty is the best policy?"

As in every profession, money does speak. Filthy rich parents, families
do give the scope to the trainee journalists who may be bores and pseudo
intellectuals with limited ability to get by, even climb the ladder but only
to a limited extent. After all there is no substitute for skill, intelligence,
dedication and hard work which pays rich dividends in the end.

So these fortunate, favoured, well placed writers, journalists are in great
demand. They can name their price, their terms and work as and when
they please. But it would take a long time to gain such an advantage, be at
the zenith end, establish contacts, have the private telephone numbers of
important people in all walk of life, like Prime Ministers and other leading
politicians, sport personalities and members of film and TV industries.

Britain is a great country to live and work, that is if you do not mind
the ever changing weather and most of the younger generation who are on
the move all the time, do not even notice the weather; that is until they
are well into there early sixties.

The saying, never trust wine, weather and women in England only
apply to weather. As for wine and women, one should know their onions,
how to differentiate the shining rock from a real gem, a true diamond.

I find English girls and women kind, caring and on most part
wonderful persons, the real English Rose, although the drink culture, the
binge drinking and such activities are ruining their names, their character
and their reputation.

I feel English girls are divided into two sections, tow groups; those who
come from the middle class are genuine and on most part a real beauty
with sensible attitude towards life and their fellow human beings.

Those who come from the Council Estates are, on most part involved
in drinks, drugs and teenage pregnancies, following into the footsteps of
their parents and grandparents where the word work is a taboo.

This is the result of family breakdown, divorces and cohabitation,
shrinking the social responsibilities, the result of benefit dependency
and the cultural erosion that loony left wing politicians introduced in
this country in the early sixties. The Flower Power, Make Love not War
generation never grew up. They were and still are Milky Bar Kids.

Less than a century ago, British people were a proud race. People
were honest, hard working, innovative, great inventors, adventurers and
Britannia ruled the waves. The sun never set on the British Empire which
was greater than the Roman, Greek, Mogul and the rest put together.

How come we have descended so low, become a non entity in less than one hundred years, out performed and out manoeuvred by Germany and Japan, the countries we defeated in two world wars?

Fortunately the dependency culture applies to a tiny minority, at least so far. But even one rotten apple in a barrel is enough to spoil the rest. According to Kavi (poet) Surdas, there is nothing blacker, darker than a stain on one's character.

There was a time when one would prefer to commit suicide, end one's life rather than go bankrupt, put a stain on one's character. How the time has changed!

Now money can erase any stain, buy any favour and acquire any honour! Do the title Sir and Lord has the same meaning, same value as it was during the hay days of British Raj! Then the title was earned on the battle field while serving the nation, not bought with donations to political parties and influential politicians.

Britain is today a genuinely multicultural society. It became that way not through dollops of tokenism but because Britishness involves a sense, a spirit of fair play, generous accommodation and live and let live attitude that is absent in most Western countries.

For most Indians, especially the older generation, Bharat (India) is our ancestor's Janmabhumi (birth place) while Britain is our Karmabhumi. (Future) Janmabhumi is our mother while Karmabhumi is our father which deserves equal respect and equal loyalty.

Our black footballers are even booed and jeered with monkey calls in European countries like Spain and East European countries that were once under the influence of the Soviet Union. It seems their liberation is merely rhetorical, not genuine or practical, at least not so far.

In return, we, the Hindus give our undivided loyalty to our adopted country who has given us home, security and a good standard of living. I believe that the patriotic action lead to the elevation of soul. Our golden cultural legacy is helping, benefiting us and our adopted motherland equally.

This is Hindu doctrine known as Karma that we all get what we deserve, one reaps what one sows. If you keep a cow, you get the milk. If you keep a donkey, it will carry your burden and if you keep a cobra, you will be bitten, lose your life. There is some truth in the saying that a person is known by the company he keeps.

Multiculturalism can best be served by ensuring equality of opportunities and leaving people alone to get on with their lives, not rewriting history to suit expediency or putting some one on a podium that one does not deserve, merely based on one's skin colour, religion and ethnic origin.

No ethnic minorities, nor gays and lesbians are hounded in this liberal country, except by other, more orthodox members of our own ethnic minorities who are bent upon destroying the unity of this beautiful nation. This is like renouncing the world which is full of God's children for a fool's paradise! We easily forget that all that glitters is not gold nor every white liquid is milk.

In Britain, Hindus have readily assimilated themselves within the mainstream culture, taking advantage of the efforts made by the host community to encompass us, the ethnic minorities of Hindus, Sikhs, Jains and Jewish people, making the best of both the world.

Although many Hindus have synthetic belief, most Hindus are expressionist and in many ways down to earth people. We believe that taller we grow, deeper the roots we need to steady ourselves, not to be blown away by the fierce wind and hurricanes of change, selfishness, greed and material wealth. This is the age old wisdom installed in us since the days of Lord Rama and Lord Krishna some ten thousand years ago.

I divide my six to eight weeks' holidays in visiting my sisters in America and Canada and I spend at least two weeks in the lap of luxury, an all inclusive holidays nearer home, visiting Spain, Portugal, Greece, Madera and Canary Islands.

I would like to relax on the beach, write my books and taking excursions to beauty spots like Mount Teide in Tenerife, volcanic peaks in Lanzaroti, Andorra, a mini Switzerland tucked between Northern Spain and Southern France and jointly ruled, a place where the famous movie, *Sound of Music* was filmed.

The Portuguese island of Madeira, a floating garden with three thousand peaks, is one of the most beautiful places on earth but not yet appreciated by Westerners who travel thousands of miles in search of sea, sand, isolation and beauty.

I found all these in abundance on our own door-steps. One of the best beaches are on the island if Fuerteventura, natural beaches regularly supplemented by sands blown from Sahara, sand dunes, giving it a Sahara desert look, as the island is only separated from the coast of Africa by the waters of Atlantic Ocean, no more than forty miles away.

One may find complete isolation on Formentera, a mere couple of miles off the coast of Ibiza but a million miles away in atmosphere created by mass tourism on the Balearic Island of Ibiza. The beauty of Madeira and all inclusiveness of Cyprus are also not too far away from British shores.

I am not a great spender. I neither smoke nor drink and only eat at expensive restaurants when entertaining some one important who would be a help, a source of important and exclusive news items. I dress modestly and there are no Armani suits in my wardrobe. I feel my exquisite manner is my greatest asset, much appreciated in a fast changing world with cut-throat business ethics.

But I like to travel business class, especially on long haul flights. For me air travel is not a pleasure but a necessity, a means of going from A to B. So I would like to make the most of it by travelling business or even first class if the circumstances demand.

I am not blessed with the most robust health. I have to take care, live within my physical means.

The longest holiday we can take is during Christmas weeks when every business more or less comes to a standstill, although newspapers are off the shelves only for a day or two. But they are watered down editions to keep the advertisers happy.

A week before Christmas, I found myself on a plane bound for San Francisco to visit my two sisters who always get together during these holidays.

In America, a vast and open country, they are practically next door neighbours, as **San Francisco and Vancouver**, both on the **Pacific coast**, are separated only by a few hundred miles, a couple of hours by plane. My parents had already preceded me three weeks earlier, as they would like to spend as much time as possible with their grand children.

Rightly or wrongly, my parents believe that too much time spent apart from their children and grand children simply zapped them out of their children's affection. Perhaps they are right, as we say "out of sight, out of mind."

It may be an old fashion belief in fast changing world but the one that keeps us united, in loving, caring relationship. Neither the time nor the distance could dent our family unity, our deep love for each other. So often my sisters still treat me like a cuddly bear, to my slight embarrassment. Then the old habits die hard!

After all they were in their early seventies and it was only a question of time when they may not be able to travel long distances, although they were fit and healthy, especially for their age. They always tell me that ageism is a mind game. One is as young and healthy as one may feel, one may look. If every one believes in these healthy ideals, it would certainly put plastic surgeons out of business.

As usual, I had a window seat. Surprisingly the plane was only half full. So we got the best seats in the first row with plenty of leg room and reclining seats as comfortable as beds. But then first class is never full, like the economy class, even at such a busy time of the year.

Perhaps Britons would prefer to travel to warmer climate during the harsh winter months, like India, Far East, Australia and New Zealand rather than to San Francisco, some what a colder place in December.

The person sitting next to me was an American girl. She was slim, pretty with long golden hair, perhaps in Indian, Hindu style where most girls have long, beautiful hair, an age old tradition but disappearing fast under pressure of work.

It is much easier to manage a short hair, especially for a working girl with little time for make-up. Most such girls visit a beauty saloon once a month that takes care of their needs on the hygiene and beauty front. She looked much younger for her age, hardly out of her teens but so often looks are deceiving. We can never judge a book from its cover!

Journalists, on most parts, are talkative, have power of observation, good judge of character and easy to get along. It goes with the territory.

When travelling, I always keep a copy of my book *Ivory Tower* and a copy of the magazine *India Link* handy, as I have my own column *"From Far and Near"* in India Link. So often it helps me to break ice and start a conversation.

Like the girl whom I came to know as *Genevieve,* I am some what slim, almost thin, may be due to all the running around I have to do in my profession.

Although I have some what fair skin, my looks are typical, that of an Indian. But that was not a disadvantage in any way. I have, on rare occasion, even experienced positive discrimination.

I look much younger for my age. Unfortunately age and mature look is an asset in my profession. No one would take me seriously, especially politicians, that is until they come to know me better.

It seems I have to fight all the way to gain supremacy. I may look young and innocent, as if butter would not melt in my mouth. But underneath my boyish appearance, there is a steely determination to succeed in my chosen profession. I have to, as I feel I have no other option.

After all I come from a family where every one sits on a podium. I can not be an odd one out, especially when my parents gave me the right of choice, the right to opt for an alternative medicine if the traditional one does not work for me.

There is a misconception among Whites, Europeans that an Asian, Indian can not master English language.

So most people find it difficult to believe that I am a journalist, writer and an author, at least to begin with, that is until I show my Press Card, issued by the Charted Institute of Journalists and copies of my books.

They forget or are ignorant that some of the best authors are Asians, mainly Indians and that include Salman Rushdie, Arundhati Roy, Vikram Sheth and V. S. Naidu, a Noble Prize winner whose book *A House for Mr. Biswas* is one of my all time favourite. His second novel, A Bend in the River also gained much praise.

My fellow passenger, Genevieve was busy reading. So I did not get the opportunity to talk to her until drinks were served. When she put the book on one side, I noticed that it was a copy of Holy Bible. I was surprised that such a young girl was reading Bible, that also on a plane!

On the whole, Christianity is in decline, especially in the West and amongst younger generation. Gay and lesbian lifestyle, even among the clergies has not help the church in any way.

The outdated thinking among Catholics, backed by the Pope neither to use contraception nor to allow abortion under any circumstances has divided Christians,

Churches have damaged their standing, especially in the developing world of Asia, Africa and South America where most live in poverty with half a dozen children.

The gay lifestyle is seen as an affront to humanity, anti Christian. Surely gay lifestyle is a luxury they can not afford, as it would make them an outcaste. Moreover it goes against what they have been taught from childhood, not only by their parents but by the church, at Sunday services most attend like clockwork.

When this charming girl gave me a smile, I sized the opportunity and politely asked her what she was reading. She proved to be more amiable and friendly than I first thought. She put the Bible in my hand and said, "I know you will be surprised to see me reading Bible.

But it is part of my thesis. I am reading Christianity as part of my PhD course. By the way, my name is *Genevieve* but my friends call me *Jenny.* May I know your name?"

It seemed my long plane journey will not be a dull affair after all. I was indeed charmed by her beauty, slim, tiny figure, smooth, silky skin, accompanied by her sweet and gentle voice, not to forget her long, slightly curly golden hair and her designer glasses that some how gave her face a lift, an unexplainable charm.

But I have to readily admit that Jenny could not be every one's cup of tea, as when boys' or rather young men first look at a girl, it's inevitably at her chest and that keeps the plastic surgeons in the lap of luxury.

But for me, for my taste, she was a glass of vintage champagne! Perhaps I may be an odd one out, exception to the rule.

In my profession, I have meet so many sophisticated and bulging beauties, but on the whole mature ladies out of my league, physically if not socially. So such a young and amicable beauty with similar physique to mine was a pleasant surprise, a well deserved diversion, some one to concentrate on and with a bit of luck we may even click.

How true it is that a beauty is in beholder's eyes, as Jenny had more or less flat chest, no visible curves that normally attract male attention in the first place. I am some what different. I look at girl's eyes, her hair and her dress sense rather than her bulging breasts and tennis player's thighs, the William sisters' scenario, the so called sexual attractions.

Intellectual ability and good manner is my main attraction. Sexual attraction may wane with age, health and circumstances while mental superiority, stimulation, quick thinking brain, witty and charming personality usually is life long gift that may stay with the person until death do us part!

"My Name is **Naimesh** but my friends call me **Neal**. You may be surprised but when I studied for my PhD. I chose Hinduism to write the thesis, although my main interest is journalism.

Then journalism is a vast and varied subject that encompass, benefit from the knowledge on any and every subject, including religion."

"Genevieve is an unusual name. Could it be French?" I wanted to prolong the conversation, strike the iron while it was hot and not let her go back to her Bible studies.

"Yes, you are absolutely right. My grand mother is French. My grandfather met her during the Second World War. It was a war time romance that stood the test of time and triumphed in the end.

We have maintained the war time connections and we often travel to France to meet my grandma who is well into her eighties." It seemed Jenny did not need any encouragement to prolong the conversation. She was willing and even proud of her family history.

Then picking the book I was reading, I had placed on the meal tray, Jenny said, "Are you an avid reader like me?"

Looking at the back page of my book ***Ivory Tower***, with the description of the book and my photo with background information, she could not hide her surprise and perhaps her delight as well.

"Don't tell me you are a journalist, writer and an author? Sorry, it is all in black and white at the back of your book. But to be honest, I could never have guessed that you are in such a demanding profession and by the look of it, a successful one as well."

She knew that only successful businessmen and professionals could afford to travel first class. We talked and talked until the lunch was served some two hours later.

By that time Jenny knew every detail about me, my family and my two sisters, one living in San Francisco who is a gynaecologist. This was a coincident that would play a crucial part in my life, indeed shape my life in a manner I could not have imagined even in my dream.

She was indeed impressed with my family background, my and my sisters' achievement, as she was also living in a close knit family with traditional Hindu, Catholic values.

I could not help but wonder why a complete stranger wanted to know so much about me, my family, my future plan and my ambition in life. Was this some kind of co-incidence?

Then perhaps when some one is studying for PhD, curiosity automatically becomes part of one's nature. Then there was no harm in me assuming that perhaps there may be some sort of chemistry between us. If so, I must explore it as I believe in the saying, nothing ventured, nothing gained.

I was also puzzled how come I told her every thing about me without any hesitation. Did I wanted to impress her with my educational qualification, my work as a journalist and my success in the cut throat business of publishing, with my two novels making waves, even a Booker Prize nomination was not out of question?

Normally as an inquisitive journalist, it is I who ask questions, intrude into other people's privacy and try to find skeletons in their cupboards, my chosen subjects. So often I even feel guilty, trying to lead a lamb to a slaughter house!

Perhaps that may be the reason I was eager to become a successful novelist, a playwright rather than an investigative journalist. Could this be a love at first sight!

I may not be Lord Krishna but Jenny was certainly my Radha! Perhaps my fertile imagination was taking over my normally cool and calm personality.

I had to admit that it was difficult for me to take my eyes off her beautiful, ever smiling face, with her long, curly hair and look elsewhere. But I was careful not to offend her, let her know that in a way I was staring at her.

Then perhaps she did not mind. She may have even enjoyed all the attention she was getting from a young, good looking, well educated and eligible bachelor!

Perhaps she may have realized that I was admiring her intellectual beauty rather than the physical one which she may believe, some what erroneously that she was distinctly lacking, with her flat chest and lack of curves in right places. But for me she was exquisite, beauty and joy, a thorough breed and not a plough horse with muscles! She was my Audrey Hepburn, not Liz Taylor!

I did not need some one to plough my field but to plough, cultivate my heart, my home and my emotions!

* * *

Chapter Three

Genevieve

Now I felt it was my time to ask questions, know about her as much as I possibly could. But the question is, would she oblige? Well, I have to seize the bull or rather a sheep in this case, as Jenny is so delicate, fragile, by the horn and hope for the best. But I have to be careful that I may not become a classic case of folly catching up fools. I should not let my euphoria rule my heart and mind.

It was time for the Empire to strike back, in a gentle, kind and caring manner that would not frighten Jenny away. Brevity is the soul of wit and secret of success.

I was hoping that what may sound mundane may assume the colours of destiny, colours of a rainbow by the time this journey is over. The beauty of rainbow is that it represents all three, rain, sunshine and clouds, a rare combination of beast and the beauty.

It is always more interesting, benefiting to live in hope than despair, in perpetual happiness than imaginary disaster. So often the time we may spend on travel is more interesting, intriguing than the time we spend at our destination.

I do not know how true it is but some newly married do say that thinking of honeymoon is more stimulating, rewarding than the honeymoon itself. Perhaps this is one subject I have no opinion, as I am neither married nor in love and certainly not on a honeymoon. But I can live in hope. Can't I?

The audit of hope and expectation sounds impressive, even in difficult circumstances. But this was a pleasant, enjoyable and hopefully a productive encounter that one may experience but once in a life time. Perhaps this was such a journey or was I jumping the gun! Was I seeing stars in the bright daylight!

The malign impact of social, cultural correctness has been worsened by a care ethos that seems to have abandoned all contact with modern world, the common sense that should be the guiding principle in such a chance encounter.

As we say, God works in a mysterious ways but we have to give, even God a helping hand. I had a golden opportunity to impress this wonderful American girl with whom I may have unwittingly establish a repartee that I did not manage with any one else.

Now it was entirely up to me to make the most of this God send gift, opportunity.

Surely I would be lambasted, reprimanded in God's eyes if I fail to follow my heart and make the most of God's gift, albeit in a strange, unexpected manner.

We were only some four hours in the flight, some where on the Atlantic Ocean. Our first brief stop would be the city of New York, on the east coast, before we cross the American continent and land at San Francisco airport, on the west coast, the Pacific coast.

It was indeed a very long flight, as I could not get a reservation on a direct flight from London to San Francisco that would have cut the flying time in half, as it flies over North Pole, the most direct route that the advances in aviation technology during the last two decades has made it possible.

Then such direct flights are always in demand. One has to book well in advance to secure a seat during Christmas holidays. It is a mystery why the airlines do not have more such direct flights when demands are so high and other flights go half empty.

"Well Jenny, it is time for me to know about you, as much as you know about me; that is if I am not intruding in your private life, making you uncomfortable in any way." I said with a soft voice, more of a pleading than asking.

After all I knew I had no right to demand an answer from Jenny. But defence and deterrence is not the way forward, boldness and assertion definitely is. I had nothing to lose by being bold, every thing to gain if I get the right response. If I do not try, then perhaps I may regret it for the rest of my life. Opportunity is like flowing water, it flows only in one direction.

"Neal, you are right. You have opened your heart to a complete stranger. Now it is my turn to reciprocate. But I am neither a journalist, an author, nor a story teller. So I may not be able to make my life history as interesting, as intriguing as yours.

But believe me, I will try my best, as I want to pick your brain, make a good impression, as I believe that the first impression counts most, make or break a friendship. Well, in this instance, it is the case of establishing a friendship. We can not break what is not there, at least not yet.

After all it is unwise to cross swords with a journalist, especially a handsome one!" It seems Jenny was indeed a wise and clever girl who knew what buttons to press to make a right impression.

I also knew that I am on safe ground; there won't be a bumpy landing after all, even if I ask an awkward question. Jenny is capable of handling any question, any situation with grace and panache! Perhaps she was as much interested in me as I was in her.

After a brief pause, Jenny continued. "My grandfather was a pilot during the Second World War. He was stationed in England. I believe some where in Kent, perhaps at the Beggin Hill Airport.

He was a reluctant soldier, almost a pacifist. He never talked about life, his war experience, just glad that he returned safe and sound, in one piece, as he saw so many of his comrades killed and maimed in France.

He abhorred the thought of killing another human being. He was a pure vegetarian, as he felt every living creature, how large or small it may be, has as much right to life as we, the humans. I believe this is the Hindu philosophy." Jenny was suddenly thoughtful, a bit serious but not for long.

Now I realized why Jenny had a vegetarian meal and she was well versed in Hinduism as well, a novelty in an American girl so young. So Jenny was not only beautiful but brainy and well informed as well, a rare combination of beauty and brain going in the same direction!

After a short pause, Jenny continued, "We may be supreme, at the top of the chain of evolution. But that does not give us the right to kill, either for pleasure, sport or food, as vegetarianism gives us more than enough food to satisfy our hunger, fill our bellies and even live a healthy life. After all, vegetarians are the longest living creatures on earth.

As Gandhiji said, *"There is always enough to satisfy every one's need but never enough to satisfy every one's greed."* It is the greed that is stripping our beautiful, green mother earth of rain forest, all kind of minerals and turning it into a desert, polluting the oceans and emptying them of fish and other marine animals. These magnificent creatures are a gift from God. What right we have to destroy them, make our oceans barren.

You may know that the Sahara desert is expanding at the rate of some thirty miles a year. Some of the Central African countries like Chad, Niger and Mauritania have already lost most of its water resources and people are starving, as lakes have dried up, depriving the people of fish, their main diet.

The Ural and the Dead Sea have shrunk by half and will completely disappear in fifty years' time.

These seas have been around for thousands of years, yet we could not look after our precious resources for the next fifty years.

We blame it to climate change. But who is responsible for this climate change? We, the Americans are the worse culprit, as we like our big cars, huge houses, meaty, unhealthy diet and our unsustainable life-style. Once Texas had the highest oil reserves in the world. Today it is practically a dry state. We have wasted our precious assets and now go after others.

But I should not move away from our main topic of conversation. I am sure you are not interested in geography lessons, rather eager to learn about me, that you find me, how shall I put it, interesting, intriguing and perhaps charming if not beautiful.

I readily admit I am not Liz Taylor or Sophia Loren that you people, young, upwardly mobile wiz kids admire and would like to be with, although I must admit that I have no respect if some one would like to be with the super model Jordan who has limited appeal, one asset, that is also a gift from a plastic surgeon. Then we all have different need, different taste, one man's food is another man's poison."

There was a mischievous smile on her face, playing with her hair in a provocative way that would attract any one's attention. I was tempted in joining her but was too much of a gentleman to gatecrash the party!

She knew I was interested in her, that her long, golden hair has captured my imagination. She also knew she had limited curves, few bulges in the right places that would attract most male attention.

So she was, in a way pleased that I like her, I admire her hair and her hair style, her green eyes, visible through her designer glasses, her dress sense, her simple but effective make-up that gave her a charm and beauty, affiliation and affection that can not be put in words and her tall, slim and attractive figure. So why not make the most of it while the sun shines? After all, it always rains in England.

I knew I had to intervene. Otherwise she may believe that I do not find her beautiful, attractive or sexy which was as far from the truth as earth is from the sun, that I am from the British royalty!

"Jenny, you are not doing justice to yourself. You know that beauty is in beholder's eyes. How would you know I do not find you beautiful, charming, even desirable and sexy!

Yes, most would like Liz Taylor, Sophia Loren type busty girls but there are many who would prefer to be with Audrey Hepburn. Have you seen her with Gregory Peck in the film Roman Holidays! This film is one of my all time favourite."

As soon as I finished the sentence, I felt I may have gone too far, overstep the mark. So before Jenny could speak, I quickly said, "Jenny, please don't take me wrongly. My intentions are strictly honourable and if I have said any thing out of line, then please accept my sincere apology."

"Well Neal, as long as your praise is not ephemeral, I do not mind. Stop being so defensive all the time. Have trust, faith in your judgement. Indeed I am pleased, honoured that you find me attractive and perhaps a little bit sexy. You are absolutely right. The beauty is in beholder's eyes and I hope I am euphoriatic beauty in your eyes as well!

After all, you would be a good catch for any girl, with your **BA, MBA and PhD** behind your name, a good job and a couple of novels to your name that may put you on the high podium sooner than you may think, especially if you have a full backing of the woman of your dream!" Was Jenny giving me a hint!

"Indeed your achievement is some thing to be proud of. Yet you are so modest! If you feel that I am beautiful and sexy, then I will be over the moon, as I know my assets, my limitations and my shortfalls! But Neal, when we are in love, we negate on the liabilities, concentrate on the assets. That is human frailty, human weakness.

Jenny's words were accompanied by a sweet, reassuring smile rather than a long reply in so many words. Jenny even pressed my hand gently, affectionally.

"Well Jenny, in my country, we say that the cricket should be appreciated as a sport rather than mixed with politics, political and fiscal affiliation. So my appreciation is pure and simple, an intellectual girl with wonderful sense of humour that I can appreciate and live with!"

"I am honoured that such a charming girl has so much faith in me, in my ability. Is the adulation a swansong Gaullism?" I could not help but tease Jenny mildly, even try to confuse her, as normally she would answer such comments with a sweet smile, showing the full range of her pearl white teeth.

"Neal, you are a thorough breed, not a plough horse. Let's stop praising; complementing each other. Let me continue before I lose the thread.

"My grandfather was also a proud American. He would never shun his duty to his country or his fellow human being.

Moreover the atrocities committed by the German and Japanese armies were so horrible that every civilized human being considered it his or her duty to fight this twin evil, stop it from conquering, enslaving the world before it was too late.

I could not even imagine what the world would be like if Hitler and Mussolini, Japan and Germany have triumphed, become global super power and ruled the world.

Perhaps we would have gone a thousand years back in history, in brutality and slavery may have been reintroduced. After all Germans did considered themselves Aryans, a super race, superior human beings who were born to rule the world.

We all know what happened under Roman Empire, under Genghis and Kublai Khan that ruled the Central Asia with unimaginable cruelty. History is full of such tyrants, not only in the past but even today.

Does any one know or cares how the kind, gentle and caring people of Tibet are being brutalized on a daily basis by the might of China? Today our attitude is, I am alright Jack. The rest can fight their own battle, unless there is black gold, the oil underneath their soil.

Even Mahatma Gandhi, whom I consider a reincarnation of Lord Jesus Christ, supported the British in this war. He knew the difference between Britain and Germany, Japan, especially Japan who had committed unimaginable atrocities against Chinese people.

We all know about Hitler's brutality against Jews and Russians, the concentration camps but not what Japan did in China and Korean peninsula. Some how atrocities against Asians do not count; not reported as widely as war in Europe.

Gandhiji even suspended the civil agitation, the Satyagrah, the non cooperation with the British for some time, so that the British and Indian soldiers could face the Japanese who were already in Burma, knocking on India's border.

Gandhi knew that if Japan wins the war, India would remain a Japanese colony for the next hundred years while the British were on the verge of granting independence to India, under Gandhi, Sardar and Nehru for whom Britain had immense respect.

It was Jinha's demand for a separate motherland for Muslims that was delaying the independence. Again this is a complicated and controversial subject. Perhaps you may know more about it than me.

You may wonder how I know so much about India. Well my grandfather was an avid collector of books. We have well over two thousand books in our own mini library and I have read most if not all.

My grandfather joined the war efforts a bit late, in 1943, due to his young age. By this time it was obvious that the Germany's efforts to stem the tide were as doomed to failure as the injunctions of King Canute.

But he flew over the enemy territories and took part in the carpet bombings of some famous German cities like Berlin, Dortmund and Hamburg, although he never talked about his war exploits.

Towards the end of the war, he was shot down in France. Fortunately France was liberated within three months of his plane coming down. But for three months, he was helped, given shelter, fed and nursed back to health by a French family, at the risk of their own lives.

While France, as a nation, capitulated without putting any worthwhile resistance, failed miserably to stand up against Hitler's might, the French people put up a heroic resistance, in their own way, in a manner appropriate at the time, what we may now call a guerrilla warfare. Emotions and fear became as muddled as allies and allegiances.

Any one collaborating with the enemy, giving shelter to enemy soldiers were summarily executed without trial. This French family had two lovely girls, Bridget and Marisa who looked after my granddad and nursed him back to health.

When France was liberated, it was in a sorry state. Industries were completely destroyed, infrastructure was uprooted and people could not even feed themselves. During these three months when they had to hide underground, brought Bridget and my grandfather close. She was a real French beauty.

At the young age of eighteen, most girls are beautiful, especially when confined in a small place, day in, day out. They fell in love, got married with blessings from the elders of both the families, especially from Bridget's, as they knew it would secure her future and perhaps help Marissa as well, as America was considered a dream country, paved with gold.

They moved to USA, in fact to San Francisco some one year after Germany surrendered. In any case, my granddad was a reluctant soldier, only doing his duty. He did not want to stay in the army once Europe was liberated.

My grandfather passed away some time ago but my grandmother Bridget is still alive and well. Few years back, she moved back to France, to be with her sister Marissa who never got married.

Perhaps they were both in love with my grandfather. But he chose Bridget, as she was younger and much more beautiful. In doing so, he may have inadvertently broken Marissa's heart.

My father John started his working life, teaching English literature and religious studies at St. Andrew's university in San Francisco. In a way he was a modest man, even though highly educated.

He never stood still, always studying, taking evening classes and accumulating diplomas and degrees, just as some would collect sporting trophies!

He never utilized his potential to the full, as he was not an ambitious man. He could not be lured with the trappings of the highest office, the clash of gigantic ambitions.

Still he became a Vice Chancellor of the University late in his life. In fact he had no choice, as both Chancellor and Vice Chancellor were lured away and the faculty needed some one of John's experience and loyalty to steady the ship. He could not refuse. He had to take command to save the ship from sinking.

My father had two children, myself and my older brother. Like your family, education runs in our veins, in our blood, in our family. My brother is a well known surgeon. He was a brilliant student and had scholarship after scholarship until he reached the top, earning a comfortable living with minimum input.

That is how medical profession works in America. Once you reach the top, you only have to supervise. Most of the work is done by your colleagues and trainee surgeons. But the ultimate responsibility is yours and yours only. That is why hospitals have to pay millions in insurance policies, to cover their backs.

Compared to my parents and my brother, I am lagging behind, at least on the educational, financial and ambition front. But I am young and time is on my side.

Financially I am in a comfort zone, thanks to my parents and my brother who loves me to bits. I am sure I do not have to tell you about the bond between a brother and a sister. I am sure you will like him; get along with him and with my parents if you have the opportunity to meet my family members."

I was taken back, a bit surprised. Was this an invitation to meet her family or just a figure of speech?

I should not read too much into this conversation, as we may never meet again. Perhaps this talk was like a holiday romance which ends as soon as one boards the plane home.

Why was I clutching to her every word that may only be a compliment, nothing more? Then it is a human nature to clutch even to a straw when the ship is sinking!

As we say, hope for the best and prepare for the worse. In this case the worse may be that I may never see Jenny again. But some how, even that thought was too much to contemplate!

* * *

Chapter Four

What is Hinduism?

But before I could dwell on my thoughts, trying to analyse her words and make a mountain out of a mole hole, Jenny Said, "Neal, would you mind if I pick your brain, ask you some questions on Hinduism.

I have some knowledge and I know Hinduism is the oldest religion in the world. I would like to compare my knowledge, the answers I would give to my own questions with your answers and try to analyse our differences, what would that mean, where I may have gone wrong or why we differ.

As a part of my PhD thesis, I will have to give some lectures, mainly on Christianity. But I would like to include Hinduism, compare the common heritage and how Christianity has borrowed some wisdom from the ancient religions of Hinduism, Judaism and Buddhism. I am sure this will give a different perspective and perhaps my comprehensive thesis may become a hand-book for future students, a sort of reference book.

Normally we are required to write some thirty thousand words but I have the permission to extend it to fifty thousand words; that is if I can justify it. My tutor who is a family friend will give me the leeway; even help me to achieve my goal. After all, I am his star pupil!

Hinduism is more complex, culturally rich beyond our, Western understanding and in many ways all other religions, like Christianity, Jainism, Sikhism and Buddhism have their roots in Hinduism, although we may not like to admit it. Hinduism is more a way of life than a monolithic religion.

The golden legacy is that Hindus are today, at least in the West, one of the most highly educated, law abiding, hard working and family oriented people in the world.

In every Western country and I suppose throughout the world, Hindus, like Jews, put in more in taxes and other services than they take out. They are net contributors, a rare achievement for any group, especially immigrant community. Perhaps that is the reason why they are so welcome in most countries."

"However, is there a prophet who can claim to be the founder of the Hindu faith, Hindu religion and what is your opinion about the age of Hinduism, when was it born, became an universal faith?"

"Well Jenny, I will also be honest with you. Hinduism is indeed a complex religion. It is like an ocean of knowledge. No two answers will be the same.

Yet all answers will lead to the same conclusion, like we put honey, sugar or artificial sweeteners in our tea, coffee or milk, with the single aim of making the drink sweet. So it should not matter what you use to make your drink sweet, as long as you enjoy it. That is how Hinduism works, unity through diversity.

In Hinduism, in a family of four, each individual may worship a different God and my own family is a perfect example. My dad worships Lord Rama, as he considers him to be a perfect human being who acquired the status of God through good deeds, leading as perfect a life as possible. He was a noble king who cared about his subjects more than his own family.

Mind you Jenny, there are a few critics who blame Lord Rama exactly for his devotion to his people, his subjects, at the expense of the happiness of his wife Sita and children when we say charity begins at home?

They have a valid point as well. But Lord Rama believed that a king is a public servant and his first duty is to his people, to his subjects. But on the whole Rama is or rather was an ideal king, a near perfect human being who conquered the hearts and minds of not only his subjects but millions of his followers today, after some ten thousand years, as no one else could in Hinduism.

Even Gandhiji considered him supreme and when he died at the hands of an assassin, his last words were, *"Ha Ram, forgive him. He does not know what he has done."*

On the other hand, my mother worships Goddess Ambika, a patron Goddess of most Rajput queens and loved and worshipped by every woman. There is a long and a complicated history behind the Goddess Ambika.

I have to give you a short history lesson in order to understand the legend of this most worshipped Goddess among Hindus. Originally India was divided into Northern and Southern India, the Northern residents were known as Aryans and the Southerners as Dravidians.

Aryans were more sophisticated, tall and well built people, mainly due to colder climate and fertile land that gave them a good diet. On the other hand Dravidians were shorter, darker people but intellectually superior and culturally rich people.

When Aryans started moving south, they mixed with Dravidians and adopted Ambika, the Goddess revered by the Dravidians, thus Ambika became the Goddess of all Indians, from Rajputana to Tamil Nadu.

Most Rajput kings, including Maha Rana Pratap and Maratha warrior king Shivaji were devotees of the Goddess Ambika. Her temples are found all over India, especially in hills and places of natural beauty.

One such famous temple is in the hills of Mount Abu which I was fortunate enough to visit a few years back, along with world famous Jain temples, one of the wonders of ancient India."

Before I could continue, Jenny stopped me in my tracks and said, "Sorry to interrupt you midway but I have to know your opinion on one point. Otherwise I will wonder why I failed to mention it to you.

I believe from the various books I have read that Aryans originally migrated to India in 1500 B.C. from Central Europe, what is now Germany and Austria. What do you think, who is right?"

"Jenny, you are absolutely right to raise this point. I believe there is a misconception, even motivated implantation among Western scholars that Aryans were of European origin who migrated to India, seeking a fresh pasture and better climate."

"In fact, Max Muller, who was the creator of this fascinating theory, had himself rejected it later in life. This should at least sow doubts in your mind, may make you think there may be an alternative explanation"

"Jenny, let me ask you a simple question. Do you believe that Europe was that advanced, a cradle of civilization dating back some ten thousand years?"

"Neal, you are right. The cradle of early civilization was Asia, mainly India and China, although Egypt was an exception, known as the **Land of the Pharaohs**. Most believe that Europe was still in dark ages at the time Lord Rama and Krishna made their mark, ruled hearts and minds of the people of Bharat."

"Jenny, I am glad that we do agree on one point. Yes, The Land of the Pharaohs was and still is a mystery. I believe that most early civilizations started on the banks of the famous rivers that provided rich agricultural land and good weather all year round.

So it is not surprising that the fertile valley of the Nile boast one of the earliest civilizations, in line with Indus and Ganges valleys in India and Yangtze, Hwang Ho valleys in China and Mekong in Cambodia and Vietnam.

Moreover such early civilizations have always left their foot-print, in one way or other. Egypt which had Upper and Lower kingdoms, the upper one below Assiat and Fayum district was the Lower Egypt.

The **Pharaoh Menes** conquered the Northern Kingdom and united Egypt, some 3400 B.C. They left their foot-prints in Pyramids and incredible temples of **Abu Simbel**. Some of these temples were saved from the rising waters of the Aswan dam and relocated on the higher ground.

Similarly India and China have so many such sights. The recent discovery by the American satellite of the remains of Ram Setu or Adam's Bridge between Southern tip of India, the port of Dhanushkodi and the Mannar on the Northern tip of Sri Lanka, in the shallow sea, the Gulf of Mannar has indeed caused a sensation, as heavy foundation stones laid at the bottom of the sea, to hold in place the floating bridge are clearly visible between these two points. This is the most ancient man made structure in the world, perhaps twenty thousand years old.

The excavation of the ancient cities of Harappa and Mohenjo –daro in the Indus valley by British archaeologists are other famous ruins dating back some 3000 B.C. But in reality, it is difficult, indeed impossible to put a date on such ancient monuments. I can go on and on. But Jenny, I have written several papers on ancient Indian civilization which I can email to you if you are interested."

"If I am interested? I would love to read them and perhaps include them in my thesis that is if you are kind enough to give me your permission. Of course, I will give you the full credit."

"Jenny, you are welcome to my writings, my research and every thing else. After all we are going to share every thing, aren't we?"

"I must admit Neal, you know my weakness. You say all the nice things about me, although we hardly know each other. But who is complaining!"

"You know Jenny; this is like a holiday romance. So often we open our hearts and minds to a complete stranger, in the belief that we are not going to see each other again. So it does not matter what we say. It will always remain a secret. We can not have such a talk, such openness with a friend or a relation."

"Jenny, we are being sidetracked. If we talk about ancient civilization, then it has to be a separate topic of conversation. But I presume you would like to concentrate on Hinduism. Am I right?"

Jenny merely nodded her head.

"I presume we were talking about my family and the different Gods we worship. I am an odd one out; as I am a devotee of Lord Krishna, for no other reason than that I love the Hare Krishna temple in Watford.

This place is like a mini Vrindavan, the semi forested place where Lord Krishna spent his childhood, where he used to take the herd for grazing, where he met Radha, his consort.

I feel at home here, the atmosphere is as it should be in a holy place, with children playing in the vast, open ground, cows grazing in the distant. For me this is a heaven on earth. Then I am a simple, humble person with few needs!"

"Well Neal, this is a debateable point, that is you being a simple person with few needs! Simple persons do not travel first class, do they?" Jenny can not resist. She has already put me on the pedestal. I felt like beating my chest like a gorilla! Then again, I am no Tarzan!

"Jenny, we are about to land at the Kennedy Airport. So let's have some rest, respite for us before we continue this very interesting but demanding, brain draining conversation."

"Neal, you are absolutely right. When I am engrossed in an interesting conversation, I am oblivious to time, place and the company. Let us have a good, relaxing break in the VIP lounge. I am sure you will enjoy this break. Now you are in my country. So it is my duty to make you feel at home. How do you say in Hinduism? "

"Atithi Devo Bhave, which means a guest is an honoured, divine person. In the olden days, there were no hotels. So it was important to travel, free movement was dependent in welcoming the guest. That is the greatness of Hinduism. In so many respect Hindus are fiduciary people. We believe helping hands are better than praying lips!"

"Yes Neal, I know this tradition. So many of you still practice this idealism, although it has no meaning, no relevance in this day and age, in this fast changing world. But it does keep families together.

I promise you Neal that I will not ask you a single question until we are back on the plane." Jenny realized the intensity of the topics we had on hand.

Fortunately it was a civil and polite discussion, perhaps matching our own personalities. We were not trying to score cheap points but gain knowledge from each other through civilized means. It is always unwise to discuss politics and religion, especially in such a confined space.

VIP lounge is reserved for first class passengers only who are allowed to rest and recuperate between flights with luxurious facilities to shower, change, shave and have a good meal.

After freshening up, we had a coffee with light breakfast. I was glad Jenny was with me. She was not only a good company but was friendly and affectionate, holding hands and making me feel at home. After all this was her country where she should feel at home, as I would be in England.

She must have realized that I was a bit shy when it came to female company. She took delight in teasing and embarrassing me, holding my hands, walking arm in arm like a couple. While her teasing was more physical, mine was intellectual and some of the words I uttered even surprised me. It was not in line with my character.

"Jenny, if you are going to held me so tight now, then what would happen when we are engaged, even married?"

"Neal, you are naughty but nice. You will have to wait and see how possessive I am. I may not let you out of my sight; that is until we are walking with Zimmer frames?"

"Well Jenny, this is one promise I would like to hold you to. Jenny, you should know that I am a sincere and a delicate person. So please don't make promises, give me hope unless you mean it!" I said it with a serious face and emotional voice.

This took Jenny by surprise. She was lost for words. So I had to put her out of her misery.

"Jenny, I got you. I may look innocent but I can give as much as I get. It seems you are forgetting that I am a journalist. Then looks are deceiving." The smile on my face cheered Jenny up. She knew I had one up on her but she did not mind at all.

"Neal, it would be a pity if we become strangers once we disembark. I would like to see you back in San Francesco; that is if you can find time. I know you are flying all the way to meet your sisters and family members.

"Jenny, I would be delighted to meet you, go on sight seeing tours of this beautiful city and perhaps meet your family as well. That is if you would like me to come to your home. I know you will be very busy during Christmas and New Year holidays."

"Neal, I am never too busy for you. In any case I have a small family. Perhaps you may join us for vegetarian Christmas dinner and if you wish come with us to a midnight mass. Perhaps you may even enjoy it, at least spiritually speaking."

"Why not Jenny! I am sure we can work out some thing. I know that we have just met. But I already feel at home, at ease with you, in your company. After all you said that every man needs a good woman to climb the podium. Perhaps you are my woman, the one who would put me on the pedestal?

"Thank you Neal. You know how to treat a woman, give her importance, boost her ego and this time I mean it." I was glad that Jean was taking me seriously now.

"In Hinduism, we call it destiny. Perhaps we may have known, even related to each other in our previous life, although I would hesitate to say we could be husband and wife!

But to be honest, I do not believe in reincarnation or life after death. This is where I differ with most of my fellow Hindus. I feel human life is unique, precious and one off. It comes to an end when we die"

This was the perfect time to cement our brief but fruitful friendship. I opened my briefcase and took out a copy of my book Ivory Tower. I signed it with the words:

"To my dear Jenny
I hope you have enjoyed my company as much as I have enjoyed yours. Don't be a stranger. Keep in touch.
Kind regards and best wishes for the future"
I signed the book with my full name.

"Jenny, it is my great pleasure to give you a signed copy of my book. When you have read it, I expect your comment on each and every story, as some of the stories have Hinduism and Christianity as background. I am sure you will enjoy reading the book. My card is stuck on the last page, with my email and mobile number."

Then I wrote down on a piece of paper, my sister's home address and her land line telephone number and gave it to Jenny as well. In return, she gave me her card with full details. By the time we had our breakfast and completed the exchange, it was time to board the plane. This was just a short stop-over without any changes in sitting arrangement.

* * *

Chapter Five

Unity Through Diversity

As soon as we sat down, made ourselves comfortable, Jenny urged me to continue from where I had left off. It seemed Jenny was pleased with me for presenting her with a signed copy of my book.

I was pleased that Jenny was so friendly, almost interested in me and was eager to meet me after we disembark, go our own way. It seemed this brief encounter may become some thing more tangible that may change the course of my life.

"Where was I, Jenny?" I have lost the track. I could not remember from where to start.

"Well Neal, you were describing unity through diversity in Hinduism. How your family members worship different deities, different Gods, yet live in perfect harmony, under one roof.

"Yes, I was talking about Hare Krishna Movement, ISKLCON, that my favourite God is Lord Krishna and I love visiting Hare Krishna Temple in Watford, as it is such a beautiful place, a real gem of a picnic spot, Lord Krishna's Vrindavan, one and only outside India."

"Jenny, I wish we had met in London. I could have taken you to this temple, although it would be difficult to appreciate the beauty in the middle of winter when the trees have shed their leaves, lost their beauty.

Watford temple stands on some ninety acres of land and resembles Vrindavan in many aspects. This place was donated to Hare Krishna Movement, *ISKCON* by the Beatle George Harrison when they were devotees of Lord Krishna. In a way Beatles put Hare Krishna Movement on the world stage. ISKCON is the most multicultural movement, religion in the world, having more white followers in the west than Indians.

As for my two sisters, they believe in every God. But naturally Goddess Ambika is their favourite one. In a way we all believe in every Hindu God and go to any temple we prefer.

No Hindu temple is exclusively devoted to one God or Goddess only. They all have murtis or images of Lord Rama, Krishna, Hanuman, Lord Ganesh, Shiva and various Goddesses. This is possible because we, the Hindus are liberal, latitudinarian and peace loving.

You see Jenny that is the reason why we are proud of our religious and cultural heritage. We can live in peace and harmony even if four member of a family worship four different Gods.

This is not possible in Christianity and Islam where Catholics and Protestants and Sunni and Shia could not live in one house, pray in one church or a mosque.

Iran is a one hundred percent Shia nation while Saudi Arabia is a staunch Sunni nation. The trouble in Northern Ireland was due to Catholics and Protestants could not live together. This will never happen in Hinduism.

No one knows how old Hinduism is. But there are so many so called scholars who profess to know how old Hinduism is. Some say it may be ten thousand years old while others put it back to fifty thousand years.

Every one has a valid argument that could be supported by some truths, assumptions and archaeological digs. But in reality it is only a guess work and always will be. Should that matter Jenny?"

Jenny nodded in affirmative smile but she did not put her answer, thoughts into words. Perhaps she did not want to stop me when I was in full flow.

"Hinduism evolved over thousands of years. It was not born within a few decades like Christianity, put on the world map by a single person like Lord Jesus Christ, Prophet Mohamed or Lord Gautam Buddha.

There is a misconception among followers of other faiths that a religion should have one Holy Book, One Prophet and One God and no other deities. This God is supreme and the world, every event, every eventuality should revolve round Him and nothing else is acceptable.

Our minds are so conditioned and rigidly narrowed from childhood, a shallow, a notion that anything else is not acceptable. I feel such a way of thinking should have no relevance in modern day society, in this fast moving, progressive world. But so often liberal religious discussion is a taboo in many faiths, including Hinduism.

It is a *No Go Area* especially when people of different faith congregate together for a meaningful discussion. That is why it is difficult to compare Hinduism with any present day's leading religions whose followers are geared to believe in concept of one God.

All these messengers of God were male and in a way most religions are male oriented. There is nothing wrong in it. Perhaps it reflects the time when these religions spread and acquired their followers.

It was a completely male dominated society then. In Hinduism, we have as many female Gods as male ones. We also have a God for every occasion, happy ones as well as sad occasions. The reason being that Hinduism evolved naturally rather than put on the world map by a single person.

I also feel that being a Hindu allows me to think independently and objectively, without conditioning, without being in a straight jacket. I remain a Hindu by choice, not by force, obligation or sense of duty, loyalty.

Don't get me wrong Jenny. I live in a predominantly Christian country. So I know Christians have as much freedom as Hindus, if not more. But Hinduism differs in one way.

We do not have a controlling body or one person as the head, not even one book as a guide that we have to follow without question. Hinduism is a set of beliefs and practices that have evolved over a very long period of time.

For most Hindus, *God is a divine reality*. We pray to this supreme abstract authority that is the creator of this universe. We do not rigidly believe in heaven and hell but believe that heaven and hell is here on earth.

We get what we deserve, we reap what we sow. Perhaps that may be one of the reasons why we, the Hindus are law abiding to a fault. Some may even say we are cowards, as we have failed to safeguard our homeland, our motherland which has been looted and plundered by so many nations, beginning with Alexander the Great and ending with the British.

I do not want to be side tracked again. So let me go back to topic on hand. Jenny, I am often asked why we do not believe or have one God that would make our life so simple.

Perhaps we Hindus do not believe in having a simple, comfortable life. We have a concept, abstract, not universal God. Hindus believe that the

God is omnipotent, omniscient and omnipresent. But He is kind, caring and forgiving, not out to punish the offender at every turn.

Yes Jenny, I have made God male by addressing him as He. But that is for practical purpose only. I do not want to describe the God as He and She alternatively and confused readers. But I know there is no need to explain this to you, as you are so familiar with our culture and our religion.

Hinduism is one of the most open, liberal, compassionate religions. We do not hide behind God or believe Him sending messengers, demanding us to worship one God or be punished. That does not make sense for me or most Hindus. God is not an autocratic emperor who must be obeyed, respected and worshipped under threat of punishment for the unfaithful.

Jenny, I am not trying to paint Hindu religion as faultless, a superior religion in any way. I am not that narrow minded.

We know we have many faults, perhaps more weaknesses, failings than Christianity and many other newly created religions whose followers are more devoted than us the Hindus. We are littered with superstitions but philosophical side of Hinduism negates all superstitions.

Perhaps Christianity is coming out of these male dominated religious beliefs and appointing females in high places, as Bishops, within the religious establishment.

But I do not believe that we will see a female Archbishop of Canterbury or a female Pope in the Vatican within our lifetime. But it is a certainty that one day we will have a female Archbishop and a Pope, even if it takes few decades, if not more.

It is time for Christianity to put this fiddle-faddle to rest, as Christianity is the most modern religion capable of moving with the time. Christianity has already banished feudalism and fatalism and in so many ways moved with the time.

On the other hand, most religions are stuck in the past. I readily admit we, the Hindus are living in the past, living on the borrowed glory and borrowed time of Lord Rama and Krishna.

Yet there are many saints, holy men and Bhagwan who have contributed to Hinduism. It is a common misconception that the word Bhagwan means God. It is not true. We give the title Bhagwan to any deserving person, like saints. Devo or Devta means God but not in the way most westerners think, believe.

So when we call Lord Rama and Lord Krishna Bhagwan, they are not Gods as such but human beings who have attained the podium seat through sacrifice and good deeds. In a way there is little difference between a Guru and a Bhagwan. In time, even Gandhiji may also become Bhagwan, God!"

"The word **Ishvar** means God, the way most of the world thinks about God. Even in Hinduism there is only one Ishvar that is one God in Western sense.

Let me quote a line from the famous bhagans, the devotional song Gandhiji used to recite all the time,

"Ishvar Allah Tero Nam, Sub ko sanmati de Bhagwan." Which means when loosely translated that we may call you Ishvar or Allah, the supreme God but it makes no difference? We plead you to give us common sense, make us good human beings."

"This was the time when India was united under British rule and religious riots between Hindus and Muslims were common place, especially just before independence. Gandhiji was like a holy saint both sides respected and listened to him.

This is the best I can do Jenny. I hope my answer is not that much different from your understanding?"

"Well Neal, I must admit your answer is interesting and make sense and not that much different from my way of thinking about Hinduism. But to be honest, I must admit I have learnt a lot from your answers. What I like most is the way you mix Christianity with Hinduism, as you have good knowledge of both the religions.

What I admire is your honesty. You are not trying to portray Hinduism as superior to any other religion, except in rich cultural heritage which I readily admit.

You also readily admit Hinduism has many shortfalls, caste system but what I admire is that different Gods do not divide Hindus. On the contrary, they unite you, *unity through diversity*, as you so rightly said.

Perhaps we all can learn from this unique concept of unity through diversity. If there was as much love between Catholics and Protestants as there is between the followers of Lord Rama and Krishna, then it will change the face of Christianity. After all diversity in any field is the spice of life. So why religion should be an exception! But Neal, this is just the beginning. So don't let your guards down."

As usual Jenny answered, made her comments with a smile on her face and playing with her long, silky golden hair that gave her face an uplift and beauty, at least for me.

Perhaps she knew it and making it sure that my attention is concentrated on her, on her face and no where else! As Narad Muni said, "A woman's mind is deeper than the deepest well and more fascinating than Mahabharat, the most complicated but rewarding holy book in Hinduism.

* * *

Chapter Six
The Holy Books of Hinduism

My second question is, *"I know you have several Holy Books. But which book you consider the main one, the one that laid the foundation of Hinduism, the one that influences Hindus, make you, the Hindus so successful in the cut throat Western society, our world."*

It seemed Jenny had questions ready for me. Perhaps she was preparing herself all the time for this stimulating discussion. If I was not a journalist, not conditioned to take questions, then perhaps I would have find it difficult to answer Jenny's questions on the spur of the moment.

Then again Jenny was so easy going, so adorable that I would not mind any query, any question from her. She was also intellectually capable of understanding my answers, no matter how evasive, how technical I may be.

But due to my profession, I was mentally prepared for this onslaught. I knew Jenny was an intelligent person with some knowledge of Hinduism.

So it would not be possible to impress Jenny with flamboyant answers without truth or merit. Perhaps it was better to give her an honest answer, to admit my lack of knowledge, even sit on the fence rather than try to fool Jenny with fancy ideas, meaningless notions and complicated words in a double Dutch language which would backfire, haunt me sooner or later.

"As I said Jenny, Hinduism is like an ocean. One can not lay foundation for an ocean, can we?

"Perhaps not Neal but I am sure I will get a good answer none the less." Jenny has by now come to know that I will answer her questions, one way or another, by hook or by crook without being devious in any way.

"Yes Jenny, we do have many Holy Books and thousands of philosophical and sacred scriptures, learned pamphleteers and in addition we have vedas and Upanishades, Puranas and similar holy books. Literature on Hinduism is as vast as universe.

But very few people, even among Hindus know the existence or the importance of these books of wisdom and knowledge, not only on religion but on every aspect of life, science, medicine, economics, weaponry, astrology and astronomy, a few among many subjects covered by these ancient books of wisdom.

Perhaps you may know that India, known as Bharat, was the centre for excellence for studies. There were world renowned universities which cater not only for Hindu students but international study centres, with the same reputation as Oxford and Cambridge and Harvard universities in USA.

Most of us are familiar with three books, The Ramayana, Mahabharata and most of all Bhagavad-Gita, the words of wisdom uttered by Lord Krishna, the ultimate book in wisdom, knowledge and philosophy, unmatched, unrivalled throughout.

Jenny, if you master this wonderful scripture, the Holy Gita, then you will know as much about Hindu dharma as any one of us who may call ourselves enlightened Hindus.

The fact is Hinduism is a religion of the individual, for the individual and by the individual with deep roots in our holy books of Vedas, Upanishades and above all Bhagavad-Gita.

In a way we all can have a personal God, like a personal Guru, teacher, in an individual way according to our temperament, our physical, moral, cultural and emotional need. It is as simple as ABC that is if you truly believe in Hinduism.

In a way Hinduism is a state of mind. Every thing, every notion within bounds is acceptable as there is no single authority or organization to accept or reject it, oppose it on behalf of Hindus, unless the idea, the concept is preposterous, insulting to Hindus.

Even the famous Indian painter, I would rather hesitate to call him an artist, F. M. Hussein who has made it his life crusade to insult Hindus and Hinduism by painting Hindu Gods and Goddesses in the nude, his paintings are no better than phonograph filth, lives in luxury in India. Even most of his fellow Muslims abhor him; keep a distance from him and his art! Could he insult the followers of any other religion in a similar manner with impunity?"

"Jenny, my sole point in mentioning this episode is to stress how lenient, tolerant, law abiding and fair minded Hindus are. That is why we are becoming a target in most extremist nations where politicians feed on the ration of hate and ignorance."

"Neal, I know that very well. That is why I was pleased when you introduced yourself as a Hindu. I have enormous respect for Hindus and Hinduism."

Perhaps I would not have opened up to you if you are not a Hindu. I do have a couple of Hindu friends and I know what a wonderful, family oriented and decent people they are.

Another quality I admire in you Neal is that you are proud to call yourself a Hindu. I am afraid that is not the case with all Hindus. But that situation is being rectified fast, as the world recognizes the quality of Hindu way of life."

"Yes Jenny. I am proud of my Hindu roots, our rich cultural heritage and our divine reality in our scriptures or Smrithis that influence our way of life.

Many of us, even those who believe that they are not religious pray to the supreme abstract authority (Para Brahma) who is the creator of this entire universe.

So in short I would say our book Bhagwat-Gita and our superior cultural heritage is responsible for our success in the cut-throat Western world."

"Neal, I have noticed that Hindus do not want converts, not in the way, in a manner other religions like Islam and Christianity do. I have never come across any one stopping me in the street or knocking on my door and explaining to me the greatness of Hinduism, asking me to convert to Hinduism. Why is that so different from the norm?"

"I see Jenny; you want to master this complicated but rewarding religion in one flight. When you fly next time, let me know in advance so that we can continue this fascinating conversation to the end."

There was a mischievous smile on Jenny's face. I knew she was going to pull my leg, make me feel uncomfortable, that is if she can. But by now Jenny should know that I can give as much as I can get.

"Neal, do you think we need a second flight to continue this absorbing conversation? Why can't we have it in our lounge or even in our bedroom?" Jenny could not help but giggle like a school girl on her first date. Perhaps it was an escapade for her with some one she may consider worthy of it, as she must have realised that I was not an equivocate person.

This easy going girl with a slim, almost a schoolgirl figure and a wicked but nice sense of humour was slowly but surely stealing my heart and she knew it. In a way I was Jenny's prisoner but at leas the prison was of my own choosing. Could it be my over fertile imagination? I was sure it was not only my imagination but it was not a *"One Way Street."* either.

"Well Jenny why wait that long? We can do it on our honeymoon night, that is if and when we are physically exhausted and need a break, can't we?" I thought I had cornered Jenny.

"Well Neal, I don't think we would have much time even to eat, let alone have a serious discussion. I don't think you have any idea what I am going to do to you on our honeymoon night. Have you Neal?"

"Promises, promises, that's all you can give!"

"Neal, don't tempt me. I can be naughty but nice and perhaps too hot to handle for you." Jenny who was resting her hands on mine, grabbed my hand and took it as near to her partly unbuttoned chest as possible, without pressing against her barest. It was the temptation she must have thought I could not resist, especially as it was at her invitation.

It surely raised my blood pressure. I thought it was time to give in before it became too hot to handle for me. After all I was not in the same league as Jenny when it came to having a relationship with the opposite sex. Perhaps I was the unwitting victim of shibboleth of the Western strategy.

"OK, Jenny, you win. I will surrender to your every demand, on the beach, under a bush and in the bed, no matter how exotic, unusual or painful it may be."

"Neal, you know I can never heart you, although the word "hurt" is a contagious issue, like one man's food is another man's poison. But let us continue our discussion. We are being side-tracked so often. But then it gives us a light relief. I like teasing you, as you are so nice, so adorable. You are my *Teddy Bear* I can take to bed every night, keep you between my twin towers!

To be frank Neal, I can never talk to any one so freely, so openly with any of my male friends, although we the girls have ten times more sexy discussions when we have few drinks and are in such a mood."

"Jenny, this is a big Teddy Bear. You will have to build up your twin towers if you want to prison the bear in your towers!"

"Oh Neal, how am I going to deal with you! You are impossible. Then I love a challenge. I will grant your wish in six months time."

There was a long pause and we had a drink, a glass of white wine before we resumed our discussion.

"Jenny, We, the Hindus believe and in my opinion some what erroneously that we are born Hindus, that no one can convert into Hinduism, as it is a way of life acquired from childhood.

One may either have it or not. But Hare Krishna Movement has changed all that. This was a narrow minded, defeatist attitude that has cost Hinduism dearly.

Now ISKCON and most Hindu organizations openly seek converts, especially those Hindus who have been lured away from our Sanatan Dharma, either by force or bribe. In the old time, we used to drive away such people who were forced to convert at gun point.

They were barred from resuming their Hindu rituals and that short sightlessness has cost us, the Hinduism dearly. I am glad to say that in the West we attract converts from the upper, higher and middle class people.

Most of them are professional people, doctors, scientists, lawyers, accountants and their kind of well educated people who choose to come into our fold without pressure from any one, any kind. These people are the gem, the real Hindus who will keep our tradition going well after we are gone."

"I can tell you Jenny that if you are looking for a salvation or a meaningful life, then there is no need to move from one religion to another, unless you are unhappy at certain aspect of your chosen religion.

I do not believe in going from one cult to another, from one Guru to another, jumping like a monkey from one branch to another. Rolling stone gather no moss. Deep roots are the best form of insurance not to be blown away in a storm.

The salvation of the soul is within you, within us, if we can discover it. I find peace, inner happiness and joy at Hare Krishna temple. So I visit it as often as I can. I believe the Bible itself gives guidelines when it states ***"Kingdom of God is within you."*** How true these words of wisdom are today, as they were in the ancient time and always will be.

I am sure you are well aware of Jesus Christ's teachings about love we have in our heart for our fellow human beings. That is where one can find the true meaning of life and salvation. That is why I say that there is similarity between Hinduism and Christianity, that most recent religions have their roots in Hinduism.

It is a pity that not only most followers but even learned historians and academics are not willing to admit that there is any connection between Hinduism and their religions.

The proof is in front of us, as most Christian books, sculptures are full of passages taken directly from holy Hindu books of Ramayana, Mahabharata and Vedas.

Well Jenny, it is human nature not to give in, especially when it comes to religion. I am so glad that we are able to discuss the most contagious subject with civility and understanding.

You may be young Jenny but you have a cool, calm and mature head over your young shoulders. I feel I can talk to you freely and without inhibition." Neal's voice was sincere.

* * *

Chapter Seven

India, Cradle of Early Civilization

Jenny, if you do not mind, I would like to deviate from the religion and explore the ancient history of India, albeit in brief so that you have as much understanding of Hinduism as any Westerner.

The word Hinduism is derived from the word Hindu, a mispronunciation of the word Sindhu, river Indus of present day India, now in Pakistan, a stolen land from the ancient people of Bharat.

All aspects of life practiced in and around Sindhu valley were termed as Hindu way of life. But these days the word Hindu is equated with religion and spiritual aspects.

Therefore the word Hindu is more geographic than religious. It denotes the area between the old rivers Saraswati, Indus extending up to central Afghanistan, as mentioned in Mahabharat. The whole area, a huge landmass was known as Saptsindhu, the land of seven rivers.

These rivers washed fertile silt from the Himalaya mountain range to the planes of these rivers, making it the most arable, cultivable land, producing rich and varied crops, more comfortable and regular source of food than hunting in forests.

Leisure created by easy life gave rise to sages, in the land of plenty, who had ample leisure time to reflect, study art, science, astrology, religion, medicine, yoga and every subject known to mankind.

The religion that evolved from the planes and valleys of Saptsindhu and spread throughout Central and South East Asia was named as Sanatan Dharma, more a way of life than any dogma.

510

The Sanatan Dharma derives its authority from comprehensive but detailed compendium named as Vedas, the word simply means knowledge. The four Vedas are: ***Rig Veda, Sam Veda, Yajur Veda and Atharva Veda***. These Vedas laid the foundation of Sanatan Dharma, popularly known as Hindu Dharma.

These are cornucopia of data about macro-cosmos, planets and galaxies. It mentions about matter, both physical, metaphysical and energy. Vedas lay down ways and means, rites and rituals to master and manipulate these for wellbeing of all, manifest and un-manifest matter.

Now that I have laid the foundation of Hindu religion, I would like to tell you about the famous universities Bharat had some 3000 B.C. which were the cradle of education, civilization, not only for Indian students but an international study centre as well.

Students from all over the ancient world were flocking to these universities to study science, earthsastra or economics, archery or use of weapons in wars, ayurveda or medicine, yoga, that is discipline of mind and body, astrology, sociology, even space travel and many more subjects that may astonish even today's most accomplished scholars.

The early life of Jesus is shrouded in mystery. His teenage years to early adulthood are missing, a blank period. Some historians believe that Jesus spend this time studying humanity, religion and faith healing at the famous Takshashila university in India.

This may just be a theory without relevance but it is worth considering for your PhD thesis. Perhaps this may give you an edge over other students if you put it in such a way that no one is offended, as you know religion is a touchy subject. I believe we have to learn from each other, from religions other than what we practise"

"Thank you Neal. I would indeed explore this possibility and would have a lengthy discussion with my professor, as he is liberal, not easily offended, even if we may not agree on some aspect of Christianity."

"According to ancient Hindu literature, the city of Takshashila was named after Taksha, son of king Bharat after whom the country was called Bharat, the present day India. The University of ***TAKSHASHILA*** is a byword in ancient history of Bharat, a place of learning unmatched in the history of the world.

I know that I am once again drifting from the topic on hand. But I am sure you will appreciate this piece of conversation. It is important to know what Hinduism has contributed to our every day life.

Takshashila was the capital city of Gandhar, the present day Afghanistan, a country that was in the forefront, an articulate, peaceful and prosperous nation. I could not help but wonder, compare today's war-torn, backward country with its past glory. What changed this once great nation? Could it be religion, conquest or subjugation!

The impressive ruins of another place of learning, *"Nalanda* University" a short distance from the city of Patna, a one time capital of the vast empire build by warrior king Chandragupta and his grandson Ashok, the greatest, noblest king in the entire history of Bharat. This university was also part of Buddhist teaching, culture, as well as Hinduism.

Another excellent centre of learning was the University of *VALABHI,* in present day Gujarat, near the Bay of Cambay with capital city of Valabhi.

The famous ancient city, Lord Krishna's Dwarka also stood on the Gulf of Cambay, now under water. The ruins of this city have recently been discovered on the sea-bed, in the Gulf of Cambay.*

Other famous universities of ancient India were *VIKRAMSHILA* in present day Bihar, under the reign of Pala kings. The ancient *BANARAS* University was situated on the banks of river Ganga, the present day city of Kashi.

There are at least five more famous universities that were the centre of excellence as far as education is concerned in the ancient, holy land of Barratversh. Most of the records were destroyed, along with buildings, temples when Mogul invaded Bharat and ruled it for some four hundred years, with iron fist. This was the most destructive period in the history of the world.

In many ways, universities are the Bastian of civilization where science, arts, commerce and architect thrive. These places of learning need teachers, scientists and professors. The ancient India had such talent in abundance. In fact it was an ocean of knowledge, an oasis in the desert.

I must mention a few, famous names and their achievement in order to understand the immense contribution they made, in our present day progress.

Acharya Aryabhatt, (476BCE) Acharya means teacher, guru, professor and researcher. He was a master astronomer and mathematician. He was born in Bihar. In 499 BCE, at the tender age of just 23, he compiled a text, wrote thesis on astronomy and papers on mathematics titled *"Aryabhatiyam."* He was the first human being to announce that

Earth is round; that it rotates on its axis and orbits the Sun. The earth is suspended, a free standing planet in the outer space.

His most valuable, even spectacular contribution was the concept of Zero, the basis of modern day mathematics. Without zero, modern computers would not have been invented.

Acharya Kanad (600BCE) He was born in Gujarat, near the city of Dwarka, the city founded by Lord Krishna.

Kanad is the father, founder of ***atomic theory*** known as ***"Vaisheshik Darshan"*** one of six principal philosophies of India. He was the pioneer expounder of realism, law of causation and the atomic theory, some 2500 years ahead of the present day exponents.

Acharya Sushrut (600 BCE) Born to ***Sage Vishwamitra*** of Ramayana fame, Acharya Sushrut wrote a unique encyclopaedia of surgery. He is considered to be the father of plastic surgery.

He developed skin-graph and facial plastic surgery so much in demand by the Hollywood and Bollywood stars of today, to keep them young and good looking for eternity.

Acharya Patanjali (200 BCE) He was born in Gonda, in Utter Pradesh. No wonder ***Guru Ramdevji,*** the present day saint and noble son of Bharat considers Acharya Patanjali, the father of Yoga, as his Guru, his aspirant and the driving force behind his success. No wonder Ramdevji has named his vast, famous Ashram, the Yoga Centre as after Acharya Patanjali.

He developed some 86 yogic postures which enhances the efficiency of respiratory, circulatory, nerves, digestive and endocrine system. He will always be remembered as a pioneer of the science of self-discipline, happiness and the goal of self-realization, a modern day psychologist.

Bharat was rich, blessed with such noble Acharyas, Gurus, professors, teachers, scientists and inventers who made Bharat such an advance nation thousands of years before Europe came out of the Dark Age.

Acharya Bharadwaj was the pioneer of aviation technology, ***Acharya Kapil*** was the father of cosmology, ***Bhaskaracharya II*** who was genius in Algebra, ***Nagarjuna*** was a top order chemical scientist, inventor of the faculties of chemistry and metallurgy, ***Acharya Charak*** was the father of medicine. His work, ***"Charak Samita"*** is considered the encyclopaedia of Ayurveda. ***Varahmihir*** was an eminent astrologer and astronomer. All these great sons of Bharat were born between 200BC to 3000 BC.

So Jenny, Barratversh was a great nation, perhaps as advance as we are today, if not more. How and why this civilization was destroyed is a mystery and will always remain so.

Jenny, I believe in many ways religion is a curse on humanity. It is responsible for so many wars, deaths and destruction. But in a way it is not religion but their followers, our fellow human beings who are responsible for this mindless thuggery.

They use religion as an excuse. If it was not religion, then it would have been some other excuse. Helen of Troy and Cleopatra, the queen of Egypt are also responsible for many wars.

It is said that the beauty of Helen is responsible for the launch of a thousand ships. A war has no cause, only an excuse.

The destruction of Lord Buddha's giant statues in Afghanistan by Taliban is the prime example of human intolerance for any thing that do not fall within their narrow define of culture, religion or way of life.

Religion is like having a life partner, a husband or a wife. We can't live with them or live without them.

Seeing me getting serious, Jenny intervened, "Neal I assure you that we will not have such a problem. I just can't live without you, full stop!" There was a smile on Jenny's face.

"Jenny, I was carried away from our main topic of discussion. But all these subjects are so interrelated that it is impossible to keep them out. It would creep in from time to time, no matter how hard we may try to keep it out.

"Neal, I really enjoyed the information you parted with about Barratversh being the cradle of civilization, with so many world renowned universities and so many scientists, inventors and professors. I am sure one day this mystery will be solved. Perhaps it may not happen during our life-time, not even in two hundred years. But ultimately it will, when space, inter-planetary travel become a reality"

"I was surprised why Jenny was so confident. Has she read some books that I may have not? Today internet is the source of knowledge. It is easy to access, knowledge on our finger tips.

"Neal, my next question is simple. But please do not side-track on this question, as it is a vast, infinitive subject without boundary"

"Please tell me about Hinduism in general, as if you are talking to some one who has no knowledge about this fascinating religion"

"Jenny, at last I will be at ease, as I can talk what I want, what I feel and not obliged to project any aspect of Hinduism. But you are right. It will be so easy to be side-tracked. So I promise you that I will keep myself on a narrow path.

Hinduism is referred by scholars, by learned people and most saints as Sanatan Dharma, the eternal faith which has laid down the conduct, the code of life, a lose principle Hindus should follow.

Hinduism expects its followers to be honest, truthful to oneself. We believe, Hindus have no monopoly on idealism, good governance, education or creating, accumulating wealth.

It is open to all, should be within the graph of every human being who is willing to work hard, earn one's keep, abide by the law of the land and be loyal to the country where one resides, earn one's keep and where his children are educated.

For Hindus, the religion and the land of our forefathers come second to the loyalty of the land where we live. In my case it is **Great Britain**.

As I have already mentioned before, we believe in one God. We call Him Ishvar who is expressed in different forms, as per one's imagination, thinking. God has no form. He is omnipresent, he is timeless and formless.

The Shivelinga, a rounded stone so often present in Lord Shiva's temple is the symbol of formless Ishvar, the eternal truth and cosmic laws. These idealism, knowledge and way of life is open to any one who may like to seek peace, fulfilment and Mox, the ultimate liberation of soul, escape from the routine of birth and death, as most Hindus believe in reincarnation.

So often believers treat their religion as a commodity, big business and try to expand, increase their share by conversion, so often by force and deceit.

Hinduism, Sikhism and Judaism are notable exceptions. But the fastest expanding business in today's materialistic world is spirituality and I am afraid Hinduism is no exception, although Hinduism uses softer approach, less aggressive means compared to other religions.

I also feel that Hinduism is one of the few, if not the only major religion that promotes vegetarianism, non-violence through *"Ahimsa Paramo Dharma"* which means non-violence is the duty, obligation of every Hindu.

I am afraid this notion favoured by Gandhiji is fast becoming obsolete in this fast changing violent world. Today's slogan is just the opposite, *"Ahimsa Kayar No Dharma.* Non violence is the religion of the cowards. They feel it is the duty of every Hindu to protest themselves when under attack, as in Kashmir, Pakistan, Afghanistan and many more countries where non Muslims, even Muslims who may not belong to the majority are not tolerated.

I have many loyal, decent Muslim friends who come from Daudi Bhora, Ismaili, Ahmedia, Shia Ithna-Asheri and Kokni Muslims whose lifestyle is very similar to ours. Like Hindus, they believe in educating their children to the highest standard. They are as law abiding, hard working, career minded as any Hindu. So it would be wrong to put all Muslims in one basket.

I have talked about Ishvar, the one and only God for Hindus. But it is not that simple. As I have said before, Hinduism is one of the most complex yet culturally rich, a scholarly religion with millions of words written in our holy books that can not be surpassed singularly or united by any other religion.

Ishvar has created three Gods who do His job. In a way Ishvar is the boss who has delegated his work to Brahma, the Creator, Vishnu, the Administrator and Mahesh, the destroyer.

In a way, it makes sense. We do not expect our doctor, the GP to look after our teeth, operate on us, as well as dispatch the medication. We have dentists, pharmacists and surgeons to operate on us.

Even the surgeon specialises in one section of the body, the heart, kidney, liver, brain and so on, so that he is expert in his field. After all it is not possible for one person to know every thing. So is in the kingdom of God.

This theory, the principal is divided and subdivided again and again so that we have a God for every occasion, even an individual has a personal God, just like a personal trainer.

I would not like to go too deep, as it is a complex subject. I believe every Hindu has some reason to be a Hindu. No religion is perfect but there is some good in every religion. It is up to us how to interpret, differentiate between good and the evil and use the religion for our advancement rather than letting it hold us back.

One can absorb what one may need from Hinduism and use it to better his life, his family, his country and ultimately the world. It is not necessary to understand, adopt or believe in every principle, every word written in Hinduism. Then no one can digest some one hundred words.

Every question has an answer and every argument has a counter argument, every point can be proved and disproved by an intellectual. Like in half empty bottle, both are right, the one who says it is half empty and the other who may say it is half full. Hinduism is that liberal, that accommodating, a great ocean of knowledge and satisfaction."

"I hope Jenny; my answer may mean some thing. It is now up to you how to interpret Hinduism. It is practically impossible to explain the intricacies, the integrities of such a vast ocean of knowledge. To understand Hinduism in its entirety is more difficult than to find a needle in a haystack.

* * *

Chapter Eight
The Ultimate Book of Knowledge

"**Well** Jenny, are there any more questions you would like to ask me? You know we are coming to the end of our journey and to be honest, I feel my brain is empty." I was hopping this would be the end of our stimulating but exhausting discussion.

"I know Neal that I have taken up so much of your time. But I hope you have enjoyed our stimulating discussion, my company as much as I have enjoyed yours. In just one flight, albeit lasting some fifteen hours, I have learnt more about you and about Hinduism than I could ever learn by reading books. You are even better than my professor."

"Jenny, flattery would get you every thing, take you every where. But remember even Lord did not made this universe in one day. He has designated Sunday as a day of rest.

I know we have just scratched the surface, talked about Hinduism in general term, not gone into any Holy Books of Hinduism which would be impossible in such a short time. But if you are not too tired, I would like to know more about Bhagwat Gita, the book that dominates the Hindu religion."

"Jenny, in order to talk about Bhagavad-Gita and Lord Krishna, I have to talk about the great book of Mahabharat which incorporates our *holiest book "Bhagavad-Gita."* The book is simple, yet complicated which can be interrupted in many ways, as most holy books can.

It was some ten thousand years ago that Lord Krishna spoke these words of wisdom, to his loyal devotee Arjun. Each word is a gem of ultimate wisdom.

The mischief makers, the small minded people can even use it against Hinduism. But on most part, every one who reads it or rather studies it, is impressed and appreciates such a book of wisdom that is beyond reproach.

The story of Mahabharat is the struggle between the good and the evil, the rivalry between the noble Pandavas, five brothers, sons of Queen Kunti. The eldest brother was Youthister, a noble, caring king but some what naïve and too trusty who was manipulated by the evil Duryodhan, to the annoyance of his four brothers.

The second brother was Bhim, a huge figure, built like a wrestler and expert in the use of Gada, a heavy weapon with a big, round, solid ball attached to a long handle. It was also the favourite weapon of evil Duryodhan.

Bhim was the reincarnation of Lord Hanuman, the Ape like devotee of Lord Rama who was also expert in the use of Gada, the most effective weapon in close combat fight. Many believe that Bhim was the reincarnation of Lord Hanuman.

The third brother was Arjun, the intelligent, charming and sophisticated warrior expert in archery. He was also married to Lord Krishna's sister Rukhmani. Arjun was a disciple of Lord Krishna and the most accomplished, respected among five brothers.

The two youngest brothers were Sahadev and Nakul who are some what silent characters, not in the limelight in Mahabharata.

On the other hand, Kuravas, one hundred brothers, were the sons of King Dhrustrastra and Queen Gandhari. The king was blind and the queen, in order to understand her husband, King's handicap, covered her eyes and willingly accepted permanent blindness.

Duryodhan, the eldest son, the Youvraj, the heir to the throne and most evil son of Dhrustrastra was in charge of his vast kingdom, for all practical purposes, besides being Commander in Chief of King's vast army.

The rivalry between Pandavas and Kuravas was so intense that ultimately it came to a war when Pandavas lost their small kingdom in an illegal game of Chess, were made homeless and banished to the forest for twelve years.

Even after completing their exile, Duryodhan refused to give Pandavas a single village, forcing them to declare war on the King and his evil son. This was a tragedy of Hercules proportion and as usual, the king turned a blind eye, refused to stop his evil son from the impending disaster.

The other elders pleaded with Duryodhan but to no avail. He was drunk with power, knowing that with Acharya Dronacharya, Karna and Lord Bhishma Pita, the unbeatable warriors on his side, leading his army and Lord Krishna would not fight, he would only agreed to drive Arjun's chariot, victory was assured.

Jenny, Mahabharata is a complicated book of over five million words, from beginning to the end. So I have to be brief, just touch the surface and concentrate on Gita, which contains one of the greatest, most sophisticated and philosophical dialogue known to men-kind.

When the two armies were facing each other on the battlefield of Kuruksetra, Arjun, who was suppose to fire the first shot, release the first arrow, refused to do so when he saw his Guru Dronacharya, in his horse drawn carriage, standing only a few hundred feet away on the opposite side.

Guru Dronacharya had taught him all he knew about use of weapons, made him an ace in archery that no man could compete with him except his Guru.

Arjun also saw his elder brother Lord Karna, who was the illegitimate son of Queen Kunti, born before she was married, described as a virgin birth and one of the noblest characters, along with Bhishma Pita, the oldest man on earth, a grandfather like figure for five brothers.

There were so many friends and close relations in the opposite camp that Arjun's heart was in turmoil. How could he kill all these noble people and enjoy his triumph, his victory. Was a piece of land worth so much bloodshed?

Arjun also knew that most of these noble warriors were fighting for Duryodhan out of loyalty, being on his payroll or being bullied by the might of this evil Prince.

Even though Duryodhan's army outnumbered Pandavas' army by five to one, the victory was more or less assured, as none of these great warriors like Lord Karna, Guru Dronacharya and Bhisma Pita would kill any of the five brothers. But there were many petty kings and rouge princes who would readily kill Arjun and be famous, be darling of Duryodhan.

But most noble and respected elder statesmen would willingly sacrifice their own life and let the truth, honesty and human values triumph over evil, selfish and manipulating Prince Duryodhan.

Jenny, I do not know whether you have a copy of Bhagavad-Gita by ***His Devine A. C. Bhaktivedanta Swami Prabhupada.*** If you have, please read it. I have a copy in my luggage that I can give to you when we meet again. It is a masterpiece, uses articulate language to match the true spirit that this gem of a book conveys to the readers.

Whatever I tell you is based more or less on this book, as I have read it word by word. This book is my Holy Bible which I keep at my bedside and read it as often as I can. To be truthful, it is not that often, as we all lead a busy life.

Swami Prabhupada has written many books and each one is a jewel, masterpiece in its own right. But unfortunately only a tiny minority, very devoted followers would read all these books, although I know Bhagavad-Gita is the third most wisely read book, after Holy Bible and Holy Koran. ISKCON runs classes on Gita which are well attended.

This Holy Book is divided into **eighteen chapters**. The **chapter one** of the Bhagavad-Gita describes the battle scene, the observation and the composition of the opposing armies, how Arjun is struck by grief, his heart in turmoil, bleeding from inside.

If Arjun refuse to fight, then the evil would triumph over good governance, the country will be ruled by one of the most evil kings who would enslave and rob his people.

The Ram Rajya that Lord Rama built and sustained by his sons and grandsons may revert into the kingdom of demon king Ravan that Lord Rama slain after building the Adam's bridge to cross over to the island of Lanka.

The **second chapter** deals with how Arjun submits to Lord Krishna. In order to convenience Arjun that it is his duty to fight, that he owed it to his subjects to liberate them from the clutches of the evil dynasty, he recited Gita, the book that contains Lord Krishna's words of wisdom that convinced even Arjun to fight and if necessary, to kill his dearest and nearest ones, even if they would not fight back, try to kill him or his brothers.

It deals in detail the difference between the body, a temporary materialistic structure that is disposable and the soul, the eternal spirit that is ever lasting, that no one, no weapon could destroy.

Lord Krishna also explains the process of transmigration; the eternal journey and that we are but transit passengers on this earth. Some learned people, disciples, scientists and astrologers even believe that science and technology was so advanced that even inter planetary travel was not out of question.

After the devastation of the war, an all out nuclear disaster, it is believed that the five Pandavas who lost all of their children travelled to another planet, to escape the radiation fallout. Before they left, they fired the ultimate weapon, the rain bomb that brought continuous rain and cleaned the air over a long period.

I am sorry Jenny, I am not trying to confuse you but merely state the beliefs, even facts how advance the civilization was and what this war did to mankind, how devastating it was for the world.

No wonder some, indeed many believe that the Battle of Kuruksetra took place, not ten thousand years ago but indeed some fifty thousand years back. It took the world all these years to come out of the nuclear holocaust.

Other chapters deal with Karma-yoga which means every action has a reaction and how to liberate the soul and attain Mox with the transcendental knowledge of one self. It is a spiritual knowledge of the soul and the close relationship between an enlightened devotee with God which purifies and liberates body and soul.

Bhakti-yoga is most selfless and expedient way to be the disciple of Lord Krishna, attain pure love and live a spiritual, happy and contended life, without being materialistic or selfish.

The most important chapter of Bhagavad-Gita is chapter eighteen, the final chapter. Many devotees can recite the whole chapter, which is in verse, by heart.

In fact the Bhagavad-Gita comes to an end in the chapter seventeen. The final chapter is the summarization of every point, every doubt raised by Arjun and Lord Krishna's reply, his teaching and clarification.

Lord Krishna explains the meaning of true renunciation, the words in Gita is the ultimate conclusion and the religion is absolute without having doubt, if and when.

If you seek complete enlightenment, liberation and freeing of soul that leads to the heaven, to Lord Krishna's eternal, spiritual and ultimate abode, then Bhagavad-Gita is book one should read, digest and take to heart. There is no substitute, at least not for me."

* * *

Chapter Nine

The Happy Landing, Happy Ending

*"**Neal,** sorry to interrupt you but soon we will be landing at the San Francisco airport. So let us recuperate, refresh and be ready, be prepared to land. I am sure you must be exhausted and I am indeed sorry to put you through such an ordeal. But Neal, I will make it worthwhile, sooner or later, depending upon you."*

The audit of promissory note sound attractive, especially when it comes from such a charming girl.

As usual, Jenny was right. We needed some time to wind-down; freshen up, as it might take a while to clear the customs, especially for me, as Jenny being an American passport holder and a white girl, will pass the custom without much scrutinizing.

It would be a different kettle of fish for me. But being a journalist and having been to the States many times before, it should not take too long, as their computer records are so up-to-date.

Jenny, to her credit, decided to stick to me and her presence, her company indeed helped me to pass the custom at the same time as Jenny, although we had to use different exits.

When we met on the other side, a long walk before the final exist, some what isolated, as every one was in a hurry to leave, Jenny stopped me and said, "Neal, I would like to thank you for your wonderful company and stimulating conversation. How can I thank you?"

"Jenny, it was my pleasure. There is no need to thank me. In any case, this is not a final goodbye, is it?" I was a bit worried, in case Jenny may say a final goodbye here and now.

"Neal, this is far from a final goodbye. Do not under estimate yourself. But I can not let you go without showing my appreciation."

Jenny who was holding on to me and dragging her bag at the same time, suddenly stopped, grabbed me and before I can react, took me in her arms and gave me a long and lingering kiss that for me at least, lasted a long time. She would not disengage; let me go until we were both out of breath.

"Well Neal, this is my gift, first of many I hope. I know you have fallen for me hook, line and sinker. Believe me, it is not one sided. If you love me, then I am sure your love will be reciprocated. Just tell me the truth. Would you like to see me again, take this further?"

"Thank you so much Jenny. You are right. I have fallen in love with you, although it may sound strange, as we have known each other for only few hours. But I know that this in not a mere sexual attraction for a very beautiful girl."

"Jenny, I would call it love at first sight, a destiny. Perhaps Lord Krishna has found his Radha. My prayers have been answered. We have so much in common and yes, I would like to take it further, to its ultimate goal. Let's see each other as much as we can. I am here for three weeks. So we have plenty of time."

If Jenny had given me such a kiss outside, in view of the waiting relatives, it would have been difficult for me to explain it to my sister. In any case when I met my sister Priti, Jenny was still with me, holding my hand. But it was a pleasure to introduce her to my sister. It seemed Priti was pleased to meet her, taken to her straight away.

When we were comfortably seated in the car driven by my brother in law, Priti could not help but ask me a straight question.

"Bhaiya, Jenny seems a nice girl. You would make a perfect couple, at least physically. How well you know her?"

"I know sis what you are hinting at. Yes I like her but we have just met on the plane. She is American and lives here in San Francisco. We had a wonderful time on the plane and had a discussion on religion, namely Hinduism. She is reading Christianity for her PhD."

"Bhaiya, please don't get me wrong. But I feel, I know she loves you, in her own strange way. But the question is how much you love her!"

"Well Sis, Jenny has invited me to go to her home for Christmas dinner and meet her family. Her brother is a famous heart surgeon, so perhaps you may even know him.

But you have to admit these are early days. I have to wait and see which way the wind would blow. It is too early to start building castles in the air. But you know the saying that no girl is perfect until you fell in love with her.

Jenny personifies idealism that is dear to us, our family and our Hindu tradition. It seems our friendship, however brief is holistic, an integrated set of ageless principles based on our religious books of wisdom Vedas.

I had to dampen my sister's enthusiasm before it goes out of control yet keep her guessing. But sisters are sisters; we can not limit or chain their eagerness, happiness or over imagination in any way. Why should we?

"Yes Neal, in our world, we know most top people. I am happy that you met Jenny.

At least you will not feel lonely when we are at work. Perhaps you may even come to visit me more often. Won't you?" Priti was over the moon, perhaps reading more than even I could imagine. Then all sisters are the same when it comes to their brother's happiness.

The next day, even before I was out of my bed, I received a text message from Jenny. "Hi darling, did you sleep well. Give me a ring when you are out and about. Love, Jenny."

Due to time difference, I had a long stay in bed, some fifteen hours. When I got up, Priti had gone to work. So I had a leisurely breakfast with my parents who were glad to see me.

By the time I had a shave and a shower and was able to go out to get a newspaper, Jenny had a long wait. She was pleased to receive a call from me.

"Hi Jenny, sorry to keep you waiting for so long. I am not a good traveller, even as a first class passenger. I need a long stay in bed before I shake off the jet leg, be myself."

"Neal, I really miss you. I have told my mum all about you. She is eager and looking forward to meet you, as she has so much faith in my judgement. We are more like two friends rather than a mother and a daughter. I am indeed very lucky to have such a supportive family. But I know it would not be possible for you to meet me for a couple of days.

Neal, I was looking in the map and you are only half an hour away from us by car. In America, you are practically our next door neighbour. So I can drive to the nearest Moll and pick you up as well. So let me know when you have recovered and ready to go."

"Jenny, what about day after tomorrow? I would like to meet you before the weekend when I may become busy."

"It would be fine. Give me a ring tomorrow in the evening. I am going to the Uni to collect some papers and see my professor."

Our conversation lasted some half an hour. Jenny was sweet and as charming as ever. Deep in my heart I knew this is the beginning of a new life, ever lasting friendship for me.

I was determined to embrace every moment of my time in the exotic, stimulating and charming company of this angel of a girl Jenny, a God send gift without fancy packaging?

Our every minute together was intellectually stimulating, spent on contemplation on the loftier issues, mystical life in our rosy family garden, watching sunrise or the stars dancing in the moonlight sky, way above any thing else.

On looking at the map of the city, I realised Jenny was right. We were very close. My sister had her two storey impressive town house on the outskirt of San Francisco, in ***the Dale City***, a parsley populated place with beautiful rolling hills of San Bruno in the neighbourhood and Bayshore Ferry Terminal not too far away.

Jenny, who was living with her family, had a beautiful bungalow in the ***Sterling Park***, ***Westlake area,*** not too far away from the majestic Pacific Ocean and the San Francisco State University.

On Friday at lunch time, Jenny picked me up from outside the house, as I felt it was too early to introduce Jenny to my parents. There were not many places where we can spend time, especially in December, in the middle of winter.

However there was a small Shopping Moll with some thirty shops and in the centre there was a Food Court where Chinese, Mexican, Italian and American food was the prime attraction. It was Jenny's favourite place, being in her locality, near her home but in between or equidistance from our two residences.

Being vegetarians, there was not much choice except pastas, salad, omelette and various types of sandwiches. Unlike London, where vegetarian restaurants are plentiful, America is lagging behind, as most Americans are meat eaters and love their big steaks and half pound burgers.

But chips and milk shakes, cakes and croissant with coffee served us fine when we could not have any thing else. But when we had each other, nothing else matter. Jenny was my appetite, my food!

My three weeks passed so fast. I enjoyed Christmas dinner and the Midnight Mass at Jenny's local church. Meeting her family, her parents and her brother and his family was a joy.

As it happened, Richard, Jenny's heart surgeon brother knew my sister Priti well, as they so often met at special dinner parties organized by the Food and Drug industries. As they say, in America there is no entertainment, parties like the ones arranged and paid for by the representatives of the drug industries!

When I introduced Jenny to my family members, my parents, sisters and their families, they felt Jenny was already a close friend, a member of our family. They were pleased with my choice, as Jenny was almost a Hindu, all but in name, not that it mattered.

By the time I left for London, I had been to Jenny's home, even to her brother's home many times. I used to meet Jenny practically every other day. If we can not find a lonely, deserted place, then we will just sit in her car and talk and cuddle.

"Neal, I know how much you love to kiss me. You have even placed your hands on my breast so often. But you always shy away at the last moment, as you are such a gentleman. There is no need. I want you as much as you want me. So do not be shy, don't keep me away in any way."

Even before Jenny could complete her sentence, I grabbed her and gave her a kiss while unbuttoning her blouse. Even I was surprised at my boldness. Then it was my heart, not the mind that was controlling my feelings, my desire and my actions.

This time there was no holding back. The crampness of Jenny's car, a convertible sports model with little space, even in the back seat, brought us together like two adults sleeping in a narrow single bed when climbing over each other becomes a necessity rather than a luxury!

Jenny indeed had such tiny breasts that she could get away without wearing a bra, unless when she was wearing an almost sea through top, with so often colourful bra, black or red, but always broad ones that would cover most of her chest.

In any case her top was never than transparent. After all Jenny's father was a part time priest and Jenny was a regular church-goer. She was a conservative girl, a convent girl immersed in the Oasis of enlightenment and rich family tradition.

To my surprise or perhaps not, Jenny loved it even more when I played with her limited assets.

So often she would drag and press my face against her breasts, not letting me disengage until I really suck, bite her nipples to the brink of her pain threshold.

It was a cohesion as well as coherent. After all Jenny was a logical person. Why should she do not enjoy such a close sexual encounter when she is in the company of a person she admire and adore so much?

"Neal, I must admit that I am still a virgin at my age when 90% of the American girls lose their virginity by the time they are eighteen. Perhaps not even one in thousand girls may be a virgin on her honeymoon night.

But I am proud of my virginity. It was my choice, not the lack of suitable candidates. I feel, perhaps erroneously that a girl's creditability decreases as she becomes loose cannon ball on the sexual front. In my book modesty is a virtue and self control a sign of maturity. I would not like to remain a **Milky Bar Kid** all my life?

I would like you to be one and only man to have me, on our honeymoon night, a virgin bride. You have the privilege to shape our relationship, on moral, ethical, professional and sexual front. As you implied, I am your beautiful Radha. Now you will have to be my Lord Krishna to deserve me!"

"But Neal, don't be apprehensive when you make love to me. You know Neal; I can read your mind. I am a Catholic but that does not mean I am a convent girl. Am I?"

"If we have to cross that thin blue line between making love and having sex, it would not be the end of the world, at least not for me. I am neither a pertinacious nor a philandering person. But I have to tell you that I am not on pills and I would not like to be pregnant outside marriage, under any circumstances." As usual, Jenny was sweet, sensitive and above all practical. It would be difficult not to agree with her.

After a long pause, Neal said with a smile on his face, "Jenny, if it happens, then we can get married the next day, can't we?"

"Neal, you never take me seriously. Do you!"

"On the contrary, I utter each and every word with caution. I would like to keep my words sweet, soft and tender, because tomorrow I may have to eat them!"

"Neal, you are like a Greek who comes bearing gifts, but a sincere Greek. Am I contradicting myself?"

Jenny can not help but laugh and laugh until tears were flowing form her eyes, rolling down her face, her rosy cheek and spoiling her light make-up.

"Jenny, I will be serious, responsible and adult after we get married and have a couple of children. Until then I want to be a bundle of laughter. I am sure you would prefer me this way than a serious person, loaded with the worries of the world, a bundle of nerves. You don't know how demanding my job is."

"Seriously Jenny, you should know by now that I would never put you in such a dilemma, give you heartache. So be assured, lower your defences and dismantle the deterrence.

As my father used to tell us back at home, there is no shortage of love in the world, only the shortage of a vessel to put it in. You are a perfect vessel for my ocean of love, in the sea of tranquillity.

Do not cage your mental or sexual enjoyment. You will never find yourself in such a situation, pregnant before time of your choosing. So let us put aside our emotions and allegiances and enjoy each other to the limit."

Jenny was not only pleased but also reassured that I not only respect her views on sex and sexuality but I also share her idealism and values.

This was indeed rare in the Western culture where cohabitation is a byword. Couples have children first and then get married, like an after thought.

No wonder family life is falling apart, divorces are as common as marriages and children are raised in one parent families, mainly by their mothers.

So often without a father figure, these children fell prey to drug trade, paedophile and petty thefts, controlled and used by older members of a gang, including adult gangsters.

While America is trying to police the world, bring civility and freedom to four corners of the world, under the futile nostalgia, make believe idealism, the country is falling apart, with mounting debt and falling, crumbling infrastructure. How the Mighty has fallen!

As the time came for me to say goodbye to Jenny, she was distressed. She felt I gave her more love, understanding and respect in just three weeks than she received from her friends in years. Ours was indeed love at first sight, unbelievable but true. Such pure, true love is only a myth, at least for all but a lucky few, more for the romantic books and on the screen than in real life.

Jenny's education was coming to an end. Once she submits her thesis by June, she would be free. There was no question of failure, as her work was regularly checked.

I emailed Jenny my various articles on Hinduism and a couple on Christianity as well, especially my favourite *"The Black Madonna of Montserrat."* she made a good use of these material that also gave me publicity and made my name famous, at least in her university, to the delight of Jenny, who was by this time my fiancée.

We got married, in traditional Hindu ceremony, Jenny wearing a red, traditional Sari, just nine months after we first met on the plane.

Soon afterward, I moved to San Francisco with my parents, the city where I already had my family members. Now Jenny and her family was an added attraction.

My parents were nicely accommodated in a **Retirement Home,** a luxury beyond imagination only a few decades ago. As it was just a stone throw away from where we live, we were able to visit them on a regularly basis.

With the help and influence of Jenny's parents, her brother and my sister, I soon found a well paid job with a prestigious newspaper. I wrote my third novel, based on our love story with a title *"Genevieve"* with Hollywood in mind, with the background of this beautiful city of San Francisco and the State of California as the added attraction to the intricate plot and a happy ending.

I wrote several more books, plays, TV scripts, based on my books which became my full time job, profession, the work I can do from home. To the delight of our every family member, especially my two sisters, I was sitting on the podium, my name became as famous as any one could have imagined.

Jenny followed into the footsteps of her father and became a professor, teaching Economics, English and Religious Studies in Hinduism and Christianity.

She proved to be a wonderful wife, a caring mother, more interested in Hinduism than me, to my embarrassment. We have three wonderful children, **Radha, Meera and Krishna.** The girls are so beautiful, the exact copy of Jenny, at their age but even more charming, more beautiful that it hurt us to let them go.

But one can not cage another human being, not even their own children. Inevitably they will fly away as soon as they develop wings. But our children are homing pigeons who return to their roots from time to time, at special occasions and above all, in our hour of need.

Yet, Jenny is as slim, after giving birth to three children and as beautiful today as she was when we first met on a plane, a chance encounter, a match made in heaven.

True to her words, she does not let me out of her sight, making love to me as if every night is our honeymoon night. I could say with confidence and without contradiction that I could not have found a better partner, a more loyal wife, companion in our own, culturally rich Hindu community.

Today we do not have our parents with us. Even our children have grown and flown the nest, to build their own; making their way in the world that is more ruthless, competitive and overflowing, bulging with humanity.

But with our help and guidance, the cultural heritage from our noble Hindu and liberal Christian religion, they are earning a good living and making their mark, leaving their footsteps in the right places.

We enjoy our retirement in a luxurious development beyond our wildest dream where our every wish, every desire, even our craze is taken care of.

When in the evening, sitting on the sofa, watching TV and having a drink, so often Jenny in my arms, I just wonder was it Kismat, just good fortune or Lord Krishna's blessing that I met Jenny under most unusual circumstances, love at first sight became a life long love and a very happy life together, a *Chance Encounter* became a permanent, a life long encounter.

We will soon be celebrating our 40th wedding anniversary and looking forward to our 50th. Who says life is a one long struggle, a bed of nails! For us, life is a one long happy dream, a bed of roses. We are a firm believer in the saying that whet you saw, so you reap.

If you pursue happiness relentlessly, it will elude you. But if you focus on your family, colleagues, friends and the needy, then the happiness will find you, even pursue you. In God's kingdom, justice may be occasionally delayed but it is never forgotten.

It is only a question of being positive. I remembered my father's words of wisdom, although uttered a long time ago. He used to say that even if he fails a thousand times, he will never say he has failed but that he has discovered a thousand ways that can lead to failure!

If you reach out and touch some one's heart, stand by him in his hour of need, be humble to those who are less fortunate than you, then people will love you, admire you and stand by you in your hour of need. Lord always reciprocates and rewards good deeds.

It is a pity that too many of us treat life as a burden. So often they give up, die in their twenties and are cremated at eighty. We should only bend down, stoop low when some one needs our help to get up, when we would like to give a helping hand, make them stand on their own two feet, Lord Krishna's hand helping Radha!

I feel Angeles have walked besides us all our lives and they will always do. They are our Guardian Angeles who look after us, protect us, guide us, a kind of our own private security force?

We have only sawed love, brotherhood, friendship and shown kindness, helped those who are less fortunate than us, the qualities installed in us by our parents that have yielded such a rich harvest, served us, stood us in good stead, as well as our children and hopefully for the future generations.

* * *

APPENDIX

Dwarka, the lost city of Lord Krishna.

Those sceptic who have always argued that our holy scripture, the gospel of Hinduism, the epic tale of Ramayana, Mahabharat and Bhagwat Gita are nothing more than mythological tales, now have some thoughts to ponder about, some relics to look at, study and to revise and enlighten their thinking on the scientific line.

The undersea exploration recently carried out and still in progress, in the gulf of Cambay, off the coast of Gujarat, by the prominent Indian archaeologists, in association with Western experts, have come to the conclusion that a city similar to the relics of the ancient cities of Harappa and Mohenjo-daro, found in the Indus Valley, three hundred and fifty miles apart but joined by the intricate network of roads and canals, may have existed in Gujarat, some five thousand years ahead of Indus Valley civilization.

The bay of Cambay, where Lord Krishna's capital city of **Dwarka**, built by **Lord Vishvakarma**, supposedly erected in a very short span of time, provide a perfect archaeological sight but it may be far predating the **Indus Valley civilization**, making the sunken city of Dwarka, some ten thousand years old, placing it at the time of Lord Rama and Lord Krishna's reign, thus putting the cities of **Ayodhia, Hastinapur, Indraprasth and Dwarka**, in the realm of reality rather than a fiction or mythological tales as most Western scholars would like us to believe.

It is difficult for the advanced nations of Europe that the civilization began in Asia, not Europe that Europe was still in Dark Age when these civilizations enjoyed such a high standard of life, with advance technology.

The archaeological sights of Harappa and Mohenjo-daro, now in Pakistan, excavated during the early twentieth century, revealed a city of some twenty to fifty thousand inhabitants, with two storey buildings, built from cut and shaped granite stones, revealing a stone masonry work of the highest standard.

The large, spacious houses were equipped with communal baths, running water, enclosed courtyard, for comfort as well as safety. The roads were paved for goods transportation by bullock carts and horse drawn carriages for pleasure as well as for use on the battlefield.

But these carts and carriages may be mechanically driven vehicles running on fuels not yet invented by the Western scientists.

It is a pity that these sites of great historical and archaeological importance are being neglected and allowed to be vandalized, as Pakistan government is not interested in preserving any heritage that predates Islam.

The unwarranted destruction of the giant statues of Lord Buddha at Banyan in Afghanistan is a prime example of how some countries do not value their cultural heritage and the ancient civilization, as we do in the West and in Bharat. It is difficult to understand this unwarranted destruction for any reason but there is no saying for taste, tolerance and appreciation.

Although the exploration of the sea bed in the gulf of Cambay is in it's early stage and the fierce tidal current, the underwater, fast flowing river, makes exploration not only difficult but life threatening as well, for the deep water divers, it is hoped that this exploration will continue and may yield scientific proof to put Lord Rama's era firmly in the history book.

The exploration of the Palaeolithic sites, dating back ten thousand years is mainly carried out from the surface vessels. The acoustic images of the sea bottom, revels a settlement on both sides of a river like channel, with geometrical structure and antiquities of great archaeological interest, have been discovered along the river bank.

The dredging of the sea bed have revelled artefacts of stone and wood that put the civilization in the reign of Lord Rama and Krishna, although these sites will never be excavated to the extent of those sites that are on land, easily accessible.

The great British author and archaeologist Shri Graham Hancock believes that an advanced civilization with sophisticated technology capable of building great cities once inhabited the earth, some ten thousand years ago and may have been destroyed in the floods that engulfed some twenty percent of the land, at the end of the ice age.

The professor of archaeology in the Deccan College of Pune, Shri S. N. Rajguru believes that this breakthrough represents a great opportunity in the offshore archaeology, to explore a site dating back at least 7000BC and a golden opportunity to peep through the golden era that may be of great value and importance not only for the people of Bharat but for the world at large. It may enhance our understanding of the world, the civilization that predates our own and may be more advance than our present day civilization.

The Indian Ministry of Science and Culture, headed by the prominent and popular politician, Dr. Murli Manohar Joshi, is planning to establish a working committee of prominent scientists and archaeologists from the best research institution to explore the site and to examine and date the artefacts, compare them with other sites in the area.

Although Palaeolithic sites dating back some twenty thousand years, have been unearthed in the Andes mountain range of South America and on the Mexican coast, this is the first time such an ancient sight has been discovered on the continent of Asia.

Although the Western scientists and archaeologists put forward melting of ice, collision of a meteoroid and similar theories as a reason of the lost civilization, some of the Indian scientists, archaeologist and theologian have different theories, including one of a star war type third world war, the battle of Mahabharat, the Mahasangram, an all out nuclear holocaust which may have destroyed the civilization, except in small pockets, in underground bunkers, some fifty thousand years ago.

Any one who may have read the ten thousand verse poem of Mahabharat, which describes the weapons of mass destruction in vivid detail, some of which are not even on the drawing board, may incline to agree with this version, this theory.

Well, what do the articulate, intellectual and well informed readers of this prestigious publication think?

Mahabharat: Myth or a legacy of Lost Civilization.

Since the serialization of *HINDU* religion's epic poem *MAHABHARAT* in 97 episodes by BBC, it has aroused immense interest among Hindus and also among indigenous, intellectual people of Britain and the West.

Even after the series was over a long time ago, numerous other plays and serials were and are still bring produced in Europe as well as in America and in fact throughout the world.

The Mahabharat has just been published in China, in the Chinese language, an atheist, Communist country where religious places are routinely destroyed, where religion has no place in public life.

The first edition was sold out within weeks in China and the second edition is already due to come to shops before Christmas. It seems Chinese people are now looking to India and Hinduism to reignite their cultural and religious awareness.

It is interesting to know how the Western world tries to explain about the civilization that may be a thousand years ahead of our present day achievement, our advancement in this day and age but not able to establish a base on the Moon.

The following paragraph is from the *"Unexplained World Mysteries"* by *Pam Beasant and published by Collins.*

"The Mahabharat is a long Indian poem, written during the second centaury AD. In it, there are many accounts of battles which seem to contain references to weapons and equipment which were not invented until the 20th Centaury. The hero, Lord Krishna, for instance, uses arrows that behave like anti-ballistic missiles. Lord Krishna also kills his enemies with what sounds like "Smart Bomb", which seeks out its target, using sound waves. Some of the equipments are so futuristic that they are still to be invented.

The most frightening part of the poem seems to describe so accurately the effects of a nuclear explosion. It tells how the hero Ghaloth Katch threw missiles against three cities, from his flying machine. It contained all the power of the universe and rose up in a single column after exploding, destroying every thing in the cities.

The poem further describes what sounds like the after effects of a nuclear radiation. Hair and nail fell out, food was contaminated and people threw themselves into the water to try to wash off the poison.

The accuracy of this description makes people believe that the poet had a vision of terrible weapons we possess today."

Well, how could any one describe so accurately the advance of science in ten thousand years' time, unless it was the description of the war that took place some fifty thousand years ago and the knowledge was passed on, from generation to generation, until it was recorded in a poem form?

Could it be difficult for the Christian European nations to accept the existence of a **Hindu, Asian civilization** with such an advance technology, which even to-day the West is unable to match?

Such an advanced scientific capability defies logical explanation. Could it be possible that a **"Star War"** type third world war completely destroyed such an advance civilization, leaving only the pocket of human existence which had to start from scratch and it took some ten to fifty thousand years to advance to where we are to-day?

The word Baan (arrow) is very similar to word bomb. Could to-day's weapons be the legacy of the past? Could **Agni Baan** be atom bomb and **Varsha Baan** a rain bomb not yet invented, used to clear the atmosphere of the radiation fall out? What about the Baan that darkens the sky and plunges the day into perpetual darkness, lasting indefinitely?

Could it be earthquake, a **volcanic bomb** which releases dust particles on a massive scale, obstructing the sunlight and plunging the earth into perpetual darkness, destroying practically every living thing except those people who were fortunate enough to take shelter in a nuclear bunker? Could the caves of **Ajanta and Elora** and many more found **in Mount Abu**, **Himalayas and the Mountains of Western Ghats** be such nuclear shelters, later on converted into work of arts by the people trapped in them?

Well, such an explosion, comparable to the war of Mahabharat occurred some thirty million years ago, when a large comet collided with earth, releasing billions of dust particles and leaving earth in complete darkness, for hundreds of years, bringing ice age and destroying all living things, including **DINOSAURS ?**

At least that is the explanation put forward by the scientists, for the disappearance of dinosaurs who once monopolised the world. Some of the weapons used in the war of Mahabharat are not even on the drawing board to-day. What about the **Nag lock,** a civilization that existed along and at the time of Mahabharat who build their cities, either on the sea-bed or under the sea-bed. Could it be a foresight, to avoid being annihilated by a nuclear war?

If so, then there must be a technology capable of building such cities and it is not possible to do so without nuclear power or harvesting Sun's energy in a way we have no idea, slightest inclination at present.

What type of an advance technology one would need to build a city beneath the sea? The capital city of Lord Krishna has been found on the sea- bed, in the Gulf of Cambay. Was it submerged under the sea or was it deliberately built by Lord Krishna on the sea-bed, as he foresaw such a conflict, a nuclear holocaust that would destroy the great civilization?

Could civilization of Mahabharat be a couple of thousand years ahead of us? Even inter planetary travel is mentioned in the poem of Mahabharat.

When the war was over, Pandav were so devastated physically, mentally and morally, at the destruction of unimaginable proportion to their cities and the tragic loss of lives of the people they loved and admired most, including the father of the nation and a grandfather like figure of **Bhisma Pitamaha**, their noble elder brother **Lord Karna,** their teacher, **Guru Dronacharya** who taught them every thing they knew about weaponry and all their children except one, that there was no joy in their victory, only a relief that truth had triumphed over evil.

The five brothers left every thing behind and went to the highest peak in the Himalayas and left this earth for a while; may be until the radiation was washed away from the atmosphere? Could it be a space travel?

Ironically Lord Krishna, their best friend, their Guru, their inspiration, remained behind, perhaps in the under water city of Dwarka, a foresight on the part of Lord Krishna to build such a city for such an eventuality?

It is the fervent wish of the American theme park industry, to create an illusory palace to match the one built by Pandav in their capital city **Indraprasth**. A visit to this magic palace by Duryodhan was the cause of the greatest conflict ever recorded in the annals of the human history.

In this illusory palace, full of laser effects, the evil Duryodhan, walked straight into a swimming pool, imagining it to be a beautifully designed marble floor and then lifted his dhoti (trouser) to walk on a marble floor believing it to be a shallow lake.

This gave rise to the famous phrase, **Andha Ka Beta Andha** and planted the seeds of the battle to come. The entire account of this eighteen day war, was narrated by **Sanjay,** to the sightless king **Dhruthrashtra**, in his own palace, watching the whole episode on TV perhaps?

The most advanced and amazing weapon used in this war, was the **Sudershan Chakra**, a Lord Krishna's favourite weapon. Could it be today's Tomahawk Cruise missiles so devastatingly used by USA in Gulf, Serbian and Afghan war?

The Tomahawk cruise missile is the most spectacular and technically advanced weapon ever used in a war. It's highly complicated radar and guidance system can be accurate to within a few yards, over fifteen hundred miles range, fired even from a submarine, while submerged some one thousand feet under sea water.

The missile hugs the ground as it flies, searching it's way from the Digital Terrain Maps, 3-D pictures showing every contour, with satellite plotting every hill, every tall building and street corners.

This is a mind boggling technology that most people are unable to understand, appreciate. This advance in technology enables America to attack other nations with impunity. Yet compared to weapons used in the Mahabharat war, the Mahasangram, the ultimate destruction, our weapons are primitive; we are in the Bronze Age.

The Tomahawk missile is so accurate that it could be fired from the island of Malta, in the **Mediterranean Sea** and make it land in the fountain at Trafalgar square, avoiding all the high rise buildings.

Could Sudershan Chakra be tomorrow's Cruise missile, even more advance and sophisticated, yet a fraction in size, seeking out not only military targets but human beings as well which were used to target some villains who were fleeing the battlefield after committing atrocities, breaking the code of conduct normally used, respected by all parties? Such a weapon we may not be capable of developing for another few hundred years or so?

The Western countries could not be convinced about such an advanced Eastern Hindu civilization, without any physical evidence. But as we have often experienced, truth is stranger than friction, as the recent events have proved.

May be we should seek the evidence in the ruins of Japanese cities of Nagasaki and Hiroshima. Could any thing survive an attack, a million times more destructive than the atom bombs dropped on these Japanese cities?

Only a very few and privileged people, in isolated pockets, perhaps in underground bunkers, may have survived this **Maha-Sangram**, to pass down the details of this stranger than fiction storey of Maha-Sangram, the mother of all battles, the *"**Battle of Mahabharat.**"*

Every Asian of whatever nationality and religious affiliation should take pride in the storey of **Ramayana and Mahabharat** that such an advanced civilization existed in Asia, some ten to fifty thousand years before the birth of the **Holy Child Jesus Christ**, who gave us **Christianity**, one of the noblest religions to emerge since Buddhism.

* * *

Black Madonna of Montserrat

Our experiences have made us realize that the best enjoyment, most memorable moments, enchanting or unforgettable events in our lives happen when least expected. It is just like falling in love without a warning, without a premonition.

One can not plan, instigate or choose the time and the person to fall in love. It just happens, so often when least expected. Otherwise we will all be marrying Ashwaria Rai, Rani Mukerjee and pretty woman Jody Foster.

So when we booked our annual holiday to Costa Doroda, one of the most beautiful parts of Spain, we had no idea, no inclination that one of the most revered Christian holy place, "The Monastery of Montserrat with the famous statue of Virgin Mary, popularly known as The Black Madonna will be on our door-step.

Montserrat means a shorn off mountain and looking at the sheer cliffs surrounding Montserrat, one can understand why it is called Montserrat. Black Madonna is a patron saint of the people of Catalonia and is said to have a mystic healing power. Madonna is a beacon of hope and joy to millions of her worshippers among all faiths.

We only came to know that a visit to Montserrat is one of the excursions on offer when we attended the get together meeting on the next day of our arrival, a normal practice on package or all inclusive holidays.

As we have lived happily and prosper in England, a Christian country, for the past thirty five years, we consider ourselves honorary Christians. The beauty of Hinduism is that we can be flexible and can accommodate, mingle with and even participate in the holy, religious rituals of other religions, especially Jainism, Sikhism, Buddhism and Christianity, without diluting our Hindu faith in any way. We feel at ease in any religious confinement that is the greatness of our culture, our up-bringing and Hinduism.

The three most important holy places on the Christian calendar, at least for me, that we wanted to visit are, the Lourdes in South West France, again a world famous Christian shrine dedicated to St. Bernadette which has a reputation for miraculous cure, which we visited back in 1974.

Our second choice was The Basilica of Bom Jesus, in our favourite holiday destination of Goa which we visited in 1996. The basilica contains the tomb of St. Francis Xavier in a glass cabinet and is lowered for public worship every four years.

To be present on this holy occasion with a million people who come from all four corners of the world, gathered outside to witness this miracle. This is an unforgettable experience difficult to describe.

One has to be there to catch the spirit, the atmosphere and the rituals.

And now in 2004, we have fulfilled our last desire, to visit Montserrat and hold the hand of holy Madonna.

Perhaps we left it last, as it is on our door-step and with all the globe trotting, we can now appreciate it better than at any other time in our life, as Montserrat is the centre for dissemination of culture.

The Excursion:

So the first excursion we booked was naturally to Montserrat. I was a bit apprehensive as the excursion was a whole day outing, lasting some ten hours and a bit exhausting, especially for me as I suffer from chronic fatigue.

The long steep walk and numerous steps would not help me but our rep, a lovely girl called June, when she learnt that I am a hobby journalist and would like to write a piece on Montserrat, assured me and even arranged for a wheel chair to be on the coach, in case it is needed.

But I should not have worried or harbour any reservation. With my unshakable faith in my noble, culturally rich, tolerant, progressive and peace loving Hindu religion, as well as faith in Christianity, which incorporates all the noble characters of Hinduism, besides having their own noble traditions, I should have known that I will come through this ordain with flying colours, with a bit of help from above?

On The Road To Montserrat:

The coach arrived outside our Donaire Park hotel at 7am. After collecting passengers from several pick-up points in and around La Pineda, we were on our way to Montserrat by 8am taking the coastal highway, passing by the coastal resorts of Cambrils, Salau and Tarragona, the ancient capital of Spain and still a thriving city with numerous historical sights worth a visit, that include amphitheatre and Roman ruins dating back 2000 years.

Our guide was a lovely young and beautiful Catalan girl named Pillar, a very popular Spanish name. She was a walking encyclopaedia and like most guides, she loved to listen to her own voice. I must admit her voice was sweet and sensual and as she had lived in London for few years, she spoke perfect English.

When she saw me taking notes and when I introduced myself in perfect Spanish, may be not so perfect, I instantly became her favourite disciple, most favoured passenger on the coach, allowed to ask any question, on any subject, although my favourite subject was Montserrat throughout.

Pillar even had a good sense of humour. She told us her favourite comedy programme in London was Faulty Towers and she introduced the coach driver as Manual from Barcelona?

The History and Evolution That Created Montserrat:

The area of Montserrat was part of the Mediterranean Sea some 25 million years ago. Gradually the sea retreated, dried up and rock formation was created, so often accompanied by volcanic eruption and violent earthquakes, which was an every day occurrence in the beginning. The present day Montserrat is a long process of evolution, perhaps a minor miracle for Virgin Mary?

The incomparable mountain of Montserrat is unique in the world, in its particular silhouette and formation and stands some fifty kilometres from Barcelona.

As Montserrat is practically on the French door-step, it has a troubled history. Our guide Pillar, a Catalan patriot, did not mixed words when she narrated history.

She described in detail how French army, under Napoleon Bonaparte, the Emperor of France who introduced centralised despotism and ruled

France with an iron fist, destroyed Montserrat more than once and converted the buildings into a military fortress.

Montserrat is perched on a precipice with a bird's eye view of the plain below and can be easily defended from the rampant, patriotic Catalans who hated French.

The French army vandalised the monastery and destroyed not only the monastic life but destroyed and looted the artwork; ancient treasure and burnt thousands of books, along with the library buildings. French destroyed in just two months that has taken centuries to built. It was a mindless, thuggish and unwarranted act of vandalism akin to Attila the Hun.

The statue of Black Madonna which has been carved out of Oak wood was taken to Barcelona for safe keeping. It took another thirty two years to rebuild Montserrat which became an abode of monks who were erudite historians, physicists, students of science, music and philosophy.

The popularity of Montserrat, the culmination of this period of splendour for the holy place was reflected into the construction of new monastery buildings to accommodate the growing demand from the modern day pilgrims.

Being a Hindu, I know that no Hindu king would ever destroy a Hindu temple, a Hindu place of pilgrimage where other Hindus worship. There are so many sects in Hinduism, worshipping different deity but there is no conflict what so ever between them. So I was at a loss to understand why a Catholic king of France would destroy another Catholic place of worship where Catalans pray.

So when I asked this question to Pillar, she had no logical answer, an acceptable explanation except that Napoleon was not a religious person and the military conquest was more important to him than religious sentiment.

Moreover it was the character, the requirement and the tradition of the time when colonisation was a byword for progress.

Nearing Montserrat:

By 10am we were within the striking distance of St. Jerome Mountain and the mass of sandstones and conglomerate rocks with a serrated spine rising to some four thousand feet above the surrounding plane.

This is where Montserrat is located. The last half an hour's drive took us through turning and twisting narrow roads with breathtaking scenery, deep valley on one side and steep rock-face on the other. Fast flowing tiny rivers and picturesque chocolate box hamlets that look so enchanting from a high vantage point.

Where the land was not cultivated, the valley and the mountain slopes were covered with Alpine pine, ash, birch and maple trees. As we go higher, the vegetation became richer, varied and dense. I wonder what animal life cohabit these mountains.

Our guide Pillar pointed to various rock formations that resemble to a monkey, a gorilla, a maid and a bull. If one has a varied imagination and some faith, then it is not impossible for you to see a rock formation of any shape and size resembling our favourite Gods.

May that be Lord Krishna or Lord Rama, Lord Hanuman or Ganesh? In my case I saw Lord Krishna in a rocky Vrindavan. Perhaps I was the only one to see an image of my favourite God Lord Krishna?

In Montserrat:

Our coach was in its parking slot by 11am. There is a long walk from the car park to the Montserrat Complex. As we were going to spend some four hours here, our pace was leisurely. We were lucky that our guide Pillar accompanied us throughout and continued to give us the benefit of her immense knowledge of the area.

The roads, lanes and foot-path surrounding Montserrat have existed ever since the mountains were inhabited by humans dating back some two thousand years, around the time Lord Jesus was born.

But Montserrat became a holy place, a spiritual centre for Christianity when a monastery and a basilica were completed in 1592, although the foundation of the faith was laid back in 1025AD.

The basilica is the home of La Marc De Dev, the mother of God. It is a small wooden statue no more than five feet high, blackened by the smoke of millions of candles lit at her feet over the centuries.

That is why it is known as The Black Madonna of Montserrat. The statue is kept in a glass cabinet but her right hand is outside the cabinet so that a pilgrim can hold her hand and make a wish, in the privacy of a tiny cabin that can accommodate only one person at a time.

It is said that if you are sincere and have faith, your wishes may be granted; your dreams may become a reality. That is why so many sick, disabled and disappointed pilgrims make this pilgrimage. It is famed of rumours that include cures for the sick and dying. Some pilgrims have been so impressed that they abandoned their worldly possessions, gave it all to the Montserrat and went there to live, devoting the rest of their lives to Virgin Mary.

By the time we reached basilica, there were already 200 people in the queue, which is a waiting time of over three hours, even if each pilgrim takes only a minute to pray at the foot of Black Madonna. Fortunately our wheel chair and people with crutches gained us an instant entry.

It was an emotional moment for me when I hold the hand of Black Madonna, prayed and made a wish, although I would not like to disclose what my wish was and to what extent it was fulfilled. The fact that I have faith is my reward and the fact that I was able to undertake and complete this gruelling and extremely exhausting excursion without any ill-effect was a minor miracle in itself.

Even today one can light a candle, not at the foot of Madonna but a few feet away, in a basement room, where hundreds of candles are laid out, along with postcards and such other items for the use of pilgrims, with a suggested price list and a donation box.

While in the basement, I met a young Afro American girl named Monica, who had converted to Buddhism and taken up the name of Meera. She was very intelligent, charming and a highly educated person, with a PhD in Economics, working as a professor in one of the Deep South University.

It was her routine to visit every year, Lumbini in Nepal, Lord Buddha's birthplace and Buddh Gaya in Bihar, Bharat where Lord Buddha became enlightened while meditating under a banyan tree and of course Montserrat where she feels at peace with herself and the world.

It was a chance meeting, as we were the only non white pilgrims in the sea of humanity. My curiosity to know her overcame my shyness and when she realised that, like her we were non Christians, she was as eager to know about us as I was about her. But alas! We had only twenty minutes together before we had to Part Company. Who knows, one day we may meet again, as she visits Montserrat every year.

After lighting the candle, we came out from the back door. By now I was dying to know more about the statue of Black Madonna and Pillar obliged me with the following story:

The statue was carved by St. Luke and brought to the region by St. Peter. When Moors landed in Spain in the 8th centaury, the statue was hidden in what is now called Santa Cove (Holy Cave) when discovered in AD 880, it could not be moved.

A shrine and a chapel were built to give her a permanent place, until AD 976 when Benedictine Monastery was established which has now become an influential centre of culture and religious activities par excellence, with donations pouring in from all over the world.

The Complex, which is being extended and improved regularly, has an accommodation for 300 resident monks and their visitors. There is also a hostel, shops, restaurants and other modern comforts that the present day pilgrims expect.

La Escolania Choir:

After the reopening of the monastery, the music school did not function until the arrival of Father Gozman who was responsible for the reconstruction and restoring the fortune of the music school.

The monastery is also the home of thirty young boys who sing in the Boys Choir known as La Escolania Sings.

It is a privilege and an honour to listen to these boys who are not only so talented at music but are the best brain in the region. Most of these boys go on to climb great heights and make themselves famous in different walks of life.

May be the Monastic discipline and the holy atmosphere is responsible for their progress in life, not forgetting the blessings of Virgin Mary, the Black Madonna of Montserrat. It is no wonder that a place on the choir is most sought after and so often accompanied by a large donation to the monastery?

The Library and the Museum:

The library, with some two hundred thousand books, some older than the monastery it self, is the hub of activities for the young residents. The walls of the museum and the art gallery are tastefully decorated with the works of Caravaggio, El Greco and other great artists, past and present. The painting by L. Limona depicting the adoration of Catalonia for La Morenta, the Black Virgin of Montserrat is in itself worth a visit.

It is a wonderful recovery in the prosperity and popularity for a monastery that was so often looted and destroyed, community dispersed and the sanctuary abandoned.

It is the reputation of Black Madonna's healing power and the attraction of the monastic life in an ideal location that has restored the reputation and the popularity of Montserrat. It is indeed a Sangri La of the Christian faith that even the mighty Napoleon failed to destroy, one of the most destructive force in the European history.

Montserrat is more than a mere mountain. It is the spirit, the soul and heart of the Catalan people. Now Montserrat, just fifty kilometres away, can be reached by train from Barcelona.

It is now possible to spend a few days in the comfortable hostel and young couples even come here to get married and spend their honeymoon. It is said that a marriage blessed by the Black Madonna rarely ends up in divorce?

We took a vertical cable train that took us to the highest point, with most magnificent views of the surrounding countryside, as far as eyes can see.

The End of a Dream:

By 3:30 pm we were ready to leave, albeit with heavy heart and every bone in my body aching, as I had not walked so much for a very long time, even with the help of crutches but our spirit was lifted, having fulfilled one of my main ambitions, a dream come true.

The second part of our excursion took us to one of the largest plantation in Europe, growing grapes that produced Spanish champagne, popularly known as *Cava.*

We were taken to the underground storage space where the wine is left for a long time, until it acquires maturity, taste and aroma of true champagne. But even though Cava may be better in taste, it can not be called Champagne, as the grapes that produce it is grown in the French region which gives the name champagne, a restrictive practice to protect regional interest. Then perhaps it is right that traditional names should be protected.

But after Montserrat, every excursion was an anticlimax. My one disappointment, point of contention was the lack of facilities for the sick and the disabled pilgrims, some of whom were suffering from a terminal illness.

As Montserrat is visited by more than a million pilgrims and donations are pouring in from every corner of the world, I sincerely hope that the authority will rectify this glaring fault, in their otherwise perfect management of Montserrat. They should make it more disabled friendly with easy approach, even providing buggy, motorised wheel-chairs.

We were back in our comfortable hotel in time for the evening meal and the soft, comfortable bed that was awaiting us.

* * *

Lightning Source UK Ltd.
Milton Keynes UK
UKOW041126230612

194921UK00006B/26/P